Published 2020 by The PARVUS Press.

The right of John Whitbourn to be identified as the author of this book has been asserted by him in accordance with the United Kingdom Copyright, Designs and Patents Act 1988.

This is a work of fiction and any supposed resemblance to persons living or dead is purely coincidental.

All rights reserved. No reproduction, copy, adaptation or transmission of this work may be made in any form without the written permission of the publisher. Any person who violates the Copyright Act in regard to this publication may be liable to criminal prosecution and civil claims for damages.

Copyright © 2020 John Whitbourn
All rights reserved.
ISBN-13: 9798653224669

ALTERED ENGLANDS

Or

CONFESSIONS OF AN ENGLISH COUNTER-REFORMATION GREEN ANARCHO-JACOBITE

COLLECTED SHORT STORIES

By

John Whitbourn

DEDICATION

To:

To Archie, Tilly, Minnie, Hannah and T.B.A.
The next chapter in our story.
Signs are it'll be a good read…

ABOUT THE AUTHOR

John Whitbourn has had fifteen novels published since winning the BBC & Victor Gollancz 'First Fantasy Novel' prize with *A Dangerous Energy* in 1991. They include his *Downs-Lord* 'triptych' concerning the establishment of empire in an alternative, monster-ridden, England; *Frankenstein's Legions*, an extrapolation of Mary Shelley's gothic tale; and *The Age of the Triffids*, a sequel to John Wyndham's SF classic. Whitbourn's works have received favourable reviews in The Times, Telegraph, and Guardian, amongst others. *The Encyclopaedia of Fantasy* (1997) says he *'writes well with dry wit'*. A rare press interview with Whitbourn in 2000 was revealingly entitled *'Confessions of a Counter-Reformation, Green, Anarcho-Jacobite'*.

AUTHOR'S NOTE

As with the Wheel of Dharma (see above) oft depicted in this book, its contents may be approached from any direction. In other words *'Liberty Hall'!* Start wheresoever you so please, and then proceed likewise. It matters little. So little does. I wish you joy!

And thank you also to fellow son-of-the-South, artist Eric Ravilious (1903-42), for the opportunity of a cover featuring *'The Long Man of Wilmington'* (or *'Giant'* as Mr Ravilious prefers), who has cameoed (at least) in much of my writing. An enigmatic hill figure, of unknown date but certainly the largest depiction of the human(?) form in the eastern hemisphere, he(?) has come to represent the presiding spirit of the beloved Downs Country.

ALSO BY JOHN WHITBOURN

A DANGEROUS ENERGY

POPES & PHANTOMS

TO BUILD JERUSALEM

THE BINSCOMBE TALES—Vol. 1. Sinister Saxon Stories

THE BINSCOMBE TALES—Vol. 2. Sinister Sutangli Stories

THE ROYAL CHANGELING

DOWNS-LORD DAWN

DOWNS-LORD DAY

DOWNS-LORD DOOMSDAY

FRANKENSTEIN'S LEGIONS

THE TWO CONFESSIONS

NOTHING IS TRUE…—THE FIRST BOOK OF FAROUK

EVERYTHING IS PERMISSIBLE—THE SECOND BOOK OF FAROUK

THE AGE OF THE TRIFFIDS

BABYLONdon

FORTHCOMING

AMY FAITH & THE STRONGHOLD

AMY FAITH & THE ENEMY OF CALM

PRAISE FOR JOHN WHITBOURN

A DANGEROUS ENERGY

'John Whitbourn's first novel… is a humdinger. … a terrifying story, marvellously inventive and written with great power and conviction.'
The Times.

'A work of brilliance. Never was a prize more richly deserved.'
Starburst magazine.

POPES & PHANTOMS

'Terrific, cynical fun.'
The Times.

THE ROYAL CHANGELING

'This is alternative history/fantasy at its very best—sort of C17th meets the X-Files… An excellent read, well-imagined, intriguingly constructed and extremely well written with a rich vein of underlying humour.'
Historical Novels Review.

'Alternative history pulled off with panache and no small amount of humour. Whitbourn's wit is both unforced and splendidly droll.'
The Daily Express.

'Gutsy, witty and time-twisting.'
The Daily Telegraph.

'Somehow in the West ... we have lost the ability to take in the sacred and the secular at the same time, to be both intensely serious and extremely light-hearted, even rude, without loss of genius in either form.'

Kate Chisholm. *'Pure Purcell'*. *The Spectator*. 16th March 2013.

'Multitudinis imperitae non formido judicea; meis tamen, rogo, parcant opusculis - in quibus fuit propositi semper, a jocis ad seria, a seriis vicissim ad jocos transire.'

'I do not dread the judgements of the ignorant multitude; I ask, however, that they spare my little works in which it was always the design to pass in turn from jests to serious matters and from serious matters to jests.'

John of Salisbury a.k.a. *'Johannes Parvus'*—*'Little John'* (c. 1120-1180). *'Policraticus'* (1159).

'¡Viva la Muerte!'

José Millán-Astray y Terreros (1879-1954). Bridge player and Philosopher.

CONTENTS

PAGE 13.	1. A SHORT INTRODUCTION BY JW
PAGE 15.	2. INTRODUCTION BY PROFESSOR E. J. GRIFFITHS
PAGE 21.	THE 'MODERN' or 'ALLAH' SERIES
PAGE 25.	3. IN THE NAME OF ALLAH, THE OMNIPOTENT?
PAGE 40.	4. IN THE NAME OF ALLAH, THE COMPASSIONATE?
PAGE 59.	5. IN THE NAME OF ALLAH, THE MERCIFUL?
PAGE 79.	6. 'EXCUSE ME...'
PAGE 96.	MISCELLANEOUS STORIES
PAGE 97.	7. 'YO ENGLISH! DR DEATH!'
PAGE 114.	8. 'THE WAY, THE TRUTH...'
PAGE 130.	9. 'I CAME TO COMPTON...'
PAGE 142.	10. THE SUNKEN GARDEN
PAGE 154.	PORTS & PHANTOMS
PAGE 159.	11. A PARTIAL CURE
PAGE 171.	12. THE FALL OF A DICTATOR
PAGE 179.	13. 'LIBERTY! AH, LIBERTY!'
PAGE 201.	14. ONE FOR THE ROAD
PAGE 213.	THE MOUNT CABURN STORIES
PAGE 216.	15. BURY MY HEART AT SOUTHERHAM, (E. SUSSEX)
PAGE 227.	16. 'THE HILLS ARE ALIVE...'
PAGE 235.	17. FURRINERS
PAGE 248.	THE STALINSPACE SERIES
PAGE 250.	18. DEMOCRACY
PAGE 267.	19. OLIGARCHY
PAGE 278.	20. MERITOCRACY

PAGE 290.	THREE NIGH NOVELLAS
PAGE 291.	21. I NEED HELP BAD MAN!
PAGE 319.	22. A PILLAR OF THE CHURCH
PAGE 350.	23. DOING THE CHARLESTON
PAGE 393.	THE SIR ROBERT HOLMES PAIRING
PAGE 398.	24. MERCY ON NONE
PAGE 416.	25. THE PROTESTANT WIND
PAGE 432.	MISCELLANEOUS STORIES
PAGE 433.	26. JUST HANGING AROUND
PAGE 443.	27. JUSTICE WITHOUT RESPITE
PAGE 455.	28. WALK THIS WAY
PAGE 465.	29. INGRATITUDE
PAGE 479.	30. PROGRESS
PAGE 483.	31. CULLODEN II
PAGE 498.	32. ENLIGHTENMENT
PAGE 517.	33. CONSUMER AWARENESS
PAGE 529.	34. *MEBYON* VERSUS *SUNA*
PAGE 552.	35. YOU MUST BE COLD
PAGE 573.	THE BINSCOMBE TALES: CODA & CONCLUSION
PAGE 575.	36. PUBLISH AND BE DAMNED!
PAGE 592.	37. UP FROM THE CELLAR / ENGLAND EXPECTS!
PAGE 618.	38. AFTERWORD & FAREWELL

PREVIOUSLY PUBLISHED STORIES.

The Modern / Allah Series
'In the Name of Allah, the Omnipotent?'. *Interzone* no. 135, September 1998 & *Nowa Fantastyka* (Poland), September 1999.
'Excuse Me…'. *Shadows & Silence*. The Ash Tree Press. 2000.

Ports & Phantoms Series
'A Partial Cure'. *Transactions of the Doppelganger Society*. 1990
'The Fall Of A Dictator'. *All Hallows*. The Ghost Story Society. No 4. 1993.

Mount Caburn Series
'Bury My Heart At Southerham (East Sussex)'. *Midnight Never Comes*. The Ash Tree Press. 1997.
'The Hills Are Alive'. *Interzone* no. 165 March 2001.

Stalinspace Series
'Democracy'. *Nowa Fantastyka* (Poland), March 2000.

Other Short Stories
'The Way, the Truth…'. *The Magazine of Fantasy & Science Fiction*. USA. Jan. 2000.
'The Sunken Garden'. *Acquainted With the Night*. The Ash Tree Press. 2004.
'A Pillar of the Church'. *At Ease With the Dead*. The Ash Tree Press. 2007.
'Just Hanging Around'. *Ghosts & Scholars*. No. 31. The Haunted Library. 2000.
'Justice Without Respite'. *Ghosts & Scholars*. No 15. The Haunted Library. 1993.
'Walk This Way'. *All Hallows*: The Ghost Story Society. No. 7. 1994.
'Ingratitude'. *All Hallows*. The Ghost Story Society. No. 15. 1997.
'Culloden II'. *All Hallows*, The Ghost Story Society. No. 23. 2000.
'Enlightenment'. *Exotic Gothic 2*. The Ash Tree Press. 2008.
'*Mebyon* versus *Suna*'. *Terror Tales of Cornwall*'. Telos Publishing Ltd. 2017.
'You Must Be Cold'. *Terror Tales of the Scottish Highlands*. Grey Friar Press. 2015.

ALTERED ENGLANDS

JOHN WHITBOURN

1~

A SHORT INTRODUCTION BY JW

Or

A DRIVE-BY SHOOTING *'HELLO!'* FROM THE AUTHOR.

✾

'Altered Englands'? My title should speak for itself, revealing all like some shameless Jezebel. No cigar for sussing that bit out.

Granted, the title of this book has been interpreted liberally—in the old, now nigh obsolete, sense of that word. Some stories within are set far from England, in both miles and centuries. Yet the prevailing spirit in them all is in close accord.

Plus, the pen that wrote these pages was indissolubly formed and forged in that… interesting Nation. *'What's bred in the bone comes out in the meat…'*

> *'Be England what she will,*
> *with all her faults, she is my country still...'*
> Charles Churchill. 1731-1764.

But what about the subtitle though? Cor, blimey, guv'nor! How does that lot hang together?

Well, *'English'*, should also be obvious. We're the largest stateless nation in Europe—but the jolly giant is stirring from a three-century sleep buried under 'Britain'. It's early days but a good time to be part of the tribe. Our best is

ALTERED ENGLANDS

yet to be.

But what about *'Counter-Reformation'* or *'Anarcho-Jacobite'*, let alone *'Green'*? How can anyone find in those things grounds for *'Hoping something better comes tomorrow'*, to quote quasi-official English genius, Ray Davies of the Kinks rock combo fame?[1]

All I can say is that it's an instinct thing, which I believe to be a miles better tool with which to grapple with Life than what Omar Khayyam rightly termed *'old barren Reason'*.[2] It's arguable that Reason stands in relation to human Life as do the rules of cricket. Handy—essential even—for playing cricket, but of limited application further afield.

Otherwise, as per the words of the 1960s Mod anthem, I:

'Can't explain'.[3]

Therefore, patient and sweet-natured reader, I implore that you kindly let these stories speak for me instead.

And concerning which, as my namesake and role-model John (*'Honest John'*) Wilkes (1725-1797) was wont to say: *'I wish you joy!'*

Finally, knowing as I do what is to follow, I also wish to echo the immortal words of another English genius, the late, great Vivian Stanshall (1943-1995) of *Bonzo Dog Doo-dah Band* fame:

'It's awfully jolly nice to see you all—and I deeply apologise...'[4]

JW. Binscombe. 2020

---

[1] *'Better Things'*. The Kinks. 2002.
[2] Astronomer poet, died 1123. *'The Rubiyat'*. *'I... divorced old barren Reason from my bed'*.
[3] *'Can't Explain'*. 'The Who's first (but not last, alas) single. Released 5th January 1965.
[4] To the audience at *'Jazz Bilzen'*, Belgium, 1969.

JOHN WHITBOURN

2~

INTRODUCTION to *ALTERED ENGLANDS* BY PROFESSOR E. J. GRIFFITHS.

❈

JW INTRODUCTION TO EJG INTRODUCTION

On occasion, throughout my various publications, in introductions, 'Afterwords' and footnotes, I have taken the liberty to quote the *'great'* [JW] classicist and philosopher and *'Celtic Marxist bon viveur'* [Times Literary Supplement] Professor E. J. Griffiths. Naturally, motivated solely by common courtesy, I sent him copies of my works, and wholly understood that—he being an extremely busy man, working under enormous pressure—commitments prevented him from acknowledging them.

However, a chance encounter with one of Griffiths' former fiancées, *'Jam of the Month Club'* founder and chairlady, Mrs Joyce Morgana Preston (to whom all due thanks), sparked off a correspondence between myself and Professor Griffiths. It transpired that he had, whenever time permitted, followed my writing with some interest and, I am gratified to say, appreciation.

Accordingly, it has since been my enormous good fortune to have the eminent Professor as a patron of my humble efforts. This connection was crowned when in 1998 he was gracious enough to gild one of my books (*'Binscombe Tales'*, Ash Tree Press 1998) with some introductory words.

For all my million+ words published since 1987,[5] I am not verbally qualified to adequately express the honour I now feel that he has been persuaded to do so again.[6]

---

[5] And so modest too!
[6] I am also sadly obliged to add that some otherwise reliable bibliographies of my work, such as the 'Internet Speculative Fiction Database' (isfdb.org), suggest that

ALTERED ENGLANDS

As honorary keeper of the 'Whitbourn archive'—a task which increasingly diverts me as I wait for my area of academic research to regain its rightful pre-eminence—I am pleased to have been asked to introduce this collection of short stories by Mr John Whitbourn. I feel he is a promising writer of some ability (by English standards) and deserving of encouragement.

The archive I refer to started many eventful years ago with unsolicited copies of the *'Binscombe Tales'*, mere fan-folded dot-matrix print outs to begin with, which I kept in a suitcase in my palatial 'Worker's flat' overlooking the Danube at Bratislava. In due course and as both the corpus and my appreciation grew, the top of the case was armed with a sealed envelope containing the then unpublished last Binscombe Tale, which promised to 'reveal all'. In the event of a NATO/Warsaw Pact showdown, I hoped to make it back in time to learn the final secret of Binscombe and Mr Disvan and co., meanwhile toasting the end of things in East German vodka. What better way could there be (if not in intimate company...) to go?

Alas, Bratislava is now in a different country and that happy (for me) era is part of history, as is the visiting chair of Marxist Studies I once occupied. In contrast however, the Whitbourn archive has continued as very much a living thing, steadily augmented over the years by a stream of novels and short stories as Whitbourn secured publication and moderate recognition.

Those Binscombe Tales were the earliest of the Whitbourn short works I am aware of, with most dating from the mid 80s to the mid 1990s. I know for instance, that *'Let the Train Take the Strain'* has its origins in a curious incident on the M3 during 1987, which I chanced to witness and report to Whitbourn. Finally, the entire corpus was splendidly collected by the Ash Tree Press as *'Binscombe Tales'—Sinister Saxon Stories'* and *'More Binscombe Tales—Sinister Sutangli Stories'* in 1998 and 99, but I see that this volume contains a new but definitively

---

'Professor Griffiths' is a pseudonym, constituting what I believe is termed a 'sockpuppet' for my own words. Accordingly, I take this opportunity to state (and give my word, should it be required) that the Professor is not only actual but that I have met him 'in the flesh', so to speak—albeit just once and some years ago now. On which occasion (as she later confided to me) he saw fit to pinch my wife's bottom. And yet in her specific case who can blame him? As I affirm above, Professor Griffiths is but flesh and blood...

final Binscombe tale, a coda to the series and a curious tale with an equally curious tale attached to its commissioning. I never thought to see such a thing and welcome it as I would a receptive Ph.D. student, with open arms.

What other joys await you, dear reader? Well, happily, the present volume now brings us up to date with an assemblage of all the 'post-Binscombe' short stories, from the 1990's and into the new millennium. That time span of almost three decades allows us, I think, to trace Mr Whitbourn's development as a writer. My remaining words will cover both what he's been writing and what I conceive he's on about.

There are several recurring motifs in these stories, which can be traced throughout as they mutate and gain in both depth and strangeness. Many of these stories also prefigure important themes in the succeeding novels, such as the prize-winning *'A Dangerous Energy,'* and *'Popes and Phantoms'*, *'The Royal Changeling'* and the *'Downs-Lord'* triptych. I could name, for example, my own favourites strands: the 'Downs Country' of southern England and those pesky English themselves, Whitbourn's chilly but charming elves, stoicism in the face of death, despair and eternal night, the driest of gallows humour, and so on.

However, first and foremost I think it should be said that a sense of place is what drives many of these pieces, wherever that place may be. I should also say that as well as being rooted in the past, the stories hold a promise for the future. The avowedly English political-cultural revival has now penetrated even the fashionable chattering classes but its early roots are visible here...

There is no doubt that the writing develops over time (which is intended as praise, since the *'Binscombe Tales'* were such that is worth *this minute* seeking them out, should you have no copy of your own!). The final Binscombe Tale was, I believe, written after some of the stories presented here and I think its power to move was in part a result of the author's growing ability to engage with the reader's deeper sensitivities. As an example of this process I strongly recommend *'Bury My Heart at Southerham, East Sussex'* and the Mount Caburn 'sequence' of stories which it opens. I am convinced that here was the starting point for the author working at a whole new level.

Likewise spread-eagled for your delectation are sets of stories on particular themes—those concerning the English expatriate port-producing community in Portugal, collectively described as *'Ports and Phantoms'*, being an early example. I'm pleased also to see two of a series themed around the Isle of Wight retirement years of the piratic Admiral Sir Robert Holmes, an actual historic figure (1622-1697). Or perhaps these are really about the Isle of Wight?

ALTERED ENGLANDS

To digress slightly, what is it about this jewel off the southern coast of England that inspires such devotion, in my beloved Karl Marx (*'This island is a little paradise'*—letter to Engels, 15/07/1874) no less than myself? I ponder its inverted triangular plan, its seductive slopes and luxuriant foliage; I consider its periodically tropical climes and its reputation for mouth-watering seafood—yet precise explanation for its seductive power remains elusive. Doubtless it will come soon. Such things do... Meanwhile, Mr Whitbourn's tales set therein only tempt me to return to probe those mysteries anew.

Lately, Whitbourn's writing has achieved a sort of synthesis of all these aforementioned themes, conjoining them in stories like *'Excuse Me...'*. Is this a ghost story or an elegy for something lost? If so, I think what's missing might be within the reader, not in the landscape. The connected *'In the name of Allah...'* series are of similar mettle, if darker, taking the ghost story to parts of the modern world not previously on its itinerary.

A note of caution: these last mentioned are very powerful pieces and via the supernatural confront the reader with a level of reality most people would prefer to remain comfortably hidden. When I say *'do not read them alone or late at night...'*, I am not engaging in the customary build up of spine-chilling anticipation. Have company and something of the warm and vital world about you when you start on them.

As if that were not enough—or too much!—*'Excuse me'* is also a very moving statement of English identity and English loss. I believe this and its sibling stories will be one day come to be well regarded beyond the ghost and fantasy genres through their sheer quality of writing. It is a sad comment on the literary world that such genre stories are not automatically considered as high literature.

One another digression: given Mr Disvan's perennial, and perhaps prophetic, choice of reading material throughout the 'Binscombe Tales', maybe an Islamic themed series should come as no surprise?

What else? Many will be pleased to find that some of the stories spring from 'Alternative histories'—which as anyone who has seen the Oxford University exam paper in *'A Dangerous Energy'* knows is something in which Whitbourn delights and excels. By the by, speaking of the novel sequence *'A Dangerous Energy'* and *'To Build Jerusalem'*—and now the belatedly published *'The Two Confessions'*—my privileged position as archivist and advance-viewer allows me to say the last named is the best of all three. Which is saying something...

Plus, lurking among these tales of historical byways and 'Altered Englands', I'm especially fond of *'Yo English! Dr Death!'*; a tempting vision of how Whitbourn's nation could and should have been.

And, of course, there are ghost stories galore, both traditional and modern. Not a few of these were originally contributed to Rosemary Pardoe's *'Ghost's and Scholars'* (which did so much to revive and sustain the genre) or benefited from her comments. John informed me that the esteemed lady and her *'Haunted Library'* merit wild applause. As ever regarding the fair sex, I am happy to oblige. And, out of respect, will abstain from any *'clap'* jests.

And another thing...—but no: time I think for some concluding words, before this turns too much towards literary review. In short, these are extraordinary, strange, unique, deeply felt, funny and unsettling stories, which will bring immediate delight and lasting reflection. I envy you, dear reader, about to skip this spiel and read these stories for the first time, or perhaps encountering them for the first time in mob strength. Fortify your spirit <u>with</u> spirits to <u>meet</u> spirits by uncorking some favourite vintage; then plunge right in and devour the lot or save each for special enjoyment, as you will! Either way, as Whitbourn is wont to say: I wish you joy—and I do not think you need fear finding it. Prepare also, however, to meet other and far worse fears...

Meanwhile, in the inspiring words of my family motto, in both of my native tongues (Latin and Welsh):

Fundi Elevare! / Penol Fyny![7]

Professor E. J. Griffiths.
Prestwood, Buckinghamshire.
13th December 2019.

---

[7] Bottoms up!

ALTERED ENGLANDS

JOHN WHITBOURN

THE *'MODERN'* or *'ALLAH'* SERIES

'Islam is in fact the last refuge for those conservative Western intellectuals who wish it were true that the Renaissance, the Enlightenment, the Industrial Revolution, the French Revolution, in short 'the modern world', had never come about. Islam is, indeed, the only remaining mental space in which these events have not yet happened.'

Ibn al Rawandi.[8]

INTRODUCTION:

The above sounds like criticism until you survey the landscape that those juggernauts Mr al-Rawandi mentions have trundled over. A refuge is not necessarily always a bad thing. Indeed, in some circumstances it can be the sensible option. For instance, who sneers at 'refuges' when bombs are dropping?

Once, a senior civil servant confided to me that in his far from humble opinion what Islam needed was its own Reformation. There was the strong temptation to grip his lapels and shout at him—*'What? Are you mad? Look what ours did to us! It stranded us in a spiritual desert! Left us stripped as helpless prey to amoral Capitalism!'*

Of course, I said no such thing. It's not the done thing. And even if

---

[8] A modern writer sheltering under a nom de plume borrowed from a noted Islamic heretic of the 9th Century. Formerly a Sufi, he has now seen another light and is the author of such persuasive secularist works as *'The Quest for the Historical Muhammed'* and *'Islamic Mysticism—a Secular Perspective'*, both published 2000.

that was what I *actually* thought (which it *wasn't*, naturally) he would never have known. As I recall, I said *'Really?'*—which is a truly wonderful English word with about thirty different meanings depending on tone. You have to be a native to pick up on more than three or four...

And to think some people say the English are duplicitous...

We're not really (that word again).. It's just a survival mechanism. You see, according to no less an authority than a former UK Home Secretary,[9] the English are an intrinsically violent bunch—and who am we to bandy words with such a respected statesman? If his exciting theory is correct, the English have narrowly avoided murdering each other in their overcrowded island home by:

ITEM: Being aggressive to the Scots.
ITEM: Exporting their homicidal urges to make an Empire.

and, my own personal addition to the thesis:

ITEM: Restricting conversation to uncontentious subjects.

I have to admit it all fits the facts. It explains the Battle of Flodden and all the other Scottish defeats (though strangely enough many were fought on *English* soil...), it offers a motivation other than lucre for the British Empire, and it certainly covers our reputation for always talking about the weather.

Yet there's method in our alleged madness. Think about it—if you start an acquaintance with *'Hello, nice day, isn't it?'* it takes a particularly perverse person to reply *'No it bloody isn't! Yesterday was way better. D'you want make something of it mate?'*

Mind you, I have met people like that. Then you know you're in a free-fire zone.

In the words of John Le Carre's great creation, the spymaster George Smiley, Englishmen are:

'... the greatest dissembler on earth... Was, is now, and ever shall be... nobody will charm you so glibly, disguise his feelings from you better, cover his tracks more skilfully or find it harder to confess to you that he's been a damned fool. Nobody acts braver when he's

---

[9] Jack Straw. Who wouldn't lie to us.

frightened stiff, or happier when he's miserable; nobody can flatter you better when he hates you... He can have a force twelve nervous breakdown while he stands next to you in the bus queue, and you may be his best friend, but you'll never be the wiser.'[10]

Again, I think it's meant as criticism, but must confess my own breast swelled with pride. I'm amazed that after all that's happened to us, and so much ruling class disparagement, that we remain such a talented people...

There's a stark school of thought that we come into this world alone, die likewise and the intervening period is broadly similar. If so—though *I* certainly don't think so—then there's something to be said for facing the facts and living accordingly. Be self-sufficient, hear all, say little and show nothing. Again, not that *I* think in that stark and terrible way, naturally, but figures as prominent and widely spaced apart as the ancient Greek philosopher Diogenes and Sherlock Holmes' brighter brother, Mycroft, seem to have come to such conclusions...

Moslems and other monotheists think differently. Their personal universe is predicated upon a beneficent Creator who cares about each aspect of that creation, right down the pecking order, so Scripture assures us, as far as common sparrows, and even mere individual sparks of humanity.[11]

Hmmm. Such a view does at least take the chill off the Universe. And in contrast to the thoroughgoing materialist standpoint that ultimately *nothing* is important, it posits the mixed comfort and concern that very *few* things are important—but those few things are *very* important.

Who knows? Well, as our Muslim brothers maintain: *'God alone knows the truth of it...'.* In time, we shall, each and every one of us, see.

If it's any guidance, as Professor Griffiths perceptively notes in his forward to this book, throughout the Binscombe Tales Mr Disvan is often spotted dipping into the Holy Quran, albeit in the less than suitable surrounds of the *Duke of Argyll* pub. All I can say is that as an unbiased onlooker to the events those tales described, Mr Disvan always struck me as a sensible sort of fellow...

Three of the four following stories have been collectively dubbed (by others) as the *'Islamic series'* or *'Allah series'*. I quite can see why, if only because

---

[10] *'The Secret Pilgrim'.* 1990.
[11] Luke 12. 7. *'Ye are of more value than many sparrows'.* Which is good of G-d when you consider our relative merits.

of the linked titles, but I have another private name for them, which it is best not to name here for fear of giving the game away. Suffice to say, it has something to do with that much misunderstood man, Mr Kurtz...

However, as a small recompense for forgoing that correct naming, I respectfully request that a fourth story be accepted into the series as its author always intended. *'Excuse Me...'* is far from Islamic in location and theme but springs, I promise you, from the same well. I ask that you welcome it into your hearts and homes in the company of the others without discrimination. They may look and sound different but share similar DNA.

And if this be granted, in that same liberal and tolerant spirit kindly embark with these intrepid Islamic explorers in their fragile craft, as they travel up the winding river into the Heart of Darkness formerly known as Christendom.[12]

Bon voyage. See you on the other side.

---

[12] A word regarding the setting of the second story, *'In The Name Of Allah, The Compassionate?'*. Lest I be thought insensitive in basing my tale around an actual place and awful event, I take this opportunity to say that it arose from reports of just such physic disturbances in the relevant locality. Likewise with *'In The Name Of Allah, The Omnipotent?'*, which follows directly. Under pressure from its staff the Tunisian Embassy made formal application to leave their Malaya Nikitskaya Street, Moscow, accommodation. The cellars there were subsequently sealed.

3~

IN THE NAME OF ALLAH, THE OMNIPOTENT?

'I saw the vulture face of Beria,
Half hidden by a muffler,
Glued to the window of his limousine
As he drove slowly by the kerb hunting down
a woman for the night.'

Yevgeny Yevtushenko (1933-2017). Soviet poet.

She was in lustrous fur, against the Russian autumn and against the old ways. The girl carried six months workingmen's wages on her swaying back. Its thick silver armoured her. She didn't see the old *babushkas* selling their last possessions on the street, the state workers all threadbare and stoic. They were invisible. All sunglasses and bare legs she was a different breed altogether. No trolley bus or metro for Moscow's new rich, oh no. A black foreign car would be round to pick her up.

Muadh ben Moussa saw her every day. He tried to avert his eyes but it was very hard. Satan sprinkled allure over his chosen *houris*. Even the pious on their death bed could be distracted by the gleam of flesh. And Moussa was weak and tired: his day was already old when this Mafia moll quit one bed to go to another. He asked the Almighty for control over his eyes, and the feet that always seemed bring him to this window at this time. God blessed him with the strength to scamper away down the long corridor.

It was puzzling. There were parts of the Embassy that made him prone to lustful thoughts: not just the typists' pool but also empty rooms and ordinary windows. Perhaps *Jinn* lived in them, ebbing out wickedness over the decades till it oozed from the very bricks and mortar. In future he resolved to avoid them as best may be. It would be difficult but he would try. Ben Moussa knew he could not confide his fears to the other Embassy staff: he was already the butt of laughter for his old-fashionedness. They rarely prayed or kept a fast. Only old women and *fundamentalists* were observant, they told him: which was he?

Moussa never answered: he was not clever enough; not like the smart boys and girls who did the real work here and who'd go on to great things. Ben Moussa made the tea and filed letters and was grateful for the glamorous job luck had gained him. Five times a day he thanked both the Almighty and Madame Afra Salimah for all his good fortune. The Ambassador's wife had taken pity on him and his dying shop in Tunis. Her kind eyes saw he was marching fast into poverty: a clumsy dreamer at life's mercy. She rarely prayed either but ben Moussa was determined she should pass the gates of Paradise. He prayed her prayers *for* her, an extra fifteen minutes each time he could.

One thing he did know was that he must not be a *fundamentalist*. They belonged in Algeria and Libya, Tunisia's unhappy neighbours. They were a threat to... well, everything apparently. They carried bombs and did not have the love of Allah before their eyes. The Government imprisoned them and worse. No one really suspected poor ben Moussa, for all that they teased him, but he kept his attempts at holiness to himself. He prayed in cellars and cupboards.

Like this one, for instance—or rather he used to pray here—for this was another place of bad feelings. Yet more evil *Jinn* probably. Its temper fits explained the wounds on the walls most likely: great rough gouges at regular intervals all round. The others joked that there'd been chains, proper slave-manacles, embedded there when the Tunisians moved in. Naturally, being a civilised people, they'd ripped them straight out. Ben Moussa didn't know which version he preferred to believe: neither gave birth to happy thoughts. He just wished his packets of tea and coffee could be kept elsewhere, but when he'd asked they'd not understood and he hadn't the right words. The girls in the encrypting room had giggled at him. They only stopped, ashamed, on seeing the tears well up in his eyes.

He would not ask again but would be *strong*. His father, peace be upon him, had always urged him to be that—and then would sigh.

There was a reception this afternoon; representatives from the Kyrgyzstan and Tajikistan and Turkmenistan embassies were calling. Newly liberated and all Moslems together, the Central Asians would be celebratory and open-hearted, amenable to influence away from the *fundamentalists*. Nothing must go wrong, that had been impressed upon him. His role was to ensure that the coffee was perfect and free flowing, proper Arab style. If a cup lingered empty or grew too full of dregs the Ambassador would frown at him and that made ben Moussa cringe.

Then the Devil sent him a thought of the Russian houri, just when he was counting his coffee pots. He fought it and so she became Madame Afra Salimah, only younger and naked and disporting herself, inviting him between spread legs. Worst of all was his urge to surrender. It was almost stronger than he. Ben Moussa screwed up his eyes, cursing the disloyal vision. This was not him; he was a romantic; he wished to go home one day and marry a village girl and be kind to her. What would she, the girl he didn't yet know, think on learning he carried such thoughts, secret in his head? These torments had not troubled him before: it was a new problem, sent by Allah in His all-wisdom to test him.

'*O Allah, I seek protection in You from filth and impurity!*'

He slapped down his improper arousal, glad and deserving of the pain.

'I seek refuge in Allah against the accursed Satan!'

For a second more it continued, another presence in the room thrashed around, striking terror from the walls. It was angry.

Ben Moussa gathered up his supplies and fled, not shutting the door. The room's scent of fear and lust admixed pursued him—but he now knew it was not his alone.

✵

'Tea!'

The *Rus* Mafia and 'businessmen' in the queue for holiday visas smirked at Ben Moussa. These new-style rich *Franks* didn't like being kept waiting by brown-skinned races. They welcomed his scurrying arrival with the tray of cups. It re-established the proper order of things.

'My guts think my throat's been slit,' said the visa clerk, mock stern and snatching the drink without thanks. 'I called ages ago. Where have you been, ben Moussa? Playing with yourself?'

He wished they would not talk like that, not in front of women, not in front of all the *Ivans* and *Tanyas*. It made him blush.

'You are a very rude man, Aziz Mohammed.' He spoke softly from under averted eyes. 'I do my best.'

That only made them roar with laughter: a sheep had growled at them.

"The tea, I grant you,' chuckled the smooth youth, 'isn't bad: usually. As to your other habits I can't say. Off you go, father, go and practise whatever it is you do when people aren't watching you.'

He left them the tray; unable to face their company any more. It put acid in his stomach, tormenting a digestion already ruined by Russia's rations. The tea-things could be fetched later when they'd all finished for the morning. He could have rare confidence that nothing would be returned to his kitchen. No one lifted a hand to shorten his long days.

Escape lay through the *Ivans*: all a head taller than him, even the women. They were not the few, grey, bad-suited ones of years ago: the only old-style Russians who came in now were those who swept up and shyly asked for food. Ben Moussa pitied those, both for their plight and disbelief: he gave to them from his own rations. This lot, by contrast, had nothing to ask of him. They were the scum risen to the top of a new-poured bath: *disc-jockeys* and *directors* and their bedfellows, male and female, desirous of spending big money in the warm. Ben Moussa's country would do: it had no *fundamentalists*. They looked down on him as he threaded a way through.

Though he tried not to see, he was still a man. If his downcast eyes encountered beauty it was a struggle not to raise them. He was used to the *Tanyas*' lack of modesty and even sympathised, knowing harsh necessity drove them to spray-on clothes and skirts like belts—but this one drew a gasp. Her legs went on for ever: no dress arrived. She was naked!

Ben Moussa's hand flew to his face. He had *looked*—more than he ought—and asked forgiveness for it. He expected uproar and the problem dragged from his hands—but nothing came. Even in these degraded days surely nudity aroused some response, some shame? Could no one else but he see her?

His question to himself, suddenly understood, froze him. Allah's animating breath faltered. Ben Moussa spread his concealing fingers.

She was still there. No one else *could* see her. She was naked and all... disappointment.

The young girl looked at ben Moussa, her long yellow hair following her head with bewitching pause. She could see him. He howled distress. The *Ivans* stared.

She was beauty itself but he ignored it through compassion. It had bought her no joy. For a moment she had beseeched him—but it was fleeting. She did not hate ben Moussa but she was disappointed—with him or life or the return on beauty he could not tell.

Pity replaced fear and ben Moussa made it welcome: the one came from God, the other was man's creation. He gathered strength to speak.

She would not have it and walked away. Her stride was firm, resolved, but not of her own choice. She walked under compulsion.

Ben Moussa watched and understood. The girl was headed for the cellar, the worst of cellars. The locked door did not delay her.

He wanted to help but *there* he would not follow, not even if Allah Himself commanded.

※

'... *one night at Kuntsevo, when Stalin and Beria were very drunk, particularly Beria, he suddenly turned to Stalin and said in Georgian:* 'You know, Master,'—*he never called him Comrade Stalin, always* 'Master'—'*You know, Master, there is only one thing wrong with the Soviet Union.*' *And when Stalin asked what that was, Beria replied:* 'That a man like me can reach the position I have!'

Stalin laughed all night—he thought it a tremendous joke.'
Alan Williams. *'The Beria Papers'*. 1973.

※

It took two days but in the end ben Moussa obeyed his Lord. Allah commanded kindness and the poor girl, even though beyond the veil of this earthly life, required his help. He could not withhold it and remain Muadh ben

ALTERED ENGLANDS

Moussa. The village girl awaiting him, all unknowing, in Tunisia would expect it—otherwise he would not be worthy of her love

He prayed for restored control over his insides and divine scaffolding for his courage. Then he descended to the cellar.

Even the clever boys and girls in the Embassy half-joked that it was haunted. Ben Moussa noticed they never went down there themselves, instead commanding some *Ivan* lackey or himself to go on rare errands for an old file. There were festering piles of them dumped there: closed cases and abandoned projects from Allah knew when: damp hillocks illuminated by naked bulbs. Early on in his Moscow days ben Moussa had thought his prayers would protect him and ventured those stairs without doubt. He'd planned to put some order in the *'archive'*, boxing the stuff up in case it should ever be needed again. Occasionally word did come from Tunis, saying a Soviet was of interest and asking what did he write on his visa application? Ben Moussa wanted to discourage people just chucking files down there from the top of stairs. It was a bind having to mine through a random avalanche of paper.

Once *down there*, he'd had more sympathy with their laziness. The place ate away at you; it was an icy abode of *Shaitan*. Ben Moussa did not think it was just the Russian winter that made it its home. His thoughts were never more indecent, never less sure of Allah's essential benevolence, than *down there*. He always took a bath, work permitting, as soon as he emerged. Yet for hours or days some taint still clung on, lowering his spirit. It could not be lingering, invisible, cobwebs for he'd noticed that even spiders shunned the place. Ben Moussa worried that part of the cellar came back up the stairs with you.

Now he would return it; shedding the stain along with the sin of cowardice. Ben Moussa had thought to pass through life without entering battle but Allah had decreed otherwise. He would therefore play his part like a man.

The lights worked, a sickly dawn reaching the furthest corners of the void. His earlier efforts, the narrow green boxes, were stacked man-high into shapes, like house walls or barricades, harbouring rock-pools of shadow. Against them washed foothills of unsorted files, pale hummocks of paper; poultices absorbing the damp of the floor.

Ben Moussa cursed and admonished the bad that was there and sang sweet words to whatever it imprisoned.

'O Allah, I seek refuge in You from male and female devils. Do not despair, this is a cleansing from sins, if Allah wills.'

The boards creaked under his careful tread. He recollected each wooden protest. Few ventured here but he and this was his signature. Whatever lived here would recognise the song of the stairs and know it was ben Moussa.

'Allah suffices us and He is the best Guardian.'

He reached the bottom. Cold communicated itself through the thin soles of his shoes. That chill was constant, year-long.

The cellar was rank with decay, from icy floor to grimy roof vault. All the paper abandoned there, once briefly important, now less than nothing, offered up the scent of its pulpy origins into the air. It was not hard to visualise fallen trees, dismembered on the forest floor.

'Miss? I am here. Please show yourself.'

She did not. He pondered the torment that must be her flesh in this eternal winter. She must have become a creature of ice.

'Miss? It is I, ben Moussa. You sought my aid. I am here.'

There was no sign: no peak or trough in the place's malignity.

'Move on. Seek the light of Allah that calls you. Do not linger in this terrib-...'

Ben Moussa could not be sure. His hearing was not so good: his father had loved to box him round the ears till they rang. Yet was that an intake of breath, hope given voice—or a snarl?

It came from the direction of the highest piled boxes. He remembered standing on tiptoe to stack them.

'Move on. The afflicted, the crushed, have nothing to fear from Allah...'

That came from the heart: as a child he'd lulled himself to sleep with it. School for a skinny, tearful, poor-boy had been a trial.

Again that sound. Ben Moussa felt surer of its source.

'I am here. I mean you well.'

He surprised himself. Unhesitating steps took him to a three-sided redoubt of boxes. He laid hands on the nearest stack.

'I am not afraid. You will be rescued. I will tell you the truth to your face.'

She had been a *Rus,* a *Frank*, he felt sure: the blue eyes and straw hair proclaimed it. In life she had most likely never heard the facts of Allah and His benevolence. That lack—and some tragedy—had trapped her in the merely material world. She simply didn't know there was a better place awaiting her. He could tell her.

Ben Moussa lost patience. He struck the remaining clammy boxes away with his arm. A window was cleared.

She was not there—though her sob was. Ben Moussa heard it distinctly, coming from the damp, empty air. He had not expected this. How could one comfort the invisible? The enclosed dark space held nothing but her unhappiness.

Ben Moussa swallowed hard—and leant in.

'My child,' he beseeched her, 'speak to me or I cannot help.'

And she was there; suddenly, overwhelmingly so. She was *too* close, thinking that the only thing a man might want from her. She was both delectable and waxy-cold.

Ben Moussa staggered back, freeing his face and hands from temptation.

'No,' he told her, unable to keep horror from his voice, 'you do not understand!'

Nor did she. She *thought* she had but no longer. He'd puzzled her. She looked on him with widened, troubled eyes. She was worried that she'd done wrong.

The girl was naked and marked: grievously marked. It was *she* who had been wronged; ben Moussa now saw that.

'I am here to-...'

Another sound came from behind her, from the darkness cast between two box walls. It was a beast's snort, a porcine sound rough-fashioned into words from far away.

She turned her head to it. Now she really feared.

'Seek the peace of Allah, I beg you. Look for the smiling face of-...'

Her face was not smiling. She looked on ben Moussa with hate. She hissed and spat at his help.

Ben Moussa recoiled before such innocence transformed. His prayers on her behalf dried and died upon the lip. She did not want them.

Then some unseen hand slapped her back into the grave. She fell back, stiffly, like a lever, to lay in a shallow scooped trough below the floor. For a second ben Moussa could see both it and her and the earth and stone above till, through God's mercy, the image faded. Then there was just flat, slimy paving— but ben Moussa knew what lay beneath.

The beast-roar spoke again. It was still remote but coming closer: a vast distance travelled at speed. He thought he heard his name, all mangled in mockery. Before it could arrive he left—but the cold of the cellar went with him.

❈

'When Stalin's secret police chief, Lavrenti Beria, spotted a girl he liked, refusing his desires was not a very sensible thing to do. He liked to send bunches of flowers to his fancies. One beauty unwisely turned down his advances but thanked him for the bouquet. Beria's answer was 'It's not a bouquet. It's a wreath.' So it turned out to be.'

Simon Sebag Montefiore. *'Times'* review of *'Beria: Stalin's First Lieutenant'* by Amy Knight.

❈

He ambushed her. She traversed *Malaya Nikitskaya* street past the Embassy every day, twitching her birch brush over the gutter, doing little good but no harm either. She was old—*she* would know. The younger *Rus* didn't *want* to know: their own past; their history, was just blood and poverty: a burden to be shrugged off.

Also, she was a *good* woman: mistaken but good. Time and time again she'd leave off her road-sweeping to cross herself: especially outside the Embassy.

'Take and eat, mother. May Allah bless you.'

She'd shrieked when he'd offered her the warm rolls. In modern Russia old *babushkas* were not used to being addressed. She'd assumed this *Moor* meant her ill.

For his part, ben Moussa had not been mistaken. The old girl held his gaze and perceived he was no harm to anyone. Likewise, her clear blue eyes went clear down into her soul. She was mere months away from streaking straight to Paradise.

'And may Christ smile on you, *saracen*'

She was famished, that was plain: the state pension was a couple of packs of cigarettes nowadays, but still she paused, giving mumbled thanks to God before biting.

'I need something, mother.'

For just a second she doubted him afresh. Cold commerce was the only expected transaction between humans in the Motherland she found herself in in old age.

'I have nothing, *saracen*. This brush, an empty state flat, these few clothes...'

'And memories.'

Her faith in him rose again.

'Ah *those*; in those I am a rich woman.'

'Spare me a mere rouble or two of them, that is all I wish. I am in the cause of Allah: there are things I must know of this place.

He reversed his thumb to indicate the Embassy behind him. The *babushkas'* eyes would not follow.

'You select bitter fruit from my stall, *saracen*. Almost everything else is better than that.'

'I do not choose the meal set before me—but God commands me to eat.'

She nodded understanding. Doubtless she'd dined on some fetid meals herself: a child of the revolution and then the famine and influenza scourge; a girl of the purges and the *Great Patriotic War*, and then marriage and babies and queuing and more purges—the only thanks the workers got for heroic survival.

'Beria lived there,' she told him—and spat into the dust she must soon sweep away. 'In there he ate green fruit.'

❀

'Beria was also a rather short man... He too was somewhat plump, greenish, and pale, and with soft damp hands. With his square-cut mouth and bulging eyes behind his pince-nez, he suddenly reminded me of Vujkovic, one of the chiefs of the Belgrade Royal Police who specialised in torturing Communists... a certain self-satisfaction and irony mingled with a clerk's obsequiousness and solicitude.'

Milovan Djilas. *'Conversations with Stalin'*. 1962.

JOHN WHITBOURN

'It was already my opinion that Beria might divert the progress of the country from a Socialist to a capitalist course... He was very skilful at anything that was filthy and treacherous... Later we were given a list of more than a hundred girls and women who had been raped by Beria... interrogating Beria, we found ourselves faced with a really awful man, a beast to whom nothing was sacred... Not only was there nothing Communist about him—he was without the slightest trace of human decency.'

Nikita Khrushchev. *'Memoirs'.* 1970.

'He particularly liked very young girls—between twelve and fourteen. His entourage used to call them 'green fruit'...

Alan Williams. *'The Beria Papers'.* 1973.

☸

Times were really changing in Russia if you could buy this sort of book, quite openly, from a metro stall. This 'Count Tolstoy'—an Englishman with a *Rus* name!—didn't spare you anything. *'Stalin's Secret War'*: here was all the dirt you could stomach and more. Ben Moussa had sipped gingerly at it, a few pages at a time. He knew some of the dreadful stories would never leave him.

His English was not good. He had tried hard to learn but Allah chose not to give him a nimble mind. Still, what he had sufficed: he could pick out the main words enough to understand. If anything, ben Moussa wished Allah has blessed him less: sometimes there was joy in understanding nothing.

Often he thought the girl—or girls—read with him, looking over his stooped shoulders into the lamp's pool of light. That, even more than the contents, would explain the chill generated. Yet when he turned to look there was no one there: just half-heard giggles from the dark. Ben Moussa suspected they—or someone—were playing with him. He kept his mind and fingertip on the current page.

Beria moderated the great purges but, newly head of the secret police, did not twist the taps to stop the flow of blood. He'd stood there for twenty more years, watching it pour. His hand had not moved, his lips only smiled. The mass deportations, the labour camps, the great GULAG, fifteen million strong, were his. The 10,000 Poles forever in Katyn Wood were his, and so was Stalin's atom bomb.

He had been a busy man and at the end of the day he liked to relax at home—in his own way.

They'd shot him—and bin Moussa was glad, urging the bullet on into his head—when he lost the post-Stalin struggle. One version had him killed, taken by surprise, at a Kremlin Politburo meeting. His body was kept in a inner sanctum for days till it began to stink and then they smuggled him out in a crate.

He'd had a guard, 200 Georgians back at his country *dacha,* who worshipped him like a tribal chief, like the old style Berber warriors back home. They'd died to a man, irreconcilable, shelled to pieces in a proper battle. The worst could sometimes beguile the best.

Beria loved music: had the finest record collection in Russia. Music by someone called Rachmaninov moved him to tears with its beauty...

Ben Moussa put the book in the bin; it had served its purpose but he did not wish to be troubled by it again. It contained information but no solution.

There was another book that would really serve, the best book in the world or anywhere else: a book that cost nothing but submission and carried wisdom, not horror, in its pages.

Forewarned, forearmed, to the best of man's poor abilities, he went to fetch it.

☸

The cellar looked pregnant like a sow; slight but obscene bulges in the floor—noticed but not understood before—now screamed out at him. The heavy air *down there* felt equally expectant.

For once the stairs did not proclaim his arrival. Their wood was too saturated with damp. Instead of their usual tune there was the faint crunch of murdered ice-crystals.

Ben Moussa bore the *Book* before him. He had faith and, now, hope. The terrible frigidity seemed to retreat, abate, before the Holy *Qur'an.*

There was no need to open its stiff cover; ben Moussa knew the comfort therein by heart.

JOHN WHITBOURN

> *"In the name of Allah, the Beneficent, the Merciful.*
> *Praise be to Allah, Lord of the Worlds,*
> *the Beneficent, the Merciful.*
> *Owner of the Day of Judgement..."*

'*Al-Fâtihah*', 'The Opening', the essence of the Qur'an, smoked him out, like vermin from its hide, straightaway. Beria raised his victims at the same time, to divert, but ben Moussa would not be distracted.

He ignored the poor girls, sat up like tombstones in their graves. The Monster had amplified their beauty and glossed over the tokens of death. Their nakedness, the unnatural allure, reached his loins but not his head. Ben Moussa advanced on the half-seen figure lounging in the shadows.

Beria was cool and smoking. His *pince-nez* reflected the electric light so that he had no eyes. The lens were focused on ben Moussa. What they saw only made him smile.

Ben Moussa brandished God's word. He noticed, from the corner of his eye, hope lighten the faces of the slaughtered. He pushed the book at Beria.

'Here is power!' His teeth were chattering, he wished to urinate, but the words emerged clear. 'Here is truth! Go to the judgement told within!'

Beria's voice was amused; ironic. It came from a faraway place.

'No.'

Ben Moussa would compromise: he did not care when precisely this abomination went to eternal fire.

'Release those you have offended from the terror of your servitude.'

'Sorry, no.'

The women's faces fell. Ben Moussa saw their second death.

'Take your sick spirit from these walls, haunt here no more!'

There were others with Beria now, he had support. Grey forms in uniform clustered respectfully round him. His retinue had lingered in loyalty.

'Again no. This is my house. You came later.'

Then suddenly he was controlled no more. It had been a mere facade. The cigarette fell. Spittle flew everywhere. It scalded. His words came in gouts and torrents, a spluttering foul tirade. He had been mad before he died.

'There's a telephone in Stalin's coffin. He rings me. I pass on orders to Kim Il Sung, and Fidel, and Saddam! Can't have Russia? No? I'll have here. A little kingdom. I'm the Tsar: Tsar Lavrenti of *Malaya Nikitskaya!* War! Fucking War! Warhead! *Warhead!*'

Beria advanced a step further into the light. Ben Moussa countermanded his feet's wishes. From somewhere there was piano music—calm and soothing—but mixed with screams.

'Red Army out of Berlin and Poland, that's what I'll do. Kiss and make up with Tito. Collective farms are crap! I'll *liquidate* them—they're gone! Let the peasants blossom. Yes! The West will love me: let me be. Russia will prosper and in the evenings we'll eat *green fruit!*'

He beckoned over one of the slain. It was the girl who'd made herself known to ben Moussa, the one who'd silently sought his help. Beria bent her over, splayed her legs and then ploughed away, treadling her like a farm animal. Her eyes would not leave ben Moussa and were all the sadness there had ever been.

The dead mass-murderer noted the little clerk's distress. His grin was like a rictus

'What's the matter with you?' he laughed, still pointlessly thrusting. 'Are you some sort of *Communist?*'

Ben Moussa had no words: they had not been invented. He still held out the *Book*.

Beria sneered.

'Sort him, boys.'

And as the grey shapes advanced he threw back his prick-shaped head and screamed: it was the stockpiled evil and anger in him and it went louder and higher than ben Moussa could believe. It was able to fill every corner of heaven and earth.

There remained only protest:

'In the name of Allah, the Omnipotent! I command you...'

The nearest shape grew a face, a flat, thoughtless, peasant-soldier's face. A plate-like hand it already had. It used it to strike the *Book* from ben Moussa's grasp.

The most precious thing in ben Moussa's life went tumbling to the defiled floor.

In tears and terror he turned to the stairs, abandoning it.

The view seemed infinite, a red haze stretching away without end. From here there was almost nothing—a few salt pans, a few rocks—between ben Moussa and the deep Sahara. That appealed to him.

The little town lay behind: the next lights were in Timbuktu. Tourists came here, to the very edge of things, to gawp and then go back. Ben Moussa had stayed. Here he could await the dark. Here he could contemplate the void.

In the evening, after work and prayers, ben Moussa generally sat out on the restaurant's flat roof. There was shade and some old white plastic chairs. No one bothered him, knowing he was a man of few words and deep thoughts. He was honest and worked hard for a pittance: that was all the owner asked of his waiters.

His wanderings had stopped here: to go further required a caravan or a jeep and Ben Moussa had neither: he was alone. There had never been that little village girl. It had seemed unkind to inflict himself upon her or anyone. He had lived alone. A short walk away lay the graveyard and its tumbled pottery markers where he would rest alone.

Now he was old he had mostly forgiven fate. Brick by brick, he had rebuilt some peace. Evenings like this were when he constructed another course or checked, for the thousandth time, the foundations. He still believed. Out here, in the arid emptiness of the desert fringe, it was easier to believe. Accordingly, he could never leave.

Ben Moussa's thoughts were lost amongst a ravine of shadow in a large clefted rock: some stray offspring of the high Atlas mountains to the north. It was dark in there: the waning sun could not bless it with light. Maybe only at noon...

'In the name of Allah, the Omnipotent....'

Ben Moussa still believed: he believed that Allah was omnipotent. But he'd learnt that God tolerated zones of shadow.

4~

IN THE NAME OF ALLAH, THE COMPASSIONATE?

❇

A typical day. Regulated by prayer and poisoned with duties.

At noon, it being a Friday, I accompanied the Prince to the mosque, escorting him to the front of the faithful. My deputies ensure none of them murder my master whilst I pray alongside him.

I sometimes wonder what His Highness thinks of when he pretends to address the Almighty. Or conceivably he is genuine and craves forgiveness. It does not matter. Either way Allah will not hear him. That much I am still sure of.

As for me, I go through the motions, I bow and kneel and my lips move but words will not come. The remnants of my integrity.

Of course, having met one ghost back in Sarajevo, I now see them everywhere. What a gift! What a prize! What favours the Power-in-charge pour upon me!

They infest the city streets and skyscraper stairwells. For instance, a hanged man accompanied the Prince. The fresh work of his *Mukhabarat* 'police' I presume; some blameless democrat in all probability. Even our speeding Cadillac could not shake him off.

Slack jawed, broken necked, he stood before my Master all through prayers, eyes bulging. Yet he did not take part himself. The dead do not pray, I observe. Which is instructive.

But I am past shocking. My indifference knows no bounds. Let the restless dead stand and silently accuse. Just so long as they are silent.

Meanwhile, behind us stretches a sea of living bowed backs—thousands of freshly laundered Friday-best *thawbs*. I snatch glances. The sight always fascinates since it has the semblance of cleanliness. Spotless garments masking corruption.

Soon enough the attitudes of prayer spoil that beauty. They arise and I see that it is not beautiful after all, but only an illusion, like all beauty. I see that they are *people*.

Nevertheless, whilst it lasts, I seize that sight. There are few enough refreshments to the eye in this wasteland of sand and concrete and refuse. Even the fortune my prince poured into the mosque could not command comeliness. It is vast, even magnificent, but not pleasing. The architects did not have the love of Allah in their hearts when they planned. The structure is their arrogance made manifest. Its dome punches rather than reveres the sky. Inside is only *shiny-shiny* splendour of the sort which beguiles children or savages.

Outside is worse. In the brief interlude between air-conditioned mosque and air-conditioned infidel limousine, the eyes are assailed by wind blown newspaper and fast food wrappers. Above, concrete canyons march in confident advance to their present front line with the desert. You do not need to be a prophet to see which side is winning. The tower blocks' inhabitants soil the desert fringe with nappies and rubbish.

I travel with the Prince. I am foremost amongst his protectors against his own people and those who rage with pretended zeal for Allah. I am permitted a gun in his presence. He bought me the best, an Uzi (irony of ironies, forbidden *haram* of haram) that hangs perfectly beneath my specially tailored jacket. The Prince says that Jew guns shoot straight and therefore Allah will forgive him.

I sleep with it beside me and desire to sleep with no other.

A typical day, as I said, and typical duties. In the afternoon I dealt with the aftermath of my Prince's post-prayer fun. The Filipina maid was shocked and bruised. She asked for a priest—which made me laugh. How long had she been in the Kingdom?

Instead I offered her *šljivovica*, fiery Bosnian plum brandy, from my own personal store. More *haram* I know, but it is all I have left to remind me of home—and to blot it out.

ALTERED ENGLANDS

You're wondering: *'But surely this is Saudi?'* Listen and learn. The *Mutaween* religious police sell it to me. They in turn get it off the Border Guard who confiscate it off—oh, but does the precise chain of sordidness matter? It is available, like everything.

'Here,' I said, 'drink this and forget your sorrows.'

I could have added: *'Drink the whole bottle; be blessed with understanding nothing.'*

But she refused the plastic cup and wept bitterly, huddled like a broken thing, clutching her violation with both hands.

The Prince is not a gentle man even with his wives, and the *'no'* of a maid from the *Dar al-Harb*, the heathen House of War, is as nothing. If they do not part their legs at his whim he orders them prised apart. Screams often echo through the palace and no one pays heed.

The position of her hands, plunged between her thighs, suddenly struck me as obscene parody of Christian prayer. I witnessed it back in Sarajevo. An old man and a young girl were kneeling beside a roadside shrine in Proletarian Brigade Boulevard (or *Sniper Alley* as it was renamed). Seconds later such a sniper saw them. I think only the girl died but it is hard to recall. There were so many deaths, they all run into one.

The Filipina was still sobbing. What did she want of me? Could I return her innocence or hymen? In no way. No more than I could... give her a new face if the old one was blown off.

I looked inside myself for sympathy—both for her and for me—but found none. That particular storehouse is swept clear. Instead I offered her the Prince's money to soothe her bruises and shame. And the address of a discreet doctor. He was used to timid knocks on his door.

Do I feel ashamed? Do I feel guilty? In no way!

I am become as compassionate as Allah who put both me and the Filipina in this position, who puts all men in this predicament.

The day passed. Evening came and with it our final prayers before sleep.

Sleep! If only! Sleep flees from me. My television with its hundreds of satellite channel remains silent, the books I brought from home and the Qur'an they gave me here are equally dusty. Thanks to that constant companion, air-conditioning, there is not even the cold of desert night to drive you to bed.

So tonight I shall close my eyes in drunken stupor, thanks to the brandy the maid spurned—foolish child. It will be the same when, some night hence, Allah finally gathers me to Him. My last sight shall be this scene of concrete and desert, not the green of my homeland.

Which is for the best. And in keeping. The new view matches my soul.

It was not always so. Not so long ago.

Saudi was some way off: those days when I could say my prayers but didn't. In Sarajevo I was willing but unable.

The instruction leaflet wouldn't stay open. I had to keep interrupting my prayers to fold back the right page.

It acted like the Wahhabi missionaries who gave it to me. They were fervent and generous (to their own) but deficient in detail. The pamphlet was so stapled that the thick creamy paper strained to close. I was getting confused. Were you meant to kneel and look left and right *before* the second *rakat* or after?

Eventually I went to find books to weigh down the corners but all I could find were trashy paperbacks which didn't seem appropriate. Some of the covers were indecent. There was my new Qur'an, from the same source as the leaflet, but placing that on the floor would be just as wrong.

My eyes felt red. I wasn't used to dawn prayers—or any prayers—or regular anything. What I really wanted, speaking as a man, was either coffee—good traditional unfiltered Bosnian coffee—or, better yet, bed. Neither, as I understood it, were permitted.

Humans find excuses and rush to delude themselves. Whilst searching my flat for paperweights I 'chanced' to see the clock. I was late. My amateur attempts at... *Salat-ul-Fajir* (and I had to consult the pamphlet even for the name) morning prayers had stretched the suggested twenty minutes into thirty and still I wasn't finished.

But I'd shown willing. I'd tried my best and was hopeful that the prayers of my heart would be acceptable to Allah, even if the motions of my limbs were deficient.

'*Pavlic,*' I told myself, '*leave what is God's to God and go and do what you are good at.*'

So I strapped on my gun and went out to be a policeman.

ALTERED ENGLANDS

❈

The *PAZIR SNAJPER*, *'Beware Snipers'*, signs were still up but becoming faded. That was good to see. There was a school of thought that wanted them left up, preserved even, so that Bosnians—and the whole world—would remember.

They were a minority. Most people don't have an eye for history. Their eyes see the signs and their spines chill. Still.

I felt guilt and haste. Two things my religion were meant to save me from. Incompetent devotions had frazzled not calmed my start of day and I barely made it to the barracks for parade. There was no question of slipping off for a *šljivovica* 'sharpener' and smoke first, like we would have during the fighting. Now, when we need it less, strict discipline is insisted upon. Timekeeping is 'part and parcel' of it, as the English say. Our British trainers are tigers in that respect—and many others.

I see both sides to the argument. Maybe if we had been more like a normal army we might—eventually—have lifted the siege of Sarajevo by our own efforts. And thereby biffed the Chetniks' noses. But then we would not have drawn in the old men and girls and boys who rallied to the Lily emblem. You cannot drill and order such volunteers and without them we would have been so much less—and not just in numbers. *With* them we held the line long enough for the UN to finally shift itself. Question: could we, the young and fit have left the rest in that hopeless situation? Answer: a real army obeys sensible orders and would have pulled out long before.

Instead, in winter 92 the old amateur *Teritorialna Obramba* had to become Bosnia's saviour *Armija* without pause for breath. We fought the best we could and it was probably for the best.

I do not put this point of view to my instructors. They see the world differently. The British are still a puzzle to me. They did not wear bowler hats and talk of tea as I foolishly expected, but their knobbly faces seemed so soft. And yet they can suddenly *turn*. If they have been drinking it is ten times worse but always it is there.

There was one man, a Scottish sergeant, who actually hit recruits that answered back. He punched them on the jaw! Goodnight! We called him the *poison dwarf* but when he was recalled we gave him a crate of scotch whisky.

'*Here*,' joked our Bosnian commander, '*with our love. Drink it all at once and kill yourself!*'

And the Scottish man actually wept. That is another difference between his kind and us: sentiment. He is a professional but Fate has been kind to his country. He has seen less than us. Many of us no longer have tears to shed.

Please do not think me a brutal man. Neither am I soft. I fought with the Chetniks: hand to hand with them on several occasions when they tried to strangle Sarajevo. I make no apology for the things I did. There was a city of women and children behind us and we all knew what they did to civilians. The Chetniks ran '*rape factories*' in Foča and Sušica—girls as young as twelve. I believe the UN even prosecuted a couple of guys—who must have been busy boys to rack up the conflict's estimated 50,000 rapes. But enough bitterness and sarcasm! Sometimes you have to tell the past '*shut up! Be silent!*' Otherwise it possesses you like a djinn. Lines must be drawn. Now I just wanted to be normal again. To once more be the Pavlic who loved kittens and kindness, who liked children who liked him in return. The happy-go-lucky deejay off the radio who gave great discos. The man who used to shift snails off pavements to save their little lives. In short, I wanted to do good, as a conscious decision, and thereby sluice the muck off me.

An English policeman over here to train us distributed a handout. There was a quote at the top:

> '*Being a constable is a glorious opportunity of doing all possible good*'
> 'Observations on the Office of Constable' by Sanders Welch. 1754.

It made my dried-up heart open like a flower.

I treasured that moment, that memory. I tried to keep it with me when the world went sordid.

Like that day. The plan was to raid a brothel. We marched through the odd mix that was modern Sarajevo: some ruins still, and the smell of shattered sewers alongside signs of EU largesse. You learned to focus on the one and not the other: the glitzy future rather than the shitty past. Which of those were we heading for that morning? A debatable point. The whore-house would be full of trafficked girls: some Bosnians but increasingly other pretty blooms plucked from the old Soviet sphere. There must be villages in Moldova with no young women left! Therefore where will the next generation of Moldovans come from? This flow of females is not only the new slavery, the fair sex sold in their *millions,* but it is also genocide of the less lucky nations.

I digress. There were British soldiers to come with us, and a British Immigration Officer, under UN auspices for what *that's* worth, to show us how it should be done. New times, new methods. In the old days we would have kicked the pimp's head, and maybe marched some of the punters home to their wives and daughters. Shame still meant something in Sarajevo then.

Like I said, by and large we liked the British, though they were *horrors* under the skin. They cracked jokes—bone dry, gallows humour—and yet somehow the job got done. They also stopped us overreacting. It was different from patrolling with the Egyptians or, Allah forbid, the French or Ukrainians. With them almost anything could happen—though mostly nothing did. With the British there'd be days when we barely fired a shot but still arrested a *bag* of bad men.

The immigration man I knew to speak to. He was called Murray—another Scottish volunteer.

'See this knocking shop we're gonna spin?' he said to me as we marched.

But how could I see it when it was still kilometres away? The British do not speak the English I was taught. Also they do not trouble to explain their idioms.

However, I nodded.

'Well, it's gonna be ace. We've had red hot info. More gurls than yu could shake a stick at. And mebbe some of the UN guys who run 'em.'

This was not unlikely. UN personnel not only patronised the whorehouses, they actually bought women like cattle. For resale. Except that cattle are more expensive.

'So we nick the foreigners and the owner fust. Especially the Euros. Then any underage gurls. Get their passports for me to look at—they'll probably be stashed in the safe. Then and *only* then do we rub down the local punters. Gottit?'

This is what it had come to. The British had already worked it out amongst themselves. Their sergeant soldier knew what to do. Murray had been deputised to convey what would be to the poor native muscle. The local fig leaf on foreign justice.

But it *is* justice and foreign justice is better than none till we can make our own. So I agreed.

'Insha'allah,' I said. 'If it is God's will.'

Murray smiled.

'Aye, insha'allah...'

We chatted as we marched towards Markale marketplace. The plan was to appear just a normal patrol before we lunged for our real target.

'Why do you repeat *'If God wills it'*?' I asked him. 'You tell me you have no God.'

Murray wobbled his right hand in equivocation.

'Mebbe I do, mebbe I don't. When I'm oot with armed men then any extra protection is welcome...'

He patted his Kevlar jacket but I knew what he meant. It was an opening, an opportunity to prove my new character was sincere.

'You said, Murray, that your... *Reformation* killed religion in your country, but I think there is a spark in you yet. Allah abandons no man, instead man must spit in Allah's face. Maybe I will convert you, yes? You will go back to Heathrow having submitted to Allah...'

He crinkled his face. The British do this a lot rather than show their teeth in a smile.

'Mebbe, Pavlic old pal. Or mebbe I'll convert yu. There's a powerful lot to be said for a life of ale and ladies...'

He joked but I had made him think. A seed had been sown and it was for the Almighty to decide whether to bless it with growth.

Murray looked about the market place, my subversion doubtless working in his mind.

'*Insha'allah*, is it?' he muttered, softer even than normal. I had to strain to hear above the bustle. 'And was what happened here God's will?'

You'd never guess from the new cafes and smart people smoking *Marlboros* round pavement tables, but this place once was the throne of Satan. The Sarajevo marketplace massacre.

Survivors said it was a single shell incoming, the big screamer type from a 120mm mortar. You could expect a hit around five seconds after the noise: no time to do anything meaningful. In those days everyone, even pacifists and little old ladies, were artillery experts.

It had been the height of the siege, but the middle of the day, when people had come to expect a truce. They'd sidled out from the bunkers and ruins of their homes to buy whatever was on offer from the food stalls. The Chetnik on the hill with his binoculars chose the perfect time. Sarajevo in its natural bowl was spread before him like someone in the Sušica rape camp.

Luck made the bomb land right where it could wreak maximum harm. The scenes were extra terrible apparently. Metal splinters, splinters from the wooden stalls, bone splinters. I didn't see because I was in the trenches all day, but people told me it was worse than anything at the front. Mostly because of the children.

Blood everywhere, of course. There's a lot of that in 68 dead and 200 wounded. And limbs—a maximum score of four each. They were finding those high up buildings and strung across phone lines for days after. *'Trucks of dead, plus legs, arms, heads; as many as you want,'* said a young Kosovar hospital worker to me soon after. Even those who walked away were missing parts and never the same again—and not a combatant amongst them.

The Sarajevo Markale marketplace massacre. It was the bloody straw that broke the camel's back, the red feather which tipped the balance. Pictures of it, suitably 'scrubbed up' as Murray would say, censored and prettified, went all round the world. Leaders of the various factions chanced to be discussing 'peace' nearby at the time. 'Dr David Owen' from Murray's country was presiding. He saw the sickening scenes.

Because of it the UN warplanes were let off the leash. They poured Hell on the Serbs' heads. We were saved.

No Sarajevan would revisit the subject. It was the dark before a dawn we did not expect to see. That day haunted our nightmares with a sea of screams in which loose limbs bobbed.

I girded myself.

'Yes,' I told Murray, 'even that was Allah's will. Since *everything* is. We submit to it as we do to Allah. We do not understand now but soon, perhaps sooner than you think, we will. We shall understand all.'

Murray wrinkled his nose as if he could still smell the blood.

'Aye, well, I look forward to that.'

But I could tell he was not convinced. He, like many of his countrymen, are spiritually *dry*. It is not their fault. I prayed for his enlightenment.

When we arrived at the whore-house, Allah's ways became even harder to comprehend.

They'd been tipped off. The owner was smug, his 'bar' was decorous. Rank with the scent of lust and cigarettes but strictly legal. I've been to wilder parties at my aged aunt's. All the dead-eyed teenagers had been shipped out to alternative sweaty sheets. The information must have cost him but at least he wouldn't have to restock from distant Moldova.

Murray was beside himself with fury. You could tell by the way he arched an eyebrow.

'Right!' he accused us. 'Who leaked this to the fucking French?'

❇

'Dutch soldiers!' the bar-owner shouted at Bogdan.

Bogdan is a joker, a waster, but has a way with words. Fixed to the bar like with a ball and chain, he gives good value for the price of a brandy. Our sozzled court jester. The regulars collapse in stitches. Just give him a subject and he'll spin a string of crazy metaphors.

'Dutch soldiers?' He didn't even have to muse. 'Dutch soldiers! As much use as... an ashtray on a motorbike...'

The red-faced old boys roared and banged their glasses on the tables. There was history in their amusement because of what happened at Srebrenica. The city fell without one shot from its UN 'protectors' in July 95. Then the massacres began.

Mind you, I hear two Dutch soldiers later killed themselves out of shame and sorrow.

Anyhow: 'More!' cried the drinkers. 'More!'

The idea was to catch him out, to find fault in his invention.

'As much use as a paper prison!' Bogdan bawled on. 'As a U2 lyric! As a mud bucket! As a glass hammer...'

'Wrong!' said an enormously fat man—a rare sight in Sarajevo even now. He rang the word like a bell. *'Wronggg!'*

Like most jokers, Bogdan is actually a proud man and therefore suffers much. His wordsmithing is all he has.

'And why's that, tubs?' he pouted. 'What so *'Wronggg'* about that?' Bogdan taking offence is like a sheep growling. 'Tubs' could have flattened him to atoms by just advancing. He wasn't worried. His fat rolled in laughter waves.

'Because,' he answered, 'at least you can use a glass hammer *once*!'

ALTERED ENGLANDS

'Score!' they all cried. General mocking hilarity.

Recalling the scene I now wonder about some of those present. Especially those hunched over drinks, backs to me, never turning. What were *they* about? Maybe the nightmare started earlier than I thought.

But back then I just flicked my newspaper open and tuned them all out. I was a policeman, a respectable person. It wasn't right to smile at clowns for too long.

The paper showed me the new and serious Bosnia, of *'gays'* and laptops, of *'Human Rights'* and *'Personal Development Plans'*. I pretended to be absorbed.

Then someone tapped it, putting a dent in the politician's picture I was studying—Mr Ashdown from England, come to solve all our problems with his craggy *'I-feel-your-pain'* looks.

Someone short. No head could be seen over the paper's edge.

'Hey, careful...,' I said, and lowered my shield. 'Oh, *you*...'

I couldn't say too much. She knew my Mother and had seen me in short trousers. All the same, Tilda-the-crone was a pain. She had this *thing* about people taking their glasses back to the bar—which was what she was paid a pittance to do. Added to her pension it just about kept her going—but for what?

'Yah, yah, grandma,' I said. 'I won't forget...'

But that wasn't her beef: not today. It was about us, in general.

'Call yourself men?' she asked *me*, not all the other louts. 'Muslims sitting here with your brandies and your shouting?'

I doubt she was ever beautiful or loved. I was only kind to her for my Mother's sake. And because of what Allah says we should do, naturally.

If nothing else, that brandy thing struck home. It had been a long hard day. I couldn't be expected to keep *all* the rules right away. So she got the newspaper treatment too. Flick, flick; I blocked her out.

'Cut me some slack, Tilda. I fought for the likes of you. So did quite a few here. Show some tolerance...'

A claw came over the top, rude as you like, dragging Mr Ashdown down.

'Time enough to rest your arse when they're settled,' she told me, her one clear eye beaming bright. 'I live over the Markale market place. I hear them at night still complaining. They don't let me rest.'

For a horrible moment Tilda imitated female despair from a voice far younger than her own. It sounded authentic and awful. My stomach turned. Advantage Tilda.

'So,' she went on, 'maybe you bold soldier boys didn't do your job, eh? Too tired, too tipsy, to gather them all up: is that how it was?'

The bar-owner spotted he was about to lose a customer. He came over and intervened, his hairy hand actually on her shoulder.

'Collect glasses, Tilda, and leave this nice gentleman alone.'

Overreaction. Everyone knows she's a bit skewiff, right from even before the War. I was just going to ignore her. A virtuous man accepts slights from those touched by God.

'Leave her.'

It was an order. I could do that now, even in other people's places. Stripes on my arm said so. Ditto the *licenced* machine pistol.

A bit miffed, the ham-like arm lifted. Then, to soften the blow, ignoring her in favour of *important* him, I asked:

'What the hell's she on about, Darko? What's the problem?'

With that little gift we were comrades once again. The bar-owner shrugged his vest.

'Who knows? She hears 'sounds': cries and groans from the marketplace at night. You and I—we say, hey, there's some couples at it, bashing the furry hoop, if I may speak so plain. We would wish them luck. She, *she* goes to the window and sees things. People, women, a girl wandering. I say to her, Tilda, what do you expect? Not all young lovers have a house to go to. Mind you don't peek too much, or maybe you'll see something you didn't bargain for!'

'That'd revive a few memories, eh gal?' contributed Bogdan. 'Take you back to the old Ottoman days. Of being *taken* by the old Ottomans probably! Mind you, the stories say they didn't like it plain and simple...!'

And all this time old Tilda's eye was still on me, her claw still buried in my paper. She heard the stuff from the bar and her employer but wasn't receiving. It washed over her head.

I felt sorry for her. A long life should end in some dignity, no matter how crabby.

'If it's ghosties you fear,' I said, putting on my policeman voice, 'I can put your mind at rest. And thus you at rest. Because you need your sleep.'

ALTERED ENGLANDS

'Yeah, beauty sleep,' roared Bogdan. I shut him up with a look and resumed.

'Tilda, there are *no* ghosts: when their time comes souls are gathered to the Seat of Judgement. Every single one, without exception. There we must give account of ourselves, for our stewardship of the life Allah graciously gave us.'

I admit they were not my words. The Chief Imam of Sarajevo gives mass tuition to 'returning Muslims'. We sit in ranks to learn what our parents should have taught us. No matter: the words were fine and true.

But was she even hearing my second-hand sermon? More like she was reliving her 'sounds'. Her face was unappeased, her lips dismissive.

I mustered my pittance of pity.

'Tilda, Allah does *not* leave strays. He gives life, he harvests it. There are djinns and demons; the Holy Qur'an tells us this, but no *human* strays.'

I was inspired by the Book which is the fount of all wisdom but she still demurred.

'You are a *child*, Pavlic. A child of this wicked world and a child within it. A drunken child at that. It is a blessing from above that your mother is not here to see you!'

I was flushed with drink and supposed faith. My hand chopped the air.

'Enough! There's none so deaf as *won't* listen. Woman: I tell you Allah gathers all souls to him. *All*.'

She left me and so did the rest. The banter was declared over. Tilda went to collect glasses, the others did what they were doing before. They were frightened, I could tell. Apparently, when roused my face can have an evil aspect.

If only her words would have departed the same way. The paper blurred before my eyes, my thoughts trod dangerous paths.

It could not be. It would not be *kind* to leave bits of human soul wandering. Lost, pained and puzzled. A merciful Deity would not permit it. Otherwise, what did that say about the Universe?

If Tilda heard things it must be the wicked games of djinns instead. Had to be.

I resolved to prove it to both her and me.

☸

The only thing haunting the Markale market place was myself. For a week I made its security my business and volunteered for all the night duties.

Murray taunted me with it and said there must be a woman that I met there. Which was perceptive of him in ways I hope he did not know.

I sought Tilda's 'girl' in both bright lit places and dark shadow but found only whores and beggars. There was weeping, but only when I sent them on their way with a boot. The sole ghostly face I saw was when a pimp came hustling up, cursing, and I shoved my gun up his nose. He went white as a sheet, thinking I would fire—as did I for a red second. But mercy, which comes from Allah, restrained my finger.

His *fizzog* was it as far as the spectral-looking went. All the evil there was of man's making and I sent it packing. The Market was clean when Pavlic was on duty. Shopkeepers tried to give me presents. I could have amassed dozens of dollars and masses of (Bosnian) marks but rejected them as insults. Officer Pavlic was about Allah's work. A volunteer not a mercenary.

I'd resolved to give it one more night. A cursed resolve. The girl in the leather coat greeted me *right* at the end of that shift. Which was a wickedness on the part of whoever permitted it.

I heard her before I saw her. A sob sounded right beside me from nowhere and no one. What was it I said to Tilda? There's none so deaf as *won't* listen. If only I had *gone* away instead of rationalising away.

Even so, I wasn't really alert. When someone strolled in sight I no longer suspected anything but flesh and blood. Whores though, those I was on the look out for. No respectable girl would patrol the market at three in the morning. There wasn't even a boyfriend with her.

'Hey, blondie: come here!'

She had her back to me. It stiffened. She almost turned her head.

'I *said*, come here!'

The United Nations people would have us arrest prostitutes and fine them in court. But what is the point of that? What is the one means they have of paying their penalty? They are straight back on the streets and then straight on their backs. So when UN eyes aren't on us we tended to just give them a slap that shakes their teeth and then a lecture. Especially good Bosnian girls. They are disgracing their nation and scarring their immortal souls. Moldovans though, they just went in the pen to await our immigration people. That poor meat is usually beyond correction.

But this girl looked like one of ours. Even our loose women have style. She wore a jaunty beret and carried herself well.

'If you make me chase you, you'll be sorry. I'll break your pimp's legs.'

A stupid thing to say actually—most working girls would welcome that. They'd probably want to video it. However, I'd been on my feet all night and wasn't thinking clear. Cotton wool lined my skull.

Then adrenaline melted it like acid. As soon as she moved I had never been so awake in my life.

The girl did not shift her feet, the red high heels stayed still. Yet she went like lightning, though stock-still and arms limp.

I saw her in instalments, between invisible instants. First here, then there, without troubling the terrain in-between. It was like a film I once saw where the reel jumped or clips were missing.

When did I lose all wisdom? Against the Serbs I had run towards the gunfire, this horror I ran after. And yet God surely understands our weakness. Would He condemn our feet taking a more sensible direction? But still this curse of *duty* and *bravery* is hardwired into everything that is me. I shall never be free of it.

'Miss! Miss!'

A pathetic thing to call, but I could not think what else. She had my respect now—and sympathy.

For I could hear Tilda's weeping. The sounds of men and women with broken hearts and bodies. It came from all around, from everywhere and nowhere—and from the girl. She wept bitterly. Her shoulders heaved under the brown leather of her chic coat.

She had her own means of transport but I can shift fast too. Under the streetlight of an apartment building I caught up with her—or she let me. I skidded to a halt mere metres behind.

'Miss... what is the matter? What... are you?'

She did not look like a djinn, though I am aware that they can assume shapes to deceive. Yet this figure did not have that sense of mischief. There was no whiff of brimstone.

She could hear me, I observed that much. Her tears abated and she seemed poised to look round.

I already knew in my heart what she was. Though there was flesh beneath that coat she should not be here. Not any more. Her time was gone and she had been called. For some blasphemous reason that call had been ignored.

'Go to Allah,' I said. 'Find peace. Find forgiveness. He awaits you in Heaven...'

And then she turned.

There was no face. Just the bloody hollow that the mortar had torn.

Yet she could still speak—and scream.

'Give me back my life!' she pleaded. *'Give me back my life!'*

I date my death—my inner death—to then. Compared to this battlefield scenes were just scratches on the soul. My emotions went into overdraft beyond hope of repayment.

Ghosts are supposed to vanish after saying their piece. She did not. She remained there accusing me for my lack of help. Her hair streamed in the long gone blast that was her eternal present.

'I want my face! I want my legs!'

But I could no more return her life or legs than fly. That was Allah's job—and He chose not to.

'Begone, djinn!' I whispered, like a little child. 'In the name of Allah, begone!'

It was no use, to me or her. I backed away into the lobby of the apartments. One of the glass double doors cracked under the impact but then they parted to let me through.

She followed, in her flitting way. The double doors swung back and hit her. Unmoved, there she stayed, a girl without eyes staring at me.

Then she began to smear her face against the glass, in wilder and wilder circles, coating it with lifeblood.

I do not remember starting to scream, only my difficulty with stopping.

Years later a door behind me opened. A shuffling old man emerged in dressing gown and slippers.

'I... she...,' I started to say, pointing. But she was gone. I looked back at him.

And though he was living he was of a kind with *her*. His eyes had seen all the horror there ever was to see and he would rush to meet Death when it came—save for fear that it might not be eternal rest.

'I know,' he said to me, in a voice run out of feeling. 'I know. She walks. She was my daughter. My beautiful daughter...'

ALTERED ENGLANDS

✦

Time for another hammer blow and so Allah awoke me.

Murray was standing over my hospital bed. The sheets were made too tight, like a shroud.

'Nurss!' he called, looking down with a smile. 'Nurss—the lazy bastard's awake at last.'

And while the medical staff attended me he sat beside my bed, eating the grapes he must have bought and reading an English newspaper. I remember it had pictures of naked women with boyish hips but the breasts of nursing mothers. It is curious the things that the mind latches on to.

Eventually I was free of the white tormentors' prodding and questioning and they departed. Murray put down his paper.

'So Pavlic, I dinna suppose there's the slightest chance of you spilling the beans, is there?'

I had come across this curious phrase before. It has nothing to do with cooking. A shake of my head confirmed he was right. I would never speak of what had happened to me. Not even to myself.

'I thought not. But it wassna assault, right? Not retaliation by organised crime, or some senior Sarajevo pimp yu pissed off? Only my people need to check that, see?'

I put his mind at rest. This was something I could be legitimately angry about.

'If any Mafia dared touch me I would *crush* them.'

My fist rose from the bed to demonstrate.

'Aye, and I'd help ye,' said Murray with apparent sincerity. It was the closest I ever heard him come to sentiment. In his own country display is frowned upon—which must make for a lot of misery.

'I know you would,' I said. 'You are like a brother.'

He snorted, embarrassed.

'Well, I wouldna know about that. My Mum might have something to say aboot it. Anyhow, I gotta go and file the news about yu. Can't have our protégés being bumped on the heed with nothing done aboot it...'

'I fell,' I said—which was true. 'That is all.'

'Fair enough. Reet then, I'll love ye and leave ye. Oh, there's one other thing—something yu might want to hear since you're so fascinated wi that market...'

I wanted to hear anything and everything right then, to postpone thought.

'We've just got the UN report on the massacre there. You know, our artillery guys came down and had a shufti, took away the shell remnants and all that. Way back. A glossy document's finally come oot of it...'

I caught my breath. A premonition. The bed turned cold as a tomb.

'Yes...'

'Turns out it was your blokes. Aiming for international sympathy. Nowhere else that salvo could have come from, plus mortar rounds definitely exported to you. It was timed for the arrival of that UN peace meeting so they could see the carnage. Worked a treat too. Wasn't it just after that our planes went in and zapped the Serbs?'

I nodded in silence.

'S'happened before, too, here and in Tuzla: maybe four or more times—exactly the same sortta thing. I reckon yu got some ruthless bods in your high command—bodes well for your country with guys like that in charge, if you see what I mean...'

I gulped, straining my chest against the bedclothes bond.

'Therefore...,' I measured my words, not wanting to reach the end of the sentence, 'you're saying that *Bosnians* showered death on the crowded market place. Deliberately. At a time when they knew...'

He cut in, seeing I was distressed.

'Aye, Pavlic, your ain folk...'[13]

'Are you sure?'

Murray looked at me with that bold blue-eyed shamelessness that only Europeans and/or wicked men can muster.

'Positive pal.'

My breath was sucked from me till it seemed my lungs would shrivel. I shrank, the blankets no longer constrained. Something even more vital than breath left too, spiralling down and out through my feet till I was left a husk.

Who was I working for? What had I fought for?

---

[13] This allegation is now disputed and, a growing consensus would say, discredited. Given their recent history, the heroic Bosnian people do not deserve such falsehoods.

ALTERED ENGLANDS

'Allah did *not* make the world this way,' I told Murray—once I could speak again, more convinced than I had been of anything for *years*. 'Allah is *good*.'

He was looking towards his newspaper again and the few remaining grapes. *'Franks'* cannot remain focused on spiritual matters

'If yu say so, mate. Whatever.'

This would not do. I had to know.

'But what do you think? Tell me. It is important.'

He made that peculiar Christian lip-pursing expression I knew meant *'no strong feelings either way.'*

'Well, if yu ask me, Pavlic—and ye did—I reckon one of your own heretics got it right. I read it somewhere. Some Muslim bloke way back, founder of the Assassins or summat. He says, okay: *'Nothing is true and everything is permissible'*. If yu get my drift...'

I did. And he was right. Absolutely right.

An irony. The girl without a face was not a djinn. My 'friend' Murray was—though he did not know it. She was a mere victim like me, whereas Murray was an (innocent?) agent of Shaitan. I had hoped to convert him but he had converted me.

'Nothing is true and everything is permissible.'

It sounded right and eminently reasonable. It fitted all the facts. It sauntered into my broken open heart and made its home there. I was converted.

Soon after I applied for the job in Saudi.

❈

Sometimes I sit and watch the Saudi sunset. There remain some angles between skyscrapers where you can glimpse it.

There is still beauty, in retreat but lingering yet. It must come from somewhere. Or someone. I wonder.

Day and night I wonder. Have I finished with Allah? Or He with me?

❈

5~

IN THE NAME OF ALLAH, THE MERCIFUL?

Poison added to poison! The Haji-Imam put water in his *haram!* Vodka *haram* to be precise: local home-made *'eye-burner'*. And local well-water too!

Some dilution was necessary, for the hootch was lethally strong: but did it have to be drawn from round the poor polluted Aral Sea? Apparently so: the Haji-Imam seemed beyond caring. He said all the chemicals added *'zip'*. Madness!

The Little-Imam advised against both liquids, for the sake of his boss's soul and stomach, but the Haji-Imam only laughed. Then he usually threw things: like bottles and abuse.

Guidance is only granted to those whom Allah chooses. So it was written. But that is a hard ruling for the tender-hearted to take. The Little-Imam persevered.

Some things the Haji-Imam *had* to care about. He couldn't afford to lose his job. What else did the Soviet Republic of Uzbekistan hold that was half as cushy? So for form's sake his 'pick-me-up' was poured into a teapot: in case one of the faithful should see. The Little-Imam saw, of course, as did Allah, but neither counted for much to the Haji-Imam.

The Little-Imam asked forgiveness of Allah for both of them, for the Haji-Imam's sin and his complicity. He did so night and day, including today as he repeated his transgression.

Off he set from the kitchen, pushing the *haram* away from and before him. The service trolley was rusty and protesting, its wheels screamed. Like the

ALTERED ENGLANDS

Haji-Imam it dated from Stalin's time—he who'd shut the Mosque down for a while; till the Nazis threatened. Just like him it brought the soundtrack of Hell to echo round the Mosque's empty walls.

Nobody much came to study or pray outside the prescribed hours any more. Which was as well in one way—given the shame those walls regularly saw. But bad in every other way.

That morning the Haji-Imam's face was black as sin and thus a closed book to the Little-Imam. Literally. Hence his failure to forecast the brewing storm.

It was a gift from Allah, the Little-Imam realised, this being able to view what men had done with their souls. Since earliest youth he'd been blessed with reading people via lightness and shade. It was that which steered him to his present profession and the guidance of those in sore need. Which proved Allah bestowed gifts with good reason. Yet the Little-Imam was also glad the power was periodic. In modern times too clear a view of humanity was a mixed blessing.

Like now, for instance. The Haji-Imam's visage was a writhing sheet of ebony. Doubtless the result of listening to Western *'rock'* music on headphones: probably his favourite *'Fab Four'* or *'Rolling Stones'*—*'Their Satanic Majesties.* Surely their names alone should have sounded an alarm? Either soulless insects or self-confessed servants of the Evil One! What was wrong with a bit of decent Sufi chanting?

The tape leaked into the room as hiss and bass. A seepage of aggressive noise. The Haji-Imam shouted over it.

'Morning tubs! Made my *tea* good and strong did you?'

The same ritual every day.

'Turn aside, master, I beg you. Life is short, eternity long.'

'Screw you—and your mother!'

A full ashtray skimmed the air atop the Little-Imam's skullcap as he ducked. Though not the slimmest of Allah's creations, his time at the Mosque had turned him nimble.

Even the Haji-Imam's prized imported *'Walkman'* and *'the Beatles'* came second sometimes. There are hierarchies of *haram*. Satan's gadget was stowed away into a desk draw, out-seduced by faster acting liquid ruin.

Today the Haji-Imam made a special point of drinking straight from the teapot's spout, to prove some or other point. His face darkened with every gulp.

'By Allah, *that* hit the spot, tubs. And now get rid of these blasted files that want signing. Mountains of shite! I can't be arsed. When? *When*? Well, just any old time in the next three frigging seconds would be fine! And another thing: *you* can conduct the noon prayers. I'm expecting a guest.'

Satan wrote the script. Even as the Haji-Imam spoke there was a hesitant *tap tap* on his door.

It was a *Natasha*, one of the local ethnic-Russian girls tugged by poverty into whoredom. Liquefied allure in an Uzbek *atlas* silk dress. For the moment *her* young face was a white oval that shone save in specks—but the specks were winning and the shine flickered. The Little-Imam saw beneath paint and lipstick to perceive what pimps had done.

She was also anaemic, like all Aral Sea women. Possibly a consequence of all the chemical weapons testing that went on there in the 70s. Or maybe all the strontium in the soil. The early stages of sickness falsely enhanced her charms. *'Pale and interesting'*...

'Mmmmmmmm!' said the Haji-Imam, licking his lips.

'Oh no!' appealed the Little-Imam, to both parties, to the walls of the Mosque, to life.

'Oh *yes*!' answered the Haji-Imam, proud behind his freshly cleared desk.

Though not yet out of her teens, the *Natasha* understood the world well—far better than the Little-Imam. She crossed the room to kneel between the Haji-Imam's legs.

The now file-filled trolley slowed the Little-Imam down, robbing him of any residual dignity. It squealed like a stuck pig (not a fit thing to mimic in a mosque...). Even the *Natasha* laughed as he fled. An easy target, the Haji-Imam got him on the back of the head with a cigarette lighter. Being big and brass it hurt.

The Little-Imam looked back but said nothing.

The Haji-Imam's face was now an entire absence of light. Allah's sunshine poured in but none escaped—like the alleged 'Black Holes' the Christian astronomers preached.

'Where's your big-eye-in-the-sky now, eh?' he jeered after his assistant. 'Eh? Nowhere is where! 'Cos there is no God! And no one is his prophet!'

ALTERED ENGLANDS

☸

Boats and quays and net-sheds, all useless and crumbling; left high and dry. Very dry. The sea was a dozen kilometres away and wasn't coming back. Barring a miracle.

However, the Little-Imam believed in miracles. Surah 36 said when Allah decreed a thing He need only say: *'Be'*, and it *is*. Thus anything was possible, even miracles. Those desiccated boats need not despair, nor those who surveyed them.

Stubby legs dangling off the end of a jetty the Little-Imam looked for that miraculous tide sweeping in from the horizon.

Not today. All he saw was a far off storm, whipping up the dust and salt that was once a sea. A fragrance of DDT preceded it to the former shore.

Never mind. If the miracle wouldn't come to the Little-Imam he would go to it. To that greatest and most dependable of miracles: one portable within the bounds of a book.

He let his Holy Qur'an fall open at random. Except that a devout man knows nothing is random.

Surah 47. Verse 4: *'When you encounter the unbelievers strike off their heads. Until you have made a wide slaughter amongst them, tie up the remaining captives.'*

Hmmm … Wisdom from another age, one the Little-Imam was privileged to be born after. His thumb grip loosened and let the pesticide-scented breeze flip more pages. Until:

Surah 55. Verse 26: *'All this will pass and there remains only the face of Thy Lord'.*

Better. Much better.

The Little-Imam looked up again. There was no cause for concern or rush. The storm was hovering, like storms rarely do, cursing the Kazakhs instead of the Uzbeks. Even if it contained cunning clouds, inscribed with the Little-Imam's name, he would still have time to scuttle indoors before they struck. The mosque's shutters would keep their scouring sand from his eyes and lungs and pores. Mostly.

Was it bad to be glad that his Kazakh brothers were imprisoned instead of him? Probably, but only a little. It was human... The Soviets' legacy of environmental meltdown blessed them both equally. The Uzbeks' turn would come in time.

Speaking of which...

The Little-Imam now had time to think and process this morning's horrible scenes. And thereby to forgive and forget. *That* must be the purpose of this fall of events. Allah offered the opportunity to cleanse his mind with a little perspective. The kind gift must be seized.

'All this will pass and there remains only the face of Thy Lord'...'

The Little-Imam thought of Lenin. Then Stalin. Then General Secretary Leonid Brezhnev. Names to be conjured—and be careful—with. First the bald bonce sheltering a huge *brain*. Then the moustachioed butcher. Today the current one with all the medals and a tractor fixation. Equalling six or so action-packed decades...

What were they compared to the long view? What was Marxist-Leninism but just another tide on the sea of history? It roared in and washed upon the shore: full of drama at the time to be sure, but soon to be forgotten. Before that had been the Tsars and Mongols and Alexander and all the rest. Where were they now? Answering Allah's pointed questions was where, whilst their monuments on earth crumbled to dust.

Surah 3. Verse 49: *'Surely therein is a sign if ye did believe.'*

The Communist tide had shaped the span allotted to the Little-Imam. Nothing in him had escaped its touch. Yet to Allah it was a mere instalment and perhaps not even that. Less than an instant, a footnote in the recording angel's book. What was permanent remained.

Which apparently excluded the Aral sea. The Communists' crash irrigation schemes, products of the lust for cash crops like cotton (*'white gold'*), had seen to that. Year by year it leeched away, leaving disaster. The fourth largest lake on Earth reduced to puddles and saltpan: maybe that might be their lasting legacy. That and disordered seasons and a cancer epidemic.

Funnily enough, the Rus had even shot themselves in the feet. The growing season now was less than 170 days. Cotton requires at least 200 frost-free mornings to prosper.

Last year an up-and-coming Central Committee member called Gorbachev had upped and come to see. Apparently, he'd had responsibility for agriculture at the time. The Little-Imam witnessed him and his entourage strutting and fretting beside the shore, but nothing followed the fine words. Not even roubles to console people.

ALTERED ENGLANDS

So Aral region grass continued to kill the beasts that ate it. Their bones, along with a fine salt dusting that looked like snow, continued to whiten the fields.

Too much *today*. Too much recent horror which killed calm. The Little-Imam adjusted his perspective controls for a wider view. He tried to recapture the grand narrative and visualise its majestic sweep bringing the empires of man to rise and fall on this dry shore. Ebb and flow. An endless coming and going of construction and crumbling, ultimately leaving only the Truth.

He was certainly visualising very *well* today. The phantoms he'd summoned seemed almost solid, causing the Little-Imam to wonder at his amazing powers of imagination. Or had he caught a whiff of the Haji-Imam's morning 'tea'?

Just in case, he shook his head to clear it.

No, he was definitely seeing them: a snapshot of each succeeding era. In swift succession towers and mosques and churches arose as complete constructions, with little people buzzing round them, living sped up little lives. From birth to grave and empire to decadence occupied only seconds. Yet the picture-show seemed every bit as real as the cinema film the Little-Imam once saw in Tashkent. More real in fact, because that had been about tractor production quotas.

Bactria was followed by the Parthians and Sassanids who were displaced by the coming of Islam. Genghis Khan arrived to shake the Faith and after him Tamerlane adopted it. And so it went on, right up to the arrival of the Rus. Soon enough they turned from Christians into Communists and the Aral started to shrink.

Naturally, the Little-Imam averted his eyes from the grislier details and so noticed the backdrop and common thread. All through the petty dramas camel caravans plied their way across the scene, loaded with spices and silk. Which went to prove the old Uzbek proverb: *there are two eternal roads in the Universe: the Milky Way in the sky and the Silk Road on earth.*

There should have been comfort in that but the Little-Imam knew the caravans had died out before his time. Silk was made in Soviet factories now.

Instead, the Little-Imam grew anxious. The present day was well known to him, and it wasn't nice. He shook his head again, threatening his *duppa*'s hold upon his crown. He closed his eyes against the display.

When he unscrewed them again, the visions were gone, proving they *must* have been mirages. Which was a relief—of sorts. The shoreline was defunct once more. Normality restored!

More or less. Except the Little-Imam didn't recall so many spectators. They dotted the 'beach' as individuals and groups.

Very strange. What was so special about the far off storm that fascinated them in such numbers? And how come so many had so much time on their hands?

The last bit was easily answered. Since the fishing industry finally gave up the ghost in '81, Aral Sea unemployment was 50% plus. And that was just the official figure! Many—and not just the Rus but Muslims too—had become the sort of drunkards who lolled around all day, killing time and their brains.

Yet the Little-Imam had never observed any such idlers so intent before. Prolonged study was normally beyond them.

They would have been better served coming to prayer—which would be soon. The call from the minaret explained explicitly.

> *Come to prayer,*
> *Come to success,*
> *Prayer is better than sleep...*

Why could people not see that? What were these loafers watching instead?

A chill sidled over the Little-Imam. He closed the Qur'an and gently hugged it to his chest.

In truth he already had his answer. They were too many, too still. The DDT-breeze did not trouble them or stir their hair. They were not as he was. They were seeing things the Little-Imam could not.

Except...

Out of the storm advanced a single figure. Black against black.

Either the Little-Imam's eyesight had improved beyond recognition or else...

The figure was heading straight for him, really travelling, yet with ordinary seeming strides. A man. Maybe. His gaze was fixed on the Little-Imam like a sniper—but how come the Little-Imam could tell at that distance? Or hear footsteps crunching the salt crust?

ALTERED ENGLANDS

Some of the gawpers were bowing. People only did that to Muftis or high-ranking Communists.

Panting heavily, the Little-Imam shifted his bulk. The jetty's unmaintained planks groaned *'gently, gently...'*. Or maybe *'stay'*...

The Little-Imam's brain advised differently. His legs agreed.

❁

Back in town the Little-Imam got a grip. His breath moderated from pre-coronary to merely puffed-out. Then the Mosque's crackly tannoy spoke over his head.

Allah is most great, Allah is most great!
Come to prayer,
Come to success,
Allah is most great, Allah is most great!

Mosque funds didn't run to a proper muezzin, not with the Haji-Imam's inroads into them, and the Little-Imam's soft voice would have been laughed at by all save Allah. So an ancient sellotape-repaired cassette tape did the job instead.

No matter. It *did* the job—after a fashion—and right then it was like rain in the desert. The Little-Imam's universe was reoriented and set aright. Nothing happened that was not Allah's will and doing. Nothing could. The figure out of the storm—even if it really existed—was one of God's creations. Likewise the serried spectators.

Thus the Little-Imam had a reminder of what was what. And of where his duties lay. How could he ever have forgotten? Guilt made him falter.

'Get a move on, fatso!'

The dirty Rus beggar was impudent but right. Even if the Little-Imam really motored he'd be late and winded for the noon *Zuhr* prayers. It was all those visions' fault ...

The Rus vagrant had moulded himself into a gap between two dustbins. A bottle and upturned cap sat before him; both empty.

The man's face was in shadow, mostly of his own making. The Little-Imam could barely see his features for the evil-doing they'd seen and done. He felt a wave of pity for the judgement looming over a being Allah intended only for joy.

Abuse or no, the Little-Imam knew his duty. That this was an infidel only filled the well of compassion. His hand went to his purse.

The beggar beat him to the draw. Suddenly the lined face shone like a saint's. There was an entire absence of transition.

He'd also found someone else better to talk to. The Little-Imam couldn't see them.

'Him? *Him?* Are you *sure?*' the beggar asked, stiff with scorn.

With an agility old soaks shouldn't have, he lurched forward and tweaked a roll of fat round the Imam's midriff.

'Not one built for the long run, I should have said. Or running at all. Some *'catalyst'*! Still, you know best...'

The Little-Imam looked right round to find the silent third party. Only there wasn't one. Or, when he looked back, even a beggar.

☸

The Little-Imam had boggled, but only a little and not for long. The world was full of wonders and there was no call to give yourself headaches over them. All would be revealed in due course, whether in this world or the next.

Besides, there were bigger, more pressing, problems. Fewer than ever had answered the crackly tannoy call. Those faithful few looked like the endgame of a long chess match when set amidst the Mosque's expanse. It could hold three thousand with ease, but never did, not in the Little-Imam's time, not even for Friday communal prayers.

The Little-Imam marvelled when he considered it. What was the big alternative draw? Television? Vodka? *Communism?* What was the matter with people? What thing constrained by three dimensions could beat communion with the Almighty?

Post prayers the Haji-Imam was ratty and hung-over. The Little-Imam happened to be with him, collecting papers and insults, when the phone rang. His boss snatched it up.

'Yep? I mean, *Salaam Aleikum*. Who is i-...'

The Haji-Imam went pale and rocketed to attention. His leather chair hit the back wall.

ALTERED ENGLANDS

'Good morning, comrade Secretary. Yes, comrade Secretary. Indeed so, comrade Secretary. Absolutely! I couldn't agree more, comrade Secretary…'

He slipped a hand over the receiver.

'Get me a drink, tubs,' he hissed. 'A bloody big one!'

It was still being prepared when the Haji-Imam emerged from his office, whiter than any Aral Sea anaemic. On the phone he'd been mild as a lamb: now he roared like a lion.

'They're coming! They're coming!'

The Little-Imam was gazing out of the window. He'd noted his mirages were back. There was water and boats and mayfly civilisations and they were *most* absorbing. But not as much as a boot up the backside.

His boss's sandal propelled him back into today.

☸

The Haji-Imam's ancestors must have reacted the same to news of the Mongols, but things had improved since then. Communists didn't leave cairns of skulls—well, not nowadays—but they could easily lose you your job.

'Paint that. And that! And for Vlad's sake clear those cobwebs. Haven't we got any better prayer mats?'

No. The money for them had gone on *Natashas* and suchlike transitory joys.

'Right then. Here's the feast I want laid on to stupefy 'em. First, mounds of *shashlik* on skewers—succulent mind you, no gristle. And *non* breads—hot-hot-hot and fluffy. And meat pies, plus noodles and pilaf rice. Be sure you cook everything in mutton dripping as well. Then there's got to be pomegranates and pistachios. Oh, and *loads* of those edible icing sugar flowers. That should slow the *kuffar* down…'

You would have thought he'd had prior notice of the Day of Judgement rather than a visitation from the Party. The Little-Imam was saddened it only prompted a spring-clean, not an audit of the soul. Whitewash was applied straight over neglect as if that sufficed. Corruption had a thin mask applied.

The men from the *Dukhovnoe Upravlenie* Religious Board Committee were only men, and men can have wool pulled over their eyes. Thereagain, they were men who believed in this world only and so their gaze upon it was intent. Either way, the Little-Imam felt only sympathy for such afflicted creatures.

On arrival their eyes showed no similar sympathy for him. They came early by design, in a black stream of *Zil* limos. Their suits were sharp by Soviet standards and their scrutiny sharper still.

'When was this last painted?'

Twenty-four blue Slav eyes fixed on the Uzbek defenders of the gate.

'Yesterday,' answered the Little-Imam, in all honesty—and the Haji-Imam groaned. Blue eyes flashed disapproval.

The Imams were tired, having been up most of the night, and one of them had risen for the dawn prayers too. The Haji-Imam had plumped for much needed *zzzz* instead. He should have been marginally the more awake.

Not necessarily so. He'd gotten flabby, inside as out, for vodka doesn't just cost roubles. His younger brain would have guessed the Communists didn't want spick and span. They thirsted for dust and desertion. Religion was meant to be an *ebbing* tide.

'Hmmm,' said the third-senior apparatchik, and made a note on a clipboard. A bad start.

The plan was that, post-tour, they should oversee the Friday communal prayers, viewing it like angels from the internal balcony. Up there they'd also hear the Haji-Imam's *khutbah*. He'd sweated blood on a text lauding *'Peace'* and the *'Progressive nations'* role in reaching it. The milk-and-water Allah that the Soviets tolerated would presumably approve...

'I'll show you the schoolroom next,' blurted the Haji-Imam, trying to regain the right path. 'It's hardly ever used...'

Then, in a side whisper.

'Tea, tubs. Good and *strong!*'

✵

'And what do *you* do?'

This Rus must have split off from the main delegation to find his own signs. One of the younger, keen types, with a reputation still to make before he got his easy-street-for-life appointment. Possibly therefore a *persecutor*: what dissidents called a *'Komsomol creep'*. His spectacles were wire-rims, like the hardcore Marxists wore. The Little-Imam suspected they held clear glass.

He'd chanced upon the kitchen and the Little-Imam busy in it. Fortunately, Haji-Imam's *'tea'* wasn't yet underway.

The Little-Imam answered the query without betraying his boss. A litany of his normal day, minus the *haram* low points. Already thin Rus lips compressed still more.

'All *Allah* stuff then?'

'What else is there, sir?'

'So you actually *believe* in it?' A rhetorical question fortunately. The Little-Imam's face replied for him.

The young Rus rested his bony behind on the serving trolley. It screamed but didn't shift. Then he surveyed the scene before him. So young but already so *sure*.

'Our last port of call,' he said, 'was the Shah-i-Zinda shrine at Samarkand. People make pilgrimage there because Qasim ibn Abbas, a cousin of the Prophet, no less, was beheaded on the spot whilst at prayers. And oh yes, he then put his severed head back on—as you do—and jumped into a nearby well where he lives still and answers petitions. So tell me, do you believe *that*?'

The Little-Imam shrugged.

'Allah knows the truth of it...,' he placated.

The Young Communist smiled.

'Latest sociological research separates Soviet Muslims into seven categories. A continuum from 'firm believer' to 'committed atheist'. Whereabouts on that do *you* reside?'

The Little-Imam never paused in washing up the breakfast things.

'The first one, I hope and pray.'

That got a smile like the grill on a tank. An advancing tank.

'Hope where there is no hope,' said the Young Communist. "Prayer' said into a vacuum. What a waste of years. Not to mention social-space. Once you would have earned a bullet not a salary. We grow soft.'

In reply the Little-Imam was going to quote Surah 109:

> *'I worship not that which you worship*
> *Nor will you worship that which I worship.*
> *To you be your way, and to me mine...'*

but that would have been provocative, even foolhardy. The Communists might not foam at the mouth any more but they still occasionally *silenced* people. The Little-Imam's mind was willing but his flesh was weak. Not the stuff of which martyrs are made.

'We must agree to differ, sir.'

The communist arose, the trolley exhaled.

'Must we? Not really. But carry on earning your thirty pieces of silver as an opium peddler...'

He left, already purging their conversation from his brain. Encounters with the tenth century were simply lost time to an upwardly mobile modern man.

Those parting references flew right over the Little-Imam's head. He'd heard of both the Bible and Marx but couldn't claim close acquaintance. To be polite he pondered the words but whichever way you turned them they made no sense. The Little-Imam was paid in banknotes, not precious metals. And opium was highest *haram*.

Unbelievers said the strangest things...

The sentiments came through loud and clear though. For an infidel instant he envied the Young Communist. If only he could be as confident of *any*thing as the visitors were of *every*thing.

Or maybe not. Such confidence could come from the devil. For example, some *Wahhabis* hung round the mosque: wild-eyed fanatics. *Their* Islam had become a red mist permanently before their eyes. Hell seemed their likely destination.

Whereas the Little-Imam believed Allah's way was the middle way. Its paving was kindness—the Qur'an's oft-repeated *Ihsan*. Feeling that underfoot was surely unmistakable sign of the right road.

But now it was time for his daily diversion from that straight path. First and furtively, the Little-Imam checked the corridor outside. No one about.

Out came the hidden bottle of hootch and the teapot to hide it in. For once the Little-Imam ignored the Prophet's (peace be upon him) advice about haste being Satan's ally. The deed would have been soon done had not the Beggar walked straight through the wall.

'Wotcha, fatso!'

The Little-Imam was frozen in mid-pour: struck comical. The kitchen's walls were solid brick: moreover they were second floor high.

ALTERED ENGLANDS

The Beggar took the Little-Imam's poised hand. His grip was iron and ice. A second before it had been in interstellar space.

'No water today. And let's be generous, eh?'

He tipped the bottle till the teapot overflowed.

Compassion overcame the Little-Imam's fear. Up till then he'd had nothing to say except *'but but but...'*

'No! Neat will kill him!'

The Beggar shook his head.

'But me no *buts*, wicked imam. Fancy feeding your boss Aral region water! Pesticide and poison! But don't worry, his liver's as tough as old boots. I've just checked.'

'Begone Djinn! Leave me. I ask Allah's aid!'

The Beggar-demon's face was alternatively pitch black and blinding white. He laughed and showed a mouth that was damnation-red.

'Dimwit! What d'you think you're *getting?*'

The Beggar poised one hand over the pot. Instant mushrooms sprouted from the dirt beneath his fingernails.

'Next, add some special sparkle...'

The fungi dried at his command so that he could crumble them into the liquid.

He sniffed over it: in role as a dosser connoisseur of rotgut.

'Hmmmmmm! *Wow* even!'

Then he whistled, like a shepherd marshalling his dogs.

'Finally, let's have your friend back...'

There was no interval between him saying it and not being there at all. The species in-between men and angels are full of such tricks.

Such as summoning people like sheep. Aware or no, the Communists heard the Beggar's call and the whole delegation answered.

The kitchen door crashed open. The Young Communist was foremost, loud in mid-pronouncement.

'... just that tubby little dogsbody.'

Shocked and shaking the Little-Imam was caught red-handed. Vodka-handed.

'*Aha!*'

'Oh *ho!*'

They weren't angry, they were amused: delighted even. Foxy smiles all round. Few things are so pleasing as prejudices confirmed. They assumed the Little-Imam's shakes derived from his drinking habits.

'*Thirsty* are we, comrade?'

'A bit *early* one would have thought...'

The Young Communist was almost impressed. Almost.

'You had me fooled, comrade. Completely. There might be a future for you in mosque... management.'

Wiser than he knew. Sometimes men's words are not entirely their own...

The Haji-Imam swept in, flustered. The delegation had given him the slip, disappearing off as if answering a summons.

He also swept up his morning 'tea', meanwhile scatter-gunning apologies. The Little-Imam's protests—extra vigorous today for some reason—were ignored as usual. Black scowls from the Haji-imam had to suffice, but if they'd been alone there would have been blows.

The witnesses from the newer, superior, civilisation smiled knowing smiles.

☸

'Uneducated peasants, irreconcilable kulaks, obscurantist charlatans, self-appointed mullahs, parasites, crooks and vagabond fanatics...'

The spectators on the balcony ticked off the faithful into precise social segments as they arrived. Then, like a line of Elvis Presley impersonators in Soviet suits, their lips curled as prayers began.

> '*God is great!*
> *Glory to you, O Allah, and Yours is the praise...*'

The Haji-Imam had been sipping throughout. Today his tea tasted *extra* more-ish. It also had, as practised drinkers say, *bones in it*. Perhaps that was why the first few drinks made him splutter. With repetition it became easier and slipped down like a sixteen year old.

ALTERED ENGLANDS

Then, as the faithful recited and dwelt on the world to come, other worlds started to dance before the Haji-imam's eyes. And they were... *wonderful* worlds.

He was speechless and rigid and rapt, and in private all would have been well. However, outside his skull, in the normal Universe, time still plodded on, pedestrian-style. It arrived at the appointed moment for the *khutbah*, his weekly homily packed with pearls of wisdom. Coughs and other prompts drew his attention to the fact.

A fish rots from the head. For the moment the Haji-Imam's extremities, such as hands and feet, still answered the helm. He made it to the microphone.

The Haji-Imam studied the cross-legged horde. He looked at them and they looked at him. The exchange occupied what seemed like *ages*. Minutes dragged by in boots of lead.

Up in the balcony suited shoulders stiffened. This was unscripted. The awful fear arose that things were turning *dissident...*

When the Haji-Imam finally spoke it provoked sighs of relief all round, a whispering tidal wave washing round the mosque. Most people are kind at heart: few actually *enjoy* embarrassment.

'Today,' he bellowed, 'I want to talk to you about our beloved Motherland. I refer of course to The Union of Soviet Socialist Republics. The USSR....'

The balcony relaxed, the congregation fidgeted.

'Yes indeed, the USSR... the good old USSR...'

A bit colloquial, a bit over familiar, but within the bounds. Just.

'You don't know how lucky you are: to live here I mean. You don't know how lucky you are... *boy,* back in the... USSR...'

Hang about... Above and below people pricked up their ears.

Too late to do anything about it, the dam burst. All propriety got swept away in the flood.

The Haji-Imam might have been to distant Mecca—hence his name—but now he was orbiting way beyond anywhere Star Trek had boldly gone. Unheard by anyone else, the *Beatles* supplied his soundtrack.

He squared up to the congregation of golden giraffes arrayed before him. The teapot went up to his mouth like a mike. To his credit he didn't spill a drop.

It transpired he was a tenor. Not a very good one, mind, but very *committed*.

> *'I'M BACK IN THE USSR,*
> *YOU DON'T KNOW HOW LUCKY YOU ARE, BOY.*
> *BACK IN THE U.S. !*
> *BACK IN THE U.S. !*
> *BACK IN THE USSR. (YEAH! OH BABY!)'*

In the murky labyrinth of his mind, the Haji-Imam had gotten lost and confused between the Beatles and Elvis Presley. Choreography came courtesy of the latter.

It seemed like Elvis tributes were suddenly all the rage. First, none at all throughout the Mosque's long life, and then suddenly two in the same day.

The Haji-Imam's version was pretty convincing—for a dumpy drugged drunk man. He *frugged* and *twisted* as best the podium confines permitted. No one could criticise his zeal for 'getting on down'. Some of those hip gyrations and pelvic thrusts might have come from the King of Rock and Roll himself.

The Little-Imam had been delegated to stay with the delegation and *'not let them out of your sight'*. True to his mission he watched their jaws gape and eyes bulge at the display unfolding below them.

Inwardly, the Little-Imam shrugged. It can be a great comfort to believe that many things are simply *'Maktub'* or *written*. And what Allah decrees it is surely pointless to strive against...

Besides, the Little-Imam *had* warned of the dangers of listening to Western tapes. He derived no joy from being proved right.

Alas, not wanting any of his hard slog composing a *khutbah* to Communist specs to go to waste, the Haji-Imam had ordered that a faithful translation be made from the original Uzbek. The Little-Imam was also strictly instructed to explain any technical terms to the infidel. So the Little Imam did.

'He says—or sings—that he flew in from Miami Beach, B.O.A.C.—that's an airline I think. He... didn't get to bed last night. Um, and on the way the paper bag—the vomit bag I presume—was on his knee. Man—man? I don't know why he said that—man, he had a dreadful flight. But now he's back in the USSR. Apparently we don't know how lucky we are... boy... Back in the U.S., back in the U.S.—he's repeating himself here—back in the USSR!'

ALTERED ENGLANDS

The Little-Imam was doubly puzzled. How come the Party visitors seemed so familiar with this patently decadent Western capitalist song? Surely they of all people hadn't indulged in forbidden *'rock'* music? And yet recognition was written all over their furious faces. Plus blushes and guilt.

In the Little-Imam's humble opinion the lyrics were rubbish, a careless appendage to the raucous music. Did people in the 'Free World' waste their freedom in actually *buying* this stuff? Any old Uzbek ballad of love and loss and death knocked such nonsense for six.

"Back in the USSR' has been repeated three times. With an exclaimed *'Yeah'*—see when he punches the air?—on each occasion. And apparently—please excuse me—the Ukraine girls *'really knock me out'*, they... um... leave the West behind. And, um, Moscow girls make him scream and shout. And Georgia's always on his *'MI-MI-MI-MI-MI-MI-MI-MI-MIND!'*

And so on.

The faithful had put up with a lot over the years but there are limits. Though subsequent verses would have been equally good, touching upon such subjects as 'SNOW-PEAKED MOUNTAINS WAY DOWN SOUTH' and 'KEEPING COMRADES WARM', they just *didn't* want to hear them.

> *'I'M BACK IN THE USSR,*
> *YOU DON'T KNOW HOW LUCKY YOU ARE, BOY,*
> *BACK IN THE U.S.!*
> *BACK IN THE U.S.!*
> *BACK IN THE U.S.S.Aaaaaaaaaaaaarrrrgh!'*

The rioting and shots and baton charges continued far into the star-studded night.

❦

'A drunken wastrel, a bourgeois broken reed and a conscious anti-Soviet element and provocateur,' said the Young Communist. 'Whereas *you*, you are merely a drunk.'

The Little-Imam meekly accepted the falsehood. His only alternative was to malign the memory of his poor departed boss.

The Young Communist had survived, a bit charred and minus one lapel, but otherwise not visibly harmed. Or chastened.

'I tell you candidly, our first intention was to close this... mosque, to bulldoze it flat. Centres of obscurantism we can tolerate but not anarchy!'

The Little-Imam's sloping shoulders sloped some more at the thought.

'However, it retains a role to play. Our essential requirement is for someone to *guide* such institutions. To pacify and make socially useful the objective forces therein. You might provide a suitable... example to the unenlightened. Till we found out your... little weakness,' one flicked hand mimed a tippler's wrist, 'I would have advised otherwise. The Soviet Motherland does not like pious people in its places of worship!'

There was no answer to that, so the Little-Imam didn't even try.

'But given what we now know maybe you will do. Expect your letter of appointment shortly. The salary should keep you in vodka forever, but keep it within bounds. Hypocrisy, yes, informing certainly, maybe even a little scandal from time to time will suit our purposes. But no degenerate *Beatles* songs, understand? And definitely no rioting!'

The Little-Imam signalled he would do his best. His view over the Young Communist's shoulder now took in the mosque. It suddenly seemed more solid, more likely to reach tomorrow.

The Beggar-Djinn (someone the Young Communist appeared quite unable to see) clapped the Little-Imam on the back.

'Result!' it exulted.

The Young Communist, who did not hear, interpreted the Little-Imam's spasm as a further encouraging sign of alcoholism.

It was just like the Rus Christians said, realised the Little-Imam: there's none so blind as those who *will* not see.

❁

It was another of those days when the Little-Imam *saw*. The shore was crowded. No sea still, but many people from many eras. They smiled into the distance. Their times, their painstaking constructions, came and went, magically revived in the distance, but their souls remained.

'They testify,' explained the Beggar-Djinn, 'They come to testify!'

'That the past and present and future are one,' amplified the Little-Imam. 'And are as nothing in the eye of *the* One.'

The Beggar-Djinn doubled up in glee.

'Good boy. Good *boy!*'

He executed a wild round-the-imam jig.

The Little-Imam was compelled to speak what he now understood. It was too great to contain as a private insight—he would burst.

'They await Judgement here, because they wish to. There is no fear, no anxiety. A delicious drowsiness drives out both. They—we—are warmed in the smile of the *One*. I now know. I know that, above all, Allah is... *merciful.*'

Silence. Djinn are driven creatures. His work done, the Beggar-Djinn was gone to guide or destroy others.

No matter. He *had* been here: that was the thing.

Because of it, the Little-Imam had spoken true. How could he not when coached by *the* Truth? Past, present and future were mere convenient fictions: concessions made to hard-of-understanding humans. All time was one.

Here was visible proof. The Little-Imam saw a version of himself waiting amongst the others on the shore. He looked much older but quietly confident.

That confidence was born there and then, and started to grow: confidence of giving—and therefore receiving—mercy.

It was tempting to stay but he had things to do.

The Little-Imam trudged back up the 'beach', back to the years and duties allotted him.

6~

'EXCUSE ME...'

✵

'Oh, save us! What *do* you want?'

Nothing apparently. No repetition.

'Come on, don't be shy. We don't bite.'

Nothing.

An exchange of glances with the officer facing. He hadn't heard. Puzzled looks.

'Listen.'

He did: non-understanding grew.

'I can't...'

And for once, what was wanted came when it was wanted. The voice; again.

'*Excuse me...*'

'There! Can *you* see her?'

The other immigration officer on 'European Control' was an old timer by the service's standard: *'an experienced IO'*, five years *'experience'* in and getting cold eyed; thin mouthed. He had the better vantage point, the acuter angle to the arrivals ramp she spoke from. He ought to have her in view.

'No.' Then tetchiness. 'What's your game?'

There was camaraderie in adversity but also limited patience for *created* problems. They had more than enough real ones. Gypsies awaited allocation from an earlier Czech flight, imminent were an *Alitalia* from Milan: the

ALTERED ENGLANDS

'beautiful people' in welded-on shades, then an *Olympic*: Greek scowls and survival-of-the-fittest queuing. More than enough.

'Can't you 'ear? She keeps on saying it.'

Shared troubles or no, the IO still had no time for fuck-wits and wind-ups. He abandoned the desk and took the ramp, tiger-like. At thirty-going-on-seventy he could still hack a fair burst of speed. She'd not leg it before he got there.

'*Look*, love, either say what y-...'

No one. The arrivals landing was not a people place at the best of times. It was only ever fleetingly occupied, a God-forsaken space for passengers, '*paxes*', only. All day, all year, fluorescent light kept it unearthly. An old, forlorn, *'Blue Peter'* competition-winner *'Welcome to Britain'* poster failed to. The hordes had scattered gaudy *'spend-your-money-here'* leaflets out of the rack and over the carpet. No one would linger unless lost.

The escalator down to the lounge. Nothing. Stairs to the gate-rooms: deserted: anticipating the next flight. Unless she'd thrown herself down or had a rocket up her...

'You all right?'

A call from the comrade left behind. He ignored it.

Down the escalator was a *'Heathrow Airport Ltd.'* security point. Unoccupied HAL boys and girls lark-flirting round a luggage scanner. There was sort of cooperation between them and *'Immigration'*: the same side, sort of. They brushed themselves down.

'Anyone come through? Youngish girl?'

The looks told everything. Time—minutes—had passed since they put 'official' on. They were relaxed *'saarf Londoners'*.

'No. Why? Want us to keep a look out?'

'Don't matter, ta.'

The way back was slower: self examining. He *had* heard. She *had* spoken. But the stairwells and corridor and ramp were sterile: *pax* free.

He resumed his podium-desk, fiddled with the date-stamp and keyboard. His oppo was going to say something but thought better of it. The shift was on short fuses, mucked-about by management.

Then the Greeks arrived, without gifts. There was forgetfulness in crap-issue passports and fending *go-die* stares.

JOHN WHITBOURN

⚓

Life, civilisation, England: everything, started *after* the staff bus, beyond the five football pitches of the staff car park and the sad plane-spotter infested perimeter road.

They abutted it at some points, green fields and sheep and horses right up against the runway; at others a scorched zone of dead, litter-land separated the concrete-and-exhaust festival that was Heathrow from life—real life.

He was the only one who *came* from here, the only real Heathrower in the Terminal. His folks had been here before the airport was cheated upon them, parachuted onto the land under cover of WWII and killing it. Every other *'colleague'* was from somewhere else, Scotland mostly, and longed to return. No one *came* from Heathrow: you went to it, under protest, and went away again. He'd tried explaining—early days only—but no longer could be arsed. It was a printed card job, even if anyone were interested—and they weren't.

Straightaway, not two songs worth on the radio, you were in Cranford, a baggage-handler's gob from the M4 Air-Cargo exit. A humpback bridge over the Crane, God-forsaken St Dunstan's church, the stables of long-gone Cranford House. He gunned the motor through there, hardly noticing; autopilot. But there were people there: living, walking—and greenery too! His mind started to revive from the shift-slumber. It was a queer old route home, ten minutes extra at least; quite a detour but vital: reaffirmation.

Off Cranford Lane: a housing estate, *HAL-ville*: security boys and girls and baggage-Neanderthals: *'Tels'* and *'Shels'* and *'mad-Mickey'*s, shell-suit, sovereign-ring and lager-land come days off: *geezer* country. All very tasty in its way, but not his, not entirely, not yet. Then another country: deep country. The airlock of a proper genuine *wood*. Another old Middlesex humpback, second gear and careful with it, then open fields to Harlington. He whizzed by St Peter and St Paul's there every day. He'd visited it once when the jumbos boomed over and made the twelfth century stones quake. The Norman door jambs were carved cat's heads, their tongues twined in a scroll. Mum said he was christened there.

Sipson Lane was real rural: lined with Lombardy poplars:, guardsmen to either side. Tractors worked the furrows beyond. He could put on a bit of speed then. There was little traffic save in the blue above, and that just the locals who knew the way. Outsiders didn't come here: no point—they thought it was Heathrow and steered clear as they would an HIV rottweiler. *Good*.

The arrival of Mordor had frozen all; flash-freezed it into a time-warp. On the periphery, farms, manors, churches, fields and lanes survived the hammer-blow at random and then stayed there. No one wanted to buy a gaff right under the roar-zone and be shaken to bits, day in, day out. The before-people stayed—having little choice. Some of them worked at the alien arrival, though early on it still seemed a bit of a betrayal. But that had soon passed. Not everyone could be a 'carrot-cruncher' working the ravished fields. Need drove the natives to beg favours from the invader. And he paid good money. A curry and club every weekend, *up-town*: gold chains and toys for the kiddies. It helped that the mortgage was cheap too. Property went for a song here—but it didn't often *go. It stayed in the family, din' i?*

Harmondsworth had a village green, three old pubs—one thatched—a church and tithe barn—though surrounded, cut-off like under siege. The M4 was a rumble, everlasting, but it could have been worse. He'd seen what survived of Burrows Lane: a couple of houses and gardens left on a spit of land between the main runway and a sewage plant. Here you were laughing compared to that. So he laughed and pulled in to *'The Five Bells'* at speed, used to it, slewing to a halt beside the cattle-trough.

Here there were humans and smokos and lager to wash away the day.

There was no need to worry. The *polis* didn't come here, save for 'domestics' on a Friday night. They hardly knew the place either, were out of their depth, had enough on their plate-hands anyhow. The *'Northside Station'* boys just toted carbines to impress the *2F's ('fuckin' furriners')*, or purged the winos back out where they came from. Boozed-up crusties were bad for business and image—top priority job. Either that or they cruised the perimeter roads, north and south, hassling the spotter-nerds or nicking staff who'd been on the sauce. Whereas the IO never drank at work, even though the bars were 24 hours. He always waited till here.

Breathalyser-carefree, he drank enough to drown out her voice.

☸

'I was 'ere before it was and I'll be still 'ere when it's gorn. That's the way I looks at it.'

They were looking at it from the edge of the runway. Uncle Eric's fields flinched away from its very lip. A margin of grass beyond was aviation-fuel singed.

'No you won't, you daft old bugger. You'll be dead and gone. Dust.'

If he'd told those not in-the-know there were actual *oh-aaah* yokels not a mile from the duty-free palaces, they'd have laughed at him. So he didn't tell them. Yet Uncle Eric and all his brothers and cousins really were genuine old *we-wunt-be-druv* Saxon-stock. They'd seen *their* Heathrow, a medieval village, annihilated by the airport, rammed through under the false pretence of war needs when it was known that'd never be. Not a single RAF plane had ever flown from the murdered fields. They'd watched their houses bulldozed at a week's notice through deceit—and nodded over news of an Iron Age temple discovered beneath the main runway site: proof of continuity being lost; embarrassing evidence hurriedly buried forever.

The younger man knew second-hand: he'd seen it set out in black and white, in a local historian's, best-he-could-do, self-published book. There were documents plain-stating it was a civil airport they always intended—but wouldn't have got under peacetime considerations. Even Churchill was lied to, had the wool pulled over his D-Day distracted eyes. The scandal was there screaming in your face if you did but look. But it didn't make any difference; no one noticed. It was too late. The mandarins got what they wanted, like usual, and a couple of thou displaced yeomen wouldn't even put a stroke on their Saturday golf. It was always the way.

The official Heathrow guide on sale in the airport had an introductory chapter. It said the area was *'sparsely populated waste'* before the godsend airplanes came, instead of the best bloomin' market-gardening land in England, that's all. The IO kept his outrage quiet and never revealed it to the family. Still, he was blood of their blood. He always rumpled that page when he had a moment and thought of it. He'd lost them a lot of lying sales over the years.

So Uncle Eric and all the other Uncle Erics had just carried on, hauling their ageing tractors across the fields left to them, dipping up and down the furrows, as though there weren't pandemonium at their elbows and occasional rain of fuel and iced passenger piss. He almost envied them that mad obstinacy, half-hoping, half-fearing it weakened in himself.

The old farmer screwed his eyes up, looking either at the control tower or some private future.

'Happen dust and bones I shall be—but me kith and kin won't. I'll see it through their eyes.'

His nephew snort-laughed, as he always did, but recognised the old fossil might even be speaking true. Maybe one day, when there was *anti-grav* and spaceships...

It was right enough that the family weren't going anywhere in a hurry. They were chained by work and affection and a dead property-market. To himself, he rather liked that, the perseverance in spite of all that'd been thrown at and over them. But because he was young and fancy-free and a bit *jack-the-lad*, minor protest was almost expected.

'What makes you think I'll stick in this dump? If the locals interbreed anymore they'll be knuckle-scrapers soon. Where's the crumpet round 'ere to keep me?'

Uncle Eric smiled. They'd done this old routine many a time before. But it bore repeating, even though the younger man was *'on early'* tomorrow. It was sort of cement for the family.

'You stick it where you chose, boy, and I wish 'ee much joy of it. But when you're done just you make sure you drags her back. I want my lot to see them plough that tarmac up. I'll be lookin' down, never fear. You mark my words: if you're missin' when that day comes, I'll come back and *haunt* 'ee, so I will.'

The IO did mark the words, he certainly did, all of a sudden. They called to mind other words. Then: fresh reminder in stale air.

'Excuse I!'

Beer before dinner always gave Uncle Eric the burps nowadays—but he never normally apologised...

'Are you all right, boy? You're struck comical...'

He'd heard right enough but was distracted. Like a missile out of the airport shot recollection of another expression of regret, a different apology. He remembered—with strange clarity—a polite girl's voice calling for *his* attention.

'Excuse me...'

It was only memory—he was almost entirely sure of it.

He was also glad when the evening Concorde drowned all possibility of thought or reply.

JOHN WHITBOURN

The day at 4:30 is dull pain; rising a triumph of the Judas will. *Will* takes you from bed and girl and home and oblivion, takes you hunch-shouldered, old-man shuffling, from bed to bath to car, betraying you. If it were weaker then there'd more warm hours in the sack, maybe early passion—and probably the dole in the end—but at least no rising with the birds and milkmen.

First memory, first half-way pleasure; a 'Heathrow breakfast': strong coffee and a smoko. That gets you to the motor. Next memory the place itself. The prospect wakes you up.

Same seen/not seen route through the concourse. As always, an imaginary grenade rolled into *Air France*'s offices. Today one of them is lolling about outside, looking smug. Big spoilt brat, olive goo-goo eyes. Then they beheld the man. The mood changed. The two had history: nothing unusual.

'Morning, cunt!'

He understand *that* much English. The Frenchman muttered something soft in return.

Too many: too many witnesses—a departure hall piled chocka full of paxes.

'Yeah, yeah, you're very brave in company. We'll meet up in a corridor someday. Depend on it.'

An Agincourt salute had to suffice, the age-hallowed two-fingered *V* greeting between the two nations. Still, it set him up for collecting a radio and *mayfly*, and all the unavoidable *hello*s and *wotcha*s to colleagues. Then another snaffled wake-up coffee out of the detainees' room, a mini-pack of *bourbons* liberated from *'asil'*-seeker maws. Then flights and foreigners. Another bloody day.

Only it wasn't. It was different.

Pier two was cold. Even the early business arrivals, the dead-men walking, Basle and Zurich *Euro-suits*, noticed. They clenched their thin shoulders as compact as their hearts.

He could have guessed but wouldn't have it. When the sun got up it would be different, he said. There would be warmth. This was such a dead place, the Airport Chapel forlorn and forgotten; Darwin and Dawkins the real presiding deities. It was easy to disbelieve contrary evidence.

He saw the Frankfurt unload, queried some of the Lagos connectees, took some flak, gave it two-times back. He stopped two Sri Lankans—passport free zones—off the Toulouse: the Toulouse! Who reckoned they didn't know where they'd come from—but they did have a solicitor and his mobile telephone number was...

Then the lull before the *Aeroflots* and guttural Russian: *'Two days business—what is problem?'* and the Paris and another Frankfurt and and and and...

Sandwiched between two slices of crap even *nothing* seems very appetising—the more nothing the less crap. He embraced that void. He pondered on the desirability of a *Burger King* and felt guilty. That was *airport food*—but it tasted good...

Normally he wouldn't care about strays in gate-rooms, whatever *'total-quality management'* Security practice might say. People wandered; found their own cosy corners in which to wait. He didn't blame paxes shunning the **BUY! BUY! BUY!** of the lounge, all the posh shops you'd ever heard of, all the things you never knew you wanted till you had time on your hands, cash in your pocket and were in *indulge-yourself*, holiday mood. Animal metaphors occurred. The pax herd were sitting ducks in the lounge, willing to be sheared chilly. By that score any maverick explorers were cheering evidence that a few of the travel-cattle still had souls, weren't entirely consumerism-BSE'd.

This one though, she merited a look, a word. Odd: promising. His legs did his thinking for him. Later on, he realised he must have known, plunging in fully aware she was the heart of the cold amidst Heathrow's cold heart.

Her back was to him, a little figure looking out over the concrete and tarmac fields. She had a saucy—but innocent—bum; a nice girl's one, tight wrapped—but not calculatingly so like Brazilian beauties in tie-die cotton. She didn't realise what she was doing. The thick flaxen ponytail confirmed that. It still happened in some rare places where the body wasn't a commodity like any other. He felt free to admire God's handiwork.

The morning sun illuminated the dress and her, resurrecting dust motes in spiralling columns. It was... very pleasant but she really shouldn't be there. Until her flight was called she belonged in the lounge. Also he wanted to speak to her, to exchange words as their life-lines crossed only to diverge forever. He wanted to see if the eyes were innocent too.

'Excuse me...'

He'd said it. The very thing, the absolute anti-matter of what he intended. Whatever possessed him? It was no longer a phrase available for his free use. Someone else had appropriated it as their own. In his voice it assumed awful significance, heavy words beyond any conceivable meaning, cracking the frigid air.

Then he saw that the rising sun really did light her up; it shone through, penetrating her even as he wished to. A Swissair taxied up, visible through her abdomen. The grey towers of distant Staines rose behind her face. She was transparanced, transfigured, petite head to toe.

The girl turned. Sudden, surprised. The innocence was there—but only by its fingertips: stamped upon. Worst of all she recognised him. Cobalt blue eyes: recognition, then last-legs longing: desperation. A drowning woman sighting something better than a straw.

'*Excuse me...*'

He didn't want to hear her say that. He did not want her to expect help from him. He wasn't worth it.

She'd seen a gentleman: an English gentlemen. She'd remembered something and had hope.

Then she saw his back.

He tore his favourite black suit as he cannoned through the stiff double doors. The traitor latch was left with its cloth trophy. A pax and his trolley got knocked over and never knew what hit them.

The cold followed him but could not catch up. It faltered for lack of encouragement and ebbed sadly back home.

☸

'What? Not *many* there ain't!'

'Yeah?'

The HAL man hadn't had a human to speak to for ages; just lost paxes bumping up against his security point. Home and TV were miles off, retirement further still. He welcomed the IO's enquiry, able to converse in slipper-comfy natural dialect, happy to offload his years of experience in machine-gun delivery pure *Saarf*.

'Yeah. Loads of em have topped 'emselves here, I tell yer. I know the feelin'. There was that *polis*, Special Branch, a few years back: didn't pass his detective exams or summink. Drew a shooter and then bang! in the embarks office. Girls won't go there now: says it's cold and makes em cry. You know the Arrivals Control? 'Course you do. Some Yank queen slashed his wrists right in front of everyone: sprayed 'em all: fought the first-aiders off. And there was that little au-pair in the loo here: one of your punters: wouldn't go home, so stayed permanent. Oh yeah, loads...'

He'd lost his audience but didn't notice. He chuntered on in happy airport-anecdote mode.

'We had a snake missing here once—it was in the papers: never found him. Baby then but grows to 'firty feet, apparently. Reckon he's up in the roof cavity eating rats and MacDonald's cockroaches—and maybe the punters wot go missin'. You imagine: wanderin' along some fuckin' corridor, then, wallop! Down from the sky comes matey, bites yer head and pulls you up: no one the wiser. Someone misses a flight, bloke never turns up for work, who cares? Not here. No one cares or gives a fuck 'ere, do they, mate? Oi! I said, do they?'

※

She'd fallen amongst illegals: came to see England but found another, newer, country. The au-pair agency proved dodgy; had delivered her into the hands of *Olufemi*'s—Nigerian? Ghanaian?—and an *Alsabah*. Kuwaiti? Saudi? He knew more about *their* names than he did the origin of his own. That was the sort of schooling he'd had, him and all his generation.

Anyway, she'd copped a queer mix, quaffed a heady cocktail—and probably one or two up that pretty tail too. They wanted a working-girl not an au-pair—and, to be fair, doubtless made a good offer. She'd been pretty. It was only after the first *No!* they might turn nasty. Three lemons on the one-armed bandit of cacky luck, poor love.

It was odd how much misfortune could tumble out of a slim pink file.

If Heathrow was a universe of its own, unrelated to the surviving green around, then *Room 104* was its outer limits. No one went to the *Lay-by* room bar clericals in the few months before they realised what a shite job they'd landed and moved on. The IO barely knew the way there: it was just legend to him, dimly recalled from a tour round on his first day, long ago: another person.

He let instinct guide him, through doors he usually ignored, along *Dalek*-style corridors, down a iron staircase and out onto the apron. The baggage trailers rattled around him as he saw a far door that stirred memory. It was open and a fumble on the wall allowed there to be light. Wire cages full of sad paperwork stretched before him on either side. This was *'Lay-by'*. Room 104: hello again: how have you been keeping this last decade?

He had a few names, half-recalled by colleagues, and her best-guess nationality; enough to drag some likely reference numbers out of the Port Admin System. He also needn't have bothered. She was there.

Without the sun to substantiate her, she was flimsy: a trace-element of human, unwilling, unable to go. There was an outline of girl, a pool of milky luminescence. What strength she had left was put into the face. She could see and wanted him to. He forced himself, leaving nail half-moons in his palms.

It was horrible. The IO had never observed such sadness, not even in his job. Still worse, she'd exchanged life for subtler faculties. The girl looked within him and discovered hope in his dry husk. That he didn't want. Softer feelings meant pain and then the grim process of shedding them again.

She was just a girl: even in unnatural outline: lovely and blameless. He didn't doubt her Mum had packed her case and seen her off to England. Hard-working Dad had probably gone to wave goodbye, not knowing their darling wasn't coming back. Her adventure had gone septic, ending as ghostly dust in the dust of Room 104.

She had just enough for one storm left, before she faded into mere disquiet. Her tears poured upon him and his inner desert bloomed.

He couldn't stop himself: try as he might. He wanted to help, even more than he wanted to *go* and forget and mind his own business. She'd not been wrong about him, not from that first call for help on the European Control. She'd seen true. She'd seen truth.

And knowing that, she could leave, taking her acid *'Ladies'* aroma and death-chill with her, back to wherever she spent the long days and nights since hanging herself.

※

No need to search the fetid archives. Her pink *'Refusal'* file was right beside where she'd appeared. Even a *gentleman* can do with a helping hand in the right direction.

It was all there in the *Q & A* notes, the photocopied letters, her toothy smile in the passport. The IO wondered why that hadn't been returned to… the Embassy or someone. He supposed no one needed it, not now—she'd not been

'Removed'—he knew that better than anyone. It was going to live a few more years than its owner, awaiting the inevitable shredder down in lonely *Lay-by*.

> *'Q: Max stay?*
> *A: Six months, please, if that is possible.*
> *Q: Why you come?*
> *A: To be au-pair, and to see England. It is my dream.*
> *Q: How know sponsors?*
> *A: Through my agency—only through agency. But I don't want to stay with them. They were cruel to me and laughed. I thought the English were all gentlemen but they are not. I would like another family and look after their children. Could you suggest one, please?*
> *Q: We are not here as an au-pair agency...'*

Indeed not. He knew the IO dealing: a lovely woman—sweet personality and swaying hips to die for—but ten years in, over-lied to, once too often mucked about, and thus—in the Terminal—as compassionate as a pike. The girl was dead-in-the-water immigration-wise even as she spoke and it was recorded. Her 'choice' of sponsors and address lit up the *Suspect Index* screen. If she'd gone back the same day it might have turned out different, but it was late, the interview schedule heaving with half of Eastern Europe's gypsies, knowingly ethnic-cleansed by their own governments out to generous old Britain. Two week's *'Temporary admission'* had allowed the sponsors to make their pitch and do whatever else they did.

She came back for *'casework re-interview'* with a modesty-edited tale of woe—and doubtless a tail of woe too. A fish-in-the-barrel *'knock-off'*—if you wanted it. Someone did. He sympathised. Your 'Annual Staff Performance Review' demanded a through-put of *stats* whatever the Home office might say to *'The Independent'*

'YOU HAVE ASKED FOR LEAVE TO ENTER THE UNITED KINGDOM AS AN 'AU-PAIR' FOR SIX MONTHS BUT I AM NOT SATISFIED THAT THE ARRANGEMENT COMPLIES WITH THE DEFINITION OF AN 'AU-PAIR' PLACEMENT AS SPECIFIED IN PARAGRAPH 88 OF THESE RULES, AND FURTHERMORE I AM NOT SATISFIED THAT YOU WILL LEAVE THE UNITED KINGDOM AT THE EXPIRY OF ANY LEAVE TO REMAIN OR

THAT YOU WILL NOT TAKE ADDITIONAL EMPLOYMENT OR RESIDE WITHIN A BONA-FIDE AU-PAIR ARRANGEMENT.

I ACCORDINGLY REFUSE YOU LEAVE TO ENTER THE UNITED KINGDOM.

I HAVE GIVEN DIRECTION THAT YOU BE REMOVED FROM THE UNITED KINGDOM ON FLIGHT...'

Preceding her and that already yellowing document was a *denunce* letter from the sponsors, covering their own arses. Apparently she was a *'whore'* and not at all suitable. They'd seen her trawling the streets and getting into cars, *'believe me, officer,'* and written to her parents to that effect. Then Customs had her for a while and tested positive for speed and *Es*—which may or may not have been of her doing: not voluntary anyway.

Any or all were enough to get a big black hot-cross bun stamped in her passport. More than. Come back another time—but get a visa first—and good luck with getting *that* lady...

Only she wouldn't and couldn't and hadn't any. A night's detention amongst... interesting people, and early flight next morning was more than she could take—that and the shame. On the way to the plane, under *Group 4* escort and any passerby's curious gaze, she'd asked to use the *Ladies*. And she had.

Her skinny belt, the door jamb to one of the traps. It was simple if you had the nerve. A little pain and then an end to pain—or so she thought. The IO pondered the horror of waking again to a nightmare without cease.

He left *104* and its still lingering taint of *Izal*. He'd read the file, he was up to speed. In his heart of hearts, he knew what the spirit had wanted, even when still encased in flesh. It was up to him to provide it. A *gentleman* had no choice.

❀

He called her by name—and being a nice, polite girl she came. There was nothing in her weary patrols of Terminal 2 to detain her.

She had her eye on him in any case, even when he did not suspect. She'd followed him to the *Five Bells* the night before—and her faith wavered. This very day, she'd heard what he'd said to the—admittedly arrogant—

ALTERED ENGLANDS

American businessman, and she'd feared. Her time was not long, her energies diminishing. Soon enough she'd be just... unhappiness swirling in Heathrow's upper air, along with all the rest. They called to her, saying come and play. They spoke of concerted attempts to down planes, whispering contagion in pilots' minds. They were many and increasingly clear. There was urgency.

She walked from the *Ladies* along the length of pier two, just a shimmering refraction of the florescent light, flash-freezing the pax hordes who brushed against her. For a second only, holidays were forgotten, hot-dates dreaded. She had thoughtfully brought every scrap of her misery along with her, not wishing anything to remain..

He waited in gate-room 8: well chosen—a south prospect and mostly Swiss Air dedicated: crazy in the rush hour, forlorn outside.

Doors and row of seats did not trouble or delay her. She came to his side.

'Excuse me...'

'No, excuse *me*. I'm... sorry.'

He had to force himself to speak out loud, to clench his eyes against the half-sight of her beside him. That shoulder was ice-gripped.

'I-know-what-you-came-to-see. We're not all like that: honest. You just hit a real bummer... I mean, stinking luck. You gotta believe me. Do you?'

She wanted to—he felt the yearning as a front of warmth—but she couldn't.

'It isn't *all* this.' He indicated the dead world around and then the wider one beyond. 'Look!'

He'd prepared, done his homework, made a mental inventory. Gate 8 had windows you could fling open if you didn't mind the noise outside. The IO had chosen his time too: it was a quiet spell: merely frantic. He could actually speak, not shout.

'Look, go on, please?'

He felt her despair edge slightly forward. Did ghosts need to stand on tiptoe?

'There's stuff beyond this. Forget central London. *Babylon*—*Babylon*don, we call it. Can't you see the green?'

There was no disagreement—all the encouragement he needed.

The IO detailed the medieval churches, spire by spire, tower by tower: Stanwell, Bedfont, Hounslow and Feltham and others he just made up. Those you couldn't see he described anyway. Stanwell's was crooked, St. Mary's, Harmondsworth, had a cupola. He touched on Cranford House's stables, surviving despite the odds, the red pillar boxes, the stranded farms and troughs and fences: all the things he suddenly realised he loved. He even told her about Uncle Eric's poor old fields. He warmed to his theme, forgetting time and place, relapsing into native tongue.

'There's that much surviving even here! And when you get further, right out in the sticks, it's even better. My bruvver, right: him and his dogs can be in deep woods just two minutes from his gaff, not thirty miles away, right? *That's* England, the place you never got to see: not here. But you can now. What's stoppin' yer? Fly and see, no ticket required. You're not bound here. *Here's* the thing you fear. Get out of here and you're free! Free as a bird! Go anywhere you want, my love.'

The doors swung open behind them. The intruder *Alitalia* rep paused. He saw only a mad IO before a window, in full flow to no one. And the place reeked like an arctic lavatory.

'Fuck off! *Fuck* off or I'll chin you!'

It was not abnormal converse between Her Majesty's Immigration Service and the Italian State Airline—particularly since the Kosovan incident and the Somali deceits, but those little unsettling extras tipped the balance. Italy's finest retreated. They were left alone.

'Sorry. *Sorry*. I had to! I've got to say this. It's important. It's all for you. Not me. I'd *like* you to see my country properly. They ain't killed it all yet. There's some of us left... Honest. Word of a gentleman: English gentleman. *Trust* me.'

Nothing. A pause. And then a chaste girl's hand brushed his rough cheek. She *did*, after and despite everything.

The girl allowed herself to be drawn through the window, out into the distant green and pleasant haze, arriving in seconds. Heathrow was left far behind, a blot on the landscape, no longer so huge seen from a new perspective. She felt better already. Finer days and sights beckoned. And then home: real home. The girl felt its pull for the first time now she was free from Hell's outmost bastion.

The welcoming golden light called from the horizon—but there was no hurry. God was love and all indulgence. Ample time for a holiday in England first.

ALTERED ENGLANDS

Another head nodding session. Ever since she'd made him think, he treasured them more than he used to. Uncle Eric wouldn't always be around. He was company and history and told good stories—the same ones, admittedly, but worth a regular outing.

'I was 'ere before it was and I'll be still 'ere when it's gorn. That's the way I looks at it.'

Again they looked at it from as close they dared. As a boy the IO had once wandered onto the runway and a policeman had come to see the family. A curtain-twitching festival for the village. Not only that but the planes almost made his ears bleed. His head rang for days—though that might just have been Dad's hard hand.

He no longer laughed at *'The Prophecy of Eric'*, as the family called it. He hoped it was true, so why should he mock? He'd done too much of that for too many years past, slow becoming the thing *she'd* run foul of. He'd neglected the seeds of decency all that time, assuming them useless pinned under the concrete. Now, with just a little attention, they already showed fresh growth. Like him, they'd just been awaiting some encouragement, the end of the long drought.

'You go for it, Unc—and if it's not you, then maybe me. One of us'll see the bulldozers tear it up.'

It was music to the old man's ears. His sermons had borne fruit. He could go down to rest happy now, reassured, reconciled.

He set his hand on his nephew's shoulder.

'You're a gent, boy'—and he'd never said *that* before.

There proved to be such a thing as gentle*women* too.

Because air rushed by the IO's ear, tousling his hair. It was not a bird or the by-wash of a plane but something more substantial and interesting than both

She had come to say goodbye, off to the holiday that lasts forever, and blessed him in passing.

For just a second he saw with her eyes, freed from the shackles of linear time, soaring high above the meandering river of history.

Heathrow was green—entirely. A man stood surveying his fields. It was not him—but not far off, not radically separated.

All either could see were farms and lanes and curious houses, half thatch, half plastic-wood, but not too many of any. The Churches were in good nick, if more mosque-like. Far—very far—above, starships twinkled in the sky. In one distant corner a little museum held a few rusting planes.

The IO blew her departing shade a kiss. A gossamer peck was returned in kind. Few men could say they'd had one of those.

Then she was gone and took the vision with her—save in his memory. It and she would only ever be sweet recollection. Nothing looked quite so bad now.

'It's just temporary,' he told his Uncle, indicating the airport with averted eyes. "Ere today, gone tomorrow. Not like us.'

Uncle Eric nodded agreement and the two gentlemen turned for home.

MISCELLANEOUS STORIES

COMPRISING:

'YO ENGLISH! DR DEATH!'

'THE WAY, THE TRUTH…'

'I CAME TO COMPTON…'

THE SUNKEN GARDEN

JOHN WHITBOURN

7~

'YO ENGLISH! DR DEATH!'

INTRODUCTION

Someone commented that there were enough themes in this here tale to make a novel or two, never mind a short story. Possibly so, but that's what happens when you take a point in history and twist it. If you pick the right point then everything changes. Otherwise *what's* the point? Who would wish to read, let alone write, a story hinging upon whether Arthur Sidebottom, junior billing clerk with the Gas Board in Guildford, Surrey, England, has either tuna or 'egg n' cress' sandwiches for his lunch on Friday 26th March 1976?[14]

Therefore, an 'Alternative history' has to be expansive, encompassing as many familiar-things-made-strange as possible. Indeed, I think that is the

---

[14] It was tuna. Which was 'off'—the fish's revenge for its murder and the truncation of its happy aquatic life (tuna can live to be 15-20, if left alone). Poor Arthur was soon as sick as a dog and had to go home early. Consequently, he didn't dispatch the gas bill that would have been the final straw in the financial troubles of a Guildfordian who would have hung themselves Saturday lunchtime—before finding out they'd won the football pools that day and were now filthy rich. Meanwhile, Arthur had to spend the whole weekend *'chained to the mahogany'*, as we say in England, i.e. in sprinting reach of the bathroom; and so couldn't go to the barndance and meet the girl he would have married and had three children with. One of those offspring would have grown up to be the greatest naval commander England ever had, Nelson included. However, since she never lived, the Battle of Cairns (2048) was lost and the Neo-Caliphate went on to...

core of their appeal, shifting the ground under the reader's feet in the same way that a ghost story should, by perking up the prosaic.

More indulgently, it offers the opportunity to convene a historical court of appeal and correct the aberrations of reality. I've always hoped that Paradise offers that facility, and that when harp playing and praise palls there's a 'What If?' history machine to play with. Which is to rashly assume I'll ever get to find out.

Presumably, the other place reruns all the things you wished had never happened. Which could mean we're all already there but don't realise...

If some elements within seem perceptive, even in bad taste, I can only plead that the story was written in 1998, i.e. before the tragic events of September 11th 2001. In this world, Osama bin Laden, if he exists at all, pushes a pen in his father's Saudi Arabian construction company and plays the playboy at weekends. *If* Saudi Arabia ever got going that is, and, if so, *if* it was ever worth a bin Laden leaving their native Yemen for—and so on, *ad infinitum*...

Nevertheless, it is interesting that this history and our own, so different in many ways, should have converged in some respects...

JOHN WHITBOURN

'YO ENGLISH! DR DEATH!'

Or

WHATEVER HAPPENS...

☸

... Q : Are you an enemy of America?
A : 'No'
Q : If 'Yes', specify what type,
A : 'Not applicable'
Q : Are you an arms smuggler?
A : 'No'
Q : Are you a munitions smuggler?
A : 'No'
Q : Are you a revolutionary?
A : 'No'
Q : Are you, or have you even been, a: Luddite, neo-Luddite, United Englander, Saxon-Brother, or Anti-Yoke party member or sympathiser?
A : 'No'
Q : Are you of Red Indian race, blood or otherwise descent?
A : 'I am not a First American'
Q : ...

The uniformed man pushed the card back at me.
'Answer the damn question properly or get to the back of the line.'

ALTERED ENGLANDS

I said nothing and meekly struck out my considered reply, composed during the hours of waiting.

Q : Are you of Red Indian race, blood or otherwise descent?
A : No, I have no Red Indian affiliations'

Flights of every nation had been processed whilst the British Airways passengers were held back. A lot of powerful people had fumed and complained but I stood aloof. I had no wish to spend even longer in the hot and sordid arrivals hall, or worse, be spat back, a refusal stamp in my passport.

'That's better. How long do you wanna stay?'

'One week, maximum.'

'What for?'

'A holiday, that's all.'

'Where?'

'Boston.'

'Come for the warm welcome, eh?'

'I'm told people are very friendly there.'

'Yeah, I'm sure they are. You Brits stick together; like shit to a blanket.'

'I'm English, actually.'

'Whatever.'

'Have you ever been to Boston?' I spoke most courteously; being genuinely interested.

'I ask the questions here, man.'

'I beg your pardon.'

'Just Boston? Going anywhere else. Canada maybe? Beyond the United States?'

'No, just Boston: one week maximum.'

'Sure you're not one of these guys come to collect his feather?'

'No.'

'Money.'

I showed him the contents of my wallet. It plainly held enough dollars, but not so many as to arouse suspicion. My travel agent had warned me to give thought to that.

'Go.'

He stamped my passport like it was my face, and waved me past. I headed for the baggage hall before there could be a change of heart. I bore the young man no resentment. Probably he and his had suffered from the actions of me and mine.

※

'Major Reno's squadrons are here'. The General's gloved finger stabbed the map. 'He can join us from the south. Captain Benteen's command is to their rear; an easy march. *So*, there's more support than sunshine, gentlemen. If we gain the high ground now, it'll be like sweeping dung from the stable.'

The soldiers round the trestle table, career cavalrymen all, appreciated the metaphor—though it was years since they'd performed that task themselves. The expected polite amusement was shown.

'What did General Crook's Crow and Shoshoni see? Who's first for the cleansing broom?'

'Sans Arcs, Miniconjous, some Hunkpapas,' answered an aide. 'They've all cosied up by the river: nothing special.'

'Any Sioux?'

'Not in the nearest line. Probably though. They've been trickling back from Her Majesty's hospitality.'

That also got a laugh. Newspaper cartoonists depicted them taking afternoon tea in china cups, and puzzling over *'toad-in-the-hole'*.

'Oh, la-de-*da*,' said the General, in strangled, fastidious accent. 'Perhaps we should send a calling card.'

'I've got mine here!' said one officer, and thumped the sabre hanging from his belt.

The General approved, nodding his long blonde locks—the boy would go far.

'I don't know about dear Queen Vicky,' he said, 'but in *my* experience sword-talk's the only language our friends out there understand.'

Finding no disagreement the General headed for the door.

'Let's do it!'

※

ALTERED ENGLANDS

'And I, Thayendanega, a true worshipper of the Great Spirit-and-His-Son, say this: a vision and blessing came to me though I had hardly begun to fast. Deep in the forest I knelt and saw and it was as real before my eyes as the view from my lodge when I rise each morning. No strength was required from me to lift the message across the gulf. It came like a rush of the great waters to the east. Therefore I take no credit from it, though it has made me King and will, I declare, preserve us in health on our Earth till we are called away.

The White Queen sat before the world tree, and she was fat and had more breasts than a woman has, but she was also beautiful and I desired her like a loyal husband might. There were many children gathered to her and she sheltered them with strong arms and light in her eye. They were happy and safe. None but a mad man would approach her to hurt the beloved children. I saw with my inner sight that the Great White Queen tore the enemies of her children limb from limb, like a cougar-mother, and opened wide their throats.

She spoke to me, and her words were strong. I dared not dispute them. She said the tree's name was Yggdrasil and she had sat before it for nigh two thousand years and she would never leave that place till the Great Spirit commanded her onwards. She said that though I could not see it, a ravenous beast was behind me. It frothed at the maw in its hunger. It would not be content until every particle of my flesh was devoured.

I asked the White Queen how I might be saved from the beast and she said, 'Be my child and come unto me.'

I replied 'How can this be, for my skin is red and yours is white? All men will dispute your parentage.'

She answered, 'I adopt who I will. I love who I wish. Let those who mock come close to my teeth.'

And so I went to her, for I had become small, like all her other children, and I was comforted at one of her breasts and drew strength to live for many thousands of years. This was not the case before. My destiny had been much shorter. At first I held on to fear but it passed. I was made welcome among her tribe and I forgot my skin made contrast with theirs.

The vision receded back into the deep woods but I also say that it has never left me.

My sons, my sons' sons, take with you what I have said. Now, when I am called to go and be happy forever with the Great Spirit, this—and not my soldiers and cannons and Kingdom—is what I leave you. I do not know who this White Queen is. She did not come in my time. But you must await her and then speed to her maternal embrace. Otherwise the People will die. This the Great Spirit does not wish.'

JOHN WHITBOURN

The Last Will and Testament of Joseph Brant, also known as Thayendanega, given at the Mohawk Royal Summer Palace, Lake Ontario. The Year of Our Lord 1807.

❂

'Here, gingernut, have a feather.'

I rode the reference to my hair; the barman had sampled his own wares and meant no harm.

'A bit soon, surely? I thought only the Peoples gave them out.'

'And aren't we just like 'em, kith and kin and all that. Englishmen in my bar get a feather: go on, put it on.'

I did so, clumsily, not wishing to show practice. The tall eagle feather found precarious hold behind my right ear.

'Only you'll have to give it back, when you leave like: sorry about that but we just keep a few in a jar and...'

'Don't mention—it's a nice thought.'

'And the first drink is free, put yer money away, boy.'

'Great stuff, cheers!'

'God save the King!' said one of the Irishmen, as a toast, and then we all drank together.

'Are you going to see the Peoples? They'll give you a feather.'

I was casual but firm. The Boston-Irish might brim with love for my kind, but the Americans had them infiltrated.

'No. No time.'

'Pity that; you'd get a rare welcome.'

'And sure now,' I said, really putting it on, mimicking their thick Hibernian, 'haven't I had that here already?'

It got a laugh, which blossomed into delight when His Majesty's money bought drinks all round.

❂

ALTERED ENGLANDS

'In this park once stood the Tower of London, of vile memory in English History, wherein the Ancient Regime held and tortured and killed its enemies. Established by William the Bastard as a visible sign of the Norman Yoke lade upon our beloved Country until recent times, this blood-soaked fortress witnessed scenes of unspeakable cruelty inflicted on those brave men and women who dared to challenge AUTOCRACY and ARBITRARY RULE. Saxon freedom fighters, Lollards, Recusants, Levellers, Luddites, Chartists and United-Englanders all languished here as the people's mounting fury grew. Waxen-mannequin cameos from these despicable times may be seen in the Chamber of Horrors attached to the Chapel of Perpetual Lamentation, Seething Lane.

The twin statues of St. Richard Challoner and the Blessed Tom Paine now stand on the spot where the infamous 'sleepless gallows' once stood. Pray linger awhile in the surrounding rose garden and silently ponder the example of our NATION's martyrs whose lives ended here. The revolutionary guards are empowered to enforce decorous dress and seemly behaviour in the sacred precinct.

For those who wish to envisage former vistas, a short length of outer wall was saved from the demolition process for this very purpose. It may be found behind the Chapel of St Patrick, donated by the people of United Ireland in gratitude for acts of famine relief and armed solidarity. Observe the tokens of Chartist cannon fire from the first revolution of 1848.

Otherwise, the black shadow of the Tower, like that of its creators, no longer looms over our happy Commonwealth. For which we thank God (however men conceive Him) and ask that He:

Bless the REVOLUTION!'

This plaque was unveiled in the presence of His Royal Highness, Guy, Prince of Wales, under the auspices of ÐA ENGLISCAN GESIðAS Society.
The 23rd day of March, the Year of Our Deliverance 1994.

Snow was coming and we knew what to expect. Last winter saw the first signs of change from war into wickedness. We had suffered grievously.

A white man of special cunning had come amongst our enemies and made study of the Peoples, all the better to kill us and take our land. He took counsel and said that there could be no victory in the bluecoats chasing a fleet and warlike folk through country they knew like their own children. The Peoples would fly and hide when they chose and turn to fight only when advantage was theirs. The bluecoats lumbered over the earth like a noisy beast, he said, heralding their coming in noise and smoke and smell, and thus found nothing. Sudden death from afar and ambush was their fate and this war might continue a thousand moons without resolution.

The cunning man had then said: 'Let us change our ways, let us kill the buffalo in summer so that our foe shall starve. And in the winter, when their horses show their ribs and are weak so that they must make long camp, let us descend on them on our sleek horses, fed from the Eastern lands we have already stolen. Let us be few but chosen men, silent in approach, sure guided by turncoats from amongst the Peoples. We shall fight at dawn or the ending of day and shoot and slash the tepees, not caring who is within—for the Peoples are but fighters, or breeders of fighters, or fighters-to-be.'

And the horse-soldiers listened to him and agreed that his plan was good. I have not heard that any amongst them spoke of the meanness of their plan, not even the representative of the Great-Spirit-and-His-Son who accompanies all their fighting bands. And so they made the plains black with slain buffalo; more meat that all the Peoples and the soldiers could eat in a thousand feasts. Then, when winter came and our children put their fingers in their mouths to placate the ache of their stomachs, the cavalry came and brought short end to much misery. Even in that first year of the change, warriors, brave men and no traitors, came to me and said we must make peace. I replied that there could be no treaty made with men who said words and then forgot them, even before the noise was gone. I have learnt this from other tribes; that this is the manner in which they geld the Peoples.

So I recalled Thayendanega's words to his descent, and my father's last words to me. I looked about for the White Queen and prayed that the Great Spirit would send her in my time, and open my eyes to see her. My prayers were answered. I read one of the white man's guns and my prayers were answered.

We set out that very day, heading north like an arrow from a bow, through the snows to Canada…

ALTERED ENGLANDS

'Martini-Henry Type 23 'Far-Killer'. Product of Her Majesty's Commonwealth Grand Consolidated Peoples' Armouries, Woolwich.'

'Is this the actual one?' I wasn't able to keep the awe out of my voice.

'The real McCoy: *'Sitting Bull's inspiration'*'

'Wow.'

'As employed at Little Big Horn and the Sweep East.'

I rose from my study of the glass case. We'd agreed on Boston Republican Museum just as somewhere vast; anonymous. Interest in the exhibits wasn't on the program. But even so...

'How come they've got it here? Number 1 medicine, surely?'

My contact, a short, angry looking man; one of the security staff, shrugged his *Barbour* covered shoulders. 'His tribe's with the trads: they don't accumulate stuff. King Joe III gave it to Boston. We just had to ask. There's still a mountain of gratitude out there.'

'I should hope so; they were close to the edge.'

He didn't like that. 'It was our fraternal duty; nothing more. Sing a different tune when you're... out there.'

As if I wouldn't. Fanatics always think they're the only trustworthy ones left.

The gun in the case caught my eye again, spooking me. An old, rusty useless thing, fit only for hammering nails with—but once upon a time the world had pivoted round on it. Our State schools are pretty heavy on history, so these notions have resonance.

He was staring at me: I had to say something.

'It seems strange—I mean, just a rifle. You always imagine them using our Maxims...'

The emissary scoffed.

'Behave yourself. D'you reckon they all had one each, every last brave?'

'No, I suppose not. Sorry, I wasn't thinking.'

'No, I should say you weren't.'

Back home I'd have had my *seax* knife out, but here I took it. 'Our People Abroad' were famously touchy about upholding the image. Each and every Briton had to be stoical, subtle, cultured: the whole stereotypical collage. Being far from home for long years the Revolution's Diplomats often turned into 'Guardians of the Flame' types; proportionally disappointed by any lapse.

'The N.A.s will pick up on things like that,' he nagged on. 'They have certain expectations.'

'Talking of which...' It was time for me to call *him* to business, to show the steel and crack the whip: pick your cliché. 'Beneath the mild exterior' and all that. I was the professional and he the mere delivery boy. Maybe that was the root of his problem with me.

'They came through in the diplomatic bag today,' he confirmed.

'How many?'

'Two dozen.'

'It'll do. Take 'em to the drop point. I'll go over the border tonight.'

He had to look at me anew. I might be on my final day, he the last Englishman I'd see this side of the grave.

His hand came forward: we shook, *huscarl*, Saxon-brother, style, and all was now well between us. He left without farewell, as is proper. For we hold that the best feelings are those unspoken.

❊

One of their *'Minutemen'* fired blind at me in the night—our side of the border too. Not for that but because he was so close I had to top him with my hand. And thus make drama where I desired low profile.

The trouble is, they rage at losing one of their own and take time to forget, often visiting comfort-revenge on innocent parties. It's all wrapped up in their intensely me-first, solipsistic-individualist ideology. Anything happens: it could have been them and so everything's always personal. That's not so. The overweight American border guard was too trigger-joyful and premature and forward-of-station, but I had nothing against him—except the edge of my hand. I needed to cross the line and that was that.

Later I heard they flame-bombed a brace of Cree villages for what I had done. They were nearby, true, but nothing to do with it. Some Cree even scout for the Americans. Not any more they don't. Shameful.

❊

'Her Majesty directs and commands as follows:

Item: that the Native Americans under our gracious protection be accorded all the respect and fruits of citizenship due a proud and much wronged nation.

Item: that their own law shall have primacy save in the case of capital or counter-revolutionary crimes. In such instances an elder of the Native Americans shall sit in judgement as one of the three Tribunes of the People.

Item: A new law is decreed. Herein after this date, any man subject to Her Majesty's jurisdiction convicted of supplying strong liquor, be it for gain or not, to the Native Americans under our protection shall, for the first offence, be subject to confiscation of all assets; and for the second, be shot to death.

Item: All matters appertaining to the refugee camps situate in the military district of Fort Bushby-the-Martyr shall henceforth be deemed subject to Revolutionary-discretion-of-the-first-water. All persons there presently situate shall apply to the Imperial-Revolutionary Citadel in New Brighton for residency permits WITHIN SEVEN DAYS FROM THE DATE STATED BELOW. Heads of Families and Englisc Folk-chiefs may register block applications.

By order of Her Imperial Majesty Queen Victoria I, by grace of G-D and permission of the PEOPLE, monarch and director of the English Union and its possessions, free-affiliates and protectorates, this third day of June, the year of our Lord, 1875

Relayed and approved for publication by Philip Grimes, Revolutionary Governor-General for Canada, Newfoundland, English-Quebec and the Inuit peoples.'

☸

'The Ladybird Book of English Heroes'. Dictated for use in Primary School and Cadre Pre-school institutions, as part of the National Curriculum-History & Ideology.

'In those days, poor men and women had to work very hard indeed, much harder than your mummies and daddies do, and still they did not earn enough money to feed their families. People often went hungry though they toiled all day long. The people of England were very angry but it seemed like things would never get any better.

JOHN WHITBOURN

Many of the rich people, who were called 'Bosses', were very wicked and wanted to pay even less wages. They did not care if their workers were thin and unhappy. Some bought machines to do all the work on their farms or factories and then there was no work at all.

In a village called East Preston in the County of Sussex in Southern England (what we now call Wessex) there was a very bad farmer called **Mr Olliver**. One day he went out to hire some men to thresh his corn and the first one he spoke to was a brave worker called **EDMUND BUSHBY**. When he heard how little money Mr Olliver would give him for labouring long hours he said 'How can I live on this?' To which Olliver replied 'That is not my concern.' The others workers heard this and were as cross as Edmund was.

Later, Mr Olliver decided he would not hire anyone, but buy a steam threshing machine and so not pay wages ever again. Soon after he met Edmund who said he should care about his fellow Englishmen and pay fair wages, not cause them to starve. Mr Olliver said bad things to Edmund and told him to mind his own business. Edmund replied with these famous words: 'If I cannot have work by day, then I must work at night!' Mr Olliver was very frightened.

That night one of Mr Olliver's hayricks was set on fire. The **REVOLUTION** had begun.

In those days the rich people were in charge of the Law. Mr Olliver had Edmund arrested and he was sent for trial at Horsham. Liars were paid to say they had seen Edmund light the fire. They also said they had heard him wish Mr Olliver would burn as well. No one was allowed to defend Edmund, even though he was a plain and simple man who could not read or write (for in those days poor people were kept from learning!). The cruel judge was determined Edmund should die and put on his black cap to say Edmund must be hung by the neck. Perhaps you could draw a picture of brave Edmund standing before the cruel judge?

Edmund was hanged outside Horsham Gaol on New Year's Day, 1831.

Mr Olliver was given a £500 reward for what he had done. With it he built a school for poor children in East Preston. But the villagers would not send their children to it...'

Nihil Obstat.

Commissioner for Educational Vigilance: Wessex, Babylondon, Kent and Vectis. Ms Sophie Nettle. 14/05/96.

ALTERED ENGLANDS

'... They [the south-east English peasantry] *took an active part in that last of all peasant movements in England, the 'Captain Swing' riots of 1830 when, according to the Surrey county historian, 'The south-eastern counties began to wear the look of a country where revolution was in the air'...'.*

Daniel Green. *'Great Cobbett: The Noblest Agitator'.* 1983. p 36
.

※

'Yo English! Dr Death! Hi!'

It was the Americans who first called us that, implying that all Englishmen were gunrunners. The name both stuck and changed and now every young N.A. hailed us thus. We don't mind; it's even become rather cool. Rather that than the feathers.

I was just glad he and I had converged. This was the centre of Pow-Wowville: as busy as it got and almost like an American city. Modern buildings, 'European-mutated', were all sides for half a mile before the timber stuff, and then the tepees, began.

'Have a feather, Englishman: wear it with pride.'

He was definitely a mod: smooth, Anglo-Saxon influenced, and so anxious to be worldly-wise. By definition most of their government people were that way. It was a sore point with the grateful-but-keep-your-distance trads, which occasionally warmed up into real friction. American agents breathed on the sparks. His kind got called *'potatoes'*; dark outside but really white within.

'I've already got one actually. The hotel manager-....'

'So wear two. Here—I'll fix it.' He then stepped back to admire his work. 'Ace! Sitting Bull or what?'

Flame-light played over his face. The paintwork was too neat and sharp edged, barber applied rather than his own work. It didn't look... right, no more than the bird plumage on me.

'Thanks. They're ready for collection.'

Asiatic eyes widened in the copper face. 'You surprise me, Doc. We thought this might mean a hitch.'

He nodded towards the pyre; centre square. I'd arranged the meet for the Ambassador's funeral, full knowing there'd be crowds and uproar. The wild scenes could shelter our bubble of discretion. His side had interpreted it as preparation for bad news. We often found them like that. Soc-scientists were working on this cultural pessimism, meddling away like Capitalists, but a century of victory still hadn't washed away the pre-emptive cringe.

'No way. A death only makes us grit our teeth.' I demonstrated. He was impressed. As befitted the occasion my locks were stand-aloft, spiked with clay. The rune-scars on my face and hands were filled with pigment. Tonight it was the suit that seemed incongruous.

The Americans had offed our Ambassador to the Indians, caving in his head in feeble imitation of street crime. They knew we were abusing the diplomatic routes—though not to what purpose. This was their warning. Baseball bats were employed: that was their signature. They need not have bothered: we would have known. Such laziness! Such self-deception. There is no 'mugging' in Pow-Wowville: murders and duels and drink-stuff but not money-snuffling like that. Humanity here can be tigers to each other—they're not perfect—but neither are they social-cannibals. Contrast-wise, the Americans' arrangements make everyone that way. Come nightfall their cities are pure Darwin. I've seen it.

No, they could have saved themselves the slur and killed him openly; honourably. He knew, even as he went. The Ambassador had time to use his *seax*. We found blood. He was one of the old breed and left recorded the wish to go to his maker in a coat of flames. Good man, true Saxon! He will be recalled in winter stories. *Wassail!*

'We are not squeamish like them,' I told the young brave. He knew who I meant. 'The Folk believe in something greater than themselves. They are willing to make—or be—sacrifice.'

'Like Mad-dog-Diane,' he said, much cheered. He knew.

That was long ago but well remembered. It proved even non-believers can cheat death via glory. *'The Girl Wot Lit Up The White House'* that Marie Lloyd sang about, lived on. We fondly imagine intrepid aviatrix and President eye to eye—for a second or two, across the Presidential lawn—before bomb-rich plane met august office. Historians pooh-pooh that, saying it all happened too quick, but illustrators take no notice. The image is in all our schoolbooks.

Turning the White House black and red turned history too—and turned them back sharpish from their *'Manifest Destiny'* revenge war. One Welsh girl was all it took. They left their neighbours alone for a while after that. If need be we can go again: the breed is still well up to it. They're aware of that, for all their 'improved security'. And this explains our history; all the feelings between us and them. Truly, deep down, people come to hate what they fear.

ALTERED ENGLANDS

'Just like Diane,' I agreed sagely. 'And she has never ceased to fly.'

That flicked the switch. 'When can we collect, Dr Death?' There was eagerness: an old style zest for combat, for all that he wasn't a trad.

'Whenever. Main station, left luggage: here's the key.'

It was done in a second: sleeve to hand, hand to hand, hand to sleeve. I know it was not observed. We were just two men from different continents, happenstance side-by-side at a funeral in the dark. Only God and History know the truth of things, but I declare that we—I mean the Folk and Revolution— had been skilful. No one saw or perceived we were starting a war.

They had set the frontier ablaze of late. Snipers and raids made misery in the provinces the Americans wanted back. And, if permitted, that would just be the start. The N.A.s were few and poor, reliant on solidarity. The infrared night-sights I had brought would even up the odds.

The Commonwealth was not exactly awash with wealth either, but we had spirit, which is almost as good. Our secret workshops in the mountains taught the Peoples best-of-science gunsmithing. The armouries on the Thames donated generously. If need be we would volunteer to come over in our thousands, as before, to physically assist the cause of good. We do our best.

On reflection, I do not like the name *'Dr Death'*. It isn't fair. True, I criss-cross the world dealing in arms—but really my business is justice.

❁

Custer and the 7th Cavalry dissolved in rapid fire. They had time— just—to note white faces and straight ranks amongst their foe, but cavalry against Maxims is a brief and to-the-point business. No horseman got near enough to wield the sabre. Half weeping with shock and betrayal, the remnant shucked up behind dead horses and loosed off with carbines. They caused the 'Indians' their only losses that day. Soon enough though, the machine guns hosed the valley quite clean of American life. There wasn't even time for a last stand.

After that came a great silence and the tribes looked down on what they had done, almost frightened at such presumption as to have *won*. Then Sitting Bull, Acting-General of Her Majesty's Revolutionary Army, stepped forward. In halting words he saluted his braves and quietened their consciences over easy slaughter. What had been visited on the buffalo, he said, had come full circle and fallen upon the wanton killers. It was not pretty or honourable; no one had counted *coup*—but it was just.

He next thanked the English and Irish and Canadians who had fought alongside them, but for the most part they did not hear. They were busy soothing the hot Maxims with buckets of water, and preparing for Major Reno's column, fast heading their way. But the *'Indians'* heard—and stored the words and gratitude in their hearts.

Old habits revived and some braves swooped on the fallen to scalp—as the Americans had taught them—and pillage. They even took up the dead men's guns, though now they had no real need of them.

Sitting Bull found there had been Irish on the other side as well. A Captain Myles Keogh perished in a coat of blue. Pope Pius IX had given him a *'PRO PETRI SEDE'* medal when he fought at Rome, a volunteer Papal zouave, against Garibaldi's nationalists. He'd survived that, and then Gettysburg and Atlanta fight, only to be torn apart at Little Big Horn. Sitting Bull took the disc and honoured Keogh by donning it. Many years later, the Chief would return it in person to His Holiness—but by then he was a King in his own right and laden with many other honours.

In Rome he sought and found absolution for the deeds done in the 'Great Reconquest'. God's representative on Earth granted recognition of the Peoples' new state, and blessed both. America withdrew its Ambassador in protest, but without effect, for it was no longer a nation of great account.

King Sitting Bull next proceeded to the Fountainhead of the Revolution, and was received at the Court of St. James. There he met Thayendanega's *'White Queen'*, though by now she was a little old widow in black. They got along famously.

Belloc, the Revolutionary Poet Laureate, composed a poem in commemoration of the day. He declaimed it in ringing Franco-Sussex tones, provoking laughter with the lines:

> *'Whatever happens we have got*
> *the Maxim gun and they have not.'*

Both Sitting Bull and Victoria were amused.

8~

'THE WAY, THE TRUTH...'

INTRODUCTION

'Prediction 63.
The theory of Evolution will be scientifically debunked in your lifetime'

Scott Adams. *'The Dilbert Future'*. 1997.

I have a problem with Evolution. There: I've said it. Exhorted as I am from many quarters to believe, I nevertheless cannot knock out of commission sufficient parts of my brain and reasoning faculties to accept Evolution, hook line and sinker. Sorry. So *very* sorry. But I'm not a *bad* person...

'It is absolutely safe to say that, if you meet somebody who claims not to believe in evolution, that person is ignorant, stupid or insane (or wicked, but I'd rather not consider that).

Richard Dawkins. New York Times book review, 09/04/89, repeated and expanded (to include *'tormented, bullied or brainwashed'*) in 'Free Enquiry' Magazine vol. 21, no 3, Summer 2001.

That is not to say I have a shiny, complete and ready-to-go theory to put in its place that fits all the evidence. I cannot be a 'Creationist' for reasons surely too self-evident to recount here, although protagonists of Evolution seem to say that is the only possible alternative position. No, it simply seems to me that accepting Evolution as currently posited requires too great a leap of faith on incomplete and flimsy evidence. Therefore, whilst awaiting more conclusive proof, I'm content to just say 'I do not know'—which in my innocence I believed to be the correct scientific stance to take. Apparently however, that's not so, and if forced to accept my Dawkinian motivation I think I'll take *'stupid'*, as the best of a bad choice...

However, plodding on in that rut of stupidity, I will say that one of my major non-scientific objections to Evolution is the manners of its exponents. They seem to invariably 'go for the man' in the argument, not the facts. Anyone was dares to say *'but...'* is immediately written off as a snaggle-toothed and probably incestuously inbred hillbilly. Now, that might be true of *me*, but hardly seems fair applied to some of the other, seemingly quite intelligent, people who've poked their heads over the parapet of late.

Also, in my experience of life, those who foam at the mouth from first off and go for the person not the facts are usually covering up for a weak argument. I mention that for what it's worth...

And, it being me, I have to confess to a more mischievous motive to my stance. Three bearded secular deities preside over the modern age: Marx, Freud and Darwin. The first is fallen, his dying creed confined to hothouse academia. The second is teetering and increasingly recognised as a charlatan. Which only leaves one idol to go...

But having said all that, here is a 'pro-evolution' story!

It stems from a family holiday in England's West Country and my discovery of Mary Anning's grave in Lyme Regis. There exists a photograph of serried junior Whitbourns gathered round Mary's headstone in strong summer sunshine, humouring yet another of Dad's obsessions. The thought of fish and chips to come, then the beach with Aunty Dolores plus tribe, kept them smiling.

Yet, as (nearly) always there was Machiavellian method in my madness in gathering them there and delaying dinner. Because I wished for them to remember Mary Anning in later life and let her be an inspiration to them: as she should be to us all. For Mary came from 'nothing', as her 'betters' would have seen it, and clawed her way to 'something' by sheer will and brilliance. She even

ALTERED ENGLANDS

survived being struck by lightning *and* encountering horror-fiction authoress Jane Austen!

For me, the moral of Mary's story is that there's no obligation to let your beginning dictate your end...

In which case, good on you, Mary! Go for it girl!

JOHN WHITBOURN

THE WAY, THE TRUTH...

'Mary Anning, probably the most important unsung (or inadequately sung) collecting force in the history of palaeontology... made an astounding series of discoveries, including squidlike creatures with associated ink-bags, a plesiosaur in 1824, and a pterosaur (flying reptile) in 1828. She directly found, or pointed the way to, nearly every specimen of importance.'

Stephen Jay Gould. *'Finders, Keepers'*. 1992.

'What name d'ye give this child?'

There was no love lost between the Pastor and Richard Anning but occasion demanded the baby be handed over. It was accepted with broad, gentle hands. Outwardly, all looked well.

'Mary,' said Anning, as though challenging any to deny it.

The mutton-chopped Pastor's head loomed over the infant.

'Mary,' he repeated, and paused in thought as he trailed two thick fingers across the font. 'So be it. Mary Anning, I baptise 'ee. In the name of the Father and the Son and the 'oly Ghost.' A watery cross now shone on the smooth and innocent brow.

'And, in those same 'oly names,' thought the Pastor to himself, *'I curse thee for thy father's sake. May Almighty God's fiery vengeance come down upon 'ee and spare ye a long life in this vale of tears.'*

The infant, blessed with knowing nothing, said nothing. It lay uncannily still looking up at the Pastor's pale face.

That gaze grew strangely prolonged. He was glad of the excuse to break it. A fleeting black figure distracted at the chapel door. He looked to see but it was gone.

The Pastor shook his head, accounting it a mistake, a trick of deceiving light. He had *not* seen himself standing in a sea of horrors. It was not *possible* that he be in two places at once—nor be accompanied by monsters.

⁕

Elizabeth Haskins shrieked as the rain drove into every crevice. Even at home she disliked thunder but in an open field it was like the voice of an angry god.

The equestrian exhibition that was the cause of her presence was given up for lost. Each rider shifted for himself. They hurtled past, a wild mixture of water and noise, making for cover. She knew she must do the same. Her charge was a weakly baby in any case: one chill or cold would finish the job.

Elizabeth attached herself to two others she half recognised. They seemed to know a way to escape the deluge; pointing, shouting each other towards refuge.

A tree loomed out of the downpour, a sheltering elm. Any port in a storm.

The little group found the tree just as the lightning found it and them. The electric fork stabbed the earth but they did not see it. Crisped and black they left the world behind.

⁕

Fifteen month old Mary survived the hammer blow of Heaven. Prised from the stiff dead arms of her nurse the rescuers found her unconscious but alive. She was revived in warm water and with droplets of (smuggled) brandy. In time those grave little eyes reopened and so there was a gem of rejoicing and legend extracted from the dung of tragedy.

The Pastor came to see the Annings and bestow his blessing. He was frightened, not knowing whether Jehovah had granted or spat upon his prayer.

Once again he looked down into that miraculous gaze—and stepped back. There was new wisdom there and he did not care for too much wisdom.

❈

'... but the babe alone survived and soon recovered, and from that time... got better health. The physicians say the shock the Child received must be like that from an electric-fluid machine, thus it may be said that the death of the Nurse was the life of the Child.'
Letter from Elizabeth Haskins' widower, twenty years after the event.

'She had been a dull child before but after this accident she became lively and intelligent, and grew up so'
Charles Anning, Mary Anning's nephew, writing in 1847.

❈

The Pastor's unhealthy hacking cough betrayed him. He announced his own presence on the clifftop better than a master of ceremonies.

Mary Anning knew that rasp well: it punctuated the psalms and scripture and sermons of every Sunday's chapel. She wished to avoid it: then and always. The Pastor had taken against her, even more than any other of the *'noisy sinful children'*. She didn't know why and even sought to show repentance, but it did no good. He still glared blackly on her and would cuff her if Richard Anning was not around.

Best of all was to avoid him and glide along, invisible, in the shy, sly, slinking byways of life. Even at the age of ten she was good at that.

Her hunt for 'curios' put into respite, Mary remained low amidst the clifftop brush and knew he would not see her. For the moment he had eyes for one thing only.

Along the new turnpike road the coach and four drew nearer. It looked well laden.

The Pastor spoke against the *'incomers'* most Sundays. He warned against their manners, their money, the way they talked and most of all their lascivious appearance when they emerged from the bathing-machines. The yearly growing influx of pleasure seekers to Lyme threatened all piety and peace and might even in time extinguish the native Dorset tongue. The Pastor told them to boldly speak their own dialect to the rich and lazy incomers—if speak they must.

Mary was sure he was right but thereagain the grander arrivals were such fun to watch with their funny clothes and speech and manners that it was hard to tear your eyes off them. And if they spoke kindly to you and offered a farthing for directions...

Father sold these 'holiday' people the things he made, or else mended what they broke. He could turn his hand to anything in the carpentry line. Then there were the 'curios'. On Sundays, when the grander Lymians were in the Anglican church, he set up a table outside his shop beside Cockmail Prison and the incomers would buy some of his finds chipped out of the cliffs and foreshore beds. Without that income things would be even harder...

The coach bypassed the Pastor in a rumble of hoofs, its breath raising his last rattails of hair. As it went by he raised his fist and thoughts against it and its contents.

Unaware they were being cursed, Jane Austen and her family and all the other passengers continued down into the fashionable seaside resort of Lyme Regis.

❦

'We called for a native tradesman, a Mr Anning—and a Chapel Radical Jacobin if ever I saw one—to repair the darling little box-lid but I thought his asking price of five shillings beyond the value of all the furniture in our room altogether. I dismissed the rude beast without further ado.'

Now I am here I am so longing for balls...'

Jane Austen writing to her sister Cassandra. 14th September 1804.

❦

''I am the way, the truth and the life'.'

The Pastor fixed the congregation with a lifetime of experience burning behind his eyes. 'Therein be the entirety of the gospels: all else be commentary.'

It was a pleasing notion. Richard Anning was partial to complex things put in a nutshell: disparate wood cunningly jointed into a useable whole. He'd been raised on Cromwell's 'Good Old Cause' and the Levellers demanding the entirety of the Law shoe-horned into one book, understandable to all. Christianity most appealed to him when it was just God made graspable and *'Do as you would be done by'*.

The Pastor knew their every little foible. They'd made their way to him in years of confidences and moments of distress. He'd made it his business to know. A shepherd should understand each sheep's plaintive *baa*.

Richard Anning he could strip bare with just a look. The man was a *radical*, a ringleader rioter in hungry years past. He was fired by grievance, not religion, that peasant anger slow-burning since the Norman Conquest. *He was here because this was not the gentry's church.*

The Pastor accepted him for his tithe and presence—for he loathed an empty pew—but he *knew* him. The man spited Scripture with his pre-Flood 'curios', raising *doubts* in those who beheld them. A bad influence he was, a millstone to those who heeded him. His children heeded, that was plain: they listened in love. They were being misled to Hell.

Joseph (the eldest) and Mary Anning leaned towards their father: they did not fear. Nothing was as it should be. The Pastor disapproved and glared.

"'The way, the truth and the life'.' He said it loud for emphasis and closed the Bible likewise. Sermon ended. The *word* would find God's elect and bounce off the damned. It was not his task to distinguish between them but to shovel out promiscuous salvation. All the same, he knew which was which.

Richard Anning was tossing an idea back and forth. He relished the exercise: there being need for the lower orders to hone their only weapon in life's harsh contest. '... *truth and the life'*... Interesting...

Yet he resisted the temptation to softness: you had to keep a stone in your sling.

'I know another *way*,' he informed his offspring as they filed out, 'A way that's hard and treacherous. I'll show you now.'

The Pastor knew where they were going and cursed their path.

ALTERED ENGLANDS

Another, later, Sunday—but much the same. Poverty set an iron pattern on their lives.

Sundays: when they weren't selling curios they went hunting them. The proceeds of the little table meant meat once a week and thus Joseph's inch or so advantage over his playmates.

Sometimes they watched their father traverse the perilous cliff ways, showing them the safest and the best. Other days—as now—they scoured the low tide beach, a relaxing holiday from risk.

'There,' Richard Anning pointed straight up. 'Black Ven: the way, the truth and y'death if ye be not mindful. Her's your best bet—stacked full of curios but she'll have 'ee if ye relax a mite. Climbing her's good but sweetest be when her face crumbles: get to the fall afore the tide and her'll be fuller of curios than a plum pudding is o' currants. But mind ye, old Blackie, she'll be waiting for ye: the half-hanging remnants up above, ready to drop on y'bonce like vengeance. She guards her treasures. Leave her to I jus' yet—promise?'

Mary and Joseph confirmed they'd never venture that particular cliff unsupervised.

'Good. The beach has riches enough for ye just now. Follow I and learn.'

The morning bled away, an hour of head down wandering for every find.

'Now, these,' he told Mary—she was the more interested, 'these be called *'dragon curls'*.' The shallow tide water covering the spiralled fossil was brushed aside. 'See? They lift easy and take a shine. Mum can do that. You'll get a tuppence for they.'

A spell of teaching and then they re-split to search. As in everything else the Annings went their own way.

Richard was driven, Mary was absorbed: only Joseph could be distracted by the scenery. He straightened up to watch the clifftop black cortege wind by.

It was the reason they were excused chapel today. Anning wouldn't have the Pastor make a hypocrite of him from beyond the grave. The man's funeral could thrive well enough without his insincerity.

A sudden, sharp-edged gust made the three Annings blink. It raised their hats and coats before dispersing over the sand like disapproval.

Richard didn't recall so many twists up Black Ven. According to his reckoning he should be near the top now, yet the path—such as it was—ventured on. Gathering dusk and fright made him abandon even the pretence of a fossil search. He was cursed today in any case, his hip-bag hanging limp, empty of any saleable specimen. Home seemed far away and correspondingly attractive.

He fingertipped his way round a rocky protrusion. It crumbled under his touch like he'd become Samson. The tussocks and loose stones underfoot felt greasy. From nowhere came the desire to just... push, to extend his arms and *push* and fall away, free at last, free from the earth and care, out into the open air.

A voice whispered in his head telling him to... fly—and die. He abused it as not his own—though it sounded like him.

Round that corner was another, even sharper, and the path narrowed further still. The bitter bile of panic was definitely washing round his taut mouth now. He'd never seen or trod this stretch before. Either he'd taken a wrong way or...

'You did!' the Pastor answered his unspoken question. 'You have!'

He stood barring the way, confident beside the yawning abyss. Having already traversed one great divide Lyme's cliffs now held no fear. A pocket of frigidity surrounded him.

Anning whimpered but could not avoid those dead eyes. He was confronted with all his errors.

The Pastor remained stock still but his cold advanced. It had fingers and enveloped Richard Anning. Gently, grip by grip, surface by surface, they detached him from the cliff.

'Down ye go,' said the Pastor by way of blessing, 'and fare ye well.'

Richard went out into the night and had his few seconds of liberty—till earth came up to embrace him.

ALTERED ENGLANDS

It was Joseph Anning who found the 'crocodile'. Its giant staring head caught his eye at the very edge of the foreshore. But for it being the cusp of the tide he'd not have been that far out. It was God's benevolence. The family had been 'on the parish' ever since their father's death. There'd be a buyer for a big find: maybe an upcountry bigwig making *'science'* of it—they paid extra well.

Dad had always said look for the *'ar-tic-ulated'* curios: the more stone bones the more pennies. This one looked promising. If that skinny neck was connected…

It would be a race. The thing was already half inch deep in sand and water. Mistress tide was on the turn. Joseph got down on his knees and began to scrape.

There *was* more: its coffin bed of stone was nigh flat—not like those frustrating few that directly dived deep below. It went on and on.

Joseph spared a second to look into the empty saucer eyes.

'Welcome back to the world, fishy-boy,' he told the two hundred million years deceased. 'Now, pardon I but 'tis time for ye' to wake.' He raised his father's chisel.

The back of his neck froze. Ice descended on it from on high. He clapped up an involuntary hand. The flesh there was corpse cold.

He was going to mark his find anyway, to align it with some shore feature so it could be found again. So there was no shame in standing to turn and confront the great fear that had draped itself upon him. It was just possible there might be a madman behind him, sneaking silently up with evil intent.

In a way there was. He knew the distant black figure upon the cliff. He knew its name and opinion.

Joseph turned again. There was enough of his father in him to protest.

'T'ain't none of your business. Not no more. 'Tis ours.'

Then the coldness was coming off the water like an incoming fog. The Pastor had moved from clifftop to sea and now stood upon—and against—the tide. Joseph could feel him, could glimpse his floating gaitered feet, but he would not look up. He'd reached the extent of his defiance.

The slab feet stepped forward, propelling Joseph one pace back. The cold and hatred were like awaking in a winter grave.

Two more steps, in swift succession, and he had relinquished the fossil.

With it—and all it might mean for the family in food and fuel and rent—went the last of his resistance. He somehow knew that the Pastor was preparing to *tell* him things. He could not bear to hear them. He ran.

The chill beach was left to the dead.

Soon after Joseph signed papers to become an upholsterer's apprentice. It was steady money.

He told all to Mary, now a sturdy, plain, little eleven year old—and told it with a warning. Thereafter, she hunted alone.

It took nigh on a year but she succeeded.

Joseph had given good directions but he'd not venture on the beach again. He had his head buried in the gentry's sofas. Mary had commanded and cajoled but his mind was set as hard as the fossil she sought. His experience had put years on him and glass behind his eyes. He'd sketch her a map but no more.

So, there was a year of paddling about on the turn of tide, a year of wet dresses and salt rash and her Mother's reproaches. A twelve year old girl's labouring wages weren't much to lose but they were something. Mary had endured all, stony faced, and God was now pleased to reward her.

The sand was scoured off by a brisk receding tide. She doubted it would ever be plainer than today. Her practised eye discerned its full extent, twenty feet or more from giant head to snaky tail. And were they four flippers splayed out at the sides? This was something new and wondersome.

She paused, focusing on the now harmless rows of teeth. It had once been ravenous, relentless. Those blank eye sockets had looked out upon a cold and... devouring age, somewhen unrecorded in Scripture. It was a monster from a monstrous time now revealed to her in stone. She was teetering over a chasm back into time. The thought froze her.

Mary shook off such silliness. First and foremost this thing was *money*—and salvation from parish charity. Her father's hammer and chisel came out of his battered curio bag.

ALTERED ENGLANDS

The sand shifted under her feet—a tiny motion but enough for pause to her attuned senses. She was wary of the tide that curled quiet in behind you, the cliff waiting to fall on your head. They betrayed their murderous intent with subtle heraldings.

Mary wrenched her hopes from off the beach. She almost wished it was only the sea come to thwart her.

The Pastor had been withholding his presence. Released, it chilled to the bone. She clenched her eyes, clenched her bladder. He was standing very close.

She'd always quailed under his gaze even when he was alive. Now it was also indecent just to behold him.

The grave had not been kind. His flesh was waxy, the mutton-chops false looking. That familiar stare came from somewhere far away and awful.

'Wicked child,' he hissed. 'Desist!' His breath smelt moss-tinged and decaying.

Deep within, some other Mary was crushed and whimpering on the sand, or else a little girl running home. Those possibilities was ignored—scathingly ignored—in favour of the victorious and sinned-against whole.

'Why?' she challenged him—and looked him in the eye. He was not used to that—in life or now.

What was left was not up to rational debate. There remained only fixed opinions.

'Blasphemy!' he told her, and pointed at the fossil.

'No!' she answered. 'Pennies! Food!'

The Pastor drew in breath he did not need, nostrils and dead eyes flaring alike. There was a flame in them that was not his own.

'Thirty pieces of silver!'

Mary did not grasp the reference. Dame and Sunday school had largely washed over her: she'd been too tired.

'Maybe,' she replied in a voice that was hope-touched. 'Pounds and pounds maybe!'

He paused. She looked. Could sympathy at last have entered him—saved up until the afterlife?

Obviously not.

'The faithful dead condemn you,' he said, a whispered fury trembling his big frame. 'They rise to *condemn* you!'

With a gesture he exhumed the beach-buried dead: the shipwrecked sailors, the paupers and murders, the infanticides of all the ages. They rose like levers from their shallow scooped graves and, as one, regarded her with the residues left to them.

Mary had not eaten breakfast (there was none)—and that was as well. She'd been unaware Lyme beach was so replete with death.

They looked at her and she at them. There was horror and weariness and pain—but she did not discern condemnation. Their grievance was not with her but myriad, individual, others. The Pastor had raised an unwilling, conscript army. Mary stood her ground. His shot had misfired.

He realised it and swept the dead back into decent concealment. He seemed at a loss—and desperate enough to reason.

'Consider, child,' the kindness failed even to convince himself, 'the past you would unleash...'

Suddenly he was surrounded by new monsters; not the vestigially human ones of a moment before but a flapping, snapping, reptilian host, kith and kin of the 'crocodile' at Mary's feet.

They swam about him in the invisible water of another age. They were soulless and devoured each other: constantly: horribly. Mary, who knew all about just where her food came from, was still repelled.

'Do ye prefer *this*,' he indicated the mindless feeding frenzy all around, 'to the reforming beauty of Scripture? Would ye drag this forgotten Godlessness to today?'

Mary wavered. She had a good heart. She didn't want to be a cause for ill.

The point was hammered home with passion.

'Would ye be recalled as the Mother of all *Doubt*?'

All she wanted was freedom from want, for herself and her family. She wanted an end to patched dresses and street taunts. But Mary Anning wouldn't buy those regardless of cost.

The tide was turning; for the first time she noticed that her boots were inundated.

The Pastor rode high above both sea and uncertainty.

'*He* is the way, the truth and the life! No other wisdom is necessary.'

Mary wavered. The chill of the water joined that of her company. Her hammer and chisel felt like weapons.

'Satan's child: do not risk another thunderbolt!'

ALTERED ENGLANDS

She knew that story as well as he. She'd never understood it till today. The little she had been touched by Providence.

Then, as she moved to stow her tools, there came that touch again. Lightning struck twice: a second bolt: another blinding flash—this time purely internal: just as searing but entirely benign.

'The way, the *truth* and the life,' an inner voice told her. It was both her's—and another's. It was God-like: all-consuming.

The backwash touched the Pastor also. He understood—and understood all too well.

His face was twisted with disappointment. He wept. For the first time Mary pitied him.

'Betrayed!' he howled. '*Betrayed!*' His last words. Then he—and his fears and visions—were snuffed out. He was taken away to learn—in love.

Mary Anning shook her head. She too understood—and understood the truth. She'd been told that truth was best and—with faith—*for* the best. All else was commentary.

Twelve year old Mary Anning took up her tools and began to dig.

POSTSCRIPT & CODA

'... It is certainly a wonderful instance of divine favour—that this poor, ignorant girl should be so blessed, for by reading and application she has arrived to that degree of knowledge as to be in the habit of writing and talking with professors and other clever men on the subject, and they all acknowledge that she understands more of the science than anyone else in the kingdom.'

Lady Harriet Silvester, after visiting Mary, 17th September 1824.

Henry Henley, Lord of Lyme Manor, paid Mary £23—a year's income to the Annings—for her Ichthyosaur when it was eventually raised, intact, from the Dorset Lias. It may now be seen in an honoured place in the Natural History Museum in London. Mary went on to become one of the founding mothers of the science of palaeontology.

The facts are as I've recounted them. All else is (my) commentary...

9~
'*I CAME TO COMPTON...*'

INTRODUCTION

Compton is the next door village to Binscombe. On the south side of the chancel arch in St Nicholas's Church, its thousand year old place of worship,[15] is a depiction of an 11th or 12th century knight, scratched by an amateur hand. Beside the figure is carved a 'Latin cross', surmounted at some later point (maybe ten seconds, maybe many years) by a 'St Andrew's cross'.

One interpretation of it—and I favour no other—is that a knight of the area, perhaps one of the local de Polstede family, clad in full armour, carved the figure with his sword during a night vigil in St Nicholas's before going on crusade. The first cross is the registration of a vow, the second a symbol of its fulfilment.

Who knows? Happily, the truth of the matter is now lost to us and so is proof against either proving or debunking. Anyway, it is a beautiful notion and since there is a deficiency of those in this world I choose to believe and write about it.

As to the site of the story, that sylvan cross-roads, even the saucy tree (in shape if not spirit, at least) actually exist. So too does the possibly prehistoric

---

[15] And maybe older still. The base of its Saxon tower is studded with Roman tiles doubtless sourced from two nearby villas: Limnerslease and Binscombe, or the temple at Wanborough..

sunken tracks that lead off from it. Certainly, the area has the atmosphere of having seen too much to really register mere single human lifetimes...

Likewise, just a bowshot away are two small hills once known as Robin Hood's Butts—probably the southernmost example of place names inspired by the great man, whoever he was—between which local legend[16] says a victory was won by locals against the French. No medieval record mentions it, nor does any known French invasion seem a likely candidate, and I wonder if we have here preserved the memory of a far older clash: against the Vikings perhaps, or even between Saxons and Britons?

Anyhow, for the reader who has made it thus far, my secret should now be out, and I am obliged to confess an unfair advantage for my humble literary attempts for which I never (well, rarely) forget to give continual thanks. Springing from such deep accumulated soil, my difficulty is not in *finding* ideas for stories, but batting *off* the numberless hordes...

And, in addition to reeling in that admission, meanwhile ponder if you will the curious and comforting thesis that not all crusades are fought far from home...

---

[16] Rescued from expiry and recorded just in the nick of time by Cecilia Lady Boston in her wonderful *'The History of Compton in Surrey'*, 1933.

ALTERED ENGLANDS

I CAME TO COMPTON NOT FOR GLORY BUT TO SAVE MY SOUL

✸

'Compton Church is unique in possessing a gorgeous upper sanctuary above the high altar, a first floor as it were, presumably to house a relic now lost even to the memory of legend. Doubtless destroyed during the Reformation.

... Examples of medieval graffiti abound. Scratched with charming naiveté into the clunch chalk (quarried from the majestic North Downs, a bare stone's throw away) of the Chancel's south side is the figure of a knight in 12th century style armour. Beside him a cross of St George is superimposed by a Jerusalem Cross. Experts have weaved the delicious speculation of a knight from Compton, perhaps one of the local and still flourishing Polsted family, carving them as symbol of his resolve to embark on Crusade. Later, safely home having smitten the Saracens, he then engraves the second cross atop the first as token of a vow fulfilled.

A scrumptious theory but, alas, perhaps a tad too pat...'

Miranda Folkington. *'Surrey—the County that Hides from Man'*.
'Escape London Magazine', 'Surrey Special', 2002.

✸

A sacred place since childhood. He'd played here often. It *still* felt sacred, though now was childhood's end. A time to put away childish things.

Four sunken lanes converged, foot-and-rain carved through the pre-Downs sandstone. Old trees weaved over them beautiful as a wedding canopy. Dappled sunlight arrived like wedding gifts.

Where the lanes met was a space. A space in which to pause and think. An in-between place popularly known as Polstede Cross.

Did his family take their name from it or they from the place? No one could say. Time had eaten the answer.

Wulfwy de Polstede paused out of respect—and other emotions. Spring morning sun or no, he felt winter coming at him from all four paths. The trees shook in sympathy and a murder of crows rose, cawing dismay. His horse stirred, unconfident.

The preceding night had been spent before the altar of the Almighty, making vows that could not be broken. He'd even carved a visible contract into the body of God's house. Therefore he should be *stiffened*.

However, in the private chapel of his heart prayers were raised for permission to turn back. It was only a tiny part of him: not zero, that concept Crusaders would carry back from Arabic algebra, but a whole lot less than added up to mastery. Just the human portion that none save saints could whittle away. Barely a sin at all.

Impermissible. Plea denied. Those who'd just said goodbye, all those who were anything in Compton or anything to him, would not smile on so swift a return. Years of absence was the pious hope, not half an hour. Those eyes would not look kindly on him, then or ever again. Fulsome farewells would turn into candlelit reproaches. To be followed by a *little* life until merciful release.

De Polstede could no more regain his home than retake Jerusalem single-handed. He needed help for both; a crusading army's worth—and a long span between *now* and *then*.

A green-gold flitting figure caught his eye. Or possibly a trick of the light. It flicked half-seen from tree to tree, hugging the edge of vision, to journey's end behind an oak made bulbous by a huge canker at its base.

De Polstede waited for something to emerge—whilst quite confident nothing would. Be it playful sunshine, poacher or elf-form, each had its own reasons for shunning him.

Particularly the last. Intercourse with the older cousins was increasingly discouraged. Nowadays, some priests wanted it reported to the Sheriff as well as confessed. It wasn't like in his grandfather's time, during the days of ignorance when they were considered lovely. What was it the old man used to say in his cups at Polstede Manor, making prim people tut? *'Ælfscine'*—as beautiful as an Elf.

Just in case imagination wasn't responsible, De Polstede politely averted his eyes.

A crossroads and a turning point. Or rather a no-turning point. Ahead equalled over the edge of the Downs and all the world he'd ever known, into the blue beyond and allegedly, eventually, London. Waiting there was some ship that would ferry him across Ocean to the Holy Land. In his mind's eye the future lay under purple, threatening skies, entirely unlike the present one.

De Polstede had known these trees since earliest days. Now, for the first time, they almost spoke to him plain. Via the dancing of branches and the wind's whisper they had a message for him.

'Go, stranger,' he was told. *'Take your fear with you. Come back without it.'*

Wulfwy's whitening knuckles gripped the reins.

✦

The rest of him was browner now, though his knuckle-joints still paled at restraining many men's weight worth of war-horse.

Back again. Only this time pointing the other way—and with every justification. No reproachful eyes to greet him now, only joyful ones. The wanderer returned—a moment to savour. Polstede Cross hello!

Suddenly he decided not to ride straight on down to Polstede Manor and home. This once-a-lifetime homecoming should be a *considered* pleasure.

So he might divert to the inn in Compton village first and clad his insides with the English ale he'd dreamt of when the Sun was a Yule-bonfire right before your face, and to touch your armour was to raise blisters. When the Saracen arrows *thwickered* in from the brazen sky seeking weak places in that armour. Involuntary, unbeknownst to him, Wulfwy's gauntlet played over the dents in helm and mail where they'd almost succeeded.

De Polstede could visualise the very bench in a shadowy corner of the inn, safely tucked away in a place that was *almost* home. The thought of it, never far from his mind these last years, made him smile. And if his smile was twisted now after a Syrian sword's crude surgery, that only meant he deserved indulgence all the more.

He'd swear the innkeeper to secrecy and sneak up on the Manor from an unexpected direction. Then the homecoming would be on de Polstede's terms. Unlike the last few years.

Years—a trio of them—that were actually like nothing. For in fact today was no success, not really—save on the level of a lost dog finding its kennel. The craven pleasure of finding a bolthole and crawling within.

He was *still* astride a horse at Polstede Cross and prey to every kind of weak wondering. He'd gone to Palestine not only to serve God but to shake off his settled gloom: that *thing* which both held him to home and yet wore him out from the inside whilst there. However, contrary to the forest's instructions, it had come back with him.

So, though his saddlebags were stuffed full of presents from Palestine, Wulfwy de Polstede himself was as empty as when he went. He might go and carve his second cross on the Chancel arch but much good would it do him. Human vision was one thing, but God could not be deceived.

Unfortunately, whilst he was away de Polstede had seen things he hadn't wanted to see. And some things, once seen, can't be *un*seen.

There'd been Englishmen at Constantinople the same as him: *Varangians* from the Emperor's Guard—which came as a shock. The cunning Venetians who'd ferried and incited them to that diversion hadn't chosen to mention that. When the first Crusader assault on the walls failed Wulfwy went with an embassy allowed into the City. There'd been a double line of English axemen all in gleaming mail lining their route from port to palace.

Then he'd fought hand to hand with the same men at the Seaport Gate when the City fell. A second sack of Rome and a de Polstede was with the barbarians...

Much later, on the Holy Land's holy soil, a Saracen prisoner told him *'I came to Jerusalem not for glory but to save my soul'*. Honesty had poured from that face as subsequently blood did. When the King ordered all the minor captives killed the Saracen awaited the knife without obvious fear. *'I go from you to a better place,'* he'd said as his last words, *'and to a kinder judge'*.

De Polstede didn't think such an infidel would be barred from Paradise but that turned out to be a minority opinion, best kept to himself. He'd been shouted down and eyed with suspicion.

Nor had Wulfwy de Polstede seen what he wanted to see. He'd entered—on his knees—the Synagogue at Nazareth where Christ himself had taught. Wulfwy de Polstede's feet trod ground where *those* blessed feet might have stood. And yet his eyes saw only a empty room, whitewashed, round and bare. If Christ had ever been there he'd taken all of himself with him when he left.

Also, to celebrate, a Spanish knight had killed a Jew outside and his blood had ebbed over the threshold. There proved to be a surprising amount of gore in such a little man. His brood of children had wept and diluted it.

De Polstede sighed and knowing himself to be alone allowed an anguished face out from beneath its mask.

'Where were we?' asked the cankered oak. 'Oh yes: still frightened?'

Thus De Polstede learned that it had been elf-kind after all. They had waited for him. Time was not the same to them.

The green and gold figure was sometimes part of the tree, at other times separate. There was no single second when you could say the one was true and not the other. Being was not the same to them.

When it could be seen the figure's face was white as cream and neither male nor female. Sex wasn't the same for them either, nor did they have a soul to imperil with it. De Polstede now saw what his grandfather meant. They truly were... beautiful.

There was no point in deceit. Those almond shaped eyes of gold could see through as well as see. Also, though a knight should not know fear or even be accused of it, it was better still he speak the truth.

'Yes. I am. Frightened.'

There were shapes in and round the other trees now. De Polstede did not feel surrounded however. They were the forest. It was only natural they should be here and listening.

The Elf smiled. A smile can be more unkind than a snarl. The King had smiled such a smile when he ordered the Saracen prisoners killed.

'Frightened of what?'

De Polstede loosened his sword in its scabbard. Not as a precaution but through acquired habit. There were deep nicks in the blade right up to the hilt.

'This life. Of what I am. And shall be. Of one day failing each day's tests.'

The Ambassador from the older race acknowledged the truth of it. Though truth was not the same to them.

'But surely,' he or she asked, from the depths of the oak, 'you went on crusade *'to save your soul'*...'

It borrowed not only the sentiments but the very *voice* of the noble Saracen. For an instant, de Polstede was back in the killing pens before Jerusalem's walls. He shivered though it was high summer.

They knew. Though God chose not to grant them a soul to reach eternity with, He saw fit that they should *know*.

De Polstede straightened his back in the saddle. His ancestors had fought at Hastings—and survived fighting on the wrong side. They'd kept their lands by sword and guile—and guts.

'I *have* fulfilled my vow,' he said firmly, 'as you are well aware. You saw me go. You waited for my return.'

It was open to him to just leave. To amble down the path and go on into all the years ahead. Elves cared nothing for politeness; there would be no slight. Yet de Polstede couldn't. This was one war he wouldn't swerve.

An elegant gold arm emerged from oak bark to wave dismissively with improbably long fingers. Thin white lips sneered over pointed teeth.

'You are *no* crusader!'

And de Polstede, a pious knight, dared not disagree.

'You were not then,' the Elf twisted the knife. 'Nor are you now.'

To tell the truth was to imitate the Almighty. De Polstede nodded slowly.

'But in your heart, warm-blood, do you not wish to be? Not still *wish* to crusade?'

De Polstede thought. Yes, he did. The *little* life yawned open for him like the Gates of Hell. He wanted a holiday from being himself. If possible, a holiday that lasted a lifetime.

He nodded again.

'Then bide here and I shall bring one to you...'

The Older Race were descendants of Cain—or possibly the giants that once ruled Britain. They had offended God but were still his servants. They had not been spared the Flood for no reason. So de Polstede waited.

Compton village was only a mile away. A third of an hour across the fields. Less if you sprinted.

Eustace the bailiff had sprinted. He was heaving for lack of breath and understanding. From under a mop of shaggy hair and heavy brows he studied de Polstede without savour.

'My Lord! Welcome!' he greeted him, in a tone devoid of welcome. 'I... We... You are *home*...'

De Polstede acknowledged him but said nothing yet. There'd been trust if little friendship between them before he left. Eustace managed de Polstede's estate in addition to his own growing farm. He'd done so well and honestly. His was a coming name in Compton. He could read and write and the common sort came to him for advice.

Eustace shook his head as if to clear it.

'What I do not understand... Lord, is how I came here. And why. Why I should have these?'

He lifted the falchion in his hand in puzzlement, the shield in the other likewise.

'Only God knows the truth of it...,' De Polstede 'agreed'.

Wrong. The Elf knew too. It fed the two men pictures in their heads, like the Bible stories come alive—only with Eustace starring. A lifelike full-colour Eustace acted out in the broad daylight of Polstede Cross the things he thought done in darkness.

Eustace cheated and stole. He robbed the de Polstedes blind even before Wulfwy left. Coins stuck to his fingers when he counted them and the fruits of de Polstede fields did not all make it to their barns. And that was a joy to Eustace, for he hated the de Polstedes with a deep hatred even though (or because) they'd shown him only kindness. He lived for the day when he'd stolen enough to supplant them. Then Eustace of Compton would be the big man roundabouts!

The seeds of that dawn had been sown at the assizes and courts of *pie powder*. Preliminary words had been whispered in the right ears and gold dropped in the right pockets.

Eustace's smile was a secret smile and as cold as any elf's.

When the ignorant came to him for advice they went away owing him money—with interest. De Polstede's going on crusade allowed Eustace to advance his plans sharply. His rule now ran in Compton and it ran a tight but not happy ship. He had burly churls to enforce it and the welfare of widows and orphans did not rank highly. Polstede Manor lay under economic siege.

Whereas Eustace prospered. Then prosperity begat confidence and confidence begat indulgence. Eustace graduated from raping farmstock to servant-girls. He lusted after the outline of Lady de Polstede's hips all through

Sunday Mass. When her husband either failed to return or languished a debtor in Guildford gaol, Eustace intended to *have* her.

A long and sordid story that somehow only took seconds.

De Polstede dismounted. 'So there,' he said, 'is an answer to your questions. You are here to fight for your cause. As I will fight for mine...'

Eustace never stood a chance. He was bigger, fiercer and a better bully but de Polstede now had a cause he could put his heart into. After only a brief exchange of blows it allowed him to put his sword into Eustace's heart.

The ruined organ commenced becoming as cold as people said it was. He sank to the ground before the bulbous oak.

The ground accepted him. Accumulated leaf mould went to make a shroud whilst Mother Earth enfolded him like any mother would her child. Roots rustled round the man in ever tighter embrace. Swiftly he was lost to sight, gathered in like harvest home.

In some barely perceptible way the local sunshine seemed brighter. It gave out a tiny portion more joy.

The tree or Elf spoke in a voice of rapture.

'*Delicious...*'

De Polstede never knew *how* he knew, but was made aware that under Polstede Cross there'd form a root which would grow exactly Eustace-shaped. Something... memorable to remember him by.

There followed other moving pictures. Very moving. Specifically, Wulfwy de Polstede was moved to sadness.

Eustace was by no means the only wicked spirit in Compton. Though by far the worse and foremost in acting on it, he was far from alone.

De Polstede saw some surprising faces, people he'd thought pious. He saw them in their chambers engaged in petty infamy. Outdoors, ever hugging the shadows, their feet ran fast to do mischief. There were those who rejoiced in the tears of others. Some delighted to open old wounds. Still more relished the cowardly blow that could not be traced. In their hearts they had said *'There is no God'* and revelled in that freedom.

Compton could either take its tone from them or the good hearted. It was up to the actors in this little play performed beside the eternal Downs. They each had their time upon the stage. For the dark to prevail all that was needed was for the kind to abstain.

ALTERED ENGLANDS

So it turned out there *was* a crusade to be fought in Compton: a quieter one where no one—else—need have their blood shed, but that Christ might actually approve of.

Accepting its call took no thought at all. Wulfwy de Polstede cleaned and sheathed his sword and remounted.

Though of a humble spirit he was used to authority. The knight employed the voice he used to command men against city walls and certain death.

'One other thing...'

'Naturally, warm-blood. Ask away.'

The Elf was wholly of the tree now, its face shining through from just beneath the bark.

'Why?'

It did not answer directly. Legend said that their knowing so much meant they weren't permitted to.

'I am the oldest in the forest,' answered the voice of liquid honey. 'I am the custodian of memory. My kind do not slice Time as your kind does into past and now and future. I see the day of my fall just as I recall my seeding. Right now, besides talking to you, I am revelling in my first sunlight and also lamenting imminent death. It is all one. You will not understand but no matter.'

'And?' asked de Polstede, impatient. He was aware that for all their powers the elf folk were inferior creations to Man. The Almighty had smiled on one but not the other.

Elf-kind were not jealous of it. They bore the discrimination bravely.

'Suffice to say I see that we and you—and yours—will be together for some while; travelling alongside in the years given us. Your seed will bide here as will mine. It will be better for us if you stay. You will love the trees and revere this place. Therefore the spirit of this place wishes peace with your spirit—which will be your children's spirit also. We simply wished you to be aware of it. A soldier fights better for knowing the reason why...'

De Polstede looked around and looked within. And in that way he saw. He saw himself within the hour enjoying ale in Compton. A memory that would warm him the rest of his life. He saw one cross carved atop another beside the image of a knight—a true knight—in Compton Church. He was made aware of that symbol of his faithfulness being remarked upon eight centuries later.

He also saw himself that very night laying alongside his wife with long stockpiled love and lust combined. Even their sweat would merge and two selves connect until there was no separating them—not till their time came in the fullness of time. Maybe a son would come of it. Then there would be someone to follow him. Someone else to fight the good fight when he was laid to rest in Compton Church.

Not a bad prospect. And a manly and holy task fitting to a life well led. He vowed himself to it.

Meanwhile the Elf was gone. There was no one there but a knight. Or leastways no one you could see.

Wulfwy de Polstede finally set off on crusade, spurring his horse down the path into Compton.

10~

THE SUNKEN GARDEN

INTRODUCTION

As it said in the biographical notes to the Ash-Tree Press' *'Acquainted With the Night'*, 2004:

> *'I am indebted for the setting to a 'True ghost stories' book—title and author alas forgotten—read long ago'.*

I thus freely admit that with this story you are handling sort-of stolen goods. Fairly innocent stolen goods though, as I shall explain.

Since University days, maybe even a bit before, I've kept 'scrapbooks' of press clippings, photocopied snippets, inspirational pictures and reports of high strangeness as a sort of 'idea compost heap' for the literary 'career' I must have had some presentiment of following. Which is good, excellent even, except for the carelessness of youth in failing to record source details. Therefore, until a shockingly few years ago, for the most part I haven't the foggiest idea of when and where the stuff comes from. Sometimes yellowing headers or a distinctive typeface, or even a lightning flash of memory, supplies clues, but not often...

Which is the case with the setting—but setting only—of the following tale. Therefore to the unknown author of that book long ago I acknowledge indebtedness and crave indulgence. The rest however, including the tormenting of its decent but uptight protagonist, is all my own work...

ALTERED ENGLANDS

THE SUNKEN GARDEN

✸

I wanted to take her away before all the madness began. Which is a bit ironic really, given what happened. Especially when you consider my actual words. *'Let's slip away for a few days,'* I said, *'before we're trapped'*.

I think there's a malevolent scriptwriter above us, putting words in our mouths for us to trip over later. For a laugh.

That wasn't always my belief. Far from it. Such sentiments wouldn't have seemed right from the pulpit each Sunday. It's what I affirm now though: *'Firmly and truly'*, as the hymn says.

Courtesy of a loving family, a head-spinning schedule of anniversary celebrations was planned, culminating in the 'surprise gift' of a week in Minorca. However, their supposedly 'street-wise' generation lacks the attention to detail instilled in us by a World War. The travel agents had *my* name when they rang up about a change in flight times.

'What holiday?' I said. *'News to me!'*

The girl twigged instantly. *'Oh shit!'* she exclaimed—and then *'Sorry Reverend.'* I think she meant about spoiling things rather than the *industrial* language.

Still, it's the thought that counts. We never let on to the family.

Don't get me wrong. It's not that we weren't grateful for the impending carnival of revelry. I'm sure our sons and daughters and their spouses (and bevy of ex-spouses—because they'd all been very 'civilised' about the splits) put a lot of time and trouble and £s into it. We'd have worn a fixed grin whatever was arranged.

It was simply that we—or maybe *I*—fancied catching our breath beforehand; to convert what was coming into a *savoured* pleasure. And once conceived, that idea just seemed... right. Golden weddings aren't exactly ten-a-penny at the best of times. On the contrary, in today's world of 'serial monogamy' and vows-taken-lightly they're an endangered species. Ours might be one of the last our stricken culture sees, and therefore not an event to be entered into *'unadvisedly, lightly, or wantonly, but reverently, discreetly, advisedly, soberly, and in the fear of God; duly considering the causes for which Matrimony was ordained'*, to borrow from our Anglican brethren's (criminally neglected) Book of Common Prayer.

Once you phrase it like that, there's little need for debate.

So I visited the Internet (because I'm no Luddite: my grandchildren called me *'techno-granddad'*) and booked us a weekend at a hotel near Stratford. The wife, a retired drama teacher, likes Shakespeare. I'm not so sure. Some of his sonnets are positively indecent. You realise they're written to a beautiful boy, don't you? Also, some of the plays shouldn't be handed over to an unsupervised child.

Anyhow, Stratford-upon-Avon leaped from the screen to my eyes. The hotel website was user-friendly. And blessedly accurate. The place proved to be clean and airy and generally... nice. A nineteenth century manor house, now part of a national chain. All other things aside, I'd recommend the place to you. If I were composing this some years from now when I shall be nothing but bitterness, I might even supply its full name and address. Just be thankful for my mercy.

Everything went swimmingly, from taxi there right through to evening meal. Afterwards, I rang senior son from reception to say we'd absconded but would be back shortly and not to worry. We're having a wonderful time—pass it on. Wish you were here, see you soon.

Two untruths, but only the first deliberate.

Next day, well fed, well rested, I went to explore whilst my wife still dozed. I do not sleep so well as her—one of the myriad pains of encroaching old age. Therefore, saying my morning prayers in the hotel grounds (post a full English breakfast) seemed a good use of wakefulness, as well as one of the little treats of life. I understand that Judaic theology believes each soul called before the Throne of Judgement must account for every—permitted—pleasure missed.

ALTERED ENGLANDS

There was a back garden with a paved path leading to an ornamental pond. Mock-classical statuary was dotted about in hedge alcoves. I should imagine it wasn't so different in lay-out from when a family lived there over a century before—all corseted lawns and herbaceous borders. The business that ran the place had a reputation for catering to the classier end of the market, rather than sales reps. This 'England meets Greece-&-Rome' effect was presumably part of the image.

When I got there, in no hurry, the pond proved to be shallow and time hallowed. A silent Neptune-fountain rose from the centre. I walked round its circular avenue. Fish darted about in a few feet of greenish water, living careless, innocent lives—or so we're assured.

It was going to be a sunny day. Possibly even hot. Ideal for a lazy day in Stratford while my lady wife sight-saw and I browsed bookshops. A spot of light lunch, maybe even a cream tea, and then back to the hotel for another grand repast. Food becomes more, not less, important to you as the years go by, you know. Other 'treats' aren't so readily available any more.

The good omens buoyed me up; I was inspired to bravery and exploration. So, when the lawn ended in a wall and shrubbery, I went further.

The wall had a gate in it—and what else are gates for? The worst that could happen was a groundsman saying, *'Sorry, sir, this bit's private.'*

Not so. Beyond was more lawn, apparently open to all, with a sundial in its middle. Well maintained if not exactly well frequented. A fence at the further end marked, I assumed, the conclusion of hotel property.

Wrong again. I didn't need to venture the gate in the low fence to see that there was more. A set of steps descended steeply into an archetype Victorian sunken garden. It was a wilderness now but an oval path still cleaved round the perimeter. Ionic type pillars and yet more cod-classical statuary peeped out of the jungle like a miniature lost city.

I saw no reason *why not*. And how many things, from the Garden of Eden onwards, have gone awry for mankind due to that same reckless spirit?

The gate was creaky but co-operative; the steps intact. I descended.

Down below had a micro-climate of its own. The morning sun had not yet penetrated and night's chill remained. Damp in the air was made heavier yet by the perfume of massed vegetation, some of it rotting.

I tested the patina on the nearest bust. My finger left a moist smear like a snail trial on the brow of a Roman emperor.

Any beauty that might have detained me had left soon after the last gardener many years ago. A quick stroll round the circuit of the path would finish me with here forever.

Halfway round, the sky fell down on me. I had never felt such desolation. All colour fled out of the world and life, swirling away down past my feet like water from a bath.

I could barely lift my face. Tears streaked it for the first time since boyhood. Yet lift it I did. That tiny movement took more courage than forcing myself ashore at Sword Beach on D-Day.

To find nothing. I stood in no especial place. Just another portion of path like any other. No statue loomed over me, no pitfall threatened. Nothing to justify feeling so utterly *lost*.

Yet there *was* power here. I had plugged into it the same as sticking wet fingers in the mains. It had noticed me for an instant before—praise be—passing on. Just space enough for the flicking open of a malign eye.

Never before in a long life with its fair share of sloughs had I considered suicide—until then. Though it was summer for the rest of the world I was in winter and shivering. The rational part of me, clambering to reclaim the steering wheel, said I must be going down with something bad.

Yet what sickness was there so 'bad' as to still the breeze and silence the birds? Alerted by an awful silence save for my heaving breath, I listened for them but both were gone.

I certainly would be sick, sick as a dog, if I stayed. Aged legs became youthful again to propel me out of that abysmal place.

Nothing could induce me to retrace my steps but through desperate eyes I saw a means of escape at the sunken garden's far end. The fence atop the high bank was pierced by a door.

The only way up to it was via a slope out of the question in normal circumstances. Yet I took it like a teenager, ruining the knees of a new pair of slacks, and roughly took the apparent virginity of the door latch.

I found myself beside a busy road, gasping and paper-pale. Doubtless I looked a ghastly sight to the motorists streaking by. What was with that old boy wobbling on his heels where pedestrians weren't meant to be?

I didn't care. Right then I loved that fume-soaked, litter-strewn bit of kerb like I loved my own fireside. Like I loved my dear lady wife.

I was reassured. The world was like this—and increasingly so. *This* was reality. And reality—however degraded—seemed sweet.

ALTERED ENGLANDS

I made my way back to the hotel hugging the untrod fringes of motorway and roundabouts. Drivers peeped their horns at me. En route I decided not to believe it. Or rather I *preferred* not to believe it. Once back I told my wife I'd got lost in a maze of strange streets. And fallen. Which was true enough, sort of.

At dinner that night we met a delightful couple from Yorkshire—very level-headed and down to earth. Plain speaking types but good company. I'm ashamed to say they were ideal for my purpose.

Over a brandy (my first since *VE* Day!) at the bar afterwards, I mentioned the sunken garden to him. In fact I skilfully reeled him in, like an angler playing a fish, though I say so myself. I hinted at enough of my adventure to make it a challenge to him without ever being explicit. A man of the cloth learns much about humanity in the course of his vocation—and not all of it to the species' credit. Accordingly, the temptation to tug upon people's strings is a sore trial. I succumbed to it.

I crave the reader's forgiveness. I was still shaken—shaken to the core. Core values were part of that shaking.

And the next morning they both went there, as I knew they would, with him leading. I watched from our window, skulking behind the net curtain. When they returned they were no longer so friendly. I 'happened' to meet them in the lobby. They were heading for the bar.

'Why did you send us down there?' she demanded of me. Her face was drawn, his dotted with sweat.

'Shut up,' he told her. 'Just bloody well leave it, woman. I need a drink!'

I wasn't invited to join him, nor did we dine together that night. In fact they cut us dead. My wife thought that very odd.

So it wasn't just imagination, or leastways not just mine. I didn't know whether to be pleased or pained.

On the way to bed I cornered the manageress at the reception desk. Her type of job teaches insight just as much as the ministry. Subtleties in my face must have told a tale

'Are you enjoying your stay, Reverend? Is there anything wrong?'

'No, not at all.' My voice was mock sunny. 'Except that I noticed your sunken garden today. I was wondering why you don't make more of it? In the brochure maybe...'

'It's just an overgrown plot,' she said firmly—and so betrayed her own reply. 'A weed trap. Our maintenance contract doesn't include it. Why d'you ask? Did you go in ? I hope you didn't fall...

... 'No, we've never thought of restoring it. No, tell a lie, I did ask our local handyman to clear the worst bits once, so it wouldn't be such an eyesore. He refused. He left.

... 'Me? Two years as manager and two before that as assistant. Yes, I went to look at it once, when I first arrived. Just from the top of the steps: just a glance. No, never actually *in* there. This place keeps me far too busy. Are you sure you didn't trip over? No? Good.'

Her fears of being sued and all the associated paperwork receded. Then the small part of her not yet owned by the business could peek out its wan face.

'It's just a jungle,' she repeated, almost wheedling. 'There's nothing down there—is there?'

✵

I must have been mad. Except that I know I wasn't. I was *famed* for my sanity. Doubtless my *'Methodist Recorder'* obituary and funeral oration touched upon my renowned rationality.

So what then drove me on? What self destructive urge led my feet to visit that place again? There was the open door before me of just checking out as per booking and driving off. I could have gone and forgotten—eventually.

My theory—which I've had ample time to hone—is that a lifetime of careful virtue isn't natural. Though I was not conscious of it, the human part of me was *bored*. Bored unto death. Nature—human nature—will out, whatever straitjackets we strap round it. A coiled up spring sprung and propelled me to the sunken garden.

Or maybe it was just simple curiosity. The sort of laudable spirit that spurred men out of the caves and towards the stars.

Or fascination with the opposition. I'd devoted my life to one faction alone. It's natural to develop an interest in your opponent. Perhaps I secretly speculated whether *He* was actually as awesome as was said?

Take your pick of explanations—each equally likely. I no longer care.

It was late afternoon. We were leaving. The weekend had not been a success, for she knew I was out of sorts. Even in light and airy Stratford, amongst all the cultural homage, the sunken garden was with me. I carried its cloud on my back and in my head. The knowledge would not leave me that *there* occupied the same planet as Anne Hathaway's Cottage, and the pub where I picked at an excellent ploughman's lunch. I lied to my wife and said that I felt feverish. With five decades of unbroken honesty behind me she simply accepted my words.

Her concern was characteristically unselfish: there was the imminent anniversary to gear up for. She wanted me at my best for it—for my sake. I took her proffered paracetamols.

We almost escaped. The bags were stowed in the boot, my navigator had the AA downloaded route resting in her lap. Then I lied again.

'Actually, darling, I think I left my driving gloves in the lobby. I'll only be a minute...'

They were snug in my blazer pocket and pressed against me like thirty pieces of silver as I walked.

Reception was empty but there was a pair of teenagers canoodling in the bar area. Today I found that reassuring rather than shocking. At least there'd be witnesses to my whereabouts—just in case.

It didn't look as if the sundial lawn had been trod at all that day. Most guests had 'better' things to do than appreciate God's creation. Less than half, in my estimation, were actually married to one another. Likewise, I'd observed that the television in our room offered no fewer than four 'adult channels' for a small additional fee. Accordingly, someone immune to such attractions could be alone in the great outdoors. I reached the sunken garden, doubtless unseen, and teetered on the edge.

I checked. There were birds in the sky, wending homewards (as I should be doing) but they were distant. Or silent. Imagination made me manufacture an anticipatory quiet seeping out of *there*...

A hesitation at the gate, but only a slight one. Anything more would call into question what I believed and based my life upon. And what I believed, in my innocence, was that there was a protecting power over me, stronger than anything the enemy could manifest.

Down below were pockets from which last night's frost had never fled. The grass to which I descended was crisp beneath my brogues. It provided the only sound.

Once round the path was my intent. To justify myself and prove all sorts of things. That there should be nothing was the maximum result. For it all to have been naught but fancy so that I could enjoy a celebration before the celebrations.

My finger print was still upon the Roman Emperor, overlaid by a fresh patina of dew or stone-sweat. Proof of some sort. I *had* been here other than in nightmare. I had left my mark.

And now to take my leave. I brushed jostling foliage aside and rounded the far end. The scrapes left by my scrambling feet still scarred the bank. Up above the door swung loose just as I'd left it.

Which should have permitted traffic noise to invade. Surely the motorway beyond never slept...

But my breath was all I could hear. I tried to regulate it. Alas, the pounding of my heart was beyond control.

Before me the sunken garden waited like an adventure. There was only me and it in the world, and above us only sky. Which is now becoming my dark suspicion...

I stepped—no, *strode*—forward.

All the statues smirked simultaneously, animate for a fleeting second. Eyes flared red with borrowed vitality and... something saw through them. Just so that I would *know*. That little was ample.

I'd seen some spirit older than I, older even than my mayfly civilisation and faith. Something with roots back into a past I couldn't conceive—nor would ever want to.

Everything in every history book I'd read, or even in the Book of my religion, was as one transient lifespan compared to the life I glimpsed then. It was confident of the future too, the far far future—and it *knew* it. The garden was more sunken than hitherto. It had a lower level that I should certainly have recalled—and *certainly* should recall descending into. A mirror image of the one above. Yet there I stood.

Adrenaline coursed through me like a train. I looked wildly round.

Steps led up to the higher strata but my way was blocked. I was not alone.

The figures were insubstantial. Men and women: faded shadows of what had once been, dressed in clothes of every era. Regency gowns and lace, Victorian top hats and watch-chains. Even some wartime uniforms.

The doleful procession did not just pass me by, it passed *through* me.

ALTERED ENGLANDS

They left a great cold behind. Not the sort to raise goosebumps, but frostbite of the soul. God alone knew how many times they'd trod that path. What else was there for the poor devils to do?

But that did not explain their anger, nor their looks full of hatred for me. Once kindly faces were now twisted.

I raced for the way out but was thwarted. A glass ceiling barred me from the upper level. The dread place of mere minutes ago now beckoned like Paradise itself.

Neither of those locations were options. Not for me. Not now. I recognised that like swallowing lead. One was visible, the other hoped for, but both prohibited. Even the slightest step to either was forbidden.

So, all that was left for me was to turn and take in my new home—and eternal destination. I somehow knew its master would introduce himself sooner or later.

Before that though, my wife 'found' me, along with the rest of the search party. The manageress and two hotel porters held torches but wouldn't enter in.

She did though. Brave heart! I called and called to the soles of her shoes directly above me, but of course she couldn't hear.

It touched her: that much I saw. Yet only the externals applied, unable to get under the skin. My wife shivered but no more.

I now see with exquisite clarity that she is—or was—a *good* person. Whatever ran the sunken garden could find no purchase on her. She was a greased pole to its talons.

Whereas I was hooked, heart and soul. Now, what did that say about me?

Watching her retreating back was a wrenching pain like no other. Or so I deluded myself in my naivety. However, it proved a pinprick compared to what came soon after. But concerning that it's best you know nothing.

I often wonder what she did about the Golden Wedding gala. I'm promised all eternity to ponder on it.

Apparently, the first few centuries are the worst...

JOHN WHITBOURN

PORTS & PHANTOMS

INTRODUCTION

'Port—a red fortified wine produced in the mountainous Douro region in the north of Portugal and shipped from Oporto, whence its name.'

A dull-dog definition in an encyclopaedia that shall be nameless. How true—but also how inadequate to describe the liquid joy accidentally discovered by Englishmen in the 18th century and the world's first demarked wine region!

These stories attempt in their own infinitesimal way to gild and propagate that joy. As per (supposedly, allegedly):

'Wine is visible proof that God loves you and wants you to be happy.'
Ernest Hemmingway.

Which, if correctly attributed, just goes to show that truth springs eternal, even from poisoned ground...

Surely no other apologia is needed for these tales, except perhaps that they involve both the exotica of my countrymen making themselves at home in a far away place, and that they star a drink that I once loved till it fell out of love with me and my tastes started to outstrip my means.[17]

---

[17] Pinpointed as a bottle of the 1960 vintage consumed in the mid 1980s, the precise price censored to prevent mariticide. This emissary from Paradise cost more, alas, than I could in all conscience ever again spend on one bottle. And yet left its subsequent but lesser siblings seeming a bit *'After the Lord Mayor's Show'*. Icarus

As the cynical old saying has it: *'when poverty comes in the window, love flies out the door.'* True, how true, but there is the small comfort that love can sometimes have an afterlife, returning to haunt a human as affection. And affection, laid down in the private cellars of the mind and periodically turned with care, has been known to mature into a vintage even finer than the palate-thrilling powers of younger wines.

The series also constituted a rising to the challenge of a clipping I found in my 'ideas for some future date' scrapbook, alas unsourced and undated, but presumably drawn from a review of Rose Macaulay's (1881-1958), *'They went to Portugal'*, 1946. It said:

'There is one significant omission from this new tale of the British in Portugal: the wine shippers of Oporto, who still constitute the most important and influential expatriate community in that enchanting country.'

Macaulay explained the reason for this in her original preface:

'What a magnificent story for nearly three hundred years is theirs, how picturesque their calling, how excitingly beautiful its setting, how rich their history in characters and incidents. Not a theme that can be adequately dealt with by an outsider. It must be written by an Oporto pen.'

The review continued:

'But no Oporto pen has yet come forward and, in any case, in spite of her modest disclaimer, Macaulay could have done it better than anyone else. The loss, alas, is ours.'

Well, since everyone else was so shy, a Binscombe pen, in all humility, stepped forward lest the job never get done.

I followed the intriguing literary recipe below:

ITEM: Take one stiff upper lipped, privately educated Englishman
ITEM: Marinate in vintage port wine.
ITEM: Civilise by contact with Catholic Civilisation.
ITEM: Season to taste with the Mediterranean 'great life-cycle' outlook.

---

had flown too close to the sun…

ITEM: Bake a under fierce sun.
ITEM: Serve as a fully rounded human being when ready.

The proof of the pudding is in the eating and you, the paying customer, must be the judge of that. For my part and to my taste buds, I consider that the finished product, Tobias Longhurst Esq. is a trifle highly spiced, perhaps even something of a rogue, or leastways he develops into one under the influence of his trade and foreign climes. Nevertheless, I conclude that the recipe is basically sound insofar as he remains, I trust, a *loveable* rogue.

By the by, the concluding tale, *'One for the Road'*, is set in what was to me then the misty future of 2012. Accordingly, the reader's indulgence is sought over its (presumptuous or daring?) ventures into prophecy regarding language, societal norms and… Life.

However, *'Quod scripsi, scripsi'*, as someone[18] once said when in far hotter water than I: *'What I have written, I have written'*. For good or ill these words were scribed and the die thus cast. Let them stand.

All that remains is for me to launch Tobias into the wide world and wish him joy of it—and you of him.

Cheers!

---

[18] Pontius Pilate, in John 19:22. Someone who (taking the reported facts only) always strikes me as a much maligned but well-meaning man, obliged to deal with fanatics. I would have been a lot less patient. It also bears mention that, courtesy of the Christian Creed and the liturgy in every Mass said, every day, all over the world for nigh two millennia, this otherwise unremarkable provincial governor is now the most celebrated Roman of them all…

JOHN WHITBOURN

PORTS & PHANTOMS

Being the curious memoirs of Tobias Longhurst, Port-wine Shipper and connoisseur, *bon vivant*, expatriate Englishman and general good fellow.

COMPRISING:

1) A PARTIAL CURE
2) THE FALL OF A DICTATOR
3) STOP PRESS! *'HANG ON, I'VE FOUND ANOTHER BOTTLE!'*
4) *'LIBERTY! AH, LIBERTY!'*
5) ONE FOR THE ROAD

☸

'How long, how long, in infinite pursuit
Of this and that endeavour and dispute?
Better be merry with the fruitful grape
Than sadden after none, or bitter, fruit.

You know, my friends, how long since in my house
For a new marriage I did make carouse:
Divorced old barren Reason from my bed,
And took the Daughter of the Vine to spouse.'

Kwaji Imam Omar Khayyam (Died 1123).

☸

'Port is the wine for a mood of philosophical meditation. A vintage port, ponderously weighted though it might be... is scholarly but never pedantic, and, as the decanter goes round, conversation should glow like the wine with a rich and seemly solemnity, and good-will should expand round the table with growing intensity, as the bouquet and aroma of the port released

ALTERED ENGLANDS

from the prison of the bottle <u>stretches</u>, rejoicing in the freedom of the air. Port cannot be the friend of upstart theories which are born and die in the ephemeral life of a butterfly Moselle. Its optimism is based on the eternal foundations of Aristotle, Plato and Plotinus.'

H. Warner Allen. *'Sherry and Port'*. 1952.

✺

'Port strengthens while it gladdens as no other wine can do; and there is something about it which must have been created in pre-established harmony with the best English character.'

Professor George Saintsbury. *'Notes on a Cellar-book'*. 1920.

✺

11~

A PARTIAL CURE

'Port is the cure for all ills save death.'
Portuguese proverb.

'If we don't get a decent growth out of them this year,' said Piecrust, with gentlemanly sadness, 'they're for it. That's it, *c'est tout*, the end of the show, old boy. 1962 will mark the end of our acquaintance with them.'

I gave him the opportunity to take another trip to his glass before replying. Giles Piecrust agreed with the 18th century Olympian figure of his trade, Percy Croft, that *'any time not spent drinking port is a waste of time'*. Even by that exacting standard, Piecrust was no time-waster.

As for me, a relatively junior partner in the ancient Slovo House of Port Shippers, I thought the maxim a trifle overstated. It was just arguable, I would have said (but I *was* young-ish then, remember), that perpetuating the family name—or maybe getting to heaven—were of marginally more import.

'So,' Piecrust continued, a ricochet of his encounter with fortified-wine paradise hitting me in the form of a beaming smile, 'that is why we're asking you to toddle up to *Quinta dos Malatesta*, young Toby. Inspect the premises, test the usual things and generally read the old riot act, dear boy. If they're still in defiance of proper authority and good wine-making practise after that, then open fire with our blessing. We can't face another batch like the '61, Toby: it tasted like... well, I'd rather not say but you know...'

ALTERED ENGLANDS

'A Scottish sparkling burgundy?' I hazarded.

Piecrust winced and took another long sip to ease the memory.

'That's about the shape of it, dear boy,' he said. 'Another like that and we'll have to strike them off our list and they can go to Brazil or tobacco growing or whatever. It's a pity but one just *has* to be ruthless, I'm afraid. There's the good name of the House of Slovo to be considered.'

He looked to me for support in this *'ruthless'* stance and was relieved to find it in my wholehearted nod. The harsher aspects of modern business did not come easily to men of the old school like Giles Piecrust.

'A train leaves Oporto in two hours or so,' he went on, tentatively, 'to go up the Valley. Be on it, will you, there's a good chap.'

I looked wistfully out of the office window even as I indicated my dutiful agreement. The red-tiled roofs of *Vila Nova de Gaia* and the taste bud titillating signs... *Sandeman, Croft, Cockburn...* surmounting the great shippers' lodges, the vivid sails of the *barco rabelo*[19] on the River Douro, even smoky and industrial Oporto on the far shore, seemed awfully attractive at that moment compared to the proposed trip.

But... as Piecrust had said, there was the good name of Slovo Ports (established 1736) to be considered. I could no more ignore that call than walk away from my children.

'Mind you,' said Piecrust, jocularly, relaxing now that the matter was in supposedly safe and fiercely loyal hands, 'I advocate a modicum of care, Toby. Our glorious founder, old Sir Ralph Slovo—he died whilst touring up at Quinta dos Malatesta, you know—in the French Revolution year.'

'Really?' I said, with more interest than I should perhaps have shown. It was widely known that I brought the same loving care to my personal safety as I did to the blending and tasting of Slovo Port.

We found ourselves, without prior thought or arrangement, both staring up at the smoke darkened founder's portrait on the wall. Old Sir Ralph's superior, contented smile looked uninformatively back at me as it had done so many times in my ten happy years with the House.

'Well, he *was* eighty,' said Piecrust, defensively, 'and drinking a pipe[20] a year.'

---

[19] Traditional and colourful single-sail boats once used to transport the young port down to the shippers on the coast.

'Oh *well*...,' I smiled.

Piecrust frowned, suddenly troubled by his explanation.

'Just the same as me,' he said.

✦

'My wife,' said Senhor Pompal, 'has lit so many candles to the Virgin that a chandler in Lisbon has written to thank me. He now holidays in America whilst I, I am still faced with ruin. And my mother, sir, she creeps around hiding iron ingots everywhere—God save us, I even found one in my mattress—to scare away the 'elf-folk' that she says spoil our wine. But still it goes on, Mr Longhurst; I am at my wits end. If only it were some living thing, something that you could squint at, then my five sons and their five guns would blow it to the devil. But no, it is some invisible, creeping curse; nothing you can stick your knife in!'

Matters were getting a little too passionate for my liking—possibly because we were obliged to converse in Portuguese. Not only that, but one should be mellow and prepared to make peace with imperfect life after a magnificent meal such as we had just enjoyed. However, the owner of Quinta dos Malatesta still bore bitter resentment enough to shake his fist at the sky.

'Do you think my wife should pray to Saint Jude, Mr Longhurst?' asked Senhor Pompal, fervently. 'He being the patron saint of lost causes…'

All the serried ranks of Pompals gathered around the great dining table were looking raptly at me, hanging on my answer.

'I'm not sure,' I stuttered, a little embarrassed, 'I'm C of E myself, so maybe I'm not qualified to-...'

Senhora Pompal looked dismissive and said something I fortunately didn't quite catch.

'Then maybe, Mr Longhurst,' continued Pompal, 'if I vary the superphosphate proportion in the March-time fertiliser... Or experiment with the fish-meal to humus percentage. My Grandfather always swore-...'

'All the damn time,' commented Senhora Pompal. 'He never stopped!'

---

[20] Traditional measure. A pipe = 720 bottles of port.

ALTERED ENGLANDS

'... by a high humus percentage,' concluded Senhor Pompal, giving his spouse a murderous look. 'And he, as you'll concede, Mr Longhurst, contributed to some of the very finest of the Slovo vintages!'

After the cabbage soup, the grilled sardines with lemon, the dried codfish in garlic and mustard sauce, the steak, the eggs and heavy country bread we had consumed, I would have been content to bide in the cool *adegas*[21] or bask in the evening sunshine on the veranda with a bottle from the Quinta's happier past.

The Pompals, however, perhaps understandably since they were facing professional death and possible enforced emigration like so many of their peasant kin, to Brazil, were anxious to conversationally press on. Or rather it would be truer to say they were anxious, driven by need, but only up to a certain point—and thereafter strangely reticent. At one and the same time, torn by some collective inner conflict: like a happy vicar on a vice charge, they both did—and did not—want their quandary resolved.

Insofar as I could, I liked to steer clear of matters involving emotional undercurrents; particularly amongst the Mediterranean type peoples unafraid of display. Accordingly, I tried to restrict things to the strictly businesslike and we traversed the litany of the port-wine business, from vine-craft to vintage, seeking a solution—whilst Senhor Pompal grew more and more agitated.

Finally, as my stately instructional progress reached the crucial necessity of clean feet for the treading, Pompal's endurance snapped.

'It is the *balseiros!*'[22] he shouted, interrupting me and raising a cry of horror from his family. 'It is the balseiros, Mr Longhurst. God forgive me for telling you but it had to be said!'

There was a babble of impenetrable dialect from the other family members.

'Oh yes it must!' roared Pompal at them in reply. 'Are you looking forward to jungle clearance in Brazil? Do you know there are spiders out there that can eat whole *birds?*'

This effectively quietened his tribe and allowed a little reason to re-enter our converse.

---

[21] Farm or building associated with the quinta.
[22] Large wooden vat, with small entry hole in the side, used to mature young port.

'Oh well,' I said comfortingly, 'that's a problem easily rectified. It often crops up, though usually with just one vat, not the whole lot. What you need to do is give them a 20% carbonate of sodium solution wash and then...'

'And what *you* need to do,' said Senhor Pompal, stony-faced, 'is to come and see for yourself. Then will be the time to talk of remedies.'

So I allowed myself to be drawn from the table of cheerful memory, out to where the great squat, generations-old, upstanding vats of Brazilian mahogany stood, awaiting the newly created port. It was their job to steward the wine for a year or so, before its removal to Vila Nova de Gaia down on the coast, for blending and shipment to the awaiting English.

'Which one is worst?' I asked.

'Any or all,' replied Pompal, fatalistically, handing me a battery powered torch. 'It doesn't matter.'

I wasn't having any truck with all this emotional portentousness and stuff o' nonsense and, ignoring the assembled Pompals' burning gaze on the back of my neck, I strode up to the nearest balseiros.

The tiny *portinhola* in its side was easily opened and, hammering on the vat's side in the prescribed fashion to raise any latent fumes, I flicked on the torch and leant in.

Whereas once a fair few inches of port were left in each year to keep the balseiros 'sweet', a good sized sulphur stick now did the same trick. The interior smelt pure and neutral as it should. No problem here, I remember thinking.

Then my torch beam picked out the white and eyeless... person hanging in mid-air inside. Who slowly 'looked' up and, bony claws outstretched, floated towards me—and I left the world behind.

☸

'Come and join me, dear boy; I insist!'

The cheeriness, the sheer exuberant bonhomie of the invitation proved sufficient incentive to draw me up out of the lagoon of black treacle into which I'd succumbed. I cautiously opened my eyes and was granted an intimate view of the dust of Quinta dos Malatesta. So, not only was I still alive (presumably) but also I'd escaped transportation to... wherever. In fact, it became abundantly clear I'd merely fallen over. Given the circumstances there was unusual comfort in that.

'It would be terribly nice if you could shake a leg rather, young fellow,' came the jolly voice again. 'You see, I'm not sure how long I can hold things.'

Reflex-bred by education and culture to obey polite requests, I picked myself off the ground and turned to observe the speaker—as mere good manners would dictate.

Sir Ralph Slovo (1709-1789) smilingly raised his (empty) glass to me from the bench at the brow of the steep slope down to the Douro River.

Very much the second thing that I noticed was that all else bar he and I were still. The Pompals were frozen in the act of turning to run, and even the mighty Douro was suspended in its course. Oddest of all, individual beams of sunlight, illuminating floating trails of dust, were stilled in flight. The Universe was absolutely at peace.

I, however, was very far from such—as Sir Ralph quickly appreciated.

'Don't worry, dear boy,' he said affably, 'I haven't *stopped* time, so much as *expanded* a particular second to ridiculous proportions. It's something we departed can do—for a while anyway. Oh, and sorry about alarming you just then. You caught me unawares. That was merely a guise I adopt to tease the natives. Personally, I wouldn't dream of hurting a soul—not unless it became necessary.'

'That's quite all right,' I heard my voice saying by way of auto-response. 'Please don't mention it.'

Courtesy had also given me courage enough to cross over to where Sir Ralph was sitting. After all, I repeated to myself like a mantra, we couldn't go on shouting at each other from a distance in such a boorish manner, could we?

He was no longer the drowned-rat nightmare figure of a moment ago but the very image of the portrait in Giles Piecrust's office—a sprightly old dandy of a gentleman, plainly come at last to a comfortable *understanding* with life.

'I'm *so* glad you're here,' he said warmly, observing me over the top of steepled fingers, 'but before you sit down, I wonder if you'd care to do the honours regarding refreshment? I just so happen to know that Senhor Pompal has a secret cache of the Slovo 1912 vintage in his cellar. He's hidden it beneath a bin of the execrable 1959; along with his collection of Parisian postcards. Be so good as to decant a couple of bottles, would you?'

And I found myself doing so; perhaps on the principle that activity was a better policy than actually trying to think through what was happening. In due course, I emerged from the *adegas* (having resisted anything more than the most cursory glance at the naked French ladies) with two decanters of the incomparable '12.

Sir Ralph's face lit up at the sight of my cargo and, as though it were the most natural thing in the world, I joined him and poured us each a generous glass. Perhaps it was the proximity of port, my everyday stock in trade, that did it, but somehow, from somewhere, I found the courage to stay around.

'To you, young Toby,' said Slovo, raising his glass to me in a toast, 'with profound thanks.'

'You know me?' I gasped—but was hushed to silence.

'Not now, dear boy,' he said, gently, 'we are in the presence of greatness. Business can wait.'

The port wine, secluded for almost fifty years in reverent peace, blushed to find itself in company and gave up to the air the fragrance of a long lost southern summer. In sight matured to warm tile-red, it retained the taste of a sturdy purple tide that did not merely hint, but plainly spoke—just like the works of Purcell—of the existence of... higher and better things.

Transported for a precious moment (the sort one should stockpile for old-age) I forgot the place and occasion until recalled by Sir Ralph Slovo (dec'd)'s voice.

''Go fetch a pint of port," he quoted,
''but let it not be such as that
you set before chance-comers,
but such whose father-grape grew fat
on Lusitanian summers'.'

'Tennyson?' I guessed.

'Quite so,' he murmured, still a little removed from events (insofar as an ambulatory dead man can be said to be involved at all) by the sheer... whatever of the wine. 'I've kept in touch with the modern poets, you see—not bad some of them...'

We looked out over the steep and narrow terraces of vines, stretching down almost to the river's edge and marvelled at the beauty of the scene in the late sunshine. Eventually, it was Sir Ralph who broke the peace by signalling that another glass should be poured.

'Oh yes, I know you,' he said, belatedly answering my question of some time before, whilst looking on me with palpable kindness. 'Naturally, I retain an interest in the old firm and pop down to Vila Nova from time to time to see how things are. 'Seen you there lots—always beavering away—very commendable.'

Despite the warmth of the evening, a cold sensation arced up my spine at the thought of these invisible, unsuspected, inspections.

'Though for the most part,' he continued, 'I linger up here.'

'And why's that, sir, may I ask?'

'Well, it was up here that I was killed, you see: and the rules of the game seem to dictate that I can't stray too far or too long from it; not if I want to hang on at all. Your health, dear boy: cheers!'

'*Killed?*' I said, alarmed—even at so many years remove. 'I didn't know that you-...'

'You wouldn't, Toby; it was never revealed. Things were made to look like I'd shuffled off the coil naturally.'

'So your killer got away with it?' I said, astounded. It seemed the Company history required radical revision—for, like every Slovo product, its integrity had to be strictly protected.

'Scot-free,' smiled Sir Ralph.

'And your unquiet spirit cannot rest until justice is done, is that it?' I suggested helpfully.

'Not exactly,' replied Sir Ralph in an easy-going tone. 'I'm as quiet a spirit as they come. Somehow it didn't seem quite fair for me to take vengeance from beyond the grave or try to inform the authorities. To be perfectly frank with you, I had a lot of sympathy with the man. Actually, I rather asked for what happened...'

'Oh...'

'Do just what you will—but don't grizzle about the bill, that's my motto and always was. You see... adultery... one knows it's *wrong* of course, if one is properly brought up, but she was such a... ripe little thing: pint sized, black hair and mocking slate colour eyes...' He smacked his lips. 'Lovely...'

I felt moved to protest—partly out of pre-emptive jealousy.

'But you were eighty years old, Sir Ralph!'

'Well, I know, dear boy,' he said, mock defensively, 'but that sort of consideration is really all in the mind. And the cellar was so cool and she was so plump and... helpful. And what with the bottle of the '75 vintage...'

'The very first!' I exclaimed.

'... we'd shared (I confess I even poured some on her naked form) one just couldn't help oneself. You're a man of the world, you'll understand that such... sweet interludes can be forgiven...'

'*Oh no I won't!*' I thought. '*Wasting the Holy Grail of the Port World on some rustic hussy? Unforgivable!*'

'Sadly,' Sir Ralph went on, 'her husband (who'd observed our disportings) was less liberal. The next day, whilst I was inspecting a balseiros—just like you were doing—he pitched me in and shut the portinhola. Of course, the fumes were so strong, one was overcome within minutes and I passed on. Mind you, I'm not really complaining; if one happens to be a lover of port, it's not a bad way to go.'

'Oh, that's all right then,' I said, calming down a little.

'Yes,' agreed Sir Ralph, 'it doesn't do to get worked up about things like that, does it? I was getting on a bit anyway. So, when they hauled me out and made it appear like a seizure or the like, I didn't bear a grudge. At least that way there was no scandal. I mean, a shipper shouldn't really treat his growers like that, should he?'

'Well, no,' I said, reasonably, 'but growers shouldn't murder shippers either.'

'I suppose not,' mused Sir Ralph, 'but it was a long time ago and everyone concerned is dead now.'

At last I saw the verbal opportunity to steer discussion politely round to the one area where Sir Ralph might legitimately be subject to a modicum of criticism.

'But, if I may *say* so, sir,' I said, hesitantly, 'the other people involved, being dead, are no longer around; whereas you...'

'Ah, yes... I'm glad you mentioned that, Longhurst,' said Sir Ralph, rousing himself. 'That is a very apposite comment. I suppose I *have* overstayed the allotted span just a bit.'

'And those other people are not lingering on, frightening the living, are they?' I added, pressing home my point.

'Or spoiling the wine,' contributed Sir Ralph—to my utter dumbfoundment. 'Oh yes, that's me, I'm afraid: another one of my minor post-mortal abilities. It appears I can slow time, ruin vintages, drink port, spy on the ladies bathing, in short do most things people would like to, except—and this is crucial—open bottles or learn Portuguese. That's why I had to create this fuss and get someone like you up here.'

I was mortified and for once not concerned about displaying its outward signs.

'But... but *how*, Sir Ralph: how *could* you? And why?'

'I'd rather not go into the mechanics of spoiling wine, if you don't mind, dear boy; it's a trifle indelicate. As to why, it's all due to cursed so-called progress. I was quite happy up here, you see, until recently. I got on with my modest afterlife, living in the balseiros and not bothering a soul. I could enjoy the heavenly fumes in the vats or take a sip from someone else's glass from time to time. But then people had to go and change things—and for the worse, I might add. Heaven knows, I don't want to appear unreasonable, young Toby, but I tell you straight: until affairs are returned to as before, Quinta dos Malatesta produces only Scottish sparkling burgundy! And yes, don't look so surprised: I *was* at your meeting with Piecrust. In spirit. It's rather rude, I know, to eavesdrop but, after all, my essential interests were involved...'

Enlightenment was starting to dawn on me.

'It's the sulphur-stick cleansing method,' I said. 'That's the problem isn't it?'

'I don't know *what* that beastly black-magic stuff is called, dear boy,' replied Sir Ralph, with real feeling. 'All I know is that when a decent portion of port was left in the balseiros it not only kept them sweet but gave me something to enjoy as well: about a pipe or so a year like I'm used to. Whereas now that old Pompal scrubs them out and puts those smelly sticks in, I'm left high—and more to the point—dry! Like I've told you, I'm too ethereal to be able to open bottles—it's all I can do to lift a full glass—and I wasn't able to tell anyone as they don't talk my lingo (which is a damn disgrace when you think about it). Similarly, I couldn't get anyone to stand still and talk to me so I could learn theirs. Back in my day, *all* the growers had to speak a sort of English but I suspect our influence in the trade has declined...'

'Only 50% of production now,' I confirmed, sadly.

'Well, there you are, Longhurst. What else could I do but keep spoiling the wine so as to eventually get an Englishman up here to sort matters out?'

Slovo eyed me beadily, his judgement hanging in the balance.

'And sort matters out you will, won't you, young sir?' he said, with just a touch of ice in his voice.

He need not have feared the decline of the breed. There was not the slightest element of doubt or hesitation in my reply.

'No more sulphur at Malatesta,' I said firmly. 'I'll see to it personally.'

Sir Ralph beamed at me. 'Good man,' he said. 'And to show I'm grateful, I'll use my influence and ensure you get a damn fine vintage next year. Buy early and not just for Slovo House—put up your own money as well. Then sell half your stock in the late '80's, early '90's, and you'll make enough to keep yourself in vintage port for the rest of your natural. You listen to old uncle Ralph, dear boy; he'll see you right.'[23]

My normally decently restrained heart swelled with joy at such familiarity from a fountainhead of my lifelong obsession and vocation. What a pity, I thought, that the honour could not be recounted to my colleagues. Sadly, there were the constraining considerations of my reputation and remaining working years with the House. Perhaps I would tell them at my retirement party—when I was eighty or ninety or so.

'Well, it's been jolly nice,' said Sir Ralph, 'but you'd better be off shortly. Don't worry about the rest of the '12, I'll polish it off, never fear. It'll keep me going until you've arranged the continuance of my port-drenched limbo.'

'Well, if it's all the same to you, sir,' I said swiftly, 'I don't mind hanging on. If it's not an imposition, I'd like to acquire some of your vast knowledge of the early years of the trade...'

Sir Ralph shrugged his velvet-clad shoulders.

'It's all the same to me, dear boy—but maybe not to you. Close proximity to my sort isn't good for the living. Apparently, every hour or so with me takes about a decade off you. Well, the energy to manifest me has to come from somewhere, doesn't it?'

'Oh...'

'The natives instinctively know that, which is why they'd never stop to listen to me. You, however, being educated, weren't aware and so I was able to get my message across. I hope you don't mind; you've been awfully decent so far.'

---

[23] Sir Ralph was as good as his word. The 1963 was one of the three or four truly great vintages of the 20th century.

'Er...'

'It's only that my need was great, you see. Some might call me selfish for not moving on, I know. I'd only have to surrender to the gravitational pull I constantly feel and I'd be off to the next stage like a shot, I realise that. But life was... or is, *so* beautiful and what follows it so uncertain, you can hardly blame me, can you?'

'A *decade* did you say, Sir Ralph?'

'About that. It's greatly comforting, you know, to find my House still has dedicated people like you in it, young Toby. If I *was* to decide to move on, I'd be secure in the knowledge that Slovo Port was in good hands like yours—well, for the time remaining to you, anyway...'

Sir Ralph looked benignly on the setting sun and studied its rays through the purple prism of his glass.

'Meanwhile,' he said, lazily, 'I think I'll hang on here. After all, I've got no certain information about heaven and judgement, and I'm fearful of the latter (what with the wench in the cellar and so on). Whereas, on the other hand, I *know* I love port...'

12~

THE FALL OF A DICTATOR

From the top of my palatial new home, I could hear the sound of the Atlantic breaking gently on Espinho beach. The brazen silver moonlight, seemingly peculiar to maritime Portugal, discreetly illuminated the deserted sand three storeys below me and traced an enticing fool's-path out to sea. It was a moment to savour without reservation.

'*Well done, Toby Longhurst,*' I said to myself, *raising my glass in a toast,* '*you've arrived. The struggle (such as it was) is over. 1968 ushers in a more... expansive age for you, dear boy.*'

And just to prove it, I poured (yet) another goblet of the unsurpassed (unsurpassable?) '45, the nirvana experience of twentieth century Port. Hitherto a rare and precious treat, now merely my just deserts. And mere dessert—in the dinner sense—as well, if I felt like it.

'*God has been good to you,*' I recited. '*A seat on the Board, a palace to move into and Slovo Ports in better shape than the company's been for the last two centuries. You have a sweet, easy-going wife (divorced and safely back in England), healthy children with intimations of discernment and—<u>and</u>—probably the finest collection of vintage ports in private hands. Should life be compared to a machine,*' I concluded, '*then, Toby, you are streamlined, unstressed and amply supplied with the sublimest of lubricants. From now on, it's just free-wheeling down to meet the grave...*'

Hubris! As if I'd not been warned! By ancient Greeks endured at prep school.

So, of course, alas, alas, the echo of my premature pride and glee reverberated abroad into... other realms and called down vengeance. Feeling undervalued and slighted, the grave came hurtling up the years to meet me.

Behind, the door of this upper room slammed shut with ferocious strength. As I turned in alarm, sounds of infinite, bestial, distress rose abruptly from the wine cellars far below and percolated steadily up through the house to chill the air with despair. Without anything more than the pressing evidence of my electrified neck-hairs, I somehow felt that the great house, and I in it, had suddenly been severed and removed from the world of men. The dark beyond the window now seemed absolute.

And yet not quite... From where the sea had once been emerged trails of grey... something, at first laboured and strained, then more freely and at speed. They flew like tracer or a zooming camera-shot straight towards me and... instantly the window was filled with faces.

That they had died unhappily I knew beyond doubt, for their histories were written plain in lines and bloody wounds. Squashed against the glass panes, jostling for position, the faces looked for me, possessed with inexpressible hunger.

The table, the port bottle, the glass, went flying as I fell into a chair and hid my face in my hands. Kindly overload was reached and time became relative.

Eventually there came along something bearable; a single discernible voice, distinct in the silence that now reigned. I raised my head in response.

'Hello, English,' said the speaker. 'So you survived then?'

He was seated in an antique chair across the room, one that no one ever sat in. An angry looking, black-bearded man in overalls, sprawled at an angle and manner that was not quite... right. Normal, intact, bodies could not emulate my surprise companion's flowing adaptation to a seat. My thoughts on the subject were read.

'For sure,' he smirked, 'your Fascist pals made a meal of me: broken spine, compressed pelvis, a whole page of stuff on the autopsy. On the plus side, it makes me look a lot more relaxed—now that I'm dead, that is,' he added, cruelly.

'I see...,' I said in a feeble whisper, that being all I could construct with certainty of it surviving from brain to mouth.

'Yes, and about time you saw,' said the man. 'You've spent too long looking the other way. Now we've come to stand before your very eyes where you can't miss us.'

'But...'

'It was in my mind,' he went on regardless, 'that my comrades from the lime-pits and shallow graves would finish you off with sheer shock. However, since it seems you are tough stuff, English, you can regard them as just the garnish on a nice cold *gazpacho* of revenge. We're going to go through this thing in full!'

I had recovered just enough to take exception to his tone, a grievance that was sufficient rock (for want of any better) on which to make a stand.

'Now look here-...,' I started—but the angry man interrupted.

'No, *you* look,' he said with quiet, commanding confidence. 'Look there.' He pointed to the window and I saw, in a brief second before shudderingly averting my gaze, that the faces, a seething wall of eyes and teeth, were still present.

'And here too,' he continued, catching my rebounding glance to indicate his twisted frame. 'Tonight it is *your* turn to see things clearly.'

Actually, I had already seen more than enough and wished for matters to end—as a dream, as a disturbed night and too much port—anything rather than sickening reality.

'I don't... understand,' I said to him, in all honesty. He was similarly reasonable in return.

'And why should you?' he replied. 'You are a wealthy man, a director of an ancient House of Port Shippers, an Englishman, a gentleman. Why *should* you understand things from outside your own world? Why, I ask, should you consider the price paid for the stability of trade, the cost of the status quo or, for instance, who and what might have preceded you in this,' (and he waved his hairy hand to the ceiling), 'glorious palace of yours?'

Now this was something I *did* comprehend.

'I've got *your* number,' I said triumphantly (for to date things had not been going my way). 'You're a... Communist!'

'Was,' the dead man corrected me. 'Politics are put into proper perspective in the afterlife.'

'Well, either way, why are you bothering me?' I protested. 'It's not as if I'm especially anti... In fact, I was a bit that way myself at Oxford and I treat my

ALTERED ENGLANDS

workers well. The Port trade's not like a factory, you know. It revolves round a product that can only be created with love, not forced through toil...'

'Yes, I realise that,' said the dead man, momentarily softening. 'I used to be very partial to a drop of port; particularly a chilled old tawny and...' Suddenly he recovered himself. 'And that is *not* the point!'

'Then what is?' I asked. 'I mean, I know old man Salazar[24] and his P.I.D.E.[25] boys give your lot a hard time... But what about Stalin then?'

'What about him?' spat the dead man, leaning forward aggressively.

'Look, let's not get on to all that,' I said, eager to placate both this... spectre and the prying eyes—of whom I was painfully conscious—behind my back. 'All I'm saying is that this doesn't seem very fair. And besides,' I went on before I could curb myself, 'what's a Marxist-Leninist doing returning from Heaven? You shouldn't be there in the first place.'

The dead man regarded me with a burning expression.

'Heaven,' he said in a controlled, clipped tone, 'has been nicer to me than ever this world was. Its gates are not barred against the poor and broken as *your* house and garden doubtless are—Christian though I'm sure you be.'

'Well, C of E,' I said, defensively.

The dead man shrugged.

'Near enough. Like I said, from this world, from Portugal and P.I.D.E and Salazar and people like you who've done well from it, I got *nothing*. From the Greater Power, however, when I recounted the story of my life I received only kindness—which is extra kind when you think of all the things I used to say about Him.

'"*Because of your hard life,*" I was told, '*because your wife denounced and divorced you for so called 'Tito-ist deviationism', because of your long hours at leaden meetings and attention to dry munitions manuals, because you were betrayed and beaten to a horrible death and Communism is going to collapse in 1989 anyway, we will make amends with a special gift. Little went right for you in your pilgrimage on Earth,*' <u>He</u> said, '*and you blighted your life in the pursuit of good as you saw it. But now, before you move on, you may make one wish and what you desire will be made true'.*'

Despite the dire circumstances and the new deep fears for my future I was understandably entertaining, nothing could stop me swapping places with

---

[24] Dr Salazar, 'Prime Minister' or Dictator of Portugal from 1932.
[25] Much feared secret police set up with Gestapo assistance.

the dead Marxist in fantasy. What, I wondered, in all the Universe, would *I* choose? A case of the 1775 or 1912 vintage? An impossible choice.

'I had to give it thought,' said the dead man, 'since Marx contained no guidance on such a question. I wanted a revolution in Portugal, that was clear—for what else had my life been about? On the other hand, I also longed for something more to human scale, a sweet and personal twist on the knife of revenge. And who better for that than some foreign capitalist, someone sleek and prosperous from the Salazar years, a person now in insulting occupation of my childhood home...'

'But there's *twelve* bedrooms,' I protested, 'and a billiards room! What sort of background is that for a Communist? Besides, I acquired it legally, bought it for a fair price—from the Government.'

'Who took it from me,' said the dead man, brutally, 'and evicted my aged mother for good measure: just another episode from life you *'didn't see'*—or perhaps didn't *care* to see, eh? Anyway, what's *fairness* to do with things? First, a Leninist in Heaven, now an all-too-rare prime slice of class-justice; the wonders just go on and on whether you like it or not.'

From behind me came the sound of heartless chuckles from the dead man's concentration camp comrades. My blood froze afresh.

'But how to greedily combine my two wishes,' mused the dead man for my benefit, 'that was the question. How to kill two vicious reactionary birds with one stone? I sought advice from some well-disposed angels and gradually all became clear.'

I suddenly felt sadly let down and isolated. Surely the Angelic hosts were meant to be solidly on the side of chaps like me. After all, I quite often went to evensong at St. James...[26]

'The Fascist Dictator likes presents,' recounted Beardy, 'and capitalist bloodsuckers like to curry favour with Dictators. Salazar likes the sunshine and so Slovo Port Shippers (established 1736) see fit to present him with a nice special deckchair to bask upon. Result? Slovo Port gets carte blanche to carry on exploiting the proletariat and Salazar can cut a dash, tanning his lizard carcass in a polished mahogany, brass-embellished chair. There was even a nice little plaque on it, wasn't there? I wonder *who* drafted the inscription?'

'Well..., in business one gets asked to do all sorts of...' I stuttered, looking the while for a half decent defensive stance.

[26] The Port Shipping Families' English Protestant Church in Oporto.

ALTERED ENGLANDS

"IN RECOGNITION',' intoned the dead man, *"OF HIS NATIONAL ACHIEVEMENTS: TO DR SALAZAR. WITH COMPLIMENTS FROM THE HOUSE OF SLOVO (T. LONGHURST—MANAGING DIRECTOR)'.*'

'Rather uncontroversial, I thought at the time...,' I said.

'So what would transpire,' continued my tormentor, 'I finally asked, if the Greater Power were to sabotage this wonderful chair and cause it to spectacularly fall at some opportune moment: what then? *'Salazar is an old man,'* came the reply. *'He would surely hurt himself severely, and in his absence his whole bloodstained pack of cards would fall'.* 'Ah, <u>good</u>,' I said, *'but what else, what else?'* 'Why then,' I was vouchsafed, *'the rabid dogs of P.I.D.E., in their fear and anger, would cast about for cause and scapegoat. They would find cunning and deliberate flaws in a certain deckchair—and beside them a little silver plaque...'.*'

'Preposterous,' I said. 'It... they... wouldn't...'

'It happened this afternoon,' smiled the dead man. 'Salazar hit his head and had a stroke. His brain is damaged—he may survive, but he'll not rule again. Tanks are on the streets of Lisbon and P.I.D.E cars are on their way to you right now.'

As if on cue, the sound of sirens disturbed the night air and the unseen faces behind me burst into mocking laughter.

'Oh those electrodes!' said the dead man. 'Those rubber mallets! I don't envy you them, Mr Longhurst: the pain becomes insupportable—and then increases. Why not use the window and escape what is to come?'

'But we're three floors up,' I protested, 'above a stony foreshore!'

The dead Communist acted as though the soul of reason.

'Exactly, Mr Longhurst,' he said. 'I think you are unduly limiting your concept of *'escape'*. Which can take any number of forms for mortal men. However, once you are in *their* hands, and strapped to *their* tables, the more easeful options will no longer be available to you.'

And, at last, I saw that there was some truth in what he had said this evening. I *had* heard tales of the dreadful things done in the camps on the Azores, and I knew full well I could not face it. I further knew, my status notwithstanding, that the P.I.D.E. would not even listen to any words of explanation.

'But it's so... *unfair*,' I said.

The dead man agreed.

'Certainly. My life: unfair, me in Heaven: unfair, my vengeance on you: unfair. You've left it late, my friend, but at the last you now appreciate what others learn early: life *is* unfair.'[27]

The muffled sound of his infernal friends echoing the word *'Unfair... Unfair...'* infiltrated the room.

'I'd go so far,' he went on implacably, scenting post-mortal victory, 'as to offer up unfairness as a sign of earthly authenticity. However, that is mere philosophising; concerning the matter in hand, they are coming for you, they are near. Would you rather be defenestrated now by your own hand—or months from now as a nameless, bloody wreck from a helicopter over the Atlantic?'

I have always prided myself as a reasonable man, not the sort to whine about the inevitable. Accordingly, my English (or Wessex) stoicism was sent into battle against the ultimate foe—self-preservation. It emerged scarred—but covered with honour.

I addressed my feet to the window. The grinning faces made way for my run.

---

[27] It certainly is. Salazar survived, albeit incapacitated, for two further years—apparently unaware of his succession by Marcelo Caetano. The dead Communist's desired revolution was delayed even longer: to 1974. And then fizzled out.

ALTERED ENGLANDS

STOP PRESS!

'HANG ON, I'VE FOUND ANOTHER BOTTLE!'

Close readers of the impending story *'LIBERTY! AH, LIBERTY!'* (see below) may puzzle over the fact that Mr Longhurst is shortly to be found, apparently alive and well, enjoying port wine in 1974. From the concluding section of 'FALL OF A DICTATOR', set in 1968, said readers might well be forgiven for assuming that he intended to end his life via the sin of suicide and the act of leaping from a high window.

Heaven forfend!

In actual fact, as those who know him well might have guessed, at the final moment his common sense and residual religious convictions (and the thought of his unconsumed collection of vintage ports) reasserted themselves. Though expensive in terms of wealth and dignity alike, a narrow escape from the hands and electrodes of the men from P.I.D.E. was secured by his natural charm.

The Englishmen of the Port trade imbibe the preservative qualities of their alcoholic product—and are thus not easily disposed of...

13~

'LIBERTY! AH, LIBERTY!'

1974

The day had started well. Matins at St James' had been replete with consolation and, emerging from the Church's shade into Oporto sunshine, I was further reminded that the world was *meant* to be a nice place. There was really no need to feel guilty about happiness.

The very mention of that emotion led on to thoughts, never very far away, of port wine, my lifelong love and calling—and the next assignation in my passionate affair with it. Being responsible, I could either read yesterday's *Times* in the English Shippers' 'Factory House', or perhaps return to my House of Slovo office and shuffle some even more tedious paper by way of work.

On the other hand, being *ir*responsible I could happen to recall that the newspaper would be full of distressing information about Harold Wilson's election win back in the Home Country. Similarly, I knew full well my desktop held some stunningly overdue letters awaiting reply.

How much easier it somehow seemed to recall that Giles Piecrust, my mentor and 'Consultant Director' of Slovo Ports, generally imbibed his morning 'heart-starter' around this time of day. It would surely be, I mused, an act of selfless charity to ignore the call of Mammon and provide the old boy with a visit from his protégé, Toby Longhurst, and share his bottle of chilled Tawny.

'Dear Lord,' I said to myself, smiling, 'for what we are about to receive...'

ALTERED ENGLANDS

'No thank you,' I said, tersely.

'I beg your pardon, Toby?' asked Giles Piecrust, incredulously, leaning forward in his chair and cupping his ear. '*What* did you say?'

'I said I won't indulge, thank you all the same.'

'That's what I thought you said but I simply didn't believe it.' Piecrust shook his snowy head.

'Are you okay, Dad?' asked Rollo, my son, from his studiedly languid pose against an oak and brass filing cabinet. 'Are you like sickening for something, man?'

'*Yes,*' I thought, '*sickening for you with your 'Dads' and 'Mans' and the way that preposterous fringe of yours keeps flopping over your face. The sooner the Army gets ahold of you, my boy, the better!*'

From some deep reserve I summoned up a mild chuckle—Rollo's dual English/Portuguese citizenship, and consequent National Service requirement for the latter, was a little secret I'd not let him in on yet...

'That's better, man,' he drawled. 'It's not like you to get the blues.'

'Or to refuse good port, dear boy,' added Piecrust, still evincing concern.

'Or any port at all—in a storm: ha ha!' said Rollo, who fancied himself the Oscar Wilde of his generation.

'I'm perfectly well, thank you,' I insisted. 'It's merely that I don't particularly fancy this new fangled single-*quinta* stuff'.[28]

'Well, that's most extraordinary,' said Piecrust, apologetically. 'I could have sworn I observed you drinking some of the *Offley Boa Vista* at the last Wednesday Factory House dinner...'

'And I thought you were all for the single quinta trade amendment,' said Rollo—who knew encouragingly more about the beloved trade than his image let him show. 'Who was it that represented the Shippers to the I.V.P.[29] on that very subject last year?'

---

[28] Port from a single vineyard. Comparatively rare when Longhurst spoke but now increasingly popular as the (discerning) Common-man's vintage port.

[29] The all-powerful Governmental 'Instituto Do Vinho Do Porto', whose iron hand regulates the trade.

'It's *most* odd,' continued Piecrust, sadly, having reached the age when most things were either odd and/or sad. 'Your antipathy must have slipped my memory: I'll open another bottle *tout de suite*.' A cherubic smile then alighted where puzzlement had sat—he had found a plausible excuse to prolong and expand the festivities. 'I've got some Slovo '48 decanted over there on the stand: will that do you?'

'It certainly will,' I said, gratefully. 'The good old '48—*'firm but fair'*.'

'Yes... that about sums it up, dear boy,' Piecrust agreed. 'Firmer than the glorious '45 but not near so fair. A shame about the *Quinta de Mallefloria* though; it's a passable little drink if you'd only try it.'

'No, I'm quite sure on that score, thanks,' I repeated, crossing to the decanter tray. 'You'll just have to finish it yourself.'

Giles Piecrust leant back in his armchair beneath the ancient oil painting of the House's Founder, Sir Ralph Slovo, plainly content and without a care in the world. The centuries melted away and for a moment the two gentle old rascals appeared hatched from the same egg—happy nonagenarian testimonies to a regime of a pipe[30] a year and relaxed attitudes to things that didn't really matter.

'The oddest thing of all,' mused Piecrust to Rollo as he poured himself another glass of purple cheer, 'is that it was your Father that got us Quinta de Mallefloria in the first place. He was the one who acquired it for our House—though Lord knows how.'

I paused, decanter in hand, as a shadow suddenly came over my day and life.

I was all too afraid the Lord *did* know the ins and outs of that particular matter—hence my prayers that morning in St James'...

---

[30] A gentle reminder: traditional measure equalling 720 bottles of port. Phew!

ALTERED ENGLANDS

❂

1956

'Will you do us the honour of starting the march, Mr Longhurst?' said Senhor de Mallefloria, flashing his perfect teeth at me. I had been warned to expect an Errol Flynn look-alike but, even days after my arrival at the quinta, Mallefloria's filmstar looks, (plaid shirt and battered felt hat notwithstanding) still had the power to shock when his profile or smile was encountered unprepared.

I stepped forward, feeling rather awkward, and, wielding the tiny hammer provided, struck the triangle proffered by a piratic-looking youth. As the puny-sounding ring produced faded away into the shimmering air, the drummer and accordionist struck up and then the whole caravan set off to their tune.

De Mallefloria and I waited until the long line of grape-laden ladies had passed and then we too shambled along behind. In a rare and much longed-for indulgence, now being out of sight of the natives, I permitted myself the removal of jacket and tie.

A comparative junior in the firm back in those days, I'd been assigned a junior sort of job in overseeing the vintage. Only too proud to be a part of the Shippers' September exodus from Oporto up into the Douro Valley, I'd kept secret my hopes for a more significant quinta to monitor as the annual miracle of the grape's transformation into the makings of Slovo Port was performed.

Quinta de Mallefloria was small, privately owned and decidedly old-fashioned; and in my early flush of Slovo fanaticism none of those qualities were designed to appeal. What I then thought (and how I blush to recall it) was that all the quinta needed was rationalisation, consolidation, modernisation—and any or all of the other *'ations* and *'isms* sweeping across the world like anthrax at that time. In those far off days, these were the words that got people—me included—excited; they still do—but now for more healthily negative reasons.

Accordingly, with such bright ideas poisoning the calm poor Humankind is entitled to, the ageless stolidity of Quinta de Mallefloria seemed irksome to me. One might reproach oneself about the emotion—like resenting blameless pavement-hogging by a doddery old lady—but it was always there nevertheless. Now, it is one of the more sensible regrets of my maturity that I wasted those precious days in impatience and groundless feelings of superiority rather than close observation. For this was before the African colonial wars, before the arrival of cursed television and economic migration to the towns: it was the tail end of a priceless—but doomed—way of life. It had survived from the Dark Ages and hung on in order for me to see its finale. Its like, for good or ill, will not return.

Senhor de Mallefloria, being the personification of both pre-hurry-sickness and pre-industrial courtliness, had striven mightily to make me feel at home, and at times he, together with quantities of the local *bagaceira*,[31] had almost succeeded.

Indeed, charmed by sufficient portions of each, there were moments when I could have forgiven the museum-style methods—but for his incongruous, unwarranted looks. Young men, being urgent, lack charity and easy acceptance of the good fortune of others.

Mallefloria doubtless detected this but did not allow it to influence his manner towards me. Aside from good breeding, he was fortified by his independence, his Family's ancient ownership of the land, and the sure knowledge that if the house of Slovo did not buy his excellent wine, there would be plenty of other shippers only too glad to elbow us aside.

'So,' he said as we walked along together, 'have you enjoyed your day, Mr Longhurst? Do you approve of what you see?'

Both questions were mere politeness. My enjoyment or otherwise was irrelevant, my knowledge insufficient to justify open criticism of another's practices.

'Yes, thank you.' I replied. 'It's all been most instructive. Everyone works very hard.'

I had some minor guilt feelings in this regard, for in the quintas it is all hands to the vines at vintage time, and even Senhor de Mallefloria had been out plying his secateurs through the heat of the day. However, my own inexperience and soft hands had no place beside the hardened *Rogas*,[32] three generations of each family working alongside each other, and it was embarrassing to see mere striplings and wrinkled ancients slaving efficiently away whilst I stood idly, uselessly by, 'observing'. Very shortly I gave up even the pretence of

---

[31] Ferocious white spirit distilled from the leftovers of the port process.
[32] Professional harvesting gangs.

involvement and 'observed' little more than the ample, saturnine charms of some of the lady *Rogas*.

'We do work hard,' agreed Mallefloria, gravely, 'but neither do we forget the purpose of work which is life and joy. Tonight there will be celebrations of equal vigour to our labours, you will see.'

This sounded promising and cheered me for the remainder of the long winding journey down the precipitous, gunpowder-blasted terraces of the river valley to Mallefloria's *adegas*. The *Roga* moved without great haste, the ladies amongst them bearing on their backs huge panniers of grapes, each as heavy as one of their menfolk. Said gentlemen, shamelessly conserving their energies for the ordeal to come, strolled along at the front behind the band, gossiping amongst themselves. All (or so I fancied) seemed blithely aware that this was just part of the great life cycle, without beginning or end (or meaning) and without, therefore, any urgency.

It was a nice, naïve, notion to muse upon in the evening sun and one I preserved for a few years to come—until disabused by the speed with which a threatened harvest could be gathered. Neither peasant nor master, I then found, saw virtue in taking one's ease when storm clouds menaced the grape and thus livelihoods. When circumstances demanded, they could move with a speed to gladden an American 'Time-and-Motion' man's heart—always assuming he had one.

Still, at present, as I say, they all seemed happy enough despite the dawn-to-dusk travail; above and beyond the cheer generated by de Mallefloria's liberally distributed drinks and cigarettes. For this too was something that had not escaped my slightly disapproving eye: from the pre-work *Mata Bixo*[33] for the men, and the previous year's wine for the women, to the garlic-drenched bread that brought proceedings to a temporary close, their Master had seen to it that his people were more than amply provided for, fortified and refreshed. I had heard about the legendary wine capacity of the *Roga* from my colleagues, but Mallefloria's generosity tested even that to the limit. He had also, in his kindness, provided sweeties and sticky lemonade for the younger in years or heart, and, though my experience was yet scant, I still knew that such consideration was rare. Amongst the port industry's propertied class there remained a tendency to a more rough-and-ready feudal view of things.

---

[33] Literally *'bug-killer'*!

In return, the workers clearly loved him and repaid the debt with the very best of the skills given them. There was a lightness in their step exceeding that of contentment with their place in the World, beyond the inspiration of the rackety musical trio at the procession's head. De Mallefloria sensed that feeling, drank it in and revelled in it.

'I love the vintage,' he said to me, in a quite passable English, as we walked along together. 'It is a time for thankfulness and welcome effort; a season full of... possibilities. When you are older, Mr Longhurst, and have seen a few more such, you will come to love it almost as much as I do.'

I politely agreed.

'I don't doubt what you say is true, Senhor. It's probably much the same feeling as we English have about Christmas.'

Mallefloria looked troubled.

'I rather doubt that,' he said, reluctant to appear contrary. 'Christmas is a religious festival, is it not?'

'Well, originally...'

'Whereas the vintage, Mr Longhurst, is most definitely of this Earth. It is a celebration of material bounty with little of the spiritual about it.'

'Yes, rather like our Christmas, ho ho,' I ventured. My 'jest' received the same (I should imagine) reception accorded to pork pies at a Bar Mitzvah.

'No, not at all, Mr Longhurst,' said Mallefloria, attempting to conceal his puzzlement. 'That is what I am trying to convey to you...'

'Yes, yes, I see,' I said swiftly, trying to pull our conversational plane out of its death-dive. 'Absolutely.'

'My people love it too,' he gamely pressed on, only a morsel of suspicion left over from the misunderstanding, 'and they gain such pleasure in the process. My one joy is to enhance that, as far as it is in my powers, and then, well... feed off it, so to speak.'

I smiled my approval.

'And hence,' I said, 'the frequent breaks for food and wine and smokes, Senhor.'

Mallefloria shrugged his shoulders.

'They are traditional and universal, Mr Longhurst; without them the *Roga* would not come to me and my grapes would rot on the vine. No, what I try to add is a prevailing spirit of paternal love. Now, you may laugh at that, young sir, coming as you do from a country riven by class-war...'

'I wouldn't dream of it, Senhor—and actually, England isn't really-...'

'However, romantic anachronisms that we are: this place, this trade and I, the older sensitivities live on. Do you understand what I am telling you, Mr Longhurst? I say that here things live on beyond their time.'

'Absolutely,' I said again, somewhat taken aback and for want of anything more relevant.

'I wonder if you *do*,' he smiled, his voice losing its momentarily pressing tone, 'I wonder. However, you must indulge me if I say, with all solemnity, that I see these people as my children. And that being so, we are bound with many ties of surpassing strength. I wish them nothing but good, Mr Longhurst.'

'Well, I can see that, Senhor Mallefloria,' I said. 'And if your excellent wine is the product of that relationship, the House of Slovo can only approve.'

Mallefloria laughed good-naturedly.

'Can they now; can they?' he said. 'Well, I will drink to that!'

'And why not?' I agreed, cautious of any injection of jollity after the previous debacle. 'You could hardly be in a better place to do it.'

'Yes, you are right,' he nodded, sagely, 'I am. And so are you. Therefore you must join me.'

'Well, yes,' I 'agreed' again. 'I'll happily join you—in a drink, that is.'

'In a drink, yes; what else, Mr Longhurst? And as chance would have it, I have *just* the potion to do it with...'

☸

'Well, I can't say I'm not honoured,' I said, 'but I never thought to be drinking madeira in a port quinta.'

Senhor de Mallefloria smiled indulgently.

'The unexpected is the truffle in the stew of life,' he said, gesturing to the fragrantly loaded bowls before us. 'It is the morsel to be searched for and savoured.'

'Except,' I ventured, joining in with the spirit of things, 'that sometimes that *'truffle'* is pretty rancid, ho ho!'

'No!' shouted Mallefloria, in considerable agitation, his English slipping slightly. 'Is not possible! I collect them myself!'

Then, to my acute embarrassment, he began to probe about in my dish with his finger, angrily looking for the imaginary offending fungi.

'I will skin the cook!' he growled. 'I told him—'*Only the best for the Inglês!*.'

It took some time to restore order and correct understanding and I resolved thereafter to speak only plain Queen's English, stripped of all the Noel Coward-ish fancy stuff.

'But concerning the madeira,' said Mallefloria, eventually, 'you surely cannot complain. I have been saving it for a person who might truly appreciate its virtues.'

'Indeed,' I said, in all sincerity. 'I am lost in praise of it. Outside of port, I've never encountered such... maturity.'

De Mallefloria looked about to deliver some long considered judgement but was interrupted by the arrival of a burly *Rogador* at our table.

'Senhor,' he said, falling on one knee, 'everything is ready. I come to ask your blessing.'

Mallefloria flashed his amazing smile and laid one elegant hand on the man's grizzled curls.

'Then begin with all benisons, my child,' he said, and the *Rogador* rushed away.

'It is time to begin the treading,' Mallefloria explained, 'the second and equal part of the day's labours. I think you will find this interesting.'

Our meal had been taken out on the porch of the *adegas* and so we were in prime position to observe proceedings. The great concrete *lagars*[34] were mere paces away across the yard and already the men, clad in traditional blue, their trousers rolled up to their thighs, were clambering into the purple sea. Contrary to the reassuring words we shippers put out to the world and confirming Piecrust's whispered warning, I noticed there was no question of a Spring-clean of feet and legs before setting to.

Split into two lines, the men linked arms and began to methodically march. The captains started up a slow, hypnotic chant for their bodies to obey, a song that may have been old when used in Roman galleys, and the lines advanced and retreated like parts of a machine.

'It is strenuous work,' said Mallefloria to me, 'but necessary to extract maximum colour from the skin of the grape. Even with four hours on and four hours off, it is by no means a game.'

---

[34] Huge granite troughs used for treading the grapes.

ALTERED ENGLANDS

'So I may imagine, Senhor. One presumes that's why the ladies don't participate.'

He laughed.

'Our womenfolk are tough, Mr Longhurst; life makes them so. In fact I cannot conceive why the army does not have commando regiments of them. No, no, they are more than equal to the work, young sir, but superstition forbids it. Actually, it is one of the oldest rules I know of. Winemaking is very much like that, Mr Longhurst; its laws and ways reach back into times beyond writing and enlightenment. There are many... survivals involved with it—and who is to say which are valid and which is not.'

'Who indeed, Senhor?' I said—whilst thinking *'modern go-ahead types like me, that's who'.*

'Tradition is the benevolent distilled advice of the unlettered dead to their descendants, Mr Longhurst. We may not understand it all but... each man's life is too short to establish all his own rules and precepts. Besides, the trial and error learning system is so painful.'

'Absolutely,' I agreed, this time sincerely—remembering an unsuitable engagement I'd contracted at the tender age of eighteen, in the teeth of patriarchal opposition.

'And the women still have a vital role to play—as you see.'

As bidden I looked and saw that the ladies of the quinta and the female *Roga* had gathered to clap and sing and urge their menfolk on. Shortly after, the band I'd dubbed the *Quinta de Mallefloria Ragtime All-stars* arrived and struck up as joyful a tune as drum, accordion and triangle can muster. Less musically demanding than I, the ladies were plainly delighted and, from granny to toddler, began to gracefully dance together.

I'd heard of such things occurring in certain Russian fishing-fleet towns (albeit in less innocent circumstances) but had never seen the like. I was entirely charmed.

'Honest toil, wholesome pleasures and easy sleep,' commented De Mallefloria, indicating his people with a sweep of the hand, 'things that millionaires cannot buy or dictators command. How very lucky we are, Mr Longhurst.'

No young person ever thinks themselves lucky, not even the most gilded and fortunate youth, but I hypocritically nodded my concurrence.

'And those lines of little holes at the top of the *lagar*, what are they for?' I asked. 'Oh...'

'Someone has shown you the reason,' laughed Mallefloria. 'The treading cannot be delayed for mere calls of nature, Mr Longhurst. Would you like some more madeira?'

It was one of those nights, the foundations laid by happy circumstances and topped out by warmth and starlight, when almost any amount of alcohol can do no harm. How much more true that was then when the liberating chemical concerned was a wine beyond price.

'Pour on, maestro,' I said, just the slightest bit tipsy. 'It may not be port but tonight you dispense the liquor of the gods.'

I caught de Mallefloria's sly glance of approval. Was it fatherly I idly wondered—or something more sinister?

'Madeira is most interesting,' agreed Mallefloria, 'a serendipitous discovery of the busy age of mercantilism. Who, I ask, would have conceived that a rough, cheap wine; afterthought produce of a tropic African isle, could be so... transformed? Considered fit only for shipping to undiscerning, penny-wise American colonists in the hot and pungent bilges of an *East-Indiaman*, it did not die but was reborn—and in most glorious form! Madeira is a masochistic wine, Mr Longhurst: it flourishes on ill treatment. I understand that when wisdom dawned on the merchants concerned, it was even sent on round world trips on sailing ships just to achieve its miraculous rough ageing. Today, the same effect is gained by stupendous temperatures in storage; but these bottles we see here, they have suffered in the traditional manner to bring us our pleasure. The seals on the cap, they are dated 1835.'

'Good Lord!' I exclaimed, genuinely interested—for no amount of befuddlement could disable my wine-knowledge collecting faculties.

'I have also tasted an 1825, Mr Longhurst, first shipped to Charleston and then, newly appreciated, lovingly gathered home to the Old World. It was just as fine as this, perhaps even a little better. I can assure you, young sir: still more than cognac, madeira is an almost immortal wine. So tell me, what do you feel about immortality?'

Amidst all the music and chanting and imbibing and the sheer... whatever of it all, I missed Mallefloria's sudden change of conversational gear and fresh seriousness.

'Immorality? Well, I've been tempted to stretch the old marriage vows once or twice but...'

ALTERED ENGLANDS

'No,' said Mallefloria, firmly, 'immor*tah*ty.'

'Oh, *that*,' I replied, devil-may-care, chuntering on in chatter-freefall. 'Well, I wouldn't mind a spot of it, I suppose. That way I'd get to see all the port vintages till the jolly old planet blows up or we all go Muslim or something. And it'd be nice to see the Longhurst line trundling on—assuming it does. Mind you, there'd be the tedium problem. I mean, Sunday afternoons are bad enough as it is. And every story's got to have an ending to have a meaning, don't you think? So, if I *have* to go, I'll board my fiery chariot when I'm a hundred, two bottles a day all my adult life, Director of the House, a great-grandfather, sat up in bed with my new nineteen year old mistress and a decanter of the legendary Slovo 1912: how's that?'

Secretly however, underneath the armour of alcoholic confidence, I felt a tiny bit ashamed at my reply. Would what I termed a *'nice girl'* really want to be in bed with a merry centenarian? Would I be prepared to introduce her to my mother (though she'd be 130+ herself by then of course, and past caring)? And boring truth to tell, I'd always actually fancied going to the sound of the 'Book of Common Prayer', 1662 style, surrounded by the manly farewells of friends—only that didn't sound such a 'jolly dog' sort of thing to confess.

For a long while de Mallefloria said nothing, though smiling on approvingly, and I must have dozed off—doubtless exhausted by the labour of my day. The next thing I was aware of was being gently prodded awake.

'The shift is nearly finished, Mr Longhurst,' said de Mallefloria, making allowance for my slow surfacing. 'I thought you might like to see this.'

'Oh, good,' I slurred. 'Thanks. Er..., see what?'

The answer was supplied by unfolding events for, just at that moment, the great chant (which I'm sure was in no small part responsible for sending me off) ceased. Suddenly, the orderly lines in the *lagars* broke up and gave way to wild, orgiastic dancing. The Quinta de Mallefloria All-stars tried mightily to supply an appropriate backing and even in the *adegas* yard, the womenfolk were seized by the mood change and performed a passable Portuguese peasant version of the jive.

'The last ten minutes of a shift are always like this,' explained Senhor Mallefloria. 'They call it *'the liberation'*—listen.'

The men all broke into lusty song and even my haphazard grasp of the dialect got the sense of it.

JOHN WHITBOURN

'Liberty!' they sang, *'Ah, liberty!*
Only to the few you're known.
If only I had the liberty
to call my feet my own!'

De Mallefloria got up and put on his jacket.

'The night is young, as they say,' he told me, 'and the rest of it is yours to use since I have business elsewhere. Meanwhile, this is for you.'

He handed me a brimful decanter and my highly attuned nose detected something painfully delectable.

'The legendary Slovo 1904, Mr Longhurst. I believe even your own House's cellars have a mere six bottles of it remaining. Drink it tonight and use it well.'

He smiled one final time upon (or at) me and then walked off into the night.

I was stunned. There's such a thing as generosity—and also **GENEROSITY!** Better than a douse in the Douro, I was sobered by the magnitude of the gift. I knew full well that only the rectitude of our House permitted us to reject the extravagant American offers which regularly arrived for our remaining half-case of the 1904. For a comparative stranger therefore to give a bottle away...

In honour of the occasion's munificence, I felt I should retire from mainstream life, and a nearby vine-terrace soon afforded the necessary dark and privacy, together with a suitably remote view of the treading. I still thought I should remain in vicarious contact with humankind—but at a distance appropriate to the transfiguration to follow.

After thanking the Good Lord (and the local deity, with the smallest drop of the precious elixir), the first glass was almost to my lips when I realised I was not alone. Straightaway I wished I hadn't dismissed Piecrust's advice on the necessity of carrying a sword-stick whilst up in the demarked region (*'It's still 500 years ago there, dear boy.'*).

In the event, I need not have worried or (oh-*so* carefully) laid down my glass. The arrival was a sloe-eyed young *Roga*-ess stealing upon me, her country vision better attuned to the starlit night than that fitted to my town-dweller's head. However ungentlemanly it may be to admit it, her saucy curls and ample form had recommended themselves to me already, in my covert appraisals earlier in the day.

'Forgive me, sir,' she said (in quite civilised Portuguese), 'but may I join you?'

I also blush to admit that the visions of my wife and the hard-by decanter which occurred to me as I stumbled over my reply, were simultaneous and without priority.

'Well, yes,' I said, 'depending on what... well, what you want.'

She did not reply directly and moved lithely up beside me so that not a *rizla*'s space divided my cavalry-twill from her cotton-clad chassis.

'It is a wonderful night,' she said eventually, turning (I sensed) to address my profile. 'Is it the vintage, you think, that adds extra sparkle to the stars or the other way around?'

'Neither, I don't suppose,' I replied, the decanter's sublime whisper tormenting my palate and making me tetchy. 'The stars are too far away to affect or be affected. What exactly do you-...'

'Even so,' she interrupted, 'they are silent sermons for us; speaking to man—and woman—of a more... generous doctrine.'

I had always been told that the *Roga* were educated to pick grapes and drink the product and very little else. Accordingly, all this provocative philosophy came as a surprise.

'The stars are just balls of gas engaged in nuclear fusion,' I said, primly, 'so I don't see what-...'

'To me they speak,' she persisted, smoothing down her bright thin gown. 'They say that life is short and man is... small; that death is oblivion and we are fools not to grasp every pleasure within our reach...'

'Um...,' I said, hesitant, thinking stellar observation a shaky sort of revelation to build a religion on. 'Perhaps...'

'No!' said the girl, breathing sweetly in my ear. 'For sure!'

Either side of me I could feel objects demanding my full, unswerving attention: namely a cotton-constrained thigh and a decanter—but the struggle between the two was brief and a foregone conclusion. I reached over to my neglected glass.

'Look,' I said, 'do you mind if I just-...'

'No,' she whispered, misunderstanding my intentions, 'I do not mind. Take me! Take me like the pagan Northern love-god that you are!'

Before I could protest, two brown arms had snaked round me, and her bodyweight pressed me back to the ground. On my other side, struck by her questing hand, unseen but still felt, something sickeningly gave way.

I hurled myself upright, thrusting the girl away like a straw doll, just in time to see the toppled decanter and glass offload the last of their cargo into the grateful, thirsty soil.

Silence ensued for some considerable time. However, my blazing eyes must have been eloquence enough, for the *Roga* girl shrank frightened away from their gamma-ray barrage, all amorous intentions abandoned. She did well to do so for, as they say, one should beware the anger of a patient man...

For a moment I did not think I could control the beast inside and would so far forget culture, creed and chivalry as to strike her. Fortunately, the first alarming tide soon ebbed and became second-by-second more manageable. Even so, the sense of loss I felt was quite... devastating.

'Just... go away!' I said to her at last. 'You... you... *silly* person!'

And so she did but in her place another figure rose, dark and menacing against the lights of the *adegas*. I seized the forlorn decanter of bitter memory as a weapon.

'Do not be alarmed,' said the warm, reassuring voice of Senhor de Mallefloria, 'instead be pleased. You have passed the test and a great future now awaits. You are what passes for a gentleman in this age: in their fury most other candidates both took her and then booted her behind.'

'Is true!' came the girl's confirming voice from somewhere in the dark. 'I was black and blue. You a *nice* man.'

'You are what we have been looking for,' agreed de Mallefloria.

✸

'I was a Carthaginian when I first came here, I think,' said de Mallefloria, reflectively. 'However that was a long time ago and the details have became rather fuzzy. Since then the years have simply flown by and now I am ready to depart. One can have too much of a good thing.'

'Can one? Are you sure?' I queried, the *bon vivant* in me interested despite present circumstances.

ALTERED ENGLANDS

'Beyond all doubt,' replied Mallefloria, sadly. 'Although my innings, as you English would say, has been a longer one than normal. Here, have some more drink. You have had a shock, young man.'

'That's true enough,' I agreed, accepting another glass of joy. 'I never expected to meet a vampire.'

'And how ill-prepared you were—through no fault of your own—to do so,' said Mallefloria. 'Modern society instils such discriminatory anti-undead views, you know—like that Bram Stoker fellow and that libellous *Nosferatu* film for instance. It sets people against us before we've even made acquaintance. In reality, I'm not so bad, am I?'

'Well no,' I was obliged to say, being a truthful sort of chap, for I could hardly complain about my treatment.

After the incident up on the terrace, de Mallefloria had escorted me back to the *adegas* with all consideration. The black-haired houri whose charms I'd resisted preceded us and informed all and sundry of events. Accordingly, upon arrival I was greeted by loud acclamation: the bellowed cheers of the men and the ululations of the ladies. Even the Mallefloria All-stars struck up a just recognisable version of *'For he's a jolly good fellow'*.

'He is the one!' announced de Mallefloria. 'He is the one we have waited for!'—whereupon the noisy welcome redoubled.

A special dish of *feijoda*[35] had been prepared and was bubbling away in a vast and ancient cauldron, and decanter after decanter was borne out of the *adegas*' cellars to be set before me. In the end it would have seemed miserably churlish to talk about the unease and concern I still felt.

As I was royally served with yet more refreshment, the treaders returned to business and de Mallefloria and I were left in comparative peace at our table. It was then he made his confession and though I say so myself, I think I took it rather well.

'You can see I am no monster,' he explained, aided by the charm of his smile, 'from the love my people bear for me. I give them a kindly guiding hand, command them with liberality and, by dint of my longevity, supply a sense of continuity to their life.'

'Ah, yes...,' I said, dubiously.

---

[35] Beans, black pudding and large lumps of pork fat. A delicacy to the Portuguese and an ordeal to most others.

'The proof of this pudding, as you would say, Mr Longhurst, is in the eating. Not once in all the long years have I ever been betrayed to the authorities or the Church—and yet anyone could do so, for all are free to come and go as they please. All I have ever asked in return from my people is occasional... sustenance from the more young and beautiful who can well afford to spare it. Is that so different in essence from the voluntary blood donor system which I know operates in your country?'

'Um... no, I suppose not. I mean, you're not what I imagined...'

'Oh, the old mirror and daylight-shunning business, you mean,' laughed Mallefloria, pleasantly. 'The garlic and running water rigmarole—no, I can't conceive where all that came from. And as for the coffin lined with native soil that should, I suppose, be concealed in my cellar; well, it's been so long I can't even recall where my land of birth was. In any case, I should be most surprised to find that it still exists; for a good few empires have come and gone since I left. No, *this* is my native soil, Mr Longhurst, if I have any, and I have loved it dearly.'

'I don't blame you,' I said, freely surveying the modest but homely *adegas*, the faultless terraces soaring away into the darkness and their incomparable produce held in the glasses to hand.

'Indeed. However, young sir, sad to say, in the end *'tout passe, tout casse, tout lasse'*.[36] It transpires that there is such a thing as a superfluity of experience—however wonderful. Perhaps every piece of brain storage is now fully stocked, I do not know—all I am aware of is that I have had enough. That being so, perhaps you would kindly examine the small box the maid has brought to the table. Lift the lid but do not show me the contents.'

Usually, my well-developed caution would have made me hesitate but, on a night already so derailed from normality, I felt no compunction in complying. Inside the cheap cardboard container was a plain silver-plate crucifix; quite modern, the kind that could be bought in any church.

'Not your cup of tea, I would have thought,' I said, jocularly, and de Mallefloria smiled at my feeble, humour-clad bravado.

'I should think not,' he agreed. 'It is, curiously enough, the one part of the vampiric tradition with a basis in objective truth. For my part, I cannot understand the animosity the 'other side' bears my kind: we do not attack churches or preach an opposing gospel—and I have had many reasonable,

---

[36] French Proverb: *'Everything passes, everything perishes, everything palls'.*

civilised discussions with the local priests as they've come and gone over the centuries. Still, there it is; the power represented by that emblem you hold has decided to invest certain... capabilities in it—and who am I to argue? Suffice it to say, you could riddle me with bullets or pincushion me with stakes and I would do no more than arise and remonstrate with you. The contents of that box however, applied with ill-intent to my form, would hurl me to final annihilation—it is as simple as that.'

'Well, I'll take it away then,' I said hastily. 'I mean, I'm a Christian and all that, but you seem like a good sort (and your port is excellent), so there's no call for any unpleasantness between us.'

De Mallefloria grasped my wrist. His hand was fish-cold and gripped like a hawser.

'But there *is*, Mr Longhurst,' he said, earnestly, 'and the call is mine. I am tired and want to sleep. It is your job to supply the lullaby. None of my own people will do it—even after my (unmeant) threat of torture. So *you* must.'

'I'm very sorry,' I said, 'but I'm not going to kill anyone. I had enough of that in Korea.'

'This envelope,' said de Mallefloria, ignoring my sincere moral stand, 'contains the deeds to Quinta de Mallefloria—lock, stock and myriad barrels, Mr Longhurst. A document of assignment to your goodself, already witnessed I confess, awaits my signature in the *adegas*.' He then swept his free hand to encompass our setting. 'All this wonder could be yours, young sir,' he enthused, still holding me fast, 'or perhaps the House of Slovo's if you are excessively loyal: for you, for them, for all your descendants ever after. And in return, all that I ask is one small favour; that you bring my stage-curtain down.'

Beside us, the treading, chanting, dancing and music continued as before but I became aware that every rustic eye and ear was slyly focused upon our conversation. Pressure stepped up to make a troika with Fear and Temptation in assailing me.

'But why me?' I asked desperately, attempting to prevaricate.

'I do not need to elaborate on the beauty of this place,' said Mallefloria, almost resignedly it seemed to me, 'the labour it represents, the quality of its product—all these things you know. They are yours for the asking because you have been found worthy of them. You see, although I am going into peace and darkness, I wish first to be assured that my people, my children, will have a new master who is as kind to them as I have been.'

'Oh, I see...'

'Ah, but do you, Mr Longhurst? I think you are a plain and shallow soul, happily occupied with the little (and therefore important) things in life. For you, family and good company and port; they are enough. You are not infected with ideals or ideology and thus not afflicted with the cruelty that comes in their train. The only abstraction I detect in you is the connection to your Slovo House—and such gratitude is a good thing in a young man. In short, there are no hard edges to you, Mr Longhurst: you are one of the sadly rare, soft and rounded variety of humankind.'

'And am I to take this as some sort of compliment, Senhor Mallefloria?' I queried, somewhat huffily.

'Most certainly. True, I would not care to feed off you, preferring more spice in my repasts, but as a *Quinta Master* we could ask for no better. I tell you, no other that I have tested fought off the hot appeal of our peasant girls with thoughts of a mere wife.'

'Ah, well, actually...'

'No one else controlled his anger at her "clumsy" loss of a precious vintage. The worst expression of your wrath and horror was that she was *'silly'*, was it not?'

'Yes—but inside I was...'

'You are the one, Mr Longhurst. Consider the matter and then attend me in my office. Bring the... religious artefact.'

De Mallefloria took a final sip of his port and then rose, slowly looking his last at the little world he'd made. Whatever were his thoughts, they must have been pleasant ones for he departed with a smile.

An animal howl escaped from the workers in the courtyard, a sound of quite inconsolable pain, and, to my amazement, I saw tears freely coursing down the faces of hardened treaders. Then, being true sons and daughters of the soil, knowing instinctively that life really *is* just shipwreck and would always be so, they moderated their grief and carried on almost as cheerfully as before.

I like to think that it was the sense of responsibility I now felt for this tribe that sponsored my decision—but it wasn't. Temptation matured into greed and delivered knockout blows to Fear and Conscience until it stood alone and triumphant. Port was the ocean on which I wished to spend my life, the House of Slovo the ship in which my family and I would travel. Metaphysics aside, there were no other calls of loyalty for me to answer to. I *wanted wanted wanted* the Quinta de Mallefloria (or what it made) and I would damn well have it!

ALTERED ENGLANDS

Senhor de Mallefloria was sitting in his book-lined study, toying with a paperweight. He saw my decision written in my averted eyes.

'Thank you,' he said. 'Here is the document of assignment, together with a copy for my lawyer in Oporto. If asked, merely say that I have gone away—my people will confirm the story. It is nothing but the truth in any case...'

I nodded, continuing to avoid his face, pretending to peruse the serried ranks of theological titles along the walls.

'Um, what exactly... do I...?' I stumbled, waving the little box in his general direction. Fortunately he took my meaning.

'There must be some semblance of ill-will, as I've explained,' he said, calmly, *"Get thee to Hell, foul fiend!"* is, I believe, the verbal formula.'

'To *where*?' I started, fresh doubts arising.

De Mallefloria tried to reassure me.

'Believing as I do,' he said, 'that the Deity is both merciful and understanding, I do not expect that... place to be my destination. I hope in fact to find eternal peace in the oblivion of nothingness from which I came. If, however, I am wrong, I shall just have to discuss matters, won't I?'

'I'm still not sure...,' I said, in all truth.

'I shall make it easy for you,' replied Mallefloria, 'and rush to meet the oncoming quiet with open arms. It will not take long, Mr Longhurst, but do please hurry: this is all extra experience and more insupportable to me than any pangs of dying.'

And so I did that dreadful thing and said those awful words and I hope that a sense of compassion formed at least part of my motive. That desire for justification has remained with me throughout the years that followed. It has formed part of my prayers ever since, right up to Matins at St James, hitherto described.

Senhor de Mallefloria did not depart easily. The flesh of his brow smoked at the touch of the silver cross for all the long time it took him to travel down the years to his beginning. However, he bore it manfully (although he was not a man) and even reached out to steady my hand when it was like to fail at its task.

His outline wavered and shimmered and different hairstyles came and went, but otherwise there was no outward sign of drawing to the end of the ordeal. One moment he was there, gritting his pearly teeth against the pain—the next he was dead: dry dust upon the chair. From nowhere, final words spoken in his voice, echoed softly round the room:

'At last...'

And it was done.

ALTERED ENGLANDS

1974

I am older and probably wiser now, and my actions that day—in contrast to their consequences—trouble me ever less as memory fades. The acquisition of Quinta de Mallefloria, albeit unexplained and mysterious, more than secured my position in the House of Slovo and formed the solid foundation of my subsequent good fortune.

What else could I have done? I ask myself, when at worship or *'in vacant or in pensive mood'*. Who else would have sheltered the people of Mallefloria and preserved their traditional ways in the change and tumult of 1960s Portugal?

Time and again I pose these questions but receive no final answer to them.

Yet... and yet, I will always feel that that night I fell somehow short of the standards to which my House and Line subscribe. Like a fox with a chicken run, where ruthless greed has once forced an entry it will most surely come again. The only cure is to wait, ever vigilant, at that precise spot, poised with a gun.

This I have done, placing a penance on myself, one so onerous and well tailored as to be an hourly reminder of the reason for its imposition. For from the day of my acquiring it, till I stand on the other side of the grave, not one sip of Quinta de Mallefloria port has or shall pass my lips again.

Oh, the torment! The daily torment!

Even so, hope springs eternal. After Judgement, if in Heaven I remain, I am looking forward to a rapid making up for lost time...

After all, what else is Heaven for?

14~

ONE FOR THE ROAD

2012 AD

'Dad's flatlined the network again, man!' said my son, Rollo. 'It's totally palestined this time...'

'I'll be right up,' replied Rebekah, my daughter, at the other end of the vide-link. 'Don't let him touch anything else.'

In this interlude Rollo had regained control of his wild emotions and, despite everything, scratch-constructed a smile.

'Don't contemplate it, man, Dad,' he said, tapping my arm reassuringly. 'It could happen to anyone. A week's orders—so what? We'll ride it. It's elegant...'

I looked at him and he looked at me—two aliens wondering if they were surveying sentient life.

'It said *'System default—okay?'* I protested. '*Okay* means all right, doesn't it? It does speak English, doesn't it? It wanted me to push that button!'

'Computers don't commit suicide, Dad,' replied Rebekah, coming through the office doorway like a smart-missile. 'You just had a conception mismatch, that's all. It's elegant; don't worry.'

'*'Don't worry, don't worry',*' I spat, bitterly. 'That's all people ever say to me now.'

'Well, maybe they're right then,' commented Rollo—not unreasonably.

ALTERED ENGLANDS

'I *want* to worry!' I blustered on. 'The day I stop worrying about Slovo Ports incorp., you can nail the bloody coffin lid down!'

There was no dutiful answer to that and Rollo and Rebekah addressed their full attention to the accounting network I'd sent to a better place. Plugged in and tapping confidently away, my daughter, all jacket-padding and sharp lapels, was transported into the virtual-reality world in which she was solely and truly happy.

'I think I can save some tail-end gear if I move fast,' she said, maybe to us, maybe to herself—or maybe to her beloved computer. 'Leave me.'

Rollo—who was more the sales side of the business and I who was... damn all—obediently left. Outside, he turned his mirror-shades upon me and I was presented with identical-twin images of the confused old buffer he was studying.

'Don't worry, man, Dad,' he said. 'Why not hit the balcony and score a nice bottle of something? It's about that time of day, anyway. It'd be elegant...'

He was suggesting I go and get even more confused somewhere I could do no harm. In the circumstances it seemed like a moderate request to make.

My presence at work was no longer required, was increasingly barely tolerated; yet still I allowed my feet to carry me there each morning. For most of those fifty years of mornings, there'd been a spring in my step to match the lightness of my heart. Now, after more than a fair run, the latter was going to join the long-gone former. If I wasn't still nominal Managing Director of Slovo Ports (due to stupid reasons like pride and not facing facts) they'd have barred me from the place long since. A few more days like today and we'd be talking boardroom coups and legal injunctions to achieve that same end. I didn't want to go that way. On the other hand, I didn't want to go at all. My *'coffin-lid'* speech had come straight from the heart.

Nodding at Rollo, I sadly made my way through the automated processing plant, through the paperless *'client-services'* office, out to the people-teeming *'Corp-Image'* department. No one said hello to me; I dare say fair few of the here-today-gone-tomorrow, silver-suited Corp contractors even knew who I was.

The one oasis of inefficient human-scale space was my office, tucked away now, excommunicated from the all-important 'Corp. data network', and safe only as long as breath remained in my body. I could sense the *'Floorspace*

Utilisation Officers' (we had three!) had sworn blood-feud on this room, a passion gnawing away at their guts (if they had any) until a nice sensible *'workstation'* could be slammed in. I took offence at that; just because you didn't have a *'workstation'*, didn't mean you didn't work...

'Well, they damn well won't have it!' I said to the smirking oil portrait of our founder, Sir Ralph Slovo (1709-1789), hanging above my desk. 'Not bloody likely!'

Then I reflected that actually it was extremely likely. I'd already overshot the Biblical quota of years and was nudging the EU and Israel-Co-Prosperity-Sphere average. All the *'Floor-Ute'* officers and other sundry barbarians had to do was bide their time.

As good as his word, Rollo sent up one of the front-shop flunkies with a bottle of something pleasant, already decanted. I indicated that the uniformed young man (another of the American economic refugees, poor devils) should take the fragrant potion out onto the balcony table.

'As you wish, sir, damn your eyes,' he said.

'And you—and your mother,' I replied. 'Get out!'

He'd never forgiven me for the business with his wife (a saucy little minx—but the *accent!*) several years back. Ever since (it being a bit unsporting to sack him in the circumstances), I'd had to put up with something less than silver-service.

Sitting out in the sunshine, observing the clean and healthy City of Oporto across the river, I told myself I had no reason to be thus waltzing with melancholy. Mine was a decent old innings, with more than its fair share of boundaries. Slovo Ports had never been more prosperous, not in all its three hundred years of life, nor were its prospects ever better. Neither, I flattered myself to think, had its renowned product fallen, in the very *slightest*, from grace. Also, now that Government was everywhere rational and reasonable, tax would remain low and revolution out of the question. The future seemed quite assured.

Tasting the Slovo 1980 provided me merely confirmed all this. It had power and grip and yet subtleties enough to beguile a whole evening away in chasing their definition. Even the teetotallers (a distressingly fast-breeding brood) could have appreciated this wine. Its foreplay of mature colour and enticing bouquet could well seduce even the most joyless and strong-willed into a memorable bout of passion.

ALTERED ENGLANDS

The thought that I was responsible for bringing this message-from-God into the world still had the power to swell my rackety heart with pride. My life was not been entirely wasted then.

And there was also my little tribe, Rollo and Rebekah, plus one or two other faithful apprentices-grown-old, who would carry on my mission and, in all probability, surpass its previous highs. True, I found them slightly... colourless and—like so many young people in the new Europe—lacking in the 5% or so of irresponsibility required to make a fully rounded human being. Yet, I had to admit, in their narrow and over-focused hearts, there lived what now passed for love for me and Slovo Ports. I shouldn't complain.

Down in the City there seemed to be a festival on in the Islamo-Germanic quarter. A restrained number of firecrackers were going off. I could be entirely confident the noise wasn't that of gunfire, for that just didn't happen anymore; not within a thousand miles. Mine was the last European generation to commonly know what a small arms exchange sounded and felt like. And a damn good thing too, I thought.

In fact, everything was good, for the best and what we had all hoped and fought for.

And I was bored.

※

There had been a choice of *'trains'* as people persisted in calling them. One, the more normal, went at some phenomenal speed, not wasting a second of increasingly precious time. The other was designed for tourists and past-it folk like myself, who could bear to stop at small stations and look at scenery as anything less than a blur. I wasn't going anywhere special and was in no hurry to get there, so the latter option seemed appropriate to my purpose.

It was a *'purpose'* I had been unable to explain to my bewildered children—or indeed to myself, truth be told. The fact was that I'd merely been seized with a powerful urge to leave home and perhaps revisit some scenes from youth. If a man couldn't do it now, when the Grim Reaper was looking up his phone number, then when could he, for goodness sake?

Finally, Rollo and Rebekah got quite... parental about forbidding it—until that is, I waved my (sheathed) swordstick under their surgically altered snub noses, whereupon they sent me on my way with blessings.

Doubtless they would arrange a pursuit posse of discreet private doctors with sedatives and oh-so-liberal policemen, but I had a few hours start on them. Come to think of it, at my stage of life, I had a few *decades* start on them in terms of indifference to the law and public opinion. At the end, all it had taken was an adjustment to thinking and, hey presto: free of all constraints!

The journey up the Douro Valley was one I'd performed each July/August of my adult life until quite recently; up into the port producing areas to supervise the vintage. There'd also been innumerable out of season visits for reasons both social and commercial. At my journey's end I'd always encountered the epitome of Portuguese country hospitality and seen the fortunes of my beloved House ever increase with each year and practical improvement. If now I was going to take stock of Tobias Longhurst (1932 to date), there was nowhere more auspicious or appropriate in which to do it.

I am all for progress (well, generally I am…) and had welcomed the changes that had stripped the port process of backbreaking labour and crippling uncertainties. No longer did women have to carry whole grape vintages down mountainsides or producers face ruin at the whim of a freak frost. One would have to be a Bourbon Monarchy Restorationist (though there were a growing number of *them!*) to disapprove of that.

However, it had come into my mind that if there were to be a final visit to the *'Demarked Region'*, I wanted it to be to somewhere where a ghost of the traditional ways lingered. That narrowed my destination options down to one place; *Quinta Mallefloria*, my own private estate,[37] where, in keeping with an undertaking made in remote youth, I'd preserved as much of tradition as seemed practical and humane.

So it was that, before long, I was inside my 'train', hurtling alongside the tamed and traffic-free River Douro. Beside the steep river-valley sides my educated eye picked out each estate and its owner: *Cockburn, Morgan, Croft*…, all the old names. Accompanying each came a blessed memory of flavour and perhaps an associated event: a wedding, a christening or just idle drinks in good company. Time passed painlessly in a cheerful reverie.

Then I realised that, aside from my fellow passengers, I'd seen no people. The only movement amongst the vines on the valley terraces was that of the spider-like robot tenders—and somehow that was saddening.

Tilting my panama over my eyes, I composed myself for sleep.

---

[37] As acquired in *'Liberty! Ah, Liberty!'* above.

ALTERED ENGLANDS

❇

The guardian spirit of my senile odyssey woke me just before the correct station and my body was kind enough to rally and make the short walk to Mallefloria a pleasant one.

I could have *'vided'* ahead and thus ensured a warm welcome but it suited me to come unannounced and see what spontaneity, that obsolete quality, might inspire. Thus it was my own fault that disappointment followed from finding the gates barred and only yet another robot to greet me.

'Hello, Sir Tobias,' it said from within the confines of the gate-pillar. 'How are you? I am surprised to see you.'

Just to emphasise the point, I heard the whirr of zoom eyes trying to get the full measure of me.

'Hello Jeeves,' I replied. 'I'm fine; never better. Signal ahead I'm here, will you, there's a good chap.'

'That may be inadvisable,' he/it answered, 'but since I am programmed to obey recognised persons I will do/have done so. Please enter in. Welcome.'

I could have asked *'why inadvisable'?* and so on but have never got used to conducting conversations with cyber-sentient walls and such. Besides, it was a tidy walk up to the *adegas* complex and I'd long trained myself to conserve energy on the 'need-to-know/ask' principle. All would doubtless be explained in good time.

In fact it wasn't. There was no one at the *adegas*, no sign of life in the 'production zone'. Tokens of recent occupation: half a meal, half a balance-sheet, were in abundance, but of their recent owners none at all.

That wasn't quite so adrenaline-rich a situation as it might otherwise be. Even at Mallefloria, modern methods meant staffing was minimal compared to the labour hordes of not so long ago. It was possible something pressing had drawn everyone away for a while. They'd be back soon enough.

I might perhaps have strolled down to the nearby village and investigated further but it was too much trouble over so minor a matter. Awaiting their return I could make myself comfortable without them fussing around. On reflection, it seemed the gods were smiling on my outing.

Fetching a decanter from the manager's office (Slovo Tawny '91, I'd swear) and half a round of fresh country bread from the kitchen, I took myself over to the ancient bench-seat which overlooked the steep fall to the river below. That spot had long been my favourite and I'd proposed to my third wife (and often, in another fashion, to her informal successors) there. From it could be seen the full spread of the Demarked Region: God's own Country (apart, of course, from England's *Home Counties*, excluding London) and the scene upon which I had chosen to lavish my humble life and talents. In the distance, its eco-friendly hiss fully muffled by row upon row of vines, ran a toy-like 'train', just such as I had arrived on. It was one of the fast variety though, full of busy people, their lives still ahead of them. Would any of the passengers be able to say they'd been as happy and lucky as I? I hoped so—but doubted it.

Taking a drink of the soothing, unassertive oak-port, I studied the play of light on the nearest vines and sighed with pleasure.

'Paradise,' I said quietly.

'Yes, it is,' answered Sir Giles Piecrust, my old friend and mentor at Slovo Ports, coming to join me on the bench. 'Absolute *paradise*.'

'Oh, hello, Crusty,' I said. 'What a pleasant surprise seeing you here. Hang on though... aren't you dead?'

Piecrust contrived to make his naturally benevolent little face even more amiably amused. Somehow, there just wasn't the material there to construct any fear out of.

'I should jolly well hope so, dear boy,' he replied, 'you arranged my funeral! And tastefully done it was, too: *Crimond*, *'Abide...'*, the full 1662 thing—very English. I haven't had a chance to thank you up to now...'

'That's all right,' I said. 'Too busy I suppose?'

'No,' mused Piecrust, 'you were.'

'Really? By the way, you never told us about your 'D.S.O. and bar' at the Somme, you dark horse. We were all very impressed when the Guards' representative turned up.'

'Well, I didn't like to mention it,' smiled Piecrust. 'It was a long time ago and a nasty business. Least said, soonest mended I thought.'

'Modest as ever. Oh well, so now you're a ghost then?'

'In a manner of speaking, Toby—as are you, you silly sausage!'

'I *beg* your pardon?'

'You died on the train, Toby: quite peacefully: of old age and the English disease—melancholy. You've rested a few days and right this moment they're burying you at St. James. Rollo's gone to endless trouble to turn up an Anglican priest—and a male one at that—for you: 1662 again; all very moving.'

ALTERED ENGLANDS

Surprisingly, it seemed entirely easy to accept termination. Not feeling 'dead' presumably helped. Equally bizarre, there were overtones of joy to the notion. I had, I supposed, long deserved a holiday from being Tobias Longhurst.

'I think I'd like to see my funeral,' I said, calmly. 'Is anyone upset?'

'You'll be able to later, Toby,' replied Piecrust, looking straight ahead, unblinking, at the orb of the sun. 'And yes, those you'd want to be are distraught—in a dignified sort of way, of course.'

'Of course.'

'There'll be sufficient salt-water shed tonight, never fear, when the family's in private.'

'But when I come to think about it,' I said, 'I don't *like* the idea of them upsetting themselves—not when I'm sitting here in such cheerful shape. It makes me feel guilty.'

'Would you prefer the alternative, dear boy?' asked Piecrust, gently. 'A cold disposal of the carcass for form's sake, and then life as normal? They can't see you any more, Toby, not for a while anyway, and they loved you; allow them to do the decent thing.'

'Well, put like that...'

'No, no one can see you now, young man,' said a new voice. Sir Ralph Slovo[38] signalled I should budge up and make room for him. 'No one except your own kind and robots. That's why there was no greeting at Mallefloria. When the cyber-Jeeves rather puzzledly announced the arrival of Senhor Tobias Longhurst (deceased) all the staff hightailed it to the hills. It'll cause a bit of a rumpus for a few days but nothing will show up on the Jeeves' video record: people will forget soon enough.'

I nodded, trying to take all this in.

'So am I in Heaven?' I asked eventually, half fearing to put the vital question.

Piecrust shrugged.

'It's *our* Heaven, Toby, a version of reality; perhaps an ante-chamber to the real thing. This seems to be a paradise kindly constructed just for people like us. And we can always move on and up when we've had enough...'

---

[38] Slovo has evidently wandered off from Quinta dos Malatesta since the events of *'A Partial Cure'*.

'Precious little chance of that, ho ho,' said Sir Ralph, liberally helping himself to my port.

'So I've come to my reward!' I gasped, half-remembering some phrase from prep school chapel. 'I've passed the test?'

'Was it ever in doubt?' replied Piecrust, laughing gently. 'With your kind heart, you were never a candidate for the other place...'

'*Is* there one?' I asked nervously, worrying that my pass could still be cruelly revoked.

'Apparently,' said Sir Ralph. 'And similarly tailored to suit individual tastes as per here. Chap called Sharp told us about it. Did you know him?'

'What, Sharp of *Cipfaria* Ports? Shiny-faced chap: two-faced too...'

'That's the one—absolute *swine* apparently; cruel to children on the quiet, so it turns out. Which doesn't go down too well with the Management—*'the tears of infants...'* and all that. Anyway, he's allowed in here for a minute a year—just to rub salt in the wound and to show him what he's missing. That's how we know about... the other place.'

'Yes indeed,' continued Piecrust. 'It seems that people with our likes and preferences wake up on the Tokyo Metro—in a heatwave rush-hour—squeezed between a sumo and a war-criminal. The train then perpetually conveys them to a hotel bar to drink *Watney's Red Barrel*—a whole *Party Seven* each. Prior to bed with Claire Rayner: twelve hours minimum. And then-...'

'No, *no*, enough!' I shouted. 'I don't want that knowledge in my head!'

'If you like it can be deleted,' said Piecrust. 'Every wish can be granted here. However, if you'll take my advice, you'll hang on to that info and thus make this place seem all the sweeter...'

'You see there's *everything* here for us, dear boy,' explained Sir Ralph, idly brushing his pink silk lapels. 'Time is overthrown; what was once our tyrant is now our servant. You can sample any vintage from any era, look invisibly in on your family: ancestors, current or descendants—play games with the whole sweep of history!'

Here he aptly swept his arm through the air and, by way of illustration in a space of instants, a few ordered millennia passed wonderfully by in review before my very eyes.

'Those men in red coats,' I stumbled, ecstatically. 'Who...?'

'The first English merchants along the Douro,' explained Piecrust, 'about to discover the wine that would one day become our vocation.'

'And in the boat down there, on the river; is that *really* Forrester?'[39]

'Yes, Forrester, Joseph James; on his mapping expeditions of the middle 1800's.'

'He was my hero,' I said, no longer caring how adolescent that sounded. It happened to be true and from now on I could have the joy of speaking only truth.

'You can meet him shortly. He was very impressed with your 'Slovo 1992', and that 'Late-Bottled-Vintage' range you launched. *'Sturdy'*: that was the word he used, wasn't it, Ralph.'

'That's it: *'sturdy and agreeable'.*'

My breast swelled with overwhelming gratification but the expected, associated, heart-pains didn't arrive. I was free of them as well.

'And the savages?' I asked. 'The ones with the war-paint and shotguns, and feathers in their hair. What are they doing in Mallefloria?'

'Far future, Toby,' said Piecrust. 'They call themselves the *'Englisc'*—a happy and confident tribe: our race's direct descendants, as it happens. You see, history didn't turn out quite as dull and uneventful as you feared, dear boy. Once again, as the *Englisc* Empire spreads, they're rediscovering port…'

'Likewise the hard-faced chappies in black, with the bodyguards and harems,' said Sir Ralph, looking even more naughty than usual. 'They're still further future: *'The Weaponlords'*—a load of *bad lads* in many ways—but very appreciative of good port...'

There was much else and Sir Ralph went to fetch more wine to accompany our talk, and the beautiful sunset lasted as long as we wanted it to.

✹

And thus it was I learnt that I need never have done all that worrying and that everything turns out for the best in the end. I tried all the known vintages and met Baron Forrester and some charming *Englisc* folk, and lots of others too. I saw my grandchildren arrive in the 'real' world and in due course, Rollo and Rebekah came to join me in the really real world—the 2060's having come round in an absolute flash.

As in life, but no longer separated by fear and ego, we were all borne along together on a mighty river of purple port wine, to wherever it might lead.

[39] Baron Forrester (1809-61), the English 'Renaissance Man' of the early Port trade.

Only now we could be confident that the ocean one day awaiting us would be a welcoming one.

THE END

ALTERED ENGLANDS

JOHN WHITBOURN

THE MOUNT CABURN STORIES

☸

INTRODUCTION

'God gave all men, all earth to love,
but since our hearts are small,
Ordained for each one spot should prove,
Beloved over all.'

'Sussex'. 1902.

'I'm just in love with all these three,
the Weald and marsh and the Down countree.
Nor I don't know which I love the most,
The Weald or the Marsh or the white chalk coast.'

'A Three-part Song' in *'Dymchurch Flit'*, from *'Puck of Pook's Hill'*, 1906.

Rudyard Kipling (1865-1936).

☸

ALTERED ENGLANDS

❇

To me, Mount Caburn simply means Sussex, or, more accurately, SUSSEX! Those suggestive green curves signal I am either on my way into or heading out of there—both occasions with poignant sentiments attached. Alas, humans can only live in one place at a time[40] and people blessed or cursed with a highly developed sense of place must stoically resign themselves to highs and lows with each hello and goodbye.

But I digress. To the probable minority who even notice it as they whizz past along the road or on the train to Brighton, Mount Caburn is that precipitous treacle-pudding shaped hill that looms over the valley of the Ouse and gorgeous, pouting, Lewes, county town of East Sussex. At best, even to many modern sons and daughters of Sussex, I suspect and fear it is only that green blur that briefly blocks their side view as the fleshpots of Brighton (or maybe Beachy Head) beckon. You also go past it to get to the opera house at nearby Glynde—and thankfully the opera-going elite do just that: go past it... At worst, to planners and politicians, Caburn is the under-utilised chalk lump blocking desperately needed widening of the A27, courtesy of sentimental tree-huggers, Luddites and other sundry enemies of progress. For the time being...

Whichever view you take, what's undeniable is that Caburn is an outpost of the South Downs, that mighty range of chalk hills uplifted at the same time as the Alps, which run broadly east-west across southern England from Winchester, once and future capital of England, to the sea. Looming some 491 feet above sea level (and thus technically not a mountain at all) Caburn is a packed cabinet of history, crowned by the ghosts of past human activity from Bronze Age burial mounds, through a Iron Age hillfort, to World War II slit trenches, the last forming part of a hasty 'stop-line' against an invasion which, praise be, never came.

Less tangibly, there are also legends from the misty past, about 'Gil the giant' who cast his mighty hammer from Caburn's top (at who? To what end?), and the knight in golden armour buried beneath the sward (to one day rise again? To resume what name and to what purpose?). On the next hill but one

---

[40] Unless the stories about St. Padre Pio and Henry Kissinger's bilocation antics are true, but not being either sainthood or anti-Christ material, that is neither here nor there (geddit...?) to me.

away lies 'The Long Man of Wilmington', the biggest depiction of the human form in the eastern hemisphere (just), carved into the chalk Lord knows when and why. A connection between him and Caburn is suspected, even likely, but can never be proved...

In short, and taken in conjunction with neighbouring Lewes town (*'Zion of the Downs'*), Caburn is an island of numinosity rising above the joint desert and sea of bland that is the 'shopping-&-f***ing' driven post-Christian modern world. It is moot whether that desert is encroaching or sea level rising, ready to swamp Caburn, or whether both have passed their high (and thus low) point. Leaving me in hope of living to see new land liberated by their ebb.

But I digress *again*—though if you can't do that here, in a spiel preceding your own story, where else can you?

Meanwhile, back on earth, as an officially recognised 'Site of Special Scientific Interest' and protected as a 'National Nature Reserve', Mount Caburn is now also the stronghold of more rare plant and beastie species than you could shake a stick at. Better still, in the present car-confined age it is largely left to itself, the haunt only of hikers plus a few gaily (and gayly) clad paragliders proclaiming to the world that they want to die NOW by launching themselves off the top towards the road and railway and powerlines.

And sometimes, of course, though not often enough by any means, there is mere me...

And when I'm there or even sadly just passing by, that strange and lovely place gives me pause for thought. Quite often the thought I pause to think is whether it is only human activity and human ghosts that 'haunt' Caburn? I wonder what grounds for certainty exist that the distant dark figures standing still on the summit are exclusively *people*? And who, if anyone, is in a position to say *what* precisely goes on atop Caburn when the light fails or the clouds descend, or on a wild wintry night?

15~

BURY MY HEART AT SOUTHERHAM (E. SUSSEX)

I'd never seen quite so many Land Rovers. Every time my ramble route crossed a road, there seemed to be at least one thundering along at inexplicable speed. Furthermore, a suspicious proportion were in East Sussex County Council livery. What had so stirred the Local Authority's anthill I idly wondered—for all of two seconds—before resuming the amiable coma that is the great attraction of long-haul walking.

Just beyond Lewes a veritable convoy of them, 'enlivened' with some olive-drab examples as well, left me with no choice but to pause and ponder. Their furious passage along the A27 blocked my path for a good minute or two, causing me to wake.

Even so, I tried to ignore the traffic tornado—the very thing I was attempting to escape—and looked to the hills for restored peace (or shut-down) of mind. Beyond the road reared the uninvolved, uncaring slope of Southerham Camp—aka *'Mount Caburn'*. Like a giant sponge-pudding, this afterthought of the South Downs rose sheer and improbable above the road and nearby farm; today hiding its (to continue the analogy) treacle-topping zone in cloud-wrapped mystery.

I was looking forward to climbing it. Therein lay the hope of a holiday from the world of Land Rovers and busy *'A'* roads, and, who knows, up in the quiet of the unfrequented summit, perhaps a break from the grind of… being me. That prospect well warranted the fag of actually *getting* there.

Once across the road, I found a little reception committee awaiting me and blocking the footpath. They were in variations of south-east English traditional dress (ancient *Barbour* and flat cap) and draped on and about the gate to what I presumed to be their farm.

One (the largest) scowled and spat heartily after the departing Land Rover convention. He then turned to study me.

'That's *all* we need,' he said, 'a bag-rat!'

We ramblers all know about the charming name the country aborigines have for us. Familiarity doesn't make it any more pleasing though.

'And the same to you,' I replied. 'And your mother.'

They all laughed (which was a relief).

'Pass friend,' smiled the offending half-man, half-tractor, and he even went to open the gate for me.

'Na!' said the lively-looking girl beside him, seizing his ham-like arm. 'It's not a good day: *they'll* be celebrating. It's not *his* fault.'

The half dozen of them looked from one to another in a telepathic exchange I couldn't fathom. Used to the ways of the shotgun and scrumpy classes, I hefted the weight of my (yes, I admit it) backpack and waited patiently.

'It's no good, Trace,' said another of the young men. 'We've argued it with 'em till we're sick to death.'

'S'right,' said a second girl. 'They've gone and done it now and so it's gotta start sometime.'

'Might as well be him, maightn't it?' chipped in the *'bag-rat'* wit, in a *stands-to-reason* tone.

'Trace' thought long and hard (for her, I suspect) and eventually shrugged her waterproofed shoulders.

'Mebbe so,' she said, resignedly, and cleared the way.

'On y'go and fare ye well!' said their hulking leader, bowing low as I passed.

Right through the farmyard my neck-hairs informed me they were seeing me on my way—but to quite where I was no longer sure...

☸

Up beyond the chalk-on-blackboard effect of human interactions, I felt a whole lot better—as always. Below me, reduced to toy-proportions and silence, were the farm and road of recent memory. I illogically felt that it was the effort of my arduous climb that had cut them down to appropriate size and, such a struggle deserving some reward, I took a rest.

Within moments of sitting down, only halfway through the ascent, I had achieved a state of detachment that, procured through pharmacology or eastern-religion, would have been pretty damn expensive. I *knew* it was just another work day tomorrow, but somehow that just didn't seem to matter any more.

Spread out for my delectation like the best Christmas stocking *ever*, was the wonderful world of the *Weald*, a patchwork of fields and woods and isolated villages where just about anything might be going on, stretching down to pancake flat Pevensey Levels and the sea. This is the place, I thought, where I came to be, and was now, after travel, the only place I wanted to be. There was enough here to keep me busy and my imagination alive for the rest of my days, and, the Good Lord willing, I would never have to go to *BABYLONdon*, nor cross the Thames, again.

I sighed with pleasure and leaned back on the springy turf. My lazy gaze swept the blue beyond and ticked off Alfriston and Pyecombe as present and correct. There too were the Observatory domes of Herstmonceux and the windmill at Polegate; all places I'd trod and knew and loved. Further out, with the eye of faith, one could just discern the vague locales of Wilmington, with its hillside Chalk-Giant, and Pevensey, where all England's invasions—Saxon, Norman and the maybes of Napoleon and *'Sealion'*—converged into a nexus of make-or-break history. Unbidden, the word *'perfect'* sprang to mind.

'Give me men,' Oliver Cromwell had (more or less) said, *'who know what they love and love what they know.'* After long years of existentialist uncertainty I had at last come, accidentally, to that happy Cromwellian state—and was very glad of it. What could possibly spoil this moment?

'Well,' reported the less-of-all-this-happiness-nonsense section of my mind, *'how about these two fellow ramblers, for a start?'*

Of course, they had just as much right to be ascending Caburn as I, but it was a nuisance all the same. Not many people came up here, so why did they have to choose this particular time? I hadn't come all this way just for chit-chat with my fellow man, and couldn't repress a flicker of irritation at the imminent arrival of company. Fortunately, most ramblers were of like mind and, being in all probability English to boot, there was a good chance of getting away with just a polite nod and grunt. Even so, it was a pain. No one likes their chomp at a ration of cheer, however defined, to be interrupted.

I straightened up and composed myself into reception mode—relaxed but not suspiciously so, guardedly friendly but not to the extent of sociability—and tried to enjoy the view once more.

Sad to say, my eyes kept on straying to the couple labouring up the hill. They weren't hanging about by any means, but I'd misjudged their e.t.a. There was still a fair while yet before I was caught up with; time enough to press on, unseen, up into the cloud zone, should I so wish.

Thereagain, I reflected, that way we'd only end up meeting on the summit, where an avoidance of communication would seem downright rude. And besides, why should I be rushed by this stroke of bad luck? Let them pass me by and then I'd continue my day as before.

I was trying to locate Michelham Priory out in the far haze when the intrusive duo hoved into sight again and caused me to note that they weren't wearing the rambler's uniform of garish *cagoule* and pack. *'Free Country...,'* I answered myself and returned to the previous search. Yes, continued the internal nuisance whisper, it *was* also curious they were all in black or brown—but that needn't unduly distract me. Why shouldn't goth-rockers go in for a bit of hiking?

There was too much cloud to see anything of Brighton (no great shame given the present state of the town) and... come to think of it, I'd never seen ramblers with staves before: golf umbrellas, shooting sticks and fancy canes, yes, but never great big pole things. I had to admit that use of them made the two very agile. They were covering the precipitous gap between us like nobody's business, eating up space at spider-speed—or so it seemed to me. I was even tempted to break the rules of my own game and actually speak to these people when they arrived. *'Where did you get the idea about the striding sticks, then?'* Or something like that.

Certainly they now seemed very interested in a meeting, never taking their dark faces off me as they clambered ever nearer. And there was another innocent oddity: I didn't recall ever encountering a coloured rambler before.

The sun went behind a cloud and sudden gloom fell on the scene. Simultaneously, the hikers vanished in a fold of the path up and, temporarily, I was alone again.

Someone once said that, on a good day, you could see all three *'Shire'* counties (Surrey, Sussex and Kent) from here, and I half-heartedly looked for proof of this. It might even be true I concluded, for county boundaries exist only in the minds of men (and Local Government) rather than on the ground. Who's to say whether some particular fuzz of grey or green wasn't just over the Sussex frontier into Surrey or wherever? It was just one of those nice thoughts and so I chose to believe it.

'Those walkers are taking their time…,' said an unsolicited message—or was it that I was impatient to see them and then see the back of them? As if in response, I caught brief sight of the two again and realised they were doing the best they could, now coming on at nigh frantic pace. For some reason I felt a sudden desire to get up and move along at just as fast, if not faster, speed than they. However, that seemed a silly thing to do, so I sternly showed the impulse the door.

By now, I could hear them, scrabbling along the loose chalk rubble of the track, exertion causing their breath to hiss. They were an implacable lot, I mused, racing along like that without a word. Maybe it was a timed route—I'd heard of some hardcore ramblers doing so.

I was feebly trying to convince myself I should look for Arundel when they arrived. There was a rasp of stones, a grunt of effort, and then the first breasted the hill just below my station. My hello aborted on my lips.

He may have been a hiker for all I know, but not any sort the Ramblers Association had as a member. There was no woolly hat or walking boots to be seen. The biped leathery thing, all twisted and spindly like some animated bog-corpse, fixed yellow eyes and myriad-rowed pointed teeth in my direction and… hissed in triumph or hunger.

Then, as I turned to go, it threw its spear at me.

❂

It's amazing what you can do when you have to. If someone had previously asked me to sprint up a 1 in 4 slope, impeded by a flint-tipped spear sticking out of my *Tupperware* padded backpack, *faster* than two pursuing wild things, I'd have had to decline. Yet, there I was, maintaining the distance between us, albeit breathing like a bellows, zooming up to the cloud-coated top like a mountain goat. I didn't know if my tormentors were impressed but I certainly was.

The only fly in the ointment (save the whole situation) was that I had no clear plan in mind. Wonderful as my unsuspected survival batteries were, I felt pretty sure they weren't *Long-Life* ones. Somewhen quite soon I would dramatically revert to being just an ordinary middle-aged office worker, and, a second or two after that, *they* would be on me. This sad thought, and knowledge of the remaining spear, kept me going, but I knew how it would end: up on the hilltop, or maybe a little way down the other side, but certainly well before I could reach the world of men. I remember thinking *'I hope they don't actually eat me—anything but that!'*

As we reached the summit my every gasp was the drawing in of white-hot lava, and, just behind, I could feel the fetid, peppery breath of my silent enemies on my neck. The finish line was mere paces away and if I had the strength left I would have screamed—a last gesture to make their dinner that little less pleasant.

Then, as my shoulder blades conceptualised a spear poised to strike, we rounded some sort of gorse bush into a clear patch in the mist. And someone discharged a firearm right beside my ear.

Death came so suddenly and definitively that the... thing behind me had no time to comment on it. Now that I'd spun round about, deafened, away from the shot, the creature lay at my feet, its face caved in; no longer a problem to anyone.

Fearfully, I raised my head and came face to face with the second whatsit. Five feet off, I looked at it and it looked at me. Then, a long second later, a number of arrows blossomed in its chest, sponsoring a permanent loss of interest in proceedings.

Apart from the ringing in my ear, all had returned to stillness and, too blown and afraid to about-face, I was left alone with the bodies in the grass, studying through gaps in mist and powder smoke the world below that I'd thought lost.

Of course, this couldn't go on forever; however much in my combined joy and fear I might wish it to. There seemed the possibility of just... walking away down the hill, of rejoining life where I'd left off, and confining the last few minutes to blessed forgetfulness. This route had its many attractions but, reason slowly returning, I doubted I could misrecall so well. There was the danger of a lifetime bitterly wondering *'What if?'*

So I turned and, silent behind me, sitting on the turf, were more than a hundred... beings. I was going to say *'people'* but a second's glance revealed this was not so. People are not almond-eyed and pure-white skinned, nor are they all so long limbed and self-possessed. This was some older and more elegant species.

Huddled against the mist under blankets, those nearest looked at me without curiosity. One, whom I took to be my saviour, was reloading a flintlock pistol.

'I'm obliged,' I wheezed.

He smiled, his sharp white teeth being the only thing visible to me beneath the brim of his hat and a fall of long fine hair.

'So you are, bag-rat,' he said, in a voice like the sweetest of chimes. 'If only your folk knew the depth of their obligation, we would not have come to this pretty pass.'

Those around also smiled, but without mirth.

'We have killed our last *asrai sith*, our last *padfoot*, our last *Downs-tiger* for mankind,' he added. 'Perhaps it is now time to turn our attentions to you...'

He raised his head and fixed me with the full glory of his pupil-less yellow eyes. I took a step back.

'Do not concern yourself, walker,' said another, wearily. 'He jests. We have left it too late. The time to fight your kind was when they first arrived—but we did not. That would have been bow versus bow, axe versus axe: a fair fight. Now we are too few and weak and we are... what is their word?'

'*'Re-dundant'*,' laughed the one who had first spoken to me. 'Which means, we are told, *'of no further use'*. It is something to do with a thing called *'budget-cuts'*. Our protection of the Free Lands is no longer needed. They will deal with it themselves they say.'

'Tell me, man-walker,' said the second speaker, 'how can this be that a living person, a nation, a *folk*, is *'of no further use'*? To whom? Who takes upon themselves such authority to say thus? We live, we breathe, we cleanse the Downs of pre-human vermin-life, as per the ancient bargain, so that you may walk upon them safely. We are of *'use'* to ourselves and the Great Spirit!'

'And they say we are *'wild'*!' chipped in first speaker. 'And so we are! They say there is now no room in the world for both Downs-folk and *'ramblers'*. They say *they* will deal with the *asrai*; they will somehow prevail in the secret war waged over these hills since the Great Spirit breathed life on them. Well then, I wish them much luck!'

He subsided into resigned silence and rested his chin on his knees. None of them seemed to have anything more to say to me.

I looked over the dejected gathering: mostly youngish 'men', but also womenfolk and little-ones, and they resembled for all the world some defeated tribe awaiting its inevitable end. The mist grew thicker.

'I don't understand,' I said, humbly.

The first speaker, perhaps what passed for a leader amongst them, raised his head again.

'Do not try to,' he said (or sang). 'It will break your heart.'

The second spokesman laughed harshly.

'Then let it be broken,' he said, 'like ours are broken. Let him take back to his world a fragment of the pain in *our* shattered hearts. Tell him!'

Number One looked at me. The silent study stretched uncomfortably.

'They have taken the people of the Downs in their *Land Rovers*,' he recited. 'They do not *'rove'* the land in these things, but keep to the dead, animal-slaying, road instead—but still, that is the name they have chosen for them: Like you, I do not understand. But I *do* understand that your 'Land Rovers' will hold my people and hurry them in secret to the *Reservations* you have constructed. These 'Land Rovers' are good enough to end a story that was old when your kind first stepped ashore. What you see here is all that remains of once great realms. Bassion, Rhegged, Britta, Agned... Annwn; they are no more.'

'But who *are* you?' I stuttered, as the memories of my earlier traffic problems were recast in a new and sinister light. 'I mean, what's it all about?'

'What is truth?' replied number Two. 'Who knows or cares? What we are we know already, but your kind cannot comprehend it. Now, here at the end of things, we are the remnants, the refusers, the last to tread Mother-Downs. We will not succumb to your threats and persuasions to go. We cannot live in *Nissans* on Kilda or Gruinard or Mann, as you wish. Only here are we what we are. So let us die here.'

'*Die*?' I echoed weakly, my voice further distorted by its passage through the mist. 'Why die?'

Number One smiled again.

'Why not? We are long-lived, but not immortal. Even Elf-folk have a final moment. To some comes the joy of death in battle. Others chose to go in the fullness of their days. I could be happy with either; the blades of the *asrai* and their humans allies, or singing my death-song beside my own hearth. What I will <u>not</u> do is cough out my last, confined in wire compounds constructed for our discreet departure from the Earth. None of your *'old People's home'* for us! Here we stay.'

'He is right,' said Number Two to me. 'And we few have followed him. The rest, the old and tired, have gone on. *'You cannot fight the dull-eyes,'* they said—and they were right also. For we cannot touch iron: only our few half-breeds and changelings from intercourse with you Sussex-English can handle the antique fire-arms allowed us—and only then at the price of pain. What chance has our ancient armoury got against the machine-magic you muster? No, we are *re-dun-dant*, as the men in grey suits told us. The myriad tribes are *out*: died-out, wiped-out, sold-out, and now... moved-out.'

'But it's not *'magic'*,' I protested, 'and we wouldn't...'

'We labour under no illusions,' stated Number One, still steadfast. 'We never did. But all we are now is despair, a last sighting to some stray human, a coda composed by the Great Spirit who gave us life. Though maybe, even at this late stage, He will not desert us...'

'We *are* deserted,' said Number Two, firmly. 'The old magic is departing. We have summoned the gate of the Shadowlands but it has not answered. Even our retreat is barred.'

Their resignation touched me with infinite regret. I felt that I was witness to some irreparable loss whose full significance I could not yet appreciate, yet wanted desperately to prevent.

'There's somewhere you could go?' I asked. 'Some hope?'

'None it seems,' replied Number One. 'Look.'

I followed the line of his torc-ringed arm but could see nothing but mist and air. I said as much.

'Doubtless so,' answered the second speaker, 'but our eyes are, as you note, different. We can view afar and in detail. I now see what your people call *'The Long Man of Wilmington'*: what we know as-...'

'I *have* seen it though,' I interrupted in my eagerness, 'before today—the chalk giant, that is. He's striding across the hill with a stave in each hand and-...'

'Not staves, bag-rat,' said Number One. 'Not staves but door-jambs. He holds open the gateway to Sheol. There, as in times past, we might be safe beneath the hill. Until Man is dead—or more tolerant.'

I had stood beside the 'Long Man' (contrary to the posted instructions) many a time, and knowing now what I had rested on on that lonely hillside, I shuddered.

'But as related,' One continued, 'our strongest spells have not stirred the gatekeeper or sprung the ancient lock. Perhaps our God *has* forsaken us...'

'Unless this rumbling is him,' added Two, cocking his ear. 'Better late than never...'

I listened. At first cloud and mist muffled everything but soon enough I could hear too.

'No,' I said. 'It's a helicopter... or helicopters.'

'And what might they be?' asked Number One, calmly. I gestured like a mad man with my arms and they got the picture.

'Flying machine-magic?' said One, and for brevity's sake I just said yes. The noise was growing louder.

The Elf-residue were scrambling to their feet, offloading their blankets to reveal finery of green and gold. Bows and spears and—here and there—muskets were pointed aloft. At that juncture airborne searchlights hit us. And a loudspeakered voice was saying something I couldn't catch—and then all was chaos as they approached from every direction.

Out of the bathing light and mist, speaker One loomed tall above me, seizing my arm with unanswerable strength.

'You must go, fortunate-born,' he said in my ear. 'Away with you—to your home. This is an age for Man alone. Much may you enjoy it.'

I couldn't decide whether to flee or fight, but then the mist was mixed with gas and we began to choke and fall. There was sporadic small arms fire and screams.

Then, as awareness receded, laying prone on the turf, my closing eyes beheld gas-masked, camouflaged figures with rifles advancing through the smog. And I heard a beautiful voice say;

'It is done.'

☸

East Sussex County Council, or whoever was hiding behind them, must have found my incongruous, senseless figure and kindly left me by the roadside to sleep it off. But I never shall.

ALTERED ENGLANDS

I had been given a last glimpse of what I'd always half suspected, what I'd sensed and what had led me to go walking in the first place. I had been shown that, in my lifetime, I had trodden *living* hills. Then, also in my time, they had been cleared of life and become dead.

So, what point in walking them anymore? I'll go no more a-rambling.

AUTHOR'S CODA & AFTERWORD

It was only some years after this story was written that I read in the Sussex Archaeological Society's newsletter[41] an article making the case that *Avronehelle*, the old name for the Doomsday Book hundred containing the Long Man of Wilmington, possibly derives from Old English for *'Hill of the Elf-mystery'*...

Of course, there is speculation, then wild speculation, then cosmology, then economics, and finally—requiring binoculars to even glimpse—English place name studies. Yet all the same, it is an odd synchronicity...

'There are signs for those who would see'.[42] The emphasis being on the volitionary *'would'*...

---

[41] Number 90. April 2000.
[42] The Quran. Surah 30, *Al-Rum* (Byzantium).

JOHN WHITBOURN

16~

'THE HILLS ARE ALIVE...'

'The Hills are alive...'

Ascending the Downs in sunlight, I couldn't fend off the feculent image. Sussex's green answer to the Alps crying out for Julie Andrews to sweep over them, singing saccharine.

Armed with earplugs I wouldn't have minded. Some female company—even an ex-nun—would have gone down well.

Memories of the sixties and *'The Sound of Music'*: saving up my pocket money to take Mum to see the film—and her dozing off halfway through. Still, it's the thought that counts...

I didn't fancy *thoughts* and thinking at the moment—or any time, truth be told. The way I see it, they only make heavy weather of life, prodding and poking the thing we're meant to just enjoy.

Sadly though, right then I couldn't practice what I didn't preach. From waking alone in the hotel, through breakfast-for-one, and now, facing the day solo, two *thoughts* were at me like a dog with a bone and wouldn't give up *grrrring*.

'I like you as a friend'. The female Armageddon option, thermonuclear end of everything, leaving only megadeaths and mutations behind. A hastily arranged extra single room for the night, tongue pie and cold shoulder for supper instead of cognac and condoms; then her icy early departure on the first London train this morning. *'Have a nice life...'* A 'South Downs Way' walk for two now turned solitary and celibate. *Quel bummer*.

ALTERED ENGLANDS

The alternative mental chewing gum was *'alive'* with what...?' Of the two it was—marginally—preferable.

With *'music'*? I couldn't hear any, not even tweetie-bird song. My preference would be the Sex Pistols (or even Sussex Pistols—geddit?) at concert pitch, but they weren't on tap and other hikers might object.

With *people* then? Hardly. I was the only bag-rat (= Sussex dialect term for full-attire hikers [derog.]) in sight. A distant tractor circled Arlington reservoir but, otherwise, aside from the sleepless A27, that was it. Yet there *was* a feeling of *life*, underfoot and all-around, even to my TV-dulled nerve endings. I'd felt it since rising, hungover, lone and little in a wasted double bed that morning. *The Long Man*, Wilmington's looming chalk hill figure, oversaw my departure with added enigma. He'd looked ready to rise off Windover hill, sticks and all, and follow us. If he had it might have scared milady up the scale beyond 'friendship' and then none of this would have happened.

That feeling persisted, whispering *numinous, numinous* in my ear, nipping my taxi-transported 'Doc. Martin' heels all the way to Glynde. I wasn't used to it. Not where I work. *Numinous* stopped at the airport boundary. Probably Heathrow Airport Ltd. have a by-law on the subject.

People say *'I never felt more alive'* (usually something to do with adultery or Colombian snuff) but today it was the landscape telling me—and those easy options weren't open to the English landscape. *I* was the odd one out; the Quaker at the wife-swapping party, the queen in the brothel. All about me the joint was jumpin' and I the conspicuous abstainer. Which was a first. Weird.

Lady*friend* had left via Glynde station. Ever hopeful, ever opportunist, I'd accompanied her in the tense taxi from *The Giant's Rest* in Wilmington. Only on the tiny platform and after a peck on the cheek worse than a slap, did all hope die. I strode off without a backward glance even before her train pulled away.

Something—but certainly not her blessing—followed me down the road. Something close and curious. I felt it in a clenching of shoulders and twin hot spots on my neck. Suspecting a poncey opera-goer en route to nearby Glyndebourne, I span on my heels, a cheery *'What d'you want: a photo?'* half way across curled lips.

No one. Not even an *Independent*-reading precious on their way to *Die Zauberflöte* and a hamper. I half wished there were. But no, nothing. The street, the bridge over Glynde Reach, were empty. A bit soon to panic yet though: no call for *'Survivors'* or Crusoe thoughts: commuting does empty some Sussex villages, eight till six, Monday to Friday.

I'd already been unfaithful to the South Downs Way by motoring Wilmington to Glynde, doubtless missing out on some *'peerless views'* and *'air like champagne'*. No wonder Mum Nature was filling the ether with static similar-to but more-effective-than my ex currently training it to Mordor. Yet something unthinking made me resolve to do the decent thing and slog the rest of the day's specified portion. Equalling a debt repaid—post a luckless flutter on the wheel—before back to the straight-and-narrow...

Doing the right thing did me no good—as ever; a lesson I relearnt time and again and always forgot. The adverse feeling increased to chalk-on-blackboard proportions. Quite an appropriate metaphor really. What else were the Downs but chalk protuberances, moulded into feminine curves by the Almighty in saucy mood? It was walking on them for the first time that had given me ideas last night. And what was chalk but the calcified shells of billions of little marine martyrs, drifting slowly down to rest at the bottom of a prehistoric sea? That ocean was now gone, the chalk thrust up and lightly coated with sheep cropped green—and that was how *'Downs'* got here. If any hills should feel alive underfoot these were they.

I kept that in mind like a mantra all the way to the base of Mount Caburn. I hummed it during a local ice-cream (recommended) refuel at Glynde post office, just by the base of the prescribed path up. Yet perform it how you like, it still didn't account for the *feeling*.

Every stile and fence conspired against me almost to entity-level, making me look cack-handed. I had to nigh on hurl myself over each. The springy turf underboot resented my stride, turning super-springy and sapping my strength. Even the Sussex sun on my back conspired in the high weirdness. Its beams held back at the last moment after their eight minute journey from the nuclear fires of home. Instead, their warmth faltered and died a few feet over my head, forming a chill canopy under which I laboured; a fly confined under an invisible dome.

I carried this personal parasol with me, struggling against the stiff slope. Eight hundred feet later (said the Guide) was a Iron Age camp, excavated by... *blah, blah blah*. The book got stuffed back in my bag, careless of dogearing. More interested in the notion that my path was dogged, I looked back down towards Glynde for the umpteenth time, semi expecting to see a wake left in the sward.

ALTERED ENGLANDS

As before, there was nothing of the kind—bar a certain knowingness to the breeze driving me and events before it. Down below, *'Grecian-style'* St. Mary's church, the stone wyverns outside Glynde Place, even distant Glyndebourne Opera House, spoke of normality—or what passes for it in Sussex. I both didn't believe a word of all this—and yet at the same time had to accept it...

Currently capable of only low wattage duck-and-weaves, I resolved on a simple dash over the brow of Caburn to take me out of sight and thus out of trouble. Feeling like the entire focus of Creation's infinite eyes, I went for it.

Oft-times there were hang gliders atop Caburn's cap; I'd seen them when driving past: gaudy butterflies defacing the scene. Right now they'd have been as welcome as a wench, but I somehow knew—revealed as if in a dream—it wouldn't have benefited me. Something had opened a chasm between me and the world this day and no mere socialising would overcome it. I doubt they'd have even seen me.

'Elf ointment!' said a wicked voice beside my ear—and chuckled. Then it brushed past, no respecter of space or person, and went ahead of me. That breath of passage—again both accepted and rejected by dint of double-think—trailblazed my path in advance—although I didn't yet know it.

Over the hill—well, I didn't reckon *I* was yet, and so mentally girded the loins—over the hill was a whole new rolling harem of green curvature, eventually leading down to Lewes and the River Ouse. *'Bible Bottom'* and Lewes Golf Club said my retrieved, mistreated, guide, then *'Zion in the Downs'*, County Town of East Sussex. *'Lost Galedin'* as per the *'Iolo Manuscripts'*, *'founded by survivors of a drowned land, probably Atlantis'*—which settled the book's hash. I flung the useless New-Age thing away to mislead some other mug punter.

There were precipitous chalk tracks, treacherous stiles and gates, a paucity of unvandalised signs and the usual bag-rat entrancing stuff like the phallic *Lewes Martyrs* Memorial, but I'll spare you the details—as I did myself. Shields raised, warp factor nine, and running essential systems only, I put all pretence aside, acting like the real me. It felt better: more comfortable all round. Nature's wonders passed by without me rudely staring at them. I was a man with a mission. Chapel Hill and then Lewes High Street here I come.

The *White Hart Inn* had an open fire and heated pool. The *Lewes Arms* nearby came with a rave review from a drinking acquaintance. I was prior booked for the one and destined for the other. A bath, a swim, a talent survey and then serious lager abuse. Stuff hiking and the *'Way'*. If my mood or love-life didn't improve before tomorrow, I'd ring ahead to cancel the remaining stages.

The warm water of the *White Hart* swept away all care and lingering doubts. I became again the sleek beast who knew what he wanted and loved what he got—often. The improperly active Downs had the town surrounded but you could still, just about, shut them out. A mere stroll down some of Lewes' distinctive short-cut *'twittens'* was the *Lewes Arms*. The spirit of head-down, no-nonsense, mindless hedonism lent wings to my boots.

It was small, harder to find than expected: a cheese segment end of a building, car-*verboten*, only approached by twittens. You accessed the bar via a hallway like one in some aunty's house. Then an… uncompromising Town coat of Arms—four foot by four foot square—confronted your face before any danger of a beer. It was crowded but not overly so: company, not claustrophobia. Rooms span off the main bar at odd angles: quiet alcoves for those who wanted; a regulars' hurly-burly at the hub. Around the walls were ancient pictures—never mind what they were, I liked their dust. I liked everything. There was even a fire.

'A *Stella*. No, make it two.'

Having once known a Stella I only wished it were her. But cold beer would have to do instead of a hot woman.

The bullet-head barman flicked a look for company, didn't find it, but caught the *'just-do-it'* in my eyes and poured on.

I took the golden glasses to beside the fire, licking my lips. A few feet back from the bar-melee there was space for me at a table. The only other partaker looked like he minded his own business—which suited me. Clad in Downs Country ethnic dress (old *Barbour*, cap and wellies), seated before a mortally wounded pint, he seemed the type to keep his opinions to himself.

Wrong, wrong, wrong.

'I'm here for Bonfire,' says he. It could only be to me.

''Triffic.'

'You don't know what Bonfire is, do you?'

'Nope.'

Despite the lack of encouragement he told me, and despite myself I listened. A whole week of misrule in an English town, centred round Guy Fawkes's brave try: homemade fireworks, processions, subversive tableaux confined to the flames, flaming tar-barrels flung over parapets. You joined your particular Bonfire society at birth and stayed there to journey's end, a wild fraternity that would see you right through thick and thin. It sounded like the idealised *Saarf London* concept of *'he's family, innee...'* I wasn't so keen on outsiders pinching my culture.

'Bit early, ain't you? S'not even November yet...'

Matey wasn't fazed. He scanned the sock-interior-like surrounds. It had got really cosy; like there was only him and me here.

'I like to be around *long* before. To drink up the atmosphere.'

And he did drink up, draining his glass till froth-lace decorated his goatee. Whereupon… it refilled itself, from base right up to rim. He drank again, relishing the replenishment and set down another empty. Then that too did the decent thing.

I let myself accept that the *cosy* thing wasn't pub ambience but that same giant finger from off the Downs—destiny giving me its undivided attention. It was all a bit *urgent* of the scriptwriter upstairs. He could at least have let me make love to my *Stella*.

'Who *are* you?'

His eyes were lively as a fox in a henhouse; oval, naughty.

'A gamekeeper.'

'Yeah, sure...'

'Of sorts.'

We exchanged glances, but not of equals.

'HELP! HELP! HELP ! HELP! HELP! HELP!'

I ought to have guessed and saved my dignity. They couldn't hear me: we were removed. And even if they could there were better distractions than some weirdo hysteric. A proper parade of small arms fire broke out outside.

'Bonfire Society officer's birthday,' explained this 'spirit of the *Barbour*'. *"Lewes Rousers'*. Absolutely illegal, of course. Home-made incendiaries, unlicenced...'

The lovely smoke-and-cordite smell drifted in: take it or leave it.

"Sweet', says he, *"is the smell of powder, in the cause that is righteous'.* So said Guy Fawkes. Top man!'

There was a window for obvious questions; like what *cause*? And why? And so on. But that was just footslogger stuff. Instead, like a sensible fellow, I buried my lips in *Stella*.

He recognised the urge to wisdom and raised his immortal glass to me.

'You're the *game* I'm keepin' at the moment. I've been herding you over the Downs and—oh, slow, slow, *slow...*'

'Sorry.'

He gurned his nut-brown face; the first expression of disapproval.

'Different creed. Keep your repentance. See her?'

A hairy hand singled out a vision by the bar. Petite—you might even say elfin. Sussex-aboriginal. Brunette. Saucy corkscrew curls. Early blooming, probably long-lasting: all cotton-summer-dress and likely lively late nights. Maybe *'Let's stay up all night!'* I was even privileged to overhear her name: *'Elaine...'*

Which sounded sort of... Arthurian.

'Got her,' I confirmed.

'Yours if you like...'

And in a vision he showed me we-two's Lewes future together—something-or-other happiness: modest but tapped into deep roots. Fruitfulness also. Fetching barrels from *Harvey's Ltd.* for the boys' twenty-firsts at the rugby club. The girls' white weddings in a Downs church. Final days with it sussed, looking up at green hills though too feeble to climb them. A *1662* send off at St Michael's, School Hill; my ashes ascending Caburn even if I couldn't.

'Could be worse,' I conceded. 'Or?'

To give him credit, he showed no preference. In my throbbing skull I beheld a black and chrome winebar, the sort of more-me place I'd go. Probably Croydon or up-Town. A peroxide blonde was dancing: a trouser-crowder but brainy with it, going places whilst spreading ripples. Choppy ones probably. I saw the upshot also. An edgy alliance, accumulating *things*. No debates over *Heinz* or own-brand baked-beans there!

Success in Babylon or authentic littleness? To be or half-be?

'Why me?'

He showed me his teeth and they were white and sharp and shiny.

'The Choice, son of man. Everyone has it, without exception. Only you're so brick-thick it has to be shoved right in your mush. But even you understand now, right?

Sure I did, but wasn't going to admit it. I shrugged, real admirable *I'm-in-charge-of-this-mere-meat* stiff upper lip.

'All bar who you are,' I said.

He sighed and peered round, like he could see inside my head.

'Nature abhors a vacuum,' he reproved me—and stretched out a leg.

ALTERED ENGLANDS

I was wrong about the wellies, misled by under-table shadows. What emerged from the moleskin breeks was hairy and cloven. It drummed a frenzied solo on the parquet.

Returning to vertical I still displayed some disbelief.

"*Great Pan is Dead!* he recited, merrily enough. 'Plutarch: *'De Defectu Oraculorum'*. Not a lie, but not the whole truth either. Wounded, he lingers on. And still welcome—in a few places...'

I looked. He wasn't a bad lad—more a friend-cum-fiend. Levelly, older-brotherly, he returned the gaze.

'The big question now,' he laughed, 'is whether he's welcome in *your* life?'

※

Wife number four—all bottle-blonde hair and surgically-lifted clefts—was finding a native to hook up the yacht. Imperious tones from the foredeck suggested success. I left her to it, still residual-sensitive to *memsahib* manners. And besides, the Harbour Bar beckoned. I hadn't had a scotch for *minutes*.

Because the Aga Khan had sailed in that day there were fireworks later, and they made me think of England. These were better, more expensive certainly, but not, I suspect, made with mischief in mind. Let alone love. I missed those in my life.

Here, November didn't bother us. We could still rely on ample sun to further lizard our skin. Wife Four wouldn't compromise re that. I daren't so much as mention Lewes to her. She'd consult lawyers rather than venture that gig, even for a daytrip, and my poor, triple-bypassed, heart wasn't up to combat. Not even in a *righteous* cause.

So, *Bonfire* and Lewes would have to do without me, as they had done, without noticing, every year ever since.

And yet, and yet... as I watched from the deck, seeing rockets ascend to heaven, I did wonder, I admit. Some got there, but others, the more flashy, seemed to expend themselves en route, falling short.

※

17~

FURRINERS

'Oh Wilfred was a Sussex man, a Sussex man was he,
He might ha' bin a furriner, but no sich fool was he,
Says he, 'I'll be a Sussex man, no better men there be!'
So sing hurrah for Sussex men and Sussex by the Sea!'

Arthur Beckett (1872-1943). *'Song O' The Sussex Men'.* 1921.

'*Ut* of my road!'

Ayling shoved by the Farmer with two fistfuls of beer-jugs. His plate-like hands were up to four apiece with ease: no trouble. Two *Barbour*ed shoulders jarred but he spilt not a drop. It was deliberate: a ram. The Farmer had the worst of it and was nigh spun round.

When he returned to view the smile was still upon his face—and that was a relief. The singing had faltered just a sliver but now resumed, lusty style. Fridays was *'Sussex Songs Night'* at the *Selmeston Arms*; something looked forward to, and they didn't want any trouble.

Thereagain it came as no great surprise. The Farmer's face was all curves; born to smiling: its natural state of repose. No one expected ill of him, come what may.

Ayling was seated on the long settle again, packed in with the men he'd gone to school with, who knew him and his father and father's father, back right into the mist. He drank and listened and communed with the songs of his homeland and the blue of his eyes was that of the sky upon the Downs—and just as free of doubt or charity.

'I know a song,' he called. 'And a good 'un. Cop this.'

He had a fair voice, deep-rooted and powerful. It courted—and got—joining in, even though all knew where it was leading.

> *'All folks as comes to Sussex*
> *Must follow Sussex ways,*
> *And when they've larned to know us well*
> *There's no place else they'd wish to dwell*
> *In all their blessed days.*
> *There ant no place like Sussex*
> *Until you goos Above,*
> *But Sussex will be Sussex*
> *And Sussex won't be druv!'*

It both was and wasn't in the spirit of the evening and the Chairman called intermission. The round-singers gladly buried their hot faces into beer. Ayling looked up and *suspected* what he saw.

'Where were it you say you come from?'

The Farmer was easy with answers, though he, no less than all, could tell curiosity from baiting.

'I told you. Brighstone, originally. Born and bred.'

'A?'

'Isle of Wight'

'That's Hampshire.'

'S'right.'

'Overseas.'

'Over Solent, if you like.'

'I bin there,' said Brazier, a nice old boy. He could just remember the real shepherds: out on the Downs half a year, unused to people save for Lewes Livestock Fair and church at Easter. 'A Holiday. Lovely it was! Sunshine all around yer! They got Downs there too. Same as ours.'

'Naturally. They're a geological continuation,' said Moorcock, a Brighton academic. He never missed a *Songs* night and loved tradition—but less so when it got... tense, like now. 'The Solent's only a recent-...'

'They call _us_ 'Overners',' said Ayling, interrupting. 'Foreigners like...'

Moorcock with his Arran sweater and weird-beard was only on the bench under sufferance. He could still be frozen out any time till he stayed put and bred. And he knew it.

It wasn't the only thing he knew. He looked and considered and for the umpteenth time decided against. Ayling wasn't a great one for books: would probably never consult a dictionary of surnames—which was for the best.

'_Overner_'s just a jest,' said the Farmer, and there was proper jest in his voice, despite provocation. 'You don't hear it much now. Only the old 'uns, the stay-at-homes...'

'So why bring yer sheep over here?' said Ayling. 'Ran out of Downs there 'ave you?'

Bluntness, yes—but that was getting real close to _not Sussex_, to rudery: Glasses were being set down.

'There's only so many freeholds and good tenancies,' answered the Farmer, though he needn't have. 'There's them and then Yarmouth and the Needles and the Sea: they can't graze there!'

Ayling drank and—maybe—said '_Should try!_' into his beer.

'Me brother's the oldest,' added the Farmer, still unperturbed, 'so he takes over and I move on. That's okay. I like it here.'

Ayling approved the sentiment but sensed outsiders laying claim to his own. It was deep down, a subterranean feeling, and all the stronger for it.

One good heart tried to defuse the air.

'I saw your flock offloaded at Glynde station,' she said. 'Caught my eye straight away. Makes a change when I sees them on the Downs...'

'Ain't _Southdowns_, are they though?' said Ayling; a statement not enquiry. 'Not special bred to and for here...'

'Near enough,' said the Farmer, even willing to bear aspersions on his flock. 'A Vectis variant of the same stock. They looks a bit different now, granted, but they're kith and kin. They'll do all right.'

Some more information spilled, unsolicited, from Moorcock's brimful brain. 'John Ellman, who developed the Southdown sheep, is buried in Glynde Churchyard, you know. In a lovely classical mausoleum. My partner and I sat beside it only the other day and ate our-...'

'That queer looking Church?' asked Mr Pothecary, a died-in-the-wool Calvinist and patron of Jireh Chapel, Lewes. 'Foreign?'

ALTERED ENGLANDS

'Well,' said Moorcock, perplexed. 'It's got a golden cupola—but, you know, C of E all the same. That was the Eighteenth century fashion. Inside, there's this marvellous Mediterranean feeling of light and-...'

'They don't look a *change*,' said Ayling, and he wasn't talking of churches. 'They don't look the right sheep. Not for 'ere. You keep 'em away from mine.'

There was a sad hush that could have been unpleasant, until:

''Ere, Baz,' said Ayling's neighbour, who was bigger than he and so dared say, 'happen your Dad neglected to 'ave a word with you.' He was grinning as broad as the grille on his tractor (itself the envy of all present). 'Let me explain. You see, Mrs Sheep, she can't... you know...' He shuffled one stiff finger into the receptive tube of his other fist. Pothecary and Moorcock looked away. 'Old Mr Ram, it's he does the business, you see. But he don't roam the Downs tupping: he's kept locked up...'

'Yeah—in a test tube,' said Moorcock, frowning. Unbeknownst to any there, he'd inaugurated a *'Compassion in Farming*' branch at his polytechnic—and no one turned up.

'S'right,' agreed the beefy speaker, enthusiastically. 'Dead handy. Anyhow, Baz, let I put your mind at rest. You needn't fear no interbreeding! Now, them lesbian sheep: that's another matter!'

They all laughed, for they'd come there by boot and bike and four-wheel drive (and 2CV) for a laugh—and had been cheated of it these last few moments.

'Lezzybians?' puzzled old Brazier—who knew full well. 'Didn't they do the Lockerbie bombing?'

'Noooo,' the beefy neighbour mocked. 'You're thinking of the place the Israelis invaded. Back in '82. Sat and shelled Beirut; the capital of Lezzybian!'

'Then what's their sheep doing here...,'—and so on and on.

And though it only occupied a short while till the singing resumed, to Ayling it seemed a lifetime of scorn, personally addressed.

'*Noel! Noel!...,*' Moorcock started up, as mischievous as a sociologist ever got, knowing it would spite Pothecary and the spectre of prejudice.

> '*... Noel! Noel!*
> *A Catholic tale I have to tell!*

*And a Christian song have I to sing
While all the bells in Arundel ring.'*

And though it was not Christmas, those who loved the spirit of it joined in.

*'I pray good beef and I pray good beer
This Holy night of all the year
But I pray detestable drink for them
That give no honour to Bethlehem*

*May all good fellows that here agree
Drink Audit Ale in heaven with me,
And may all my enemies go to hell!
'Noel! Noel! 'Noel! Noel!'*

Good honest laughter followed. Even Pothecary forgot the Reformation and the Lewes martyrs, done to fiery death by *Bloody Mary*. It *was* 19**, after all.

But there were several seasons and centuries operating in parallel in the *Selmeston* that night. Scowling and songless, Bazza Ayling conferred with his.

❈

'**Ayling** : *Trad. Southern shires particular. A descendant of* Aelle *(died 514?), founder of Sussex, the Kingdom of the South Saxons: the* Suth-Seax, *and first paramount King or [Anglo-Saxon]* Bretwalda, *of England. Thus: of Sussex royal blood and lineage.' From* Aelle, *proper name, and* lytling, *Old English, child.'*

'Count the Stars If You Can. Such Will Be Your Descendants'—*A Dictionary of English Surnames'*

Dominic A. Elias *OUP*. 1997 pp 1223/4

❈

ALTERED ENGLANDS

Ayling and his dogs took to the hills and the land was theirs. A glad dawn.

Lewes, *Zion-in-the-Downs*, was just waking below. From the depths of Bible Bottom, up onto Saxon Down and Ranscombe Camp, the light was sweeping in like revelation. Mount Caburn shone under a glorious new day.

With the eye of faith—and Ayling did not lack it—could be seen the sea sparkle at Newhaven. Before that were Firle Beacon of Armada fame and Wilmington with its chalk hill giant, tutor godling of the Weald. Sunlit wonders before breakfast.

His flocks had already reported for work, fattening themselves and close-clipping the sward, making it perfect for a carpet of rampion and milkwort. Thus keeping the Downs as they were. He approved.

King of the hill, monarch of Caburn, Ayling surveyed and the royal blood he was unaware of warmed proprietal. He heard, even if he could no longer understand, whispers from the Dark Age kings, warriors in their dragon-boats standing off Pevensey. They granted him patience even as they fired him up. Time: all was time.

The Lewes Golf Club and A27, mere temporary intruders, could be overlooked. Even the *Didecoi* camp at Southerham was tolerable. They understood; were a—just—acceptable frayed edge to his tapestry. When the gypsies took one of his sheep for a feast he'd shoot a brace of their dogs. If that hint didn't take, the sides of their caravans would be peppered by night. Once a man lost an eye that way. He and his were gone before dawn. Aelle tactics.

Distant hills had other *Southdowns*; far-off flocks: Ayling gave them wary blessing. But closer home, strangers spread. He saw them and somehow all was... marred.

The Farmer's flock of Wightian stock were there from Glynde. Ayling watched them spreading, spreading like a stain. They weren't close, not yet, but coming, maybe. Coming ever closer. If they did, the aggressors, then they'd be sorry. A right royal welcome would be waiting.

※

Straightaway, the Farmer noticed them hobbling. At close of day they were clear outlined against the skyline: shambling: rendered comical.

Sheep were funny things: would stand out in the rain with a tree nearby, drop dead at the drop of a hat or in a gentle grip. Yet, hack their hooves off, even so recent that blood still flowed, and they'd carry on cropping like nothing was amiss. Funny, contrary, creatures.

So there they were, a stoic band like Romans of old. Not a *baa* of protest at fate or their loss, stolidly grass fixated, stumbling crack-limbed from patch to patch, undeterred. A round dozen who'd go no more a-wandering nor grow properly fat: invalids from now on, fit only for quick sale at a loss, or else mollycoddling indoors, their feed brought to them, room-service style.

It was an affront and cruel to boot: insult piled on injury, but he could have ridden the warning. The Farmer wouldn't have let them roam so free in future.

The little packets settled it though. Tied round each fleecy neck was an envelope formed from winter-feed wrapper, now well-stuffed and stained red. The Farmer enquired within and grew wise.

So there it was and there they were. Hoof tips. Nothing had actually been taken from him, nothing stolen, his property was merely... rearranged.

Still and even so, it wasn't a very nice thing to do. Time to have a word with his neighbour.

⁂

'And the word is... goodbye.'

The Farmer lowered Ayling down the shaft. Twists upon the lamb birthing hoop around his neck guided the body past tricky bits until gravity took control. Then the Farmer's straining arm released.

'Down ye go...'

Aelle, blueprint of the breed, would have noticed a man approaching with murderous intent—even a neighbour. The stiffness of his sleeve alone should have shouted *axe!* to Ayling. Fifteen centuries of near-peace had lulled regal seed to sleepiness.

'And fare ye well...'

Now that sleep should be eternal—or so the Farmer devoutly hoped. Though resolute still, he'd no wish to account for axe-play on the lovely Downs. Thoughts of Judgement Day would henceforth be the one thing that could cancel his smile.

Still, that was a chance he'd to take: an unselfish gamble to stay on the Downs with honour. There were those who'd come after to think about. If his kin wanted centuries here as there'd been on the Wight, then it merited some sacrifices—like easy sleep, stainless conscience and maybe eternal damnation—for one small sprig of the family tree.

Sound of the dead man's descent ended in a long postponed splash. The disused (till today) well took Ayling to its heart; a welcome that would last till he dissolved into component parts. No one visited here. No one enquired. Perfect.

Thought of parts reminded the Farmer. He searched in the dark and gathered up Ayling's severed hands. Now was too soon, too easily traced, but years on, when nicely mummified, he'd return them to the Aylings. A surprise parcel in the post for the widow or grown children.

For the Farmer had standards. Justice yes, even murder if really necessary, but stealing? No: never.

It would also help put their minds at rest: after a fashion. And graft on a moral. *'As you sow, so shall ye reap'*. A farming family, of all people, ought to appreciate that.

Only the chalk *Long Man*, prone on Windover hill and oddly illumined by a harvest moon, observed the Farmer leave the scene. He'd looked on, way back, when there had been a holy well, the recipient of votive swords and virgins. Amidst his slow and swirling thoughts, he approved that worship be revived.

Likewise, only Long Man saw the Farmer followed home to his supper.

❈

He was back. A lone conspicuous figure skylined atop Caburn. Black against blue. Very still. Where he'd always stood at close of day, monarch of all he surveyed.

The Farmer stopped in his tracks, did a double-check. He couldn't pretend. There was no mistake.

A void lay between them—not only the valley of the Ouse but a greater abyss—as well as thankful distance. Too far to tell just what he was watching but the Farmer could guess. He stared back.

A flicker, an instant, and suddenly *he* was closer, without ever passing in-between. Still a matchstick silhouette but plainer. The gusting wind did not raise his coat or hair—but most likely both were sodden.

Now he was beside the river, down among his former flocks. Yet though he was amidst them the sheep did not register him. He was no longer *master*.

One further jump might take him to the Farmer's land. It would not be defended. The Farmer had never sought confrontation.

As he turned to go ice slid between his shoulder blades. They clenched, his feet faltered, he was both chilled and burnt by its intensity. Somehow he set off again but that hatred accompanied him all the way, impossible to shrug off.

Without word or backward glance, the Farmer hurried home to warmth and family and dinner, leaving the figure to its hill and lonely dark and cold. Later that night it would rain.

Someone still had the best of the bargain.

※

The Farmer didn't stay to see if his territory was invaded but decency certainly was. Spectral severed hands followed him, cool but active and wondrously dextrous, to invade the marital bed. Happily, Mrs Farmer mistook them for his and he chose not to disillusion her.

'Lord, but you were like an octopus!' she reviewed him later, when breath returned. *'Even better than normal—saucy beast!'*

The Farmer smiled in the darkness and dismissed the presence.

'Boy, you'll have to do better than that...,' he told it and prepared for sleep. The bed, his wife beside him, were cosy and comforting.

What was left of Ayling departed via the keyhole, back to his bitter resting place.

※

He was there again, like every morning and dusk, the would-be topping and tailing of all the Farmer's days.

ALTERED ENGLANDS

Down he came, onrushing from breast-like Caburn's nipple zone, shifting through portals invisible save to him. The Ouse could not delay Ayling, nor the Farmer's fence deter. Within the space of fearing it, he was mere paces off, glaring from the corner of a sheep-pen. Truncated arms were raised: accusation and challenge combined.

The Farmer's only escape ran right past him. Left and right lay the Ouse and A27 and certain death: drowning or collision. Backwards meant mere surrender.

The battlefield was thus selected, the climatic moment come. As in another Dark Age, long before, both indigenous and incomer wanted these fields, but only one could have them.

The Farmer squared his shoulders and set off.

The chill got worse closer to. Energies Ayling required to thwart the tidal pull on him needed leaching from the living. Round him the turf crisped in unnatural frost and the Farmer was subtracted from to have *doubts*.

'*Cold's cheap,*' he told himself. '*It gives in to a jumper*'. He kept going.

Face to face there was no avoiding the eyes that peered out from where no live man went. They held knowledge but couldn't impart it. There were hints though, and none of them pleasant.

The Farmer simply averted his gaze—and suddenly Ayling was only wet boots and soggy corduroy to him. It meant he had to restrict his view, to lose perspective. Slower now, grown cautious, his feet pecked like hens at the downward vista. Ground was still being covered, but at a dawdle, postponing the awful moment.

However, you could look at things another way. So the Farmer did. Like Ayling, he rose again, albeit only with his eyes. Mercifully brief was the arc holding the Ayling vista: drowned-rat, axe-ruined, nothing but soaked suffering. Then came merciful release: the sky: blue, eternal, a reassurance.

The Farmer hadn't had so bad an innings. First the Isle of Wight and now here: he'd gotten to see good things. He had sons: he'd go on come what may. And there was something else. Despite himself, Ayling confirmed it. For good or ill, nothing was just *the end*.

Those glad tidings took him right to Ayling's station. The Farmer could have been by and off with only a shift of stance. But he would not. *Could* not, not if he was to earn his new homeland.

Shoulders collided, as in the *Selmeston Arms*. Dead man's waxed-jacket clashed with that still serving life.

Ayling was inert but the Farmer carried God's animating spark. He and it proved stronger.

'*Ut* of my road!' Farmer told Ayling (dec'd)—and no longer feared.

The ghost was brushed aside.

☸

'More beer!'

'*Monstrous* beers!'

The Farmer was the man with what they wanted: a brimful tray-full, jugs and tankards enough for everyone—for a little while.

Ayling would have brought them grasped in huge hands, more manly-style, but no one commented. The Farmer's ladylike tray would do them.

He sat down at the crowded bench. There was no significant chasm, no *in memoriam* gap. The space was well filled.

'So, beer-man,' said Moorcock, 'start us up one of your Isle of Wight songs!'

He was tonight's elected *Chairman of Song*; a signal honour for one who'd not yet shone a patch on his customary pub seat.

'Yeah,' another seconded, 'we *likes* being on the Isle of Wight!'

That birthed a real laugh all round. That Island's triangular, bushy, nature, its often tropic climes, were supposedly suggestive of another intriguing zone, one altogether more feminine and intimate. The Farmer had earned infinite points in confessing the Islander in-joke.

'I don't know none,' he answered, above the roar, and because they knew he did they liked him all the more. 'But how about this 'un?'

> '*For it's good to live in Sussex, the land o' the brave and free,*
> *Where men are bruff and honest—such men as you an' me;*'

He started—and others carried on.

> '*So if you weren't born in Sussex, whoever you may be,*
> *Then come an' die in Sussex, sweet Sussex by the Sea!*'

ALTERED ENGLANDS

And so, God willing, the Farmer would!

Which conviction let him rise with easy conscience. He crossed over to the window.

Where the Farmer drew the curtain against the sad figure standing outside, forlornly looking in.

☸

JOHN WHITBOURN

ALTERED ENGLANDS

THE STALINSPACE SERIES

✹

INTRODUCTION

When the Polish SF magazine, *'Nowa Fantastyka'* wished to publish the first of this *'Stalinspace'* series in 2000[43] they requested a forward to explain to their readers the oddity of how an Englishman should come to know such things. To introduce the stories I can do no better than repeat my words here...

'For reasons too tedious to relate, I grew up with a close knowledge of Communism far from typical of Englishmen of my generation. By the time of my delayed University years I'd devoured the works of Marx and Engels and Lenin—and the counterbalance of Solzhenitsyn's masterpieces likewise. The definitive, three volume, 'Main Currents of Marxism' by the great Polish scholar, Leszek Kolakowski (who I had the privilege to meet and thank) were well-thumbed items on my bookshelves. Andrzej Wajda's *'Man of Marble'* and *'Man of Iron'* were no strangers to my video machine.

Then, whilst working on an archaeological excavation in the middle of Southern England's Ashdown Forest, the events of the 'Solidarity Summer' of 1980 were day by day avidly recounted round the mealtime campfire, courtesy of newspapers fetched from the nearest shop, a six mile round trip away through the forest. Elsewhere and elsewhen, I heard opinions of events from

---

[43] An honour all the more signal had, like icing on a cake, the promised payment ever arrived.

UK-based Solidarity supporters and Ukrainian nationalists and also perhaps the last generation of Communist true-believers alike. My honeymoon was spent in Brezhnev's Moscow—which was interesting...

In short, the issues being settled, by word and deed, on the far side of the Iron Curtain just seemed... bigger and more important to a certain young Englishman than those on offer back home. I now know different but, as I say, I was young then.

Then, years later and as an author, I started thinking, what if? Post 1989, Communism's 'internal contradictions' are now held to be obvious and inevitable but I don't subscribe to such 'historical determinism' or any other of the relics of Marxism. If God saw fit to throw the dice another way then it's plausible that the—equally unappealing—Capitalist-Disney-McDonalds world culture might have succumbed to its own cancers within—as it still might. Suppose then it was a Soviet civilisation, fossilised circa 1950, never de-Stalinised and increasingly reliant for stability on his divine memory, which finally—in whatever delayed and ramshackle form—reached out into space? In the swirling snowstorm of energies and possibilities that is our life in this universe, nothing is impossible—or so it seems to me.

I thought on. Maybe the heavy hand of totalitarian government could have kept things controlled and pure close into the homeworld, but further out older social forms might well re-emerge to meet new needs—just so long as they nominally tipped their hat to the commissars. Who can say what other arrangements might have been tolerated on the fringes in the long years between visits from home?

To find out, I drafted in the stylish but appalling Slovo dynasty, who repeatedly haunt the fringes of my books, from Renaissance Italy to 1960's Portugal—and, now, icily thriving as ever, standing aloft among the stars.

'Democracy' is the first part of a triptych, comprising three inter-connected glimpses of a alternative future. It is succeeded by 'Oligarchy' and then 'Meritocracy'. I am grateful for the opportunity to present them to a people who have experienced something of the substance of that depicted...'

18~

DEMOCRACY

'*Cadres decide everything*'.

Joseph Stalin. Address to the Graduates of the Red Army Academy, 04/05/Year 18.

The Hit failed. It was an expensive embarrassment to all concerned.

As I later dictated to the Family poet; *'Democracy weakens the predatory faculties'*. He was meant to fashion a statecraft-ode out of that but things got confusing after and he got lost so I never heard it. Grandfather would have approved, I'm sure. Shortened up, he might have had it lasered onto the black walls of Castle Slovo—alongside his all-time great: *'Smite your neighbour (that the stranger will fear you).'*

These glasnostniks must have discussed my death, chatted through the options, maybe even taken a vote on it(!). Their failure was thus, of course, assured.

The laser flick-ball was a newish sort of toy (last Party catalogue but one) and hellish pricey. It was maybe a third of a standard-year revenue off the coal or iron Slovo sub-planet that financed the junior branch that spawned the traitor that hired(?) it. The random generated fire-fields are supposed to give total coverage of a standard prefab conference hall in... well, damn fast. Far too fast to lumber-foot away from. As for the average ship corridor; coverage is even faster: in theory the victim shouldn't even know he's joining History.

However, all this cunning tech is to no avail if you discuss your plan and the icy, frightened whisper of a traitorous traitor reaches my security network. It's no good at all if she's then taken apart and examined for every morsel of information. My people are so good they even put her back together convincing enough to last until the move was made. We knew the time and date and I could sit listening to the Mozart-guy's *Requiem* on my 18th birthday present tape-deck, waiting for the game to start. It was all very elegant.

Consequently, their laser bomb hit a decoy, some prole sufficiently like me to fool a drone's brain. I threw in a couple of my retinue to make it specially convincing, as well as my second best Noble-House, Party-status red cloak. It quite upset some of the more starchy Slovo retainers to see it draped around the prole's unworthy shoulders—before he and it got torched.

The flicker sent out a mission accomplished signal before closing down and all over the ship the conspirators declared themselves. There were some surprising names amongst them; even family and probationary-family. My purpose thus achieved, we went in and started what the golden age dialect and the older hands call a *pepirschina*: a hot purge. It's less considered and surgical than the real thing but, all in all, more fun. Most of the time it was just the straight arrest of shocked little liberals, leavened with a few real *enemies-of-the-people*; genuine elitist glasnostniks. To put some bone in their ideological jelly they'd also got some real men; proper soviets—family or Party trained—and they were good sport. So, right at the tail end we had a decent fight on; a scamper down the corridors and room by room sort of thing.

Well, that's all fine in normal circumstances. *'The steel must be tempered'* as my Grandfather says whenever the body count is accumulating and the Family accountants look more pained than normal.

However, it's like this: the Party-Spacers don't land divided Houses. I wouldn't dream of querying the sense of this policy: I can see there's no merit in exporting civil wars to new settlements. The next Party inspection might be standard years off and Vlad knows what ideologically deviant winning side might have emerged by then. Anyway, that sort of business is evidence of indiscipline, lack of vigilance and all those kinds of bad words. You don't export that either.

Our sensors were old, purchased during Grandfather's young manhood from the remnants of the old Grand Guard Fleet, and we can only give them

ALTERED ENGLANDS

Family-tech maintenance, with all that implies. So, when it was reckoned there was maybe 500 of these degenerates holding out, plus or minus 100 can be tacked on. The analysts postulated them as mostly Glasnostnik cadres plus families and sub-family retinues with some suborned ethnic mercenaries. They also had some bits and pieces of reasonably heavy stuff and the luck to be holed up in a tight corner of the Family transporter with heart-warming fields of fire and stacks of cover.

My second-rank cousin, Bolshevik 30th conference Anti-neo-Kulak, Slovo, went in first with my third best unit of Sikhs and came to a horrible end despite all the finest fieldcraft. The traitors seemed to emerge from all over and mowed down the rushes or picked off the pauses. It was a strikingly appropriate metaphor for such vermin's position in society, said the Family poet—the bourgeois democrats and so-called reformers lurk in the dark and neglected nooks and crannies of human life and emerge to strike down orthodoxy from behind. I hate him being present at battles for his eye misses nothing and he might note my odd second of non Soc-Stoicism. Sadly though, my Father liked him so he couldn't have a nice accident.

I was waiting, back in the safety of an only 95% fire-free-potential corridor, watching Cousin Eighth Five-Year-Plan Collectivisation Slovo go down in flames, with, I must admit, reasonable cheerfulness. But then I noticed the glances of senior Family folk upon me and saw, behind their eyes, the great black shape of Castle Slovo and the judgement waiting within. Because of the ancestry, because of the place that ancestry got me, certain things are expected...

My squire slid me into some heirloom battle armour, all tiny reflector mirrors and age-old burns, and I went in with a mixed unit of Family retinue, Jews and Sikhs. We got thirty metres further than cousin Bolshevik 30th conference Anti-neo-Kulak Slovo (he was still smoking in situ) but that was just for form's sake. We walked back, though that cost a few extra, thus keeping the Family's good name.

'Tucked in too snug,' said the mercenary tactician Grandfather had hired to come with me on voyage. He'd been with us, off and on, since his Bar Mitzvah and, given the Old Man's personnel methods, must therefore have been both good and lucky.

'You're not paid ten grain pods to state the obvious,' I replied as the minions unbuckled me. 'What else?'

He pointed his black beard down towards the enemy and smiled.

'I see an impossible position, my Lord. I see a nice mix of arms and plenty of powerfeed facilities. I see desperate men with their dependants. I see textbook multi-interlocking fire-fields. That's the thing about inter-ship fighting, my Lord; you can actually get stalemates.'

He turned to face me again and turned off the smile. 'They won't let us land,' he concluded.

My strategist, another old Slovo Family hand, looked aggrieved. That was his field to pronounce on, it was he who could speak on the wider aspects of things.

'We will not be permitted to land,' he said, as though the news was new, 'if this nest of vipers remains unpurged. The Party will allot the fief to another Noble House and your Grandfather will not be pleased at the loss of face.'

'And your loss of face,' said Volodya, my fat old, half pure-Soviet blooded, personal advisor, 'will probably be actual—and engineered by laser.'

He's been around so long and earned so many points (and more importantly, remains so useful) that he can say straight things like that. Aside from that, I had no grounds on which to disagree. Childhood recollections of being forced to watch my twin half-sisters' execution sauntered through my mind. Things like that ever remained a distinct possibility unless I could clamber up the Family league tables and get near the top. These counter revolutionary filth were hindering that process.

I loosed off a couple of wild shots down the corridor in their general directions to show the way my thoughts were moving.

'And so?' I asked with a snarl.

'There's only one thing for it,' said Volodya brutally. 'We've got to get a mortgage.'

☸

'Are we ready?' I concluded, looking round the full Council. They all nodded obediently. 'Right; patch them in.'

Volodya flicked the monitor on and the Party Fleet Captain appeared in all his chilly glory.

'Sub-Lord Electrification 3rd Conference Slovo,' he says, 'Fraternal Greetings.'

ALTERED ENGLANDS

Now, that was nonsense, for I am to he what my boot-shine is to me, but I replied properly. There is a lot of this pretend in the world we have constructed.

'I have received your request,' he goes on, 'and it is not beyond the realms of possibility. Our costing of your requirements is a shade over 3000 standard credits—or twelve-fold of official exchange rate if you wish to use local currency such as the Slovo-Rand. As an additional service, I can also offer the wiping of the relevant log sections for an additional 125 credits.'

Hiding my horror deep down out of sight somewhere, I looked at Volodya and he indicated we should accept the lot. We were talking such irresponsible, fantasy, sums that it felt surprisingly easy to pass the message on.

'Okay,' I said (okay, admit it: croaked) to the monitor. The Party man smiled like it required splitting his skin.

'Excellent, Sub-Lord,' he says, 'We suggest a model seven year mortgage, funding as per details currently being fed to your Info-tech team—plus an initial two year profit reversion guarantee on proceeds accruing from our destination: all to be secured on your estates on Slovo Prime and Sigma. Happy?'

Again Volodya shrugged (or part withdrew his head into his body) suggesting that I should be joyous or whatever.

'I understand that this is your first time away from home,' said the Captain, mock social. 'Your first Family undertaking, so to speak. How doubly unfortunate therefore, that these difficulties should have arisen.'

'Quite so,' I said, recalling my youthful Soc-Stoic training.

'And yet, ultimately, how educational it will be,' this silk-arsed spaceman greased on. 'One day you may see this time as the foundation of a more... spacious era.'

'Quite.'

'However, at this point Sub-Lord Slovo, I'd like to bring on a third party who, I'm told, has just tapped into our exchange-...'

'Cut it!' shouted Volodya at the Family-tech people standing round the side of the Council room—but it was too late. The shiny, virtuous face of some minor cousin Slovo (the shame!) now occupied half of the screen, side by side with the Party Captain. Just looking at a Glasnostnik makes me feel sick; they effect me worse than believers.

'Our funding credentials are being fed to you at this moment,' he smarmed. 'I offer 110% of whatever has been agreed for a comparable package plus shipment to any suitable, off-lane frontier planet.'

'Hmmmm,' said the Captain appreciatively. 'What do you say to that then, Sub-Lord Slovo?'

'One-one-five per cent,' answered Volodya, taking over the negotiations given the gravity of the moment. 'Plus our guarantee of no memory-drone ejection, containing full records of your criminal fraternisation with anti-Party elements.'

I couldn't help a certain dislocation in the old breathing rhythm—never having heard anyone threaten a Partynik before—let alone a Spacer aboard his own ship.

The great man paused, reflected and then pressed on.

'We could very probably torch the drone on ejection,' he said, 'or linger here and search at our leisure. It is true that we're on-lane but the chances are still rather against its escape and eventual retrieval. Still, you have disturbed me, I will grant you that. Tell me, fat-man, are you part Russian, real *Old-Earth*?'

Volodya nodded proudly (his father went there once for a conference) and the Captain took due note.

'I haven't heard the accent for many years now,' he said, 'and I find your 115% equally impressive. Any response to that, Glasnostnik?'

That blonde vision was sweating a bit and consulting with people over his shoulder—a good sign perhaps, but maybe they do that about every little thing.

'123%' he said eventually, turning back to the screen.

'I'm informed by my analysts that you cannot top that, Sub-Lord Slovo,' announced the Captain. 'Your credit lines appear exhausted...'

A serpent of commendably controlled panic slithered round the Slovo Council chamber.

'... unless, that is, you ante-stake the 18% inheritable portion of your mother's dowry ship, *Iskra-in-London*—but that may take very considerable explaining within your Family...'

'It will be explained,' said Volodya, swiftly. The Party Captain looked down at some computational device we could not see.

'And you thereby triumph,' he said at last. 'I can see no feasible counterbid in your opponent's financial portrait. I take it that we do business, Slovos?'

I shouted 'Yes!' partly through relief, partly to drown out the shriek and babble coming from the traitor's side of the monitor screen. Blondie was making some kind of emotional appeal and other heads kept hoving erratically into sight. Then somewhere in the Party Ship someone hit a switch and cut them out.

'The documents are coming down the line to you right now,' said the Captain, once again attempting his *smile*. 'And as good fortune would have it, we possess the facilities to hardwire the details of our transaction onto your life-card. I will make the necessary arrangements to have that done but meanwhile...'

The screen went dark and a great, deep klaxon, like the voice of *Stalin-of-the-Ages*, commenced its roll. The Family Council and I sat tight, thinking our own thoughts, listening to the hollow booming of bulkheads and emergency doors as the rebels' section of the ship was first isolated; then bled of air and its contents spat into cold space.

'I am, it seems, now the economic equivalent of a prole or Neo-mus,' I said directly to Volodya. 'Aside from my title, the clothes I stand in and the gun at my side, what am I left with?'

'What more do you need?' asked Volodya, wide-eyed. 'For Vlad's sake, you're a Slovo! That name's good for help or revenge on ten thousand planets. We're still breathing, boy—that's all that can be asked for. Don't have a breakdown on me now please.'

'I'll try...' I no longer got hot blooded about (private) references to my little lapses. Nerve trouble was just one of those things.

'Try hard,' replies Volodya, pressing on mercilessly. 'Wait till we're off-ship and I can cover for you. Up here we're under the all-seeing Party eye and being weighed in the balance—like with this trouble with the cargo...'

'Is there trouble, Vlady? First I've heard of it...'

'Wanted to allow you to rally a bit, drink a bottle, visit the wives and that. You might be a bit one-thing-at-a-time just now, after losing your capital. Yes, there's fair trouble: started after the *enemies of the people* got spaced. They knew there was something going on but not what. We've lost three pacification teams down amongst them—though judging by energy issue monitors, one of them's holding on.'

'Anything we can do to get them out?' says I.

'Not really,' replies Volodya, screwing up some folds of face in annoyance, 'not economically. They're North-Amer ethnics anyway; we've got plenty more.'

'Okay, so what do you recommend?'

'I don't. It's time to earn your ship-key, boysie.'

'Oh...'

'Don't worry, I'll veto anything too stupid.'

'No you won't,' I said, flush-facing and all the words coming most natural. 'Master-servant; servant-master—understand? Please do understand, Vlady: I know you're a childhood memory and all that, but... well, you can't breathe empty space any more than a Glasnostnik: take my meaning?'

Volodya smiled in wreathes, clearly proud of something.

'You keep on passing the tests your Grandfather set,' he wheezed. 'Congratulations; you're still in charge.'

☸

So, I have words with people, feeling just a bit more tigerishly Slovo than before. I had to spend yet more future-money, inducing minor Party spacers into viewing **WHAT IS TO BE DONE** (I actually put that Lenin reference in when talking to them and must have clicked) in the same manner as me. At the best of times, when you're in flight nothing can be done without these insects and the lowest of them acts like a Noble House warlord. It's them who allocate us our compartments and lock us in. We have to ask permission if we want to get out to visit anything but immediate Family quarters—as today when SORTING OUT the cargo; which is my own property for Vlad's sake!

Anyhow, they provide guides cum escorts all along the twisty corridors and stairwells of the mighty ship. Up, way, way above us is where they live and work; down below is where our fleet of atmosphere craft has been mothballed the last six standard-months. In between is room for 1000 times us and Steel-man knows what else.

An interesting point—I notice that they always have their own security when they take us walkies: more than adequate quantities of hungry looking types. Now: is that for fear of us, or something else I wonder? It got so that I reckoned they didn't really know the full info about what they were flying. I mean, it predated them all, a living relic of the *Outreach Time* when the Party flexed its muscles and spread the word off-planet. There was years and room enough for the ship to have plenty secrets. For example: legend (which is worth nothing, I know) says they just lose individuals they don't like and let them wander the rest of their life in the dark—till they fall down something or whatever. It could even be true.

Generally though, they leave us to get on with things and don't interfere; seeing us, I suppose, as just slightly superior freight. They would have even landed the triumphant Glasnostniks had their hit on me succeeded—the task being just to ferry some stuff about and spread the Stalinspace frontier. If they didn't feel inclined, they wouldn't enquire about the type or quality of the merchandise being landed. I'd heard that often: the Party isn't just one big thing; it's *lots* of big things with occasionally different ideas. That's why Earth-Central need to purge, more or less random.

After about an hour's walking, we ended up in the shadow of a pretty big Lenin statue (1000 metres maybe) lying on its side. Come to that, it looked like the one my 3rd sequential, 2nd ranking, brother bought so he could call his fief planet civilised—except this one had a hat.

'This'll do you,' said the Party tech in charge, indicating a stadium-sized floor hatch alongside. 'I can give you a standard hour. After that a new man comes on monitor duty and he'll have to be paid to be unobservant as well.'

I said okay and set my people to work as soon as the tech somehow started the hatch to slide.

It was like looking down from my favourite atmosphere craft; down-side was a sort of landscape spread out before me, taking up a whole section of ship curvature. If any of the proles had been so-minded, it would have taken them two light periods to walk from side to side (a handy deterrence-to-revolt sort of distance). Of course, in practice, they didn't have leisure for such antisocialness, being too busy trying to scratch life out of the materials provided (such scarcity being part ploy, part economy).

I could just make out little groups of dwellings and those horrible temporary *mosques* they always throw up (the right word) and maybe, just maybe, little dots that were crowds of them up to something.

Last indications were that the American pacification team were still hanging on down there, so I let that general area have the first fire sweep—to put them out of their misery (and prevent the proles getting their horny hands on too much hardware).

After that I let the artillery boys pretty well compose their own tunes so as to spread the **TERROR** as wide and random as only low level intelligences can do. When it was reckoned we were approaching two per cent kill-rate (more than eight thou smoking meat units would apparently upset the eco-balance down below), I also had a selection of the *god-houses* fired to make a point and maximise the social trauma. Oh yes—and we tried out some of the vacuum bombs Central Slovo research had recently launched at Prime-Planet main auction. Later on I could commission an effect analysis for sale at next year's weapons party. Just now, however, it would have been impolitic to prod around downstairs; feelings ought to be running high.

Since every tale must have a moral (or, to *Golden Age* it: practice must be related to theory), the finale was a pamphlet burst, in sufficient quantity, with sufficient spread, to reach most of the historically retarded wretches below us. Rather than use a standard-form or leave it to our poet, I'd composed the thing myself—and just by grunting, Volodya had approved it.

I left in the usual preamble from *Stalin-of-the-Ages* about the need for class vigilance and far-sighted perspective and all that stuff. Then, in my own words (*Golden-Aged* by computer correction), I said they'd better shape up before planet-fall or else we'd not be let off—and I was *expelled* if I was going to ship the whole crowd back for nothing. Basically therefore, we were talking an off-loading 30 kilometres up situation—in which case they could still serve history/Party as sky-falling fertiliser on the new world allotted them (me). Then, more conciliatory-wise, I hinted they'd *'clearly'* been incited by agent provocateurs, reactionary elements etc. etc. So, they could redeem themselves in the Party's eternal eye by delivering same up for swift class justice: delivery being expected by planet-fall plus one: say two thou *enemies of the people* being sufficiently convincing repentance.

Then I ordered (well, asked) the hatch closed and left the cargo to it.

I've never quite got rid of the paradox feeling thing about the hard line we take with our charges but, like the Party teaches, I suppose it's only suffering that makes a prole a prole—hence our Historic sympathy for them. It makes a kind of sense if you concentrate.

ALTERED ENGLANDS

Back home, Volodya said I'd done okay. Father or Grandfather would have been more... robust, but moderation in youth, he conceded, was sometimes a good sign.

❂

If we were alone in the Universe (and we're working on it), planet-fall would be a joyful, festive sort of thing. After you've been cooped X standard months at the mercy of the Party-Tech spacers, it cannot fail to be nice to zoom out over a world-curve and see a real dawn or whatever. What double-joy then, when that world is both terraformed and yours!

However, given the RAGE-war's been a thing since Vlad knows when, every move outside fortress world perimeters or transport-space bubbles, is a bit fraught. Being incompatible (of course) and in competition (it seems), we bust their home worlds and they bust ours. Or, even worse, they hang around places we're prone to go and liquidate new arrivals fresh out the bubble. It used to be called an *ambush* though the parallel's not quite strict.

Now, whilst the Party-tech have a lot of leeway and loopholes for a bit of Kulak-ish private enterprise, they're prone for a purge if they don't establish *some* humanity on the designated target. It's a question of *the greater mission* and all that. Accordingly, at the final briefing they tell us that once the transport bubble bursts and the Slovo Fleet is flying, they'll hang about for a decent while. That way they'll be around to try cope with any RAGE presence that might have sneaked in. There's no nicer thing, one told us, than to cauterise a helpless RAGE colony to make room for your own kind. It makes you feel part of the *Species/Polit* process.

Of course, the same could happen to us in due time. It's like this: we get settled, our escort departs and then one fine day a RAGE sponge-ship arrives, packed with its own colonists. Then we get fried or eaten or whatever it is they do with us; right down to the last prole-brat.

These are not nice thoughts to ponder, even sitting poised in your own ancestral atmosphere-fighter (all patched up and temperamental, but painted blood-red and cared for), waiting to acquire your primary governorship. There all are sorts of stories about what RAGE do to their prisoners. No one really knows of course, but in a funny way that only makes it worse.

JOHN WHITBOURN

The proles took three days to load onto freighters, shepherded about by the Party-Tech opening and closing doors, killing the lights and starting slow, noisy, air-bleeds. The masses then get the message and shuffle off to where we want them to be. It gets a bit tight and stuffy in the freighters once loaded but that's both energy efficient and useful. It's conducive to class solidarity too (so the Family text books say—but they're full of dry humour) and also hinders them organising anything.

Meanwhile, all the freighters and family ships were serviced, tooled up and programmed to fly in one of the set patterns that the Slovo Tacticians (retainers born and bred: one doesn't trust mercs with such stuff) dream up. Sometimes you get the odd decent pilot who objects to the pre-planned formation discipline; who says they'd do better letting initiative flourish. This is doubtless true if style-flying/fighting was all you had to worry about. Just as important however is keeping your tech-people on a tight rein. Imagination in one thing leaks over into others. They might start thinking about individual flair in more than just flying. I hate it when such people start in on such questions—it's a shame to lose them.

Anyhow, the great day dawns (sort of) and we strap up and wait.

Aside from the major rainbow and atmosphere friction effects, the main sign of a transport bubble bursting over a live planet is a sound like the god-thing on a gong. You don't get to hear it on board but it was kind of challenging to imagine it going as all the crucial red lights suddenly came on.

Now, piloting is something I like to do for myself (though a grey-maned old vet sits beside me just in case—Slovo bloodstock is too valuable to risk overmuch), and Grandfather had arranged for me to do it well (or face Family demotion). So, I reckon I was one of the first to hit lower atmosphere at reasonable acceleration and so among the first to see the RAGE thing.

After that I didn't see it for a fair while since I was nigh tearing the wings off with some special diving. Behind me though, I was oh-so conscious of the great golden globe and the daylight stars it had made of some of my formation.

The intercom was going wild so I turned it off. Nobody would be listening to me for a while anyway. With the RAGE thing occupying a fair section of the sky, it's possible to forget considerations like Slovo and Party loyalty.

Thus, my first look at *my* new planet was pretty perfunctory. Thereagain, you see one bit of a terraform-standard and you've more or less

ALTERED ENGLANDS

seen it all. This was to be a grain world, 95% prairie, with all the lumps and bumps levelled out. It being a Party as opposed to Free-Corp bought, eco-terraform prog, I'd expected a few rough edges, so to speak, and soon saw them in the form of far more mist and fog that you'd want or expect. Still, with goldie on our tail, it could have sported sulphur volcanoes and I'd have barely have noticed.

I exaggerate. The RAGE thing (ship? machine?) wasn't on our tail. After cutting an appallingly quick flash-and-beam swathe through my little fleet, it had spotted and engaged the Party ship. Or maybe the Party ship bravely engaged it; I don't know or much care. By that time I'd calmed down to a passable skim speed over the (my) endless flatlands and was able to sit back and enjoy the fight.

Actually, ship to ship violence is, of necessity, short stuff. The relative movement, speed and vulnerability factors turn it into a spectacle suitable only for machine audiences. All I could ascertain was that they'd made a pass, exchanged compliments and then limped hurriedly on.

Now, on *our* side it was mainly the computers in charge, assessing what had been dealt out and received and making pretty pressing recommendations. The RAGE thing, though, was a puzzle. From what little was known (or passed about), normal RAGE ships look like they've been grown rather than made. However, our attacker was regular and lovely and golden, like an idealist's idea of an apple; so maybe we weren't shooting at anything *alive*. If so, the fact there was nothing illogical at the end of their chain of command might give us that useful shade of advantage. On the other hand, the Party ship, like so much of the stuff we muster, was more than long past its prime...

I put my ship's internal comms back on and got an instant flood of reports and analyses to the wordy effect there was a stand-off upstairs. The two great beasts, Party-ship and RAGE-fruit were maintaining orbital speed and keeping the planet between them. I suppose neither *knew* what joys the other was packing and didn't fancy another dose of anything HOT.

'They don't like each other,' confirmed Volodya from his specially widened seat at the side of the bridge. 'They've both got serious love-bites.' I took this to be a pleasing sign I was getting to think like him.

Our judgement might have true—or maybe not. Nobody's ever seen a RAGE or, if captured, escaped back to report. We trigger off their suns if we find one or, sometimes, selectively, *hellburn* them off each planet from afar.

Close up, ships and colonies get fried as speedy as can be before they do it to us. Whichever way, not much is left to examine.

All that's safe to say is that we can hurt them as much as they hurt us—which is a relief considering how much more tech-advanced they could have been. Less happily, the rumours are that they're a spot more committed to their work than us—which is hard to credit...

This golden thing though, was displaying caution, tracking the Party ship (or other way about) round and round my planet. It looked more or less beautiful above us, glinting and twinkling in the sun—but then I recalled no human hand ever touched it and unsympathetic eyes (if applicable) surveyed its launch. Suddenly I liked it a great deal less and the human ship so much more. To reinforce the human bond-feeling thing I turned on the main intercom system again.

A lot of piled up messages came through in babble: *Historic Inevitability* was a black hulk (and Cousin Glorious Achievement, 75th Conference a cinder within it—ho ho), the *Kim Philby* was 10%'ed and afire, the planet-fall Master had lost sight of the merc carriers *Dutt-Palme* and *Burgess* plus a prole freighter etc. etc.

This all got cut—like with a knife—by a Party-ship communication using the override facility they build into everything. Vide-link was even provided (not a normal courtesy) and I saw the Captain and the Ship's full Inner Soviet. Some of them looked a bit scratched.

'Slovo,' says the Captain, briskly, cutting all the proper *Sub-Lord* politeness business, 'I can inform you that this form of RAGE phenomenon has been encountered on two previous occasions. Proven destruction options narrow down to a close proximity approach and closest encounter full armament volley. At the same time we cannot afford another fire exchange like the last. We therefore have to maximise approach and escape speed.'

So I says 'Check, Comrade Captain' and wonder briefly what other info titbits they have in the Party access only archives—things that *I* need to know.

'Are you in visual with it, Slovo?'

'Sure.'

'Then stay in our communication shadow: we may as well go in for the rush now.'

'Makes sense,' confirmed Volodya softly. 'The power curve projections must dip pretty swift, whereas the RAGE thing..., well, that's-...'

ALTERED ENGLANDS

'Anyone's guess,' I interrupt, culling the spiel of obvious stuff and holding down the little 'interference' silencer we'd rigged on the comm control; thus getting some reasonably plausible privacy. 'So; we cooperate?'

Vlady wobbled his head.

'Why not, my Lord? Unless, that is, we want to fight it ourselves—and that I cannot recommend.'

I didn't mind the rebuff; this was inner, *inner* Family tuition, when almost anything went—even the evaluation of Party words. I let the Captain back in.

'We require route specs for a type 2 Dreadnought standard flank pass: two standard minutes time: 100k proximity,' he says.

'Do it,' I relayed to Volodya, bypassing the on-duty Family navigator and hitting the privacy switch again. 'But patch in...,' furious mental calculation with serious consequences, 'say, 3% critical error on closest approach.'

I was very proud of them all—not a tremor on any face. And you have to hand it to Volodya: surviving terms with Grandfather and Father had taught him things—not many! If I'd initiated self-destruct he'd have carried on just the same. It leads me to think our Family bank balance of fear is good enough for a few generations of influence yet.

Meanwhile: 'Flight path on way,' I said, cleaning the line to the Captain. 'We'll keep you and target in proxy contact. Good luck! Long live the Party!'

He didn't even say thanks or goodbye but cut the line and set off. We (sort of) saw it on visual as the white streak of the Party Ship rounded our horizon at max-accel—and hit the RAGE thing head on.

'Did they get to fire?' I asked the Bridge analyst, mostly to keep them busy. 'Or was it a straight ram?'

'Ram, my Lord,' says the young officer, he and all the team—fourth generation Slovo-ites minimum, smiling away, proud to be part of the achievement. We'd just killed their equivalent of the old god-person—a big deal—but their shock had been overcome. So now I knew they were mine.

I slowed the ship right down so we could watch the two great craft tumble down in a lover's embrace (or, to be boring, mutual death-grip), freely exchanging the elements for a really good nuclear inferno. It was kind-of dawn (or maybe dusk, I forget the details) and that made it really scenic as the atmosphere slowed them down into what seemed like slow-motion. The lower they came, the wilder the radio bands went, but I still managed to get through to one of our heavy-weapons craft. A baby-nuke on their eventual crash point would nicely screw up the remaining evidence in case next year's relieving Party Ship stuck its nose in too closely.

The spiral of black smoke looked okay and I could see the new Family poetess was getting inspired (such *foundational* events was what she was tolerated for). It wasn't the kind of story that could ever get outside-wise but already I had fond dreams of league promotion at the next Family appraisal night. Being cautious, it was now much less likely I'd ever be *culled* (negative scoring three consecutive or four out of five years). Thoughts like that were *so* much better than any mere once in a lifetime *view*.

'As a matter of interest,' says Volodya, already uncapping a bottle and browsing one of his old 'books', 'did the Captain ever get round to hardwiring your life card?'

I took the craft up to top speed in celebration at the sheer... whatever of it all.

'No, Vlady,' I reply, grinning. 'He was going to have it done during the official handover.'

'Ah well,' he answers, taking a mega-swig (it was that greasy prole-stuff, *Long-Live* spirit), 'dead men redeem no mortgages...'

☸

Apart from the mist, our 'afternoon-shift-before-a-festival' job of a terraform prog had also given birth to howling storms out of nothing-in-particular. Once the proles were offloaded, their first job was to dig themselves sunken huts. Otherwise day two or three would see me with no one left to do the surplus-value producing work. Simply not on! Family people either sheltered in the ships or else set to, wrapped in furs and rags, on their provided prefabs. Then, when we could venture out and the prole bodies were cleared away, before the seeding or anything, there were important preliminaries to attend to.

The proles were given a standard-day free and those who cared or had the strength, arranged the 'Neo-Kaaba' thing they always do. They build it, then they worship it, I think. Volodya says it's not that simple but who cares? Actually, technically speaking, that sort of thing is all *enemy of the people* stuff but we were a long way from Party-Prime and there's no peace if you don't permit it.

Meanwhile, my construction squads used up a lot of our fuel reserves (so, hard times and cold nights to come) in putting up the prefab Stalin (blessed be his name etc. etc.). I sat and watched by candlelight as, 300 metres aloft, the flyer topped it off by lowering the hat on.

It was only a standard pose but I'm only just starting out and can't afford flashiness. Besides, the mirror-gold effect cost plenty extra and was a nice metaphor—or so the Family ideology team had advised me. Supposedly, everyone passing would see themselves as a tiny facet of the *Great-Leader-of-the-Ages*—which, of course, they are, I hasten to add. Maybe that's why the higher Party people wear the same kind of sunglasses—all glitter and dazzle. A nice theory but, like all the ideology stuff, it *'loads no guns'* as Grandfather says.

Then, illuminated by flares and what spotlights we could muster, the proles were rounded up (their demanded quota of fifth columnists being surrendered and LIQUIDATED) and we had the election. It's absolutely required and anyway, the distinguishing mark of a civilised, established Soc-system planet.

There was only one nomination for Under-Party, Planetary General Secretary. I was elected unanimously.

JOHN WHITBOURN

19~

OLIGARCHY

Or

A LITTLE KNOWLEDGE IS A DANGEROUS THING

'It is time to realise that of all the valuable capital the World possesses, the most valuable and most decisive is people...'

Joseph Stalin. *'Problems of Leninism'*. Year 09.

For a while he thought that what he needed was a handgun. Watching the sheer number of them strapped to full-citizens walking past his window bench in Worker's Rest-Halt 82, probably planted that wild idea. But when he wasn't in panic mode, Hashem-Joe knew, had always known, that a gun was about as unobtainable as safety. Nowhere in Castle-zone, in New-Joburg City, in all of Slovo-Prime, sold guns. True, they did sort of percolate down, by permission only, through Party and Noble-House channels, but Hashem-Joe was cultures and centuries—any kind of distance you like, from proximity to *those* lively nerve endings. He was in the same position as the lowliest neo-Muslim field-hand out in the primary industry food zones, having no contacts; no favours to pull in. Owning a gun, even if he *found* one or the god-thing dropped one on his head, would have been a death sentence for him—and he already had one of those. Slovo Noble-house liked (maybe encouraged) a bit of illicit exchange at the distribution terminal's end. Presumably it gave them excuse to rough-purge anti-social elements now and again, and helpfully identified sweep-targets at the same time. The sort of non-comrade with the spirit to arm up was the sort that should talked to—and maybe dealt with—after all.

So, he suppressed that particular security wish/ambition and tried to think of more useful things. If his problems were too numerous to shoot or stab (he still had his slum-knife) away, then maybe there was somewhere he could hide; really burrow in, before the New-Joburg residence permit got *looked into* and new bribes were needed.

But there wasn't anywhere really, for, with their centuries of practice, Slovo-House and the Party whose franchise they held (clutched, embraced, half-strangled) had tied things up too tight. So, when the Rest-Halt staff noticed he was sipping his *Long-Live...* spirit and not downing it, not braindeathing before another twelve standi-hour shift, like the place and drink was intended for, and when they accordingly had the pleasure of chucking him out, Hashem-Joe wasn't really sorry. It gave him the excuse to stop tormenting himself with notions of escape.

Outside, exposed to the polluted grey-green sky and the eyes of persecutors, he felt, more than ever, atom-small and alone. It was a bit like the *tide-of-History* thing he'd been taught in Worker-school—but less comforting. There was no purpose he could see in what he was going through now, no *'progressive'* charge or impetus to it. Being one of the small percentage of units inevitably ground up by random events turned out to be less tolerable when it was your turn.

Of course, he could adopt a fatalistic attitude and let matters freewheel—but that was a Neo-mus cultural trait and he'd spent all his conscious years trying to shake that and properly Sovietise himself.

In and around shift-change the crowds in Castle-zone got really thick as people tried to fit in shopping or hit the drink. Hashem-Joe flowed with the crowd, in and out of the narrow shanty streets, trying to look like he was more or less involved in normal life. If they found him, well, they found him and that would be that—but he wasn't going to make it any easier for them. Yet really he wasn't going anywhere: just killing time till they killed him...

Then everything stopped and all the proles and shop-people and everyone stood still, watching as a fleet of ships cleared the black, glassy top of Castle Slovo, up and up to an awaiting transport bubble.

So the word had been true. The Family was stretching forth a limb, sending out Prince Electrification 3rd Conference Slovo, with everything he could finance and muster, to do or die on a new world.

Some of the ships were centuries old and looked a bit tired of life but it was still a stirring sight. Hashem-Joe derived a wonderful, reviving thought from it. Princes, it suddenly occurred to him, were not the only ones capable of risking all on one dice throw...

☸

'I very much doubt it,' said the Lower-court retainer sarcastically, before Hashem-Joe even had much chance to say anything. 'And forget the Sov-style stance: I've seen the real thing.'

And that cut Hashem-Joe (who, after all, was only 13) right down to size. He'd spent his last tenth-Rand to get even this far into Castle Slovo precincts. All around there was the inferno of trade and the crackle of exchange going on—and he was just nothing, with no real merchandise and about one second to try to sell it in.

'Information!' he started, down-mouthed.

'Buying (don't make me laugh) or selling, peasant?'

'Selling.'

'Play the vocals then, let's hear it.'

Suddenly, Hashem-Joe knew his tale was just... life, and the Slovos would back-sell it to the slums for circa... nothing, and he would be tagged, handed over and... they would *liquidate* him.

Yet at the same time he heard himself gabbling his last possession: which showed he was tired of the chase or distrustful of his reasoning—or something.

'My Papa—well, step-Papa—was torched in the Club Ivanov, two+ standi-days ago and word is it's a thorough, not a surgical, so they'll want me too, and I reckon it's them Splendid Ovations, expanding and moving in nearer the Castle and doing debt collecting (Papa owed *everyone*). Or maybe the Purity

Sejm is reviving—'cos Papa drank a deal and injected things—or maybe it was something to do with him being a Spacer or-...'

His voice hadn't finished vibrating the airwaves before the guard was away, up and walking, stony-faced and stiff-legged, his gauntlet gripping Hashem-Joe's arm like a precious possession.

Then there was a succession of Slovo *apparatchiks*, each one further up and in, who'd listen to just a taste of Hashem-Joe's data before referring him on like he was contagious. And it was so strange and drug-dream-like, and Hashem-Joe now so far into the obsidian heart of Castle Slovo with no way out, that he ceased to be frightened. Neither the *Splendids* nor the *Sejm*, nor all the gangs and movements implausibly combined, would dare breathe if Slovo interests said otherwise. For the time being, strange to relate, he was safe with these most unpredictable and dangerous of people. Indeed, his previous terror had jumped onto the back of others now (and how well he recognised the sight of it), for the Slovo men looked at him (or perhaps not exactly *him*) in awe and didn't want to hear him speak—not, that is, until he reached the lawn.

Hashem-Joe had never seen its like and couldn't work out how they'd got it in—but thereagain, what was not possible to the Slovos? The great expanse of grass and flowers was open to the sky and caressed by sunlight that never failed. There was even some sort of fruit tree and real blossom, and imperfections like weeds and bumps and stuff. It was the sort of scene that couldn't have survived five minutes in the *barrios* and was impermissible waste out in the agric zones. Only in his little-boy-time dreams had Hashem-Joe imagined such places—but now he'd seen one for real and needn't mind so much about his life—or the leaving of it.

At one end was a Golden-Age-style red-brick wall. There was an oldish—but still clearly streamlined—man sitting on a chair in front of it, the plainness of his uniform declaring that this was a real *inner*, steel-hardened, cadre. The negro-type didn't smile—didn't look like he recalled how to—but, friendly enough, beckoned Hashem-Joe forward.

And thereafter Hashem-Joe's life got amazingly better and better until the day, long distant, when it came to an end.

JOHN WHITBOURN

Malcolm M'Bow, Franchised Party General Secretary of New-Joburg City, looked on the slum youth and reflected on the irony that this mere... zero was shaking the house of Slovo.

M'Bow was a hollow man, a mouthpiece, long past conceiving any division of interest between self and Slovo. His universe was both sealed and self-sufficient. And yet, and yet... Well, why not admit it, there was just this rebellious *residue*, a remnant of prior personality, that thought itself done dealing with out-Party, out-Family, white types—*Mzungus*. His wearying career should at least have earned him that. Still, akin to the sales pitch about 'semi-sentient torpedoes' he'd just been reading in the latest Party stocklist (*'memo to Arms-wing: mortgage two tertiary planets to buy... five*), the slum youth could not be ignored. The great dictator, *Duty*, dictated that he be paid loving attention.

'Make him crouch there—no, exactly there,' said M'Bow to the scowling, resentful, inner-Castle retainers. 'And now retreat from audible range of our conversation.'

Whereupon, M'Bow questioned Hashem-Joe with exquisite care about the circumstances of his step-Papa's death, going over and over the pitiful details—and paying no attention at all.

Conveniently timed, the message came through on his internal wiring that the slumster's story checked out. Busy Slovo intelligence teams were pinching and squeezing the outer-City's nerve centres at that very moment; threatening, rewarding and hurting, to acquire a data-rich picture of just one particular death on one particular night. There was great skill in picking out the one required thread in a City-wide tapestry of random violence, and M'Bow was relieved to find his proxy fingertips still mustered the necessary sensitivity.

Despite the gravity of the moment, the story recurred to him of how one Family, another Noble-House, (Beria? Robespierre? No matter) had dealt with a High Counsellor—such as he—who'd failed them. They'd played pain-threshold white noise down his wiring until (some time later) there was a sort of... explosion.

Had it ever happened or was it just a tale designed to keep his kind ever tense and useful? Slovo-House were capable of either deed or ploy—and quite rightly so, of course.

ALTERED ENGLANDS

M'Bow thought the necessary mnemonic, so switching his wiring to send mode. To impress the *Mzungu* he also spoke aloud.

'Arrest the Splendid Ovation and 1717 gangs, plus any revivalist Sejm elements—down to third level operatives plus families—and liquidate. Full achievement expected within three standard hours. Confirm completion.'

Hashem-Joe's eyes widened and he crouched lower still. M'Bow observed it. To a slum-boy these... sordid street organisations probably seemed world-bestriders, pinnacles of day-to-day effective power—bar omnipotent abstractions like the Party or the god-notion. It did no harm, and perhaps a deal of good, to show that to a Slovo Counsellor liquidating them was of no more moment than a casual abortion.

'The people who killed your step-Papa are joining History,' said M'Bow, far more kindly than his habitual tone to his own sons (harshness to them merely proved his love). 'Meanwhile, tell me what he was like.'

And whereas M'Bow had laboured over the irrelevant story of some slumster's fiery death, he slipped in this most vital of questions as though it were throwaway whimsy.

At first, of course, there was a surge of nonsense about the man's *personality* as it was called; the way he did or didn't do things, inspiring a degree of fastidious nausea. The proletariat were acceptable enough in a philosophical and conceptual sense but there was something slightly... indecent in staking a case for individual awareness in them. Even so, M'Bow listened patiently.

.'... and once he was a spacer...'

'Really?' replied M'Bow, as polite as to a prince.

'Said so. Stopped it because of the *samagon* and needle-joy stuff he took—and the bad dreams, I think. He came here and kinda pulled out of life, never doing much, just a bit of running and gang sub-contracting. Didn't even do that, boy's work really, when he got older and got the shakes more often.'

[*Disgusting!*] 'I see...,' said M'Bow.

'Actually, he wasn't much good at anything later on—except the stories. He'd tell them when he was halfway braindeathed—but not to anyone else: just me. I think he liked me, more or less. Anyway, I said he could make some credits with them, spinning tales to other citizens—but he never would. So mostly we were serious poor and I wasn't too fused-up about him getting hit—but, y'know, it was a *thorough*, so I was-...'

'Involved, yes—and these stories...?'

Hashem-Joe made a face and brushed the subject matter aside, to show he was too big and case-hardened for such things really. It ought to have been true, for childhood ended early in Stalinspace.

'Oh, just *Vivid-and-Glory* yarns,' he said, dismissively. 'Like them films or *Komsomol* comic strips. About battleships and the RAGE-war: 'A*dventures of a vacuum-combat vet'*: stuff like that. Save he could make you, well, kind of *live* it...'

'Give me an example,' said M'Bow and then, for the first time so far, put some ice in his voice as he well knew how to. 'Give me a very *good* example, I want to be *excited.*'

Hashem-Joe chucked the ready tale that first occurred to him and dredged up something more the ticket.

'Well, there was the one about the Guard Fleet Flagship off Castro 4; how's that?'

M'Bow nodded. 'Yes,' he said, 'that may suffice.'

'It got some sort of RAGE ship crashing in on mid bow,' gabbled Hashem-Joe, 'which is as close as anyone's been to them Papa said. And it sort of staggered and died in blue flame—only everything's silent in space, he said, and there was like, crew flying out and vacuum-boiling, and when the ship hit the atmosphere it was like May Day—only better and...'

'Yes, I see,' commented M'Bow, sadly.

'... and he liked the one about sterilising Philby House Prime when this co-op of eth-mercs had rigged up a sort of homemade sub-space superfortress using stolen Party-specs. So the Party fleet had to stand off and planet-burst— which hadn't been used against humans before and...'

'*So it is true,*' thought M'Bow, '*and this gutter-bred worker is reeling off things that are the rarest, the most expensive and most dearly won of 'Rumours-Unconfirmed' in Slovo-House Gold Band intelligence archives. So it is true and therefore all plans, all the schemes and efforts of my working life come to nothing...*'

The boy was not reciting misinformation from Party sources, the Fax-mags and the *'Vivid...'* rags, but repeating what he'd heard from a man who'd been there: someone who'd flown the great Party fleets and fought the RAGE aliens and seen what it was like to burst a star and sight a brand new planet. In all of M'Bow's life and knowledge, this was a rubbing of the rawest of nerves. Space flight was the strictest of the Party's many monopolies. They had been known to relinquish parcels of power—to the Noble-houses, to frontier corporations—but of the travel secret, nothing at all—not *ever.*

ALTERED ENGLANDS

They and only they provided the Prole-freighters, the warships and the transport bubbles that carried them. For a fee, for a favour, out of Humanspace duty or for quiet reasons of their own, they would ship the atmosphere fleets of the Houses, the Corps, the eth-mercs and all, off to fight or explore or trade or whatever. But never ever was a molecule of *knowledge* allowed to fall from their table. They guarded what they had most jealously. Every textbook, every program, every spacer was accounted for and secluded from creation to end. That was the way.

Except now, this first time ever as best M'Bow knew, in this boundless opportunity and boundless tragedy, somehow, inconceivably, the Party had fallen from perfection. This one wretched, cursed man had permeated through the impermeable and come, damn his dead eyes, to drink and drug himself dead on Slovo-Prime.

'... and he said there was once this transport bubble chain that went out of sync, despite the multiple system redundancies, and the bubble went ploughing on out of line with a whole fleet in it—not Guard but pretty decent stuff—and they never found it. He said they'd be still alive but really ancient now; the same as him if he'd not been torched, about prole-expiry age or more. And he used to say about how weird it'd be on board, trying to keep things going as they slowly died off one by one or got useless...'

But it *had* happened and now there nothing that could be done to reverse events. All possibilities converged on one outcome and everything had changed for ever for Slovo-House. Even if they killed the boy now, liquidated all the retainers he'd said as much as one word to, everyone who'd ever known or met him since he could talk—or known or met his Papa—or known or met anyone who'd known or met either, *still* there was no safety in it. The Party would say thank you for the sign of good faith and then (understandably) not believe it. Why should they? Why should they take the risk? Would a viable, sharp-toothed Noble-house make contact with spacer knowledge and not try to pump it for advantage? Unthinkable.

They would have to proceed on the assumption that data flow had occurred and act accordingly. Would it be House dissolution? Disciplinary decimation of all Family members, operatives and assets? Family data-core wipe? Planetary sterilisation? Who could say? This was all new ground.

'... and he would say—frightening this—that most of the time the RAGE ships are better than us and we can't hold them and the frontier bands are just a joke and lots of them were evacuated or sterilised standi-years back and...'

Of course, it was possible that the dead spacer and this resultant prole were Party implants, a loyalty test; but in the end it all amounted to the same thing. He hadn't been torched straightaway and too many people had talked to him—so Slovo-House had failed the test, if such it was, and the Party would... act accordingly.

'... the only thing that'll touch them is a lucky shot or a suicide ram and there's not enough good and/or Jew/Jap mercs to keep that up so all you can do (this is what he said) is get towards the human-core and amuse yourself till they arrive. I'm smarter though, I know the Party is invincible. Well, it is, isn't it? Beside, that sort of talk is section 5—Spreading of Negativity, punishable by...'

Everything had seemed so coldly peaceful that morning but now all was changed. The Party would find out one day, sooner or later, maybe tomorrow, maybe a century from now—but they would know. They always KNEW the fullness of things in due course.

So, the credit reserves must be spent, discreet as can be, and the Slovo worlds filled with ethnic mercenaries, units of Zion and Secular Jews, Sikhs, Englisc, Native Americans, Maoris and KwaZulu. There would have to be a contingency for arming even the city-proles and the neo-mus workers. The ultra-secret mothballed terraformed planets must be revived as bases and refuges. Deepest Slovo secret of all, the Sun-burster catalyst corruptly obtained from Party arsenals three centuries ago must be unearthed and made ready. Slovo-House (and M'Bow thought himself such, the same as any Prince-of-the-blood) would either live—or maybe die—in a manner befitting its illustrious name.

'... liquidation. Look, maybe I can be useful: I'm good at telling tales—like Papa taught me, I suppose. Couldn't you kind of keep me on? I mean, he went on about this thing called Quantum Tunnelling they use to fly—whatever that is...'

'*What indeed*,' thought M'Bow.

ALTERED ENGLANDS

'So maybe I could tell you all that. There's no call to torch me, I won't say anything about anything. And please don't send me back out there, I've got no papers and like, if I'm put in the fields, the neo-mus will kill me if I don't convert and...'

'Oh, you are <u>secure</u>, my child,' thought M'Bow. '*I wish my offspring could have such a future. It might have been better to interrogate your Papa—or perhaps not, since he knew the value of his life-tale and only spoke of it in braindeath. However, you are all we now have and you will be cherished and educated and made to appreciate and recall the morsels of data that was all your Papa left you. We will hide you deep on some distant planet and treat you in such a way as to make you love us. There must come a time when the summit of your desires is to tell Slovo <u>all</u>.*'

This morning, a death-marked prole, this afternoon, a future Prince of the Slovos, mused M'Bow and compared that to his own hard and hardening life in the chilly corridors of Slovo power. He was pleased to find no note of jealousy—or indeed any other emotion—within him. Feelings no longer had much purchase on his smoothness: another feature of that same history

And, of course, most of the research projects: the gravity pulse weapon, the interrogator's synapse-prod and so on, would have to close. The 'volunteer' legions of Slovo people out on the frontier worlds would cautiously, return. Even the fifty year old range-war with Ulbricht-Pauker Noble-house would have to be settled with whatever loss of face. Throughout the two hundred worlds in its franchised zone, Slovo would draw in its horns. Only Prince Ec3 Slovo, secluded in a Party freighter surrounded by Party warships, all in turn within a Party transport bubble, on his way to a newly granted fief, was beyond the reach of the recall. They would have to do without him and his fleet.

Not since the last great Humanspace-wide *Reforging* random purge (the fourth, or was it fifth such *Great Reforging*?) would things be so... busy.

But still, looking on the bright side, there might be advantage to this deadly bit of flotsam thrown up on the tide of History. If Slovo House *could* glean something from the slum-youth's stream of casual revelations then... The flow diagram etching itself in M'Bow's mind suddenly became expansive—and then monstrously open-ended. There appeared notions of a deep-space ship with the Slovo emblem on its side; of transport bubbles created and directed by Slovo-tech—and no one else. It was all alien and unsettling: the antithesis of centuries of conditioning—but M'Bow realised it could become less so.

Willingly or no, Slovo House were sliding down the slalom now and there was no profit in fighting that acceleration—quite the contrary. M'Bow might not live to see journey's end but he would at least be able to add what speed he could to getting there. After all, he mused, shocking himself, not even the Party was immortal: something, someday must replace it. Why shouldn't that something be the offspring—in brazen, mutant form—of the House of Slovo?

Blasphemous thought, to be sure, but even great Stalin-of-the-ages had a successor. Why should the civilisation he created be any different?

20~

MERITOCRACY

Or

DEATH OF A SALESMAN

'What do we need in order to really win? We need three things: first—arms, second—arms, third—arms and arms again!'
Joseph Stalin. 17/10/Year -12.

'Incoming transmission, Sicarii.'

The Sicarii idly wondered what it cost the Communication woman, what it really *demanded* of her, to have two distinct personas: the clipped, efficient, razor sharp *sica* of ship-work-shifts, and the brazen jezebel of off-duty. But that wasn't a particularly profitable or joyful line of thought—not in his condition—so he sank deeper into his seat, inhaled another cigarette and flicked the switch.

The response message was all along the line average, medium tone, minimum variation, minimum inflection; as bland as they could synthesise it. Along with precautions against tracing, should someone catch its transport bubble no *clues* were offered up to the inquisitive.

'Subject to personal considerations,' it said, 'your proposal, *Project Slovo*, is approved. After-sale option one has, however, been adjudged excessively sinful. Accordingly provisionally delete. Permissible profit parameters: break-even within five standard years. Message ends. Goodbye, Sicarii.'

So there it was. The possibilities were nicely narrowed and that was a relaxing end to speculation. The Sicarii sat in his foam cocoon in the semi-darkness he preferred for his office and let the ship drift for just a little space more. Outside, the transport bubbles were being constantly renewed, rapidly building up force to undeniable proportions, urging him on to action or destruction (one way or another) in short order. The pathway between the stars was not indulgent towards pausing or reflection, and soon enough enforced submission to trajectory. Perhaps that was a hint in itself.

Even so, the Sicarii had plenty time to make peace with what was to be. And since things were the way they were, he permitted himself the indulgence of reciting Psalm 1. Then he brought Communications back in.

'It's on,' he told her. 'Take me in.'

Almost immediately he felt the ship revive and aim itself at a prepared course to the green planet of so much recent study.

There would have been opportunity, had this contract not come up, to make it back to a Home-Zion, where they could have patched up his cancer, or at least caged it for a decade or two. That option had in all kindness been offered him: *'Subject to personal considerations'* they'd said.

But the Sicarii was... the Sicarii. There would be no running home for health and extra years. He would make one last sale for Corporation Uzi.

☸

Plugged so full of strong medication that he felt suspiciously normal, the Sicarii was roused once again from his smoking, nail-worrying, aimless thoughts by the cool voice of Communications.

'We've been detected,' she said. 'What's the mode, Boss?'

'First ferocious,' he replied, 'then second thoughts. Make a decent hole for me to hide in.'

'Will do,' she said—and he could tell she was smiling. 'Actually, we've found the perfect thing for you: you'll laugh.'

The Sicarii doubted that, he hadn't really *laughed* since childhood—but he knew what she meant.

ALTERED ENGLANDS

And she knew *exactly* what he meant and the flight-crew likewise. Together, the Sicarii and his staff had the sort of empathy associated with the very best of sales teams, the sort always scaling the right type of Company graphs. Without needing to be requested, a visual was patched into his office, creating an island of light in its smoky dark. The computer co-operative net was instructed to enhance, slow and make human-sense of what was revealed.

House Slovo ships were waiting for them at the fringes of vestigial atmosphere, there for the instant the transport bubble burst. Maybe they had time to repent of their zeal before two, perhaps three, of them were sent spinning down, mortally wounded, trailing smoke and crew.

'*First ferocious...*'

Corporation Uzi, especially when equipping itself, spared nothing. Its citizen employees were not sent helpless into the realm of Amalek. '*We carry blessings—but also a sword*' was what the Sicarii was taught the very first day at sales school. The Slovo ships were maybe a century old, perhaps more: loyal family retainers, covered in history. Uzi craft were deemed obsolete after a decade, ripe for resale.

Faster and more venomous than their welcoming committee, the Uzi ship flew clean through the ambush, punching holes in hulls, fighting with not far off indecent relish...

'*... then second thoughts...*'

Before the unequal struggle became too one-sided for House Slovo to endure, the Uzi ship turned timid—passive even. Moving away from the falling hulks it had created, off it skimmed and away, giving every impression of seeking escape.

Obligingly, the remaining Slovo interceptors screamed in pursuit. Such that, amidst all the high drama and orgy of what the Sicarii termed *emotionally-conditioned* responses, the shy arrival of an (admittedly shielded) one-man-craft went unnoticed—as planned and intended.

Whilst often a welcome visitor, the Sicarii took care never to be expected, nor offered the facility of appointments.

☸

Of course, Uzi intelligence sub-Corp wing stated (unthinkable it should be mistaken) that Suslov 3 (T)(F) was a minor fief only, recently acquired by some offshoot scion of Slovo Noble-House. Therefore the ease of penetration was not unduly indicative. Nevertheless, if this hadn't been his last (and thus testimonial) sale, the Sicarii would have permitted himself a degree of encouragement.

All change upon landing however. The Sicarii had occasion to re-evaluate all preconceptions—a thrice-daily prescribed spiritual exercise for executives anyway. They'd inserted him in what was both a good and bad place to be. No one would bother him here, certainly: anywhere within miles of the great wreck of the alien craft would be lead-suit country for anyone but dying men like he. The huge golden globe-ship of the RAGE retained little of its former unhealthily attractive organic appeal—but all of its carcinogenic properties. Every moment in its awful proximity was adding nutriment and cheer to traitor cells in the Sicarii's body and speeding up the countdown.

On the other hand, he would have ample time to do what was necessary. Which was all he required.

Except... the RAGE presence was disturbing. Someone had downed their World-ship (or creature?): a thing rarely recorded in Uzi-archive (he checked) or, for all he knew, in all Stalinspace. The man or woman who'd taken this planet for Slovo might just be someone to reckon with.

But then so was the Sicarii. A sector speculative-projects manager for Corporation Uzi became highly... resourceful in their climb to the top. He was more than a match, he felt sure, even for a paladin of regressive, Noble-House, methods. And besides, the Sicarii was a dead man. There was that great advantage.

He took his samples case from the chameleon-skinned one-man-craft. One side of it mimicked the golden glow of the thing the RAGE had built or grown. The other imitated the (dying) pampas grass of the endless plain.

Above, the sky was clear of the swirls of combat, so either the Sales-ship had already escaped or else the fight had been successfully lured around the planet's far side. It amounted to the same thing and the Sicarii had every confidence in unfolding events. As it should be, the efficiency of his team left his mind free and relaxed and able to think thoughts of vision.

And yes, it *was* a good team he realised; a wonderful one. It would be a terrible leave-taking to let them down in any way.

Thus inspired, with the illusory warmth of the dead alien ship playing on his back, Sicarii set off across the prairie.

ALTERED ENGLANDS

✦

Slovo were looking for him and had narrowed the zone for beady-eyed suspicion commendably. Some Family analyst had rewound events and queried the strict need for that dramatic little tussle high above Suslov 3 (T)(F). Ulterior motives were proposed and traced home along the myriad pathlines.

Which was why, the Sicarii assumed, the first neo-mus encampments he encountered out of the carcinogen zone had already been cleared. And since it was early days in the Slovo presence on this planet, they'd felt free to employ classical prole motivation techniques to get things moving. The bodies of the uncooperative—or maybe just examples—were littered all over.

The Sicarii was well provided with shields and cloaks of brand new Uzi design and so didn't fear any of the Slovo-House family heirloom tracking devices doubtless being used to snare him. He watched from the shadow of a water tower as one village was pacified before his very eyes and then shipped off in venerable skimmer trucks. The grey clad Slovo retainers scanned and overflew with patience born of fear and generations of discipline but the Sicarii remained invisible to them. The beast was thrashing back and forth, he mused, but the modernist, progressive virus (as represented by himself) was now well and truly inside the reactionary econ/soc system.

Eventually, the search circles, 'prime', 'secondary' and *vigilance'*, were traversed and the world through which the Sicarii trudged returned to what passed for normal. The neo-mus and all the other eth-elements, Amer, Euro or whatever, were tending the prairie world as they were so bred and enjoined. The Sicarii started to see traces of stability—and yearned to set it ablaze.

Once he'd tripped the arranged signal the response was swift and subtle as objective circumstances permitted. Neo-mus field hands—who were not always or only field-hands—peeled away from the fellow faithful as the Sicarii passed by their shacks. He found himself surrounded

Using a basic hand unit (disposable, the very cheapest made on Uzi gunsmith worlds, but worth a Sultan's prize out here) he burnt some crop stacks to show both who he was—and who he wasn't. The inferno created a show-and-tell saying:

'*No, I am not suitable material for expressions of long bottled hatred. On the contrary, for you, poor downtrodden talking-tools, I, the Sicarii, am good news second only to your good book!*

And the collection party, these rag-clad *'Soldiers of God'*, they were also good news in themselves. To perform this most vital of tasks precious arms caches had been brought to surface by their warlords—and they contained gunpowder weapons, converted welders, even crossbows!

'Truly,' thought the Sicarii, *'this is fertile ground.'*

'We have already suffered grievously,' said the Mufti, 'and as the death fell on us from above, I swore that never again would I permit my brothers to rise without the means to resist.'

Uzi intelligence had already bought or stolen the news about the mid-voyage trouble and the Slovo reprisals on the helpless human cargo in the freighter holds. It was nothing remarkable in itself but some manifestation of shock seemed to be expected. The Sicarii dredged within for appropriate sentiments.

'I confess,' he said, suppressing a fruity cough, 'that these Slovos make a great meal of minor problems...'

The Warlord crouching opposite looked unfavourably on him.

'They are *soulless*,' the man said, doubt-free. 'An affront to Allah and a stumbling block to faith in providence. We wish to kill them all. That is the only reason you are here. We do not require your lukewarm sympathy.'

The Mufti looked disconcerted by such bald stating of facts and the Sicarii rushed to smooth over this loose thread in unfolding events.

'I am here to serve,' he said, 'both my masters and, for the moment, yourselves. At this time therefore, under God's guidance, there is not a knife blade's width between us.'

This was acceptably sincere and appeared to pacify the varied disquiets felt by the neo-mus inner circle. The Sicarii charitably understood that warrior-pride was hurt by the need to skulk in this rickety barn and ask for favours. Impatient to be more in accord with the nobility of their plans, they were unwilling to linger at the humble start of things.

'I am unwell,' announced the Sicarii, 'not able to do justice to you or my products with present powers of thought and speech. Accordingly, I ask your indulgence for the recording of my Company's petition. I will of course be available to answer any questions later...'

ALTERED ENGLANDS

The video-pitch and screen was already up and ready. A simple gesture with his company seal was sufficient to put it in motion. The neo-mus, deliberately starved of high-tech encounters, were straightaway entranced.

Indeed the Sicarii *was* ill. Sickbay prescriptions had ceased to bludgeon the enemy down and he felt drawn and weak. Retiring to a handy straw-bale, he lit the first of a stream of cigarettes and tried to blank out the heard-until-memorised videoed sales-talk. Before his unseeing eyes, smart clean figures paraded the latest in weaponry and destroyed targets both living and dead. It was all expertly pitched by Ad-sales division and even the Sicarii, who was wearied unto headache by repetition of it, had to fight the temptation to piece together the half-heard, random snippets caught. It was proudly said that even pacifists would buy after that commercial.

So, though *he* might not have a future, the Sicarii's works were now projected into the dreamy what-will-be. All he had to do was retain a chrome-clear mind whilst he was still able to, so that his sales would live after him. And so they must, of course, for his name's sake and for his team. He wasn't worried about any entry on his sale division's role of honour, nor the lasered bronze plaques lining the walls of Uzi-Prime College. It was more important that his people should remember him with respect. That was the way he operated.

'Sales projection, *Account Anti-Slovo,*' he said quietly, activating a recorder threaded in his collar. 'To whom it may concern; second day, third quarter, eleventh Sales-month, standard year 560.'

One of the neo-mus headmen turned to see what the Sicarii was about, but he heard nothing of interest and soon enough the engrossing video drew him back.

'Bulk sale achieved,' the Sicarii continued, 'quantity and mark to be determined. Five standi-year break-even constraint imposed by Uzi-Home. Project options (subjective) analysis by Sicarii 2323, 1st class. For use by successor sales-staff and Uzi-Home research analysts. Copy for comment and evaluation to Torah-planet Prime.'

Unlike most operatives, the Sicarii liked this part of his job. It was an opportunity to dabble in pure creativity and twist the time-lines into pleasing shapes. He would be sad to leave such work, something he could not say of life in general. This was an ungrateful thought he knew: and in the life-to-come he would most certainly be held to account for such scant regard for G-d's gift.

'General preamble. The neo-mus labour echelons are in pre-insurrection mode on fief planet Suslov 3 (T)(F) held by Slovo Noble-House under Earth Party franchise. This is despite medium level, indiscriminate reprisals against ship-board unrest during transportation to the fief. Accordingly, I am authorising release of on-demand supplies of basic level sidearms. Note my embargo on any training teams for support or heavy weapons of any type. Speculation regarding outcome of revolt irrelevant to project (pending ethical audit by qualified Torah planet) as outlined herewith:

'Option 1: Ensure all weapons supplied have one month average usage life. Rising will consequently fail. Severe repression measures by Slovo-House likely. Uzi Corp should use ensuing disruption to agri-crop production as justification for counter bid to Earth Party for franchise of Suslov 3 (T)(F). If bid is successful, Uzi Corporation will have unopposed takeover transition (viz. one month weaponry supplied to neo-mus). Break-even estimated 65% probable within five standard year constraint.'

'Further N.B. Preliminary analysis by Uzi-Prime Torah advisor adjudged this option to be excessively sinful even under survival-emergency regs and therefore forbade it. Suggest an appeal against ruling to Torah-Prime: Yeshiva Carmel or Yeshiva Epsom and Ewell.'

'Option 2: Issue normal weaponry and maintain as-needed supply up to and including self-defence by Uzi ships during delivery. If insurrection is successful the establishment of a pseudo-friendly regime on Suslov 3 (T)(F) will enable payment for weaponry supplied to be rendered (probably in wheat-produce). In addition, the blow to Slovo-House prestige (propagation of info by Uzi Ad-division) will permit pre-planned raid on Slovo quoted stock on all outer-zone business Stock-exchanges (restricted to legitimate only) and short-profit taking on inevitable price fluctuations.'

'Debit items re this option: provision against losses arising from Slovo retaliation—military and otherwise—and cost of blocking Slovo appeal to Earth Party Politburo. Also provide for cost of enhanced protection against Slovo assassination projects (speciality of the House) and associated loss of middle to higher echelon Uzi personnel in inevitable successes. Break-even estimated 55% probable within four standard years.'

'Option 3: Issue normal weaponry but curtail supplies at insurrection optimum (for timing, suggest liase with Tactical division on any Uzi Gunsmith World) upon payment of sufficient compensation by House Slovo. This will of course be regarded as *betrayal* and will lower Uzi goodwill in neo-mus eyes. It is also moderately sinful but, in the prevailing conditions of the era, I suspect it will be passed. Estimated 75% chance of break-even within an eighteen standi-month period but nil profit thereafter.'

The Sicarii suddenly felt disgustingly tired and allowed his grasp of other, more subtle, more pitiless and profitable, scenarios slip away. He knew in any case that what he'd just carved from nothing would do well enough.

'And that's it,' he added, a trifle breathlessly. 'Good fortune, successors.'

As though he had timed it thus (and he hadn't, therefore it was a sign from G-d), the video spiel ended, the screen blanked at that precise moment. The neo-mus turned to him with fire in their eyes: another sale made!

There was no reason why he shouldn't light another smoke and relax. This was all after-sale, post-coital, stuff now.

'You are not of us,' said the Mufti slowly, measuring his words, 'but we know that your people has suffered as we have. Moreover, you are akin to us, a people of the book...'

'Corporation Uzi is *strictly* secular!' said the Sicarii, swift as possible. Never ever, not even in this forgotten building on a fifth grade prairie world, not even tucked up in bed under the covers, must the Company give the impression it thought anything even vaguely anti-Party. *No* religion, not to outsiders, not even amongst themselves: Uzi-Corp golden rule 1, exclamation mark, day 1 of training and ever after. Stalinspace (which was to say: Humanspace) tolerated religion—but only as a man might tolerate ants underfoot. That toleration didn't stop the Party seeking a cure...

'... *strictly* secular,' said the Sicarii again to emphasise the point.

'If you say so,' agreed the Mufti, waving away the temporary dislocation (for, by the standards of his tribe, he had been lucky, had travelled and so *understood*). 'But you are, as I have mentioned and will maintain, *people of the book*. I appreciate what this implies and, to me, a Jewish gun is perfectly acceptable as any other. Sadly, however, not all of my soldiers-of-Allah are so liberal... What I am saying is that I do not wish to have to explain this concept of co-existence ten million times...'

(*'Ten million,*' pondered the Sicarii, rush calculating. *'This was going to be good!'*)

'We have taken such sensitivities into consideration,' replied the Sicarii with quiet confidence. 'We sell to all cultural archetypes. Your weapons will be manufactured complete with crescent emblems and an initial 25% will be gold-chrome plated and inscribed with Quranic and other suitable texts. What we suggest is that an angel directs yourself or some other notably pious person to a miraculous underground cache of the gold guns. Then, under *'divine guidance'*, you allegedly copy the balance of the firearms to that pattern in your own secret manufactories. In practice we guarantee full but discreet deliveries at any suitable point or rate. Of course, I leave the precise details of the accompanying story to your own ingenuity and idiosyncratic embellishments.'

In the privacy of their heads the Mufti and the Warlord were visibly turning dreams into tangible possibilities. With some difficulty in keeping them there alone. Once watered, the seeds of ancient ambitions of restitution and revenge—for yourself, your father and grandfathers and untold generations back—soon blossom into riotous growth not easily tamed.

'When?' husked the Warlord.

'Your communal prayers are on the fifth day of the standi-week, I believe,' said the Sicarii calmly, too old and battle-worn to be any longer impressed by bloodlust or justice. 'Why not work the tale into next week's *khutbah?* Call a *Jihad*. I'll ensure by then you'll have what you need...'

To seal the bargain (and lighten his load) the Sicarii handed the Warlord a complimentary carbine of the sort that Uzi reps distributed in abundance. To the Sicarii it was akin to Company ashtrays and pens he also carried, but the Warlord held it with love written plain on his face.

Suddenly he turned and fired his new toy, full automatic, spraying one of the barn's metal sides. The carbine's computer (for want of more inspiring instructions) dutifully cut out a perfect metre diameter circle before lapsing into silence.

The Warlord stepped back (the Sicarii frowned—there was *no* recoil!) and looked amazed at what he had done and what had done it. Then he recovered and punched his fist towards the sky.

'God is great!' he cried. 'God is great'—and all the other neo-mus joined in.

Soon enough, the Sicarii would be flying away to die somewhere, probably before this particular sale was even resolved and turned into a memory on a file. He knew what he was, had became and made of himself. Hard and icy as the Universe (Stalinspace!) in which in he moved, he had given up his name; become a mere occupation,[44] all for his people. Those of them that had survived the *Second Shoah* were often (needs be) that way. The division between Gunsmith and Torah worlds (protection and sustenance each, in their own way, for the other) was absolute. Corporation Uzi, the Gunsmith Worlds Combine, was strictly secular and that was that. Yet on the Torah planets people knew what was being done for them and prayed day and night in thanks. Somewhere, even at that moment, it was likely a pious *tzadik* was interceding for the Sicarii's soul—because of what he had to do for the sake of Life. Therefore he was in with a chance. Which was all he had ever asked for.

The neo-mus, in their fragile joy, were continuing to dance and announce that God was great.

Despite everything, the dying Sicarii smiled to himself and agreed.

---

[44] *'Sicarii'*: from the Latin *'sica'* = dagger: hence, plural, *'daggermen'*. Name and modus operandi of fanatic terrorist movement in Judea, first century AD.

JOHN WHITBOURN

ALTERED ENGLANDS

❈

THREE NIGH NOVELLAS

Or

SOME NOT-SO-SHORT SHORT STORIES

❈

COMPRISING:

I NEED HELP BAD MAN
A PILLAR OF THE CHURCH
DOING THE CHARLESTON

❈

21~

I NEED HELP BAD MAN!

'I need help *bad*, man!'

'I can see that, sir.'

The slender swaying bloke rose from his hotel bed. The London traffic hum seemed to trouble him. Likewise the wide-open curtains—as if fans, photographers and other freaks could fly this high to peep in. He swept back already standing-to-attention hair. I noted that in places it was grey and thinning. At his young age!

'Skip all that *'sir'* shit, man. I hate that stuff!'

The customer is always right, even when stoned.

'Very well. What would you prefer?'

'Just call me Jimi, man.'

I shook my head.

'No. Not my style. Not professional. Let's compromise on *Mr* Hendrix.'

His girlfriend was semi-supporting him. It looked like a full-time occupation. And looking the way *she* did, that was probably the nearest she need ever get near gainful employment. Miss Kathy Etchingham was sitting on a fortune.

So now I understood the wrecked bed, the signs of room service all over the place. Understood if not excused. The room reeked of passion and indulgence. It brought out the inner Spartan in me.

'Whatever,' she said, cutting the crap. 'Just help him. Please.'

I liked her from the start: all eyes and legs but tough-minded. Not the standard rock-chick blow-job-machine 'companion'. Within limits she might have his best interests at heart.

Meanwhile, my client was giving me the once over, his pupils mere pinpoints. Sigh...

'You're an army guy,' he slurred, 'right?'

'Was, Mr Hendrix.'

Jimi smiled—and was transfigured. I saw the ghost of the easy-going boy there'd been before the hits and hangers-on arrived and spoilt things. Looking back on events, it was probably then that I took the job.

'Me too, man,' said Hendrix. 'Paratrooper. 1-oh-1 Airborne. Did me twenty-two drops! *Hooo-weeeeeeeee!*'

He tugged at his Victorian-vintage embroidered hussar's jacket—as though that bolstered the claim.

'Hell of a long way down from a plane, man!'

I nodded, poker-faced. 'Yes, *very* steep, Mr Hendrix...'

Kathy was English and so understood irony. She smiled, reassured I wasn't just another yes-man. *Man...*

'Actually, he was: I mean did,' she told me. 'I've seen his discharge papers.'

'Like you said, miss: *whatever*. Anyway, Mr Hendrix, your manager told *my* manager you require assistance...'

Jimi freed himself from Kathy's arms, asserting his independence, swimming back to upright.

'Yeah, man, and he ain't jivin'. Yous here to help me. So help me!'

My words exactly. The star certainly needed help, but not, I suspected, the sort I sold. Time to cut it short: cruel to be kind. There was a contract going in Rhodesia. Wet jobs, but sweetened by untraceable gold krugerrands.

'I provide protection,' I said. 'Not life guidance, not rehab. Do you need protection?'

I caught the look of caution in Kathy's long-lashed eyes, but otherwise she was well in control of that pouty face. Old-fashioned stiff upper lip. Typical product of a troubled childhood—as she later confirmed.

Hendrix had doubtless gone through the same mill but not absorbed its lessons. Insofar as the stuff currently in his veins allowed, he was animated.

'Protection? *Yeah*, man, I need protection. Plenty protection!'

'From who?'

Kathy stirred. I was getting all my prompts off her now, not Hendrix. She suppressed things but I saw.

Jimi lurched forward and grabbed my lapels, part support, part emphasis. He was lucky I was on duty. Other times I'd have flicked him away. Then maybe stamped on those talented fingers.

'From these white cats,' he said. 'They *after* me!'

'What *'white cats'* are these, Mr Hendrix?'

His eyes were like saucers—which proved a coincidence.

'The ones outta the flying saucer, man...'

Sigh...

'Show.'

Kathy secured him a second chance. On the very doorstep. There's something about pleading females even cold fish like me can't ignore. Especially when she's being unselfish. I spared a life in Katanga in much the same circumstances—a pretty nun of all people. Something evolutionary, I suppose.

Stupid. Humans are free to opt out of evolution. I reproached myself for my weakness. It would be rooted out.

Meanwhile I'd agreed to humour Hendrix. 'He doesn't lie,' Kathy had said. 'Fantasise yeah, sure: but not out-and-out *lie*. Not even stoned. There must be something. He's *scared*.'

So I saw. Insofar as he was able, Hendrix had gone pale. The army would diagnose combat-shock. Maybe it was that, not Kathy, which detained me. The residual regimental bit of me was intrigued.

We wandered out of the hotel. Hyde Park was plain and pointless. I looked with a trained eye. Nothing. Just autumn leaves and people doing what they do. All too busy working to ever make any money.

Not my scene. My foster-parents were dead before their time, worn out plus potless. Leaving just enough to bury them. Oh, and two coronation mugs. Mugs for mugs.

That thought plus fresh air restored my senses. Again, I made as if to go.

ALTERED ENGLANDS

'Save your money,' I said. 'See you...'

'There's one!' said Hendrix. 'Over by the horse thing...'

Dammit, he'd *handled* me again—tugging my shoulder. The boy was living dangerously. I don't like tactile people.

However, I'd agreed a one-hour retainer. He survived. I looked.

'The horse thing...' Sigh and thrice sigh. Just G. F. Watt's *'Physical Energy'*: supreme statuary: lifetime pinnacle of the artist called 'England's Michelangelo'. Even better than all his portraiture: those limpid treatments that somehow saw spirituality in eminent Victorians.

Oh, sorry—did I just surprise you? Take you aback? An educated squaddie? Well, pardon *me*...

Since going freelance I'd had time to read, to think; to put things in context. I'd read a lot, in-between engagements. Was halfway to being a Marxist—without getting emotionally involved, naturally...

But don't fret yourself: no offence taken. I get that reaction all the time.

So, let me put it in terms you'll understand. *'The horse thing'*: an equestrian statue the size of a bus. Two tons of metal in the middle of Hyde Park. All you *need* to know. That capture the scene for you? Sufficient for your simple needs?

Hendrix was hopping from foot to foot in excitement.

'That's them, man! Them's the cats out the saucer...'

There were some herberts hanging around the statue. Difficult to see much at that distance. Skinny sorts with nothing better to do. Maybe druggies. My invisible, inward, lip curled.

Then matching it, my interest rose. They saw us seeing them. They didn't react right.

Some slipped behind the statue. A couple others were *off*.

'Catch 'em, man!' I was exhorted. 'Make 'em say what they want!'

There was a slice of my contracted time to go. So I went.

First normal pace, then, when they scattered, as fast as they. Which is saying something: I was sprint champion of the Regiment once.

It pained me but now I saw Jimi's point. This wasn't normal behaviour. These weren't waiters but watchers: *bad* watchers.

Although clued up enough to all head in different directions. And sprightly with it. I'd be lucky to nab even one.

Or maybe not even that. I saw a flash of metal. If my eyes didn't deceive me, a hell of a long blade. Almost a sword. One, the nearest, was showing he had teeth. I now had an excuse to break his arms in myriad places.

But maybe I was deterred, just a shade. Slowed even. And I did say *sprint* champ, not a marathon man. I accepted that they had too big a start on me. The scrotes soon merged into the urban biomass.

I returned, prizeless but pleased. A hundred yard dash and not even out of breath. *And* they'd scooted at mere sight of me. Any man who tells you he's not flattered by that is lying.

Besides, I'd found out there was substance to the apparent nonsense, maybe worth some more hours of gainful employment.

'Well, at least *this* one came back...,' said Kathy—concerning which I made a mental note. Something requiring explanation later.

'You see, man,' said Jimi. 'I *told* you they was there!'

As an accepted client he impinged on my senses more now. I realised I'd just checked him over to see all was okay. An infallible sign.

'So there's *some*thing in it, Mr Hendrix,' I conceded.

'Not just kids?' asked Kathy. 'Or, like y'know, fans: autograph-hunters?'

I might have guessed she'd be invincibly optimistic, sniffing for a positive spin.

'No, miss.'

'Shit!'

She stamped her white-booted leg. If that mini-dress rode up any more it'd be a belt.

Miss Etchingham then crossed her alabaster arms and shivered. A disturbingly childlike response. Suddenly I knew for sure: she was orphanage-spawn like me, or as near as makes no difference. You might think that would breed kindred spirit—but you'd be wrong. Chill descended from years ago.

Which I welcomed. Attraction is the enemy of professionalism.

Hendrix subsided onto a park bench and lit a cigarette. I'm not normally susceptible but had to admit, despite everything, he looked the epitome of cool. Right down to the smoke rings. It was all so effortless: natural.

He smiled at me through a vapour portal. Revealing bad teeth.

'I said send me a *scary* dude and, man, I got me one! Just glad you're on my side, man!'

For the moment, I was. I'd also got the impression there weren't many he could truly say that of.

ALTERED ENGLANDS

Kathy and I locked looks. Telepathy. We'd both just thought the same thing and it had arced the space between us. *Spooky*, as her sort might say.

She had the grace to look embarrassed but Jimi never noticed. When he was smoking he concentrated on just that, and then the next thing, and then the thing after that, whatever it might be.

After just a few long drags he flicked the smoko away. A pigeon hopped towards it, destined for disappointment.

His head unspoken for—for a span—Hendrix could spare me some attention.

'Anyhow, looks like you done scared 'em good, man. Them cats won't be back again!'

His take on life was akin to Kathy's joy-snatching variety. I now saw how they'd got together. It came from the happy-go-lucky kid there'd been before music-biz success landed on him like ten thousand firework displays.

'No, *sir!*' he burbled on. 'We seen the last of their sorry asses!'

'Yeah, *right*...,' said Kathy, agreeing whilst not-agreeing. Again, her Yank boyfriend was deaf to irony.

'Do you recognise any of these people, Mr Hendrix?' I asked.

He scoffed.

'Yeah, man, sure! Don't every half-dead dealer in Seattle and New York looks like them dudes...'

'So you *have* met them before?'

Hendrix tutted. He was frustrated I wasn't getting the witty repartee.

'No way, man. But they sure know *me!*'

'Yeah, just like *'every half-dead dealer in Seattle and New York',*' said Kathy, dryly.

Jimi didn't mind. He flashed her a wolfish smile. Then he realised I was just a poor sad limey who was lagging behind, not up to speed with his world.

'I'm only saying they look *like* them, man! These guys here are way worse. *Oo-weey!* They so sick they're barely *here*, man!'

Instead of all this... unilluminating stuff I should have been making myself useful, scanning Hyde Park like I had Yemen a few weeks before. Being back had softened me: green grass was now the same as sand and *wadis*. Sadly...

There were any number of hidey-holes for the evil-intended. The thing was to prioritise them and then examine each in turn; methodically, never bored, like each one was the first and there was *all* the time in the world. While

296

at the same time proceeding with urgency and remaining alert to dangers outside the field of view. Should be second nature now.

'Hey, come and have a drink with us, man...'

I heard Jimi, but like he was on another planet. Which he was really.

'In a minute, Mr Hendrix...'

Yeah—maybe a million minutes—as if I'd ever set out on the path he was stumbling down...

'Wow, like I thought you English cats never turned down a beer, man!'

'Shaddup!' I thought, but kept schtum.

Then I got it. There! The flash of a lens in a neighbouring block. Apartments, not a hotel.

I gave them the chance to be accidental but they proved fixed, focused on innocent, boring, us. I let my gaze traverse a few degrees on, so they wouldn't suspect or get scared.

It's funny how far-seers think themselves invisible, just because they have the detail and their targets don't. Amateurs.

In the *Dar al-Harb* that mistake might be their last, but sleepy London town wasn't the time or place for sniper fire. More's the pity. But maybe *one* day... Then I could walk to work for once.

I decided to reveal my hand: to shake them up; maybe make them move house in haste.

I snapped back, fixed the flash full on. I waved hello. I'm aware my face looks like a fist when it wants to.

Peeping Tom disappeared. Which was all the confirmation anyone needed. Guilty as charged.

Back in what you civilians call the real world, Hendrix was talking. Or gabbling. However, on the off-chance it was relevant I tuned in.

'Whatta day, man! I gotta get me outside some booze! And, y'know...,' here he giggled like a schoolgirl, 'maybe some funky stuff too...'

Hendrix looked up at me.

'Hey man, maybe you could go score some for me, y'know?'

'*Jimi*...,' warned Kathy.

Hendrix got my transmission half a second after her.

'Or maybe I'll go get it myself...,' he suggested, hurriedly by his standards.

I put my worst smile on before replying.

'I should...,' I said.

☸

I shouldn't. Have let him out of my sight that is. Or insisted on no narcotics for the duration. But that would have been contract's end. He was hooked. A quandary.

Also, like all druggies he was crafty. Boredom being the last thing I expected I'd been lulled into a false sense of security. Those first few days mangy street-dealers bought soft drugs *to* him. Otherwise his idea of fun was milky coffee and watching *Coronation Street* with Kathy. Ena Sharples was a major favourite as I recall.

But then the serious craving came—for fun, for the hard-stuff—and he went AWOL. It continued so long I got concerned. Another quandary: my client was up to illegality and naturally didn't want to be found. Plus he was a star and I looked like what I was. People didn't believe Jimi and I had a connection and should be re-united. In his own best interests. The candyfloss and pop-scum people I met on my travels had their own particular take on Jimi's *'best interests'*.

I imagined Kathy trying to persuade him to get in touch but once people start off down that helter-skelter there's no reasoning with them. I believe it was Lenny Bruce, the alleged comedian, who said smack was like kissing God on the lips. If true, who's going to keep any other appointment in preference? It's even so with simple wacky weed. I met these guys in Yemen who smoked great trumpets of the stuff every day all their life—it was like trying to talk to someone through a mattress.

Speaking of which.

'I *told* you once,' said Keith Moon, peeking round his door. 'He ain't 'ere. So fuck off. Fuck off and die!'

I couldn't decide what I objected to most. The *industrial* language, the *I'm-a-rock-star* discourtesy, the bulgy eyes or pink cravat. Plus, of course, *The Who* are a crap band. Commercial, insincere. Talentless in all essentials. Perm any two from the above.

So I broke his nose and then Mr Moon took me more seriously. The trademark 'madness' turned out to be just skin-deep: the skin over a soggy rice pudding. Beneath cowered the *nice* young man he'd once been. Just like John Lennon when I'd cracked his granny-glasses earlier. It was him who gave me

Moon's address. Even offered to drive me over. I declined. I drive myself, at all times, in all things.

Anyhow, I let myself in while Mr Moon sought a sink. Jimi proved to be a couple of rooms away, sunk into serried cushions as the party milled all around. There were bouncers or possibly just big blokes there but they chose to find me invisible. All the fragrant smoke supplied a fig leaf of excuse.

I felt and must have looked a little tetchy. What with Moon's blood spray and the weed fumes I'd need to get my suit dry-cleaned before mixing with decent folk again. Let alone my friends or the Law. Which was a drag. So was the music playing: Pink Floyd at their most *'experimental'*, post Syd Barrett. I'm more of a Dusty Springfield man myself.

Shoving encroaching caftans and afghans aside, the party parted Red Sea-style as I progressed.

Jimi's non-recognition was the real deal. He was viewing a different reality from this one—and who could blame him? Kathy was alongside, in her different way also *of* the scene but not *part* of it. She seemed glad to see me.

'I *told* him...,' she said. I signalled understanding and folded down into the beanbag beside her.

Jimi perceived extra company had arrived. Given his topic of conversation, he may even have had some idea who.

'It was in Hawaii, man,' he was informing the room, 'and that was like really cool, 'cos I always wanted to gig next to a volcano, man. Him and me were the same. There's so much inside us to give the world we both might blow any time...'

Kathy had heard it all before. She lit up another cigarette and puffed smoke signals at a member of Herman's Hermits.

'...and that's when I saw the saucer...'

My ears pricked up. There might just be snippets of sense to glean from this.

'Did you now...?' I prompted.

'I did, man. And a load of other cats did too, and, like, they was amazed I knew *exactly* where it was from and what for.'

'Which was...'

Hendrix drew breath for a big revelation.

'The supreme planet of material wisdom, man; on a mission of peace and love...'

Gordon and Bennett! The things I do to fund my retirement (a bar in Belize, in case you're wondering).

In rolling my eyes I noticed a white bloke giving us black looks. He was over by the door like he'd just come in or was leaving. I looked back. Pale and skinny. Not a happy man. Perma-*chagrined* probably. Plus sort of... frustrated.

Meanwhile, Jimi had more.

'Which ain't *nothing* like the saucer I saw in Hyde Park, man. Them cats came outta that ain't carrying *no* good vibes!'

My first thoughts were that Mr Starey was one of Moon's mates, or maybe a disappointed dealer. Looking daggers. But then the feeling grew that we'd already met. From a distance and not so long before. He'd been tooled up at the time and anxious to avoid my company...

Same story today. Seeing that he was observed he left. The door edged ajar and he was through it like a rat.

'Hey, you off already, man?' said Jimi, trying to focus like he was underwater. 'What's the time?'

I must be slowing down, but having to trample hippies en route hampers you. By the time I got there the stairwell was empty. But you could still sense the tension. Smell the sizzling ozone. Now I knew his number...

I returned to the beanbag. When you sank down it gave off essence of hash. Worse still, they were now playing Dylan, which only made your mind more spongy. I regulated my breathing to counter all the cack.

There was no need to check my watch.

'The time, Mr Hendrix,' I told him, 'is precisely *just* in time...'

'Cool...,' answered Hendrix, understanding nothing. Which is often a blessing.

☸

'I've been dead a long time...'

Jimi Hendrix's concluding words to the audience, abandoning a concert after only two songs. Aarhus, Denmark. 2nd September 1970.

☸

Later. When I'd got them back to the hotel.

'So, what did happen to my predecessor?'

Kathy parted the jungle in her cocktail and drew on the straw. The glass emptied in one. Wow. No wonder Jimi often wore a smile.

'He went off in pursuit,' she said, après-suck. 'Like you. Unlike you he never came back.'

I admire that in a woman—or anyone. All you need to know, succinctly said. Which left only one minor issue.

'You might have *warned* me, Miss Etchingham...'

'But then you wouldn't have took the job, would you?'

It was a simple statement of fact to a simpleton: no hint of an apology. I was really warming to this girl. Save for the high ruthlessness and high maintenance issues I'd be gearing up to propose to her. Because bigamy holds no terrors for me after all the other things I've done.

'Do you remember his name?'

I only asked because if I could identify him it might grade those who'd taken him out.

'Yeah: he said to call him *Big Joe*. He filled the doorframe.'

'Right...'

Great. It might be any one of hundreds of *geezers*. The East End and Army baked them in batches. Not any *face* known to me.

'Speaking of which,' asked Kathy, 'what's your name by the way? You never did say. Oh, sorry...'

My expression had answered for me. I pressed on.

'Do you remember where your management got him fr-. Hang on, where's Mr Hendrix?'

Kathy looked about. There was just us and a suite of rooms: I'd had him in view not ten seconds ago. And *warned* him about wandering.

'Ciggies,' she said, and extended a crimson talon to an empty fag packet decorating the end of the bed.

'Fuck me!'

Those painted-on eyebrows arched.

'Well, if you think there's time...'

I didn't even consider it. I was on duty

'*I* would have got him smokes! The *porter* would have-'

Kathy shrugged. She pitied me. As far as she was concerned I'd had my chance and blown it.

'Haven't you got it yet?' she said. 'Jimi's a free spirit. You can't cage him, not even for his own good. That's why I... respect him. It's not the music—I hate that. It's not even the lifestyle: I'd get along fine behind the counter at *Boots*. No: it's *him*. Like now. With Jimi he just has to go out and meet his destiny...'

I could have given her the Keith Moon cure. Maybe should have. These people were more foreign than any Yemeni I'd met, led or shot.

'Or to get cigarettes...,' she added. 'Whatever. It doesn't matter. Very little does.'

Suddenly I felt old. But a run downstairs soon revived me.

❂

I found him eventually—or more accurately, he found me. Before I'd got word out on the grapevine he returned. Back into the hotel bar trooped Lord Muck in his hussar jacket and cherry coloured drainpipe trousers. He caused a hiccup in the buzz of conversation.

Moi aussi. I cut the call I was making and rang Kathy in the room. She was with us in as long as it takes to touch up makeup.

My intended sermon died on my lips. Something was wrong, although Hendrix had got his ciggies. He smoked one, then another, then some more, lighting each from the embers of the last. He was ashen as their ends.

'They were waiting for me, man,' he told me, as he downed a rum n' coke—or three. 'I took a taxi; told him take me any place with shops. And they was there waiting for me, miles away! What's that tell you, man?'

He wasn't offering his *Camels* round, so Kathy proffered a *Silk Cut*. I don't usually smoke but needed cover for some thinking.

'That the taxi driver was theirs?' I suggested. A good debrief examines every byway, however unpromising.

Hendrix shook his head. It matched his hands.

I wouldn't have had him down as an impressionist, but he was. In his short time here Hendrix had absorbed more of us than you'd credit. Of course, London-cabbie is easy. I wondered how he'd do me.

'*Where jew wanna go, mate?*' Jimi mimicked in pure Cockney, screwing his face up rat-like for the full visual effect. '*I'll say one fing for you nig-nogs: you're always bleedin' cheerful!*'

I almost smiled: a career first.

'Not one of them then...'

'I sure hope not, man, otherwise they got all you cats on their side!'

'Not quite all, Mr Hendrix. Then what happened?'

'I *told* you, man! They was already in the shop—like they know everything before I think of it. So I skidooed—but there was two more in the next taxi I hopped into. They offered me smokes—my usuals—and hash: my favourite *Red Leb,* and acid too, man: you name it: any damn stuff I want they got it there wrapped and ready...'

'Tell me you didn't...,' I said, warily.

Hendrix swatted his hands at me. With anyone else it would have looked queeny.

'What kinda dumbass you think I am, man? I chucked it out the window, right in front in of their damn pasty faces!'

'What did they say to that?'

Hendrix stared at me full on.

'They told me they *did not like me,* man! Not 'cos of the dope. They just don't like me *bad!* Plus they'd come a *long* way to say so. Yeah? Well, thanks for nothing, guys! Like I couldn't see that already! They just sitting there in funeral suits, skinny as dead men. Still as stiffs too. Only thing moving in them cats is a whole lotta hate in their eyes. They one *angry* set of motherfuckers!'

I didn't 'dig' that. *Language* before womenfolk? Not nice. Even if was only Kathy. Distracted, Jimi missed my frown—which took some doing.

'Oh yeah,' he added, diving back into the cesspit of memory to retrieve something he'd rather not. 'And then they said we'd meet again...'

He should be counting himself lucky to have that to look forward to. As should I: there's such a thing as professional image and track records to consider. In my trade you just can't afford to lose clients: word gets around.

'Where did they get out?' It was a long shot but might just tell me something. In the event it told me everything.

'That's the deal, man! I know how I look—I could pass for your pale brother, right? And you know why *that* is?'

'No,' I said, deadpan. 'But I'm dying to find out...'

'I'm gonna tell, if you'll let me, dangerous-dude. It's 'cos they never got outta that taxi. I'm telling you, man, no word of a freakin' lie, they just... *shazam*!'

I curbed my mounting impatience. Just.

'Mr Hendrix, you know very well I can't speak jive.'

Jimi's brow creased and he dashed a hand through his hair. A clump came away with his fingers. Then he so far forgot himself as to take out his fear and frustration on me.

'What you on about, man? *Shazam's* circus-spiel, not brother-talk. But okay, have it your way: let me spell it out for you in pure *spook*!'

He straightened up, straightened his stars and stripes waistcoat, maybe even straightened out his thought processes (toxins permitting).

'The gentlemen in question,' he intoned, sounding like his idea of a BBC presenter, 'departed without deploying the taxi door. Or indeed, requiring the taxi to stop—or even slow. They simply transmogrified into the ether!'

I think sarcasm is the lowest form of wit. I informed my client of it—or something along those lines. Kathy shot from stage right to interpose her body between us.

'What Jimi means,' she said, her hot breath playing on me, 'is that they... like, *vanished*!'

I looked into her eyes and saw that she believed. Which left me little choice.

※

'Everywhere.'

'*Everywhere*, man?'

'Together. Everywhere. From now on.'

I caught the flash of interest in Kathy's eyes but kept my mind on the job.

'Understand, Mr Hendrix? That's the deal: the only one on the table. Otherwise I quit.'

Hendrix didn't want to be abandoned: he'd acquired that much wisdom, or been that badly scared. But you could see that fear was battling with his 'freedom' hang-up.

He prevaricated.

'You sure, man? I mean, I hang out some pretty strange places...'

Pathetic. Procrastination. He knew I'd been around, had... seen things.

'I'll risk that, Mr Hendrix.'

Eventually he smiled. His slow teeth-peeling grin, doubtless the downfall of countless pairs of knickers.

'Well, on your head be it, man. I always wondered about them Siamese twins cats. Guess now I'm gonna find out...'

Then, strange to tell, I found out there was some steel beneath the satin. I'd misjudged him. His smile hardened, his eyes likewise. Experience emerged from his lips.

'And you're gonna find out what it's like to walk in *Jimi's* shoes...'

※

They pinched, metaphorically speaking. You had no privacy; no one was sincere. The whole world wanted a piece of you and most had no sense of shame. Within five minutes I was sick of it and them. So I dealt out some sore faces in the first few days and cleared a little space.

Worse still, his life had no *structure*. Things happened at random and fizzled out the same way. I found it intolerable but Jimi muddled through. Maybe it accorded with his world-view, insofar as all the narcotics let him have one. Those I couldn't wean him off. At the time I thought it wasn't any of my business.

Mind you, having to be his daddy wasn't all bad. I had the great pleasure of refusing a patched-up Keith Moon entry to my client. Likewise, sundry other rock-star royalty and riff-raff I took against. For instance—McCartney: *yes*, but Lennon: *no*. On a whim. For a laugh.

I said had it been *Lenin*, that would be different. Ho ho. *My*, how they huffed and puffed—when safely out of reach.

Not only that, but each night Kathy made a meal out of getting undressed for bed in front of me. The minx. I was almost tempted to look—but didn't. Then every night I slept the sleep of the just at the foot of their king-sized bed. Once they went to sleep that is—which was sometimes delayed.

All in all I was getting that warm glow you get from a job well done and victories over the self. But not all glows are good. Like with hypothermia for instance. No, in retrospect I think it's better to feel you're doing so-so but not as well as you might. That might have saved me from breaking my word to Mr Hendrix.

You don't recall? Forgotten already? Typical. I'd said *'Everywhere'* and *every*where it should have been. But the time came, some while later, when I slacked off: slipped up. We were backstage after some gig and I'd already sussed the place out once, even stuck my head into each stinky toilet cubicle. However, truth be told (*shaming* truth), I just didn't fancy accompanying my client to the gents. Whilst he went I simply stood outside the door and barred the way. Which should have been good enough.

And what was it my first NCO always said to me? *'Good enough' is for civvies...'*

I don't know how they got past. Or perhaps they were already there—though I doubt it. My suspicion is that they had other means: which sort of exonerates me. Except that it doesn't—not after the taxi tale. I should have known. Only children and academics believe in or rely on Reason.

He was taking his time, but there was nothing especial in that. All the stuff he took, his stomach was often crook. Either that or he was shooting up. As was his right. So long as it didn't threaten our contract, i.e. his life, I had no objections.

Then it went on too long. Either he'd dozed off, overdosed or had a groupie in there with him. He hadn't permission for any of those.

The door was held. Not locked or barred or stuck, but secured by someone. Someone deploying superior strength to me. Which, I hope you'll forgive me saying, is pretty impressive.

At the time that shook me, though subsequent review devalued the superior muscle theory. More likely the door was taken out of time: sealed within a given second. So I needn't hit the gym or sign up with Charles Atlas after all.

Whatever it was, they had confidence in it, to the point of being casual. Cocky even. I could tell it was just one person, at ease, in no danger of a sweat. For an instant they pressed a pasty face to the frosted glass. I got to see a squashed smile. Perfect teeth but dead eyes.

This was England, so I wasn't tooled up, leastways not shooter-wise. Even with a phone to hand, getting a van load of mates was a good twenty minutes away. It was down to me and me alone. As always.

Kathy arrived. She'd sensed the tension.

'Keep trying the door,' I said. 'And scream.'

Lovely girl: no *'what?'*s or *'why?'*s. She just got on with things.

And proved good at it—should have been one of Dr Who's assistants. No sense of embarrassment either. Her banshee *blue murder* took away the privacy of whatever was going on in there. They hadn't a free run any more.

By the time I was outside and round the back of the venue I had my jacket off (never did see that again—a Savile Row suit spoilt) and sock-blade out. With that slim comfort between my teeth I shinned up what looked like the correct drainpipe. Which pretty much did for the trousers too.

The outside window was frosted. I resisted the most obvious option and scaled past it instead, then swung in feet first (scratching my handmade Italian loafers—today was a wardrobe write-off day…). By that time a crowd of ghouls and gawpers had gathered below to see the show. Mostly teenyboppers and hippies—fortunately the Filth (police, to non-Brits among you) hadn't arrived yet. Hopefully, they all headed slivers of shattered bog glass.

Inside, the place was echoey-empty. I landed cat-like and was ready for anything—except nothing. The unexpected non-event left me looking like a splayed-legged scruff suffering from a touch of the trots.

I couldn't decide whether there was just the usual smell: old *Dettol*, or something burnt too: maybe fluoride or chlorine. At that moment it hardly mattered. I was alone.

'Mr Hendrix?'

Nothing.

'MR HENDRIX!'

At that point Kathy fell in from the opposite side. Whatever prevented her till then had suddenly gone. I stowed the knife away before she could see.

'Jimi? *JIMI?*'

We exchanged looks. Kathy was a believer anyway, but I hoped she'd been in time to glimpse the face at the opaque window. It wasn't my imagination. There *had* been people.

'Stay there,' I snapped. 'Leave it to me.'

Like I said: sensible kid. No lip, just a nod.

I kick-opened each trap. One, two, three—well, you get the picture…

The last door banged not against porcelain but knees.

Thank Gawd. Jimi was not only alone but decent too. Trousers up, though face down. Then he looked at me.

Except it wasn't Jimi—or not a him I'd ever seen before. All the joy was gone. Even his Guardsman-on-sentry-duty *Afro* drooped.

I know eyes like that: long-service Foreign Legionaries, or '*Les Affreux*' for-the-fun-of-it Congo mercenaries. Basically, people even God had finished with.

'Mr Hendrix?'

Those eyes pleaded with me. Then Kathy. Neither of us proved much help.

'They *spoke* to me...,' he said eventually, *long* and drawn out. Not the usual *'Hey, baby...'* Hendrix at all. 'They... they like *told* me things...'

The silence way outstayed its welcome.

I went in and hauled Hendrix off the Scottish jacuzzi. That took all the reserves he had left. He went limp as lettuce in my arms, so I held off with any questions.

Kathy was more innocent—or ruthless. Enter outraged dolly-bird, easy mistress of wherever she moved—even a rock-venue gents.

'Told you what?' she asked her lover, combative, close up.

'Don't...,' I advised. Like I said, I'd seen similar cases. Similar—but never this bad.

Aloft only by dint of my support Jimi raised his head to meet her gaze.

Yet it was she who retreated. Those high-heel kinky-boots almost put her on her backside, down in the dubious damp.

He hadn't said a word—but Cathy had just got an inkling.

❂

'The story of life is quicker than the wink of an eye.
The story of love is hello and goodbye.
Until we meet again.'

Lines by Jimi Hendrix. 11.30 p.m. Thursday 17th September 1970.

❂

He never did say, not about what 'they' told him. Not in so many words anyway. I like to think it was because Jimi was basically a decent sort who didn't want to burden us.

But I was the one who had to sit beside his bed in the following days. Kathy couldn't take the thrashing about, the flailing limbs. Or, to be blunt, the wet mattresses. So it was yours truly who got to hear the fallout from his dreams. The only good thing to be said about which was that he didn't say *'man'* in them.

'They' were from the future, I got that much. Or so they said. And they blamed him, amongst *many* others, for the pickle they were in. Based upon rock n' roll starting the rot...

Evidently, in their days only the reckless ventured out. The streets were pure Darwin. Yet these were the very cream of their generation. Patriots even. *They* dared go out, to cooperate—like few people did any more. They used a time device and came back to prevent their epoch being born. Suicide bombers, sort of. Or *'vampire groupies from the future'* as Kathy put it when I filled her in.

Once he woke Jimi must have guessed he'd been processing during sleep what wouldn't come out as conscious speech. The shredded sheets spoke volumes—as had he. He could also see I was curious.

'Don't worry, man,' he said (back to business as usual, alas...). 'It's cool. They can't *kill* me. That wouldn't work. They said: *If it happened, it happens*. What they call *'The Grandfather Paradox'*. What? I dunno. Don't ask me, man; I didn't get it either. All I know is they gotta make me kill *myself*...'

To my amazement I saw him actually consider obliging them. He went up in my estimation then. The present they'd outlined to him must have been really something. Something worth preventing, even at the ultimate cost to himself.

Then the ethics of our own age and civilisation kicked back in. What was in it for him?

'The hell I will! Ain't *my* fault, man. I'm sorry they living under siege in their fortress high-rises, man; I'm sorry about all the granny-rapes, but, like, my *'Purple Haze'* ain't the reason for that! Wasn't Janis or Brian's fault neither! Or Joe Strummer's—whoever *he* is... or was. And, hey, like we gotta warn John!'

It's shaming but I felt a wave of compassion for him then. Hendrix was alone with the consequences of his actions in a way no one should be. Not till you appear before the Just Judge anyway. If you believe in all that rubbish...

Well, maybe I do, a bit. Off and on. Don't quote me but right then I felt like I owed the Big G something from the dross and cinders I'd made of the life he'd given me *gratis*. Fortunately the feeling passed...

However, when Hendrix looked at me in honest panic I sympathised. Even when he held my hand I didn't mind. It may have looked homo but what the hell...

'You gotta help me, man! I need help bad!'

ALTERED ENGLANDS

He was a naked soul clutching at any straw that might break his freefall.

And for once I spoke from the heart. Which was an organ I hadn't heard from in *ages*. Jimi could even have been skint but I'd still have said the same!

'I'm here for you, Mr Hendrix. *I'm* your future!'

Kathy wasn't present and Jimi's not around any more. So you and me are the only people who know I weakened.

Which is a relief. Nowadays I'd deny it. And who'd believe *you*?

✺

'I need help bad, man!'

Last known recording of Jimi Hendrix's voice. Message left on manager Chas Chandler's answerphone 1.30 a.m. Friday 18th September 1970.

✺

'I can't rest! I can't sleep!'

Kathy was on the bed beside Jimi, showing more leg than was kind and sipping from a bottle.

'Here,' she said, 'have some of this. It's what you usually do.'

True enough, but few things were *usual* at present. The move from their flat had been sudden and brutal. Because 'they' had arrived and established a cordon. It had taken my... *you-shift-because-I-won't* driving mode, and a tank-sized car reversed right up to the door, to fetch Jimi and Kathy away with minimal baggage. Revving off, I've no idea how we missed ploughing one of the black-suited brethren into the road.

In retrospect, perhaps we didn't. Maybe they died stoically and silent, leaving no trace in our time—their own dim and distant past.

It was Kathy who knew of the *'Samarkand Hotel'* in posh Holland Park—I didn't enquire how. It was ideal so I made a mental note of the place for future reference. Central but obscure, solicitous but incurious. How come I'd not heard of it before? Some of my leathery South African clients would love the place. You could be a recluse or entertain whores or nuns or both and no one would comment. Old style service—or maybe ultra modern.

Best of all, our rooms came complete with panorama. Surveillance couldn't help but be surveyed.

But then it turned out they didn't give a damn. Allegedly, no one did where/when they came from. It took them less than an hour to find us. Then they deployed the patience of the dead. Plus the shamelessness of corpses too. Seen or unseen: so what?

Hour after hour, rain or shine, they stood under the streetlights looking in. It was hard to estimate numbers, whether few or many: they all looked so similar. Yet even I could feel their intent. It was a wonder it didn't rattle the windows.

'Should I call the police?' asked Kathy.

By then Jimi and I had both moved on beyond her streamlined simplicities. He towards my world and I towards his. From that halfway house we both laughed simultaneously: kindred sour sounds

'If you like, baby,' he said. 'But ain't you better flush our stash first?'

That gave her pause for thought.

'Oh yeah...'

'Like, *yeah*...,' he echoed.

She still looked unsatisfied, so I spelt it out.

'This isn't police territory, Miss. More my field...'

Kathy edged to the window and peered from behind a tweaked curtain.

Her recalibration took just a second. I doubt she carried a sackful of 'O' levels, but Kathy had studied at the University of Life—and graduated with high honours. Far better.

'Maybe you're right,' she said, and would never raise the issue again. Probably never even think of it.

Just as well. By the next morning even my nerves were taut—and as for Jimi...

An impasse. I couldn't go out and leave them, but Hendrix wouldn't come with me. And no one knew how Kathy felt—probably not even her. Room service would do for a while but not forever. I started thinking in terms of that van of old mates and a diversion. Then we'd crash out, squish anyone in our way, and go somewhere I knew of that made Mongolia look like Trafalgar Square. A *really* secret refuge some of us had prepared in case times got *bad* bad.

ALTERED ENGLANDS

For me that time had come—though in reality I realised even then such thoughts were just wasted electricity. They'd find us on the far side of the Moon. It might buy us a breather but sooner or later they'd be there.

So, by breakfast of the second day I'd thought on. In the quiet watches of the night there'd been self-criticism. *'A man's gotta do...'* etc. etc. You don't run from problems: you confront them and give the *problems* problems.

Sorted! This was more *me*. I ordered and wolfed down a full English breakfast. If you're going to have a last meal it might as well be something iconic. And delicious.

Kathy watched me *gronff* and nibbled a stolen sausage.

Sometime after dawn Jimi lurched from bed to bathroom. His eyes were red-rimmed pain-pits. You had to wonder how long it'd been since he'd had any real rest. First of all the wall-to-wall parties and gigs and drugs, then... this mob outside. And topping the lot to keep him up and wide awake was the ever-lively Miss Etchingham. Now his body was finally presenting the bill.

'How do I get this stuff outta my head, man?' came his voice, quavering and echoey from the tiled hotel loo. 'I can't get no relief!'

My heart was touched. My temper too. But both operate under strict control. They just happened to accord with what I'd already decided. A sort of 'Amen Corner': nice, but by no means essential.

What was it Nelson's last signal said? Not the *'England Expects'* thing—the British Army kicked that out of me—but his actual *last* one: *'Engage the enemy more closely'*. Sound advice for any young man.

'Can't stand this,' I told Kathy. 'See to him, will you? I'm gonna see to *them.*'

'Gonna'? *'Gonna'*! I meant *'am going to'*. Present company was rubbing off on me. For shame...

There was another famous saying I was fond of. And safe in assuming that neither of these... children would be familiar with. Captain Oates might be an icon to me but his sort wouldn't be their *'bag'*.

'I am just going outside,' I said, loud enough for both to hear,. 'And may be some time...'

'Don't go, man!'

Hendrix's head peered round the bathroom door, his hair sodden from time under the taps. 'You *cain't* go: I'm paying you, man!'

'He'll be back,' Kathy said, at her most maternal. 'It's for the best.'

312

I nodded.

Hendrix trusted her, if not me.

'Yeah? You reckon?'

'You try and sleep,' she coaxed, stroking his furrowed brow. 'You need it. Get some rest and he'll be here again when you wake.'

But to me, not a word, not even goodbye. From either. Duly noted.

One final check at the window to see they were still there. They were. I'd sort of half-hoped not. But thereagain, only half...

Speed. Aggression. Commitment. Once your decision's made you call up those terrible triplets. Or 'Trinity', if you prefer. Moderation is rarely the best policy in life or... anywhere else.

Down in the lobby I drew breath, composed myself, envisaged some variant outcomes, then—*whoosh!*—piled past reception, crashing open the front doors. Out on the street puddles splashed dramatically underfoot.

They weren't expecting me, there was that comfort. We hadn't become total prey. Or so I thought then.

The nearest one, sickly pale in the lamplight, looked up, looked for a way out, saw there wasn't one. In a second or so we'd be having a no-nonsense chat. In the absence of satisfactory pledges re my client—non-harassment and so on—I was going to break some bones. Probably neck bones. People die in London all the time and the Coroner doesn't necessarily always hear...

Despite almost getting run over by a taxi I *nearly* had him. Before he vanished. First a fumble in his coat pocket like he was going for a gun, then an all-over shimmer of yellow, then... there he wasn't any more. Save for that burnt air odour—and something else. Something I might have the misfortune to recognise.

Though I didn't acknowledge that. Not yet. Then was not the time for reminiscing how cooked persons smell.

Instead, I explained-away: which is different from explaining. Maybe this particular one had some special futuristic means of slipping from my grasp, something *beyond* my grasp. But never mind, there were plenty more where he came from.

So I went for the next nearest link in the surrounding chain. He bolted but, looking back, saw I was gaining. And then left the scene like his chum. Timely-wise, *just* as I was at his heels.

And the same with the third, and the fourth and the.... Well, you can surely extrapolate...

ALTERED ENGLANDS

I followed. I followed a whole succession of them ringed round us. Plus it wasn't like they were hard to spot: a gaggle of junky-funeral-director lookalikes lurking around snooty Holland Park in swinging London-town. You might say they stuck out somewhat. At the time I thought that *their* tactical mistake.

One by one they flicked out like lights. I was left clutching at air.

Finally, hiding behind the hotel, I found a female of the species—not that that meant an ounce of difference to me, merely a change. I remember her hot sunken eyes and rattail hair. *Scant* rattails. Although, unlike the rest, she seemed sad to quit the scene. There were tears. Yet she also fiddled in her pocket just the same and the obliterating light came.

Her courage shamed me. I couldn't delude myself any more. These people weren't going anywhere: they were *going*. To the place no one comes back from—unless you believe in ghosts or Jesus. The trip of a lifetime, next stop Oblivion. Courtesy of some grenade gadget from their own era.

I suppose it was nice of them—and unlike them—not to wait till I was in range and take me too. Or two.

Yet overall their policy could be interpreted several ways. Either they were *so* scared of a close encounter—and I don't rate myself *that* high—or else they had purpose. Self-sacrificing, admirable, purpose...

Too late it struck me—and I could have struck myself. While the cat was lured away the mice had probably played.

Neat. Very neat. Not all ambushes are noisy.

Only a short-fused thug (which I'd not realised myself to be till then) would have fallen for it. But there I was in the street, alone, led-on and suckered in: far from my client and further still from wisdom. In short, a very silly-billy-bully. It came on to rain again. A judgment.

I looked up from my shoes. At the far end of Lansdowne Crescent, standing with a ready avenue of escape down Ladbroke Grove if need be, there was another of them. Perhaps he or she was the last. Or maybe a leader: officer class. Whatever the case, their side were still around. And smiling too, I don't doubt.

For a second I wished I could use the rain as cover and weep. But that simply wouldn't do. Maybe in the afterlife—if there is one and I make it. As a luxury denied me down here.

It turned out that 'escape' wasn't on their wish-list. The distant figure waved to me—though I didn't think it was a fond farewell. Then they shimmered, a splash of lemon-yellow light against the Holland Park dusk. Then nothing. Nothing at all ever again.

And why not? Job done; nothing to linger for. Like me, they didn't want to hang around—except their remedy was more radical.

Then I felt Time start to shudder. No other way to express it. An aftershock from a tremor far away, working its way backwards. A consequence of many people being *un*born. You'll probably find the precise moment on some seismic record somewhere.

I dashed back to the hotel room, more in hope than expectation.

'Don't disturb him,' said Kathy, finger to lip. 'He's finally drifted off...'

I feared she was right, more right than she could imagine. Pushing past I went and looked.

And pointed out the froth of vomit round Jimi's mouth. The froth that was in no way disturbed by breath. Kathy belatedly saw the significance of that.

I once was a combat-medic, for a while. I knew the proper procedures: check heart, check pulse etc. No call for that here. This was just meat under a sheet now: manifest in all the little signs you'd struggle to express on paper but were dead giveaways. So I didn't touch. Anyway, in the circs. I wanted to minimise my tracks before making tracks.

Kathy was beside me. She could see the score—and as ever, ate what was set before her without whinging. She closed Jimi's eyes.

By the bedside was a little bottle. *'Vesperax Sleeping Tablets'* the label said. Which I don't doubt they were, plus whatever *extra* our friends had added. It was empty.

'Remember when he was rooting round the bathroom?' I said. 'Maybe he got them then...'

Kathy nodded. Her eyes were moist. She used her fringe to hide it.

'There'll be questions asked,' I advised. 'And I can't be around to answer them. You *do* understand that, don't you?'

Another nod. A tear was dislodged to splash onto the shagpile. *Top girl* to the end.

'I'll send my bill to his manager. Mention it would be unwise to welch. He's got seven days: on the eighth he won't need money any more. Got that? And *I* need ten minutes before you phone the ambulance. It won't make any difference to Mr H-... *Jimi*, but might mean big grief to me. Also you'll need to put your own thinking-cap on before they arrive. For instance, why didn't you hide your medication from him? You saw the state he was in...'

Stupid. I should have guessed. Again, I could have kicked myself. My brain really was going soft, my game well wonky in this toxic bubblegum-world I'd gotten involved in. High time to head abroad where things were simpler. Deadlier, true: yet also cleaner...

'But I don't *take* sleeping pills,' said Kathy.

Sigh.

Of course she didn't. Kathy was hardly the insomnia sort.

Time for a parting gift. She'd benefit from understanding the calibre of people we'd been dealing with. Who'd *dealt* with us.

Clever people—but cruel people. The kind you could now be glad had never been born.

Because there was no *need* for their parting, Parthian shot. Totally gratuitous—and thus *them* to a tee. Kathy Etchingham had never hurt them but they were happy to hurt her. Eager even.

Marvellous attention to detail though...

'That's not what it says here,' I said—and showed her whose name was on the bottle. Typed on a proper chemist's label and all official.

Kathy gasped.

Some futures deserve aborting. Jimi didn't die in vain.

JOHN WHITBOURN

AFTERWORD

'I just don't give a damn as long as I have beautiful England to come back to.'

'... after I learned how to read and write, I figured there wasn't much more they could tell me, because I was more interested in the next world than this one—because I didn't like very much the way this one is.'[45]

Jimi Hendrix (1942-1970).

Jimi Hendrix arrived in England for the very first time on Saturday 24th September 1966, off a *Pan Am* flight from *JFK*. He was travelling 1st class and also travelling light. His possessions comprised a change of clothes, some acne cream, pink plastic hair curlers and a guitar. His worldly wealth totalled $40. He informed Immigration Control he intended only a visit.

In terms of gaining entry he should have had two chances: slim or none. However, the Immigration Officer (Stamp number 62: yes, *you*...) was either... kindly or seized by a prophetic spirit. Certainly, some that I used to know often acted under the influence of spirits. Either way, Jimi's passport was stamped and into our country he came. *Good.*

He played a club that very night (as was always his intention), in the way visitors *sans* a work permit shouldn't, and at the end of that very same evening met the redoubtable and delectable twenty year old English-rose, Kathy Etchingham. They hit it off. As did Jimi's music. Word-of-mouth turned rapidly into acclaim and stardom. He never looked back.

Up to that point, not a lot had gone right for Mr Hendrix career-wise: or any other-wise really, but from that auspicious September night onwards things just got better and better for him—until he died of the downside of meteoric success. Meanwhile, England made him and Ms Etchingham made it complete.

---

[45] Both quotes from *'Jimi'* by Curtis Knight. W H Allen 1974.

ALTERED ENGLANDS

Along the way he became an honorary Englishman, having seen the sunnier side of life and humanity here. Reportedly, he wished to be buried in London, but that never happened. As didn't many things Mr Hendrix wished and deserved.

Yet things went right for a while. Which is the most any of us can hope for whilst still abiding in *'Samsara'* (aka *'This Vale-of-Tears'* aka *Babylon*). It was Kathy (if I may be so familiar…) who provided Jimi with his first and last experience of stability and a happy homelife. Which just happened to be an upstairs glorified bed-sit in Brook Street, Mayfair. Next door, coincidentally enough, to where the musician Handel (1685-1759) once lived. Both properties, now lovingly restored and justly proud of their associations, may be toured by arrangement. Indeed, I've often done so. Supposedly, Jimi saw Handel's ghost there, as have other, suitably attuned, tourists. I'm not numbered among those few, but can nevertheless report a palpable… spirit of place.

In all probability, and (one devoutly hopes) as doubtless happened in many variant worlds in the multiverse, if Jimi had stayed with the redoubtable, delectable etc. Kathy, he might well be alive today, and still making music. As to what sort of music that might be, who can say? Other than to observe you can bet the farm it would be *interesting*…

However, it didn't turn out that way, and, as Oscar Wilde learned to his cost and observed:

'Life is a very terrible thing'.

Mr Hendrix (or Jimi, if I may…) R.I.P.

☸

JOHN WHITBOURN

22~

A PILLAR OF THE CHURCH

INTRODUCTION

'Beware the Protestant minister,
his false reason, false creed and false faith:
the foundation stones of his temple
are the bollocks of Henry the Eighth.'

Brendan Behan (1923-64). Speaking on US television talk show, *'The Open End'*, November 1960.

Bishop Beaw—or Bew, as per some records—(1615-1705) is another real-life character I've kidnapped from the past and cruelly made to dance for me. Whether he was really like this I cannot say for sure, but I rather suspect so—which is why I've disturbed his well deserved rest. If I'm wrong in that then I apologise to the Bishop here and now in this world, and trust that changed perspectives will render apology irrelevant in the next.

A clue that my depiction may be not entirely alien to the truth comes from the fact that Beaw, a fellow of New College Oxford, chucked his studies right at the start of the English Revolution[46] and hastened to take twelve of his pupils and other scholars into Charles I's service. Then, in his own words, he:

> '... *served the King from a pike to a major of horse, was wounded in the service (and on that account still halt) and kept long a prisoner of war, and at last turned out of his Fellowship and all that he had, and forced by his sword (which at first he never intended to draw but for his own Prince) to seek his bread in foreign parts...*'

Those parts including such far flung places as Muscovy, where he had an '*honourable and profitable service*', and Sweden and Poland.

However, we join the good Bishop when all that is past and when, after the restoration of the monarchy, he has come into his reward for loyalty. Alas, since that reward is the impoverished Bishopric of Llandaff in Welsh-speaking Wales some tiny particles of discontent remain...

It only remains to say that in my humble and uninvolved opinion, if the Church of England had properly cherished men of Beaw's ilk and recruited more of the kind, then Anglicanism might not be teetering on the verge of undignified extinction.

Still, as Anglican bishops supposedly so often say, 'in a very real sense' I'm sure that they know best...

And by the by, I *do* realise that, conventionally, there can only be one dean per cathedral, even in the disputed badlands of the Church in Wales. Yet in this case someone—I or the Muse or Bishop Beaw—decreed differently. No one wise would argue with those last two. Plus '*The past* [and Wales] *is a foreign country: they do things differently there*'.[47]

Dearly beloved, a reading from the gospel according to Beaw...

---

[46] Formerly 'The English Civil War'. Normally I disapprove of altering time-hallowed terminology to fit changing, often transient, opinion, but in this case I think the re-christening is necessary and accurate.

[47] L.P. Hartley, *The Go-Between*. 1953.

JOHN WHITBOURN

A PILLAR OF THE CHURCH

'A POESY OF DEVOTION TO MY OWNE TRUE LOVE'
by Bishop William Beaw, D.D. (1615-).

'My love is like a thrice-charged cannon
a' thund'ring in the breach,
her bee-stung lips more sweet
than squadrons of hors-ed men
trampling Turks to the turf,
bashing their turbaned bonces into bits:
which I've seen full many a-...'

'A dull-dog line, that,' muttered the Bishop. 'I'll slash her about later.'

'... which I've seen full many a time, yea,
before Vienna's embattled gates.
There was no chance for this 'love' business then-...'

'Come in!' roared Bishop Beaw. 'Come in, damn your eyes!'
No one obeyed. The scratching desisted. Beaw growled and returned all focus to the act of creation.

'... but perchance there <u>had</u> been time,
then my love would be like unto a hot saddle,

ALTERED ENGLANDS

fresh from morning patrol,
or wine and doxies after bloodshed-...'

'*Will* you come *in*, Dolly Daydream! Come in or I fire!'

This got a response: the Bishop had a record of pistol diplomacy. With painful slowness the study door edged open.

In Beaw's terminology there was 'Snivelling Dean' and 'Canting Dean'. When in pious mood, the Bishop accounted them additions to the classical proofs of God. It was, he reasoned, logical of a Loving Deity to construct tests of His shepherds' patience. The steel must be tempered and Bishops weaned off murder. Everything was put on earth for a purpose; even Frenchmen or the Church of England. Thus, out of charity, Beaw conjectured purpose in the Good Lord raising Cathedral and Rural Deans into being.

Setting the fact of outrageous interruption to one side, Beaw rejoiced it was 'only' Snivelling Dean. He didn't fancy scripture flung at him this early in the day.

'And next time,' the Bishop exploded, even so, 'clutch your courage, not your privy parts! I heard you scritching and scratching outside. Knock and enter like a man! I won't bite!'

To be fair, Snivelling Dean had no certainty of that. In fighting mood the Bishop was known to use whatever weapons lay to hand. Failing all else, teeth would do...

Nevertheless, his dispiriting slab-face crossed the Tiber/threshold. Less venturesome, the attached body hedged its bets by remaining outside.

'But I have only this moment arrived, Bishop...'

'Don't bandy opinion with me, you... palsy-brain! You're always lurking about—well known for it! And you whisper to yourself as well. Put a cork in it. God hates whisperers!'

Snivelling Dean plainly didn't agree but had more pressing disputes to raise.

'The time, Bishop! The time!'

Beaw consulted his pocket watch. No prior engagement sprang to mind. The cauldron of fury began to bubble...

'Time? Aye, the time that I indulge my muse, you dog!'

'No, Bishop, time for Holy Communion!'

Troubling recollection gave the Bishop pause. He put the paperweight down.

'Holy what? Oh, *that*. No, I did that... some while back.'

'Easter season comes round again, Bishop. You recall: we spoke of it—at the Chapter meeting...'

'*You* may have done,' said Beaw, grumpily, obliged to agree.

'There are certain expectations, Bishop. Your flock awaits.'

'You mean there's *people?*'

'Dozens, Bishop—and growing impatient.'

'People?' protested Beaw, lumbering out of bed, vast and naked, all the same. 'People! Why can't they take the hint? The Cathedral's in ruins, we disbanded the choir and I'm *busy*. God's teeth! Why they must bother me just to worship the Almighty I *do* not know. What's wrong with private prayer? God's equally present in an open field, even a Welsh one, and-...'

'The inestimable honour of the Apostolic succession,' intoned 'Canting Dean', ever a silent arrival like the ghost Beaw said he resembled, 'involves certain duties. The sheep must be fed, the... good shepherd must celebrate the Lord's Supper. Our Saviour commands it.'

There was no answer to that, but Beaw made moves to return to bed.

'It takes *hours*,' he complained. 'It's long-fangled.'

'I shall be there to guide you, Bishop,' purred Canting Dean.

The Bishop surveyed his high-boots, standing to attention by the commode. They were a devil to get on. It was all so... wearying.

'Bread and wine,' he muttered, in last-ditch resistance, 'a mummers' dance around the altar. You're both educated men—well, almost—surely you don't believe this popish japery?'

Snivelling Dean was shocked, cavern mouth agape; Canting Dean merely icy.

'When last I read,' the latter observed, like a soldier piking a stricken foe, 'I found it to be one of the 39 Articles of Faith, each of which you swore to uphold at your consecration. 'Tis in the *Book of Common Prayer*, quantities of which adorn your Cathedral.'

That capped it really. If one served the 'Church by Law Established', the law deployed the final word. Beaw reached for his wig and powder jar.

'Really, Dean?' he said, surrendering. 'Oh well, you may be right...'

ALTERED ENGLANDS

❦

The Bishop brightened visibly when he heard of the threats. A new haste, a skittish spring, appeared in his steps. Snivelling Dean reported that Lord Bute promised to ply his horsewhip on someone if Easter communion was not forthcoming before ten. His Lordship had a full schedule before him, a fact that—quite understandably—obliged him to wear his hunting pinks to church. Piety was one thing but disobliging *Reynard* quite another! Bute's grooms and ostlers were at that very moment ordered to the Chapter House in search of the missing Bishop. They would find him en route—and regret it.

Both Snivelling and Canting Deans stood aside from the fray and sighed as yet more fisticuffs demeaned Llandaff Cathedral.

Those lamentations—and the cries and blasphemies—ascended into the air, finding strange echo amidst the ruinous towers.

❦

'... A bishop generally had to begin with one of the poorer sees, such as Bristol... or one of the Welsh bishoprics, three of the four miserably paid and all in remote and 'barbarous' dioceses.

... their chief ambition was generally translation to one of the richer dioceses, an ambition which sometimes took up more of their attention than their spiritual duties.

... The poorer bishoprics suffered especially from this custom of translation owing to their brief tenure, particularly in the case of the four Welsh sees: in fact, of the fifty-six bishops appointed to these four sees during the century after the Revolution [of 1688], no less than thirty-nine were translated, often within a few years or even months of their appointment.'

The Oxford History of England—The Whig Supremacy 1714-1760.
Basil William's Second Edition 1962. p 79.

❦

JOHN WHITBOURN

TO: Earl Rochester. Pudding Lane, ye 23 of March, 1670.

You asked, dear friend and patron, for a lucid account of my adventures and here it is. I was born at a very early age...

... choosing to lay down my sword—and gun and battleaxe—honourably employed first for my King and then as a soldier of fortune at the fraying edge of the glorious garment that is Christendom, I came home in search of more pacific employ. Happily, the little bishoprick of Llandaff fell free at that juncture and, on impulse, I made bid for it by dint of a rare gem I had off a Turk Janissary (we having met, he no longer requiring it!). Your kind recommendation then sorted the issue.

... my taking of the cloth was necessarily much accelerated—but God allowes that this is a liberal epoch. The minutiae of my new profession were left to be acquired in the fullness of His Grace and time. I avowed that I did indeed hold to there being a great FIRST CAUSE and my inquisitors did not press me further...

... I am advised that etiquette dictates one should actually visit one's diocese, even a Cymric one, if the See is held upward of one year and promotion does not intrude. Naturally, I am hopeful to be spared that fate. As I informed you in the Cock at Southwark, sir, I am at one with Rupert's general, my old comrade, Sir Thomas Dabridgecourt, when he opined to his commander thus:

"If your Highness shall be pleased to send me to the Turk, or Jew, or Gentile, I will go on my bare feet to serve you; but from the Welsh, good Lord, deliver me. And I shall beseech you to send me no more into this country: if you intend I shall do any service, without a strong party to compel them, not to entreat them. And then I will give them cause to put me in their Litany, as they have now given me cause to put them in mine."

I have the document sitting beside me, written at Chepstow camp in the dark year 1644, and it is stained with tears. I do <u>not</u> intend that I should thus weep, not countenancing that Almighty God would so punish his humble servant.

Another thing: did I mayhap leave my walking-stick-pistol with you? I fuzzily recall your examining of it (and, do I dream, discharging same against the Tavern wall in sport?). 'Twas a grand evening of discourse and, ah, the solace of good English ale!

I breathlessly await your words of wisdom and kind reply.

I remain, John, your loving and obedient servant.

William Beaw. Bishop of Llandaff, by God!'

ALTERED ENGLANDS

'Dear Rochester.
Llandaff,
March 1680.

Forgive the unmannerly doldrums in our corresponding intercourse. I have been in low spirits—and in spirits beside—which only assuage my woes to compound them next day. Melancholia dampens me as though Satan's own best hound has pissed upon my coat. Alas!

I picked up the little bishoprick of Llandaff upon the persuasion of all my friends and in expectation of a sudden remove and quick preferment. It has been mine now for one full decade, a disease which none of my predecessors were suffered to labour under so long. If I'd known the same before, I'd have continued a jolly blade-for-hire 'gainst TURK and FROG, and like as not laid my poxed-up, nose-less, bones 'neath foreign turf. T'would be no worse a fate than an eternity buried alive here.

Even my senses begin to unravel in competition with my hopes, and I am afflicted by whispers from nowhere and alarum calls in the night. In this Celtic twilight, Reason being thinly stretched, occult forces readily venture in. I wonder that the elves do not throw all caution aside and stroll openly in Llandaff High Road. Half my congregation here are doubtless of that stock...

On the other hand, have I advised you concerning my researches amongst Wales' fairer sex? I can only conceive that the Cymric art of love is taught in some sweet and secret academy...

... It seems that literary fame offers my last hope of escape hence and to this end I enclose another batch of verse. You have not yet told me your opinion of that quantity sent before. Exalted Earl and fellow bard, pray do not be bashful with your words of praise! Rest assured I shall not grow overweening proud through your unstinting approbation.

Sir, write! Tell me what offers my work prompts from the publishers of fair London.

I await, with mounting impatience, your missive of rescue.

WILLIAM + Llandaff.

JOHN WHITBOURN

'ODE TO LLANDAFF CATHEDRAL SEEN IN AUTUMNAL LIGHT FROM A CONVENIENT TUSSOCK'

by William Beaw

'See the mossy, ancient and neglected pile,
Oh, tumbled Welsh temple by the Taff!
Fit only for stables or baiting of the bear,
(or mayhap a small tennis court in the south corner).
How low have you come,
since founder, Dark Age Saint Teilo's day,
low as the blouse on the snow-white milkmaydes that oft
frequent your precincts but never venture in to PRAY.
Those brazen hussies, all eyes and legs and winning ways,
that nought of the queen of sciences, THEOLOGY, know,
though much else of interest, true.

But I digress, oh once stately pile,
raised to the Divine clockwork maker,
how thou hast lapsed.
And in thy ruin, trapped so many good men
in the clutches of thy rubble, alas!
Like some Welsh SAMSON, bald and blinded,
bringing unseen death to conquering Philistines.
Not that I number myself amongst them
or call the parallel exact...'

English Minor 17th Century Poets, Vol. 12. University of Little Rock Press, Arkansas, USA. 1965. [N.B. verses 3 to 37, inclusive, of this poem and BEAW's other epic odes and tragedies remain unpublished but are available to the indomitable and completist scholar on microfiche.]

'What's that?' barked the Bishop. 'Come on, speak up. God hates whisperers—I've said so before.'

The altar servers were puzzled, the scant congregation misled into thinking it part of the service. One or two responded *'Amen'* and got an episcopal glare for their pains.

Beaw recognised innocence when he saw it, rare though it might be in these parts. None of those near him had spoken. Yet, unless his wits were finally in rout, someone had hissed faint words of blasphemy into his ear.

Never the type to be shackled by mere events, Bishop Beaw ploughed on with the service. It was only to be expected, he reasoned, that those who'd seized their proper share of port and claret and the general good things of life, should have some dislocation of senses by way of penance. His Uncle, for example, ended his days pursued by a green dwarf—invisible to the rest of mankind—who ceaselessly enquired: *'Do you like fish?'*. That had been a considerable distraction but he'd borne it stoically, and gained much credit thereby. It was only on the old man's deathbed that he'd deigned to reply, and told the dwarf*: 'No. Except hake'*.

That, Beaw always maintained, was the wonderful thing about life: you could do anything you damn well pleased with it. Maturity comprised quiet acceptance of the consequences. Soldiering and injury, doxies and the pox, or port and voices: with every pleasure there came a price. Whinging about the tally only demeaned the feast before.

Whisperers were preferable to green dwarves. The Bishop reckoned he'd escaped lightly.

'They kneel to no avail,' said the voice again. *'God sleeps or never was. The bread and wine is all that it is.'*

Beaw had long suspected as much but thought it bad form to say so. The proper piety of the lower orders ought to be nurtured, even at the expense of plain English speech. And, if *living* men of good standing must be restrained by such scruples, then a shade from beyond should be doubly sensitive to its responsibilities.

'Be quiet, ghost!' he ordered.

The voice, smooth and seductive as a harlot's silken gown, was unabashed. Its tone was one of pleasure in arrival, as though great trouble or uncertainty were involved. This was not someone lightly willing to be dismissed.

'I am no ghost,' it said, not offended or distressed. *'I live. My sole business ever was with this life. There is no other. I come that you may have life more abundantly.'*

The Bishop had been reading the Bible lately (for want of better entertainments) and so recognised the deployment of scripture—and a pagan's misuse of it. For all her faults, he had the Church of England to thank for his daily bread—and port and venison—and, indirectly, the milkmaids in his bed. He thus felt honour bound to defend at least the outer walls of its tenets. A soldier had to fire a shot or two even for the worst of masters...

'Leave our Saviour's words in peace,' Beaw instructed angrily. 'Mock not, you dog!'

That got a grade one funny look from Canting Dean, but Beaw imperiously waved him on with the communion service. It was coming up to the bit with the wine doling and wafer breaking, and it was usual for him to delegate that. The Bishop found it too fiddly for his spade-like hands whereas the Deans' were dainty (suspiciously so in Beaw's eyes), well suited to juggling with chalice and paten.

'One cannot mock what is not,' countered the voice, but then deferred to the admonition. There was a moment of respite.

Beaw's thoughts wandered. He had painted himself into a corner with his latest opus, *'Ode To A Milking Stool Broken By Hard Use'*. Somewhere in the incomparable English language, somehow, there had to be a good rhyme for *chimney*... He had tortured himself about it for days.

Then the voice returned, hard by, and recounted an infinitely indecent jest about Queen Mary, an orange and a hosepipe. The Bishop's helpless guffaw ripped through the most sacred moment of divine service. Its echo, returning from the west wall a second later, doubled the dose of embarrassment.

'Sorry about that, everyone,' he told the upraised moon-faces. 'I just remembered something funny...'

The canting hypocrites didn't seem disposed to believe him, but he stared them down. If you couldn't enjoy a spot of humour (God's unique gift to mankind, after all!) in your own Cathedral, where could you? What was the world coming to? Beaw blamed the Quakers.

He also blamed the voice and thereafter ignored it. Being invisible was one thing, ditto atheism: one might not be able to help such afflictions. But no *gentleman* shamed another in public. The voice apologised in vain.

Bishop Beaw turned a deaf ear and froze him out.

ALTERED ENGLANDS

❁

'A Survey of all the Cathedral Churches of England, Wales and Cornubiae'.
By Browne Willis.
Undertaken in the year of grace 1717.'

'... the poor desolate church of Llandaff...'

❁

He was quizzing the Cathedral's west front from a steep rise adorned with even older ruins. Snivelling Dean had once told him what they'd been but he'd vomited the knowledge forth post-haste. At that time he'd not been planning to linger a Welsh bishop overlong...

Bishop Beaw wondered again what it was that Llandaff Cathedral reminded him of—other than purgatory. Some similarity had been nagging away at him for years, forever teasingly *just* beyond reach (rather like Canting Dean's will-she/won't-she wife). Likewise, as with that hot-eyed minx, Beaw knew a too ardent pursuit would not advance his cause. Consummation and closing of the simile-circle would come of its own accord or not at all. *'Never run after women or coaches'*, his father had advised him as he mounted the scaffold, blessing his son with the distilled wisdom of a well lived lifetime, *'there'll be another along in a minute.'*

How true, how true. And doubtless the same applied to coquettish thoughts. Bishop Beaw turned a cold shoulder on the inner tickle—and it there and then surrendered (just like Madame Canting would one New Year's Eve a few years hence). He swiftly sampled all its joys whilst the notion was still warm and willing.

So, *that* was it! He recalled now, with increasing ease, trampling down the undergrowth infesting a mental path not travelled for three decades.

They'd bombarded the Bosnian town for days and only then, just prior to the assault, did it acquire the Llandaff look. Precise recollection was still hazy, and as full of gaps as the Cathedral below him, but the likeness was not to be denied.

What the Holy Roman Emperor's cannons achieved in a noisy rush, Llandaff had gained over quiet centuries of neglect. The 'Reformation' set that ball to roll and the receding tide of faith kept it in motion. Bishop Beaw had the greatest respect for Henry VIII—a man after his own heart—but conceded he'd been rough on wives and churches. All the old carved saints were headless thanks to him, all the gold and gilt gone to fund his forgotten wars. People turned cautious about gifts to God's house when Parliament decreed what was holy and all was chop and change. Dying men left their wealth as they saw fit nowadays, to punish wives from beyond the grave or stir up family trouble. Why endow an altar or bestow plate when, like as not, the King would have it? And since 'purgatory' was no more (and probably illegal) no one commissioned prayers for departed loved ones. The old 'Chantry priests' faded away. Today's souls were left to face judgement without defending counsel.

Bishop Beaw saw the good sense of it all, the necessity for progress, but sometimes he... regretted. There was a lot to be said against Popery but it did at least provide for Church repairs.

What he was reliably informed (and recalled!) was that the 'Jasper Tower' had lost its pinnacles in a storm a while back. True, it didn't owe them anything, being built long centuries before, but modern piety wasn't up to a replacement, so a shocking gap was left. That tumble had brought part of the nave down too, allowing the rain to come in to play. Fierce argument had then raged about the fitness of male headgear in church, and whether wet pates might be a sacrifice properly demanded by God. Bishop Beaw had settled *that* issue with some torn tricornes and thick ears, before declining congregations ensured all fitted easily in the remaining dry portions.

The even older south-west tower looked fit to follow 'Jasper' any minute and Beaw was always careful to give the thing a wide berth. Legend said it looked out for passing pagans to shed rocks upon their heads. Needless to say, the Bishop didn't regard himself amongst that number, but equally he placed no reliance in masonry's discernment. Better safe than sorry. Despite all the times Beaw had proclaimed Llandaff would be the death of him, he had no wish to be proved right.

Amongst wise men, discovery of a curl on one's lip is an order for an end to scrutiny. The engines of the face are signalling that some sight is injurious to inner equilibrium. Bishop Beaw had no exaggerated respect for his thoughts or reasoning, but he paid proper heed to the cries of *'Brother body'*, as St Francis wisely called it. Past experience told him that prolonged study of his own personal career-morass, as realised in (crumbling) stone, put acid in his stomach and fury in his eyes. Neither were pleasing to God or man, or of use in securing escape. If anything, they threatened to one day lay him low with an apoplectic fit. That would be the final irony; if death should find him stretched out in mock homage to his edifice-enemy, struck down by its invisible claws.

'That shall not be,' husked the disembodied voice, blessedly absent this last month or two. It came from close by, intimately so, but twist as he may, Beaw could find no parent mouth.

'Go away!' he said, but alone of all the Cathedral establishment it could afford to ignore him. It had no crown to crack or toes to stamp on.

'Heed me. Embrace glory. You shall not die but live!' There was a tone of urgency now, and pain also. The psalmist's phrase particularly brought out a rasp, as though each word seared.

Beaw was not to be enticed with prolongation of life: once was nice but quite enough thank you.

And besides, it never failed to shock, *shock*, him throughout his long life, that there were people so *degraded* as to make a gentleman repeat his words.

'Go *away*, vile derangement of the senses, begone!'

'No.'

Impotent anger always brought imperial-purple to Beaw's face. Various surgeons warned him against it. He tried, he really did, Canute-style against the tide—with similar success. His sword was out and searching.

'If you had ears to notch I'd...'

Snivelling Dean then saw fit to pass by, leading a crocodile of children to or from indoctrination. Every eye turned the fighting madman's way.

'Good morning, Bishop,' he said, deadpan.

'Such malice! Such deep buried bile of resistance!' thought the Bishop. At the very least this... Dean could have feigned ignorance of the embarrassing scene. Beaw thought fast—something he reckoned undignified to do.

'Away and die!' he quipped, wittily; following it up with a bit of medieval masonry. 'Don't interrupt m' fencing practice, you mollyfrock!'

Beaw didn't check to see but felt confident his refined response would fool 'em. Leastways, they hurried on and out of his hair.

Alas, a more persistent pest lingered.

'Come with me,' it implored, quite desperate.

The Bishop's heart retained a few—narrow—avenues of access. The helpless: infants, three-legged dogs and poor milkmaids, might still draw from its drying well of compassion. On the same Christian principle, those without even a body to call their own were, on the face (!) of it, deserving candidates for indulgence.

'Well...'

'Time is short!'

There they parted company, conversationally speaking. No clock span fast enough for Beaw's tastes, and save when there was a thigh or bottle to grip, minutes could stretch out dry and tedious as a Quakers' congress.

On the other—though related—hand, there *was* the slim prospect here of diversion. Bishop Beaw positively hungered and thirsted for diversion.

'Where to?'

'I will guide your feet,' said the voice, eagerly, receding as it spoke.

Beaw could not see how this might be—unless the ghostly one was already within his reasoning faculties, tugging strings and favouring one route over another. That was a de-manning thought. The Bishop gingerly checked for alien incursions onto Beaw-land, but found all graces and opinions inviolably his alone. Images of favourite things were framed—the usual gross pleasures purified by irony and manners—meeting with impeccably correct responses. All seemed well—and yet that first step forward was still a problem. Was it *his* decision or the thing's? Were there phantom tentacles about his boots biasing them this way or that? With a man of the Bishop's bulk it wasn't easy to tell; he possessing (charitably) a stately galleon gait…

Feeling, as much as ever, his own man, Beaw left the ruin capped knoll and descended to his not *quite* so dilapidated Cathedral.

Inside the North door it was dark, even compared to the merely Welsh sunshine outside, but after so many years labouring in this vineyard the Bishop knew every puddle and pitfall. He would not stumble and besmirch himself as so many other worshippers amusingly did. Long ago he'd fixed the shortest route to do what he must in that place. Once again he took it. No tremulous shade would halter-lead a Bishop of Christ's Church-by-Law-Established!

ALTERED ENGLANDS

Early on in his exile, Beaw had discovered a little oak carving of the death-bed of Our Lady. Ancient, probably foreign, it had been black-leaded and hidden against the violence of vandal bishops and Cromwell. Whereas *this* Bishop was charmed. Red eyes that generally lit only to flesh and firearms were seduced by its... honesty. The *Allemande* or *Flemm* who'd carved it had been a sinner—but he'd also loved. Mary was shown, surrounded by confident grief, on her way to a meeting all must make. Beaw found strange grounds for hope within its foot-square. He also liked the spectacles put on St Luke.

'*God's bowels but I'm partial to 'er!*' he'd said. '*Clean that gunk off and stick her up.*'

The Dean of the time, long since gone, prematurely white-haired and shaking, to his reward, had seen fit to bandy words with his Bishop, not actually *disputing* the decision, but mumbling things like '*popery*' and '*false idols*'. Those theological niceties had been overcome (with a headbutt) and ever since the restored work had hung in a place of honour in the South aisle. Beaw went to it today, as ever.

'Good day, dear Lady,' he said, also as ever, and doffed his hat.

'*I am here,*' came a reply which froze his heart—till he recognised it as 'only' the voice.

'Where?'

'*By the window, below your heavy feet.*'

Beaw took umbrage at that: he'd slimmed down a trifle after forgoing his evening third bottle for Lent. Deliberately stamping, he crossed to the general area. Beside the tall, cracked sidelight there was a wearied mat; its pattern evident only in years-defying patches. The thing had always been there so he'd never marked it. There was a wealth of such random junk scattered about the Cathedral, once of some purpose at some point—maybe.

'Here?'

'*Lift the veil and behold my beauty.*'

Having outstared Mehmet '*The Stake*' Osman, Pasha of Sarajevo, Beaw disdained to blink before some chatty hell-truant. He puffed and laboured down to snatch away the covering.

And revealed nothing worse than a gravestone, plus more dust than a Bedu-arab might cope with. The name and dates had been chiselled out, which was fairly unusual—more Henrican, Anglican vandalism most like. A line of amateurish Greek below said (more or less) '*Whom God Loves Dies Young*'.

Beneath that was a carved lotus flower, a popular emblem within living memory, symbolising resurrection and new life.

'I do hope,' growled the Bishop, his swordstick tapping the stone like it was some sleepy debtor's door, 'that you have not put me to all this trouble just so I might pay respects. One says prayers for the departed each Easter: well, *most* Easters, and-...'

'I AM NOT DEAD!' The voice was exhausted but willing to spend scant reserves on a crucial point.

'Oh dear,' said Beaw, genuinely concerned. His age had an especial horror of premature burial. Exhumed coffins evidencing *interior* scratch marks were favourite tavern talk-killers of the day. 'How have you managed for air? My poor fellow: let me summon stout labourers and we'll soon...'

'They would find naught but dry bones. I change and decay, I rest, but I do not sleep.'

The Bishop considered the notion. He knew about Heaven, and its contrary, and of the Papist invention of Limbo. This matched nothing in his, admittedly swift, training.

'Well, you should *try*, sirrah,' was his prescription. 'It must be jolly boring down there.'

'It is.' The voice didn't just agree: it couldn't agree more.

'There you are then. Recite your times-tables: when I was at school I-...'

'I welched on death. I REFUSED it!'

Beaw didn't think he should approve. If Adam (or rather, Eve) brought death into the world then one ought not swerve it: rules were rules when THE CLOCKMAKER framed them. The Bishop looked nervously round at that thought. Poor old Llandaff could ill afford another lightning strike.

Even so, he was intrigued: this might be marketable.

'How so?'

'By will. Will holds me here: will misers each last vital drop to make a scant pool of life. I sip, sip, sip at it and linger'

Beaw tasted the notion—and spewed it out.

'No, fellow,' he advised, as kindly as might be. 'I counsel against it. Go out roaring. I want pleasured wenches in my deathbed, and the clink of ravished bottles! Or a duel—with the Archbishop; that'd suit.'

'No!'

ALTERED ENGLANDS

'Blow what's left on a last shout. Say *BOO!* to my Dean one night when he molests his wife. Grant me that jape and then go on. In return I'll dust your grave: how's that? A deal?'

Up to now the voice had concealed its venom under silky tones. Now the poison welled through.

'I will <u>not</u> surrender to the dark. There is life or there is nothing. I must rise again! You must help.'

That did it. The Bishop's hackles rose.

"Must" is it, eh? *'Must'!* Must's not a word I much relish. Least of all from a bag of bones. Beware sir, or I'll hoick you out and give my hounds a treat!'

'And I should thank you for even that. A canine husk would suffice. Better even a dog's life than this cold lingering.'

Not since 'Dirty Dick' the groom confessed to pleasure in the Bishop's horsewhipping had Beaw been so disconcerted. Threats should beget cringes not smiles.

'Oh...'

'My gratitude shall have no end. And you, you shall have any end.'

It must surely have been the revenant that framed the sinful but exciting options, the views that... arose before Beaw's inner eye like mushrooms. Of his own devices he could not have conceived cameos of such depravity.

For, direct upon the voice's word, he beheld the *'ends'* proposed, vivid, pink and inviting, of several high ladies that had caught his eye—and numerous *'ends'* to life: long postponed, happy and most glorious in their audacity. And those were amongst the most innocent of the entertainments on parade!

'I say!'

'You shall say <u>YES</u>, lustful Bishop, and 'NO' will no longer disfigure your life. Now read and learn, lucky man-of-meat, read and learn, for I must rest.'

Beaw was going to say 'Rest in Peace', but in the circumstances... It did not matter though, for his companion had retired and he was left alone—or almost so.

Suppressing a monstrous erection with his stick (to show it who was boss), the Bishop composed himself. Then, leaning over the memorial he set to 'read and learn'.

And 'Canting Dean', who had privily seen and heard all (and understood nothing) crept quietly away, thirsting for pen and paper. Llandaff's few remaining (malnourished) choristers shied horrified from him. So too did some stray sheep venturing into the Cathedral to crop its grass or pray sheepish prayers. On his corpse face, a beaming smile seemed an affront to nature.

'To: His Grace, the Archbishop of Canterbury.

... has taken to conversing with thin air—as I have witnessed myself and will swear to on my faith as a Christian—all the meanwhile beating himself about his privy parts...

... the blustering iniquities of his pagan and autocratic rule mounts outrage upon outrage into a quivering and bloody pyramid of infamy whose delineation it is not fit for my pen to transcribe—though I shall attempt it for your Grace's sake...

... no woman or mayde being proof against his slavering importuning, no placket safe from his questing hand, he bids fair to populate the Diocese with his bastard progeny, raising a new generation of Amalekites in our bosom: the which I am constrained to baptise at the Chapter's expense.

And another thing...'

Out of the compassion which fired his heart, Bishop Beaw felt that Cymric postal employees were inadequately recompensed for the risks they ran. Consideration of highwaymen, tavern rations and inclement weather caused him anguish over their plight. Therefore, for years he had supplemented the wages of all the Llandaff couriers—and they were duly grateful.

Beaw gave the Dean's intercepted letter one last, withering look, before savagely rending it with his brown peg teeth.

'Canting dog indeed!' he growled. Then, shocked into exhaustion by such evidence of ingratitude, he laid down his weary head to rest beside the bottles.

ALTERED ENGLANDS

So, the Bishop had read, just as the spirit bade, and then went away to learn. An obscure chamber in the Chapter House held all the ancient records, damp to the touch and scattered any old how. Patience was not Beaw's strong point and perhaps some force other than fortune guided him to early success.

Memory wasn't just expunged from the gravestone. The man's name had also been scored from the burial register; proof positive of scandal or hatred strong enough to transcend death—rather as he himself claimed to.

Other details remained however. The Bishop's thick finger traced them out, leaving a brown trail of baccy-perspiration compound on the faded page. Only the honoured got interred inside these hallowed walls: their passing and place of rest were set down. Thereby, when time came to change things, build anew or make space, one knew who was dug up and could act accordingly. Accurate records might make the difference between decent re-interment or the midden or River Taff. Therefore, for once, Beaw approved of the modern cult of pen-pushing over every little trifle. Slope-shouldered clerks might just, he conceded, have some place in God's plan. Certainly they proved of use that day.

The voice had gone under in the martyr King's day, before even the Lord's anointed lost his head and the world did somersaults to Satan's flute. There might still be a few around who recalled him: though the Welsh diet and climate were no great incitements to longevity.

He'd outfaced both however. '*In the Ninety-third year of his life,*' said the remaining entry. So much for '*Whom God Loves Dies Young*'—unless it was his last little joke, a tweak on the tail of Mother Church. He must have had plenty of money to placate the proprieties *that* inflamed.

'*Ample,*' said the voice, right close to. Proximity was essential, its previous bold tones reduced to a strained whisper. '*And much remains, well hidden. Descendants I have none, always taking care to sow seed only in barren ground. I will share what is mine with you: all my charms and curses and bullion.*'

'How much?'

'*Enough.*'

'You don't know my tastes!'

'*I do*'—and Beaw was revisited by wild visions which proved the point.

The Bishop flushed at being so undeniably revealed

'I had a sheltered youth and must compensate for it. What do you require?'

'*Life.*'

'That comes from God alone.'

'Then renewal of it. But time is short. I need life anew'.

'How, pale shade? I know only one way to inject new life—and don't even ask!'

'Sufficient is rallied for my try. I have spirit enough but want a vehicle for it. Bring one to me!'

'Which would you prefer, a coach or sedan?'

The voice hissed in sheer hatred, at the waste of time and at mockery. Actually, that ire was misplaced: Beaw's mistake sprung from slowness not jest.

'I must have meat! A new body to assail and make my own. I must leap soon or sink again to centuries of sleep.'

'What! Would you have me act your *procurer*?'

'Yes.'

'Ah...'

Whatever he might say, Beaw's curiosity was piqued. Whenever the bottle deprived him of Venusian faculties, and mounting a horse became a matter of planning, he sometimes dreamed of regaining the tireless flesh of youth. Not that *he'd* be guilty of so major a theft, you understand, but in theory...

'What must they do?'

The voice was in a rush now, racing to the light of day, opposed by failing powers.

'Have a weak creature stand upon my naked grave. Have them be still and contemplative. I shall do the rest.'

An alarming thought surged over the parapets of Castle Beaw.

'Was I was in danger? When I lifted your mat might you have...?'

'I muster enough to board and take a trusting, unarmed ship. You are a bristling man o' war with open gun ports. Your crew lusts for battle: any battle. I have waited long years for such as you, a sympathetic ear willing to set a meal before me, but the feast itself you cannot be. With but one throw left to me I durst not hazard it on so lusty an animal.'

Even if he chose to take offence there was no means to gain satisfaction for it, so Beaw harvested the words as praise.

'I'm obliged, sir. So, what sort of beast would you have of me?'

If a disembodied voice might lick its lips, this one did so.

'A member of the quality, I insist, sir: a lady of the choicer sort: with skin of milk and pouting lips.'

'Why so?'

ALTERED ENGLANDS

'Sometimes busy love entrenches or rain doth keep a man indoors. Thusways I may still divert idle days hotly running hands over a lily-white form...'

Up to then, Beaw had been minded to deny the voice its impious wish; to accept its nagging as part of the personal cross all good Christians must in some shape bear. Now he wavered: this might be a kindred spirit he was denying to the world. And besides which: a roaring idea was leaving the womb of his thoughts...

'I'll see what I can do,' he said.

The spirit left for its stony home in a blast of stale air, troubling the pages of Beaw's open Bible. His eyes were drawn—or directed—to the newly revealed text.

'For now we see through a glass darkly; but then face to face.'

Bishop Beaw looked up, half expecting to see St Paul frowning at him through the window. But there was no saint, no help or reproach: only the reflection of a monstrous old man. Beaw resisted a full second before accepting it as himself.

☸

'It shall be done,' the Bishop told the grave. 'I will bring a soft-palmed and full-bottomed wench of the finest pedigree.'

There was no reply—in speech. But, around the crumbling edges of the slab, droplets of moisture appeared. Frothing violently, they darkened the surrounding stone. Beaw puzzled briefly—and then recognised saliva. The carpet was allowed to fall.

☸

'Why keep a cur and *woof* yourself?' the Bishop mused, rationing himself to just half a mug of smugness. 'Why house a strumpet and-...'

Wisdom: was there anything sweeter? Well, yes, there was, now he came to think of it—like port and cards and milkmaids—but wisdom was well up there, snapping at their heels. All this saved effort sprinkled spice into his evening refreshment, making wine frolic on the tongue even more than customary.

JOHN WHITBOURN

Beaw swept aside some dead bottles and smoothed out Canting Dean's second intercepted letter. It improved with re-reading, the treachery-slicked pomposity standing more boldly to the fore.

'Archbishop, if sleep were sustenance then I have fasted full sore and rimmed my eyes with tearful red in this quest. But I found the truth and all that is needful. I have him!'

Bishop Beaw showed *his* perception of the matter by slowly closing one great ham-fist, crushing an invisible manikin within.

'The Lord hath delivered them into my hands,' he murmured vengefully—and then remembered those were Cromwell's words before the destruction of the Scots at Preston field. Fine words, fine day, but the speaker! Beaw dutifully recanted the phrase and read on.

'By dint of most painstaking scrutiny I find that our false shepherd worships before the foulest of graves...

... the wizard Toynbee's vile memory lingers here like a jakes' miasma amongst the most ancient rustics. In sordid hovel and sober almshouse alike I have heard with my own blushing ears...'

'Which I'll have off,' growled the Bishop.

'... variant tales of wickedness the like of which would cause even a Cardiff whoremaster to heave. Deo volente, may the memories, grotesque furniture of the mind, be speedily excreted into the pit of forgetfulness. O Tempora! O Mores! Herod himself would have bowed the knee to this fiend in human form. Messalina have acknowledged her out-doer in slavering lubriciousness. And Nero, that prince of sodomites...

To recount the salient themes risks this page and pen bursting into flames sparked by a justly indignant deity. But I must hazard that risk and recount the full disgusting details—purely so that your Grace may be properly informed just <u>how</u> disgusting they are.

... not only that, as if t'were not enough, but 'tis said that every morning, employing wizardry to gain his way without demur, he would breakfast on baby and then, securing a bowl of blancmange and four choristers...

... to say nothing of his sorcerous skills, gained in some crossroads contract with the demon BELIAL, whereby he mounted the air (and not <u>only</u> the air, if his Grace takes (sic) my meaning in delicacy) unseen and ventured forth to storm strongboxes and maidenheads...

... first for the late King and then the rebels, chop and change about without shame, taking the heads of those he slew, shrinking them by some alchemical method to adorn his saddlebow...

... and was signatory to the cursed death warrant of Blessed Charles, King and Martyr, seeing fit to append a beaming visage thus: ☺, to his deadly autograph.

... and never paid his tithes, to his eternal infamy, nor disbursed one copper farthing to multitudinous creditors, none daring to press the matter.

God, in his infinite kindness, having bestowed a generous span of years in which to repent, at last took him from the world whilst he danced the estompe at Glamorgan Assize Ball (in a coterie of masked jezebels, none of them his lawful wife) in the tenth decade of an uniquely wicked life, the year of our Lord...

... Pray break your silence, your Grace, and inform me of the—doubtless draconian—measures proposed to free us from the twin Babylonian yoke of dead thaumaturge and his English apprentice in corruption.

Meanwhile, worshipful sir, I am in your hands and at your disposal.'

'You-most-certainly-are,' 'agreed' Beaw, and having crushed the metaphoric man in his fist, now dropped him to be ground underfoot. He then hawked mightily, a viscous admix of chewing baccy, port and the bile of betrayal, on the remains.

☸

'EXHORTATION TO A FALSE SERVANT'
by William Beaw, D.D.

'There is, G-d wot, no worse a knave
who presumes to be master,
who should be a slave.
Who full thankful should be
for the untold times,
(no sirrah, but me no 'buts'),
for withholding my blade
from spilling his GUTS.
Now, worm, wriggle no more,
for the time is nigh,

*for your gross ingratitude
the reckoning to pay!'*

Bishop Beaw thought long and hard about that last line; right through the time he should have been paying attention to the Chapter meeting. It all depended how you pronounced *'pay'*, on how swiftly it was said, how co-operative the audience. Sometimes he thought he had his perfect rhyme for *'nigh'*: other readings hinted—rudely—not. Yet some foreigner—a painter type: Lolly? Loony? Lely?—once told him that the secret of great art was knowing when to *stop*. Beaw now saw what he meant. Why strive to achieve *more* than perfection in his muse—and in that loss of time thus deprive posterity of another ode? Away with fiddling then! He had written what he'd writ and it was ready for the centuries to come. The thing was glittering and polished and certainly good enough for the tastes of this base metal age.

'Bishop!'

'Yes? What? What do y'want?'

Snivelling Dean's spectacles peered anxiously at his spiritual superior: more confident of paradise than he but fearful of gaining it early.

'You asked to be woken for this item of the agenda...'

'Did I?' He enquired within, wandering the echoing caverns of memory, braving monsters and storms till he found confirmation. 'So I did. Oh yes!' His enthusiasm paled the faces of the good men around the table. 'Yes indeed, sirrahs, let us now discuss the Cathedral repairs!'

❊

'Halfway along the south wall of this aisle may be found a curiosity akin to Ozymandius' 'trunkless legs of stone', namely the lone testament to Bishop William Beaw's fanfared "Project of Urgent and Needed Restoration" in the late 17th century. This proved to be but a fitful stirring in the deep sleep—some would say coma—afflicting the Church in that era. Launched with all the zeal of Archbishop Baldwin's preaching of the Third Crusade beside Llandaff Cross in 1158, it mirrored that stirring address only in fervour and brevity rather than any lasting consequence. For, search as I may, I find no other fruits of its labours anywhere in the Cathedral fabric. And even then, stout and lasting as this unique erection may be, it has no discernable purpose or utility. So, Beaw's best efforts proved not even a drop in the ocean of the stricken building's dire needs.

ALTERED ENGLANDS

Hints are found in the Chapter records that this paltry (and puzzling) outcome of such great expectations was the cause of long-running controversy; its cost falling far short of the sums donated by the pious. Bishop Beaw is reputed to have fought duels (!) arising from accusations about his stewardship of the appeal: by no means the least tittle-tattle attaching to this colourful archetype of his age...

... Then go straight (only joking!) to the nearby coffee-shop, where I once met this Aussie Deacon who..."

'That Man is Over Six Foot Tall. A Gay Pagan Guide to Cardiff and Llandaff. By Prof. M. Jarrett. Chapter Arts Collective Press. Maindy, 1979. p23.

❂

'Your zeal for these works is... most commendable, Bishop, but at the same time...'

'Puzzling, Dean? Bemusing?'

'Your words, Bishop, not mine.'

'They'd be yours if you had a spine instead of ice,' thought Beaw, though saying nothing. Truth to tell he felt almost sorry for the robing Dean.

Unsure of the ethics of his plan, he'd sought guidance in prayer—and receiving no plain answer did what suited him, like everyone always does. True, there was danger of homicide here: but it wouldn't be his first, and was in a good cause, and it wasn't much of a *hom* being *cided* anyway. As with everything else in life it was all a calculated risk—and he *meant* well.

Canting Dean had been dubious about the full canonicals but Beaw convinced him of the solemnity of the occasion. It wasn't every day—or indeed ever—that time and money and care was expended on the Cathedral. This auspicious project should be copiously blessed, and fervently, reverently, prayed over Wherefore the Dean was just the reverend to handle it. Full motley: alb, cope, *and* lacy surplice were the least they could do.

The harsh truth was that Canting Dean made one of the least convincing or appetising females Bishop Beaw ever clapped eyes on—and *he'd* caught the future Queen Anne *in flagrante* playing a game of flats! However, to a revenant, viewed in poor light and *'through a glass darkly'*, the Dean might just pass as a juicy young thing—to a desperate thirst.

Beaw moved on as quick as war wounds allowed, jollying Canting Dean along. He wanted him in place before the birth of notions about why *he* should have this honour, rather than the Bishop himself. Thereagain, knowing the vanity of the man, maybe there was no need for haste. Pride cometh before a fall...

For once, Bishop Beaw avoided Our Lady's wooden eye, and hastened his pace for shame. Then they were beside the waiting grave, invisible beneath its threadbare mat. Beaw stopped suddenly, as though on impulse—no mean feat for a sixteen stone man. He dissembled never having seen the spot before.

'We shall start... here,' he announced.

'Here?' asked Canting Dean, retracing his additional steps. 'Why here?'

It was a tricky moment. The Dean should have guessed, he ought to have been ware. But conceit poured water on the gunpowder of suspicion. Arrogance bade recollection be mute.

'On a circle's circumference any point's a start,' Beaw replied. It was one of his library of sufficient yet meaning-free answers that had served him well in the employ of four separate armies.

'Well, yes...'

'And look at the wall here...,' the Bishop gestured freely at the medieval masonry: as good—or ill—there as anywhere else, 'An outrage!'

'Is it?

Beaw bestowed a first-ever smile on his Dean—like a crocodile, admittedly—but the full teeth and gums thing nevertheless. He even winked conspiratorially; man to man. The Dean's desiccated prune of a heart was hydrated and opened up like a flower to the sun.

'I *know* about shaky walls,' the Bishop confided, as if to a beloved son, 'having bombarded enough in my time. *Trust* me.'

Right then the Dean did—almost—yet there was a lot of history to set against this one brief beautiful moment.

'But Bishop..., where are the congregation? And the servers?'

Beaw tut-tutted; an unaccountably mild rebuke from him. 'I *told* them, er...,' he consulted his pocket watch, '... ten past seven. Modern Christians! Tut tut.'

Canting Dean agreed with that. The slackness of the present generation was a scandal ever flaming in his thoughts—that and what dogs did when they met. Quite why the good Lord chose to permit such sordidness in his material creation was a perpetual trial to faith.

Material creation... *Material* creation: there was something about this especial spot the Dean felt he should recall. As in *now!*

'Step forward, dear fellow,' purred Beaw, 'say your piece.'

Hesitation was fatally delayed. The Dean had researched his prayers about the starting of works: choice, apposite words from *'Kings'* about the construction of the Temple. They'd sound profound, they would impress—or they would if only there were an audience.

Actually there was—aside from the Bishop. Beaw perceived it: a panting sense of tension spreading from the tomb. Sticky stress pulled at cheek and hair, the mat's edge dampened again. Canting Dean would have felt it too and thus saved himself, if, deep down, he'd been a believer. Alas, like many men who've never suffered much or lost all, he placed all his reliance in just five senses...

At the last and too late moment, the Dean *did* recall what had happened here. He considered his Bishop's partiality for this place. Yet there seemed no danger. The old brute had taken a sweetness potion, the dead were irrelevant, and these building works were *approved*. He'd commissioned some of the tenders himself—and promised work to his wastrel brother-in-law. But still...

'And there shall be a plaque,' said Beaw, observing the threshold pause, 'gracing the new wall, commemorating the new era. Your name shall be prominent upon it.'

Those last words did the trick, *'putting the wench on her back'* as the Bishop was wont to say. The only afterlife Canting Dean truly believed in lay in bricks and stone and statues.

Thus inspired, the Dean's foot stepped forward—as Beaw's boot twitched the mat away. Heel met slab—and stuck.

The noise started at the higher end of human possibilities but soon shot far beyond. The banshee *A-A-A-IEEEEEEEEEE* fled to the echoing dark of the roof, to play there awhile in private conversation, dislodging a tile or three. Then it escaped through the great choice of gaps, still sounding, to disfigure the dusk. The door-hinges of death, little used to it, had been forced back the wrong way.

Meanwhile, Canting Dean had other distractions bar the music. He'd noted the Bishop's magic carpet trick, and the unaccountable *moistness* of the stone below. Despite everything, he could not prevent inopportune, dutiful, thoughts about drainage problems adding themselves to the long list of Llandaff's afflictions. They were his last.

The damp was mixed with firefly lights; fitful evidence of life seeping up from the pit. Together they crept up Canting Dean's clothes, soaking in, mounting at speed. He was held speechless as the cloud of lights mountaineered towards his head. He beheld and belatedly understood. The man looked beseechingly at Bishop Beaw. Sad to say, that gentleman shifted himself further from Heaven with a shrug.

At Canting Dean's crutch the substance hesitated, finding first inkling of betrayal. But then, committed, it surged on. The tiny constellations, sole remnants of a stubborn soul, mustered swarm-like before the Dean's face. Obligingly, he gaped with fear and the lights dived in.

And there met the full wonder of Canting Dean—and were *appalled*. Bishop Beaw's gamble had come off.

Like a drunken sailor, bottles and doxies in hand, suddenly meeting his mother, the spirit shrank away. Then, repulsed on these frontal plains of rectitude, it tried flanking moves, lunging at Avarice and Lust—but both proved impenetrable fortresses. Pride looked promising, a weak bastion in the wall, yet on arrival the wizard found defences raised even higher than his siege towers. It tried *Trojan Horses*: Trojan treasure chests and Trojan girls (and boys), but none were taken in. They stood, ignored and absurd, before the resistant city.

Then, in fury and desperation, the spirit *banzai*-ed: a battering ram charge beseeching to come in. It did great damage—but mostly to itself.

The Dean had been known to walk ten miles to return a farthing excess change; and summons his own son for debt default. That young man now lingered in Cardiff Castle gaol. Every Sabbath eve Canting Dean delivered a frugal food parcel to him.

Pitted against this rockface (to change the martial metaphor) of probity, even a thaumaturge couldn't find finger-purchase. Slowly but surely, weeping all the way, it slid back down to its former—and now eternal—home. A frail voice spat *'Bastard!'* in Beaw's brain. Who did not disagree.

Canting Dean's clothes were left bone dry; as was, alas, his mind. The undead thing had smashed what it could not stomach. An amiable, easygoing smile now lolled across his face.

Bishop Beaw lumbered cautiously forward. It wasn't the done thing to point pistols in a holy place, but seeing how it *was* his own Cathedral...

'Dean?'

He who was addressed turned—to reveal there was no one at home. The Dean would cant no more, and, in forgetting all, had forgiven all. Beaw had seen the like before: in a Cossack confined for a twelve-month with a Swedish jester—but this was worse. Dean was now at peace with the world: that peace that comes with unconditional surrender It even included his Bishop. Beaw approved and stowed his *growler*.

'Now, doesn't that feel better, Dean?'

Dean agreed—because it was the *nice* thing to do.

Then Bishop Beaw took him by the hand, like a tiny child, and led him gently home.

From under the replaced mat came subterranean sobs, but the sound was faint, soon faded, and then died away.

※

Beaw stood before the brand new buttress and was pleased. Deluded that they were on for *years* of work, the artisans had started with enthusiasm (likewise deluded they'd get paid) and built well. Pettifoggers had questioned the need for an *internal* buttress but the Bishop soon put them straight. Now, reenergise as it might, the spirit could never rise through that weight, nor any victim tread its grave. Both possibilities were well and truly covered.

The former Canting Dean flitted by, arm in arm with Mrs Dean. He looked benignly on all things now and even his wife wore a more relaxed face under the new regime. She accompanied him everywhere lest, in his innocence, he go astray.

Bishop Beaw even got a wink off her! She didn't know what he'd done to her husband but she was grateful. Soon enough he'd be giving her extra cause to smile.

'Like I said,' Bishop Beaw continued once they were gone, 'either way I saw advantage. Perchance you'd have him and I'd gain a mettlesome companion—for a while, before I had Canterbury shunt you off to convert the Turk, or I skewered you me-self: you being a *bad* sort and so on. Or, as transpired, you'd clean slide off his shield of sanctimony—albeit putting some decent dents in it. God's teeth and tootsies! I only wish cards and dice could be so weighted in my favour!'

Beaw then blushed to recall that when *he* played they often were.

The spirit could no longer speak but, taunted, was roused to silent fury. The stones and paving *almost* heaved up; a hot blast filtered through unseen airholes in the bricks. Rebirth was thus further postponed another millennia, or perhaps forever, just as Beaw had plotted.

'What's done is done,' he admonished the exhausted shade. 'Be content. I did the right that my position dictates. There's no grounds for complaint: I kept my bargain.'

Mute abatement of the hate suggested puzzlement below.

'Yes I *did*,' Beaw maintained. 'Do try and keep up. You wished to be like me—well, that's accomplished.'

If an absence can be said to increase, the lack of accord heightened.

'Don't you *see?*' asked the Bishop, anxious there be full understanding—and a sword twisted in someone's bowels. '*I'm* a pillar of the Church...,' he smothered guffaws behind coughs and his kerchief, nodding at the looming buttress, 'and now so are you...'

23~

DOING THE CHARLESTON

❂

INTRODUCTION

'WORDS ON THE FIFTIETH ANNIVERSARY OF THE DEATH OF LYTTON STRACHEY'

'You are DEAD, Lytton Strachey,
Siren of the bourgeoisie.
The worms ravish you,
Your beard unfurls.

No more books, 'bon mots',
Boys or 'brilliance'
For you—for good.
GOOD!

Eva Tyhtsov.[48] 1982.

---

[48] The Soviet poetess Eva Tyhtsov (1925-) won the Lenin Prize for Literature in 1953 and, subsequent to her defection (along with her partner and artistic collaborator, Moldavian sculptress Stella Lykarolova), was the longstanding chair of the World Council of Churches' Cultural Advisory Committee. In the West she is probably best known for her verse published in the Brighton based and Arts Council funded magazine *'Interzone'*, which in conjunction with the BBC long acted as her

JOHN WHITBOURN

❀

Lytton Strachey (1881-1932) was a member of the 'Bloomsbury Group' and arguably the most scintillating light in its intellectual firmament. Which is an dreadful thing to say about anyone—and also inconsistent with the advice given to me by my beloved Mother (may she rest in peace) to the effect:

'If you've nothing good to say about someone, then say nothing.'

Well okay, Mum—but I still maintain he wasn't as nice as he looked...

Meanwhile, in humble obedience to parental guidance, here is the next best thing to *nothing* about Mr Lytton Strachey.

❀

UK champion. Tyhtsov's experimental and, admittedly, 'acquired taste' verse has still yet to find an appreciative mass market, but cognoscenti rank her alongside such lesbian literary luminaries as Gertrude Stein, Hope Mirrlees and Philip Larkin (when writing under his *'Brunette Coleman'* pseudonym). None of whom, however, can hold a candle to Dori Anne Steele (1956-2010).

ALTERED ENGLANDS

DOING THE CHARLESTON[49]

'Lytton Strachey—that extravagant old stage duchess whinnying and trumpeting her pronouncements over the teacups…'
P N Furbank. Biographer of E. M. Forster.

☸

'The Bloomsbury Group' (and hence 'Bloomsberries') were an upper-class social, literary and cultural avant-garde group cum collective, cum clique, cum conspiracy, active in (but radically disaffiliated from) 20th century England. Natch, I kinda dig them, but they're not everyone's bag. [50]

'Strange Sex-Gods: Strachey, Gramsci & Trotsky—OR: 'Three [Phonetic] *'Keys'* to Unlocking a Warm, Wet, Salty Society'. Myra Abzug. Cornell University Press. 2009.

☸

'Well, it's just too *too* beastly, my dears. They should be made to STOP!'

Dear, *dear*, Lytton's opposition to the War was well known. He had simply *devastated* a Conscientious Objectors Tribunal when he appeared before it in '15. *How* the red-faced colonels had fumed! Only a timely letter from myriad

---

[49] With interpretive notes by *Bloomsbury* scholar Professor Myra Abzug (Cornell).
[50] They were the subject of philosopher Ludwig Wittgenstein's sole recorded witticism, viz: *'If all the Bloomsberries were laid from end to end—I wouldn't be the least surprised!'* (Telegram to Churchill, 1940). Later his view hardened: *'My dear, they should have all have been shot!'* (Letter to Bertrand Russell, 1950).

352

sympatico doctors declaring Lytton unfit for service had saved the martial boobies from making *total* fools of themselves.[51]

'I mean,' the darling one continued, 'how is one to supposed to think, to *create*, with those ghastly things continually booming away?'

Sweet, innocent, Lytton had initially mistaken the artillery's distant rumble across the English Channel for more threatening and proximate thunder. Naturally, he was anxious lest some sudden squall curtail his afternoon constitutional. Therefore we *all* were, and rushed to allay the poor dear's fears. Alas, to no avail. Whether it be Western Front[52] or storm front, his Sussex clifftop promenade was imperilled. Who knew what sublime ideas hung in the balance between birth and abortion?

The magnificent man barely showed it but inside he was *chagrined*—and rightly so! Our cultural duty was clear and we showed solidarity: all of us present: Rafe, Brennan, Christabel, Eyeions, Carrington, Virginia[53] *et al*—the very *cream* of our generation.

At that moment one almost saw the argument put forward by certain *militant* Bloomsberries, that the beastly War was a *good* thing, serving to cull the bovine bourgeoisie and kill off those ghastly philistines who'd volunteered for it. Society—polite society—is thereby purged and purified, leaving behind only the *enlightened*. Dear *dear* Norman was going to say as much at Lytton's Conscientious Objectors Tribunal hearing, although (perhaps just as well) he proved otherwise engaged at the time, appearing in a nearby court about the usual ghastly misunderstanding.[54]

---

[51] Despite exhaustive efforts, the narrator's identity remains a mystery. Plainly, she (or he—it is never resolved) was an eyewitness to the events described and an intimate (in every sense) of all the main characters. Painter Dora Carrington would be a prime candidate were she not frequently referred to (and not always obligingly) as a third party rival for Strachey's affections. Moreover, elements within this priceless and recently unearthed Bloomsbury resource seem to reference events post Carrington's death in 1932. See, for instance, manuscript 1348(A*) *'Virginia & Vita & Their Sick-making 'Il Duce' Pash'*. Further investigative work is urgently required and requisite funds are being sought from academic foundations.

[52] Various Bloomsbury group diary entries can be taken to attribute this disturbance to the first day of the Battle of the Somme (1st July 1916). However, their highly charged, disparate—and ultimately irreconcilable—accounts preclude precision.

[53] All Bloomsbury luminaries, names too dazzlingly bright in the cultural landscape to need elaboration here.

[54] Probably to be identified as Norman Douglas (1868-1952), Austro-Scottish writer, traveller and self-styled *'Premier Pederast d'Europe'*. The cited *'ghastly*

ALTERED ENGLANDS

But Lytton, angelic man that he is, considers this too sweeping. Many of those thus occupied, he says, are perfectly *sweet*, and some of them quite *juicy*. Therefore blowing them to smithereens constitutes a terrible waste.

It was an issue that remained unresolved right up to Armistice Day, despite innumerable *Conversazione* evenings in Gordon Square[55] and privately published 'slim volumes'. Even so, we never permitted the war clouds to block our brilliance, or the rumble of guns to drown our tinkling laughter. We just closed ranks, pushed on, and were *brave*.

'I shall complain to the War Office,' Lytton pronounced, in that same spirit. 'My cousin Bunny[56] works there in some tedious but senior capacity. I ask you: must they have their beastly bombardments day and night? Have they no *consideration?*'

'None!' I said, and nuzzled his gorgeous spade beard to comfort him.

Alas, he shrank away because he was madly in love (*violently* unrequited) with our postboy and had been so since last Thursday. Doubtless he feared that gimlet-eyed Virginia (who'd conceived a hopeless *pash* on the yokel youth—whatever his dreary peasant name was[57]—herself) would run swift to tell tales. That's the kind of sweetie dear *dear* Lytton was—always thinking of others.

Freed from my passionate embrace, he recovered composure and brandished his walking cane like a wand, magically waving away the War.

'Beasts! *Beasts!*' he accused them—and they had no answer against him save to grumble on, like some grumpy Jehovah on Mount Sinai. The difference was that *this* particular wandering tribe—and especially our modern-day Moses—proposed to totally *cut him dead*.

If only those sick-making Jews had done the same back in Biblical times! Just like dear Lytton did when the local Vicar[58] called on us at Charleston.[59] Goodness, how we'd giggled at the silly goose's discomfiture!

---

misunderstanding' (involving the Natural History Museum, two young brothers and confectionary) was the culmination of a long career of same, as least as far as the British courts were concerned. Sensing the likely outcome, Douglas skipped bail and thereafter made his home on Capri, where *mores* were not so provincial.

[55] Select residential square in London, near the British Museum. A Bloomsbury group epicentre.

[56] Roger *'Bunny'* Rendel, 1879-1981. Noted balletomane and relentless raconteur.

[57] Assiduous research in United Kingdom Post Office records almost certainly identifies him as Alfred Gubbins (1899-1917).

[58] Probably the Reverend Algernon Moth (1850-1919) of St Peter ad Vincula's,

The battling armies now put firmly in their place, dear Lytton could turn to more pressing matters.

"Stands the Church clock at ten to three?", he proclaimed, rhetorically. *"And is there honey still for tea?"*[60]

How remiss could one be? Luncheon had been simply hours ago, and the poor darling must be frightfully peckish! And yet he was being so courageous about it!

'There'd better be!' I piped up. 'Or else Cook shall be dismissed!'

One *meant* well and was deadly serious, but it proved too too blush-making, because people laughed as if one were joking. So all I got was a black look from Lytton for stealing his thunder.

Speaking of which, *boom boom boom* continued the ghastly guns across the water. However, we turned our backs on them and carried on along the coast path, being brilliant.

※

'Oh, *oh!*' said dear, *dear*, Lytton, clasping one hand to his cheek. 'Oh, my word!'

My first thought was that he had been bee-stung and I positively *charged* to suck out the venom. Alas, he soon let me know that was not the case; in fact he fended me off with his stick—which rather stung in itself. But it was done so *lovingly*.

In reality, our own personal guru-cum-genius was lost in either wonder or disgust—sometimes it was hard to tell.

Folkington, East Sussex, or, less likely, his curate, Basil Beisley MC (1895-1940).

[59] Charleston, a charming farmhouse and Bloomsbury Group stronghold in the unlikely setting of Sussex, Southern England. It served as the out-of-London ground-zero for their brilliant creative explosion. Now a Museum dedicated to the group. Recommended as a delicious stop-over before the delights of Brighton. Also a 1920s dance craze and American city.

[60] Lines from *'The Old Vicarage, Grantchester'* by Rupert Brooke (1887-1915). Brooke had the good fortune to meet many members of the future Bloomsbury Group, such as G.E. Moore, Virginia Woolf, Lytton Strachey, Maynard Keynes, Juliet Eyeions and Leonard Fry, before dying in the First World War. Amusing, albeit mischievous, intrigues by Woolf and Strachey allegedly played a part in Brooke's failed engagement and nervous breakdown in 1913.

ALTERED ENGLANDS

Once again he stood like an Old Testament prophet, beard pointing in accusatory fashion, staring up at the South Downs. His elegant fingers waggled at something invisible to us mere mortals.

'What,'—he made it a general demand—'*what*, I say, is *cet objet là?*'

We did *so* look and look, keen as teacher's pets to answer, but it was that beastly tomboy and so-called painter Carrington[61] who got there first. Why does she not get the message that Lytton is *not interested*? And while we're discussing her, why doesn't she go to a proper hairdresser instead of doing do-it-yourself with a pudding basin?

'I know! I know!' she gushed. 'It's the Long Man! *Cet objet là* is the Long Man of Wilmington!'[62]

I knew that—I just couldn't believe it was what dear Lytton had in mind. Normally, he has no time for manifestations of Sussex-ness. Anything to do with *'l'Angleterre profonde'* angers the poor man into *frenzy*.

We reappraised the feminine folds of the Downs above us.

'God *damn* you, England!' said a visiting Vorticist poet, shaking a feeble fist at the figure. 'Damn you and all your history laying like a nightmare upon the living!'

Fine words[63] but unsolicited. Dear Lytton supplies the summations round here, thank you very much. We didn't invite *him* again.

---

[61] Dora Carrington (1893-1932). Aforementioned artist and serial wife/lover to various Bloomsberries—including Strachey! Prime candidate as author of this anonymous narrative were it not for her premature demise. Noted for her capricious sexuality and curious coiffure.

[62] Huge effigy carved into the South Downs, East Sussex, not far from Charleston. Belying its name, the somewhat androgynous figure stands on the side of Windover Hill holding two staves (or possibly door jambs). The largest depiction of the human form in the eastern hemisphere. Possibly prehistoric in origin and preserved in modern times by an outline of white bricks. Doubtless a tutelary deity of the Downs, dating to pre-modern deity-credulous times. No café, alas.

[63] Though not even original. The anonymous Vorticist (might it be Wyndham Lewis, before his vicious rift with Bloomsbury? The *'feeble fist'* certainly fits...) quotes—without attribution—from Karl Marx. The full reference is as follows: *'Men make their own history, but they do not make it as they please; they do not make it under self-selected circumstances, but under circumstances existing already, given and transmitted from the past. The tradition of all dead generations weighs like a nightmare on the brains of the living.'* From *'The Eighteenth Brumaire of Louis Bonaparte'*. 1852. The narrator's decision to purge him from Charleston circles is thus vindicated.

JOHN WHITBOURN

Fortunately, dear *dear* Gordon was also with us that weekend.[64] He can be a *teensy* bit earnest when it comes to Marxism, and his mad *pash* on Biffo's wife (whatever her dull bourgeois name is—and *she* only has eyes for Virginia anyway) is terribly cringe-worthy, but he *does* know his stuff.

Alas. Said shy youth set aside his pipe and positively *lectured* us. Within seconds we knew more about the silly old hillside daub than could be decently endured. Fortunately, dear Lytton delivered us.

'Well, well!' he said, and pursed his lips at the apparition. 'Rustic Sussex never ceases to surprise—as well as provoke...'

Actually, I feared the worst. As I've said, dear Lytton was easily provoked by manifestations of Englishness and its *ghastly* past. One all too clearly recalled how visiting HMS *Victory* made him physically sick—all over me and many passing trippers. The ambient patriotism had been, he kindly explained later, just too *too* vomit-making...

Today though, his indomitable soul graciously overlooked all the fusty antiquity. Instead, he embraced the spirit beneath.

In fact, an embrace might turn out to be the least of it and mere foreplay. There were signs that naughty hands would soon stray *backstairedly* to flies or bloomers. Our leader's pale, sensitive face was positively aglow. The last time I had seen him so enamoured was that Naval Cadet flag day in Brighton—which had almost got into the gutter press until strings were pulled...

He drank in the green and white titan from titanic head to titanic tootsies. He quivered whilst deliciously devouring the view.

'A *long* man, eh...?' he said eventually, when the communion was done. 'Well, you can never have too many of *those*. Least of all in stuffy old Sussex!' Then he lifted his head to address the hills. 'And what might you be up to, eh? Lurking around on the Downs for what reason I wonder, you gargantuan gorgeous brute you!'

It was obvious to anyone with half a brain that dear Lytton was interrogating the giant (the lucky thing!) rather than any mortal audience, but that clod Childe saw fit to thrust himself to the front of the photograph again.

---

[64] Almost certainly Vere Gordon Childe (1892-1957), eminent archaeologist, excavator of Skara Brae in Orkney and proponent of the now widely accepted 'Neolithic Revolution' thesis. If so, he must have been taking a break from his then studies at Oxford. A connection with the Bloomsberries was not previously suspected and has been ruthlessly excised from his published journals.

ALTERED ENGLANDS

'Well, some authorities opine that he holds twin staves of power,' said the frightful bore, pointing things out with his pipe, 'whereas others hold that they are the doors to the Underworld. Still further experts posit that...'

Gracious, *how* we all ignored him—so eager to please but *such* a tart.

Meanwhile, dear Lytton waved the archaeological ass to silence. We were all, more than ever, grateful to him.

Then he struck a pose, an exaggerated copy of dear, dear Rodin's sculpture, *'The Thinker'*. It was just too thrilling: Lytton always did look so scrumptious in tweeds and scarf and deerstalker. And he proved to have sock suspenders on—the scarlet ones I gave him last Solstice!

We were hushed and reverential, even chatty Childe and loquacious Ludwig,[65] never doubting that some superb *bon mot* was making its way towards those hirsute lips.

Oh, and how one envied those words their delectable destination! If I were they, I would linger forever amidst his moustache and lose eternity in that jutting beard... But then their ejaculation brought me back from reverie.

'Rigid rods?' said our glorious leader, 'Proffered portals? *What* an inviting menu!' He raised his hands in mock supplication to the figure. 'Dear boy! Pray come visit me without delay!'

Goodness, *how* we all laughed at the deliciously naughty quip.

At the time.

There are more tears shed over answered prayers...

☸

It was too *too* ghastly. Back at Charleston and wearied from our walk, we had to take our own boots off! Even though we called and *called*.

Further shocks awaited inside. At first I thought we'd been burgled! And the servants murdered as well. But it was worse than that: all our gorgeous things had been... *rearranged*.

---

[65] Not previously mentioned as a member of the party, but, from subsequent references, presumably the mercurial mathematician and contra-cognitive philosopher Ludwig Wittgenstein (1889-1951). An admiring but jealously ambivalent auxiliary cum probationary-member of the Bloomsbury movement.

JOHN WHITBOURN

Keynes, with that slow, slimy voice of his that oozes all over you like a snail, offered the unhelpful hypothesis of an earthquake. He observed—as if we couldn't see for ourselves—that the walls seemed to have shrugged off our myriad enhancements. Simply *sweet* portraits in oils of dear dear friends lay rejected on the floor. Likewise, myriad limpid water-colour landscapes. Many *divine* ceramics sat shattered beneath their appointed shelves.

If that had been all, Maynard might have been right. But could an 'earthquake' stave in the panels on our *avant-garde* Omega Workshop[66] *escritoire*? Or place a chamber pot atop dear Carrington's bust of Lytton? What earth tremor could cause simply *disgusting* green and gold mould to grow in every corner?

More to the point, earthquakes do not swallow servants whole. Or not in England anyway. There had been hordes of the beasts before but now not one around!

Which meant, despite it being time for high tea, we found nothing prepared for us! Not a sausage—including *no* sausages, and *no* plates of crustless oyster-paste sandwiches either. Not to mention *nil* savoury nibbles and *zero* artful arrangements of those angel-cakes that dear Lytton so loves. *Rien rien rien*! Not even *tea* brewing in the pot, to revive our drooping frames, for Pankhurst's sake! I could have wept. Lytton and Ludwig *did*.

It was an outrage! In fact, a *double* outrage, because there were no menials to berate about that outrage—if you see what I mean: oh *do* please try to keep up you morons!

As I've *said*, we discovered an absolute absence of drudges—well, all bar one—and words were wasted on *her*...

---

[66] Production company founded in 1913 by Roger Fry, artist and art theorist, and funded through its brief life by donations from arts luminaries, but not, alas, sales. *Omega*, in London's prestigious Fitzroy Square, brought together the period's most brilliant creative forces including a veritable crescendo of Bloomsberries such as Duncan Grant, Vanessa Bell and Dora Carrington, plus myriad other lovers of Grant. So-called because the Greek letter Omega appeared on all their otherwise unsigned products (ceramics, painted furniture, textiles, domestic glass and jewellery). Unfortunately, lack of business acumen and venomous internal disputes led to *Omega*'s closure shortly before its first interior design exhibition.

A mouth-watering collection of surviving *Omega* items can still be viewed at Charleston. Look out in particular for the exquisite primary-colour frenzy of the paper-mache triple-headed *'Cerberus'* broomstick ascribed to Duncan Grant and Virginia Woolf (1916).

ALTERED ENGLANDS

The bedraggled country girl retained for simple tasks (she being simple) was discovered scrubbing the scullery floor. In fact, we literally stumbled over her whilst exploring the disaster. As if things weren't bad enough, poor Ludwig got his socks soaked with soapy water that she'd slopped everywhere.

The dreary slut claimed to know nothing and plainly understood even less, although we all spoke quite sternly to her. *'Cook done set I to scrub, beggin' y'pardon,'* she said, *'and scrub I shall till told diff'rent, yer majesty…'* ('Or till the flagstones wear away', as Lytton quipped, despite the circumstances—which was so typically *stoical* of him).

One does hesitate to wield authority the way one's ghastly Victorian parents did, but sometimes, quite excusably, there is no choice. Naturally, Virginia had to be kept out of the picture because she has quite strong views on such creatures,[67] but we set dear Ludwig on the child and he soon had her blubbing. Teutonic academics just seem to have this natural wonderfully *direct* rapport with lackeys.

Alas, we were no more enlightened. All that ensued was rustic rambling, and then tears, and we were in no mood for either. This was no occasion for nonsense about *'Old Nick'* and suchlike. The working classes can be terribly amusing at times—but not at *tea*-time, thank you very much.

After a house meeting we agreed it was all too too headache-making to *understand* and therefore must be *transcended*. Lytton said such things probably happened in darkest Sussex *all* the time and we should not let them divert us from being beautiful and brilliant. I think that was so *exquisitely* put, don't you?

Bloomsbury resides in the real world and nowhere else. There were practical issues to resolve and we set about them like the cultural soldiers we were. First on the list was restoration of proper order. To this end a convoy of cars containing a positive *posse* of Bloomsberries was dispatched to the village. We fetched back the errant servantry, and I must say that starvation made us quite savage. As with the scrubber back at base we had no time for their silly stories of dear Charleston *'coming alive'* or the walls *'breathing'*. With Lytton wielding sarcasm like a whip and Ludwig wild-haired and glaring worse that twenty separate Medusas, we soon had them rounded up for ferrying back like

---

[67] See for instance *'Diary of Virginia Woolf'*, Volume 1, 1915-1919, edited by Anne Olivier Bell, p.13: entry for 09/01/1915: Woolf and her husband are walking by the Thames at Kingston: *'On the towpath we met & had to pass a long line of imbeciles… It was perfectly horrible. They should certainly be killed.'*

naughty runaway slaves. Within the hour they were setting the place to rights and gagging over mould-scraping duties. *Goodness*, how they whined about that little thing!

But one can only serve at the front, so to speak, for so long. I confess that soon after I took to my bed with a migraine and plate of anchovy toast, unable to cope any more. Ludwig's screams at the servants and Carrington's unfocussed whines followed me up the stairs and into my room until I could put firstly door and then pillows between them and me

Although, of course, the door was left invitingly unlatched. But alas, dear Lytton must have been equally drained by the day. One had no nocturnal visitor.

However, at one point one's hopes were raised by *noises off*. The rustle of vegetation, high pitched *peeps*. And were those creaks someone scaling one's drainpipe?

But that could hardly be *Lytton*, could it![68] He feigned problems over flights of *stairs*. I rolled over, disappointed.

A hedgehog orgy in the hedgerows: that was the explanation I decided. The only ones in danger of pricks that night. Lucky *beasts*.

Eventually one drifted off to sleep and dreams flayed by a fuzzy beard.

❦

'Und ze quotidian hegemony of ze absolute—taking ze absolute to be quasi-verifiable when verifiability cannot be absolute or verified or even quasi— is undeniable even to ze meanest intelligence! Unt likevise, ze proposition about a *complex* stands in an internal relation to a proposition about a constituent of ze complex. Hein? Und so ze complex can be given *only* by its description, *which vill be right!* Or *wrong!* Or neither, depending on its indescriptability. In short: *whereof all that is hereof one must accept thereof…*'

As some of us discreetly wiped spittle away, Ludwig's bulging eyes travelled round the table, demanding approbation from all.

Lytton nodded sagely, slowly re-opening his eyes from rapt contemplation. 'So true, so true…,' he murmured.

---

[68] The narrator underestimates Strachey's scaling abilities, as we shall see…

Which was good enough for us and gave us our cue. E. M. Forster, the beastly swot, even applauded.

Ludwig smiled—a bizarre adornment on his normally furious face—and crossed his arms in satisfaction.

'Only ein drooling idiot could contest a syllable of vot I have just said today,' he concluded. 'Hein?'

'Oh yes, absolutely,' we burbled, feeling privileged merely to be present. Doubtless, comprehension would follow in due course.

Whatever the case, it was always wise to simply agree with dear dear Ludwig. Not only was the wonderful man a towering genius and erupting *volcano* of wisdom, but he was prone to step in and slap faces (jolly hard!) if his audience were slow on the uptake. Apparently, there was an itsy-bitsy *scandal* on that score in the infant school where he'd taught in Austria, necessitating hurried departure from his homeland.

Well, their loss was our gain. I say some children *should* be struck regularly—like dinner gongs. I would mine, if I had any, which thank Stopes[69] I don't and won't![70]

---

[69] Presumably an invocation of Marie Stopes (1880-1958), the Scottish birth control advocate, serial church-invader and ardent eugenicist. Her most influential work was *'Married Love: A New Contribution to the Solution of Sex Difficulties'* (1918), a trailblazing title all the more praiseworthy for bring written when she was (though married) still a virgin. Stopes was a life-long champion of perfecting humanity via selective breeding and compulsory sterilisation. Sadly, this led to some unwise academic collaborations in the 1930s with Nazi 'racial scientists', and superficially friendly correspondence with Hitler; contacts which have been opportunistically seized upon by her anti-progressive critics. Stopes' beliefs also led to her forbidding her son to ride bicycles and severing all connection with him when he married a short-sighted woman (incidentally, the daughter of Barnes-Wallis, inventor of the 'Dambusters' *bouncing bomb*) on the grounds that any offspring might be similarly afflicted. Stopes worked tirelessly to validate voluntary childlessness (via sterilisation) as a liberating life choice for the modern individual. The modern organisation bearing her name, 'Marie Stopes International' works in 38 countries across the world, providing quality termination provision. A 'strong woman' and evidently a role model to the narrator.

[70] This admission of (Stopes inspired?) childlessness ought to be a valuable clue in identifying the mystery narrator. Unfortunately however, self-imposed sterility does not unduly mark him (or her) out amongst the Bloomsberries. Most tended not to breed in captivity. The movement therefore comprised a scintillating but only single-generation phenomena. Alas.

Chest and chin aggressively thrust out, though in an utterly *charming* manner, Ludwig was surveying us like conquered territory. Which, in a way, we were—although one much prefers to think of Charleston and its coterie as in the absolute *vanguard* of surrender to the new order. Rather than raise resistance our white flags were right there to hand, all ready to wave.

Would that all were so enlightened. Incredible as it may seem, certain *dinosaurian* elements at Cambridge University apparently saw fit to question dear Ludwig's brilliant *blitzkrieg* career there. Lytton has a *most* amusing stock of stories about our hero savaging the fuddy-duddy dons![71]

'Und zo,' said the genius, concluding, 'I propose a toast.'

We swiftly raised our glasses. Those who did not have one found one.

'To me!' he said.

A demi-second elapsed before dear Lytton seconded: *'To you!'* and we all joined in.

It was worth it. My word, but we'd been served good stuff! Absolute nectar—simply *divine*. Like dew from the first dawn! Or Lytton's saliva!

Aforesaid saucy liquid goosed my tongue, en route to fondling my throat all the way down. Then a backwash fizzed like Dr Freud's finest cocaine[72] in my nostrils. And so potent! One mind positively *surged*, and thoughts, previously ambling along, shot right to the end of the line and logical conclusions!

There I found awaiting me an intoxicating freedom, and with it not a little *rage*. *If*, as Bloomsbury held, everything was relative and provisional, who

---

[71] This would seem to clinch the identification of *'Ludwig'* as none other than the world famous philosopher Wittgenstein. Yet the accepted record shows him as serving in a howitzer regiment in the Austro-Hungarian army at this time, firstly in Russia and then the Tyrol, prior to his capture by the Italians(!) in November 1918(!). Likewise, conventional scholarship has Wittgenstein at Cambridge both before and after the Great War, but not during. Can it be that his god-like brilliance extended to even evading the global conflict and deceiving future biographers?

[72] At this stage, Freud was still proposing cocaine as a universal panacea for all ills, both mental and physical. This aspect of his career was subsequently downplayed when patient cases of overdose, addiction and cocaine-psychosis began to emerge. Certain reactionary critics of the tripod of founding fathers of modernism (Marx, Freud and Darwin) preposterously theorise that much of Freud's psychoanalytical theory stems from his cocaine use/abuse. In the absence of legal redress for the dead, there are no legal sanctions to prevent repetition of this *canard*—although legislation is pending re the remit of Canada's Human Rights Tribunal.

were *they* to preach to me with all their '*too too*'s and '*beastly*'s and pettifogging '*right*' and '*wrong*'s? Just as bad as Mama and Papa and Admiral Uncle Jasper, only less honest about it![73]

No! I was at liberty to love—or loathe—or stab—anyone around that table, as case may be and mood took me, without their beardy bourgeois say-so! And *another* thing...

Such dizzy-making headiness! Such strong winds of liberty that found me without anything to hang on to. Accordingly, my head—and my world-view with it—positively *span*. It was too much for me. Rather fright-making in fact...

Fortunately, distraction arrived. Ludwig had downed his slim flute-full in one before hurling it, drained, over his shoulder. As we heard its distant shatter those thin but talented lips smacked in relish.

'Zat vas *nice*!' he said.

My head cleared with the shock. Goodness, how *all* of us sat up, stunned not by the tinkle of glass, but by such unique praise. Dear Ludwig had *never* commended a single aspect of Charleston hospitality before. On the contrary: everything was normally either too hot or cold—and sometimes both simultaneously. It was the kindest—and indeed shortest—thing we'd ever heard the darling man say. Dear Vanessa, our much-loved hostess,[74] positively *glowed* with joy.

Brennan was drunk of course (easing the pain of his hopeless *pash* for Carrington), but at this early hour retained the capacity to string sentences together. He proposed another toast.

'Champagne for my *real* friends,' he slurred, eying up his love-rival Lytton, 'and *real* pain for my sham friends!'[75]

All things considered it was rather witty. We would so *miss* the lovely boy when he left us. So long as he went soon and forever.[76]

---

[73] Once again, the editor exults at such identifying detail, thinking, '*at last we have her/him*'. But no, the British Navy List for the relevant period holds no less than thirteen Admirals thus named. One could almost be excused for feeling that the narrator is teasing one from beyond the grave(?). Almost.

[74] Perhaps a waspish reference to Vanessa Bell (nee Woolf) and her convoluted serial-monogamist lifestyle, the chronicling of which, and the associated husbands and lovers (and hybrids thereof) passing through Charleston, challenges even the most painstaking of historians.

[75] An epigram often but erroneously attributed to figurative painter Francis Bacon (1909-92). It is the least of his unacknowledged borrowings from Bloomsbury.

JOHN WHITBOURN

Of course, the dear one was above such jealousy and pique. He was *impervious* to Brennan's barbs.

'Oh, well *said*,' drawled Lytton, sipping more fastidiously but with equal pleasure. 'One *so* agrees...'

He communed with the moment for a moment and we, his acolytes, patiently waited for thoughts to ferment into vintage conversation.

'In fact, Vanessa, my dear,' came the coda at last, dear Lytton squinting over his *pince-nez* like some lascivious dowager, 'I'm reminded of the immortal words of that Jesus chappie—you must know him: the Jew-boy; trainee carpenter—*'You have saved the best wine till last'*.[77]

A *gorgeous* frisson fizzed round the table at such pillaging from scripture. Normally, Lytton is rather strict on the subject and bans pious talk from our civilised table. So to hear this from him was just too too nicely naughty—like a Bishop reciting a spicy joke instead of grace...

Gracious, *how* we giggled!

Except Vanessa. She's such a dear girl, and so *generous* to keep Charleston as open house to us, but why does everything always have to be just right *all the time*? She can be so wearyingly *literal*. It's just too too yawn-making. How does dear Clive—and Roger and Duncan and Rupert *et al*—put up with it?

'But I didn't,' she said, wearing that lifeless poker-face of hers, so unfortunately horse-like at times and so unlike her *ethereal* sister, Virginia. 'I thought *you* provided the champagne...'

'Me?' replied Lytton, as flabbergasted as the rest of us. '*Me?*'

We were livid! Since when has *dear* Lytton been obliged to sing for his supper or provide his own little luxuries in life? The very idea! She'll be asking the poor man to bring his own coal next!

---

[76] The narrator had their wish. Gerald Brennan (1894-1987) departed for Spain (with 2000 books in tea-crates) in 1919, having calculated that his small war-service gratuity could be best eked out in third-world rural poverty. He ultimately spent the rest of his long life there, becoming a much honoured Spanish citizen and author of the classic interpretation of Spain, *'South From Grenada'*, as well as standard works on Iberian history. However, lest his life be thought a total failure, it should be stated that research reveals he *did* sleep with Carrington, just the once (Seven Sisters Cliffs, Eastbourne, 23rd March 1917). One can only hope that brief intimacy with core Bloomsbury sustained him through all the remaining empty years.

[77] An ironic and thus forgivable Bloomsbury referencing of Christian myth, namely the purported *'Marriage at Cana'* miracle (c. 28 CE) which began Christ's public ministry (John 2:1-11).

ALTERED ENGLANDS

'And they're not my glasses either,' Vanessa continued to plough the same tiresome rut.

Now one noticed, they did indeed seem somewhat *olde worlde*—albeit perversely so—for Bloomsbury taste. Naturally, everyone present had been too well bred to mention it, simply assuming a teeny *lapse* in dear Vanessa's taste, or perhaps an inheritance from some ghastly bourgeois blood-relative she'd been too frugal to turn down.

We looked from one to the other (noting, in so doing, so *many* brilliant, beautiful, people gathered round one mere Sussex table!), and it became clear no one had the answer to the mystery.

'Zey were here ven I came out!' contributed Ludwig, enraged by any puzzle which resisted him.

'Ditto,' echoed Lytton, and held up his empty glass to twirl it in the late afternoon sun. Its facets flashed a strange kaleidoscope of colour over his face, causing him to squint. For some reason I felt a sudden pang of alarm for the man.

'Find out!' I ordered—*ordered*—Vanessa, my zeal arriving quite involuntarily 'Find out whose they are, you beast!'

Everyone was abashed to find me suddenly severe, but Bloomsbury worships at the altar of Impulse (and no other). My command was instantly deferred to and Vanessa summoned the maid.

She was a buxom wench, plainly indigenous Sussex from hocks to homely head-thatch. Her peasant form, ordained for breeding yet more tractor-drivers, waged winning war against her uniform. I noticed Carrington's eyes narrow with ghastly *backstairish* interest.

'Dunno, your lordships,' she said, under close questioning. 'Not I. Not us. Cook only just said to I: *'gentry'll be wanting to get tipsy soon. Go on girl, make y'self useful and fetch some of them daft flowerpots they do drink out of'...*'

We graciously overlooked that reference to our wonderfully *bijoux* Omega Workshop goblets. For the moment.

'Well, it didn't serve itself did it, you stupid girl,' chided Vanessa. 'Champagne doesn't just appear from the blue!'

'Ah, well, that's all *you* know, missus...,' came the impudent reply, and before she could be stopped or scolded, the girl had the temerity to sweep up a part-filled glass and hold it to her nose. She sniffed suspiciously and for a moment we thought she was about to swig it back, as though it were that '*Ale*' beverage her kind drink. Which would not have done at all! Once the servant classes taste champagne they grow disgruntled with more *suitable* libations. It is neither nice nor kind to corrupt them.

'Thought so!' said the slattern, triumphant—triumphant but wary, if such a thing is possible. She gingerly put the glass down again. ''T'ain't no posh champagne there, missus, beggin' y'pardon. That's *Pharisees' champagne*, that is! Elderflower and… other stuff. *Unnatural* stuff. *Told* you t'weren't nothing to do with us skivvies…'

We *snorted*. To think that such Dark Age cobwebs persist after nigh fifty years of compulsory State education![78]

'Yes, *thank* you, *Elizabeth*,' said Vanessa, still surprisingly civil given the circumstances. 'That *will* be all…'

Except it wasn't.

'My grandma told I about it,' the wretched girl persisted. 'Afore she went off with 'em. I'll tell you summat for nothing, sirs and missuses: you've more guts than I! Wouldn't catch *I* drinking it—no chance! Cor! Must be perishin' cold dancin' on the Downs at night. Not to mention all them *swords*… And the *predators*. Catch y'death you would… Just like my ole gran…'

Then she left us. I wonder that Carrington's slitted eyes didn't leave twin scorch marks on the retreating b.t.m.

'Honestly, you just *can't* get the staff…,' said Vanessa. Which was true, but still rather blush-making, for we prefer to think of them as *protégés* one happens to *pay*, rather than old-fashioned beck and call servitors like mama and papa had. Reconciling that aspiration with actuality caused a teensy *pause* to dapple upon us like snow.

Then, heralding the start of a *mauvaise heure* of dark marvels, metaphor morphed into reality and I suddenly realised it *was* real snow. In high summer.

---

[78] In fact, the narrator's utterly understandable disdain may be, on this one occasion, slightly misplaced. Modern dialect research suggests *'Pharisees'* in this context to be not a reference to the Biblical Jewish socio-religious grouping, but an outsider's mishearing of the local pronunciation of *'fairieses'* (plural of *faerie*). In primitive pre-21st century thought Sussex was held to be a last stronghold of the fey race in England, with a particularly stubborn enclave on Harrow Hill, near Worthing (prior to their displacement by archaeologists in the 1930s). For an alternative and later *terminus ante quem*, see *'Bury My Heart at Southerham (East Sussex)'* in *'Midnight Never Comes'*, Ash-Tree Press, 1997.

ALTERED ENGLANDS

Flakes fell, at first just a few, but then in profusion. They were driven upon us by a high wind off the Downs: an evil breeze which seemed strangely *selective*. Thinking of escape, I chanced to look round and observe that the neighbouring farm (whose Morlock-like owner disdains our advanced views) was not similarly afflicted. It remained bathed in Sussex summer. I saw Mr Morlock himself setting off for milking, his back, as ever, pointedly turned upon Charleston.

It would have made no difference had I tried to hail him and demand explanation. The snow muffled sound as it fell, blotting out birdsong and all else. It is often said of Charleston (by admirers and critics alike) that we live in a world of own, but at that moment the charge was indisputable—and literal. When, a mere yard or so away and teetering on the edge of terror, Lytton slammed his wine glass down, I heard not a chink.

As they spiralled down snowflakes refracted the sunshine into prisms in a manner entirely new to me. Likewise, the spectra produced seemed more… extensive than any recalled. Accordingly, second by second, our little group was strobed with strange colours, turning familiar faces fleetingly alien. Lytton with a green beard and blue nose did not look *right* at all, and images of an orange Maynard Keynes constituted the very antithesis of any mental *objet d'art* one might care to acquire for contemplation in memory…

Tearing my eyes from such sick-making—yet oddly compelling—sights, I then realised that the flakes were always *almost* alighting on us, the tablecloth and ground, yet never actually landing. Instead, spurning the material world in the split second before impact—*pif!*—they were suddenly no more.

Even so, they left a legacy—for they were *cold*, colder than a lawyer's heart—and their frigid calling card lingered even though they did not. Each phantom impact was a ticket to beyond Neptune. Icy fingers probed the interstices of our bones.

And *no*, since you ask, you filthy beasts, it did *not* feel *backstairish* or intriguing in any way. It was akin to being goosed by H G Wells (something I'm sure we've all endured, my dears: a routine rite of passage in literary London): only infinitely worse and extra revolting. There wasn't even the compensation of getting your poetry published in return for not calling a policeman.

Lytton shrieked—or desired to—but all that emerged was an abortive mew. So, instead, he pointed. Possessed with urgency, the spindly limb quivered like a lance.

He had such a gorgeously expressive arm—with just a *naughty* hint of newspaper-pale flesh protruding beyond his tweed sleeve—that it was tempting just to drink in the view. But that would have been remiss when the supreme intellect directing it had something it wanted you to see. Reluctantly, I stored the scene away for later and wrenched my gaze to where bidden.

The Downs were transfigured. The hills heaved. Windover Hill shimmered. Out of that unnatural kaleidoscope I dimly glimpsed figures emerging. They started down towards us.

Detail was obscured by distance and dazzle such that it was impossible to focus for more than a second, but *impressions* developed. Those figures were tall and elegant, and clad in green and gold. They also travelled astoundingly fast for apparently unhurried people. In fact, suspiciously fast for *people* at all…

That sufficed. None of us round the table could be classed as athletes but many personal—perhaps even Olympic—records were beaten that day as we scrambled for the house.

Lytton demanded someone give him a piggyback, but for once one did not feel able to oblige. Or perhaps I did not hear correctly. Of course, Carrington—the shameless trollop—hastened to comply but straightaway fell over, borne down by his weight into an obscene tangle of limbs. Fortunately, Ludwig lingered long enough to rescue our sage and drag him the rest of the way.

It then transpired that the beastly servants had barred the front door against us, and no amount of cajoling or even outright orders could persuade them to open up. We explained about property rights and the law regulating master and servant relations *in no uncertain terms*, but to no avail. In fact, as things grew heated, in response their replies contained a lot of Sussex *patois* that I felt sure was disgracefully disrespectful. Lewes public library has a whole room devoted to local matters (though God knows why when there's not even a *shelf* devoted to *Bauhaus*!) and I dare say that a dictionary of local peasant dialect lurks within. When opportunity arose I resolved to make enquiry there, whereafter certain people might be looking for new positions without a reference! *'Crowbait'* and *'Cack-abeds'* indeed!

But I digress. At the time we all felt—but dared not look to confirm—that the strange light-show was fast approaching our unprotected backs. And the… figures would not be long behind that unearthly aura.

Urgency inspired inspiration. Dear *dear* Duncan[79] recalled that he had left his bedroom window open after relieving himself thence last night, and so we positively *scrambled* up a drainpipe in search of it like so many *cat-burglars*. In fact, in his haste, Lytton overtook me and accidentally put his boot in my face several times—but I truly believe he didn't mean to, and would be mortified to be reminded of it.

Nevertheless, despite the unseemly scrum and traversing of an alarmingly narrow roof-ridge, we made it; even portly and puffed-out Maynard—at the cost of some blush-making rents in his trousers. Eventually, after an interval that seemed both inadequate and lifetimes-long, we lay gasping like landed fish on Duncan's carpet.

Was *that* the moment, I *ask* you, for Vanessa to remind Duncan to use the chamber pot provided under the bed in future, because his alternative practice killed the ivy outside and streaked the tiles a nauseous yellow? Didn't she realise that his was a free spirit that must *not* be crushed by conformity? Hadn't the dear sweet boy's bohemian ways not just saved our lives?

Or had they? Now that we seemed safe, some of us were somewhat shamed by the madness of the past few moments. Both Ludwig and dear *dear* Jolyon,[80] who had been in the War (mobile laundry unit and travelling concert party respectively) and so had *seen* things, became quite shamefaced. In

---

[79] Presumably Duncan James Corrowr Grant (1885-1978), Scottish painter and core member of the Bloomsbury Group; founder of the *Omega Workshop* and sometime lover of Keynes and Vanessa Bell (although not, it is believed—on balance—concurrently) and numerous others (see provisional alphabetical listing in appendices 1 to 3).

[80] Not hitherto mentioned but extensive research tentatively identifies him as peripheral Bloomsbery, Sir Jolyon Adonis (1895-1975), one of the most brilliantly gifted polymaths of his generation. Initially a Dada-ist actor and impresario (e.g. the legendary improvised opera *'My Bottom is Prime Minister, Hurrah!'*. Performances: London's Aldwych Theatre: two nights, 1923, and an eventful British Council sponsored tour of Iraq, 1930). He later became a prominent architect of the 'Brutalist' school whilst simultaneously pursuing a glittering career in politics. His company, the award-winning Adonis Architectural Redevelopment Group, oversaw the 1950-60s modernisation of Croydon (city in England, UK. Allegedly J. R. R. Tolkien's model for Mordor) where he also served as Conservative MP for Croydon Central, 1955-1968. Sir Jolyon's political progress faltered after a high profile arrest in 1968. Although acquitted of all charges, the involvement of invertebrates and school premises was held against him by unenlightened opinion. Likewise, the bizarre but apparently unwitnessed nature of his death (despite occurring in Croydon High Street during a busy weekday lunchtime) attracted further, regrettable, headlines. See, for instance, the *'Daily Mirror'* of 2nd August 1975: *'I didn't know longbow was loaded says Conservationist'*. He never married.

JOHN WHITBOURN

Ludwig's case this manifested itself in banshee screaming and a compensatory savage attack on one of dear Duncan's simply *ravishing* raffia tapestries.[81]

As the massacred shreds flew, one observed the darling boy creator's lip begin to quiver, and we feared the onset of a classic Bloomsbury *'scene',* taking many years and poems to placate. But then the lights hit the house and did the trick in an instant. Ludwig fell still and silent as a statue. Duncan straightaway forgot his (and Civilisation's) loss.

The illuminations more than made up for any foregone dramatics. We *refused* to face them, but their play upon the far wall was enough. There were colours that the eye declined to accept, and silhouettes likewise. Worse still, whatever was occurring seemed to be ever increasing in intensity. When one of dear Duncan's wonderful artworks over by the window started to smoke and shrivel,[82] we decided to go downstairs RIGHT AWAY. Everyone entirely understood that dear Lytton needed to go first.

In the sitting room we found Cook sitting in shocking unconcern, reading the *News of the World*—which she knows full well I won't have in the house.

'But that's *my* chair!' I expostulated, clutching in my distress at the straw of the mundane. 'How dare you? And why aren't you preparing dinner?'

These were good questions, requiring respectful answer, but Cook insolently ignored them.

'You can 'ave your chair, and welcome to it!' she answered, pulling a face. 'Talk about bloomin' torture—s'like sitting on a spike!'

The beast! That was an *Omega* chair! Five hundred guineas worth! Every component plank was handcrafted by one of Duncan's unemployed miner chums!

---

[81] Possibly the legendary lost *'Giant Aardvark Making Love to Argentina'*, or even the likewise missing *'Painter Stanley Spencer Having His Hair Cut—Blue Bakelite Bowl'*. See *'Top Ten Losses to World Heritage—Is Israel Involved?'* by Robert Fisk, *'The Independent'*, 23rd March 2006.

[82] Could this be Grant's famous painting *'Blistered Landscape: Sussex After the A-bomb'* exhibited and judged a *'succès d'estime'* at the Institute of Contemporary Arts *'Time to Take Sides'* CND sponsored exhibition in 1963? Although unquestionably a towering genius, Grant was also known for his sloth-like indolence. Perhaps he decided to make a virtue of circumstances and claim the unauthorised alterations as his own?

ALTERED ENGLANDS

Understandably, one was lost for words but happily for good order Cook complied nevertheless. She made way for our arrival, *en mass*, clutching the small of her allegedly afflicted back as she went.

'I ain't stopping anyhow, your worships,' she said. 'I just came to give notice—for me and for all.'

As redundant reinforcement she indicated a humble cardboard suitcase in the hall. In addition to all the other horrors, the spectre of a self-prepared dinner suddenly hoved into sight.

'Our Lizzie told us about the... *champagne*,' she added. 'And now all this... The rest have gone on but left I to explain. Us can't stay.'

'*What?*' said Vanessa—it being her house, after all. '*Why?*'

In fairness, the weird lights lingering on the landing could have been answer enough, but further justification came via a knock at the front door. A loud and imperious *rap-a-tat-tat*. Cook indicated it as her entire reply to all questions.

'We likes yer wages, missus,' said the awful Sussex aborigine, 'stingy though they be. But not the company yer keep...'

Like on cue, the door was struck again: veritably *pummelled*. Its panels bulged and securing groaned. The resultant shock wave caused an exquisite china ballerina above the fireplace to commit suicide via the tiles below. That noise made Virginia jump and hit her head on a horrid low beam. She began to cry—joining Ludwig who was already well ahead of her. Light from under the front door transformed their tears into colourful crystals.

Cook proved to have a motherly heart to match her maternal figure—though one heard that heart had been broken by losing two sons to the War. Still, it remained capacious enough to contain compassion for our collective funk.

'Oh, bless ye!' she said, her bluff exterior melting. 'Don't you worry, yer'sen, lords and ladies. 'This be all woof and no bite. They lot out there can't come in unless *invited*. Not over an *old* threshold. And now, missus, ain't you glad I stopped you puttin' in that stripped pine one?'

How could one ever forget the frightful *fuss* Vanessa had endured about that! It had concluded with Cook running amok with a toasting fork, plainly in the grip of powerful emotions, routing the Omega Workshop designers—poor boys—back in wild flight to London. At the time there'd been talk of police involvement and prosecution, but since Bloomsbury exalts spontaneity, and after *much* discussion, it had seemed less... *tiresome* to just go along with such pre-Enlightenment silliness. And besides, if Cook had gone to prison we would have had the aforementioned prandial problems...

Now that 'decision' seemed vindicated. Our proletarian protectress was emboldened by the time-hallowed in situ stone threshold between us and... outside.

Cook stepped up to address the door and those behind it—so very *close* behind it—on our behalf

'Now you do clear orf,' she said, 'and leave these children be! I don't mean no offence but you be scaring the gentry silly. Or sillier. So back to yer hill you goes or I shall get the vicar to ye!'

There was a pause in the impertinent raps. The magic-lantern show under the door seemed to ebb. Many of us belatedly discovered we had been holding our breath.

'Oh *honestly*, missus!' By rights Cook had turned to and on Vanessa, but really it was a collective appeal. 'What *shall* we do wi' ye? What *was* your parents thinkin', letting you set up house on yer own? S'like givin' kiddies guns. Well, anyhow, you've bin and gone too far this time. What a pickle! Playing at being Bolshies is one thing, but them out there's *real* radical company!'

For a second she looked desperate, and then focused all the more on Vanessa, almost pleading with her. Curiously enough, I was comforted: proper hierarchy was restored.

'Look, missus,' said the menial, 'you must be *careful*. Please! Life ain't like what you think it is. 'Tis the other way about entirely. Money can only cosset you so much...'

Duncan had been lolling against a shelf, admiring an Omega Workshop porcelain toffee-hammer; half listening but learning nothing.

'Be an angel and see if the bores are gone,' he asked, languorously, indicating the door and all points beyond. 'Then tell us what's for dinner, Cookie dearest...'

Cook gave him a *look* and sighed. She re-addressed the door.

'Go!' she ordered the unseen delegation. 'You ain't invited, so go!'

There was quiet, but not the variety she evidently sought. Doubt infiltrated her.

'You *didn't* invite them, did ye?' she asked us, incredulous, not daring to credit it. '*Did* ye? Oh, Gawd, *tell* me you didn't invite 'em...'

'Well...,' said Maynard, 'Strachey may have-...'

Lytton overruled him, as he so often did, both in conversation and the boudoir.

'No,' said our leader, delectably firm. 'One—I mean *we*—did *not*. One is *very* particular about the company one keeps…'

Cook considered him and came to her own judgment on that, and though no believer in the *'sixth sense'* or any such nonsense, I just *knew* she was recalling what to her mind was a cavalcade of *'mincing lady-men, conchies, bookworms and no-better-than-them-ought-to-be sailors'*.

'Right…,' she 'agreed', after an insulting pause.

Then she turned to the door once more.

'You ask your Earl Arthur—he'll vouch for I,' she said—albeit to my eye not quite so 100% assured as she sounded.

Nevertheless, the extra character reference seemed to suffice. The phantasmagorical lights ebbed further. There was less… palpable presence than hitherto.

Then all of the door paint suddenly bubbled and blistered. The coating shed and fell like dandruff. It may well be that many of us said *'Eek*!'

In the same instant, the door heaved with one last—so it proved—thump. Not a knock, but a kick. A contemptuous kick.

Even Cook took a step back, but they—whoever they were—were gone. We could tell. My million+ goosebumps stood down. Ludwig departed to dry his trousers.

Meanwhile, Cook picked up her suitcase, poised for her own departure: a diminutive peasant figure, but for one revolutionary moment monarch of Charleston. Yet I noticed even she allowed a little interval for safety's sake…

'Don't you worry y'selves about me,' she said—not that anyone *had* expressed concern. 'They'll not hurt I. My Great-uncle Arthur married *in* y'see. Strange old devil he were. *'Randy old devil,'* my Mum said…'

And then, when that got no response: 'Well, cheerio playmates. You'll find some sausages in the cold store to do for supper…'

Well yes, we did, I suppose. *Eventually*. But they took a beastly long time to find and longer still to cook when you're not familiar with the procedure and gas apparatus.

Finally, about midnight, when we were all famished and tearful, Ludwig got it going by flicking matches at the grill.

JOHN WHITBOURN

❀

It had *not* happened we decided. That was the consensus, proposed, seconded and agreed in lengthy wrangling before bedtime. As with the 'earthquake' incident, *nothing had happened*. Not a thing—*nada!*

Or, if perchance anything *had*, it was due to *powders* placed in the donated 'champagne': substances similar to those dear, dear Aldous[83] experiments with. Or perhaps some horrid Sussex mushroom with strange powers had... somehow trespassed into our rations. Such things can produce discombobulations aplenty but, in *'ze final analysis'*, as dear Ludwig so wisely put it, they were—as *the Bard* put it—*'full of sound and fury... signifying nothing'*.

At any rate, some such possibility was far more likely than what had allegedly occurred. In short, whilst our evening might be assaulted, our wonderful and wise worldview need not be. Which was *such* a relief.

In that celebratory frame of mind, and being the compassionate creatures we are, it was decided not to pursue the fiend who had tampered with our libations. Nor to have an inquest on who had behaved well or ill. As dear Lytton said, introducing morality into everything can be so *judgmental*. Were we to preside like some beastly bourgeois magistrate over the *'rightness'* or *'wrongness'* of our actions? Was that the Bloomsbury way? Had dear *dear* Oscar died in vain?[84]

And so that was that then—*'and so to bed...'* Even to, in some *exhausted* cases, our own.

If only *reality* was so amenable to reason. Alas, facts kept dragging us back in a most reactionary fashion.

The ghastly telephone machine rang all night and there were no servants to answer it. One barely slept a wink—and not for the usual reasons. One pretended to slumber through the racket but it was no good, and

---

[83] Presumably Aldous Huxley (1894-1963), author of *'Brave New World'* (1932) and pioneer ingester of mescaline and lysergic acid. Although born in darkest Surrey he was converted by contact with Bloomsbury and moved to California to become a trailblazer of progressive thought.

[84] Almost certainly a reference to writer and Bloomsberry-before-Bloomsbury, Oscar Wilde (1854-1900). It displays typical Bloomsbury generosity of spirit that Wilde's treacherous deathbed conversion to Catholicism is overlooked.

eventually *dear* brave Duncan got up to answer. Some others, myself included, drifted down to supply support.

'Hello? Hello?' he said. 'Who *is* this? Do you know what *time* it is? What do you want, you rotter?'

Clearly they wouldn't say.

'Now see here, you swines,' he said, his splendid Caledonian brogue ascending the scales up into *castrato* realms, 'I'll have you know I've got friends in Parliament—that's right, *Parliament!*—and if you don't desist...'

Then the ringing resumed, even though the receiver was aloft. Dear Duncan's eyes widened like saucers before he threw the thing down in disgust. Laying rejected there on the ground the bakelite beast continued to emote.

By now everyone had descended, red-eyed and unamused and pyjama-clad (Lytton looking delectable in salmon-pink...) to bear witness. Therefore, we were all present to observe Duncan give way to rare wrath and wrench out the wretched telecommunication cord. Plaster flew, the cable snapped and whiplashed away. A most satisfying *coup de grâce*. Or so we thought.

Then, I suspect just to make a point, the ringing continued a whole minute more. The point being that the call would end only when the third party wished it so. And may I assure you, dear reader, that minute seemed as long as one of H G Wells' embraces—and equally invasive...

Eyes connected to the finest minds of our generation looked from one to another and for once we had no witticisms. Then the ringing stopped and the silence started. No one was brave enough to break it.

Without servants there could be no cocoa and none of us felt the slightest bit *backstairish*, and so we beat a mute retreat in dribs and drabs to our separate bedrooms. But not to repose.

Then, the whole rest of that wretched night, someone outside tested the exterior doors and windows. One after the other, round and round, until the dawn. It was just too too terrifying and tiresome. Poor Lytton barricaded himself in the lavatory with only Carrington for company.

I resolved to ring the police about it first thing in the morning—but then remembered dear Duncan's rash response ruled that out. Next, the briefest of reflections revealed that an indignant letter was out of the question too. True, some of the world's greatest writers rested—fitfully—beneath Charleston's roof that night, but even they would struggle to find words to fit our complaint into a form acceptable to Sussex constabulary...

JOHN WHITBOURN

❦

Yet, as Scarlet O'Hara would later say: *'Tomorrow is another day!'*, and I do so believe there's a lot of truth in that. Come bright new morning we found the moral fibre to decide that last night hadn't happened either. Cautious enquiry revealed no fresh new paths worn round the house, as one fully feared there might be; no virgins lay spreadeagled and sacrificed on the croquet lawn: in fact nothing material to show of the siege at all. One's sigh of relief practically hoisted the net curtains.

Wisdom returned and reassurance with it. Good taste dictated that *no more was said* on the subject, or: *'least said, soonest mended'* as the lower classes so charmingly say.

Moreover, central to the core creed of Bloomsbury is the fact that there are our five senses and the evidence they reveal—*and nothing else*. Which is quite enough, thank you. Therefore, that which does not produce tangible evidence to be perceived by those senses can be discounted—if so desired. Bloomsberries are nothing if not *scientific*.

And I don't doubt there are many *many* scientific reasons as to why all the paint should blister off the inside (only) of a front door. But no one was so boorish as to raise the matter over breakfast. There were *myriad* more important things to do, because all the distractions (which didn't happen) meant we had got *completely* behind with being brilliant and groundbreaking. Also, during the early hours, both Bunny *and* Biffo[85] had conceived mad *pashs* for Virginia, and so proposed marriage. Dear Leonard—who *is* her husband after all—was

---

[85] Conclusive identification of the two men(?) is problematic. *'Bunny'* cannot be the peripheral Bloomsberry Roger *'Bunny'* Rendel (see footnote 56 above) due to his verifiable absence at the time, escorting the Scottish National Ballet on a morale-raising tour of the Western Front. He may perhaps be the experimental chorographer David Hawkins (1888-1960), the brilliant *Chef de danse'* with Isadora Duncan's troupe, and dubbed 'Bunny' because of allegedly rabbit-like proclivities. Hawkins' amorous liaisons intersected at odd times with the Bloomsbury cat's-cradle of connections. *'Biffo'* may be more confidently ascribed to the composer Stephen Wiltshire (1890-1992) whose *'Symphony for Harp and Drums'* caused such a stir at the 1919 Prom Concerts. Curiously enough, on the demise of his musical career (despite staunch Bloomsbury patronage), Wiltshire went on to became a brewery owner and professional golfer. *Such* a waste.

terribly sweet about it, but the boys fell out and hurled specially composed verses at each other until one's head positively *span*. And, of course, Virginia had an attack of the vapours and took to her bed, periodically sending down notes to each party. Which merely served to stir matters more.

It felt so *wonderful* that things were returning to normal.

Or almost so. Did I mention breakfast? Well, there wasn't one! All the food we could find in the larder was raw and so we went without. It was too *too* ghastly and hunger-making.

We can, of course, live perfectly well without servants[86] but it just seemed sensible to get some more for the time being. The village proving strangely barren ground for recruitment, our substitute batch came courtesy of a roadside callbox and an agency dear young Freddie[87] knew of in London. They arrived en mass on the train later that day and proved a scurvy crew of Jewesses and drink-sodden dismissed butlers that would not have looked out of place in one of the Duke of Wellington's Peninsula regiments. My dears, you should have *seen* the facial scarring and five o'clock shadow—and that was just the women!

One felt soiled by association right from the start and thus the urge to just *about turn* our convoy of motor cars and maroon them there at Firle station. But it was almost time for luncheon and so one didn't. In normal circumstances things would be different, but they were *not* normal. As Lytton so wisely said of Maynard's marriage to that utterly *provincial* dago dancer, *'Buggers can't be choosers...*[88]

---

[86] *'Why we have servants I can't think. How terrible it is to be in this position.'* Virginia Woolf. Letter to her sister, Vanessa. 22nd(?) August 1911.

[87] Perhaps a precocious *enfant terrible* appearance by the future Sir Alfred Jules ('Freddie') Ayer (1910-89), the 'Logical Positivist' philosopher, academic, pundit, relentless *Don Juan* and Tottenham Hotspur soccer team fan? Like Wittgenstein, Ayer held that traditional philosophy such as metaphysics, theology and aesthetics, were so intrinsically meaningless as to merit abolition. A perhaps unwisely publicised 'near-death' experience in 1988 led him to briefly nuance his hitherto lifelong atheism, although he subsequently retracted the embarrassing revelation.

[88] If this is indeed a reference to the surprise marriage of economist John Maynard Keynes (1883-1946) to ballerina Lydia Lopokova (1892-1991) then it is—doubtless innocently—misinformed. Lopokova, who never found favour with the Bloomsbury set, was of Russian birth. Keynes' former(?) lovers, and in particular Strachey and Duncan Grant (although connection with the latter was near compulsory in Bloomsbury circles), never forgave the misalliance and subjected Lopokova to a

Their manners proved as surly as their looks. When Lytton demanded of the new cook what was the alternative to the alleged *'fricassee'* she'd just served, he was brazenly informed it was *'Lumpit'*. Before one could stop the dear sweet innocent man he replied that *'he would have a portion of Lumpit then…'*, whereupon the ranks of servantry in the room dissolved into barely concealed hilarity. The filthy beasts! One just longed to sack the lot of them there and then, and dismiss them into a snowy night without taxi transport. But, as you know, it chanced to be high summer at the time and in any case, later on, our cocoa required preparing. So one didn't.

Likewise, the next morning, as breakfast (a rather *greasy* proletarian breakfast I might add) was being served, I naturally enquired about dear Lytton's absence from table. And had to bite my tongue when the (equally greasy) maid pretended not to know who I meant. I ask you! One merely enquired about the author of *'Landmarks in French Literature'* (1912), that was all, and yet she claimed never to have heard of him! *Goodness*, how our tongues should have chastised her! But at the time we were famished and so for once held them still.

Nevertheless, it was all too plausible that none of these animals had given thought to go and help Lytton wash and dress, and so I pressed the matter.

'Oo?' 'answered' the ghastly girl, 'You mean the gangly gentleman? Wiv the bog-brush beard?'

'Yes,' I spat—and then, directly: 'I mean, no!'

'Well, make yer mind up, luv,' said the slut—doubtless the very *sweepings* of some Tsarist gutter decanted into London's East End. 'But if it's 'im you're on about, then 'ees gorn out—the messy bugger!'

'How *dare* you?' I retorted, on the verge of feisty fury. 'He is *not* messy! And he is *not* a…' I looked around the breakfast table for support but found only titters from the Bloomsbury brethren. It was just too *too* dispiriting. 'Well anyway,' I concluded weakly, 'he is *not* messy…'

'If you say so, sweetheart,' said the maid, not really deferring at all as she gathered up the plates with a clattering *completely* careless of our inner equilibrium. 'But I do wish he'd put his clothes in the wardrobe, not all over the floor. It ain't kind—not when people gotta pick 'em up and hang 'em and all

---

campaign of denigration from which Keynes signally failed to shield her. Wittgenstein also behaved abominably to her on their collective shared honeymoon.

that. It's more like a *floordrobe* than wardrobe in there! Still, he's gorn now. And in a hurry by the looks of it…'

Hurry? She did not know the *meaning* of the word—and doubtless many other simple terms. Whereas one hardly need tell you that *I* was out of that room before her lower class prattle had faded from my ears. If she hadn't been so robustly built I would have trampled her en route. Believe me, one positively *stampeded* up the stairs in one's haste. Lytton gone? It mustn't be!

But it was! Dear *dear* Lytton's room was deprived of him. The wardrobe door hung open, the bed lay unmade. All the garments (including those sweet salmon jim-jams!) lately used to conceal his gorgeous form were strewn just as they'd been discarded. But of the body that formerly graced them there was no sign, not even a polished, *piquant* note.

'*Oh Pankhurst,*' one prayed (prayed!), '*don't let us be as bereft of him as this room is…*'

But as all civilized people know when they're rational, prayers are not heard, let alone answered…

One possibly panicked for a short while; there may even have been some screaming and sundry hysterics. One really can't recall. After the events (which didn't occur) of the night before last, one's nerves were already stretched to breaking point without this total *cataclysm* presenting itself. The next firm memory that arrives is of dear Ludwig slapping one's face (with just a *teensy* excess relish one thought) and a search party being organized.

Whilst Carrington plied the repaired telephone, *demanding* that the Army be mobilised down to the last Beefeater—*and* the Air Force and Navy too, if applicable—we meanwhile sought dear Lytton in the grounds and shrubbery. For he and Ludwig sometimes thrashed out finer points of philosophy there in privacy, the herbiage positively *heaving* with the vigour of their intellectual to and fro. We also sought him in the summerhouse which contains a *chaise longue* of particular plasticity to mitigate his martyrdom to *the piles*. In sum we searched for him in circles of ever increasing size and compromised dignity, but it was not until midday that we finally found spoor.

The station master at Firle was still in a tizzy at his encounter with genius.

'Yus,' he said, displeased to see us to the point of barbarity, 'that gentleman *'as* been through, I regret to say.' His walrus moustache fairly *bristled* at the recollection. 'He caught the 9.07—and good riddance.'

Our collective shock and grief prevented us from dealing with the swine as we should, but Ludwig's bulging glare ought to have warned him he blasphemed.

But it did not: he had more.

'And next time you see your friend, you tell 'im he should keep his hands to 'iself! Ain't no call to go kissing people just for telling 'em the train times…'

Really, sometimes one concludes there is *no* hope for England!

Yet at the time one was not in any state to conclude anything other than one's life, perhaps in front of the next train, or in the welcoming arms of the Ouse.[89] In fact, one remembers very little of the ensuing distraught hours—and nothing whatsoever after the Doctor arrived with a hypodermic of sweet oblivion.

I surfaced from the arms of Morpheus (and morphine) to shortly find myself on the opposite mountain top—from despair to joy in a single bound!

''Es back,' said the chambermaid keeping vigil over me. 'Your beardy-weirdy pal. Just arrived downstairs. Jew wanna see 'im?'

One couldn't help oneself. 'Thank God!' I said—out loud and in company (of sorts)! Isn't it funny how in profound moments one instinctively blurts out the—in Bloomsbury circles—*naughtiest* of words?

Though one's legs were as unsteady as a newborn calf one took the stairs three-at-a-time. An ascending servitor bearing me some redundant medicine was quite *swept aside*.

The divine man was down in the hall, still in his outer coat and deerstalker, surrounded by luggage. One suddenly had the ghastly fear he'd had to carry it *himself!*

But no matter—court martials for that could come later. He was returned to us!

'Er, hello,' he said, and his reedy voice played me like a veritable flute—a *magic* flute! One felt reborn! 'How are you?' continued the sweet one. '*I'm* not feeling too well…'

---

[89] Primary river of East Sussex. The site chosen for Virginia Woolf's suicide (some sources say involuntarily accompanied by her pet dog) in 1941. Fascistic (probably) elements among Sussex police long indulged in suspicions of foul play by her husband, Leonard, but no charges were ever brought.

ALTERED ENGLANDS

I presume certain provincial zeros might think he should have paused for answer before updating me on himself, but I spurn such short-sightedness. I spurn it!

'Then you must go to bed!' I hastened. 'Mine is ready. I shall *minister* to you!'

For some reason that provoked hesitation and wariness in his eyes. There was something missing from the Master's customary confidence.

'*Actually*, I'd rather have my old bedroom,' he replied. 'There's something I want to show you there…'

One recalled he'd said the same thing a while ago, to the handyman who came in from the village, and quite a rumpus and scandal had ensued. However, as for me, it was just too *too* thrill-making an invitation and so one quite forgot to ask where he had been and why he had tortured us so by disappearing. Plus, on reflection, that would sound such a beastly *petit-bourgeois* line of thinking that one's glad the surge of *saucy* adrenalin swept it away.

Not even pausing to take his coat off, Lytton drew me up the staircase and I followed, little loath. Likewise, one went along with his haste, lest the mood pass or, worse still, that jealous cat Carrington see us and intervene. Happily, we made it to his former room unseen.

'After you,' he said, ever the gentleman.

I entered in and hoped he would soon emulate me. The dishevelled bed beckoned us and I only awaited the word to simply *hurl* myself in, over or even under it—should such be his fancy.

But no. *Dear* enigmatic Lytton lingered on the threshold, still encased in three-piece tweed, far from any *backstairish* state. Indeed, one might even conclude he seemed *shifty*. But surely one was mistaken?

'Goodness me!' he said from the door, pointing within. 'What's *that?*'

He was indicating the wardrobe, which gaped open just as it had been left.

'Well,' I said, trying my simple best to facilitate genius, 'it's a wardrobe: a container generally used to contain spare clothing and-…'

'No, no, *no*, you silly goose,' he said, almost tear-makingly spiteful, stamping one long leg upon the floor. 'Look inside—look *inside!*'

I did, I really did. It stubbornly remained just what it was.

'Um, would you like me to hang your clothes up?' I enquired. 'Is that it? One certainly can't trust the current staff to take proper care of-…'

'Can't you *see?* Can you really not *see* it?' he said, his tiny eyes straining against rimless lenses; so dreadfully *pained*—which thus pained *me*. '*Can't* you?'

For dear Lytton's sake I put my head right inside and looked again. And I saw...[90]

...

... that the wood forming the wardrobe's back was particularly fine-grained. An attuned eye could see simply gorgeous patterns within. It was all too typical of Lytton Strachey to draw attention to such beauty which ordinary mortals pass by without appreciating. One was so grateful to Lytton Strachey.

And then the rest of the weekend and all our years at Charleston passed by in perfect amity and normality, with nothing untoward happening at all. We were all wonderfully happy there and got on famously and carried on being the most brilliant minds in the Western—and indeed the whole—world.

Lytton Strachey also continued as our unfailing inspiration and the most brilliant of all of us, with everyone living in harmony together, thus proving the total rightness of Bloomsbury values.

Some warped and fascist minds may have cavilled at the time, but Civilisation will laud and thank us in the end.

THE END

---

[90] Unlike the rest of the manuscript, the remaining four paragraphs of this portion are typewritten and markedly altered in style. But for their consistent sentiments one might almost suspect completion by another hand.

ALTERED ENGLANDS

'NOT FOR PUBLICATION'[91]

... For dear Lytton's sake I put my head right inside and looked again. And I saw.

Oh, I saw all right! I now saw *lots* of things.

It hurts but it must be said. In the immortal words of *dear* E. M.—*'Only connect'*.[92]

Actually, *no!* On second thoughts what did *that* drivelling streak of weak tea, soft-as-shite-but-twice-as-nasty *ponce* know about *anything*? Apart from seducing lift-boys with shillings and writing piss-poor novels for old women (male *and* female)? Sweet Fanny Adams, that's what![93]

Years after this, heading out to fight for Franco, I happened to bump into *dear* E. M. on a train. Yeah, I bumped into him right enough—my boot bumped into his groin. Gave him a couple of *acres* for free, ho ho.

'Connect with this, you old tart!' I told him. 'That's for all the boring bloody books! I want my hours back!'

Laugh? I thought I'd never stop! And my fellow *Legionnaires* fell about the barracks when they heard!

But I digress.

By looking within the wardrobe I *connected*. I could see what Strachey saw. Not nice. Not nice of him, not nice to see.

Since *he* wouldn't come, they'd started on his deceased family. I saw a selection of Strachey shades dragged from the grave, silently screaming, drawn to and up through the house and then sucked into the wardrobe. I felt their agony as they went. There was no telling what fate awaited them but it can't

---

[91] Hereafter each page of the manuscript is marked—in heavily underlined script—**'NOT FOR PUBLICATION'**. In places the instruction is so impassioned and forcefully inscribed that the pen has penetrated the paper into the sheaf below.

[92] E.M. can surely be identified as author Edward Morgan Forster (1879-1970). Forster's limpid and Bloomsbury-influenced humanistic *oeuvre* is succinctly summed in the epigraph to his 1910 novel *'Howard's End'*: *'Only connect'*.

[93] The change of tone is as radical as it is inexplicable. Whilst the manuscript resumes in the same hand as before, the motivating intellect seems utterly transformed—and utterly beyond the pale. The Cornell edition ends at this point and this second section is not submitted for wider dissemination—in deference to modern sensitivities and the author's expressed wish whilst she/he was still, as the Law has it: *'Of sound mind and testamentary capacity'*.

have been good. Their fearful faces turned in appeal to him and me, but he wouldn't—and I couldn't—do anything to help.

They tried to cling on to the wardrobe's sides but their hands were insubstantial, the gravitational pull too strong. The last look was invariably a reproachful look at their traitorous descendent.

'I say!' I said. 'Isn't that your Uncle Sebastian?'

'Do you think so?' replied Strachey. 'It's possible...'

Yet to know that he'd need to *look*—and he didn't.

The last named's glare had been particularly venomous. I now recalled that he'd left Lytton a tidy sum in a trust fund...

'Oh well,' said the great *litterateur*, almost cheerful, 'at least you can see them too. At first one feared one might be going mad—like poor batty Virginia.'[94]

The stream must have been pretty constant for me to see so many in so short a space, and it was clearly catching up and getting close to the living. I knew for a fact that old Sebastian Strachey only kicked the bucket a couple of years back.[95]

But there were still bigger things to worry about. In-between ghastly ghostly Stracheys I got to see a whole landscape, nay, a new *world*, within the wardrobe.[96] As its entrance the Long Man held wide a door. It was inviting me—but it was not *inviting*. Quite the Contrary.

And as for what lay beyond *that*... I decline to say. It's best not to. I don't know you, dear reader, but I don't hate you either.

---

[94] The assertion, though less than kind, is in essence correct. Biographers differ in their exact tally but Virginia Woolf may well have been approaching her nineteenth nervous breakdown just prior to her death. There can be little doubt that she supplied inspiration for the song of that name by the Rolling Stones rock group, written in 1965 and released as a single in February 1966, reaching number 1 in the UK pop charts and number 2 in the USA's 'Billboard Hot 100'.

[95] Sebastian Strachey (1849-1912), publisher of the infamous twelfth volume of *'The Greek Anthology'* (1902). Long term resident in Capri. Died in curious circumstances during a tour of the Turkish Fleet.

[96] The 'writer' and Christian propagandist C. S. Lewis (1898-1963), had glancing encounters with some Bloomsberries in his youth. Is it possible that we have here the inspiration for his 'Narnia'? If so, how ironic that Bloomsbury should give birth to so regrettable and malformed an offspring! One is all the more grateful for Mr Phillip *'Pineapple'* Pullman's antidote *oeuvre*.

ALTERED ENGLANDS

Cold, cold wisdom! Arctic enlightenment! So *that* was what finally became of us and everything! Well, well, who would have thought it?

A discreet cough disturbed my trance. Strachey was sort of waving, urging, ushering me in!

Up to that point, I still hadn't fully twigged. But one—I mean *I*—was well on the way. The bastard had tricked me into looking inside and now he wanted me to go all the way.

Once upon a time, oh *how* that phrase would have excited me with all the power of long-frustrated lust! But now he was handing me the key to… what? Not to his bed, but his *wardrobe*. Which was as no other wardrobe…

I glanced back in and saw… I saw how life *really* is and that the comforts of philosophy don't even scratch its immensity, its sheer… size and unconcern and coldness. The joys of friendship and art—*art!*—which we conceived as the be-all-and-end-all of civilised existence don't even scratch the surface of it! The whole caboodle of Charleston and all its works were reviewed—and not kindly either. It was, as I was once wont to say: just too *too* ghastly. The horror! The horror!⁹⁷

It called to me, its grappling hooks fastened *into* me. Internally, I felt *loosened*. Into that void I saw the edifice of my everything vanish: first the superstructure: my passion for Cubism and dear *dear* Pablo's daubs, for Virginia's *'stream of consciousness'* scribbling and even Sigmund's magic mountain of sick silliness.⁹⁸

Then the underpinning: the notion that aesthetics and *connection* could constitute a philosophy of life; that *'Logical Positivism'* was anything more that a speech impediment rendering its adherents incomprehensible! Or that *friendship* mattered—existed even—and served as a justification for the slings and arrows of life. Ha!'

And last of all, like the final swirl of bath water down the plug hole, went my crumbled foundations: the capacity for love and admiration for *you know who*. Which left nothing. *Rien!*, as my former friends would say. Pretentious twats!

---

⁹⁷ A borrowing from Joseph Conrad (1857-1924) and his *'Heart of Darkness'* (1899)? Or possibly parallel ponderings?

⁹⁸ Sadly, one must assume a reference to Pablo Picasso (1881-1973). Likewise, Virginia Woolf (1882-1941) and Sigmund Freud (1856-1939). The reader should be warned that torrents of cultural blasphemy hereon ensue.

Now, where *I* once stood was left a gaping hole. I felt younger, more free. Appallingly *free*. Reality had taken all that was once best and most vital about me. The Elves had all that—and then I saw them begin to *feed*.

Merely an *aperitif*. All those losses had left me lighter, making the gravitational pull still more powerful. In a way not easily explicable, everything of me that wasn't *meat*, spent many, *many*, years lost within that landscape. Hunted by the inhabitants.

But back in Charleston only seconds had elapsed. I chanced to reel rearwards. It could easily have been different. If I'd happened to go the other way I'd have fallen in, body and all, and that would have been the last seen of me. But like I say, it *chanced* otherwise—pure blind chance—just like everything else in the universe.

Now that reality had what it wanted and was sated—for the moment—and Lytton had given it a substitute sacrifice—mere me—the portal winked shut. *For the moment*. It would be back, that much I knew, but right now it was just a wardrobe again, custodian of a few moth balls and some Lytton Strachey long-johns.

I carefully shut its maw—I mean door. The catch gave a reassuring click. Then I addressed Strachey without deigning to turn my head, my voice as frigid as the rest of me would now forever be.

'Why did you come back?'

Lytton sort of swivelled on his heels, twisting like a hooked fish.

'Well, one thought to escape it, but… the beastly thing followed me home… One didn't expect that. It was in *my* wardrobe too. And the front door was rattled all night. Windows were tapped as well: first, second *and* third floor windows as one progressively sought to escape. One's companion—though *such* a dear boy—got scared and left even before we-…'

'So *you* thought…'

The truth was ejected like a blockage in his throat: he'd rather not have people see it but out it had to come…

'Well, *naturally*, one didn't want it in *my* house as well! The idea! So I thought you might…'

'Might what?'

'Well, you know, be a dear and…'

'… and take what was coming for *you*…'

'Oh, I wouldn't quite put-…'

'This was intended for *you*. *You* asked for it.'

ALTERED ENGLANDS

Not an opinion but a blunt assertion. Strachey didn't like my tone.

'Who? *Me?* My dear, you cannot be *seriously* alleging that I, I! would stoop so far as to-...'

He wasn't even convincing *himself*, let alone me.

'Yes, *you*!' I seethed. 'You... you...' Suddenly the floodgates opened and a tsunami roared down the dried-up riverbed of common sense. 'You pathetic cowardly, mincing, spider-legged, shirt-lifting, barber-dodging, servant-bullying, postboy-molesting, legacy-living, talentless, sneering, *rentier*, parasite! You... micro-talented, maiden-aunt sounding, piles-afflicted... *Bloomsberry*!'

I do believed he rather enjoyed it. Leastways, he hugged himself afterwards.

'Gracious,' he said. 'Such passion! Such a *lashing*! If one had realized your animal depths beforehand one might have-...'

I was no longer in the market and cut across him. I jerked a thumb *thataway*...

'*Do one!*' I ordered. '*Any* time you like—so long as it's in the next minute...'

'What?' he gasped, unaccustomed to such treatment. 'But what about breakfast?' he whined. 'I know you're slightly peeved right now but I have to think of myself. I'm not feeling very well and it's a long way to the station and I need-...'

'Begone or be dead,' I said—and meant it. 'And never come back. *Tosser!*[99]

He still thought it was all a joke: just part of the much bigger and universal joke he skipped and pranced through. But I convinced him otherwise. And to drive the message home—dear reader, I kicked his arse!

'Oh, oh, *oh*!' he trilled, and did a delightful little dance, clutching the afflicted part. Which disproved what Orwell said of him: dear Lytton *could* find it if he wanted to![100]

---

[99] Again, this easy assumption of authority over entry to Charleston and Strachey's ready acceptance of it ought to assist in the tricky task of identifying the narrator. Charleston belonged to Vanessa Bell née Woolf, but numerous references to her, many far from flattering (see above, passim), indicate it is not she. If, however, the writer is a husband, partner, lover or otherwise 'significant other' of Vanessa's, the field of riders—if you will excuse the phrase—is, alas, little narrowed.
[100] I have been unable to source the implied comment by George Orwell (1903-1950) although the narrator is correct in assigning an unfavourable opinion of Bloomsbury.

I felt no impulse to join him in either dancing or clutching. The taboo of nothing but veneration for his nether regions was broken. Free at last! Free at last![101]

I then saw that I'd have my way regardless of anything I said or he wished. What had happened had expanded my capabilities: given me night-vision for the darker side of life. For a second I could see the undiagnosed cancer as it would one day be, coiled like a slug or raw sausages around his guts. It was tiny as yet, the matter of a few cells, and quiescent, but the thing knew its time would come.[102]

I thought to maybe tell him, but then I thought, *'why should I?'*

And indeed, why should anyone do anything for anyone? I had just inhaled an older—and also newer—wisdom. Showing how hypocritical was Strachey's insistence on his *petty* morality, and all his arbitrary *'ethics'*...

Strachey straightened himself up whilst rubbing his behind.

'Very well,' he said, feigning insouciance, the mask over his cold fishiness now fully slipped. 'I *shall* go—but I think you're being a perfectly unreasonable *beast* about this. And I now see that *dear* Virginia and Carrington were right about you. *'Not one of us,'* they warned one—how true, how true!'

Once that might have crushed me. Now it was a badge of honour. He sensed that and my: *how* those thin nostrils dilated.

'At the very least,' he said, 'I must first insist that not a word of the matter ever emerges. The whole saga has *reactionary* implications. So not one mention, to anyone, not ever. No one must know! Or you shall hear from my solicitor.'

My indifference knew no bounds. I may even have raspberried his hairy and astounded face. Two can play at that game: like himself and half of Bloomsbury, unwanted disclosures swing both ways. For instance, I was present when he boasted about Lloyd George and the Zeppelin raid *incident*... Some of the suffragettes involved never recovered!

Perhaps she/he had privileged access and heard the sentiment expressed privately. Significantly, it is implied that they served in the Spanish Civil War (1936-1939), as did Orwell (although not, it seems, on the same side).

[101] The narrator and Martin Luther King (1929-1968) have something in common in their use of this inspirational phrase from a slavery era Negro spiritual. And *only* that one thing...

[102] Its time came some years later. Strachey would die thereof, aged 51, at his country house in Wiltshire.

'And furthermore,' he said, playing what he thought a trump card, 'I shall excommunicate you from Bloomsbury!'

It was neither the time nor place but I confess I doubled up laughing. He got the message that I would somehow come to terms with my loss. That in particular infuriated him.

'Do you know,' he said, spitting feathers, his four-eyes boggling, 'I don't think you ever really *believed* at all! All it took was next to nothing—a *teensy* Elven intrusion, a *soupçon* of the supernatural—and whoops, you were *lost* to us! Tell me, you *beast*, did you ever truly *believe*?'

I finally caught him Full Square, fixing him eye to eye at long last, informing of him the truth I'd just learned. All *he* had was a pose, a feeble feverish fiction from a dying civilization. Something sickly. Whereas more than just me now moved behind my eyes. I had the power of conviction. Tomorrow belonged to me!

'I'll tell you what I believe,' I told him, positively *glowing* with confidence. 'I believe that *nothing* is true. And *everything* is permissible.'

No contest. Match over. One-nil!

Strachey shrivelled before me: the old retreating before the new, the effete faced by virility, fake rebel before the real thing. All unwilling, he *accepted* he and his sort should make way. Unconditional surrender!

I saw evolution and survival of the fittest kick in. His cancer commenced to grow.

※

'CHARLESTON-A-GO-GO'

The *Guardian* 'Weekend' supplement, September 2009.

'... and in an expansion of their facilities, the Charleston House Trust now offer residential weekend breaks and the opportunity to stay in rooms graced by the Bloomsberries themselves. All are en suite (plus bidet), and complete with Bloomsbury artefacts and original furniture.

So why not simultaneously expand your cultural horizons and hang your smalls where Strachey hung his?

JOHN WHITBOURN

My partner, Jocasta, felt like a totally new woman after just a short stay…'

ALTERED ENGLANDS

JOHN WHITBOURN

THE SIR ROBERT HOLMES PAIRING

✡

INTRODUCTION

As the story about to commence says:

'What was the truth then about this man whose career reads like the script of an Errol Flynn film, who amassed a large fortune and who retired and spent the last twenty-five years of his life in Yarmouth as Governor of the Isle of Wight?'

C.W.R. Winter. *'The Ancient Town Of Yarmouth'*. 1981.

Sir Robert Holmes? *Who he?*

I asked myself the same question during my first, blessed, adult stay in Yarmouth, Isle of Wight, when chancing on a reference to him in a local history book on the jumbled bookshelves of our holiday home. Priding myself on a reasonable knowledge on 17th century history (my literary stock in trade, after all...) I was surprised not to have heard of him before—especially such a vibrant figure. It was odd...

But now I consider it not odd at all—or alternatively, supremely odd, depending on my mood. As Scripture says in sundry places, there are *'signs for those who would see'*.[103] Maybe Sir Robert was saved up for me and occluded from my eyes until the time and place was right, for although I'd read books galore on Charles II, James II, Jacobitism, the Isle of Wight *et al*, up till then he'd been

---

[103] For example, The Quran. Surah 30, *Al-Rum*. See also footnote 42.

made invisible to me. But now, with rare free time at ground-zero in Holmes' home ground just when I was casting around for a new writing project, the time could hardly have been more 'right'. Thus the veil was withdrawn and someone was... motivated to leave *that* book on *that* bookshelf in *that* house, ready to fall open at *that* page when I picked it up. Leastways, that's the way I see. *Maktub*— It is written. *All* is written

And there were other synchronicities at the same time, piling on top of each other like some erotic rugby scrum. Also *Maktub*—but concerning which it best not to speak here.

So, what else I could I do but *'write'*?

Later on, with an 18,000+ word *'Chronology & Commentary'* of Sir Robert's life drafted and presented to Yarmouth Town Council, and these Holmsian stories composed, granting Holmes an extra... interesting retirement, I was moved to summarise the man to the uninitiated thus:

'Mercy on None' involves a real-life 17th century historical figure, Sir Robert Holmes, a sort of licensed pirate, who, amongst many other things, started a couple of wars, burnt most of the Dutch merchant marine, explored Africa, imported the first gorilla into England and pursued Mrs Pepys, much to her diarist husband's displeasure. He's also widely—but erroneously—recorded as the taker/renamer of New York from the Dutch. In later life he ended up as perpetual governor of the Isle of Wight off the south coast of England.

These stories depict Sir Robert at the fag-end of his career and in apparent sad decay. Yet beneath the fading embers of life, there is still the making of a fire...'

So, Sir Robert was a real-life person between the years 1622-1697—and more than usually alive if his record is anything to go by. After enough adventures to justify multiple lifetimes, he wound down his allotted span by becoming uncrowned king of the Isle of Wight.[104] Characteristically not content with mere Governorship of the Island, he turned the surrounding water into a nepotistic Holmsian sea by securing one (schoolboy!) nephew control of the mainland fort controlling access to the Solent, and a younger brother the

---

[104] An idyllic plus strategic large island off England's southern coast. The Solent separates it from the mainland and England's premier naval base, Portsmouth. Nowadays it is also a favourite family holiday destination, not least to the Whitbourn family, as well as a bastion of former, calmer, ways. *Plus*, my beloved Mum was born there—thus making me a half-*caulkhead*.

command of the Channel fleet. As another of my heroes, Mr Punch, is wont to say: *'That's the way to do it!'*

Even then, Sir Robert's 'winding down' was only relative (if you'll excuse the pun). One of the perks of the Governorship was the proceeds from all ships cast up on its shores, and amongst many accusations levelled at Holmes was that under his custodianship a suspiciously *large* number of craft came to grief nearby... Even his memorial statue, now to be seen beside the altar in St James's church, Yarmouth, was originally intended to glorify the *Sun king*, Louis XIV—until Sir Robert liberated it and its creator from a French ship and had the sculptor amend the head to depict Holmsian features.

You had to hand to him—otherwise he would simply snatch it off you. The Restoration of the Stuart monarchy had taken the man out of piracy but not piracy out of the man...

From a safe distance of three centuries I could not but admire Holmes—principally for his style and choice of abode—but also for his dangerous energies, his zest for the game of Life, for eating what was set before him, and particularly his atypical loyalty to James II when all the chameleons were deserting that monarch. So, since the fellow was safely dead and all passion spent, I could entertain the fancy that the old rascal might have been fun to meet, and not just a leathery old pirate prettified in scarlet and lace.

It was a fragile fancy however, safe only within the pages of a tale. Crane your neck and meet the eyes of the statue in St. James's, or look deep into the five-mile-stare emanating from Lely's portrait of him, and there you will see, I fear, a truer measure of the man.

Certainly, that was Samuel Pepy's opinion whenever their paths crossed. He strongly suspected Sir Robert of ambitions (perhaps even fulfilled ambitions) towards Mrs Pepys, he profoundly disagreed with him on naval (no, not Mrs Pepys') policy, but dared not broach either subject for fear of being challenged to a duel. Stuck with Sir Robert as company for the duration of a short coach journey in 1661, an appalled Samuel was moved to write....

'Good God! What an age is this, and what a world is this! that a man cannot live without playing the knave and dissimulation.'

However, even now, Sir Robert is not mere dust and memory: he moves within the modern age, and not just in the stories included here either. Recent top-notch detective work by Isle of Wight local historians seem to have solved beyond reasonable doubt the mystery of Sir Robert's daughter. Unusually for the age he had no wife, but less uncommonly had an illegitimate child, a girl on whom, as best we can tell, he doted—or at least provided for. The identity of her mother was long thought to be beyond recovery and presumed to be some rustic milkmaid Sir Robert had tupped but declined to wed. Now though, close examination of the diaries of the great scientist Robert Hooke[105] makes it as conclusive as such things can be that Hook's beautiful-but-flighty niece had the honour of Holmsian attentions. Her charms were such that she made many conquests[106] when she moved to London before her untimely death, but true to form piratical Sir Robert sailed in and out again free from capture, disease or wedlock.

However, my story was written before that revelation and so tells a different tale...

Also in the modern day, Sir Robert secured for me one of those little victories that justify hanging around waiting for natural death. It so happened that the *English Heritage* guide to Yarmouth Castle[107] stated that Holmes was Irish, not English, on the grounds that he was born there.

It was open to me to respond succinctly and save on scholarship by quoting to English Heritage the immortal, true but then somewhat daring words of Sir Arthur Wellesley, Duke of Wellington, in comparable circumstances, to wit: *Jesus Christ was born in a stable, but that didn't make him a horse...*' Yet for some reason I didn't feel this would be a productive approach. Instead, by politely mustering the record and Sir Robert's own words, in the course of lengthy correspondence, I convinced them otherwise. Then, true to their word, when the next edition of the Castle guide was published, Sir Robert was reclaimed for England, and discovering that fact gilded for me the entire family holiday it commenced. That joy I felt is probably incomprehensible to non-historians and other normal people, but was nevertheless real.

So, in some small thanks for joy rendered, to Sir Robert and the colourful script he composed out of the years God gave him, for his

---

[105] A son of Wight, perhaps its most eminent, born in Freshwater, a neighbouring village to Yarmouth. Where an enigmatic concrete cube outside a supermarket commemorates the fact.
[106] Including, it seems, her scientist uncle...
[107] Whose uncompromising bulk adjoins Sir Robert's former home, now an upmarket hotel and restaurant.

inexplicable Jacobite loyalties, to Yarmouth and 'St David's', to the events of Thursday 6th August 1998, and to West Wight in general...

Ladies and gentlemen, I have the honour and privilege to present to you:

> *'Captain Holmes, in his gold-laced suit*[108]....

Take it away Sir Robert....

---

[108] Pepys again. 1661

24~

MERCY ON NONE[109]

*'Vectis, the Isle of Wight, a blessed plot,
Made free by God of foxes, snakes and lawyers'*

Anon. Traditional

❁

'What was the truth then about this man Holmes, whose career reads like the script of an Errol Flynn film, who amassed a fortune, and who retired and spent the last twenty five years of his life in Yarmouth as Governor of the Isle of Wight?'

C. W. R. Winter. *'The Ancient Town of Yarmouth'*. 1981.

❁

'I am now soe ill of my limbs that I have not been out of my chamber these twelve daies. I want the Bath Spa as an old horse doth grass.'

Sir Robert Holmes. Letter, July 1689.

❁

---

[109] *'Heaven is just, and can bestow/Mercy on none but those that mercy show.'* From *'Fling this useless book away...'* or *'Written in a Lady's Prayer Book'* by John Wilmot, Earl of Rochester, 1697.

Old Treadwell came off the beach a saint. Sand in his hair and everywhere, but quite the saint. There was no bad left in him. Where before were just cold words and gold-lust, now were smiles and love for all.

He was no more good as a lawyer, of course. He had to give that up.

'So, Mrs Treadwell...,'

'Marble-faced bitch?' interrupted Sir Robert, 'mouth like a sphincter?'

'That's her,' confirmed Notary Ezekiel, his *'man of business'*, come to update him on all the Yarmouth gossip.

'Knew her when she was young. Chill as charity but pretty with it. I protest before the Almighty, Ezekiel, what *does* He do to us, eh?' Sir Robert slapped his bandaged legs and bit down the wince that provoked. 'Once she was a saucy baggage, now a baggy sausage. What *is* He playing at? What *can* you do?'

What Ezekiel could do was lead a blameless life, attend divine worship twice on Sundays and decline to tread the primrose paths his employer's words tempted him down. As a *'Papist'* it was just as well he expected little of life.

'What indeed, Sir Robert? But as I was relating, Madame Treadwell observed their reputation and wealth departing with the husband she knew and... admired. So she packed him off to a private bedlam at Newport. He, alas, had become so sweet he complied just to please her.'

Sir Robert smiled, a hyena's amusement.

'Clever minx! Their gentle care and rations, the high sunless cells and chains, will soon kill him off. She won't be left potless, poor darling AAAAAAA ! AAAAAA!'

Ezekiel had adjusted his seat on the bed and inadvertently dragged the heavy covers over afflicted parts. Sir Robert clenched his fists, clenched his eyes, clenched everything. Then the gout-arthritis spasm passed and he beheld his friend again. From the corner of those same rheumy eyes he also beheld the brimful *po* beside the bed. The two visions met and mated.

ALTERED ENGLANDS

Ezekiel prophesied the project in mind and spoke hurriedly; knowing a mere apology wouldn't save him. He foresaw the splitting time-line: himself piss-drenched; days of rupture in their acquaintance—or avoidance, the alternate way: well worth a betrayed confidence.

'She'll be disappointed. He's had me change his will. It all goes to a poor girl out at Thorley.'

The intelligence arrested Holmes questing hand. He'd had his own *'poor girl'* out that way. Often. Alone in his extensive love-life she'd been fecund. Naturally, he hadn't wed the wench but still acknowledged her child: even gave it the farm her mum milked on. Disturbing coincidence: and a sickening blow if he'd shared favours and orifices with a *lawyer*. It would change everything: turn the world topsy-turvy like he had the mother; worse than Cromwell or King Billy the sodomite had.

'No,' said Ezekiel, as firm as mild nature permitted. 'Not your one. Your Mary was not like that.'

Holmes had the bed well crushed under his long presence but sank still further into it. A sigh signalled his anger's demise.

'Praise God, praise God...'

'Treadwell gave detail: *excessive* detail. At length he praised her orbs and chines,[110] stating them proof of a benevolent Deity whose work is beauty, who command is to enjoy.'

'Really?' Sir Robert was late-warming to a land-pirate he'd cut dead on numerous occasions. He admired his theology.

'Worse still, he spoke to me as to a friend, not a *papist* he'd bestowed a pavement oyster[111] on a mere week before. You may depend I made due enquiry as to his state of mind but found him firm and rational. I called not two but three sober witnesses, burgesses all. Alas, *la Treadwell* will rage in vain in her widow's weeds. She'll not overturn it.'

Holmes's vast amusement, cruel homage to rough justice, was curtailed by the double doors opening. A maid appeared, preceded by a wheeled basin. The steaming water whispered indulgence.

---

[110] Isle of Wight and Southern English dialect for a deep fissure in a cliff. From Old English *cinan*: to crack. Hence Blackgang Chine, Shanklin Chine etc.
[111] A hawking forth of comment-worthy extent.

'Talking of overturning,' said Sir Robert, rousing himself and dismissing his man, 'If I can't get to Bath, damn its eyes, then one shall attend me!'

That had been his way, all through his long life.

❀

'My wife and I go to Church and there in the pew was Captain Holmes, in his gold laced suit, at which I was troubled because of the old business which he attempted upon my wife.'

Samuel Pepys. *Diary*. 22nd December 1661

❀

She clutched her guinea tighter than he clutched her. At any other time there was food for thought in that. All the gold he'd brought back from West Africa, bartered from the black kings on *Dog Island*[112] or torn from the Dutch (even out of their tulipy-breathed mouths on occasion), had both invented and baptised the new coinage. England's stirring now seeped out into the world stamped on 21 shillings of yellow metal; heralds of great things to come. In return, they made great things possible for their creator, enabling *him* to come.

Inflation was the bugbear of the age, sticking its nose into the most intimate realms. Time was when maids were cheap, or even free when brisk-arrayed in his suit of gold or hero-like back from battle. Now he wasn't such a pretty sight and only lucre could sorcerously shape-change him into desirable form.

The position helped though; helped her as it did him.

Buxom back to him, the maid bounced happily away, impaled atop his cocker-rampant. She rode untroubled by any view of his reddening mask, he by any pressure on his tormented legs. Both were happy in their different ways: her delight lay all before her in the spending—and his likewise.

---

[112] Island at the mouth of the Gambia River, re-christened *Charles Island* and fortified by Holmes.

ALTERED ENGLANDS

Sir Robert re-raised the slipping skirts for the umpteenth time. He welcomed sight of those pink pseudo *Downs* as he had their chalk originals, viewed from a Solent-treading man o' war long years before. The glorious vista, infinity of curves, a friendly Janus face, assisted the ageing lance to tourney again. He was a captain once more, steering a lively ship—only nowadays its cannon wouldn't fire without long ramming and point-blank target.

He kneaded the proffered cheeks just as earlier he'd needed them. Then: joy! Oh joy! Or was it Joanna?

After the mess and sweat of love, a bed-bath delivered by soft palms and limpid eyes was doubly welcome. Joy or Joanna—he could never recall and didn't like to ask after so many bouts—was a wonderful ministrator. She even dispensed wit amidst the dabs.

'The way I sees it,' she told him—or perhaps her conscience, 'is I haven't disobeyed me Mum. *'You beware that Sir Robert,'* she says, *'he's hands like hawsers and'll ambush 'ee like he did Frenchies in the Solent. You mind he don't lie atop you and make your poor Ma cry!'*'

Holmes shrugged. He had no grounds for complaint. *'To thine own self be true...'*. *'Ma'* had been ambushed long and often herself in the past: once bitten—or five-score bitten—twice shy... That wise-woman spoke from experience.

'So,' the maid rattled on, negotiating a tricky bit with her cloth, not wishing to rouse him again, 'I says to myself: I know: *you* lie atop *him*—let *his* Ma cry!'

Their honest hilarity was aborted by a delegation.

☸

'Holmes... a rash, proud, coxcombe...'
Samuel Pepys. Diary 16th June 1665

☸

'Where? There? Who? Is that all? Bugger off!'
They did, were glad to, leaving him to it. This was his sort of thing.

He realised he'd gotten his immortal soul all grubby—in no fit state for handing back to God—when he thought *'Only four? Four's not even a skirmish!'*

Actually four deaths or disappearances was a lot to a tiny place full of trying-to-be-good Christians. For the first time in ages he was ashamed of himself—even before the gaggle of rascally Burgesses. Their sins were little ones, clipped coins and furtive adulteries, only Yarmouth sins, beneath St Peter's notice. Whereas he...

The former *Rear-Admiral of the Red*[113] had known too many men overboard, deserving or no, to get worked up over less than a fistful of endings. He'd seen the dead spin, dukes and seaman alike, arms flailing, when beheaded by a cannonball, their dumb torso expressing the outrage and puzzlement of it all. To ask their *why* was to mimic them; to peer, tippy-toe, into an abyss that beckoned like a whore.

He agreed with Rochester:

*'Wisdom did his happiness destroy,
aiming to know that world he should enjoy.'*

Still, age had brought with it another, wiser, *wisdom*. The fault was not the Yarmouth worthies but his own. They'd not learnt better, lucky them. No way back for him, of course, but their innocence deserved to be protected.

The seat of the problem was easily visible from his windows, could almost be glimpsed from his captor bed: the low *'flats'* out to Thorley and Yarmouth Mill, the narrow *'strand'* along the shore. They were the realm of the vanishings and Lawyer Treadwell's conversion. The mob of merchants and prelates had only to point.

Now though, it was day and low tide. Lone mudlarks and inshore fishermen dotted the drear waterscape. Nothing would happen: never had—that was Yarmouth's charm; nothing since the French sacked it in 1377, save a slow climb-back to civility.

Night time was the right time. Life had taught Sir Robert that Truth is nocturnal. It never did to do ill by broad day. Otherwise the sun and its Creator would *see*.

Admiral Holmes would wait for his mistress.

---

[113] One of the nine senior flag-officers in the English fleet. Deputy commander of the centre squadron.

ALTERED ENGLANDS

❦

'Ah, Night, my beloved, my mistress, what trickster tunes we've composed together you and I...'

Only she wasn't that. Harlot rather than honoured mistress, still less wife, he'd used Night for his pleasures and then denied her hideous children. Offended, she now declined to answer his serenade. Sir Robert didn't care. He knew the trollop would always be good for another bout. Allow her her sulk: she was dependable.

Night had drawn her obliging cloak over the sack of Westerschelling. She obscured his deployment of its pacifist *Mennonite*[114] inhabitants as human shields, sent shrieking to useful death, wide eyed at the indifference of their God. She was the cover for rapine amongst the Dutch Guinea settlements and the extraction of teeth—and worse—from their traders. Night lovingly blurred the quivering aftermath of many a seafight. She was a bad man's good friend. He welcomed re-acquaintance.

He also blessed the imperative to quit his fetid room, to bandage up and hobble forth: to drink again the salt air and star-to-sea shine, not through glass but direct in your face: lived and savoured. It was not spice-laden Guinea air, nor the impending heaviness of battle-day, but the good-enough gift of the Solent, looking back towards Southampton. He kissed the draught all the way down his heaving lungs.

Darkness also threw discretion over his stumping walk. No longer the bounding cavalier that pursued Mrs Pepys, he did not like people to see his monkey gait. In January he'd sailed to Spithead to attend the Queen of Spain's state visit but the gout in his feet had prevented climbing aboard. That humiliation had actually made him weep, even as he conversed with her Majesty, head tilted up at the ship's rail like a boy to a giant. Her Majesty had thrown him her hankie. Even now the memory deeper flushed his face.

The shadow of St James's Church, where his statue (or leastways a pirated, amended one of Louis XIV) would one day stand, let him go. He left the little town behind. Tip tap went his two wooden supporters (sword-sticks

---

[114] A Protestant community, rejecting Church organisation, infant baptism, public office and military service. From *Menno* Simons (1496-1561), a Frisian religious leader.

both) along the quay. *Holmes* was on his way and thus the problem half-solved. The *problem* knew its own: he could sniff the evil and it sensed his coming. This would be simple.

Round the cube of Yarmouth Castle the tide left a little sand. At the cost of cold sweat he took the steps down to it.

There was beauty in unspoilt, untrodden sand, the blemish-free look of Eden: like moist new leather or a war-horse's flank. No one had yet dug for bait. Lesser spirits shunned the night beach now. But not Holmes; he felt more at ease than ever. He had his pocket pistols: the price of cheerful entry.

They ebbed to him like urchins to a mid-winter brazier. Patches of sand sleeker than the rest converged. Fascinated, Sir Robert observed their undulant approach. They were lovely and they loved him. He didn't even think to shoot. Musketry would draw mundanes from the Castle and *Wheatsheaf* and *King's Head* and spoil the communion.

One, the chief and best, flat and brown as a waiting Guinea virgin's belly, paused before Holmes in homage. A pool of water rose above it like saliva. Then it ate him.

※

'By and by we called to Sir W Battens to see the strange creature that Capt. Holmes hath brought back with him from Guiny; it is a great baboone,[115] *but so much like a man in most things, that (though they say there is a Species of them) yet I cannot believe but that it is a monster got of a man and she-baboone. I do believe it already understands much English...'*

Samuel Pepys. *Diary*. 24th August 1661.

※

Swaddled tight by a cold mother. Wrapped like a bed-roll. Absolute dark, abrasive sand in eyes and ears and mouth. All the time diving deep into the beach, beyond sight of God or man, down into the chill places of the earth. Bumping into other buried things: man-shaped cocoons.

---

[115] A gorilla, more likely.

ALTERED ENGLANDS

Then, invisible tentacles slithering over memories, dainty like a delving maiden's fingers. Probing, teasing—and then convulsion, a vomiting back into light.

And morning and bed and safety. Holmes reproached himself even as he embraced the day. The same dream two nights running: mere peasant predictability. A true gentlemen was insouciant; never *dwelt* on things. And to think he'd forgone cheese at supper to avoid it.

Fortunately, the company was easygoing.

'You'd dream too, Billy,' said Sir Robert. 'Mock not. T'was a disagreeable experience, albeit a brief one.'

Actually, leaving all else aside, it had done his gout and joints a power of good. For a while afterwards he'd been able to march around the house and make a nuisance of himself: a prize well worth the ruination of wig and clothes. In those few precious hours he'd felt like an eighteen year old again—and again and again. Happily that was the age of the laundrymaid he was going to compensate anyway, because of all the sand. So, she got tipped with coin *and* on her back.

The years soon returned though, descending like an anvil from on high. The Holmsian invasion had to retreat to its base, leaving a ravaged, relieved, servant army to their normal peace. There his customary company awaited.

Billy did not reply. He'd never been one for conversation even when alive.

'I'd most liken it,' Sir Robert continued, trying to find comfort amidst mangled sheets, 'to sudden descent into wet leather and the darkness of choking sand. Then envelopment in a pancake of prodigious power. I imagine my cocker braves the same buried in a cunny—though his welcome's warmer. I'll confess to you, Billy—and you alone, so tell no other, one felt just the slightest alarm...'

Billy the stuffed gorilla said nothing, was as tight-lipped as his namesake, King William of Orange—though a far more trustworthy confident.

'And then, just as sudden, it sicked me up and out, and I landed on me arse in the wet. Left me free to hobble home. It transpires I'm indigestible; too rich: even worse than Lawyer Treadwell! *'Like two brimful bowls of treacl'ed sugar'* apparently: *'over replete with rum, sodomy and the lash.'* Damned insult if you care to take it so...'

He didn't. Now he *understood*—and to understand all is to forgive all, better even than a commanded Christian.

'We talked, Billy—though I cannot tell you how. The converse appeared in my noddle and returned the same way, I suppose. Highly instructive. A most *interesting* species. Sin-eaters, after a fashion: vice as vittles. They both cook and consume the dish impartially. So that's where our fishermen have gone: swallowed whole and still down there as husks: discarded breakfasts. Treadwell was a more substantial repast: they left what they couldn't finish and sent him back for refill. Me though, I was too ample a feast: which gained me their respect—and confidence.'

The sheets heaved as Holmes's chest swelled. He liked to be well thought of, even by the worst.

'Told me all, they did: charming fellows in a way. Last of their breed, alas, or as far as they know. The poor beasts wander the ocean seeking dinner and haven't bumped into another shoal this last century or more. Didn't I mention that, Billy-boy? Oh yes, they're long-lived beasties by their account. What's that? *The good die young*? Witty point—for an ape. But no, their wickedness is rarely their own: they feed on ours: absorb it in the water or, better still, mouth to mouth—for they're linked to us in most intimate fashion. No blame thereby attaches. What do lesser breeds know of wrong? They obey Mother Nature's harsh decrees in all innocence, but only Man can *sin*.'

That gave him pause for thoughts of repentance—but it was too late and... demeaning to retread so much scarlet terrain. Sir Robert had always put his true faith in God's *mercy*—and if He were not more merciful than Man what was the point of worshipping Him? Holmes drowned the notion with a gulp of wine. The urgency of the task caused overflow onto the sheet and blankets. More laundry work for poor sore Joanna.

'Why *here*, you say? Why flock to blameless Yarmouth, home of honest sailors and fairly honest bourgeois? Another telling riposte, Billy. I wonder you don't stand for Parliament. Now, there's an idea! I've two Island seats in my gift, haven't I? One's heard worse nominations. You'd not stand out amidst the other, shaven, apes—and would tower over all in integrity. Talk about it to me later, over a bowl of punch and fruit, just you and I: for I like the cut of your jib, so I do, *William Baboon MP*. Now, where was I?'

The poor exiled corpse continued to stare out over the Solent, vainly seeking its African home—as it had so often done in life and now did all day.

'Oh, that's right. You'd just cut to the quick regarding the affliction. But think on: put that razor monkey-mind to work. If vice and sorrow were your chosen grub, what is it along this coast that'd draw you like beggars to a banquet? They said they scented it even before they rounded Normandy—and Lord knows there's ample iniquity there...'

The gorilla couldn't quite grasp it. The silence grew strained.

'Come on, hairyhead: you'll kick yourself after! What's here that leaks their favourite nutrient into the water even after a century? No? Give up? I'm surprised at you, old friend.'

Sir Robert gestured at the window, towards the sea.

'It's the *Castle*, Billy—obviously. See now? I mean, you know its history as well as I do...'

※

'... *Then came the dissolution of the monasteries and Quarr Abbey was sold to a Mr Mills of Southampton, who demolished it, much of the stone being used to build Yarmouth Castle. It may be that this was just because the stone was available on the island, but what a supreme irony for bluff King Hal—to demolish a monastery in order to build a castle to defend yourself against the very foreigners you have just alienated!*'

'*Fifty Fascinating Facts About the Isle of Wight*'
John Dowling. Museum of Smuggling History. Ventnor. 1984.

※

'It's St James Day, Mr Abbott. St *James* Day!'

With that 'explanation' of his behaviour, Sir Robert was off and on to further outrages as the mood took him. A normal day for Admiral Holmes—but also *St James's Day*.

His frank admiration—indeed exploration—of Mrs Abbott's cleavage had clapped her husband's hand to his sword. Ezekiel, who made his business to be closer than ever to his employer this of all days of the year (if only to avoid temptation himself) sidled on stage left.

'On St James's Day,' he informed the outraged bigwig, a luminary in London's '*Worshipful Company of Cordwainers*' (i.e. boots) Guild, and also Yarmouth burgess, albeit usually an absentee one, 'for reasons mainly—or indeed entirely—forgotten, licence is granted to all Yarmouthians so long as the gloved hand is flown. The law stands aside, averting its indulgent eye. An *open hand*, you see. Tis our most ancient custom...'

Together they eyed the pole-mounted red glove, proudly protruding from the upper story of the Town Hall. Mr and Mrs Abbott (though she noticeably less so...) regarded it as they would an indecent farmyard protuberance. Ezekiel took the opportunity to *go*.

Sir Robert was already at the Castle gate. The gunners hastened to admit their commander.

Here he felt even more at home than at home. This cannon-crowded, behemoth, reeking of grease and powder, reminded him of below-deck. The sea lapped at two sides. If only it could move with the swell he'd never leave.

But it couldn't. Untold tons of brick and stone moored it permanently to land. The pious labours of Quarr Abbey's builders, re-jigged, formed a lasting monument to King Henry's fears and the memory of 1377. A charmless child of the post-monastery, post-praying, world, it wasn't going anywhere. Its low squat bulk and angular bastions were ideally suited to after-*'Reformation'* times. England stood alone against... everyone. Only evil came from abroad. The garrison and cannon would not leave until 1869.

Ezekiel joined Sir Robert. The gunners' greeting coughs sounded like *'papist!'*

The tide was in, the sand and salt-levels under water. Holmes pondered their choppy shroud.

'Grimes!'

The Master Gunner's feet were swift to attend him.

'Sir Robert?'

'Tell me, sirrah, what do you know of the *'Guinea Codpiece Sponge'*?'

'I've never heard of it, Sir Robert.'

'Nor me,' said Ezekiel. Holmes sighed for form's sake.

'Tell me you two, has the Island been your life-long home?'

They both nodded. Sir Robert already knew it full well.

'Well, they say travel broadens the mind. Pray let me enlighten you then. The Guinea Codpiece Sponge is a loathsome jelly creature from *Afrique*: half fish, all teeth. I've had the misfortune to witness its depredations before. It lurks beneath the sand in order to leap and latch onto the privy-parts of Man and then devour the same. Guinea abounds with long-countenanced eunuchs thus formed. I now perceive that Yarmouth has the misfortune to be so infested. Doubtless the Pope or Dutch have diverted the affliction our way. Deal with them, if you please, gentlemen.'

Grimes had always loved his seaside home but now saw it draped in fresh sinister light. Involuntary hands hovered protectively above his crutch.

'*Codpiece sponge?*' queried Ezekiel. 'Are you *sure?*'

Sir Robert dilated his nostrils. It sufficed. The feeble mutiny was stillborn.

'You are an ignorant man, Ezekiel, priest-ridden and baby-blissful unaware of the wilder extravagances of Nature beyond this blessed Isle. Wade out and see for yourself, should you *doubt* me. T'would be no loss to Mrs Ezekiel, or so one hears.'

'I shall attend to it now,' snapped Gunner Grimes and was gone—only to directly return. 'Um... how?'

The greater hurdle of belief now crossed, Sir Robert could be avuncular. He would have draped his arm around the troubled shoulders but treacherous arthritis castrated it to a mere gesture. Still, the thought was there.

'My independent company of Foot is already en route from Carisbrooke. By their arrival next low tide, you shall have prepared a chart. Delineate it into squares and ascribe each man a portion. Have them criss-cross the flats and strand, thrusting a half-pike deep down every pace. A static line of men at the water's edge shall forestall the creatures' retreat. You will observe their hiding places, if not their demise, tokened in sleeker patches of sand. Now go to it, man.'

Grimes did so—and with a will.

Sir Robert liked to just... wander the fort: as a terror to the garrison and balm to himself. Here, *just*, he could re-imagine himself a man of account. He was at the helm, going nowhere, true, but the centre of bustle, particularly now as the gunners assembled pikes and thick wadding to thrust down their breeches. Ezekiel dutifully followed on.

In the *Long Room*, where the larger cannon waited, there was reminder underfoot. A sculpted hand, torn from a saint or Christ was sunk into the stolen stone of the floor. Ezekiel gave it wide berth and even Holmes minded his feet.

Sir Robert peered through a gunport out over the Solent. His view was bounded by hexagonal stone: exquisite pillars, spiral carved, perverted from worship to more martial use. He pondered that change, all the labour and love and infusion of prayer, and then violent betrayal and destruction; all that... disappointment seeping out into the sea. Rich pickings indeed.

First the Tudor aristocracy, feeding off the monastery lands: becoming a new class, old-looking but not keen on recollection: today's *'Enclosers'*. Meanwhile, beneath the water, that history continued. King Henry's serial marriage problems carried on providing sustenance for all sorts.

For a second—and only a second—Sir Robert sickened of life. He stepped back and inadvertently trod on the stone hand. Ezekiel flinched.

'Postpone the orders,' Holmes told him. 'Make it tomorrow. Let them first have their St James's Day.'

Sir Robert looked down at the proffered hand underboot, and then out again through the ex-church window at the sea. He gave each the full benefit of his thoughts. The waters seemed to know and shudder.

'So *there's* an end to an old story,' he told himself and the guns.

※

In River Road, by the Quay, he re-met the Abbotts and a cloud of other *overners* from England. *La* Abbott's fan flew *(fairly* fast…) to her breast but she need not have feared—not immediately. Sir Robert's smile was alligator-wide. And as false.

'*Dear* lady,' he greeted her and them all, 'my friends! Soon the tide will retreat. *Do* promenade the beach, I entreat you. It has charms all its own in the failing light…'

Relieved to find him affable, they looked likely to comply.

He felt justified in his decision, the servant of virtue. It was not right that any portion of God's creation be excluded from the revels.

'Let <u>everyone</u> enjoy their St James's Day,' he thought, '*without discrimination.*'

※

An ill-tempered summer tide was lashing the town, matching the indoors disharmony. The sea was loud in their ears.

'Good-night, Billy. Sweet dreams.'

ALTERED ENGLANDS

But the monkey's glass eyes would not let Sir Robert extinguish the candle—or anything else—not without reproach. Holmes's sailors had shot the rest of its troop. Billy had been the last of his race as best he knew. So he knew all about extinction. From beyond the grave, he *sympathised*.

'Oh, what of it?' asked Sir Robert. 'Is this any worse than the rest?'

And then, fatally, hoist by his own petard, he had to review the *'rest'*. The silent gorilla was a cunning adversary.

The true answer was *no* of course, but it proved no comfort. Sleep fled from him like an unbribed maid.

There'd been the point-blank broadside into the already sinking Dutchman—*just to see*. And the survivors left to swim home to Holland. The smell of branded black flesh on Dog Island: none of his doing but his to witness, unperturbed. The puzzled reproach in the eyes of slaughtered gorillas. These were minor things: the stock in trade of the wider world beyond Wight.

And as to *major?* Well, he comforted himself with *'Holmes's Bonfire'*: 150 sail of Dutch merchantmen incinerated in the Vlie, a history-changing kick in the parts to Netherlands prosperity, albeit marred by the easy target, gentle Mennonite town beside. They'd prayed as Holmes preyed. That was fairly bad but he'd lived with it—been knighted for it, had the bells of the City rung for him. Some said—in print, the dogs!—the Fire of London was God's judgement on the deed—but not to Holmes' face, not ever. They knew him, knew better. *He* knew better. All that mattered was that it was done with *style*, with aplomb: that had always been his creed.

And he'd had a daughter and been kind to her. She didn't have to work and was quite often visited. What *more* did people want?

And anyway it was a *war*, like all of life, cradle to grave. He'd heard that Dutch merchants would stamp on a crucifix when required by the pagan blacks and Japanese, just to gain an *entrée*. Them or the vice-suckers: they signified nothing. They had it coming to them

And just as the Dutch got their just desserts, so sleep came at last to Holmes.

The candle guttered, though there was no draught, and Billy the gorilla stared on.

He'd always imagined the senior saints as tall men, of stature befitting their stature. But St Francis proved a little fellow, towered over by all the animals around him.

Yet that was not conclusive proof. The dream had its scale all awry. Billy was his living size but stood shoulder to shoulder with a cat. It toyed cruelly with a likewise giant mouse.

Others of the company were less familiar, their proper proportions open to doubt. A terrifying green insect stood by the Saint, chittering and slicing its serrated claws over some unfortunate dragonfly. Sir Robert had seen the like in jungle surrounds but there it was less intimidatingly swollen.

A wasp raised to human scale revealed its full malevolence. It injected its venom and seed into a similarly huge grub. The poor victim writhed under the lance and then was still, paralysed, awaiting consumption alive when the wasp brood awoke within.

Yet the Monk loved them all and raised his arms to embrace all their ugliness. Even the leech-like Yarmouth vice-sucker, flapping lithely by his sandalled feet, did not draw disapproval. Only Sir Robert's disgust met with rejection.

'As you are in God's plans,' he was told, in a voice of persuasive reason, *'so are they. Evil comes from the Almighty just as grace and virtue do.'*

This was unfamiliar theology and Holmes showed it in his sleeping face.

The Saint would have none of that.

'His thoughts are not your thoughts, little man,' he said firmly. *'Nor His ways yours to comprehend. Know only this: that as they are so are you...'*

The vice-sucker coiled affectionately around Francis's feet, though it knew it would find no nourishment there.

The apostle Matthew appeared beside them and smilingly quoted from his own Gospel:

'Can you not buy two sparrows for a penny? And yet not one falls to the ground without your Father knowing.'

'Arrogant son of Adam!' Francis persisted, not angry but concerned. *'Did you really think your kind alone may appeal in prayer?'*

Then Holmes was with them and of them, was amongst them, shoulder to shoulder, shoulder to wing-case and thorax. And there was understanding amongst brothers.

ALTERED ENGLANDS

Sir Robert sat on the quayside steps and dabbled his feet. The moon shone on the congregation before him. They radiated gratitude for his mercy.

He allowed them to nibble at his toes. That probably constituted a banquet in itself—but the fact no longer troubled him. The heavy backpack of dainty conscience was thrown off, cheerfully abandoned in his dream.

'*So,*' Holmes concluded, 'no more Islanders—save in famine and subject to notice. Agreed?'

Warm approval slithered back from the shoal elder. It coated Holmes mind like syrup but restrained from feeding. They simultaneously loved and feared the canceller of pike-thrusts.

'Otherwise, take what else you like: French and Dutch and Scots: there's only ever a few but it should suffice. Plus there's always *Overners* if there's been a drought. In-between, suck monks' tears from the Castle. One way or another, you need never starve.'

Holmes disengaged his feet before they got the taste. He no longer had to care about his *sins* but the memories were still his to treasure, the freshly laundered solace of old age. Now he could review them without fearing Billy's reproach.

He arose and the vice-sucker formation drew back to perform a graceful dance of thanks. Then Sir Robert bowed his own gratitude as they swam away.

He felt warm inside. He had been *merciful*—like God was and like God would be to him. There was no cause to fear exchanging this sunset glow for just a few—a very few—foreigners.

Lame in body but light in heart, Sir Robert stumped along Yarmouth Quay, into the years to come and then Judgement.

'GO WIGHT! IT'S ALL-WIGHT!

Official Paper of the *GO WIGHT!* Campaign.

... Yarmouth: Gateway To The Island!

... and the fantabulous Lymington to Yarmouth ferry statistics just speak for themselves!

	Foot Passengers	Cars
1937:	219,000	2,400
1948:	441,000	20,000
...		
1981:	1,250,000	250,000
1998:	2,250,000	750,000

... not surprisingly, much of the traffic isn't from England but from our partners in the European Community! So the Yarmouth Go-Wight campaign says hurrah and a great big hello and welcome, wilkommen, welkom, velkommen, bienvenue, bienvenido, benvenuto, bemvindo, witamy, vitame vas, shalom, failte, croeso and '*See you, jimmy*' to all our special friends from abroad.

We can PROMISE you the trip of a lifetime—literally. For who knows? You might never go back!'

ALTERED ENGLANDS

25~

THE PROTESTANT WIND[116]

Or

SIR ROBERT IN THE MULTIVERSE

William, Prince of Orange, stood proud aboard the *Brill*. Some little of his joy crawled out from under his glacial nature to infect others. One of his passing Surinam soldiers—a *damned* attractive one as it happened—dared to flash a dusky smile.

Forgetting himself, the Prince smiled back. What was *that* black beauty's name?

The musket-crack of the sails above recalled him to duty and concealment. This easterly wind was really something. If he'd believed in God he'd have given thanks for it. The Prince felt that lack. One of the drawbacks of streamlined pragmatism was the lack of a recipient for gratitude.

He had praised it, even christened it, to counter the embarrassment of first being blown back to Holland. Now the elements were about-face, at his service, driving events on as he wanted. *The Protestant Wind* was taking them to England and holding the English in port. The Prince felt sure that when its job

---

[116] The victors' appellation for the fortuitous easterly breeze which propelled William's invading fleet in 1688 and confined the English navy to port and impotence.

was done it would retire decently to its obscure quarters—somewhere in the attic, maybe—like good servants did.

Again he studied the straining canvas and all the driven ships stretching miles on either side. A tiny spasm of stomach alarm: a hint from the Deity he doubted.

'Thank you. That will sufficient be,' he told the gusts—and then frowned as they did not abate.

'You can have too much of a good thing' thought the Prince—but then in beholding a sailor's bum-cleavage undermined his own mind.

Windward, wolfish, at the Solent's narrow neck, Sir Robert Holmes and his cannon awaited.

❇

'A knock-off?' asked Sir Robert, overjoyed.

'Clean orf!' answered his double. 'A proper kiss-the-cannonball, spray the sails red and keep walking—joy to behold apparently.'

'Whoa! What d'you reckon of that, Billy-boy?'

The stuffed gorilla by the fireside, Holmes's pioneering innovation into England, fruit of his Guinea rampages long ago, did not reply. In death, as in life, he treated the pink-monkeys' questions as beneath contempt, and continued staring after lost paradise.

Whilst not despairing of a reply one day, the Admiral turned avidly back to his more co-operative companion. 'Go on. Tell me more! Lavish me with detail!'

'People really are cack. Directly they heard, the mob lost their craving for Orange and cried *'Ho for King James!'*'

The two old devils cackled appreciatively, each framing the scenes in inner, private, theatres. Then they remembered themselves. Joy could only ever be short: anything longer was to invite Life's revenge. To business.

'But tell me, my friend,' said the first, gesturing with his gin, 'when did the new time-line commence? At the point he was beheaded or later when his legs got the message? You seem to report a decent gap...'

The other Sir Robert laughed—a travesty of a sound and an affront to merriment.

'Oh yes! There was progression all right...'

ALTERED ENGLANDS

'A second or two?' ventured first Sir Robert to his twin, hopeful of more.

'Noooo.' A brown-tooth smile framed the words: a bearing of fangs from the savannah-time. 'We're talking three or four determined paces. His arms continued to direct operations, expanding on words never-to-be spoken. You'd need a heart of milk not to laugh...'

So they did: briefly—for show. Then:

'I—we—we've seen the like before,' confirmed first Sir Robert. 'Once in Guinea and again at the *St James's Day fight*—and in the farmyard, of course. Of the two, chickens put on a better show, in my opinion '

'A function of the speed of strike and thickness of neck, no doubt.'

'No doubt. Also they have wings to flap and thus enhance the drama.'

'Just so.'

Sir Robert paused and studied his guest by the inconstant light of his bedside candle.

'Damn your eyes, but I *like* you!' he announced, and shoved the pistol further out of sight under the blanket. 'You're a man after my own heart.'

Indeed he was—and more than that. The two were identical right down to the cloaked gleam in their eyes.

Overwhelmed, drawing on their hearts' dregs of sentiment, they shook hands. The million needles of the gout caused both to wince.

They rode it: pain was there to be transcended like women and regret.

'And the time-lines?' A gentle reminder.

'*I* think,' said second Sir Robert, carefully, choosing words like ship's supplies, 'that one of them gambolled on in the pretence of life—akin to the headless Prince. But then—and here is the crux and difference, finding it sweet the imposture has been outrageously prolonged. I can only assume a saucy variant has turned a deaf ear to the call of death!'

'Well, doubtless there was much distracting noise...,' offered Sir Robert sympathetically.

'Indeed: that is the way with sea-fights, as we well know. And now, one twin bravely refusing abortion, the brethren histories have continued in affectionate tandem. The 'correct' variant, whichever it might be, has conspired with its doomed brother to preserve both. That at least is my humble supposition.'

The two men considered—identically—and then each nodded. It was the only explanation.

Another smile, careless and accepting.

'Welcome aboard!' they told each other simultaneously, and raised their gin-tins high.

✸

'I yield,' said the Archbishop, and sat down. Another had a better point than he and that was the iron etiquette of *'The Blaze of Speculation'*. The resulting quality of debate, just as much as hallowed walls, was the jewel that justified worldwide fame.

The sole sound now was expectation, the congregation waiting to listen and pounce. All the London babble, the roar of River and Embankment traffic, was filtered out. Cunning technology inserted into old stone stopped it at the Cathedral's walls; the twenty-first century coming to the aid of the eleventh: fitting mutual assistance between kin. Electro-magnetic blotting paper now preserved a temple of pure thought in the heart of the metropolis. Here all... nonsense was ruthlessly excluded. They sought the mind of God—they really did in earnest, all day, every day, bar Easter and Christmas. Interruptions were not permitted.

'I propose this thesis,' said the girl—and stood again, her full five feet augmented by high heels. Buck teeth and jewellery caught the candlelight. 'If the Almighty is *above* and not *of* time, then we've really gotta chuck the temporal-linear concept of prayer. I mean, it's counterpart's already gone out of the lower philosophies, and theology belongs at the forefront, not lagging. Read and learn, ladies and gentlemen: ask around: you'll not find a modern physicist who'll accept the straight-arrow model...'

Her pause for breath unleashed the growls. *'Counter-intuitive!'* came the chant from the die-hards in the aisles. *'God does not play tricks!'*

That was the hot line of some decades back, the last bulwark against acceptance of the troubling new. Nowadays Christendom's consensus had moved on, teetering on the precipice of hugging paradox to its chest.

'No, no,' the young priestess-astronomer persisted above the babble. *Beefeater*-Beadles with lead-tipped staffs moved to keep the heckling down to non-intimidatory levels. 'Listen! As the Father is above our perception, so too are His ways. Right? We've gotta have faith and patience and learn in time—whatever *that* might be!'

This was cheating: a mere paraphrasing of her hero's *coup de grâce* summation on *'The Sky at Night'* a century before, even down to the arched-eyebrowed quip at its end. No one minded too much. The words of the great Greenwich-Archmage Moore were always welcome at the *Blaze*.

The lighting was deliberately retro; just the same as when Edward built the Abbey a millennium back. Only candlepower did the job, even though the electric-fluid was long since tamed and old hat. It supplied a kind of *slow-down-a-moment* atmosphere the subtle minds in charge were keen to preserve. Modernity was blackballed from membership and kicked its heels, pretending not to care, outside the Saxon-carved portals.

Also, the serried banks of flaring wax that gave the place its name did other favours. For one, imperfect light glossed over some deficiencies: a plain-jane might be a goddess. Secondly, a bit of teasing obscurity was a boon to the bashful.

She didn't need that comfort. Her voice was thin but strong, the equal of their hesitation.

'Wrestle with it, Christian brothers! The struggle is worthwhile!'

That vision of hand-to-hand grappling propelled one such shy set of feet aloft. The girl gave way.

'Are you saying,' asked a fellow Doctoral student, whose sinful lust for her rode tandem with genuine pious curiosity, 'that God stands aloof from our poor grasp of time? Does He thus foreknow all?'

'He does!' said the girl, stoutly, rising to answer. 'It must be!'

The Archbishop shouted *'Amen!'*.

'Orthodox! Orthodox!' chorused the lower stalls: City slickers and costermongers whiling away the lunch hour with philosophy. The rougher elements loved to see the truth really put the boot into error.

'Then,' hazarded her would-be lover, tossing her an easy ball, 'by extension we could validly pray regarding past events: things done and gone. We could petition *now* that things *then* go differently or exactly as they did—and God hearing us *then* (which is His eternal now) would consider our requests and-...'

'You got it!' The girl beamed at him. She'd never stood so long in the *Blaze* or had such an easy ride. She recognised her questioner and warmed to him. Perhaps he too deserved some or other *'ride'*. Inwardly she begged forgiveness for the thought—but didn't change her plans.

The Archbishop—who was also an historian—rose again. His mind was awhirl with new thoughts: better than sherry. He bowed to the re-seated astronomer, profoundly grateful.

'If this be true,' he told the throng, excitedly thinking it through a second in advance of his tongue, 'we have to read our history books anew. I mean... they wouldn't necessarily be set—and sad. Hellfire! Sorry, but... you know—think of it! Mebbe we can add our pleas to that which worked well—and be thankful. Maybe we can even voice appeal against that which went for ill. It's in God's power—and His mercy—to heed future cries and grant 'em! Got to be! *Stone* me...!'

This was the Blaze of Speculation at its very best, a living culture of theology. Old intellects ran wild, enthused by youth, even as they dispensed the gentle cooling rain of hard experience.

The Archbishop pondered the history he knew and the large proportion of it he deplored. Hope flared like a sunburst within. Perhaps there really was a court of posthumous appeal—and full restitution of injustice. If enough of those not yet born had grace sufficient to care and pray...

'It could be changing,' he told himself and the huge echoing hall at the same time. 'Right now! It could be changing under our bloomin' feet! He could do it—a loving Father *would* do it! And... and! Cop this: we'd never know!'

❂

'Your head would explode.'

The babble died. The tavern gathering looked at Sir Robert. It wasn't the answer they expected—or indeed the answerer, but it was a good one.

Newton was stunned—for a moment, just a second, till his liquid intellect cascaded over, under and through Holmes's dull dam.

'Mebbe so: t'would be only just and pious—but just suppose: suppose one noddle *could* tolerate the infinite? One brain frame the thoughts of God!'

'Beyond me!' said Pepys—as were most things at that stage of the evening and jug. 'Beyond us all and forever! Who here could even memorise all the things present on this simple table: the relative positions of platters, pipes and cups?'

ALTERED ENGLANDS

Holmes had acquired the rank of hero by ceaseless and unthinking can-do. He squinted at the tavern battle-board and had a go till his brain hurt.

'No.' he concluded firmly. 'Even that bare child's play courts the risk of combustion. Master Pepys is correct.'

He gravely toasted his companion on the bench.

The Naval Secretary was glad to see and hear it. Long years had been invested in getting on the fearsome sailor's good side. That security against dying in a duel was worth forgetting the ancient business with Mrs Pepys and the younger Holmes in his stylish coat-of-gold.

'S'right,' he confirmed. 'And if we can't do that, what chance of memorising the pebbles of the seashore: even a little one: Pevensey Sluice, maybe—went there once. Not much to it—but *lots* of pebbles.'

'Pebbles on the beach...,' mused the then-unsuspected Newtonian titan, admiring an inner vista.

'Let alone the sea-spray in a typhoon,' Pepys blurted on. 'Couldn't compute that. Not a chance.'

'I concur,' said Holmes, 'having the misfortune to skirt two such in my long life. The first, off the Indies, claimed my dear comrade and mentor Prince Maurice. The second by Guinea I spurned with contempt for his sake. They are forget-all-bar-surviving are tempests: the roar of the devil around a mouth of stillness. Quite beyond cold calculation.'

'There you are then,' slurred Pepys. 'S'not possible. Sir Robert says so.'

Because of his temper there were those present who'd accept that as the final word. But stronger winds than caution—of typhoon force—were driving Newton on.

'Even so..., imagine...,' he mused, to them and himself and all futurity, 'even if for one second. The complete chain of causality, there to look at, to see it whole. Yours to understand, the how and why...' His eyes were shining, rapt, other-worldly.

'It would have uses,' Holmes conceded. 'And in times such as this, for that I'd pray.'

'Me too,' said Newton.

But because that was Sir Robert's first faithful prayer it was his which was granted.

On the Wednesday it remained an option. Prince William, a super-sleek, iced-blood, calculating modern-beast—as patient-indecisive as a dead accountant—wanted to cup it in his hands as long as possible, alongside all the other throbbing possibilities.

By Thursday dawn the continued blow demanded decision. His captains plucked up courage to seek him out, waiting outside the regal cabin, avoiding each other eyes, till the whispered orders and grunt-scuffling within ceased.

Finally, an avian, *sans* wig, head poked round the grudging crevice. One pale arm held a map for form's sake, the other maintained a death-grip on the ajar door.

'Yes, what? Leave me be. Trying I am to get on top of very weighty matters.'

One of them, the sole Englishman there, lost control of his face and blew decades of hard work, danger and exams with a giggle.

Eventually though, the Prince was roused out, and coaxed aloft to consult the wind. Everything was pointed out: the sails like swelling buttocks, the ceaseless wind, the jagged rocks of Wight approaching.

'Solent or Channel?' was the decision put to him. *'Choose whether to go or to stay.'*

William looked left: the open sea, and endless possibilities. Postponement: indecision—gorgeous temptation...

To the right, the Solent: one way: certainty, disquiet. The Island one side, Portsmouth the other. Soldiers, sailors ships and rampant, thrusting, cannon. A narrow, resistant tunnel leading straight to them.

Discretion or joy: always a tricky call.

After the decision the Captains said *'fine'*, so long as the *Protestant Wind* didn't keep blowing. The Solent funnelled urgent fleets into a narrow strait and death-dealing forts either side.

William consulted the blustery sky. All his life—up to now—he'd had just the luck he wanted, neither more nor less. The rest of success was easy: for what wasn't show was timing, plus a courtier's-conscience worth of courage.

'You have already told been,' William informed the east wind. 'Enough, thank you. Sufficiency is as good as a feast. After Cowes you may leave us.'

The elements took not the slightest notice.

ALTERED ENGLANDS

❈

'Nightmare without cease,' exclaimed Sir Robert. 'A new Dark Age!'

The other Sir Robert furrowed up, covering disagreement with a sip. He surprised himself with loyalty to his own timeline.

'Oh, I don't know. One adapts. Given time, toothache kills the nerve that pains.'

'But paper money! A *'National Debt'*! Dutch troops guarding Parliament! England as Holland's satellite!'

'T'was called a *Revolution*, not invasion.'

He clinked the bottom of the spittoon. A liquid statement.

'Heaven forfend I should be unkind,' said second Sir Robert, passionately, 'especially to you, a better brother than Father could ever spawn. But, sir, I protest! A nation of slaves, jigging to the Bank of England's tune? Mercantilism's lickspittles, applying a tongue to the City's arse? How did you bear it?'

His 'brother' was almost abashed. He spoke into his troubled chest.

'Fortunately, I'll die quite soon: 1692. Can't tell how I know that but something just told me. Shall miss the worst of it. Can't answer for the rest.'

The luckier Sir Robert graciously conceded, and showed mercy to his variant with the best bow a gouty cripple might muster.

Understandably, given his kidnapping and slavery, Billy the gorilla looked on less charitably with eyes of glass, reflecting flames.

❈

'Holy Mary, sweet Mother of God, please make this *fricassee* full-flavoured. Send, we ask you, tastiness upon this shredded swede.'

'With strawberry vinegar dressing,' added Under-Cook, urgently. He wasn't allowed much leeway with Royal dinners and wanted the Almighty informed of any input.

'So adorned,' Cook graciously agreed. 'May they who dine thereon be reminded by these fruits of God's creation—amended by man's humble hand—of the beneficence of your reign, wherein to enjoy all good things is but to obey you. May those for whom this will be their last taste of this world carry its toothsome flavour, as foretaste of your great mercy, from the heat of battle to a better place, wherein they will gorge upon such infinitely-coursed banquets as shall never be surpassed. And may Holy Mary, Mother of God, and her Son, Christ Jesus, shower blessings on this repast and all who eat it, and if we, being busy this day of trial, do dare forget you, do not, Father and Lord, we implore you with the fervent words of our mouth and meditations of our heart, forget us.'

'Amen,' said Under-Cook—and most of the galley scullions and platter bearers—for they too were Catholics: souls and services bought with gold or ignorance or indifference.[117]

Cook held aloft the great spice mill of his renowned seasoning, that secret mixture whose recipe would not pass his lips till breath was failing—if then. It was what transformed mere fuelling into transcendence, like hope's sparkle on the drab stuff of life.

'And may the Lord guide our hands no less than the steersmen and gunners above. Amen.'

And He did and Cook found himself spicing like he had never spiced before. He laid on in *unprecedented* abundance. He just couldn't stop himself.

His grinding arm was guided. Surprised but well-educated in the faith, Cook did not demur.

⚜

Sir Robert had to come when he was coming. Something made him disengage a sweet set of Isle of Wight lips just as their intimate conversation grew gripping. With curses and apologies he set the laundrymaid aside and himself on his way.

'*NOW!*' said the inner voice, his own, but reinforced: additionally convincing. Though stiff and sad the Admiral didn't argue.

He'd thought he had ample time but instinctively trusted instinct above reason. If something told him his place was on the Castle gundeck that was

---

[117] Curiously, there were probably more Catholics aboard the great *'Protestant Fleet'* than in 'Papist' King James's waiting army. As one misguided mercenary wrote: *'My soul is God's, but my sword is for the Prince of Orange'*

sufficient cause to do the 'half-on-trousers-dance' up three whole flights of stairs.

When he arrived, prim mistress Reason reasserted herself. He and She were right and the Dutch fleet still visibly way off; beyond even extreme cannon range. There'd been *ample* time to whitewash the wench's word-factory.

Holmes puzzled. Assuming this wasn't simple error—and seven hard decades had knocked those out of him—then someone owed him explanation.

'Well?' he questioned the gunners, reckoning a jog might spill an answer out of them.

They, of all people, he thought he could trust. The Yarmouth townsfolk and most of the Islanders, even the supposedly picked militia he's drawn into West Wight, were pro-Orange, that was clear. But his own men, King's wage-takers of many a year, Yarmouth cannoneers, those he reckoned as sound. And yet...

The barked query, his sudden arrival, had shaken some. They wore *bad-dog* expressions.

'You, Skingle! What's that behind your back?'

The black-bearded cannoneer had no answer. They'd sailed together, long years, ago, to Guinea and deserted St. Lucia, and the Royal Bull-stables at Lisbon. Therefore he had good, fitting, grounds for feeling guilt

'Show!'

There was no point or dignity in denial and so the man brought forth the collection of match.[118] The Castle had no others, save maybe in some far-off storage and yet to be seeped in vinegar. Without them the guns of Yarmouth would remain silent.

Now Holmes saw it, plus sniffed out faint traces of a parallel *coitus interruptus*. They'd been debating something as he boarded the saucy pout below.

Sir Robert ran 'Skingle' through with the sword that never left his side. His last breath offended the Admiral's face.

'*Proditor*: noun, masculine: traitor,' said Holmes, disengaging the blade. A little instruction for the man to ponder on en route to Inferno.

---

[118] Cord boiled in vinegar. Superseded by the flint for musketry but still indispensable, state of the art, fuse technology for late Seventeenth century artillerymen.

Betrayed friendship aside, it had to be. The man was one decision away from casting the cords through the portal, into Neptune's extinguishing embrace. Justice and necessity for once accorded.

Suddenly all was untoward urgency again.

'Light her.' Holmes retrieved one match from the now uncaring hand. Stooping so low meant fuss and ache but he was impelled. Though by no means a pious man, certain tones of interior whisper still cracked the whip.

'But... But...,' said some.

A blade, Skingle-coated, overcame any objections. One of the ever burning lanterns in the long low gun room obliged.

'Her,' said Holmes, pointing outward at a ship. 'Fire. Now.'

She was *miles* safe; oceans of time from danger from a shot. And anyhow, it was far from certain things would take that road. Though the implacable breeze blew the Fleet on towards Yarmouth and Hurst castles, those sentinels of the Solent had been studiously passive to date. Indeed, the gunners' truncated debate had touched on whether any salvo might provoke lynching by the townsfolk. An ugly mob muttered *'Orange'* outside. Odds against a firefight were lengthened by delay. Ever-mounting moments of peace and invitation were one by one building a barricade against violence.

The sixty-six year old crippled Admiral leapt over it.

'Fire! Fire now!'

No aiming, no ranging, and precious little motivation, but the culverin spoke. It's gift, once posted, already had all the guidance a cannonball could desire.

❂

'Delicious but *so* spicy!' said the Prince, dabbing his razor-thin lips. 'What came over Cook?'

Others had asked themselves the same question. Invited to the Princely armoured cabin but not privileged enough to dip into the golden platter, they had all the pain with none of the preceding pleasure.

'Oops, again. Excuse I please.'

The atmosphere now matched the richness of the dish consumed. Its consequences greened the air.

'I... must check... the guns,' said one gagging captain. 'With your indulgence, Highness?'

'One doubts we require them shall,' quipped William, poker-impaled upright in his bolted chair. 'The path to England's throne seems well greased to facilitate... Oops, pardon one...'

'But the sails, Majesty,' said another, excusing himself already. 'Peace or war, they still merit inspection...'

'Constant vigilance,' said another, rising. 'Essential. I will assist.'

'And me.'

By now even William's sliver-nostrils could no longer tune out the offence.

'Join you I think I will, gentlemen. A draught of fresh air, a spy of our new shore...'

A speedy chorus: *'No need!'*, *'Prey rest!'*, *'Do not concern yourself!'*—all ignored. The Prince thought democracy one of the less admirable legacies of Ancient Greece.

He hadn't planned venturing aloft: down-below was snug and dry and full of sailors—but also now just a few farts short of toxic.

Given wide berth, William of Orange took the ladder to a different history.

⚙

'Fire!' Stride. *'Fire!'* Stride. *'Fire!'*

Sir Robert paced along the line and each footfall was an explosion. Emerging ghost-like from the back-billowed smoke to beside each gun he bade them speak.

Once the die was cast, all joined in, even if their hearts weren't in it. There was a technical job to be done, the sole reason for long years and training in Yarmouth. Looked at from one way, it was a shame to waste all those cannon now they had something useful to do.

Hurst Castle, across the water, must have felt the same way. That was less than surprising, for the Solent was a Holmsian lake. Sir Robert's loyal nephew, Henry, commanded there. Once he'd joined in the corralled fleet was bathed in lead and chain-shot from both sides.

The invaders hadn't anticipated a torrid time but could afford some losses. However hurtful the guns of Yarmouth and Hurst might be, there were still ample ships to secure the slip-slidey throne of England.

Or there would have been, but for the head of the head of the invasion.

❈

William of Orange arrived on deck at *just* the right time: seconds after Sir Robert's first *'Fire!'* Then he—the essential he—continued his journey at more sprightly speed.

The Head of State travelled on, athwart nineteen pounds of lead going at four hundred miles per hour—though rapidly diminishing.

The mysteries of synaptic transmission permitted William a slice more consciousness than the flailing torso left behind. Like Moses, the dying light let him see the promised land: green Hampshire harbinger of his would-be realm. It came upon him fast but he fell short of both land and ambition. William's dead head disembarked from the ball whilst still over the Solent.

English fish were there to welcome him, a piscine, hungry, court he could not greet.

❈

'Well, *you've* done well of it,' said Sir Robert.

The other Holmes studied his sunburst Star of the Garter and could not but concur.

'A fortunate shot; happy happenstance,' he said modestly.

'And an Earldom.'

'Yes,' he admitted. '*Lord Yarmouth*, true...'

'And the service of God.'

'That too,' the more successful variant admitted humbly. 'Aspiration to the Deific will is the lodestar of the new regime...'

'You lucky people...'

Earl Holmes conceded it even as he sought to slay jealousy.

'We have our own problems, brother. False trails, bloodshed even. We are less rich than you.'

'But on the right path.'

He put his pipe on the fire. He'd not be needing it again. Not here.

'We think so.' It had to be said. 'Money or Spirit: *'Man cannot serve two masters'*.'

Holmes 1 was saddened but not *sad*.

'Knowing what I now do, after what you have told me, I will be glad to die in '92. This line leads to naught but piss and rubble.'

Lord Yarmouth's silence said everything.

The two old men shook hands like beloved kin, one blessed to another cursed but stoic.

'Travel well, Robert.'

'And you likewise, Robert. *'May God be between you and harm in the empty places you shall walk'*.'

'I know that one. An Egyptian blessing...'

'Another interest of ours.'

'Indeeeeeeeeeeeeeeeeeeeeeeeeeeeeeeeeeeeeeeeee-d'

An author's deceit. His final, defining *d* was never sounded or heard. The kindly circumstances had ceased and they parted.

Tides of mortality and history now longer pulled or bullied. Liberated from as yet undefined *'gravity'* the Sir Roberts could just... step aside.

Both Holmeses were freed and free: free to part and roam. So they did.

※

From the cool, marble, palace, the pyramids could be seen. Pharaoh gaped to find a fantastical be-wigged figure beside him.

'*Not* a god,' said Holmes, in reassurance, sensing all his fears—though there might have been advantage in pretending otherwise. 'Merely...'

And he told him. And... somehow was understood. As was Pharaoh when he replied.

It proved to be quite late, almost too late: towards the end of independent Egypt; nigh on Cleopatra-time. Still, the Ptolemaic twilight proved quite delightful, blessed with chilled date-wine and hot women and gasp-worthy temples in which to stroll. And though as yet seventeen centuries unborn, Sir Robert still had a role to play. With the operative word being *play*.

'Not a god', no, but...

Pharaoh strolled with God's *confidant* and emissary and received the benefits of his insight. When hobnailed History and the Romans arrived, they would find a people forewarned.

Meanwhile, another Sir Robert...

ALTERED ENGLANDS

MISCELLANEOUS STORIES

❁

COMPRISING:

JUST HANGING AROUND
JUSTICE WITHOUT RESPITE
WALK THIS WAY
INGRATITUDE
PROGRESS
CULLODEN II
ENLIGHTENMENT
CONSUMER AWARENESS
MEBYON VERSUS *SUNA*
YOU MUST BE COLD

❁

JOHN WHITBOURN

26~

JUST HANGING AROUND

INTRODUCTION

Veterans of this literary guerrilla-conflict will have noticed my penchant for titles taken from song titles. This one is liberated from early punk group, *The Stranglers*.[119] Their *'London Lady'* was the first Punk record I bought, courtesy of drinking in the same Godalming pub (a former coaching inn in sad decline—though not only because I frequented it) as some roadies for the band. And there Punk's connection with this tale ends.

Actually, the story is drawn from the experience of having hours to kill in the picturesque town of Farnham, Surrey, prior to inflicting a lecture on the transition from Roman Britain to Saxon England on my lady wife's Adult Education class. The pub being out of the question—not wanting to slur my words before the poor punters—I kept myself out of mischief by visiting St Andrew's Church to pay respects to one of Surrey's finest sons, a permanent resident in the churchyard there, just outside the church porch.

William Cobbett (1763-1835) was one of those admirable people of unstoppable dangerous energies—dangerous to his enemies and himself alike. Those same energies carried him out of humble beginnings to the highest ranks, and more kerfuffle and combat that you could decently ask of a regiment of

---

[119] Originally a Guildford-based group, *'The Guildford Stranglers'*. For many years a graffitied *'They're Strangtastic!'*, spray-canned in large letters on a boarded-up window, used to greet visitors to Guildford town centre.

men. Naturally, his English peasant-radical opinions and *'call-a-spade-a-bloody-spade'* manner appealed—but I fully recognise I'm biased. Nevertheless, I commend him and his works to anyone who enjoys crystal clear political prose and bare-knuckle polemics inspired by honestly held beliefs: a sort of proto but more pugnacious George Orwell...

I particularly esteem his brave *'History of the Protestant Reformation in England and Ireland'* (written 1824-27) which, although penned by a free-thinking nominal Protestant, put forward an argument that could have got him lynched in such anti-Papist times. My own copy dates only from 1929 but in a forward to it by Cardinal F. A. Gasquet (no less...) he says that he has taken the liberty of removing *'the occasional strong or coarse expression'*. In which case, all I can say is that you never would have guessed and what must the original be like?

All the same, Cobbett the fearless radical appears only peripherally in this tale—which must be the first time ever he wasn't centre-stage in anything the man brushed against. However, given what transpires, perhaps that's for the best...

JOHN WHITBOURN

JUST HANGING AROUND

※

I saw and heard them clearly enough. For a second there were fire and screams, red-orange tongues licking the stained glass to unearthly accompaniment. They halted me in my tracks outside the church but I chose to disbelieve.

'Weird...'

Because this was Earth and Farnham and Thursday, and the horror was fleeting, I wilfully disbelieved my antennae's evidence, favouring cheap 'explanation' instead. That cowardice in the face of the enemy was duly noted by an unseen commanding officer. I didn't know then but grave charges were preferred.

In my defence, I call Darwin, Freud and Dawkins; in mitigation I cite accountancy and the whole school system. I maintain that my spirit had never been taught to soar. True, my clothes were designer-black and new, but the inner wardrobe held only tattered rags of noble thought.

I shouldn't have lacked for inspiration to heroic acceptance and courageous rout, since the mortal remains of William Cobbett, *'Lion of the South'* and *'Enemy of cant'*, were right before me. He was the cause of my pilgrim presence—that and time to kill—and though marble now pinned him (recently renovated by the Cobbett Society), in life his yeoman spirit had roared down all fears and foes. Farnham's most famous son; soldier and MP, a self-taught champion of his class and first recorded witness of the 'Surrey Puma', author of the timeless, sandblasting *'Rural Rides'*—*he* would have done the right thing.

In my idealistic moments (ten mins. per week, max.) *Battling-Bill* Cobbett remained a residual role model, a fig leaf of naivety not sloughed off yet. I ought to have emulated his courage and dared to accept my senses' good sense. I should have shown a clean pair of heels away down 'Streaky Bacon Lane' and never returned. That would have been the valiant, intrepid, option.

Instead, I blamed the setting sun, something called *'unusual angles'* and workmen's shrieking power tools. The last named conveniently swarmed the scaffolded roof, dipping in and out of sight, industriously about the *'RESTORATION'* the appeal board before St Andrew's proclaimed. True, they bore no visible means to mimic souls in torment—but they might and could.

I didn't know them or they me, but something hardwired within forbade, *forbade*, any sign of fright before them—even if they weren't watching. For they *might* be—and might make adverse comment.

So I took the path of false bravery and tucked every ensuing second of normality under my belt as justification. The John Major-ish reasoning went like this: my lecture wasn't for an hour: the *Bat and Ball* beckoned, but I didn't dare imbibe—the Adult Education students would *know* and familiar facts might play hide and seek when I sought them—and anyway, just one pint was worse than going dry. Of course, there was always the Library, a safe and dependable surrogate-wife of long-standing, but she no longer got any juices flowing. Truth be told, I'd imperceptibly grown sick of books and their dryness, lusting after stronger meat...

I little knew then that even faithless prayers were heeded—an unfairness to me, as well as to more pious petitioners, when you think about it. The Almighty should have given *their* prayers priority.

However—and however feebly—right then an unfamiliar church was the best I could think of for diversion. God had seen fit to place one hard by and the risk of missing out on any weirdness within was the strongest draught on offer. So I took it.

Just inside the porch was all I wished to know (and more) concerning the restorations. My unengaged eyes blurred over the salient details. Rebuffed for Lottery or EU funds the local hobbits and yeomanry had jumbled-saled and tombola-ed it themselves, taking a painful age. Therein lay a metaphor, I reflected; a little wisdom for those who cared to see.

Once properly within, the place had another fleeting *frisson* for me. Hammering overhead sounded like angry footsteps—till I remembered the workmen. It continued, loud and conveniently clear, entirely unghost-like, long enough for me to examine and pin down with a label. I reproved myself for such skittishness. Restorations = works = men paid to *'hit it wiv an 'ammer'*. It was a pain that I should choose their time for my visit—but bearable. I wouldn't be staying long.

'Afternoon...,' I said—but there was no one there, contrary to firm conviction. I could have sworn there'd been a figure pouring over the visitors' book. Still, on balance, it was more pleasing to be definitely alone, and I interpreted my mistake as optic-afterburn of something seen before. My own company suited me well. More and more, I couldn't get enough of it.

I executed a swift drift around the piled-up accumulated essentials of Christian worship: as conceived of by each succeeding century and then neglected or discarded by the next. The place was fairly light and airy: a function of having purged away Victorian stained glass save for some central figures. The Deity's daylight was thus graciously allowed a peek in. You could see what you were about.

My glazing eyes were accosted by a *Royal Flying Corps* memorial: an oddity with added personal reference, since my Granddad was with them. Next to that I found remembrance of a soldier killed in the Maori wars: some local lad transported to fight tattooed men the other side of the world. I pondered that strange juxtaposition: a cavalier of the air adjoining a Farnham Victorian braving shotgun and tomahawk in tropic forests. How had one history, one little town, birthed them both? And had they reconciled it to themselves post-mortem? I couldn't and callously wandered on, forgetting them.

In the south aisle was an age-browned brass, commemorating a seventeenth century Farnhelmian who'd spent his last twelve years of life *'Dark'*: *'Dominus illuminatio mea'*. I felt a moment of distant sympathy for the long-lost blind man before easy distraction intruded. Above my head an incongruous ancient helmet protruded from a high spike. I thought *'Armada'* but an equally elderly label said *'Vernon Helmet'*—though not how so or why. It was a bit of a puzzlement; rather like, truth be told, my presence here.

Overhead the workmen had kept pace: a coincidental coinciding of our paths. They grew loud, like furious boots upon the tiles, aborting any chance of quiet reflection. I wished they'd at least concentrate on one part of the roof so that I could steer clear.

Wandering back, generally doorwards but with oceans of time, my roving eye grappled other things to detain me. I found a brass to the Vicar who wrote *'Rock of Ages'* and for the first time since School *Chapel* (and first time ever voluntarily) I hummed the tune. Nearby, a glass case held something called *'A Vinegar Bible'*—which mildly amused (the contents having always seemed vinegarish to me) but not enough to stop and investigate its strange christening. The light was fading: a convenient excuse to call it a day. The hammering followed overhead to see me out.

Before then was the Bell Tower and, despite the twilight, I saw its four walls were festooned with plaques, the uppermost lost to sight even in brightest day. The dead from Farnham's famous levitating families I quipped to myself, or maybe memorials to dear departed bats.

One of them predominated in terms of size and style. On it I caught sight of the word '*Cobbett*' and rapidly reangled my feet from escape.

In life he would have scorned so grand a tribute, and had his wishes been respected I might have been saved. Alas, in death, as in life, others used him for their own purposes. All unknowing, '*The Lion of the South*' was employed to delay/betray me—and I a fellow *Sutanglii* of yeoman stock!

Underneath the up-into-darkness of the tower, I read what I could: on tiptoe, peering:

'... *Farnham lad, self-tutored, by turn Bishop of Winchester's garden boy, soldier, farmer, political theorist and Member of Parliament. An irreconcilable foe of injustice and-...*'

Enough already. I'd read it later, maybe—if the photo came out.

Adjusting my camera to the max. to allow for poor light, I raised my aim to the unseen bells and.. *flashed*. I need not have worried. The shocking flare shockingly revealed all: more than all.

A fish-white face plummeted towards me: gaping, omnivorous, haloed with rattail locks. It was not Cobbett, nor human, nor living.

The camera flew and I raised my arms to save myself. But, well-muscled or no, they weren't up to it, even though no impact assaulted them.

The first thing I noticed, aside from continued life, was silence. What I'd thought was the 'workmen' had ceased to sound. Then the camera met the stone floor and died messily. Eviscerated, the faithful friend of numerous holidays and liaisons spilt its guts all over.

There was no time to mourn. Even the light had changed. Where before was honest dusk all now was some other, sickly, gloom. Only the sanctuary's candle continued to burn true, a lone survivor of the world left behind. I noticed that and tried to catch its dependable, winking, eye—like a man spotting one friend in a hostile mob. Alas, it was too late to learn.

'*Learn*'? said the glittering dust figure before me: he who had plummeted like a hanged man but landed like a moth. Who'd read my thoughts. *'No: I teach now!'*

His words were made from motes and specks falling throughout the church: stolen, composite, constructs. His eyes were like holes punched into a box.

The shroud and long hair were aglow, but joylessly so: no Christmas tree or faerie sparkle there. They covered mere hints and space: a void already gone ahead. Only the face retained substance: a slab of pale stale luncheon-meat, pecked and pitted by time, plus a flap jaw, loosely attached. It rose and fell, albeit with effort, failing to sync with speech. Saying:

'*Please...*'

It was both plea and spiteful command, spoken from the stone: St Andrew's omnipresence.

A spectral, star-shiny hand reached up to just... brush my face. Its fingertips retained only residual presence, sometimes material, mostly not. Yet I felt it still and what was missing imagination more than made up for. My eyes closed, I could not move. A great spider was running riot over my features, drawing strength.

He sighed and shuddered, as though dining after long famine. The head was thrown back, thin lips licked by a darting grey tongue.

'*Oh, joy...*'

A parched, sandpaper voice from far away: heavy laden with erotic pleasure. Then came recollection of purpose.

'*Learn...*'

The present leprous light was not of this day; nor the product of any natural sun. It was his own to illuminate what he would.

Though—or perhaps because—my eyes were clenched, I saw an *olde-worlde* funeral: Cromwellian figures in black and white—but not many; a sparse, dry-eyed congregation, and easy acceptance of loss. Then the view altered and all indifference scattered.

Inside the coffin everything was *fury*: a humidity of passion in the dark. The scent of unseasoned wood and rough shroud-linen was admixed with rampant decay. I caught recollection of expiry: not swift but still sudden; finality falling like an anvil from on high. Dying had been feverish and confused. Pain had prevented the thinking of things through. There were so much left undone; pleasures not yet ridden raw.

ALTERED ENGLANDS

When the pastor said the dismissal, there arrived light and air, and freedom from the awful container. Unseen to his loveless loved-ones, the spirit rose above them, answering a tidal pull. A beacon not of this world signalled clean through St. Andrew's roof.

On the brink, high amidst the rafters, he rebelled. There was shock at continued consciousness—and fear: sluggish half-wake thoughts of Judgement. The upward urge *seemed* benign: it grew more welcoming by the moment, but the spirit still retained its own opinions. In life, lack of trust had represented safety. It clung to that acquired wisdom; a last anchor to earth.

Up among the old ship's timbers and roof-space, the spirit panicked and reached out. Death grip claws found purchase. The drifting progress ceased.

In the course of dying his nails had grown long. No one had much cared to approach the sweat and cack-stained sickbed, but now their neglect wasn't torment but an ally. He recalled those talons and dug them in, and it transpired even oak beams bow to pure willpower. I dare say some half-moon nail prints are still up there on the rafters for anyone to see, should they care to.

There he came to rest, high up in the unfrequented roof, his little stock of being exhausted by effort. The barrel of vitality was almost—but crucially not *quite*—scraped clean. Fearful of what he'd done, just then and in all of life, the spirit was content to let drowsiness descend. Pinioned by the firm decision not to decide, there he would rest.

From time to time in succeeding years there were stirrings: the close passage of bats and birds, the taking down of the old candelabra and fitting of new, hissing, light sources. He roused and turned in fitful sleep, half regarding them as if in a dream. It suited him to postpone the consequences of full wakefulness.

Occasionally he would deal with intruders who grew too familiar. Priests and Churchwardens became used to finding crushed sparrows atop the pews. An electrician who came to install new fittings stayed forever when he *'slipped from the scaffolding'* and screamed all the way down to an appointment with flagstones.

And, at random intervals, he would spy, as the need for sleep grew less pressing. A cold eye was cast on many a christening, to curse any noisy babe. Jealous ill-will was sicked upon the future of bride and groom. I even caught a glimpse of great Cobbett's funeral and then successive ordinary, Edwardian,

Sundays. Where one devout mother-of-three regularly excited his lust. Sabbath after Sabbath spread over years, the blameless matron was quite unable to worship, subject to sensations of ravishment.

Then came the workmen I had seen and more disturbance than ever before. He was woken beyond any pretence. The whole roof was to be renewed and holes opened to the sky through which he might be sucked. A decision could no longer be circumvented.

I returned from my tour of the centuries as though falling from the rafters myself, slamming breathless back into my body—which no longer fitted one hundred per cent.

My scream was curtailed by the palm of a long dead hand. The empty eyes came up close.

'*You'll do, beloved.*' His jaw flopped down to say it but the words were already in my head. '*In here, no,*' he nodded back at the undiminished sanctuary light, '*but outside: free rein! I'll be waiting. On the roof. To fall.*'

There came a final caress, a soft hand cupping my chin, tousling my hair. I sensed he could do it. Free of constraints his final fling could purge me of *me*. For he loved life unreservedly whilst I often found it a drag. Even after the death of flesh, his spirit was the stronger. It would prevail and don a new coating.

'Why not them?' I pointed up to the presumed roofers. Weak, I know but forgivable(?). 'Take one of *them!*'

The ghost smiled: a stretching of skin. The enemy was delivered into his hands.

'*That is why,*' it hissed, jubilant at its find. '*Kindred spirit! Permitted!*'

The sanctuary light blinked and then I really knew I was alone.

He was gone and his false day with him. The return of even fading normality was like air to the drowning. Collapsing against the Bell Tower wall, I gulped life in.

Then the door opened, bringing with it Farnham noise. In came a lady flicking light switches with the familiarity of a churchwarden: someone come to lock up.

She took in me and the massacred camera. Though plainly not the usual cider-fiend I was still strange enough to constitute potential *'trouble'*.

'I've got a mobile phone!' she assured me. 'You'll have to go.' A short-sleeved arm indicated the way. Gaping space led to the great outdoors.

I imagined skeletal black standing atop the roof arch: vigilant, ready to pounce. Around him the workmen moved—straightforward men, innocents all and thus unsuitable food—packing up for the night: happy, unaware. His prey selected, he would ignore them, like a big cat—or *Surrey Puma*—moving with fixed gaze in on the weakest of the herd. Meanwhile, in a classroom nearby, students were gathering to hear my wisdom on the *'Dark Ages'*—whilst I explored one all my very own.

'Now, come on, please,' Mrs Churchwarden urged, hesitant from the porch, seeking to conceal her niceness. 'I'm very sorry but there's seats out there to sit on. You can't stay here forever.'

And she was right. You couldn't. It just wasn't in me to say *'I claim sanctuary!'*. It would sound silly before this woman I'd never met before and never would again. The police would back her up: jokey coppers gradually turning serious. *'Game's over, sir, ho ho. That law's long repealed. Now on your way, don't push your luck...'* Then the time for jests would pass and the officers would drag me out and that would be *embarrassing*. And the end would be exactly the same.

How can you explain such a predicament to a nice lady churchwarden, to the Surrey constabulary—to anyone? It was simply easier all round to just do as I was told.

Commendably steady, I walked into the fading day. Very soon I felt a new man.

27~

JUSTICE WITHOUT RESPITE

'And this is where your Mum and Dad got married, Joe,' I said.

'Married,' replied Joseph, confirming message received. Even at almost three years of age he mostly remained content to repeat sentence terminals, pondering all else in the privacy of his own thoughts.

'Do you want to go in?'

'O-K.'

My last visit to this place had been a bit whirlwind-ish—the minor matter of a wedding service and all that—and I'd never had a proper gander round. A swift pop-in seemed like a good idea and so that's what we did—or at least tried to. At the end of the short path through the graveyard our way was barred by a (presumably *the*) vicar.

'Hello,' he said. friendly enough, 'welcome to St Nicolas.' My name's Jagger, the Reverend Jagger. Are you visiting Pemsey?'

A welcome is always very welcome as the saying goes; but I wasn't so fussed about the interrogation that accompanied it.

'Er... yes, that's right. A memory lane sort of thing; I got married here.'

'Never mind, never mind,' laughed the Vicar, in rather poor taste I thought. 'We all make mistakes. Before my time I assume.'

''82—um, look, do you mind if we go in?'

'I got here in '83,' he replied, 'so I just missed you. No, I don't mind you going in—but you won't see much; the daylight fades early this time of year and we don't keep lights on—too expensive. You're not a Sussex man are you? Not a local: the accent's not right.'

'It's right enough for where I come from, Vicar—which isn't Sussex, it's true. Meanwhile, returning to the matter in hand, if it's as dark inside as you say, couldn't you make an exception re the lights just for us? I can make the appropriate Church funds contribution and all that...'

A visit to St Nicolas' had been the merest chance of a whim after our Boxing Day tour of the Romano-Norman Castle which loomed over the Church. However, the more I found my wish frustrated the more dead-set on it I became. What was the *point* of a Church of England if an Englishman couldn't get through the damn door of one of their churches?

'Sorry,' said the Vicar, somewhat implausibly, 'they're all on a timer; switching them on now would throw everything out.'

'Oh, God *save* us, Vicar....'

'Precisely,' he responded swiftly to my explosion. 'But look, you seem a nice person, a southerner and all that: there's the porch light on and the Lady Chapel lamp—I expect they'll shed enough illumination for you to see a fair bit. Why don't you go on in for a few minutes.'

'Why not indeed. Thanks *so* much, Vicar.'

'That's quite all right, Mr...?'

'Does it honestly matter?'

'Not really—just for possible future reference. One other thing though, how's your Latin?'

'How's my Latin what? Latin Lover? Latin-American dancing?'

'Knowledge of the Latin language, I meant.'

'Non-existent: why?

'No reason—I just wondered, that's all. In you go with your little man and have a nice look around. Call at the Vicarage next door if you've any questions.'

With that he swept off like a great black bat and we in turn swept in before he changed his mind, all too glad to shed his company.

'Say goodbye and good riddance to the funny man, Joe,' I muttered.

'Bye-bye, funny man,' he complied, a bit louder than would have suited me. Jagger wasn't that far out of earshot.

Unfortunately he been right enough about the light. Aside from a circle around the porch and the Lady Chapel and its reserved Host, the Church was in deep gloom. Doubtless, our eyes would soon grow more accustomed but I remember thinking that a thorough tour wasn't really on. That just goes to show how wrong one can be and how pitiful our reasoning and plans are before the scripts dreamt up for us.

It could just be that Joe sensed something of what was to come, for his tiny hand slipped into mine and, in his innocence, he drew closer for protection.

Making the best of a bad job, I examined the lighted area around the door: Norman font, faded Anti-Apartheid mural and a Roll of Honour from two World Wars. Three men from one family in the 1914-19 one (why was it often *19*?). Yet I happened to know, despite that pointless hammer blow, the name and line survived, still fishing the same sea as their forefathers in a small boat out of Pemsey Bay. There was consolation of sorts in that and I felt that the Church thing had been a decent idea after all. A periodic douse in melancholic cultural continuity was probably beneficial—in moderation.

Beside a half-millennium unused water-stoup, there was an ancient Church History pasted onto a handboard, and I was giving it a cursory glance (Saxon to Norman to Victorian-vandalism: the usual thing) when Joe interrupted.

'Soldier,' he said and pointed.

I knew he was keen on soldiers and war, being yet unaware of the occupational hazard of horrible death, so I allowed myself to be led to what he'd seen.

On the other side of the door to the Roll of Honour was another sort of memorial but one altogether more grand and individualistic. There, reclining in marble form, was the armoured likeness of *'Sir Walter Salmon'* (*'I bet he had a miserable childhood,'* I thought) surrounded by all the carved glorification his estate could afford.

I advanced and retreated, as one does in a picture gallery, to admire the detail or take in the whole. It was certainly impressive in an 'I-defy-you-to-ignore-me' sort of way and Joe, for one, was shocked into open-mouthed appreciation.

Some eight foot square, the memorial dominated that corner of the Church with its principal figure and deeply recessed interior. Great heraldic shields, punning on the man's name, topped the pillars at its side, and the plain symbolism of carved long-bones and skulls peeped out of the dark below. Over all sat a mock temple roof giving the impression that Sir Walter was laying doggo in an entrance way—presumably to the great beyond.

ALTERED ENGLANDS

Whilst he waited for the call to judgement, *lobster*-armour and unconvincing posture aside, he did so in comfort on a great bed of the whitest stone. The face of this was filled with a scrolling Latin epitaph for which, propped up against it, someone sometime in the dusty past had provided a helpful translation on a cardboard sheet, now somewhat damp and sad but still readable.

'Sir Walter Salmon', it read, '1550-1610. Lord of the Manors of Pemsey, Pemsey-on-the-Beach, Wallsend, Westham and Stonecross. Sometime High-Sheriff of Sussex, Master of the Musters and Director of the Assizes. He sponsored one ship, sailing out of Pemsey, against the Great Armada and strove with all his might against the enemies of his monarch; particularly those deluded by the popish superstition. Died without issue the first day of April, 1610. He delivered Justice without respite.'

A couple of unconnected cuckoos-in-the-nest: a stone trebuchet ball from the Castle moat and a crusader tomb slab, had been hauled up in front of the memorial to complete the visual feast. Whether this was to add to or dilute the overwhelming personality cult of that corner one couldn't say. In all likelihood it was an area that none but visitors frequented, a good spot for the disposing of the ancient but unwanted.

All in all, as I've said, it was very impressive. As to if it was... nice, that's another question.

'Soldier—no hands!' said Joe and, looking closely for the first time, I noticed this to be true. Sir Walter's gauntleted extremities, originally clasped in prayer, had been almost entirely sawn away. I lazily ascribed this to the ubiquitous activities of poor old Oliver Cromwell (who'd probably never even heard of Pemsey) and thought no more of it. Certainly, Sir Walter's bland and hirsute Stuart features didn't seem to register or mind the loss.

And that was that. If forced to pass judgement I would have said that the memorial was like the Charge of the Light Brigade—magnificent but not worthy of approval. There was something not particularly Christian about it, a lack of self-effacement which rendered the Church a mere appendage to *it* rather than the correct contrary. False modesty had probably not been numbered among the late Sir Walter's faults.

We then wandered off into the lesser-lit areas for a few paces until I was halted by Joe.

'What that?' he said, pointing again. It was a question repeated many dozen times daily but, educational considerations aside, I'd found that each query was worth paying proper attention. A child's eye is not yet jaded with familiarity and hurry and sees things that adults edit out.

'What's what?' I replied and crouched down to follow his gesture's line of sight. He was looking back at Sir Walter's memorial and indicating towards its very top. I screwed up my eyes and thus saw that what I'd catalogued and dismissed as 'just' an imitation temple portico was in turn surmounted by a little scarlet curtain. It looked new-ish, a judgement supported by the shiny brass rail and hooks that held it in place. Most uncharacteristically, my curiosity was fired.

'Stay here,' I said to my son and went back to investigate. Nearby were several handy stacks of plastic chairs, presumably used for the modern Church sacrament of 'Coffee', and using one I gained the necessary height boost to just reach the curtain's hem. I distinctly recall thinking at that moment that this was unlike 'me.' Normally, I would have been too polite to just go poke my nose in—and then have wondered about it ever after.

Be that as it may, my new dynamism plus some curtain drawing revealed a further marble shield fixed to the Church wall at the memorial's apex. It too was covered in deeply carved lettering, 'inked-in' in black.

I should now confess that, in my haste to be shot of him, I'd not been entirely honest with the Reverend J. It was broadly correct that I'd never been taught Latin as a language—but Archaeology as a degree study and family tree hunting in the years that followed more or less obliged me to get to grips with that dead tongue via the medium of inscriptions, deeds and registers.

Accordingly, it was the (albeit painful) work of a few moments for me to get the sense of what was written there. It took the form of a poem, a short and bitter rhyme, that I could only assume allowed me, across the gulf of centuries, to hear the voice of Sir Walter himself.

> *'AT THREE SCORE WINTER'S END I DIED,*
> *A CHEERLESS BEING, SOLE AND SAD.*
> *THE NUPTIAL KNOT I NEVER TIED*
> *AND WISH MY FATHER NEVER HAD.'*

'Lovely,' I commented and put the shield thing back into decent *purdah* behind its curtain. No wonder someone had gone to the trouble of concealing

Sir Walter's passing ray of sunshine. The fact of death was depressing enough without eternally advertising what a drag life could be.

The chair was soon enough replaced and I rejoined Joe. He seemed to share my unease and stayed close, the normal chain of *'What that?/Who that?'* temporarily suspended.

We skirted round the rapidly darkening Church, to the Lady Chapel, the High Altar and the Bell Tower with its huge framed list of incumbents since 1249. The mystery of Jagger's presence was cleared up—his predecessor survived officiating at my wedding by a mere twelve month. Then, there being nothing much left to see, it seemed time to head back home for tea.

Joe had remained silent throughout and clung even closer, often inconveniently so, causing me to stumble. There was no way we were going to make it back before midnight at this rate and so I turned to see just what the problem was.

It proved only too easy to detect. I found myself staring straight into the marble face of Sir Walter Salmon. Joe had known better than I, realising that our tour of St Nicolas' had become a (silently) conducted one.

Now, marble is a good stone to work in, so I'm told—Michelangelo didn't do so bad with it for instance—but, such exalted exceptions aside, the real subtleties of human expression usually defy the sculptor's art. In this instance however, whether it was the obscure energies that now propelled him shining through, or maybe the genius of a long-gone, unsung Sussex mason, Sir Walter's gross disenchantment with all he saw came through abundantly clear in the look he gave us.

To my horror (99%) and amazement (1%) his stone mouth split and a gale of grave-air spewed forth as he formed an accusation.

'Papist!' he hissed. *'Papiiiiiist!'* It turned out to be all he ever had to say to us.

Stupid as it now seems after the event, I thought, in my shock and desperation, that I could reason with him.

'No! No—only by birth,' I yelled. 'Lapsed—I'm lapsed!'

It didn't do me any good.

Joe was more sensible and had Salmon's number right away. He slapped the statue's leg with all his tiny might, piping *'Smack!'* as he did so, just to make his point clear. Then, finding himself getting the worse of the bargain, he sped off at his equivalent of warp factor nine. Sir Walter went in pursuit.

JOHN WHITBOURN

It is hard to properly describe the memorial's movements, for his limbs were stiff and suitably stone-like, although they propelled him with remarkable speed. You didn't catch the entirety of his progress, for he was seen as through a strobe-light, first at one place, then at another, but never at points in-between. I suppose the explanation for that lay in the probability that his time was not as ours, but at that precise moment(!) there were more pressing things for me to consider. Whilst still bemused by his appalling and unnatural motion, I was revived by the rate at which he gained upon my child, arms outstretched to... do what he would.

For the first time in my life I found myself capable of Olympic standard sprint speed, and it took only seconds for me to interpose myself between Salmon and prey. By dint of another miracle, I found I had unsuspected total recall of every karate lesson suffered through at Uni. A much-warned-against killing blow was delivered to Salmon's eye sockets—and I split my two forefingers asunder.

It turned out that consideration of minor things like insupportable agony could be postponed whilst a frantic chase ensued round and round the shadow-filled Church. The first, second and third laps I somehow managed to slip his stony clutches, scrambling heedlessly over pews or leaping choir stalls and altar rails. However, the game was complicated by it having multiple objectives. The Salmon memorial very clearly wanted to catch hold of one or both of us—for whatever vile reason—but at the same time needed to block the way to the door. Similarly, whilst I craved exit (*through* the closed door if necessary) more than *almost* anything in the world, I was (later) relieved to find that Joe's escape was an even greater imperative.

Several times therefore I inserted my cringing form between the marble monstrosity and the screaming boy, and, as mentioned, the first few occasions then contrived to writhe away. Once, I even managed to knock a fair sized chip from his polished brow by giving him some with a Churchwarden's staff. However, luck can't last forever and finally I was cornered in the bell-rope area after once again narrowly securing Joe's salvation.

Sir Walter Salmon's image (or maybe it was the man himself?) gazed on me with twisted satisfaction. He'd had three centuries of uneasy rest in which to brew up impotent hatred and those batteries of power now shone reddish through white bulging eyes. Stumps stretched forth, he leapt forward and seized his victim.

ALTERED ENGLANDS

In what turned out to be a dual raising of the alarm, my despairing arm reached out and found a bell rope. Reserves of strength implanted by Mother Nature allowed me to pull it and produce, after a not very enjoyable pause, a single solemn peal. At the same time, the pretty profound pain my action caused to two broken digits called forth a roof-raising cry of animal distress.

But that was my last stand, for Sir Walter had the unyielding qualities of stone and the fixed purpose of the unhappy fanatic. I was borne away across the Church back to his white marble lair, the journey of just a few seconds but time enough for me to notice that there was a touch more '3-D' than hitherto; its recesses darker and deeper than before. It also became plain that Salmon's intention was to hurl me into the inky black that now lay behind his vacated marble bed.

For what it was worth, inspired by the stomach-turning knowledge that Joe was still within the Church, howling pitifully and soon to be without any protector, I resisted—but to not the slightest hint of avail. An infinitely implacable stone arm was twisted into the material of my coat and one final push plunged my head into the memorial.

Suddenly all was silence and stillness.

My upper torso was projected into a place beyond normality but, though held firmly, for some reason the rest of me did not follow through the veil. So, like a man peering into a rock pool, I found myself, head foremost, staring into a dim, dank chamber that, according to the mundane rules of space and volume, there shouldn't have been room for.

Mercifully, my stay there proved to be short but I saw its grey walls with their running damp and dull, phosphorescent glow. I noted the slimy flagstoned floor and, worst of all, I saw the dim, white faces of the captives in one corner, turning eyes bereft of hope towards me.

Then, before I could scream, I was hauled back out into the world of men and fell to the floor.

The Church was flooded with light and the Reverend Jagger held Joe safe with one hand whilst the other brandished the biggest hacksaw I had ever seen against the grovelling form of Sir Walter Salmon.

'That's your *last* warning,' he said sternly to the memorial, 'and don't think you can rely on my Christian charity. Next time it won't be just your hands, but arms and legs as well! Now, go back to sleep you wicked old bigot!'

Despite my present state of disequilibrium, I still had the wherewithal to scramble out of Sir Walter's path as he returned to his 'bed' and laid down upon it. Again, in some way that is not readily expressible, he stretched out and 'clicked' back into lifeless, stony immobility in front of a perfectly solid wall, into precisely the posture we'd first seen. I doubted perfect recollection of its every line would ever leave me.

'You're lucky I heard the bell,' said Jagger, brightly. 'Normally I have Radio Three blaring out in my study all the time. If they hadn't proposed putting on a Sir Michael Tippett composition, well... I only just got here in time!'

'Er... yes,' was the best and only reply I could presently think of.

'And, on the reasonable conjecture you weren't trying to rob the Church, I must assume you found, translated and read the *'Salmon Summary'* that I keep covered up.'

'Er... yes.'

'Despite not being, by your own report, a Latin speaker.'

'Well...'

'That's what sets him off you see—or wakes him up or whatever. That or attempted robbery or desecration. So I think we can further safely assume that you're of the Roman or infidel persuasion.'

'Um..., not exactly.'

'They're the sort of people who most get his blood up—if you see what I mean—apart from robbers. I recall that we never even found the last would-be thief or thiefess. The candlesticks and plate they were intending to take were neatly placed in front of the Salmon memorial. Presumably...'

'That's right, Vicar,' I gabbled, my tongue suddenly loosened and now able to dwell on issues further afield than Joe's and my immediate survival. 'There's people in there—alive! We've got to-...'

'I always suspected as much,' agreed Jagger. 'But do we really need to trouble ourselves particularly about it? Might not their awful incarceration be rough justice for attempted sacrilegious theft?'

'What?' I said, finely attuned *Guardian*-reading sensitivities a-quiver.

'No, what worries me,' continued the Vicar, as though I'd passed his Bronze-Age ethics without protest, 'is the folk I've seen come in here and yet failed to observe leaving. For instance, there were some nice young Spanish students a few years back... Alas, I don't suppose Sir Walter would have approved of either their nationality *or* religion, do you? I mean, he's still thinking in Armada terms, isn't he? And there were these Japanese tourists only last summer: their coach driver looked and looked for them but they never did turn up to my knowledge. You see, if any of them had been unexpectedly curious *and* erudite—well, you can guess, can't you?'

'For God's sake get them out!' I yelled, forgetting myself and the place.

'What do you suggest?' replied Jagger, the very soul of reasonableness. 'Sir Walter's interaction with our world is very much on his terms and at his own volition. It's also, moreover, deeply irrational. I don't think he would be inclined to cooperate or make it easy for me, do you?'

I didn't really have a good answer to that one.

'And I *have* done what I can to minimise the problem,' continued the Vicar. 'Firstly by giving Sir Walter the Ayatollah treatment with my trusty marble-saw, and secondly by covering up the *Summary*. What else can I do if people are indefatigably curious—*and* deceptive...?' (this last with a disapproving look at me). 'In the present day climate I can hardly get away with a sign forbidding entry to Catholics and non-believers, can I? Besides, looking on the positive side of things for a moment, Sir Walter's efforts permit this to be the sole church in the diocese that can leave its doors unlocked at all hours for people's private devotions—and with complete confidence too. That's quite a consideration don't you think?'

'I think you should pull the bloody thing down!' I shouted, the developing pain in my dying fingers putting a hysterical edge on my voice.

For the first time I saw an inkling of fear enter into Jagger's eyes—but it had nothing to do with any threat of violence from me.

'Have you ever had to *deal* with the Church Commissioners?' he said, with real animation. 'Or *'English Heritage'*? Or even just the conservation element in the Parish Council when they've scented blood? You can't *conceive* the consequences of what you're proposing! I'd be eaten alive!'

I suddenly found that I had the most enormous desire to quit this Church and never ever darken its doors again, and that feeling got stronger by the second. At the same time, ridiculously enough, I found myself wondering how to explain to the wife that a simple post-lunch walk had resulted in broken bones, a traumatised child and nightmare source material for a lifetime to come.

The Reverend Jagger accompanied us in our speed-exit and out into Castle Lane beyond. I think he had somehow sensed that I was less than euphoric about my visit, and so thought better of giving us a farewell wave.

Which was as well for I would have responded with just two (albeit broken) fingers.

'I can't help feeling that you're being a trifle *unreasonable*,' he called after me.

Whatever else, I was determined not to let him have the last word, and turned on my heels to face the enemy.

'What *are* you talking about?' I said, fiercely.

'You wanted to see a historic church. For you, the attraction of a church is as a repository of history. And I agree, for a non-believer that's just so. Well, you *got* your history. So I can't understand your sense of grievance.'

'I-did-*not*-plan,' I said, through gritted teeth, 'to see its history animated for my benefit!'

'No..., you might have got more than you bargained for,' Jagger conceded—whilst smiling triumphantly, as though proving his case with a crushing rebuff. 'But really: what did you expect? Whoever told you that all our history was *pleasant*?'

AFTERWORD

The model for the (renamed) monstrous memorial in this tale may be found just within the entrance to St Nicolas' Church, Pevensey Bay, East Sussex.[120] An as intimidating a fingergrip on just this side of the grave as you'll find anywhere in England.

---

[120] Site of sundry family weddings, and resting place of my beloved in-laws, Bob and Viv. RIP.

ALTERED ENGLANDS

The probably blameless *'John Wheatley'* whose posthumous reputation I've just traduced, contributed £40 towards the fitting out of a Pevensey ship to fight the Armada—and thus also unwittingly contributed towards the above libel of his memory and memorial. There's an argument that says the Spanish Armada ultimately only wished us well, that the Welsh Tudor usurpers had as little or even less call upon our loyalty than any other foreign invaders; and that it would have been but poetic justice to see Elizabeth's (or *'Black Betty's*) ginger noddle on a spike above the captured Tower of London—as recompense for Mary, Queen of Scots, her Dad's bloodbath 'Reformation', Edmund Campion *et al*, and the other atrocities of her reign and dynasty. Also, people forget—or are deliberately not told—that there were English volunteers aboard the Armada and an English ship in its number. Tudor propagandists, whose shameless suppleness I bow to, have gone unchallenged until comparatively recently and rendered the Armada story monotone. Elsewhere in my novels, like *'A Dangerous Energy'* and its brethren, I've added back a few other colours. And another thing...

Where was I? Ah, yes: the story you've just read. Well, I can add that the memorial's depressing epitaph is *not* from Pevensey but transplanted from the original classical Greek, via William Cowper (1731-1800), English poet and hymnodist. I've also seen it quoted as an inscription from an English gravestone somewhere—details alas lost in the mists of time. If so, what a fun person *they* must have been!

The inspirational visit to St Nicolas' (without its denouement) can be securely dated to 29th December 1990, and composition of the resulting story to the following New Year's Eve. When I didn't feel like joining in with a day-long drinks-&-nibbles party. Where some plainly tipsy woman said I sounded *'Just like Michael Caine'*! And my family didn't stampede in to contradict her...

As to 'Little Joe' in the story, he does exist but is now a six-foot-something tall astrophysicist, plus built like a brick... outhouse. Plus a Dad in his own right. Nowadays, only an unwise spectre would chase him or his round a church...

28~

WALK THIS WAY

INTRODUCTION

Sometimes I had no other motive (that I'd divulge) than a wicked wish to scare the reader and season their solitary moments with a spine-chill. Up till then they might have felt secure within their own snug, bought-and-paid-for house, but suddenly there's the desire to look round, to check there's no one lurking in the larder, and maybe just see that the front door's properly shut...

Of course, sometimes there are ricochets and you end up scaring yourself too...

WALK THIS WAY

✸

'It's a tempting offer, Mr Shields,' I said, unable to resist what I call a grin but the wife terms a smirk. 'Incredibly tempting.'

'*Unbelievably* tempting,' echoed my wife, returning the 'grin' with interest. That expression might well become my patrician features but on her it looked like brassy triumph.

Poor old Mr and Mrs Shields looked discomfited—as well they might, not having done at all well out of even the *first* house sale. A bit of hard bargaining, some judicious late-in-the-day *'doubts'* re the structural report, and indeed the whole deal, had got us a bit of a bargain off them. Coupled with Mr and Mrs Shield's eagerness to sell, I reckon I'd scraped maybe 15 *K* off the price. Enough to fund some serious golf and some not-so-serious secretary wining/dining/bonking. It was therefore icing on the cake to have the vendors return after six months and offer a very generous buy-back deal.

The wife, who *can* be a bit soft, took pity on the old dears.

'Didn't the move work, then?' she asked in her *'loud but kind'* voice. 'Miss the old homestead, eh?'

'Something like that,' mumbled Mr Shields, fiddling with the coffee cup on his lap. 'Yes, we do miss it, don't we Florrie?'

'I'm surprised you still recognise it,' snapped the wife, back to her normal self, thank God, 'what with the new kitchen and bathroom, the complete redecoration...'

'Oh yes,' agreed Shields, in a placatory tone. 'It's all mod cons now, I can see. Very chic...'

'That's right,' the wife continued. 'We couldn't be doing with all the dingy old stuff.' Her voice trailed off as she realised, even for her, she'd gone too far.

'So you want to come back,' I smiled, mercilessly, 'out of... nostalgia.'

'Yes, that's about the shape of it,' agreed Mr Shields, wearily.

'Expensive business: nostalgia...'

'Well,' said Shields, agreeing yet again, 'we've had a chat and we didn't think you'd take anything less. It's our best offer, mind; we've got nothing left in reserve.'

I used the old 'wistful intake of breath through the teeth' noise (as invented by mechanics and builders).

'We'd *like* to oblige,' I said, 'to let you back: for nostalgia's sake. Sadly though, the building *has* appreciated in value since then, and we've made improvements: turned it into a nice modern home...'

'Oh, enough!' said old Mrs Shields—and quite impressively—to her husband. 'They're tormenting us, Albert. They know *just* what we're about. They've seen him!'

⚜

And so we had, almost since day one.

'*Hello*,' the wife had said, the first time, as she was feeding the dishwasher. 'Who the hell's this?'

She spoke like that to most people not honoured or bold enough to use the front door. I assumed it was just some salesman or neighbour approaching the rear entrance and carried on with my invoice checking.

'Bloody cheek!' she went on. 'Oi you! Private property!'

Then I heard the kitchen window being tapped furiously with a valuable diamond wedding ring and thought I might as well earn some brownie points by intervening. I found her leaning over the Swedish sink-unit, trying to defy the laws of science and see down to the bottom of the garden.

'He never stopped,' she said. 'He just walked by like he owned the place!'

'Who did? I asked, not unreasonably.

'This bloke,' said the wife, in her *'call-yourself-a-man?'* tone. 'I thought he was coming to the back door but he just kept going. He's in our garden!'

ALTERED ENGLANDS

'I didn't hear the passage door go,' I prevaricated.

'Are you going to sort him out or shall I?' she said, turning to face me. I could already hear the story being told, with unflattering embellishments, to her mother.

'All right, all right; I'm going...'

To my delight and relief, the garden was unoccupied. A tentative *'Who's there?'* met no response. A bolder advance up the path confirmed the diagnosis. No one could have made it across the fence into the neighbouring field and woods in the time given. Materialist that I was, that meant there couldn't have been anyone in the first place. I sneaked back to the house and suddenly loomed up against the kitchen window whilst pulling a face. The wife recoiled across the room like I'd threatened her credit cards.

I'll skip the next bit—just a torrent of abuse and an *'I saw him/you couldn't have done'* exchange, and then some more abuse. She was adamant she'd seen a shaggy youth promenade down our garden and I didn't see how that could be. A glacial chill descended on the marital home for a couple of days—but that was no great loss.

The second time was actually a bit of a godsend. A minor lapse in the fidelity stakes—nothing serious, just an office-party-plus-a-few-weeks-after sort of thing—had been discovered. As a result, I'd dined exclusively on tongue-pie and cold shoulder ever since. My every word was met with gamma rays and things had got to a bit of an impasse—not being able to contemplate divorce at that stage in my career. Just when matters were at their worst, the shaggy youth turned up again and then the cow *had* to speak kindly to me.

'He's back!' she screeched, forgetting the 'not-talking' sanctions.

'Who's back?' I asked—as if I didn't know—but she was already gone, out into the garden to vent her woman-scorned stuff on some innocent. I didn't let it distract me from my *'Independent.'*

In due course she came back, wonderfully abashed, all my sins apparently forgiven.

'Come and look,' she said, taking me gently(!) by the hand like we were at a works-dinner. *'Please* come and look...'

So I did (acquiring my putter en route, just in case) and we gave the neighbours something to talk about by wandering round the garden, hand in hand.

'No one...,' she said in hushed terms, rather stating the obvious.

'If he can make it to cover in that time,' I said, gesturing to the distant trees with my golf club, 'it's the Olympics selectors we should be contacting.'

We went back to the passage door and discovered it was locked.

'*I* did that,' muttered the wife, clearly on autopilot. 'Since the last time...'

I gave the door handle a final rattle.

'Well then, my dear,' I said, 'so what is it? A ghostie? The *DT*s? Or maybe just the 'Change of life'?'

A moment of shock—then normal service was immediately resumed. Her eyes regained their familiar steely state.

'Nothing,' she said. 'It's nothing.'

'So you're seeing things then?'

'So it seems.'

Never again, she appeared to be resolving, would she display such 'weakness', least of all to a mere man. That suited me fine.

'Let me know if 'he' returns, won't you?' I japed. 'I enjoy a stroll in the garden.'

'He won't,' she snapped, with jutting jaw. 'Because it never happened.'

☸

But he did—and it did; happen that is. I have to hand it to the wife (if I don't she'll just take it), her emotion-stomping self-control was superb, but I heard the sharp intake of breath one Sunday afternoon, not long after, and recognised the tell-tale sign.

That involuntary squeak aside, she was going to say no more, I could tell, and maybe it was to spoil her stoical achievement that I decided to intervene. Or maybe I just wanted to be kind. Anyway, a couple of swift strides took me into the kitchen just in time—I think—to see something—I think—vanish past the very corner of the kitchen window. It might have been a jumper-clad elbow, or a bit of someone's back, but certainly it was moving and material enough to convince me. In the short time it took the wife to additionally convince me that I *did* want to investigate, he, she or it could have got no further than the garden's edge. Once again though, when out and about in our grounds, I found myself in glorious isolation.

'No one,' I reported back, though perhaps with detectably less conviction than before.

'There *was*,' she said, quietly, more to herself than to me, as though trying to fix the thought in her mind. 'There *was* someone. He was young and wild looking and scruffy. He was staring at the ground and mumbling. He was walking—down *my* garden!'

'Nope!' I answered, affecting nonchalance and essaying my Tommy Cooper impersonation, complete with gestures. 'Garden empty—empty garden...'

'You saw!' she said, in tones of burning accusation, but, seeking marital high ground in all this, I was already thinking on my feet.

'What *I* saw was a fleeting bit of black something,' I smiled. 'It could have been a bird or-...'

'Or *him*,' said the wife, pointing behind me, a triumphant grin now disfiguring her model-girl features.

Reluctantly, unable to help myself, I turned, gingerly, shoulders hunched, to look.

In the field beyond our property, halfway between the old sheep-shed and the woods, there 'he' was, just as described. Having had closer encounters, the distance lent courage to the wife, whereas I, a virgin in such matters, suddenly felt a whole lot less happy.

He was... prowling in a circle round the field, head down, completely self-absorbed; the indistinctness of his features at that range turning the merely odd into something sinister.

'He *couldn't*,' I exclaimed, 'have got there, in that time...'

As neatly as though he heard us, the method was then kindly demonstrated. We stood aghast, unconsciously hand in hand, as the man moved to the woods. He didn't walk or run or jump; he just... moved, as though in strobe light or on faulty film, from one point to another without troubling to appear in-between. A few such... jaunts took him, standing still and erect, from the field into the trees and then out of sight.

Fearing the reappearance of that pale face, peering at us from the wood's edge, I fled indoors, dragging the wife behind me.

'But in the end we've just got used to him,' I said, poker-faced. 'He doesn't do *us* any harm.'

'And it's only once a week or so,' confirmed the wife, brightly. 'We can live with it.'

I was pleased with the tough and shiny united front we were presenting to the Shields. Correspondingly, they were looking at each other in some dismay.

'We wondered whether to mention it to you...,' said the old man.

'But you thought it'd bring the price down, eh?' I jeered.

'No, not at all!' he shot back, now a sitting duck of confusion. 'Me and the missus, we didn't want to move, we'd spent our lives here. We just wanted to-...'

'Do the right thing,' said female Shields, in a voice of cold-forged anger. I made a mental note about trouser-wearing roles, on the off-chance of future negotiations.

'Yes, yes, that's right,' her husband stumbled on. 'We thought... if we left, we'd just bring it to an end. We thought we were to blame. There was no telling he'd just keep on walking...'

'And we couldn't take it any longer,' added Mrs Shields. 'More than anything, we wanted rest—for him and for us. We thought it was being done for our benefit, you see. We weren't to know he'd carry on. When you said in your letter...'

We'd written in deliberately general terms, asking about any *'stories'* or *'legends'* attached to our house. The Shields had obviously twigged straightaway.

The wife, for whom my admiration (and wariness) increased by the moment, smiled meaninglessly at the old couple perched on the edge of our cream leather sofa.

'Well, this is all very nice,' she trilled, 'but, like I wrote to you, is there any chance of a word of explanation?'

Mrs Shields sighed.

'He was just our son,' she said, in a monotone, speaking from the heart. Mr Shields looked on. 'No one special; just our everything. When we had him, well, we couldn't have any more. So he got all our love—much good it did him...'

Mr Shields put his tweeded arm round her shoulders but she shrugged it off. The harsh pill of truth apparently required no sugar.

ALTERED ENGLANDS

'He read a lot, right from before school. Always reading he was—and thinking. *'A solitary little philosopher'*, his school report said. But in the end his mind was so well stocked he just withdrew inside. I expect nowadays they'd have a word for it. There was no reaching him, was there, Bert?'

Mr Shields looked into a distance far beyond our walls and nodded.

'He knew too much,' he said, 'too much to enjoy himself. And he had to think it all through.'

'Towards the end,' continued Mrs Shields, 'I think he got too deep in. He'd pace up and down for hour after hour—just the same route as he does now, along the path and round and round the field. We couldn't talk to him anymore...'

By some telepathy, Mr Shields sensed it was his job to complete the tale for his wife and make a swift job of it.

'One morning he just upped and said to us, *'That's it; now I know!'*. Then he had a final walk and hanged himself in the woods.'

'That's it, now I know'?' I queried, interested despite the more important financial considerations under consideration.

The Shields nodded. They thought there was nothing more to say.

'He didn't say what *'that'* was?'

'No,' answered old man Shields—and firmly for once. 'He learnt something, he thought of something, but we don't know what. We don't *want* to know. All we *do* know is it didn't end there for our poor boy. We weakly abandoned him to... whatever it is he's enduring, but now we want to make amends. Sell us our house back and let us share his burden—please?'

It was all very moving (excuse the pun) on a certain level, but, as my step-father always said *'Business is king!'*

'That's all absolutely fascinating,' I said, smiling, 'but the question is, can you *afford* to make amends?'

'How do you mean exactly?' asked Shields, Presumably taking the question as a metaphysical one.

'Well,' said the wife, stepping in like half of a veteran tag-team, 'like we mentioned, property prices have shot up round here.'

The wife and I aren't exactly a soul-match, more a (financial) mutually-assured-destruction pact than a marriage. Against the outside world though, we make the Corleones look loose-knit. My shallow heart swelled with pride.

'That's right,' I embroidered. 'And what with all our improvements...'

'And it being so handy for my husband's work,' the wife lied, 'I don't think we could let your son's visitations drive us out.'

'Unless it were for a *lot* more money,' I added.

'And to be frank,' said the wife, smiling sweetly and looking the old couple up and down. 'We don't think you've got it.'

Sad to say, I'd been looking forward to this *coup de grâce*, so the Shields' stoicism disappointed me.

'*It* being the money,' I said.

'And therefore the house,' confirmed the wife.

❦

The tiger-ish feeling of well-being generated by that meeting didn't last all that long—perhaps the duration of the Shields' bus journey home. Still, it was a sweet little *glacé* cherry atop the cake of upwardly mobile professional life. So, pretty soon we forgot all about the Shields and even their stay-behind representative in our midst. His ongoing hikes didn't distract us from the edifice of the good-life that we were building.

In fact, months later, I was commenting on that very structure the precise moment it all came crashing down.

'Ha!' I shouted to the wife and gesturing to the teletext screen. 'Nirex Petrochemicals are five points up—just like I predicted. How do you fancy St. Lucia this year?'

'I *might* be induced to accompany y-...' came her truncated reply from the kitchen. 'Hang on, look who it is!'

I could guess. We hadn't seen the boy Shields lately. The cooking area had become a bit neglected now that we ate out and socialised with all our contacts so much. He'd been relegated to the limbo-ish outer circles of our minds to stand alongside neighbours and parents and other such nuisances.

'Say hello for me,' I laughed. 'But don't make him hang around—'*hang*'—geddit?'

In reply, there was some muttering, and then a banshee scream came through the door. I didn't think my rare stab at humour *that* bad.

The ensuing silence went on a bit too long and deep for comfort. I hesitated but then mustered enough of scarce courage resources to go and look.

ALTERED ENGLANDS

The wife was huddled, embryo-style, in a corner by the ceramic hob. The tear-streaked eyes she raised to greet me were those of a stranger—and a feral, demented stranger at that.

'I tapped the window,' she said, her once strident voice now a lost little girl's whisper. 'He *looked* at me. He said...'

Rather than finish her sentence she started screaming again. As it turned out, those were the last sensible words she had to say to me—or anyone else for that matter.

The next morning, after a night of hysteria, I woke alone and exhausted. And found my wife doing the rounds of the field.

※

I reduced my price again and again but the cold-hearted Shields wouldn't buy. They must have guessed their precious son doesn't grace us with his presence any more. Why should he? He's shared and halved his problem, and got my wife to walk his way.

※

29~

INGRATITUDE

'It was the good of Guildford, old Guildford as it was when I was borne and my parents lived in it, that I did seke... out of love to the place of my birth.'

George Abbott (1562-1633), Archbishop of Canterbury.

INTRODUCTION

Back in the nineties Guildford Borough Council declined to fund a statue of possibly its most famous son and certainly its most generous benefactor. Some councillors said some quite remarkable, indeed unforgettable, things about the place they supposedly represent and surely ought to—well, if not love, then at least *like*...

In the end, the sum required had to be funded by private subscription and the £10 here and £5 there of the good hobbits of South-west Surrey.

This story stems from the strong emotions the episode stirred in some hearts, mine included.

Now, when my cynicism-stream is far more toxic, when far fewer things shock, and all that surprises me is people's ability *not to blush*, I envy that lost me such engagement...

ALTERED ENGLANDS

DISCLAIMER

In my *Binscombe Tales* series the Town of 'Goldenford' is said to be situated somewhat to the north of Binscombe, centre of said stories—and the Universe. Or so Mr Disvan has intimated in sundry places. So it must be so.

Accordingly, just like that variant Binscombe, Goldenford is at a tangent to the 'real world'. Therefore none of what follows really happened save on pages *wot-I-writ*, these people aren't actual, there's no such place and I made it all up.

As my hero, Sir John Major (1943-), would say: *'Oh yes...'*.

And I should know, because I was there when it didn't happen.

JOHN WHITBOURN

INGRATITUDE

✺

'Sir,

In these times of ever worsening recession and widespread 'tightening-of-belts', it behoves us all to economise and act with proper financial prudence. Does this apply, however, to our Lords and Masters: the Local Authority? It seems to me that hard times don't impinge on Goldenford Borough Council, for they are proposing to spend £35,000 of <u>our</u> hard-earned Rates money on a statue of some old bishop or other, to plonk right in the middle of the High Street. I think this is outrageous. It might also interfere with traffic. Let those Councillors vote for it who dare. We shall be voting about <u>them</u> not so long from now. It wouldn't happen in America!

Yours disgustedly,

Trevor Willington B.Sc. (Chartered Accountant).
'Chez Nous', The Mall, Goldenford.'

Letters Page, *'The Goldenford Advertiser'*, Friday 19th March 1993.

✺

'And those against?'

No one spoke or raised their hands.

'Very well,' said the Chairperson. 'I declare item 22: the raising of councillors' attendance allowances, as per attached document, pages 135 to 159, and appendices 3, 5 and 9, to be duly passed. Let it so be recorded.'

ALTERED ENGLANDS

There was a trickle of ironic applause from the public gallery. The full Council meeting magisterially ignored it.

Those weaker brethren present—the paid officers, the public and the less fanatical members, were looking at their watches as dinner inexorably merged into supper, and the margin between now and work tomorrow grew ever thinner.

'Madame Chairperson,' said one of the younger councillors, rising to his full five feet height, 'in consideration of those members of the public present, unusual as it is, I move that agenda item 43 be advanced for immediate discussion: that's what they are here for, I suppose...'

There were some polite *'hear hear'*s and even a *'yowsa!'* from the gallery.

The leader of the ruling party looked beadily at the mover of this motion. Such spontaneity, such energy: *there* was someone who might not be getting the Party nomination come next election. The Leader just couldn't comprehend why anyone should want to leave a Council meeting before it came to its stately conclusion.

Still, it could do no harm and was in currently *de rigueur* popularist spirit... When the Chairperson next pointedly caught the Leader's eye, he shrugged his enormous shoulders to signify indifference.

'The proposed statue of Archbishop Pie...,' she therefore mused aloud. 'I think that's reasonably straightforward, Councillor Layton. Very well, we'll hear the item now—unless there's any objection?'

The majority party leader sat still and so everyone else did the same.

'It is laid before us,' read the Chairperson, 'that a formal commission be given to sculptor Ronald Oak, that he create a full scale statue of Archbishop Pie as per the scale model previously supplied; full cost excluding delivery being £35,000. This was passed by the Policy and Finance sub-Committee on 5/11/92. Is there anyone who wishes to speak before we proceed to vote?'

Silence followed until, relishing the dramatic effect *just* as the Chairperson was about to move on, a lone figure rose.

'Councillor Fenris...,' toastmastered Madame Chair.

He nodded politely in recognition of his name (a sound ever fresh to his ears) and waved a well-stuffed folder at the bemused Chamber.

'I don't think,' he said, solemnly, 'I can, in all conscience, allow this item to go through 'on the nod', as it were. We are all aware of Archbishop Pie, our Town's most famous son. We have all read of his humane and masterly interventions in the vicious religious squabbles of the 17th Century; apparently a kind-hearted man set amongst bloodthirsty fanatics. We are all culturally indebted to him, to some extent, for his masterminding of that great palace of English Literature, the *'King James Bible'*. But I ask you this—are we £35,000 indebted?

'Now, what I hold here is a stack of letters received from my constituents. The question *they* ask with one voice is how on earth do we justify such expenditure during a recession? These people,'—and here again he waved the folder aloft like a brand—'the people who put us here, are angry that we should be busy honouring the dead when it's the living that need help. Must I remind you, ladies and gentlemen, of the homeless problem in this Borough; of the loan-servicing bill for the new *Kaleidoscope* Sports Centre; of the far from acceptable level of our Rates imposition? Our *constituents* don't need reminding of these things!'

On this resounding note he gave way to another gentleman who had been signalling for the Chairperson's attention.

'Councillor Chimes-Wasp,' she called.

'I belong to neither of the two major parties in this Borough,' he said, sounding almost relieved. 'So, the only axe *I* have to grind is that of a loyal son of Goldenford...'

Subdued groans came from either side.

'I am glad to hear,' he went on, fortified by years and conviction against the silver foil arrows of ridicule, 'of Councillor Fenris' appreciation of the life and achievements of Archbishop Pie. I had no idea he had any sympathy with tradition—certainly this is its first public outing to my knowledge. Be that as it may, he quite rightly alludes to an averted Civil War and the glorious gift of what is, despite many, lesser alternatives, *the* Bible. I should add that I refer, of course, to the 1611 *'Authorised Version'*, since I fear that many of those present may not be familiar with its existence, so far has the media and education system deracinated them.'

The elderly man paused and looked round. A sad survey: of a sea of uncomprehending faces.

'What *is* unaccountable,' he went on, 'is that my colleague forgot to mention Archbishop Pie's generosity to our Town and the deep regard in which he held it, however high in the world he rose. A few hundred yards from here stands *'Pie's Hospital'*, a haven for the old-in-years but short-of-purse of Goldenford. In that High Street masterpiece of Stuart architecture, maintained to this very day by the funds endowed by the Archbishop, live a score of Goldenfordians who have very good and present reasons to put our thanks to him in concrete form-...'

'Bronze, actually,' drawled someone alongside Chimes-Wasp. Who crushingly ignored them.

'The green fields of Glebe Park,' he said, 'atop half of which this Council has recently seen fit to erect the... Kaleidoscope Sports Centre, this too was bequeathed to us by Archbishop Pie: to be held in perpetuity for the people of Goldenford—as an *open space*, I might add. And, as if all this were not sufficient-...'

'More than!' said a voice from the opposite benches. 'Sit down!'

'... although I should very much hope it is—if anyone actually still doubts the overdue honour we propose to pay to Pie, then I'll close-...'

'Alleluia!' said the heckler.

'... with the words of the Archbishop's will: *'It was the good of Goldenford, old Goldenford as it was, that I did seek'*. Surely that's enough said?'

Chimes-Wasp's conclusion unwisely offered a hostage to fortune. His last words seemed shot through with sudden doubt, as if a certainty was now dependent upon someone's questionable better nature.

'Not really,' smiled Councillor Fenris, rising to reply. 'The amenity resource factors of both Glebe Park and Pie's Hospital *are* appreciated, of course. But anyone can leave something in a will—when you're dead and gone, what do possessions signify to you? What better time for a grasping man to appear generous? However, like I've said, it's the *living* that I and my party are more concerned with: people like Mrs Betty Rasp-...'

'Who's she?' catcalled one of his opponents. 'Your latest?'

'Who is a resident of my ward,' continued Fenris, unperturbed by this reference to his known-to-be-complicated social arrangements, 'and who says,'—here he read from a piece of paper conveniently placed before him by a colleague—*"I don't want a statue of this religious person—which might be offensive to members of the ethnic minorities and the non-Christian community. What this Borough needs is decent child day-care facilities."*

There were a few suspiciously prompt *'quite rights'* from around Fenris.

'Or Mr Terence Low,' he surged on, as another letter was slid before him, 'who says the relevant money would be better spent on the faulty paving he assiduously monitors around his bungalow. I tend to agree with him. And then there's Jasper Brush from Old Cathedral Ward, where the proposed statue might be... placed. He, quite rightly, says-...'

'Hang on,' called out Chimes-Wasp. 'If you're reading out all these letters, what was in that folder you were waving—and where's it gone?'

'May *I* speak?' said a compact, unhappy-sounding woman, three seats along from Fenris. The request was redundant, for she had already risen and Fenris given way.

There was a restive stirring along the lines of the ruling-party benches and their leader narrowed his already porcine eyes. Twenty-five years in the Lilliput-meets-Lebanon of local politics meant he recognised a choreographed double act when he saw one.

'It seems Councillor Fenris is willing,' said the Chairperson. 'Please proceed, Councillor Treen.'

'*I've* taken the trouble,' she said, shooting out the words like bullets—and illegal, dumdum ones at that, 'to do some research on the saintly Mr Pie. And *what* an interesting can of worms I came up with. For example, it seems he had a rather lengthy tumble from... grace after, accidentally *he* said, killing a huntsman with a crossbow. Now, you all know the trouble we used to have with the Mayoral tradition of greeting the Goldenford Hunt on Boxing Day. With that painful memory in the recent past, ought we now to be celebrating a trigger-happy slaughterer of animals?'

No one knew—or no one said.

'Archbishop Pie,' she went on, warming to her theme and using his title like the Mark of Cain, 'acquiesced in the contemporary subjugation of women by failing to take a principled stand against the misogynistic tenets of the creed he professed. He pandered to the monarcho-rightist ruling class of his day and preached quietism to the oppressed proto-proletariat and peasantry. I have also discovered that he quite openly advocated the—and I quote—*'evangelisation'* of the so-called *'New World'*, blatantly trampling on the totally justified human rights of the indigenous peoples, and recent studies show-...'

'Councillor Treen,' interjected the Chairperson. 'You are going too fast even for our highly skilled committee clerks.'

Two simultaneously harassed-and-bored-looking clerks rested their blurring pens.

'Too fast *and* loose,' said Councillor Chimes-Wasp, rising to protest. 'We know that Archbishop Pie suffered agonies of guilt for that accidental death of a servant by his hand. He atoned for a full year—bread and water only—and lifelong provided for the man's widow: there were any number of genuine signs. What my colleague says is an abominable slur. And as for the rest of it...!'

Various inarticulate growls from the public gallery backed him up.

That turned out to be the only support he would get. The Fenris-Treen song and dance act had struck home, playing a veritable symphony upon the xylophone of councillors' buzzwords. The half-dozen actually important people in the chamber were gathered in a huddle around their leader, raising record harvests from the seeds of doubt sown.

The rest of the ruling party noted this and sat passively back awaiting guidance. Their opponents were similarly observant and Fenris rose like a grey-clad matador to apply the *coup-de-grâce*.

'All I'm suggesting,' he said, the soul of reason, 'is that, in view of the anxieties expressed about the Pie memorial, and the less than fortunate aspects of the man's record—not to mention the ill-timed expense—we simply refer the matter back to committee. Let's mull it over.'

That sounded moderate enough to the uninitiated, but the councillors were not deceived. They knew that referral back was council-speak for death-by-dust-gathering. No proposal *ever* returned, revenant-style, from the limbo of referral back.

Fenris sat down and in the ice-house of his mind there shimmered headlines in the local media: *'Fenris foils the spendthrifts'* or *'Voters hail the ratepayer's friend'* and—a thrilling if ethereal vision this—*'Fenris seizes Power!'* Then he awoke from his reverie to find the (at present) Council Leader speaking.

'I must confess,' he said, slowly, with all the confidence of a man not contradicted for a quarter-century, 'I thought this matter all but settled. The dearth of statuary in the Borough was pointed out to us by the press and, being jealous custodians of our civic reputation, we hastened—after due discussion and debate—to rectify the lack. We now have the preliminary model made, the site chosen and prepared, the commission contract drafted...'

He then turned his dull eyes to the public gallery. This was all for them.

'How surprised I am,' he went ponderously on, 'to now hear the opposition raise fundamental doubts at this late stage. If only they had spoken up earlier the Borough might have been saved substantial expense. The people of Goldenford will note this and realise who are the *real* would-be profligates.'

Fenris and his cohorts huffed and smiled dismissively as was expected. The gesture was as formal and stylised as emotions in silent films.

'Still,' the Leader rumbled on, serene as a Hindu juggernaut, 'doubts *have* been expressed, albeit with singular ill-timing. My party is not one to railroad policies through-...'

'What about the Kaleidoscope Centre then?' shouted someone from the gallery.

This was a raw wound to prod but, with the thing now safely built and the correspondence equally safely shredded, the members could afford to ignore such taunts—the squeals of field mice against an oncoming *combine*. The Leader barely paused.

'The proper stewardship of the ratepayers' funds is ever the foremost consideration in our mind, as all present will confirm. That being so, let us put the statue issue to a vote.'

One of the note-taking committee-clerks, a desensitised Local Government veteran, had summarised this speech in just one word: *'Election!'*. Looking across he saw that his colleague had done the same.

The pow-wow of the inner half-dozen had decided on caution as the order of the day—something so inbred it was barely a decision at all. When the time came, the half-dozen voted for referral back and, half a second later, so did all their troops. Assisted by his own party's votes, Fenris' motion was carried overwhelmingly. He sat back and glowed with pleasure.

Councillor Chimes-Wasp, on the other hand, didn't glow—he *glowered*, though with equal passion. He rose—in the way that Mount Etna sometimes does.

'May I remind councillors,' he shouted above the chatter, 'that the sum involved is almost exactly that voted tonight for the increase in our allowances?'

It turned out he might but the desired connection clearly wasn't made by the blank faces before him.

'Then shame on you,' he said, making it sound like a curse (which in some ways it was). 'You've disowned Goldenford's most faithful son. Can you not appreciate that a town is something *more* than a collection of retail outlets?'

Some councillors looked shocked at the expression of such blasphemy.

By now the news had also sunk into those left in the public gallery and they were making their underwhelment known.

'If peace is not restored,' said the Chairperson, relieved and pleased to find a proper role for herself at last, 'I shall be forced to have the public areas closed.'

In fact, powered by disgust, the gallery was already clearing itself.

'But we've already had the plinth set up—a prime site, top of the High Street!' said Chimes-Wasp, in one last desperate clutch at a straw.

'Oh, that's no problem,' said the Leader, quietly content with an opposition ambush swerved. 'We'll put a pot of flowers on it. How much would that cost?'

The Borough Treasurer, who had been perched on the edge of his chair all evening, such was his eagerness to please, fairly rocketed upright.

'£39.40, with bi-annual replacement,' he said, smiling winningly. '£52.50 with tri-annual. Could I have a *little* time to calculate the associated cleaning and facility-enhancement costs, because-...'

The Leader imperially waved him to silence.

'A mere bagatelle,' he said. 'See to it.'

As the Treasurer signalled in every way open to him that it would indeed be done, a breeze like a sigh disturbed the Leader's vestigial locks. Several other councillors noticed the intruder as their papers and hairdos were briefly raised.

'This old place is draughty,' thought the Council Leader. *'High time we had a brand new Town Hall.'*

⚙

'So this is what it's like,' said Councillor Treen. 'What a dump!'

Councillor Fenris turned to look at her.

'Do you mean to say you've never been in Holy Trinity before?' he said, surprised.

'In a *church?*' Treen laughed: an unnatural sound. 'You must be joking!'

Fenris nodded understandingly.

'Come to think of it,' he said, 'I've never seen you at any of the Civic services on the 'High and Holy days'—they're a drag aren't they? It's one of my long-term projects to phase them out. Oddly enough, the vicar's pretty progressive and he's with me on this. I plan to say they're *'monoculturalist.'*

'Well they *are*,' frowned Treen, not getting the levity.

Councillor Fenris concealed a shadow of worry crossing his brow. Sometimes his latest conquest... worried him.

'Anyhow,' said Treen, pinning Fenris with her curiously protuberant eyes, 'church or not, it's very handy for us to meet in. Good idea. You have these little flashes of brilliance, don't you?'

Fenris grinned.

'It's town-centre but unfrequented. No one would expect to find us here...'

'But we could have a plausible reason for so being,' chorused Treen. 'Like planning a ceremony, or maybe discussing the place's demolition—if only!'

'And it won't be for much longer—all this secrecy,' said Fenris.

'You *keep* saying that,' answered Treen, moving from smile to scowl without changing gear. 'You never deliver though. What about some 'action-this-day!' That's what you shout at your underlings, isn't it?'

'You don't understand,' complained Fenris. 'My wife is not a reasonable woman—and more to the point, her people are big noises round here. I have to move carefully—it's all a matter of timing...'

'Normally your timing's good; that I'll grant you,' smirked Treen, and trailed her be-ringed finger along his five o'clock shadow. 'So, are we okay for tonight and do I need to bring a wh-... Hang on—what's *that* over there?'

'Where?' said Fenris, whirling anxiously round and adjusting his tie.

Treen pointed. Seductive to *chagrined* in two seconds.

'All those flags and banners in the corner! Are you blind or something, man?'

'No, I'm *not* blind,' replied Fenris, patiently. 'That's the chapel of the Wessex Regiment with their battle honours and memorials and all that. It's been here since the year dot.'

'Well, *that's* about to change if *I've* got anything to do with it!' fumed Treen. 'It's rampant militarism and it's got to go! We can't countenance that sort of thing in the Borough!'

'I agree, I agree,' said Treen, trying to smooth her ruffled feathers—thereby to get back to more interesting matters. 'But now's not the time—or era. They're the County Regiment: lots of local ties and so on—and they all have votes. Think of it as an ambition, darling—timing: always timing...'

Councillor Treen wasn't de-ruffled at all.

'And that monstrosity in the other corner—who's that? Some dead warmonger?'

Fenris was starting to feel a bit irritable himself. The woman's 24 hour-a-day political correctness was spoiling his little lunchtime romantic interlude. Maybe the new typing temp would have been a better bet after all.

'Not exactly, dear,' he answered, tersely. 'It's your old friend Archbishop Pie. Really, Deirdre, your ignorance of the town you represent is embarrassing. It's not everywhere that can boast the tomb of an Archbishop of Canterbury, you know.'

'My concern is with living people and their problems—not stiffs,' snapped Treen. 'God! Look at it—it's ghastly!'

She wandered over to the tomb and, still hopeful of a return on his time-investment, Fenris reluctantly followed.

'Ghastly...,' she repeated in awe, studying the monument; from its marble roof, via the recumbent effigy of Pie, right down to the dark and skull-decorated pedestal below. 'Can't we ditch it on the grounds of not wanting children frightened? Couldn't we get away with covering it up?'

Fenris regarded the yellow-white stone hands of Archbishop Pie clasped in final prayer. He had to admit (or rather he didn't—not out loud) that the deliberate gloom of the thing... impressed him. These people didn't try to hide or gloss over the fact of death. They adorned their great ones' graves with tokens of that ending, with marble bones and grinning skulls. And then they added cherubic messengers, heralding the deceased to a better place—or possibly not.

Happily, in averting his eyes from the tomb to answer his mistress, sanity returned to Councillor Fenris. *'What a load of nonsense,'* he thought. *'You can't afford these flights of fancy, dear boy—not where you're going in life...'*

'No,' he replied succinctly, enjoying giving her a categorical rebuff for once. 'You *can't* remove it. It's a listed monument.'

Her clenched face said that this was another category of things she had no time for.

'So it's a fixture,' she said. 'Shame. I'd like to *make* something of here; clear the whole place out and turn it to some *useful* purpose—like a women's refuge or a pop-in centre for substance-abusers: something like that. One day...'

'One day...,' he said, going along with her in hope of reward.

'Meanwhile,' she mused, smiling like a car grille at the marble Archbishop, 'we sorted *you* out, didn't we, you old... racist, fascist, sexist, imperialist, heterosexist, Zionist—hang on, that's not right...'

There was also something else that wasn't right but the two Councillors, now wrapped in each others arms and tongues, failed to notice it.

The black, cast-metal fittings of the tomb, the rods and struts that held and adorned its roof and pillars, were starting to seethe and melt and flow. Lost in a sweaty embrace and grope, Fenris and Treen weren't aware that Pie's sepulchre was becoming wonderfully... fluid.

They were finally interrupted by a polite cough and instantly, comically, leapt apart—like opposing-poles magnets. Councillor Fenris was already framing honeyed words of explanation to a long-suffering wife.

To their astonishment though, neither Mrs Fenris nor anyone else could be seen. They peered and craned as they smoothed their clothes but still drew a puzzling blank.

'Hello?' said Fenris at last, cautious in raising his voice, fear of discovery/exposure rendering him reticent for once.

'Hello,' replied a quiet voice from behind them. They whirled round with the speed of guilty gunfighters.

From his bed of marble, Archbishop Pie turned his head and winked at the two.

"Ingratitude', he said, a thin voice echoing in—and from—some very distant place, *"thou marble-hearted fiend. More hideous... than the sea-monster!"*

'*King Lear!*' screamed Councillor Treen (an academic by trade); her panicking mind unable to suggest anything more helpful than spot-the-quote.

'Correct,' confirmed Pie. Then he sighed and rose up on one elbow. 'Now: let's see what we can *make* out of you...'

From the tomb, a stone cherub's trumpet blew molten metal over the Councillors—with uncanny accuracy.

❦

'In the final analysis,' the Borough Recreation and Community Services Officer told the Council, 'we can't account for the statues' appearance. No donor has answered our press advertisements, no one has any clues. It's all a bit of a mystery, frankly.'

ALTERED ENGLANDS

'But you would describe the work as satisfactory?' asked one of the leading party's tame question-planting councillors. Opposite him, the opposition were curiously subdued, two unexplained vacant seats in their midst like knocked-out teeth.

The Officer shrugged the shoulders of his oversized *M & S* suit.

'Dunno. Technically, the mounting's fine and safe—or so Borough Engineering Services assure me. The Insurance Officer's okayed it. As to artistically—well, that's a matter of... judgement. It exceeds the original commission: there's the second allegorical figure, of course. But that accords well with the title found inscribed on the plinth...'

'*'HONOUR TRIUMPHS OVER FANATICISM'*,' read out Councillor Chimes-Wasp. 'It's a nice summation of Archbishop Pie's achievement. I vote we keep it.'

'And it's a good likeness of Pie,' said the Borough Rec... *etc. etc.* Officer, pressing on, inspired by thoughts of his long drive home and football on the telly, 'as best we know. In fact it's a fine piece of work all round—very flowing and lifelike. It's true you don't often see civic statues with one figure standing in booted triumph on the other's chest...'

'St George and the Dragon?' offered Chimes-Wasp.

'Yeah,' agreed the *'BR & CS Off.'*, sorry he'd raised a cavil. 'So there's an English tradition of that sort of thing...'

'How much to demolish it?' asked the Leader of the Council, bluntly.

'£248,' said the Borough Treasurer, bobbing up.

'How much to keep and upkeep it?'

'£52 per annum.'

'We'll keep it.'

'Of course,' added the Treasurer, with unheard-of bravery, 'my demolition estimate presumes the figurines are hollow-cast, not solid. Should that not be so then the scrap value would be far greater. I'd be happy to arrange a test probe to ascertain...'

'*No*,' said the Council Leader, who, for all his faults, was not slow in putting two and two together. 'Best not...'

✦

30~

PROGRESS

INTRODUCTION

Herewith, something entered for a 'Short-short' competition.

Not *too* ephemeral an effort I hope, even though it didn't win. A labour-of-love just like the rest, with proportional pen-chewing hours put in.

Plus, for what it's worth, if we as a race ever *do* make it this far in time and space, I suspect here's how things will turn out...

It's being so cheerful keeps me going!

ALTERED ENGLANDS

PROGRESS

'Death is better than shame or innovation!'

The teeming servant castes hissed approval. That was the prescribed phrase on being handed the Lordly blade. Each successive wielder, back into hazy legend times, said the same thing during the sublime ritual of gearing for war. The menial-of-the-sword was allowed, as *high* favour, to slash his thumb on its edge and then show first blood.

'A taste before a feast!' Unused to raising his voice within Castle precincts, he was both exultant and afraid. That acclamation was also strictly prescribed. Like all his ancestors before him, the salutation was his supreme privilege.

Most probably, the sword predated everything. It perhaps helped the very first Lord to win the Castle from... whoever had it before. Scribe records scarcely reached so far back, and told a sketchy tale even then. For the millions who lived in, around—and most certainly under—the thrall of Castle Slovo, there was nothing else, no time before or notions of an after to its rule.

'Behold the harness of The-Subtle-King-whose-name-is-forgot.'

The head-man of the dresser caste also got to speak. Whilst he strapped his Lord into the myriad faceted gold-and-mirror armour, a dozen bards were sacrificed to the ONEGOD, who was merciful and allseeing and pleased to make the CastleLord his vice-regent in all the planes of existence. It was sad but time-hallowed, and beyond questioning. The poets' final compositions were recited even as their lifeblood flowed away.

'May this breastplate acquire further honourable scars,' said the dresser, as he belly-crawled back. It was awesome to consider that the present Lord's ten-times-great-grandfather was thus attired when he fought at Middlezog Bridge and smote the Demon Debbi-of-the-Maw (or so it was said). The glittering golden vision reflected arrows of light to every corner. To intercept a beam was accounted a blessing.

The CastleLord stepped over the dead poets, past the crimson attired and fury-faced satraps of the inner retinue, through the terrified ranks of his children. Beside the chamber doors stood the dowager CastleLady, holding out the ancient *'Mask of Appalling Intimidation'*.

'Come home with glory—or not at all,' she advised him as he donned it, with the concern befitting a mother—and then prostrated herself creakily to the floor.

In the courtyard the higher-ranked harems tracked in stately dance, singing the shrill *'Incitement to libidinous return'* song. Their faces and forms were painted with courage inducing runes from pattern books a thousand years old. CastleLord knew each *houri* well, as they did him, and they avoided his eye.

Beyond, in the *'Gathering in Splendour'* arena, the household regiments were already mounted up, reining in eager horned steeds. It was their proud boast that every weapon they held, every item of rainbow coloured equipment, was handed down via at least three generations of honourable usage. Each chosen warrior could recite his lineage for ten times that.

Their Lord was winched astride his war-beast, to the acclamation of men and the ululations of women. He took up the lance of his forefather Impale-Him VI. Around the walls the priests blessed him and read Surahs wherein the ONEGOD plainly stated that HE was beside those who did well for HIS sake. There was no more to be done, no more that could be said. Ceremony and the ancestor-spirits and HE who saw all were placated. The CastleLord rode forth and his army followed.

The foot-troops, from mailed broadsword men right down to near-naked slingers, were waiting in successive courtyards and followed in the cavalry's wake. So many were they that it took three hours for the last of them to escape the gargoyle-shadow of mighty CastleKeep and issue into bright purple day.

These were merely the regular troops. The levies of the rice-plains and corn-deltas, the leathery half-men of the cactus lands and the forest-tribe beetle-mahouts awaited outside.

Collectively, the horde darkened the land and made thunder as they marched to battle.

ALTERED ENGLANDS

❀

Mik 23(ii) lived in a *humihab* or *capsicle* (or even *plasti-coffin*, as real old timers called them) dorm. He had only dim recollections of Mother, and as for Dad, well, not even the Navy knew. It was fairly certain he was born on Earth—somewhere.

Family, as far as Mik was concerned, were the four other draftees in his team. They went by the name (and he was *ordered* to remember this) of Marine-inf AB/34:12/23. All others were just part of the sea of faces passing through the ship without cease. Thinking on, Mik didn't even rate *Team* much. They went days without speaking.

What Mik 23(ii) did like was cocooning in his plastic nest, watching sim-porn and sucking on a high-gain nutri-bag with nerve-spice sprinkles. Doing that made the hours and days and years slither right on by. He was quite fond of his gun as well.

Mik knew no songs and would never write anything. Reading more than labels and weapon-blurb caused his lips to move, tugging painfully on his attention span. He had his uniform, a gun, some sim-porn still-prints on his coffin walls—and nothing else: no other possessions to treasure. Yet he was a happy man, as fortunate as anyone in those days. True, there was no pay, but the Navy fed and housed him—which meant a lot to a 27th century Earthman.

On the minus side they made him work, like now when a klaxon screamed through his *humihab*, calling him to battle.

❀

It required only a few teams: three at most spat out of the mothership, to *'Reincorporate'* a *'Lapsed'* colony world. Most were long-lost and had gone pretty primitive. They required reminding of the benefits of civilisation.

And thus CastleLord came to meet Mik 23(ii)—albeit briefly and at a distance. The marines hosed the charging hordes away with energy weapons, and Mik wondered briefly who that golden guy had been...

❀

JOHN WHITBOURN

31~

CULLODEN II

INTRODUCTION

The shadow of ulterior motive stalks this story's Jacobite theme, drawn from the fag-end days of Jacobitism when it was hard to distinguish from Scottish Highland nationalism. Its genesis also lies my researching resistance to Bonny Prince Charlie's 1745 invasion, in response to rude things said by contemporary Scottish chroniclers—though they'd already been paid in like coin when their turn came to be conquered by 'Butcher Cumberland'.

But what truly was in the engine room of the tale—apart from fun? Well, after the constitutional scramble of the late 1990s, the UK has a Parliament and so does Scotland and Wales, and Northern Ireland its 'Assembly'. Each nation within the UK was asked to vote on the issue. Except England, of course, which the then Government said wasn't a nation but mere 'regions'. And therefore shouldn't have a vote or any constitutional expression. And remain content to be the largest stateless... nation in Europe. *Hmmm*...

The officially very wonderful 'Campaign for an English Parliament' may be contacted at www.thecep.org.uk

I am also indebted to the likewise (when writing) very wonderful Evelyn Waugh for a paragraph of plagiarism lurking within this tale. Source: *The Loved One: An Anglo-American Tragedy'* (1948). Indeed, having got away with this literary 'tribute' or 'sampling' (*'theft'* is such an ugly word...) once, so tempting was the prize that over the course of four decades writing these stories, I saw fit to steal/pastiche it once more. As the more laser-focused (among other terms…) reader may discern.

The question also arises: should I have updated references herein from 'video' to DVD or Blu-ray, to match modernity? Faced with such a knotty problem I consulted not one but *two* former Prime Ministers, Sir John Major and Theresa May, on the subject.[121]

They both said I *should*.

So I didn't.

---

[121] In troubled dreams.

JOHN WHITBOURN

CULLOODEN II

❀

'*Our stragglers seldom failed to be attacked by the English peasants, who were implacable enemies of the prince, but too cowardly to dare to take up arms against us, though the different provinces, through which we passed, might have easily formed an army of a hundred thousand to oppose us. They were deficient neither in hatred towards us, nor in the wish to injure us, but they wanted courage and resolution to expose themselves to the swords of the highlanders.*

... For the English people make a great noise but are not fond of blows, nor of quitting their fire-sides.'

The Chevalier de Johnstone (1719-1791?). '*Memoirs of The Rebellion in 1745 and 1746*'.

❀

'*Whenever any of the men straggled and stayed behind they either murdered them or sent them to the Duke*':

David Wemyss (1721-1787). '*A short account of the affairs of Scotland in the years 1744, 1745, 1746*'.

❀

'*Highland stragglers were shot dead by a farmer and his sons on the road to Ashbourne... they were harassed by the locals who lit bonfires to signal the whereabouts of the Rebel army, the militia played hit and run on their fringes...*'.

Diana Preston. '*The Road to Culloden Moor: Bonnie Prince Charlie and the '45 Rebellion*'. 1995.

❁

'They'll be parst and gorn by nightfall, leave 'em be I say!'

'They've not harmed I.'

'Arrh, s'right. Nor I.'

'Let 'em be, arrh.'

''Tis sodjers work. Let them as are paid for it do the job.'

'S'right. We raise corn, not lay men low.'

'My grandsire, he were a Jacobite: he'd no approve of I stirring out.'

'What's German George done for we?'

'Bugger all, Samuel! You hit the nail square there!'

Of the tavern company only Farmer Jack stood aloof. The rest looked to him for his contribution. Unanimity was sought to lay niggling doubts. If everyone agreed not to rise and smite the Scots there could be no cause for reproach, not now or in years to come. It was important. Just a nod would do.

Jack never was one for words and those that did escape were doled out miser-style. He spoke to the point and then that was that: no entreaties would shift him. A Chapel elder and self-proclaimed 'Man of peace', people *listened* to him.

So they listened and waited—and waited.

Jack didn't mind them, couldn't even see them: he was communing.

Whilst they chattered he found counsel—and discourse with the shades of his ancestors. Miles and centuries from the *'Rose & Crown'* in Ashbourne he conversed with his savage, melancholic race who had spurned the altars of their old gods, who'd taken ship and wandered, driven by pursuing furies, through dissolving empires and millennial wars. It was a *revelation.*

His father had cared for nothing but root crops and beer: his mother cooked, but now distant English voices prompted him to a higher destiny. Voices which, far away and in another age, had sung of Beowulf and Grendel brooding beneath the mere, spoke sweetly to him of the shoreline of England-to-be, and armed wolfshead-ships, silent in the windless new day: the Saxon fleet at anchor and Aelle of Sussex, *Bretwalda*, spying out the land. They spoke of Aethelstan and Edmund Ironside, of *'Great'* Alfred and black-hearted Arthur. They were unanswerable.

Farmer Jack slammed his leather tankard on the bench. Beer went everywhere.

'It's like this,' he told the all-ears company, 'I reckon we're being mucked about!'

※

His rage surprised even himself. There was no call to carry on once they'd bagged an honourable tally. The Scotch rearguard would well recall Ashbourne and the murderous narrow lanes beyond. Hedgerows spouted muskets and innocent fields raised crops of snipers. Dead-ends lived up to their names. Given that the Rebels' one wish was to be on their way there ought to have been occasion for Christian clemency—and prisoners.

In principle Farmer Jack agreed—but this final cornered trio were too tempting. The *voices* spoke to him again. His world-view flushed scarlet once more.

The Highlanders looked at Jack and he at them.

'Halooo, *Sassenach*,' said one.

'Good day to you, sir,' he replied, politely.

They looked fairly lively: shaggy red-haired and armed to the snaggle-teeth. Jack's sons urged gunning them down from a distance but he wouldn't hear of it. A man of position and a father to boot, ought to set an example. The voices agreed.

Farmer Jack turned to his neighbour.

'Would you pass me that axe, please?'

※

'SCREAMING SCOTCH SKULLS SPOIL STEAMY SESSIONS!'

Complains attractive Barbara 'Babs' Spong, 23, of Councillor Drachman Crescent. 'Sometimes they're so loud my boyfriend Gary and me can't concentrate during sex. It's awful. A dead liberty. Bonking's a Human Right. Citizens Advice say we should sue. It's coming to something when you can't have a quickie without ghosts putting you off. My Gary was so upset last time he went and spent the night at his mum's—or so he says!'

A spokesman for the Council say they are powerless to serve noise nuisance enforcement notices on post-mortem entities but-...'

Deflated, Mr Bland lowered the *'Ashbourne Advocate'* he'd been waving. 'What? *None* of it?'

'Not a word!' confirmed Miss Spong, his neighbour, as heated as he though for different reasons. 'I told 'em like you suggested: *'No comment'*. I haven't even *got* a boyfriend—and I don't know anyone called Gary! I mean, you try to be a good Catholic girl—and then this! Bastards! They're calling me *'Bonking Babs'* at work! What's my Dad going to say?'

Mr Bland realised he wasn't the only one with problems and repented of his earlier annoyance.

'Sorry, Barbara. It's all my fault.'

'No, it's not, Mr B. I know you're doing your best. I hardly hear them at all nowadays.'

'Well, we bought better soundproofing, but they gnaw their way through it, you see…'

'I'd rather not know, thanks. You'll excuse me, Mr B: I've got solicitors to ring.'

'And a busy bonking schedule, ho ho…'

Mr Bland's peacemaking quip didn't just *die*, it spiralled earthwards in flames, spewing afire-fuel everywhere, to finally crash in a crowded playground.

Miss Spong crushed him under her glacial gaze.

'I *suggest* you speak to them again, Mr Bland: *reason* with them!'

He would have loved to—but they weren't reasonable men—or indeed men.

☸

'Noooo'

'Noooo'

'Noooo'

So that was it. Without dissent in the ranks there wasn't the slightest leverage he could use. The voices from the ancient cabinet were adamant: they'd *'No shut up'*.

Mr Bland's father had always advised being *'strict'* with them. *'Stand no nonsense, son. Show 'em who's boss…'* Which was all very well but how exactly was one 'strict' with three severed heads? They had no privileges to withdraw, no shins to kick. And besides, Mr Bland, a gentle soul, disliked being strict with anyone. At home, at work in the Public Library, he ruled by kindness and example. Up to now it had seemed to work.

'Not even for the children's sake?' he pleaded. 'They're not getting a wink of sleep—and Esther's got her mocks next week...'

*'Flower of Scotland,
When shall we seeeeeee ya likes aginnnnnn...?"*

they sang in horrible unison, for possibly the millionth time that day. The trio had a knack of reaching—and holding—notes that went right through you—and walls and vicinities.

'Why *now*?' he asked. 'You never used to be so bad.'

That was true. Mr Bland recalled the odd '*Screaming night*' from his childhood, but they'd been few and far between. On those occasions he remembered his Grandfather, and later his Dad, adjourning to the skulls' box room and swiftly restoring a lasting peace. But how had they done it? The knack, never explained, was now lost. Mr Bland freely accepted he wasn't the man they were. People, living or otherwise, never *used* to use the Blands as doormats.

"And rise a nationnnnnnn aginnnnnnn!"
'Aye.'
'The noo.'

Actually, he felt a bit guilty trying to wield the stick at all. What right had he to expect favours or cooperation when it was *his* ancestor that had brought them to this pass? Mr Bland did not approve of chopping people's heads off, even in wartime. And as for adding insult to injury in boiling and displaying them as 'trophies', well!

There'd been attempts to make amends but they wouldn't have it. When Grandfather tried to give them decent burial there was a house fire that took lives and still seared Bland family memory. No one had dared so much as move them after that. To be fair, they'd warned the curse would descend if they were shifted—and were as good as their word.

Apologies were likewise spurned and decent gestures sneered at. When Mr Bland put a Highland stag's head in their room, to '*make them feel at home*', they afflicted it with rampant mange that stank the house out. The fumigation bill had sorely tested an impecunious young married couple. When the ensuing little Blands put up childish tartan designs to please their guests, the trio (somehow) contrived to gob and puke mightily upon them.

The vicar attempted an exorcism after that, warning the dead heads that *'God counts the tears of children'*—but they projectile-puked on him as well.

So, they wouldn't be sent forth, nor explain their desire. Mr Bland suspected it was revenge—something so foreign to him as to resist comprehending. Instead, he persisted in thinking there must be a way to appease them—if only he persevered in good will long enough.

He also suspected they could read minds, for they sometimes responded to unposed questions. As now:

'Don't bet on it, English!'

'We'll be in guid voice toneet, the noo.'

'And every neet, aye...'

[x3] '*'Flower of Scotland, when shall we seeeeee yer likes aginnnnnnn?'*'

☸

'Spooky Olde England—'A Guide for American Visitors'

by Randy Hassleburger III

The OHM/Happy-Bisexual Press. California. 1997.

... DERBYSHIRE. (nr. LONDON).

Ashbourne. Councillor Drachman Crescent. Home of the famous 'Screaming Skulls', supposedly three of Bonnie King Charles' highland soldiers killed whilst on the retreat from Brighton during the 1745 Jacobite rebellion. The present owner, a direct descendent of their killer, retains the grisly prizes for fear of a dreadful curse that will descend on the family should the skulls ever be removed from his home. Sadly, he does not place them on display but it is said the unearthly wails may be heard throughout the neighbourhood on each anniversary of their fateful death. The neighbours all attest to this.

Do not approach the house. This author received a inhospitable welcome when he sought entry. The owner will not accept money(!) and neither do the Brit police—who were called when I persisted...'

☸

'Much better, Dad—but thanks for asking.'

Mr Bland's sigh of relief drained him of air.

Esther Bland dried her eyes and departed with an overnight bag. A spell away at her best friend Caitlin's was the Bland-consensus best option.

It had been a day of high emotion—not Mr Bland's favourite thing at the best of times, and least of all on a day off.

Esther had been jittery about her driving test to start with, even before the night campaigns and apparitions started. Knowing that, the trio had targeted her and gave the poor girl no rest. The vital 'night-before' her early appointment had been a virtuoso display of persecution. They'd screamed and whispered and threatened and revealed things thought safely secret. Morning found Esther a red-eyed, ready to explode, bag of nerves.

She failed her test.

The celebratory bottle of champagne was quietly stowed away, and Mr Bland had to wrestle with his own daughter to get an axe off her. During the polite tussle the skulls sang a ditty of their own composition.

'Oh, it's tickets and bus fares forever for you,
Just tickets and walking.
Och aye the noo!'

not the least worried by the girl's promise to split them into '*a million rotten pieces!*'

Then Mrs Bland stumbled upon the powerful sedatives in her daughter's room, sought, prescribed and taken in secret, and the row opened again on a second front. Rare disunity lightninged across the harmony Family Bland had built.

As the door shut on his beloved, beautiful—but unhappy—girl, Mr Bland wrestled again, this time to control unaccustomed sensations. Was this what is was like, he wondered, to feel *furious*?

Apparently it was: he couldn't help himself.

Bland levelled an accusing finger at the skulls' cabinet. Words came without asking.

'I'm... I'm... very *cross* with you!' he told them.

ALTERED ENGLANDS

In times past men sought sanctuary in churches but Mr Bland went to *W. H. Smooth*, the newsagents. He preferred the bigger branches but any size would do.

It was the sheer... *variety* that appealed, the solicitousness re modern society's needs. There were magazines pandering to every fad and fashion, a journal for any conceivable interest, from rose-growing to appreciation of naked ladies. Mr Bland knew the latter lurked on the top shelves even if he modestly declined to look up. They weren't for him—he only had eyes for Mrs Bland—but it was nice to know that even voluptuaries and lonely souls were catered for.

And as for the stationery and office accessories! There could surely be no cataloguing of them: such variety, such choice—things you didn't suspect you needed till you saw them. Nowadays there were even music and video departments: a cornucopia of modern solaces available for just the flash of a credit card.

Mr Bland rarely actually bought anything but in just wandering the aisles he relearnt that civilisation was getting bigger and better and... well, nicer. There was no call for anyone to be melancholic, not when even '*Airgun World*' and '*Science-Fiction Modeller Monthly*' were produced to please their tiny audiences.

There'd been bad times before—like when Young-Man-Bland had... well, why mince words?—conceived a fierce but chaste love for Mrs Peel from *The Avengers*. It had quite disturbed his equilibrium during vital Librarianship exams. *W. H. Smooth* had restored proper perspective then, and now he had hopes it would work its magic again, to heal this new and worse emergency.

In pondering *what* a lot of books Terry Pratchett wrote, Mr Bland was almost there, so very nearly restored to serenity. One more turn round the calendar section should have seen him home and dry.

He never made it. Trouble had tricked its way even into this cathedral of calming influences.

Mr Bland had already spotted the rash of new '*Unexplained*' and 'X-something' magazines, and again thought it only cheering that people dissatisfied by rationality should be so amply provided for. Which was especially nice because in general society was usually dismissive—even rude—about such unfortunates.

Then, on the matt black cover of '*High Weirdness*'—*Issue 2 FREE with number 1!!!!!*" his roving eye betrayed him in spotting three skulls—triple toothy smirks in a row.

Reluctant hands sought the slim journal. They turned to the relevant pages. Heartbeat and bloodflow faltered.

They'd only printed his full address, that's all—and even directions on how to get there! Someone had leaned over his fence to *photograph* his house—and chosen a moment when Esther was sunbathing in the garden. And his name was Bland, not *'Blind'*, and *no*, he wasn't willing to *'show visitors round at all times'*!

Some wild voice in his head told him to bite bite *bite* the bloody rag, then screw it up and clogdance on it—but people like him don't do things like that. Mr Bland carefully replaced the journal.

'*£2.99?*' commented the normal part of his mind. '*That's a bit steep...*'

'*Shut the **** up!*' answered another part, less often heard.

His dejected feet sought the exit. It lay through the video department.

And there, *flaunting* itself, bold and brassy—and tempting—as a *loose woman*, he found the solution to his problem.

The only question was, did he have the will to go nuclear?

❂

'*Beware the fury of a patient man.*'
John Dryden '*Absalom and Achitophel*' (1681) 1.1005.

❂

Esther's room was empty. She was not at home like a knocked out front tooth isn't home. The absence was palpable. A note said:

'*Sorry but I can't stand it any more. I've found a little bedsit in town. Love you to bits*'
E.

And there were four kisses, thus: XXXX

ALTERED ENGLANDS

Mr Bland looked up the stairs towards *their* door and said... nothing. If the gruesome threesome had really known him, or accounted him more than just another *Sassenach*, they would have worried about that. They most certainly would not have sung:

> "His bonnie lies over the ocean,
> His bonnie lies over the sea,
> His bonnie lies over the ocean,
> And she'll nay be hame for tea!"

Those *voices* that had once communed with his ancestor, the same advisors that had advocated decapitation, now spoke again to a Bland—and found lusty answer. Even the fictional—but convincing and leather-clad—Mrs Peel joined their throng to purr affirmation.

In his mind's eye Mr Bland saw a resolute finger stab at a red button labelled '*NUKE!*'

❈

'... *nuke the entire site from orbit. It's the only way to be sure.*'
Ellen Ripley (2092-2179?). '*Aliens*'. 1986.

❈

It was a simple matter to put a glass front on their cabinet. Then the work of mere moments, facilitated by a well-stocked and neatly arranged DIY-box, to bolt on a TV and video facing the bony trio.

What with that and his grim silence the three grew perturbed. They sensed something was up.

'Hey, English! What's wi yew?'
'We'll sing!'
'We'll scream!'
'Nae peace for yeeeeeee!' they threatened in unison.

Mr Bland confronted them. The trio noticed a difference in him: extra stiffening in the spine and ancient fire lancing from the eyes. For the first time in generations they were afraid.

He showed them an empty plastic box. Its contents were already whirring within the puzzling black machine facing them. Words were scrolling across the screen above.

> *BBC SPORTS VIDEO*
> *'England's Glory—Scotland's Agony!*
> *Football between the 'Auld Enemies'*
> *From 1961 (England 9 Scotland 3)*
> *to Euro 96 (England 2 Scotland 0)*
> *A treat for England fans everywhere!'*

'£4.99 at W. H. Smooth's,' Mr Bland informed them, in his new, pitiless, voice. 'They had a sale.'

And then the river of bile and belligerence reversed to head in their direction.

They endured bravely—for a while—till realisation came that this volcano would never run out of lava. Wicked Mr Bland had rigged up a loop-tape. The screaming began.

✼

And continued for weeks without cease. They also cursed and threatened to *'Do such things—what they were yet they knew not—but they should be the terrors of the earth!'*

Mr Bland turned a deaf ear to it. Mrs B and the younger children had retreated to her mother's, and Esther was safe in her bedsit. All the neighbours were primed. He'd told them—*told* them—that this was a war to end wars—and thus a price worth paying.

None of them argued. No one argued with Mr Bland any more.

✼

'*Yuks!*' said the little child.

Esther smiled at her grandson and hobbled forward.

'Don't be frightened,' she told him. 'We're friends now.'

The boy looked dubious. He'd been prepared for this first meeting but it was still a shock—and he almost left his skin behind when the skulls spoke.

'Aye!'

'Best o' pals.'

'The noo!'

'He's a bonnie wee boy.'

'Aye.'

'A braw wee *Sassenach*.'

After that flattery he lost his fear and chattered away freely to the severed heads. They condescended to let him dust and polish them—a rare favour—and the link was bonded for another generation.

Then, with that hurdle successfully past, the New Year's party started to go with a swing.

They'd outlasted the first video tape but fell sullen silent before it did. Then even the video machine grew wonky with repeating its identical replacements. The war bogged down into attrition: men (sort of) against machine. In such an unequal struggle the outcome, though postponed, can never be in doubt. Mr Bland was prepared to buy as many videos as need be, whereas the flesh (or bone) is weak. One day, albeit long after, they signalled they'd had enough.

Each side having suffered sufficient for honour's sake, the atmosphere became propitious for peace talks. Esther never learnt what had been agreed all those years ago but a new spirit of accord prevailed ever after.

Alas, Mr Bland was no longer around to see it. He'd played his part, reverted to his true, kinder, self, and in due course gone on to where—in strict theology—the skulls' occupants really ought to be.

What they did the rest of the year nobody knew. What—quiet—conversations they now conducted amongst themselves remained obscure. The only thing well established—if fact, firm tradition—was the trio's emerging for New Year's Eve—or *Hogmanay*.

Some male Blands—in the privacy of house and family and for a few hours only—wore kilts in honour of their guests. The skulls in turn consented to be chalked by the children with the red and white of England's flag. Each side could not do enough for one another.

And then—also for that one night only—the neighbours would tolerate the singing: an unearthly blend of Bland voices and three others, as hand in hand—or hand on skull—they celebrated another year of good accord.

"Should auld acquaintance be forgot,
And never brought to mind?
We'll tak a cup o' kindness, yet,
For auld lang syne..."

❀

The mortals could not hear it but from far away their chorus was melodiously augmented.

High in Heaven, Bonnie Prince Charlie and Butcher Cumberland and Mr Bland—reconciled combatants of Culloden—sang along.

The senior historian angel smiled on each group, both up above and still below. It was beyond high time and he took up his pen with pleasure.

Some centuries after conventional dating for the event, the angel recorded the end of the 1745 Jacobite Rebellion.

❀

32~

ENLIGHTENMENT

✹

INTRODUCTION

Akin to the German sense of humour,[122] the story 'Enlightenment' is no laughing matter. Indeed, in more melancholic mood, I have sometimes feared that this tale (in the immortal words of the Sex Pistols in *'Holiday in the Sun'*) constitutes:

'A cheap holiday in other people's <u>misery</u>…'

Nevertheless, in my defence, should defence be needed, I can only protest that my intentions were sincere. But thereagain, so were Hitler's and Stalin's. Well, okay: maybe not Stalin's…

Saying which supplies an elegant link to this searing tale about Stalin's legacy and the enduring horrors created by his students. The man himself may have died and gone to boost Hell's fuel bill in 1953, but we are not free of him and his yet…

Plus, as if all this were not vaunting ambition enough, 'Enlightenment' also undertakes the modest task of interweaving Zen Buddhism and contemporary North Korea—that is to say, from the sublime to the sickening.

---

[122] Peter Sellers said it. Blame him. He's dead.

Both subjects notoriously defy description, albeit for very different reasons. The reader's indulgence is therefore craved.

Inspiration for the tale originally stems from that great conundrum beyond which there are few greater, to wit: ultimately, who is the wisest? The compassionate or the cruel? Saints or Saddam? My humble hero herein, Park, or cocksure Kim Jong-il?

The only answer to which I know of (save pagan despair) is this: *'We shall see. One day—perhaps soon—we <u>shall</u> see.'*

ALTERED ENGLANDS

ENLIGHTENMENT

'Without a jot of ambition left
I let my nature flow where it will.
There are ten days of rice in my bag
And, by the hearth, a bundle of firewood.
Who prattles of illusion or nirvana?
Forgetting the equal dusts of name and fortune,
Listening to the night rain on the roof of my hut,
I sit at ease, both legs stretched out.'

Ryoken (1758-1831). Zen poet.

The sage must have lived in happier days than these, Park reflected, to have *ten whole days* of rice! Whereas his own larder held no more than a thin week's worth, plus some fermented tofu—which nevertheless placed him amongst the favoured few in 1990s North Korea. But as for ample firewood, well, forget it.

Park rebuked his non-Buddha nature. This was meant to be a discourse of the above-waistline portions, not a litany from his guts. Consider instead, Park told himself, in master-pupil tones, the *principles* outlined. Are you not free to copy the poet's sublime sentiments? Or failing those, at least his stance?

Indeed he was. There existed—just—room in his cubby-hole cum accommodation, and a wall to rest his back against. Relaxing from the lotus position, Park made himself comfortable. He directed his feet to the nearby cosiness: an unintended gift from the palace beyond. Park luxuriated.

Abandoning the memorized poem, he then tried hard to see reality. The one visible via the inner eye.

What Park saw was daylight dappling the room beyond in lattice form, artistry born of the windows' anti-missile grilles. Happily, the same safeguards also filtered out all the barking from the barracks and parade grounds below. Try as mankind might, there *was* beauty. The dust danced for Park, mobile motes transfixed by golden spears.

'*And HE is not expected back today!*' said a fugitive thought, then fled like a naughty child before it could be caught.

The notion was as warming as the palace radiators, but, alas, of the forbidden kind, the sort that must remain buried like some sleeping dragon, never burrowing up to show its face at the surface. Park harboured a whole tribe of them, fierce but secret and subterranean. He did not think anyone suspected their existence. In fact he was sure of it, for otherwise he would be dead by now, or in the camps—which amounted to the same thing. Park owed his survival to inscrutability. Being a second-generation lackey helped there, as did guidance from Ryoken and other Zen masters.

Today though, he might have been safe to smile. He was alone save for, in another parallel with Ryoken, the raindrops to keep him company. Park now let their pitter-patter on the palace roof form the anchor for his meditation. Thereafter, when pleasure and desires and other errant notions popped into being, the rain was there to gently wash them away.

It did the trick. Even the telephone's ring, hot and hostile, from the room beyond, did not distract. Portion by portion, Park became *mindful*, and though the raindrops hinted at meaning, maybe even a message from Heaven, just as with the telephone he paid no heed. Breathing was all and *sunyatta*, the great voidness, the universal source, beckoned. Which contained within it Truth and Nature and Suchness and Mind—and everything that is and is not. From it wafted the perfume of Nirvana.

In search of that delectable scent Park passed into *za-zen*: proper meditation. Today he did not need to contemplate the paradoxes of the *One Hand Clapping, the Soundless Sound,* or *One's Original Face* koans. *Wu wei* worked: the 'actionless action'. Without movement, Park pursued his highest ambition: enlightenment.

It was still beyond view when into the harmony of emptiness crashed noise. From outside, in every sense.

ALTERED ENGLANDS

Much time had passed. In the room beyond was the half-light of dusk, or as much of it as the grim grilles permitted. Park returned to earth on a greased slide of fear: sudden, jarring. He had been self-deluded. That had not been mindfulness but mere dozing! How else could he have missed hearing a motorcade of so many cars? Including armoured-cars!

Again, he had betrayed himself with desire. Even desiring enlightenment was still desire: lust even. Perhaps he had learned nothing, progressing not one inch towards his goal.

Unseen, the outer doors slammed back. Boots thundered across marble, a *tsunami* of boots. Shiny leather boots upon shiny stone, the slap of once-living upon never-lived. Then the inner sanctum's entrance flew open. Likewise unseen by Park, it was surveyed. Exhaustively. In silence. Long silence. Then they entered in waves.

Inspected by eyes simultaneously hot and cold: furnace-heat and fish-frigid, Park was not found wanting. On the contrary, he was found ready, bowing low. Which sufficed to save him.

Those cold eyes of the guards, the cold steel of their guns, took in Park's existence and stance, and the fact that the cubby-hole could not possibly hold anyone but he. The rice-paper carpet, which would record any trespassing from his kennel, had been intact. Which was all that was needful to know about this nameless flunkey. The boots backtracked. Park raised his eyes.

The soldiers—inner *inner* cadre—withdrew like ghosts, bearing that day's now ruined rice-paper floor with them. Then for a while there was no one, or so it seemed—but Park knew better. He could sense if he was in the *presence* or not.

In due course, in his own good time, the 'Dear Leader' crossed Park's line of view. Park bowed deeper still, even though it would not be noted.

No, he was not noted at all. Park's presence was just assumed.

'Tea!' said the Dear Leader. 'And Five Star! And TV!'

The first two were easy, practiced to perfection ten thousand times. Although each could be done *mindfully*, making repetition easier, gilded even.

First royal ginseng tea with gold-leaf sprinkle, stirred with a solid silver spoon before the Dear Leader's very eyes—because ancient tradition held that silver reacted to poison. Then, served steaming in finest translucent porcelain, proffered up from kneeling.

Next: Hennessey *Five Star* cognac, specially imported for the Dear Leader, in his favourite chunky tumbler—an inscribed fraternal gift from the *'Communist Party of Great Britain (Marxist-Leninist)'*. The rich liquid lapped against the glass and left languid tidemarks. Its heady fumes beguiled master and servant alike.

But the third and last was hard: hard on eyes and ears and soul. Because the Dear Leader demanded that the cubby-hole door be kept always open unless decreed otherwise. And whilst eyes could be closed or averted, ears remained vulnerable to the screams. And as for the soul…

After a hard day of doing whatever it was he did outside the palace, the Dear Leader liked to unwind watching footage from the camps. It was—literally—incredible what happened to the poor inmates there. Worse than any mere nightmare could devise.

There'd been a new delivery of tapes. Aware of its contents Park had gripped the first cassette by fingertips alone as he loaded it into the machine. The black stack of them beside the monster TV radiated an evil aura.

Park didn't understand—doubtless because he was just a simple man. He realized that these were all enemies of the people, perhaps even allies of the American devils, but surely a simple bullet would suffice? That would be clean and show compassion. But where was the pleasure in tormenting living skeletons? And why bother with recordings when the current famine brought such scenes almost to central Pyongyang itself? You could watch people dying in the suburbs for free.

Park comforted himself with the thought that the ways of politics were strange: a closed book to a mere worker such as he.

Back in his cubby-hole home, crouching in its furthest recess, Park's spine suddenly chilled. He'd had a horrible thought. Didn't butchers torture dogs to death to make their meat adrenalin rich and so taste better? So maybe…

No. No! *Wicked* thought! Bad as the famine was surely no one would so far forget their Buddha-nature as to become cannibals? Of their fellow citizens? *Surely…?*

Park's heart said one thing, his head another. So he plunged the notion into the ocean of universal truth and held it there till it stopped moving. Then he carefully recalled the four-fold *Noble Truths*. First amongst them was that Life was suffering; the third that suffering could be overcome. The eight-fold Right Path which stemmed from the Truths carried men above suffering. And all things, even suffering, were only temporary…

ALTERED ENGLANDS

Mercifully, the Dear Leader soon tired of repetition. This particular cassette concerned the Christians—and the camps were especially savage with them. Even Earth's supreme intellect could only take so many crucifixions, one after another. So the Dear Leader called for Park and alternative entertainment. Park scurried out at speed.

'Film!' Noun, imperative. 'You choose.' Order, not invitation.

Kim Jong-il slugged down more Hennessey. The eyes behind the round-rimmed glasses were goggled, unfocussed. 'You know what I like…'

Did he? Well, yes he did. But the *responsibility*! Park's guts froze, liquefied, then froze again. This man—if he could be shrunk to so tiny a title—sprawled behind him was the equal of Einstein and Marx combined. Presidents hung upon his lightest word. Had not a speaking swallow *and* double rainbow heralded his birth? Did he not play world-class basketball *and* golf from first attempt? His IQ was immeasurable, soaring off all scales like a rocket from his missile program. The North Korean Institute of Clinical Psychology confirmed it so. And now his gaze was burning upon Park's skinny frame, awaiting action. Appropriate action.

Park had just two seconds, three at most, before mankind's mightiest mind became impatient. Then the Hennessey-fuelled temper might flare. The Dear Leader went armed at all times: a pearl-handled pistol that could penetrate three prisoners stood in line. Park had seen it done.

Crouching before the serried video library, Park sought refuge in Zen, seeking the artless art. Simultaneously, he prayed for the opening of the *Dharma* eye. Then, fortified by faith, his arm extended and snatched.

'*Godzilla V*'.

Joy! He had been guided. It was appropriate. It was Buddha's prescribed '*middle way*', a bridge between crucifixions and boredom. More importantly, it was a favourite.

'Mmmm…' The Dear Leader purred and snuggled down, tumbler clutched to his chest. Cognac slopped over its lip to stain his silk jacket, but he did not notice.

There must be no foreplay. The Dear Leader could not be troubled with intros or slow bits. Park had prepared multiple copies, each ready to roll at various exciting parts.

Park hit the button and then withdrew, crab-like, backwards, folded in on himself, aspiring to invisibility. Meanwhile, behind him, a giant lizard ravished Tokyo.

The Dear Leader smiled.

Until the telephone rang.

It was the old-fashioned one—even by North Korean standards—that occupied centre stage on the Dear Leader's desk. It rarely rang, but when it did…

In a blur of motion, Kim hurled the tumbler aside and was on his platformed-shoed feet. He killed the film, even though homes, cars and people were being trampled. The second both hands were free he brushed his uniform down and bouffant up.

Park was already back in his cubby-hole, slamming the door shut. This time he needed no permission: it was mandatory. He knew the drill well. Then, seeking the furthest wall away, Park clamped his hands over his ears.

❂

'Without a jot of ambition left
I let my nature flow where it will.
There are ten days of rice in my bag
And, by the hearth, a bundle of firewood.
Who prattles of … of …'

Though it was only a day since he last recited it, Park simply could not recall the missing word. Was it is *'illusion'* or *'nirvana'*? *Or 'sunyatta'*? Or something else entirely?

He adjusted his lotus stance, suddenly aware of myriad minor discomforts. Plus a persistent itch above his left eyebrow. They were not there before, or if so, not noticed.

No matter. Let them be and let memory play her flirty tricks. Park would not pursue her. Another poem or *koan* would serve to slide him into proper meditation. Like, for instance, his old favourite: *'What was your original face, before your parents were born?'* That would do.

No it wouldn't. Park had been working on Ryoken and felt himself near to… yes, well, enlightenment. The poem had become a mantra, with precise wording. Anything else was … inappropriate, jarring. The right word was needed to resume the right path.

Park cudgelled his mind but it did not take kindly to blows, instead retreating defiant to some inner sanctum. *'Gentle, brother! Gentle!'* it called back. *'You will not get what you want that way!'*

Which left only one other way. Park reluctantly opened his eyes and looked up.

He could see the very volume on the Dear Leader's bookshelf, peeping out from all the paperbacks and porn, tantalizing him in its slim scarlet jacket. It was the source from whence he'd stolen those words in the first place. That precious store which had started him on the path towards enlightenment. Siren-like, it and some other Zen classics had once called to him, and he had answered to find a jewel of incalculable price. The call was no less strong today.

Park knew that this was *craving*. And craving was the subject of the Buddha's second Noble Truth: namely that craving was the *cause* of suffering. But what he craved for was the cessation of craving: so perhaps it was nevertheless right action?

It was a paradox, a *koan* in itself, which could become the subject for future meditations. Once he had Ryoken cracked.

Had he the courage? Park looked within and located it instantly, though well hidden. Everyone thought him a broken reed, a servile dog; but they were wrong—or mostly so. He'd found courage by setting his feet along the right path and courage had proved to be a faithful friend. Today it was waiting there for him, willing to guide him further on.

Park arose. He straightened and stretched his limbs, summoning them to suppleness. Then, arms aloft for balance, he danced.

He danced into the far room, the Dear Leader's domain. On tiptoe he alighted on the rice-paper carpet, but so light as to barely be there, so fleeting as to leave no trace. And so *swift!* Without pause, performing ceaseless movement, Park aligned himself with the atoms he passed by and through. He was at one with the transient nature of all things. Momentum, not will, carried him, nor by the straightest route, to his destination. The artless art permitted Park miracles.

At the bookshelf he paused, *en pointe*, on some inadvertent space left between rice-paper and floor. He drew breath, he monitored breath, he *was* breath. Breath was all: the kernel of Zen. He recharged his mindfulness. His occupation of this place, this conjunction of particles, had never occurred before and would never occur again. Park drank it in and did not pass judgment. *Mindfulness.*

Then he *invited* the book to his hand. Park felt its leather cover on his fingertips, he scented its pages as they offered up their content, their purpose. It obliged him and opened like a lotus flower at morning. To exactly the right page. A sign of *rightness.*

'Who prattles of illusion or nirvana?'

Who indeed? Not the wise. Not the enlightened.

Park closed the book and, eyes shut, stroked it back to precisely its former position. Not even dust was disturbed. Again the artless art. This reading had never been. No one would ever know.

Exhaling every particle of air and then drawing in fresh supply, Park set off home. The same dance but a different way, whirling an alternative route round the desk. Perfection the world would never see.

Except that perfection belongs to God alone. A telephone rang. Startled out of attunement, Park's arm dipped a degree. His sleeve caught the receiver. It toppled towards the floor.

Park did not have enough time for haste. There must be calm, *much* calm and total reflection.

He caught the receiver before it hit the rice-paper. First priority. Otherwise the pristine white would be sundered. A sign sufficient to secure his death. Then, expelling breath through gritted teeth, Park slowly settled his stance, relying on the padded parts of the feet to respect the virgin surface beneath them.

A moment of mindfulness, and then back into the illusion of the passing moment.

It was the old-fashioned phone! It *would* have to be that one! Park winced. Even the scarlet Yankee hotline would have been better!

There was a voice. Barking from the Bakelite. Echoey and from far away. It sounded angry.

Park brought the receiver nearer his ear: not close but nearer.

There should be no way of knowing, but there was. Wherever it was coming from was cold. But also curiously warm... Another *koan* in the making.

At first the words did not make sense, it was a mad man shouting in a foreign tongue. Though wasn't that some Russian in there? Park had studied Russian at school, before the regimes fell out. But then, bit by bit, the discourse morphed to contain more Korean.

'Death is the solution for all problems!' said the voice, screaming now. 'No man—no problem! Die, but do not retreat! War! Now! *War!*'

Then suddenly it was calmness itself, without interlude; a vehicle going from speed to stillness in an instant. Unnatural.

'Who *is* this?' it asked, all prickly suspicion. 'Who *are* you?'

Park knew that at this moment he must *not* be mindful. It was sure and certain knowledge as a free gift from the Void. Uniquely, mindfulness at this moment would be neither right-path nor wholesome. He replaced the receiver.

Park also knew about the single security hair always left pasted over that particular telephone. The Dear Leader thought Park didn't but he did. There it was, a holy relic from the planet's supreme being, lying black upon the rice-paper.

Warily retrieved, it was replaced with mere mortal spittle.

Then, lifting one foot, then the other, Park checked the floor covering. Impeccable: not a single stretch mark, not one speck of sweat. Park subdued a inner bat-squeak of pride. Pride was not right-path.

Taken literally, the right-path now was straight back to his cubby-hole home, and quick about it. Park refreshed his mindfulness and then resumed the dance where it had been left off.

Strangely enough, when he checked later, he found that Ryoken's missing words had gone missing again. Something had sucked them out of him.

☸

In due course the Dear Leader returned, with cacophony and clattering. His guards studied the rice-paper carpet, as always, but found no flaw—as always. Park sighed in relief—in silence.

Full of bonhomie, amongst other things, the Dear Leader even deigned to address him.

'Hey you! Yes, you! I've been playing golf. Round in forty-two, including five holes in one! Can you believe that? You *can?* Amazing!'

He must have been celebrating that world record in his massive clubhouse-for-one. Hennessy Five Star most likely, in a balloon glass big enough for him to swim in. Then the Dancing Team for after-golf entertainment, the Happiness Team for massage, and completion with…

intimate services from the Satisfaction Team. His Field Marshall's overalls were dishevelled and his mind likewise.

Thereafter the Dear Leader took his normal no-notice of Park, or any other furniture. Save for the old-fashioned telephone: he noticed *that*—as always. Park spotted it from the corner of an averted eye. But the plastered hair passed muster. The constriction in Park's chest could ease.

The ritual of tea and cognac and TV might well have followed had not the telephone rang. *That* phone.

The Dear Leader sprang to attention and his full five foot six inches (four of them courtesy of shoe-lifts) height. Park's heart spasmed likewise, but he couldn't let that delay him closing the cubby-hole door. Or seeking the far wall and chanting. Anything else would be noted.

Park did not fear death as such—that would constitute *craving*, and attachment—and be craven to boot. But sudden death, the sort that stole you away without time for mindfulness of it: that *was* to be avoided. He wished to have a death *haiku* ready to recite before the swirling chaos of rebirth. Something stylish and polished as a freshwater pebble. However, only two lines, the first and third, existed in draft yet (playing upon a man's first garment—swaddling—and last—a shroud). The vital connecting middle sentence was nebulous. Thus it was not yet time.

And so, for the very first occasion, Park eavesdropped. He clamped his ears, he softly chanted the alphabet and party-slogans—'*The Project to Guarantee Longevity of the Dear Leader is the Sacred Duty of all!*'—as instructed and usual, but meanwhile, strand by strand he separated each audible element till only one remained.

It was a Zen trick, and also worked with pain. By segregating each sensation, mindfully replacing it *just* off the ear or injured part, there could be constructed a riot of noise, a starburst of hurt, that, though close, was unconnected to you. What was left was the coolness of non-pain—or the single selected sound.

Away went the party-jingles about the Dear Leader and tractor production. Gone was the booming of Park's breath and whirr of myriad Palace machines. Ultimately there remained only silence—and one other thing: still indistinct.

Then Park penetrated the dead trees of the door, and his hearing was suddenly free and untrammelled, out into the room beyond. The sense paused briefly to reflect on the wonder of this, before homing in on a one-sided conversation.

'Who?
'No. No!'
'Not for some time.'
'It can't have been.'
'Are you sure?'
'Then I'll put him down. Bang! What? But...'
'Right away, boss. I'll find out.'

And then footsteps.

Park reeled in his antennae at speed. They slashed back like a whiplash, joined along the way by all the excluded frequencies. Each arrived at intervals and jostled for good order. Until they sorted themselves out nothing made sense. Park's head was a Babel where all the voices were his. Until:

'You. What is your name?'

For the very first time Kim Jong-il had opened the cubby-hole door himself. HIS hands had grasped the handle just like a common or garden human, and exerted power to alter its position. Park would never again be able to handle it without feelings of awe and blasphemy. If he was still around to have the opportunity...

'Park, Comrade Leader.'

'Park what?'

The focus and heat of divine curiosity was too much. Park liquefied and melted floorwards.

'Just Park, Comrade Leader...'

To be a second generation servant of the Korean leadership was to need no first name, no other identifier than clan. *'You!'* would have sufficed.

Enlightenment dawned on he who the Party press said already knew all.

'Oh, you're one of *them*, are you? Really? I *thought* your face was familiar...'

Then the Dear Leader lost the thread for a second, bemused by the vagaries of human intercourse, or maybe attacked by earlier Hennessys.

'Where was I? Oh yes: have you been out of your cage? But how? What about the rice-paper and everything? Have you learned to levitate? Then you should let the People's Army in on the secret: our tanks could float over the Yankees and straight into Seoul!'

Unable to resist, the Dear Leader's glasses glazed over for a second as he savoured that delicious vision. Then he recalled reality. Apparently it had a bitter taste.

'More importantly, whatever your name is, have you touched the telephone? *The* telephone?'

Prostrate, Park edged his eyes up from the floor.

'Not *entirely*, Dear Leader…'

It was the closest he dare steer to a negative. The Dear Leader descended from the *'Great Leader'*, Kim Il-Sung! He who, although tragically deceased, had recently been declared 'Eternal President' of the Democratic People's Republic of Korea. This fruit of those loins now looming (as best he could) over Park, this divine force shoehorned into diminutive human form, was both Mother, Father *and* embodiment of the nation. He could never be given a blunt *'No'*.

The Dear Leader giggled—a jarringly girlish sound. His pearl-handled pistol rested by his side, a forgotten extra finger now that he'd been given fresh instructions.

'Liar. Anyhow, Buddha knows why, but he wants to talk to you …'

'*He*', Dear Leader?'

'Yep, He. *He!* Hurry up, the line's not always reliable…'

Shrinking so as not to tower over the Dear Leader, Park followed like a dog being dragged to the pot. At the threshold to Kim's domain he heard the voice still ranting away, even though the receiver hung down beside the desk, unheeded.

'Go on.' The Dear Leader waved him through, highly amused. 'You've already met so I won't introduce you…'

Park shuffled forward and took up the instrument as he would have a turd. Likewise, he held it near but not *to* his ear.

Once again, the tirade swiftly adjusted from flowing, furious Russian to pidgin, then fluent, Korean.

'… and call their bluff! Are you man or mouse? Invade! Warhead! *Warhead!* I tell you, the Americans are paper tigers! The Europeans? Ha! Don't make me laugh—*ladymen!* Belgians? Molesters of children!'

Like all his twenty million+ countrymen, Park looked to the Dear Leader for guidance, but he received only a smirk and pistol wave in return.

'Get a move on: don't be shy.'

Park addressed the mouthpiece. It reeked of the Dear Leader and fear and adrenalin. Forcing himself, he mouthed the word *'Hello?'*—but nothing audible emerged. The voice continued unabated.

'Always remember: weaklings deserve it! Pound them! Cuba? A humiliation! That shit Khrushchev's fault! Should have smashed them in the mush! Turn cities into glass! Guevara had it right. Che was a *real* man. Pre-emptive strike! Now! Strike!'

By the end it was a scream, a madman's hysteria.

'Hello?' said Park, under compulsion. Second time around he had success, albeit a mere whisper.

'The world *wants* to be deceived!' raged the voice, unfazed. 'One man dead? That's a tragedy. But one million? Ten? Fifty? That's just *statistics*!'

Then the gears changed, crashing from bloodlust to mistrust in an instant.

'Hang on, who *is* this? Is that you again? The silent one? Where did you go last time? I hadn't dismissed you! Speak up, damn your eyes! Who are you?'

The words had to be forced out, one by one.

'My… name… is… Park. I serve the Dear…'

The voice became extra urgent, almost wheedling. It wasn't as omnipotent as it made out. And it didn't *listen*.

'What country do you run? How many tanks? Atomic bombs? Hydrogen bombs are better!' Then, suddenly plaintive: 'Can you warm me? It's cold here… Can you help an old man?'

There was indeed ice travelling up the line from the caller. Sentient ice. It was in Park's hand and questing for the vein that led direct to his head.

Park looked up, pleading with the Dear Leader. He might as well have sought mercy from the marble on the floor.

'I don't have any…,' he said—to the phone—not, please Buddha, to the caller.

Wasted breath. Whatever words he said were being selectively heeded.

'Put Mao on the line. That's an order! What's become of him? He hasn't answered in ages. Bastard! Or Castro. Not even Hoxha in Albania. And as for that fucking kraut, Honecker! What's going on? It's not *fair*! Warhead! *Warhead!*'

The caller's sanity never lasted long. It was fragile and jerry-built. The voice went from conspiratorial to complaining to rant-mode without interval.

'Have you *smashed* them? Put a bullet in their heads? Good old lead poisoning? Ha ha ha ha ha ha ha ha! You'll never sleep more calmly. *HA* ha ha ha ha ha ha ha! Good *boy!* That's the way to do it! Invade! Purge! Death is the solution!'

The laughter became almost liquid, each syllable melting into the next and ranging the octaves exactly like human voices can't. More than ever, the caller sounded *confined*, instantly resonating from nearby surfaces. And though he had complained of cold, Park was detecting heat now, organic, humid, heat…

The malignity got too much. Any minute now Park expected acid to spout from the receiver and melt his face. He hurled the phone from him like something toxic and contagious.

The Dear Leader caught it. His smile was as broad and bold as an oncoming car-grille.

'Comrade General Secretary?' he said down the line, interrupting—respectfully but with difficulty—the crazy flow. 'My humble greetings once again, Revered Architect. It is I. Yes. Yes. Er… no—the Korean one. No, Great Helmsman, not that one. His son…'

The Dear Leader retained residual humanity enough to steal an embarrassed glance at Park before continuing.

'Yes. Yes. Absolutely. Yes, I'm sure: 1997. No, *ninety*-seven. Really. What? Him? His what? I don't know—I did ask but keep forgetting. Excuse me one moment…'

The Dear Leader covered the receiver with his hand and turned to Park.

'What did you say your name was—is?'

Park humbly enlightened him again. They'd only known each other since childhood.

The Dear Leader relayed the information.

'His name is Park and he is nothing. He has been disobedient in troubling you. I'll give him to you if you want…'

Apparently there was potential interest in that, but more details were required.

The Dear Leader looked Park up and down, with wry amusement.

'No, comrade; he has no warheads *None*. And no tanks, no torturers, no *anything*. What? Pardon? I don't know: I shouldn't think so but I'll ask.'

Kim paused, his hand once again keeping the exchange one-way.

'He wants to know if you ever meditate.'

Before the Dear Leader's god-like gaze poor Park could only be an open book. No answer was necessary.

'*Really?*' Kim was astounded, as if he'd arrived home early and found a family pet playing the piano.

Then, to the caller:

'Apparently he does. Live and learn! Huh-huh. I see.'

Sunlight slatted by the window shields caught Kim's glasses. For a second the lenses were circlets of white fire. They turned to Park.

'Comrade Stalin says… Oh, what is it *now*? *Do* try and keep up, peasant! Stalin, *yes*. Of *course* they put a telephone in his coffin. How else could he keep in touch? Now, as I was saying, Comrade Stalin says he'll meet you shortly. He also says he *'looks forward'* to it!' Kim couldn't help but chuckle. 'Poor you…,' he concluded.

Naturally, Park had heard of Joseph Vissarionovich Dzhugashvili, aka Comrade Stalin, 'Uncle Joe', Supreme Spokesman of the Proletariat and etc. He'd always been a part of Park's life, woven into every facet of state propaganda. Which also consistently conceded that the man was dead…

Fortunately, Park's overalls were black, so they did not betray his onslaughts of sweat. Drenched in that and horror, Park recoiled to his cubbyhole—before being ordered there. Doubly fortunate for him, the Dear Leader did not notice his mutinous initiative. Now the comic interlude was over and the clown departing, Kim was preoccupied. He had serious matters to discuss with his special advisor.

To prepare himself, the Dear Leader was drawing upon *Communist Zen*—whose existence a mortified Park had not suspected till now. Forgetting brandy, the 2000-girl-strong Pleasure Groups, the 32 villas and palaces, and absolutely every inessential, Jong-il groped towards communion with *History*, to make sacrifice to it. One of its former high priests was on the line waiting to help him…

'Revered Comrade,' said Kim eventually, entwined with the receiver like a lover, 'I need your guidance. It's about the Counter-proliferation summit. The Americans are talking tough. What should I do?'

It was a few days later. Park missed both big toes a lot less now. Of his infinite kindness, the Dear Leader had arranged sedatives to be prescribed. *After* the secateurs.

'Don't mention,' said the Dear Leader at the time, 'but no more levitating, comrade. Keep off the rice-paper. And don't get gangrene and die on me. That's an order too. Don't forget you've an appointment to keep…'

Park was huddled against the furthest wall of his cubby-hole again, as he had been then. He sat with both—bandaged—legs stretched out, but unlike Ryoken was not *'at ease'*. He would move to eat, to attend to nature or the Dear Leader, but not otherwise. Meanwhile, his sole meditation was Stalin. And the *implications*.

Which… which were that when both ego *and* wrongdoing were stupendous enough, apparently rebirth could be defied! The great cycle of existence shouldered aside. A sort of anti-nirvana…

Which was a negation of the Buddha's Noble Truths. Perhaps even a calculated insult. For what did Comrade Stalin care about Buddha? How many *divisions* did Buddha have?

Meanwhile, the Noble Truths remained noble, certainly, but *true*…? Could Truth accommodate exceptions? It was almost a *koan*; a fit topic for meditation.

Except that Park was done with meditation and *koans*. Both were barred to him. The day after his mutilation he ventured into *za-zen*. He'd deemed it essential, because if one's soul was not burnished in *this* life, then the next must be either the same or worse. Which, like the Noble Truths issue, just did not bear thinking about…

Therefore, he'd overruled wisdom, he'd shushed caution; perhaps even succumbed to craving. Craving for solace and salvation from his suffering. Even though, as noted before, the second Noble Truth said craving is the *cause* of suffering. Another paradox that must be left to others now.

No sooner had Park closed his eyes and made his breath mindful, then *He* was there. A corpse-cold presence, perpetually questing. *He* did not have to worry about cravings, *or* conscience, *or* justice. Stalin was above judgment. The Great Helmsman was eternally everywhere and nowhere in the void for those who knew of him. And Park knew of him. As he now did Park.

ALTERED ENGLANDS

So Stalin was waiting. He had carved a niche in the Great Void, becoming infinite and eternal, populating even the great *sunyatta*. And the *sunyatta*, which is also eternal truth, had not spat him out. Which Park found instructive. Destructive but instructive ...

Park was sensed and sought for. The presence rocketed towards him, roaring. It even had a bristly moustache like in the photos.

The enmity was palpable. And his hunger? It was ravenous enough to gobble up all Park's future rebirths.

Which was not even to mention his madness. The evil madness with not one rice grain of compassion for any other being. That madness was conspicuous when talking on the telephone, but loose in the Universe it seemed to blend in nicely. Leastways, no one and no thing objected. Which was also instructive. Maybe the Universe concurred.

Park had panicked and thrown open his eyes. His spirit shot back and shut the door into *sunyatta*. Park re-embraced the material world, the mundane, and hugged it close. Since that was where he must forever after remain. Strictly. Exclusively. Until death and the yielding up of his spirit.

But what then Park wondered? What would become of him when he was no longer clothed in flesh, when he was naked in the void before rebirth? Would Buddha protect him during that vital, vulnerable, interval? There'd been no sign of him the last time...

Dusk and the Dear Leader's return and demands for tea and Five Star and films, found Park precisely where he'd been all day. Because he had nowhere else to go now, in this world or any other. Nothing beyond *now* and the present moment.

Which just so happened to be the entirety of Zen.

The thought struck Park like lightning. Suddenly, between one shout of the Dear Leader and another. It shorted out all previous circuits.

And thus Park achieved enlightenment.

33~

CONSUMER AWARENESS

✱

'I never knew Simon…'

No, you didn't. Never met. Never introduced. My choice. So, by what right did this spiky-haired… priestess presume to sum up my life? And address me by my first (or even 'Christian') name? Cheek.

'… but his family have told me some things about the man Simon was…'

I bet they had. Those few that stuck around to the bitter end that is. It was a damn thin turn-out in the crematorium. And the service hadn't even been *1662*. My will had specifically requested *1662*…

'For instance, I'm told that Simon lived his whole life here—well, they do say that travel broadens the mind…'

And some of the congregation actually tittered! Insensitive creeps. Your turn will come!

'But enough jokes…,' she went on—and on and on: blathering about that which she did not know. As per usual in her job.

'Oh, there's room for just *one* more joke,' I thought. 'And the joke's on you, pompous plump priestess. *They're* here, come to pay their respects—I saw one sitting at the back, face first into a service book. Right beside some of my dry-eyed relatives. And where there's one…'

The *crem* is a big place: with wide grounds and unfrequented corners. Ideal for them! *I'm* safe now, but not so the Anglican mumbo-jumbo merchant. It's a good job I'm no longer subject to temptation. Otherwise I'd have been tempted to point her out to them. And then afterwards, maybe in the rose garden, or unlocking her 2CV in the car park—when she thought herself all alone...

Which I, more than anyone, know is *not necessarily* the case...

✹

'It's lovely!' I said, back in the days of blissful ignorance. The last such day. 'Absolutely lovely! Buy that one.'

'Oh *Dad*!'

'No? Well okay then, how that first one you tried on? I thought that suited you. The blue one—or was it white?'

To be fair, there had been a *lot* of dresses that day, so they'd become sort of blurred in the memory. All *I* knew was that not one had been bought yet. A bloke could have selected his next decade's wardrobe by now and still had time for a pint...

Daughters aren't into fairness for Dads, not when it comes to feminine core-interests. Their Father displayed *no respect* for shopping.

Daughter 1 pouted. More patient Daughter 2 put it into words a mere man could understand.

'*Daaaad*: you're just saying that. You want us to buy any old thing to get it over with!'

Well, maybe there was a grain of truth in that. My feet were about to fall off, my knees were numb with stop-start standing. I recalled that in more civilised times past clothes shops provided seats for dead-beat husbands and dads to despair in. Now, I and my kind—the mobile cashpoints of the shopping sacrament—had to stand around like side dishes no one had ordered till time to play (i.e. pay) their part.

Hour one had been fun: a dad and daughters doing family things. Their delight in rampant materialism was transmittable. Hour two was bearable, though lightning-shot with thoughts of beer. Thereafter you became *very* conscious of passing time.

By hour four minutes masqueraded as millennia: mind-rot set in and impatience sandpapered the brain. Impatience's foul-tempered big brother, Irritation, was on his way.

JOHN WHITBOURN

Even my face was denied freedom. I was slap-bang by the changing rooms, where gaggles of women grunted and wrestled to fit actual bodies to body-image sized clothes. I was obliged to be there for when the daughters brought out each successive garment for my (ignored) verdict. In the intervals though—oh, the long lonely intervals!—looking in that direction was *verboten* for fearing of being thought a Peeping Tom. Which left a blinkered field of view.

That was how it all started. How I came to *see*. I blame shopping, I blame my daughters. Of course, I now understand all—and thus forgive all.

Back then though, I was in a visual and spiritual desert, constrained view and all. Specifically a shop: a nicely, brightly, lit sterile shop: the kind that's standard issue and ephemeral: one year a boutique, the next a coffee bar. At the slightest market spasm in came the shop-fitters and hey presto all was new—but the same as every High Street everywhere. In short, the fittings were prefab: neutral white Teflon-for-the-eyes. Two seconds flat and you'd seen all you needed to, or could bear to. Likewise, the racks of stock held no interest for me; so that just left the customers. Alas.

Surprise, surprise, they were 99% young women and therefore not to be stared at unduly, for fear of being thought a middle-aged letch. Worse still, lone males in this environment might be taken for the letch brigade's provisional wing: an active-service pervert. When the daughters were out of sight, trying things on, I wished for a sign round my neck proclaiming *'I Am Not Odd. I Have Female Chaperones.'* But thereagain that would have looked... odd. You can't win.

Anyhow, my gaze needed to be butterfly light, alighting only on walls or the occasional Mum (and even they were mostly the yummy-mummy variety) or desperate Dads like me. The latter and I locked looks and exchanged silent solidarity.

Such scattered seconds didn't help much. So, I was on my hundredth+ passing-glance-tour of the venue when I saw her.

An ordinary young girl by the standards of the species, out shopping and casually sliding things along racks for inspection. Yet she gave off that indefinable *more-than-meets-the-eye* that you can't buy or even learn, no matter what magazines tell you.

In my several seconds of permitted scrutiny, I also noted that she moved well. A certain grace and poise about the hips and hands. And her outfit suited her too, neither tart nor frump but spot on to earn a second look. And a *nice* girl besides—though how just one look might reveal that I couldn't say. Her red jacket suited her, her black boots were just the right side of racy. Suffice to say, all the parts pleased.

Take away two decades, a wedding band and family, and I would have been interested. Even burdened with them, having nothing else to do, I noted her down for a second, innocent, window-shopping, once-over next time round.

It duly arrived. Perhaps even a bit ahead of timetable. You'll have to excuse me.

She still had her back to me, poring through a rack of tops. Seeing only a wall of hair, I couldn't help but wonder what her face was like. And only because that small proportion of the human acreage is the very seat of attraction—the reason strict religions cover it up. Unless, that is, you happen to be a *basic* sort of person, or believe that coarse old adage about *'not looking at the mantelpiece when you're stoking the fire'*. Which I'm not and don't. I was just curious—which, as another old saying informs us, is fatal to cats...

It became downright uncanny how I couldn't get a look—not of her face. We were locked in a sort of Earth-Moon style orbit with only one view ever presented to me. Or else every time she turned face-on a passerby intervened. I got so frustrated I dared a full-blooded stare.

There! *Almost.* She pivoted suddenly, as though a row of dresses had called out to her. Yet immediately her long locks caught up with the motion and obscured all again, I thought I got a glimpse of chin; maybe even some brow. And any second now all would be revealed, if only she continued the turn...

A gum-chewing 'sales assistant' (ha!) interposed herself. She started to rearrange some stock and then must have sensed my gaze. Up flashed her bovine eyes.

I looked away but not before she caught me. Prior to disengagement, I registered the start of a sneer. Very embarrassing—but you can't call out *'You've got it all wrong: I don't fancy you!'* in a crowded shop, can you? It isn't *done*.

I looked at my watch (dear God! Could it *really* be...?). I studied the floor and ceiling, I did everything possible to acquit myself of the obvious charge. A full minute elapsed.

Truth be told, I didn't want this fascinating female to get away. Yet I assure you there was nothing more to it than the burning desire to find out what she looked like. It seemed intolerable to part and never know. It sounds strange I know, but once curiosity was satisfied I was confident she'd be purged from memory minutes later. On the other hand, at that time it felt important not to face a lifetime without finding out.

In my defence, there was nothing else for me to do. *'The Devil finds work for idle hands'*: another one of those annoyingly true ancient clichés.

Looking up I half feared she might have gone but no, the girl had merely moved on. Yet she had her back to me again and seemed really engrossed in a row of coats. The position didn't look likely to change for a while.

That wretched sales assistant had gone by now. The coast was clear.

I took the bull by the horns and advanced. An apparently aimless 'I'm just waiting for my daughters' sort of meander, but actually a deceptive route designed to take me within plain view. Again, I understand it must seem peculiar, but the sensitive will sympathise. You may even have experienced something similar. My life forked at this point: along one road I would *never ever know*.

I realise what you sensible folk are thinking. I should have told myself *'So what?'* And you're absolutely right—*if* Reason has the slightest relevance to human affairs. Which, of course, it doesn't. *How* old are you?

Personally, I blame boredom. Shopping and my daughters' fault again.

She was now within yards of me. Near enough. If either of us shifted stance even a little…

I paused at the end of a rack of hot-pants and was about to lean on it before noticing its… overly intimate apparel. So I checked that motion and instead checked my watch again—without actually noting the result. Then, alibi established, I took a step forwards and *looked*.

She moved, at precisely that instant. Where I should have received full frontal I got only hair. Nice shiny chestnut hair, to be sure, but not overly informative. Then the girl stepped away from me, still browsing, but with overtones of almost being through here.

That was unacceptable. I sped ahead, overtook her, and turned.

Aha!

No. Just *o-ho!*

Oblivious of me, she'd turned too, at exactly the right—wrong—moment. More cold shoulder and coiffure

ALTERED ENGLANDS

From the changing room zone, some way behind me now, I heard a familiar puzzled voice call *'Dad?'* Had, miracle of miracles, a daughter decided to buy? Or was she was just checking the walking-wallet hadn't gone walkies?

Well, he had, temporarily. Like most family men I'd cultivated a handy cover story of mild deafness over the years, which would explain me not answering the call. Naughty, I know, but I was on a mission now. Plus I'd soon be back, credit card at the ready. Life owed me a little slack.

I pressed on, getting more and more reckless.

I was sure it wasn't being done consciously, but this girl was really jerking me about now: almost literally.

Back when Christmas crackers used to contain decent toys, I once got two plastic Scottie-dogs, one black, one white, with magnets in their nose and... other end. Their poles were arranged such that they could only kiss, never sniff behinds as actual doggies delight to do. If you tried to make them conform to type one would always swing away. These then were *decorous* dogs: an example to their kind. I still have them somewhere I think: probably in the wall-rack of nonsense knick-knacks the wife has accumulated. I mention them now for a reason.

Which is that the girl and I were acting the same. If I turned she turned too, always presenting a blank view. It was like we were choreographed and in telepathic contact. Way beyond statistical likelihood I told myself. It *had* to be deliberate—and yet how could that be? She didn't know of my existence because she'd never faced me face-on. And I hadn't thrown away *all* caution: I wasn't close enough for her to sense or scent my aftershave. Not yet...

Still, it must have been getting obvious to onlookers. I noticed several shoppers noticing me. Whatever cover I'd had was long since reduced to shreds. And no matter where I stood I always seemed to be in the way of some damn woman's gaze.

'Excuse me...,' said one, rather pointedly I thought, when I got between her and a display of underwear she could never have pumped into. I got the hint. The English language contains myriad varieties of *'Excuse me'*. This was the warning-off sort.

In the embarrassing interlude the girl had shifted. She was some way away now and definitely door-wards. I had to make a decision: to know or not to know, whether to risk arrest or forever wonder.

She settled it for me by turning a corner. Once out of sight entirely I experienced the full feeling of deprivation. So, this was what it would feel like! Also, Fate was mucking me about and I was taking it!

I ploughed after her like a starship, scattering shoppers.

More *'Excuse me'*s followed in my wake. By putting emphasis on the *'me'*, you ratchet up the reprimand. Fortunately, no boyfriends or hubbies were around to take it further.

I was right about her being a nice girl. It was nice of her to wait for me.

For waiting she was. Deliberately. No longer shopping but full of purpose.

Just round the corner that had separated us we finally met. There she stood, head on, in all her glory: awaiting. We met in no uncertain terms.

In fact I almost cannoned into her. Save for an emergency-stop my face would have met hers in an involuntary snog. Which must have been why at the last instant I averted my eyes. So that I could tell the magistrate it was all a misunderstanding.

The red of her jacket filled my horizon before I appreciated it covered a heaving bust. Which was awkward. So, down my eyes slipped still further to behold boots pointing my way. Which, in terms of facial direction must mean... My stare bounced back and up.

I needn't have worried—not on the magistrate score anyway. To kiss you need lips. The girl had none.

My intended *'Very sorry...'* died away, aborted at the first syllable.

Where there should have been a face there was none. Where features ought to be an abyss yawned instead. A bottomless pit neatly framed by brow and chin and hair.

I say *abyss* and mean it. Not a mouth, not a maw, nor an orifice of any kind, but a face-shaped portal into some other place. There were vistas within: astounding vistas. Concerning which it would not be kind to tell you.

Fear froze me. I was hers for the taking had she so wished.

She did not. Not today. Perhaps she'd not long since fed. Or was toying with her food.

The girl cocked her head to one side, examining me—by what means I know not—just as I examined her. To put it mildly, she had my undivided attention, but her control was the greater—many thousands-fold so. Without a shred of evidence to go on, I would have said she was *amused...*

ALTERED ENGLANDS

All else about her was normal: her gestures ditto. She raised one upright finger in front of her 'face', signifying *'shush...'*

I was happy to obey. Any outside orders were welcome right then. My only plan had been to scream like a stuck pig. And then what?

She certainly knew *'then what.'* The silencing gesture languidly unfurled into directions stage left.

I looked and observed she was not alone. Another 'girl', new to me, was on the other side of the shop. Her fleeting glance in our direction showed she was not as other girls. If an abyss can be said to smirk it did.

This fresh creature approached a customer admiring a blouse. It pounced.

Its speed was such that even I—who saw all—doubted it. Those less fully focused would have been left agnostic about events.

The abyss had... gaped. Somehow, for a second, it was woman-wide. Then the woman was swallowed, blouse and hanger and all. She ought not have fitted but she did.

The victim had not been gulped or chewed or even simply swallowed: she'd been *consumed*. Gone. Downed in one. Her fate came swifter than sound, too swift to protest.

Where once there'd been two now was now one. Then the second 'girl' turned away from us, expertly hiding her nature in a way I'd become all too familiar with. She mingled with us normals again, unsuspected.

Too late I looked back. 'My' creature was gone. Then just in time I glimpsed her through the shop window, heading up the High Street, her face artfully obscured once more.

I never saw her again—save in my dreams of course.

Her colleague left too, and acknowledged others of her kind in the street. A small pack, out hunting. Male and female, young and old: ordinary... You would never have suspected. *You* still don't.

But I could see them now, when others remained blind. There were more of them than you might think, sidling along, window-shopping and biding their time. Waiting for hunger (or whatever drive drove them) to strike.

It astounded me—to start with—that no one else noticed, but thereagain we live such *busy* lives. We self-train ourselves into non-observation. Beggars and buskers soon become invisible, as do most everyday sights. We keep ourselves to ourselves, mind our own business. A survival technique—which *they* turn against us.

Added to which, they must have had so much practice, have been beside us so long. We, their passive flock, are too dull of brain and eye to heed the occasional straggler picked off. We have no good shepherd or sheepdog to protect us. Or leastways, so it seems.

Without asking for it, I'd been granted access to their world, the scales were off my eyes. I saw their cunning glances at humanity, sizing up their next prey. And oh, those appraisals: such hunger, such venom! But for the fact it would break their cover, they would take many more of us than they do!

Even so, that's still enough. The mystery of all those missing people you hear about was to me a mystery no more. Devoured! Brazenly taken and consumed in the street. They were so confident, we so complacent, that their dinner wasn't even wrapped up to eat later...

Truly we were a 'consumer society'—but not in the sense generally meant...

A second's worth of reflection made me realise that in this case ignorance was bliss. Yet, like a curse, I'd been educated. Panic like a thunderflash suddenly illuminated all my days to come.

How could I bear to venture out in future? Or shop or socialise at all? *They* were on the earth, in artful camouflage!

Even second-hand participation in the world was now out of the question. What price the TV news or pictures in a paper, when forever inspecting *that* figure in the crowd scene, *that* person turned away or obscured by something, for fear it might be one of *them*...?

And as for actual populated *places*...

Worse still, I couldn't tell anyone. That way led to straitjackets and padded cells—where I'd be all the more helpless if one of *them* should drop by...

Oh God, the prospect...!

Somehow, I found the strength to find the daughters, dragging them out of the changing room reckless of other feminine *'eeks'* and *'do-you-mind?'*s. I settled their bills, hurling cash carelessly across the counter, and herded them out into the street.

Meanwhile, of course, I was looking wildly around, ensuring everyone within lunging range had a face. An honest-to-goodness human *face*.

'Oo you staring at, mate?' said someone. Him and everyone was the answer, as in staring real *hard.* But I didn't say so. I was in no mood for conversation or combat.

Then I *really* shocked the offspring with the unique extravagance of a taxi home. Neither they nor I knew it then, but that was our last family outing. Once safely home I never left it again.

Well, just the once—feet first in a box.

☸

I lived too long.

In the intervening years I turned to drink, naturally. It quelled my thoughts—but at the same time started the avalanche away of family and friends. That and my hysterical pleading with them:

'DON'T GO OUT!'
'DON'T GO NEAR PEOPLE!'
'CHECK YOU CAN SEE THEIR FACES!'
And etc.

Which made me hard work to be around. Plus *no* fun at parties.

Men in white coats came, with calming syringes. Then prescriptions for sedatives that'd let you grin through Armageddon. I took some, to placate them, then started palming the things off on the dog. Because scotch did the trick better, with kinder hangovers.

On the plus side, afterwards *'Fang' WOOF*ed a lot less during the night—not that I was sleeping well anyway. He was the last to leave me.

Or I should say almost the last. A select few remained loyal: precisely those I'd rather not.

The creatures proved spiteful. Or maybe they feed on fear as well as humans. Perhaps either was why they'd spared me, then haunted the street in which I 'lived' my hermit life. For food and/or a laugh.

And, oh *how* they laughed—silently—during their fleeting visits. After a while I felt like joining in, but never did. Once you start laughing there's always the danger of not being able to stop...

Sometimes they even took prey right outside my doorstep, just to make a point—that it could well be me next time! Maybe might be!

So, as you may guess, I got through a fair few neighbours. The area developed an evil reputation and suspicious policemen came to ask me questions. There was even talk of digging up my garden—till one look at that undisturbed jungle revealed no one had been there for *years*. Not even to machete the lawn, let alone bury victims.

All sorts of other things slipped too. The curtains got patchy and eventually fell down. After which, some nights when I sat and sipped and watched the rain streak down bare windows, they'd come right up to the house. They'd just... appear and press their 'faces' to the glass, as if to say: *'You're wrong! It can get worse!'*

And also show me things...

Bastards!

Which is why I didn't die, why I didn't take the short route out of my misery via my/Fang's pills. For fear of what came after. As seen in their alleged sneak previews. *Anything* looked better than that.

All lies, of course, but I didn't know that then; any more than the priestess at my funeral knew anything for sure.

Fortunately, the creatures are fibbers as well as predators. The afterlife is not without its issues, but it is without *them*. They don't make it here—but nor do the poor people they consume. Which is hardly fair when you think about it. So I don't.

Just as I don't think about *them*, not from one aeon to the next. They're not a problem for me any more.

If only you could say the same.

Enjoy your outings, folks!

ALTERED ENGLANDS

AFTERWORD

Dear reader: it all happened—except for the denouement, naturally. Lost for diversion, indeed losing the will to live, after eons outside changing rooms during a day-out-with-daughters shopping extravaganza, I noted a young lady whose face curiously always remained *just* unseen. No matter how close she passed by or how I shifted my aching legs.

The phenomenon became first noticeable, then inescapable and, at the end, defiant of all reason and probability. But I didn't go and investigate like the foolish fellow of my tale. Instead I settled for just… wondering ever after and writing a story about it. Which was possibly the wisest course. The *sensible* and *reasonable* thing to do.

Yet what had I to fear? I had already done my Darwinian duty, as demonstrated by aforementioned two daughters. My role in getting the family genes into space was done.

The Tuareg people of North Africa have a proverb:

'Reason is the shackle of the coward.'

JOHN WHITBOURN

34~

MEBYON VERSUS *SUNA*

✦

INTRODUCTION

I've long been fascinated by the Cornish Language revival movement—all three(?) ('Unified', *Kemmyn* and 'Modern') pretty much mutually exclusive and contentious splinter-streams of it. It seemed like a laudable stab at cultural restoration and enrichment akin to—albeit with better chance of 'success'—Jacobitism.

That interest even survived invitation to a Cornish learners' barbeque. Where the company was convivial in direct correlation to the guests' genuine Cornishness—as opposed to the 'born-agains' resident in London.[123] Until my lady wife eventually went all 'Red Mist' at some final straw 'Celtic' casual racism, delivered in cut-glass English tones. Chairs may have been hurled...

I hasten to say that most of the true *Mebyon* I've met—usually in Kernow/Cornwall itself: try getting them to leave!—were warm-hearted normal people. Likewise, involvement in the 500th anniversary commemoration of the 1497 Cornish Revolt and its long march across England, was a pleasure.

As to this story: the Cumberland sausage incident actually occurred, precisely how and where stated. It wasn't me though—I was the charmless 'snake-charmer'. Little did we know at the time that we were under cold-eyed surveillance by one of my stories...

---

[123] The hosts were nice though. I don't think I ever got a chance to thank them.

ALTERED ENGLANDS

I have also partaken of the herein mentioned 'Wally's Special' cider—and, being young and foolish, in excess of the stipulated quart maximum. After which you're all set to play 'Exeter Charades.' Wherein someone leaves the room and then you try to guess who it was.

Waking the next day was surprisingly painless—until I tried to get up…

JOHN WHITBOURN

MEBYON VERSUS *SUNA*

I could have just *stepped* across. A single stride. Without stretching. No danger of getting my feet wet. But I couldn't. Because I mustn't. So I didn't.

I knew only reddened eyes awaited me there. And I don't just mean my own, swollen with tears. Even leaning slightly over, straightaway searing heat-in-the-head arrived. A first stage leading inexorably to brain-boil and death. If I wasn't sliced into slivers first.

It was more tolerable where the Tamar was wide and raced to the sea. Seeing the unobtainable far side wasn't so bad with a real stretch of water before you. I could delude myself there was good excuse to stay put.

Here though, near its north-coast source, the combined river-and-border narrowed to a trickle. Crossing from Cornwall into Welcombe in Devon was just *'One small step for a man'*. But at the same time also a *'giant leap'* beyond what was wise.

Plus there were legal niceties. A tenth century king decreed Cornwall extended to the east bank. Whereas later bureaucrats said *'centre of watercourse'*. Which interpretation prevailed? Testing that out might involve 'the trip of a lifetime'. As in never coming back...

So, the Wife and I surveyed England stretching away before us. A mere four or five hour drive and then you got to London. She liked London—in moderation. Not to live in, God forbid, but good for an occasional shopping expedition followed by a show. The first step towards which was but a yard away. And doubly desirable now it was forbidden.

England's Capital held no appeal to me—never had—but Welcombe's *Olde Smithy Inn* looked extra tempting today. At its garden tables some combined families were enjoying a pub lunch. One man was making heavy weather out of a Cumberland sausage casserole, trying to unfurl the uncooperative serpentine coil with his fork and getting gravy specked in the process. His companions made out he was snake-handling and supplied a *sssss*-ing soundtrack. Another 'friend' pretended to play a snake-charmer's pipe.

Much merriment ensued; even their toddlers joining in without fully comprehending. Children instinctively know not to look gift-horse happiness in the mouth.

All this normality occurring a mere stone's throw away! And yet also an astronomical distance. It wasn't these folk's fault, I realised, but that stone chucking option still held appeal. The selfish swine! Sitting there laughing and enjoying themselves? An outrage! Plus the *Butcombe Bitter* thing too! I saw several pints of it before them, on tap for supping *anywhen they liked...*

I liked Butcombe bitter. Once upon a time I could have strolled over and imbibed lovely Butcombe to my heart's content. *Once.* Alas, for some inexplicable reason it wasn't often available in Cornwall. Not that I was... bitter.

The Wife read my face.

'There's more tears shed over *answered* prayers....,' she said. Not exactly *'I told you so'*, but definitely biscuit crumbs strewn in the marital bedsheets.

I knew why. Yesterday there'd been a hen-debrief on her girlfriends' outing to that *'Mamma Mia'* musical. The ankle-chain-gang had reviewed it as *'miles of fun!'* Although they still thought it *'funny'* she'd refused to join them, even for the mere skip-and-jump to Bideford. Saying she'd become an *'old stick-in-the-mud'* who never left Cornwall. *'They don't eat people over in Devon, you know...'*

Actually, we *did* know. And know differently.

There ensued what the Wife calls *'One of our silences'*. Of which there were more and more these days; our relationship descending into frigid Polar peace. Which I suspect she could well live with. Apparently, silence was an improvement on (and I quote): *'Banging on about bloody Celts and Kernow and Logres. And reciting the 'Armes Prydein'—whatever that is when it's at home!'*

The Wife would never have attended a bullfight—out of compassion and principle. But standing there on the edge of *Kernow*, staring into *Logres*, she revealed herself as no mean matador.

It didn't *have* to be said. It was better left *un*said. Yet evidently I'd asked for it. *'It'* being all I'd ever wished for, other than her hand in marriage. And now I'd (we'd) got it. Wherefore *I* now *got it* from her: both barrels. Because it would have been nice to go up to Town and see a show. Just one more time before she died.

The matador-missus waggled her metaphorical cape. Behind it hid a sword-sharp *coup de grâce*.

'It serves you right!' she said. 'I've no sympathy…'

I turned to her. It was to her I'd always turned for sympathy. Where else was I going to get it now?

'Oh, get *you*, Dr Clever-clogs!' she went on. 'PhD from *Truro* College: couldn't be anywhere else, oh *no*. Cornwall, Cornwall, *Cornwall*: got to be. But someone's not so clever as they thought, are they? You thought *your* dad was bigger than *his* dad…'

Across the Tamar-trickle imagination made red eyes flare in England's every shadow.

If only it were imagination…

⚘

'Hello there! Welcome! Welcome aboard…'

I was taking inventory of my new garden at the time. Nice flowerbeds and so on, but too high maintenance was my judgement. They'd be going under concrete *toot sweet*.

Neighbourly greetings suggested an even more urgent task for my list. Such as raising the fence above chit-chat level. To exorcise the spectre of *'Hail fellow well met'* every time I showed my face.

Pending that pressing reform, some reply, sadly, seemed obligatory.

'Meea navidna cowza Sawzneck.'

That did him. As always. A very *handy* phrase. It puts proper distance between me and them every time.

The elderly man's homely face furrowed. 'Er…, pardon?'

More missionary work was required, to enlighten the pagans. Which never ceased to be a pleasure.

'It's *Kernowek*. The Cornish language, in case you didn't know. For 'I won't speak English'. But I see that to you I shall have to.'

'Oh… right… Um, well, welcome anyway…'

ALTERED ENGLANDS

He had to hoist himself up to get his handshake over the panels. Meaning he must be a short-arse. Which was a bonus. The natives need not be feared.

I shook the proffered paw anyway. No point in prematurely insulting people. The Wife had warned me about that in no uncertain terms: especially after 'last time'. I still deployed my famed bone-crusher grip though—only to find a surprising steely core awaiting. Unlike most recipients my new neighbour merely winced a bit. Which was disappointing.

'I'm Alfred,' he said, when his pain abated. 'Alfred Ayling. Her indoors is Amy. Lived here for donkey's years—man and boy. Well, it suits us. I only hope you and your lady wife will be as happy as we've been and-…'

I took a step back, pointedly terminating the *tsunami* of trivia.

'Yeah, well, maybe,' I replied. 'But I don't *want* to be here. Never wanted to live abroad—in England. *If* you can call that living. I wanted to stay in *Kernow*.'

Which bamboozled Ayling again. Which gave me a warm glow. Two-nil up already, only minutes into our acquaintance!

'More *Kernowek*,' I informed him. 'It's our name for Cornwall. Don't you know anything?'

Apparently not. Ayling pointed over my head, across the broad estuary of the Exe towards my longed-for homeland.

'But you're not all *that* far away now,' he said. 'From Cornwall, I mean. Fifty miles or so…'

'Fifty-one point two-four. I've checked.'

'Oh, right. Well, there you are then. On a clear day you might even see it from here…'

'I don't want to *see* it. Especially not from *Logres*.'

Bemusement squared. This wasn't going anything like he'd hoped.

'Pardon?'

'You call it England.' I didn't add *'dimwit'*—but it was implied. 'We Celts call it *Logres*. In other words, occupied *Prydain*—i.e. the island you lot stole from us. Both places as rendered in the original *Kernowek*—oldest language in the land. Which, as I've said, is what I speak for preference.'

Ayling's face fell.

'Oh, I see,' he said—when he plainly didn't. 'Hence the... um, *'me a navvy...'* thing I suppose. Only it's just that, um..., unfortunately, Amy and I don't really spea-...'

'Quelle surprise,' I countered. 'Don't worry, mate, I wasn't expecting much. Not in this dump. We won't be here long anyway. Soon as the Wife gets a transfer and Kernow job then back we go, pronto. Won't see us for dust!'

Ayling abandoned tippy-toes and sank behind the fence, down to only upper-features-showing level. The 'Chad' analogies made me smile. He mistook that for affability.

'Oh well,' he said, bright and breezy again, 'whilst you *are* here, should you ever need anything—the proverbial 'cup of sugar' and so on—you know where to come. Please don't hesitate to ask...'

'Neither of us take sugar. Anything else?' I was pre-turned to go.

'Um, well, no, I don't suppose so, Mr... um, Mr...—you didn't mention your name...'

Given how he walked into that one I could see how Ayling's punchbag innocence might make him my perfect 'straight-man.' A handy human-amusement-park parked next door to lighten my English internment. Allowing one's sentence to pass more mischievously.

'That's right,' I replied, heading back indoors. 'I didn't...'

☸

The Wife disapproved. Women can be so... *sensible.*

Having heard edited highlights of the over-fence sparring match and my knockout victory, she invited the Aylings round for tea. *'To mend bridges'.*

The only bridge I was interested in was the one over the Tamar, Kernow-wards. Speed the day! So, when the 'tea' ordeal arrived I wore an appropriately sour face.

Whereas *La Ayling* and the Wife hit it off, despite age and racial differences. It transpired they had things in common. One retired nurse and another still combatant paired off to exchange NHS war-stories. Leaving me to face Alfred Ayling.

It turned out he'd prepared a conversational gambit to get us going.

'After you mentioned you spoke Cornish,' he said, 'I took the opportunity to look it up. In the Library, on their interweb thingy. *Very* interesting. Though it must make things difficult there being three different versions. And their speakers not getting on. Like with that EU grant to do a dictionary business. Death threats even, so I read...'

The... complex issue of parallel 'Unified', 'Common' and 'Modern' revived Cornish wasn't something I cared to air at the best of times. And never ever in the face of the enemy.

'Irrelevant,' I bristled. 'Concentrate on the mere fact it *is* revived. You English had better get over it.'

Did I detect a slight stiffening of Ayling shoulders? I think so, but nothing came of it. *'Nice'* people are pretty plastic, ever agile to switch topic rather than give or take offence.

'I'm retired now,' he volunteered, as yet another uncomfortable silence stretched, finding there was only so much diversion to be had from teacup stirring. 'But I used to have a hardware shop down in the city. In Exeter I mean. Till it got bit a much and you had to go computerised. So we sold up.'

'No!' Tell me more. More *detail*...'

Sarcasm bounced off the Ayling amiability-armour.

'Um, okay. Um... I had it nigh forty years, bar two months. Inherited it from my Uncle Egbert—and he'd run it a half century himself, so-...'

'Hellfire! I'm hanging on your every *word* here, Alfred! It must be a pain getting pestered with autobiography offers all the time! Not to mention the film rights...'

He didn't know how to 'take' me. But someone else did. I caught a warning 'look' from the Wife.

'No...,' answered Ayling. 'Not really. Not at all, actually.'

'You *do* surprise me...'

He took another sip of tepid (appropriately enough) brew. The English think tea the sovereign cure for all ills.

'But enough about me,' he said, rallying for another go. 'What do *you* do?'

A straight answer to that seemed harmless enough. So long as I kept it terse.

'Proofreading: publishers, academic work, local press; the lot. Freelance. Which means I can work anywhere I want. Which isn't *here*, dammit.'

Ayling frowned. Not angrily, but merely concerned for poor little me. Although he found my words hard to credit. Who *wouldn't* want to abide in an identikit English end-terrace box in an identikit English city suburb?

Eventually his puzzlement emerged as:

'No?'

'No.'

'May I ask *why* not?'

'You may.'

He really was the perfect foil for fun. It took *ages* of pregnant pause for him to twig.

'*Why* not?' he asked.

I can't recall the specifics now—it being a well and oft-rehearsed recital of mine. However, despite this foreign fool not meriting excess ammunition, I still ensured he received a proper broadside.

It definitely started off with '*This hole?' Pah! Here's just where I park my car…*' And developed into '*Kernow: the proud and ancient nation oppressed by your nation.*' And how no self-respecting *Mebyon Kernow*—which I kindly translated as '*Sons of Cornwall*' lest he not get it—would choose to hang out in hostile territory unless they were conscripted. Or kidnapped by love, as in my case. Courtesy of the Wife's 'promotion' to Exeter.

'Lost capital of occupied Kernow,' I concluded.

After that I wouldn't say Ayling was exactly chilly. More lukewarm. Like all his race.

He set down his cup, straightened his cake fork and checked his watch.

'Really?' he said, not meeting my eye. Which is one of those slippery Swiss-Army-penknife English words where meaning depends entirely on inflection. I decided to take it as the interrogative mode and excuse to further enlighten the *Sawzneck*.

'Yeah, *really*. Because your King Aethelstan—*Black Aethelstan* we call him—expelled the Cornish from here. In 927. Out of Exeter, out of our ancestral *Dumnonia*. All of us: ethnically cleansed beyond the Tamar. To stay there on pain of death. Forever. In 936 he even passed a law enshrining it. Which I spit upon. Because here I am, loud and proud, part of the Celtic vanguard returned to claim what's rightfully ours. And what are you going to do about it, eh?'

Ayling wouldn't acknowledge the flung gauntlet. A being made of milk-and-water, he pretended to not even notice.

'Oh well,' he said, 'that was all long ago. Water under the bridge…'

Alas, at that point the Wife re-tuned to our frequency and picked up on the vibes. Being both a nurse and married to me, she was a dab hand at applying soothing ointment. In this case the conversational kind.

'Oh no, he hasn't got you onto history has he, Mr Ayling?'

'Alfred, please… Well, yes, I suppose he has. Not that I know much about it. But it's all… jolly interesting. I'm getting quite an education here…'

Whereas I was getting bathed in Wifely gamma rays, singeing the side of my head. Although Cornish to her Celtic corkscrew ringlets, and despite the graveyards near Land's End heaving with memorials bearing her maiden name, the Wife didn't share my born-again nationalism. Strange to relate, she preferred getting on with her neighbours, no matter who.

I don't think Alfred's words carried any subtext. Even though passive aggression is his kind's weapon of choice. Yet the Wife chose to take it so. Meaning I now knew what was on the menu for supper: tongue-pie and cold-shoulder.

But I wasn't that hungry anyway. It had been worth it. Another evening-up of the 936 AD score.

The Wife consulted the nurse's watch gracing her front.

'Goodness!' she said. 'Doesn't time *fly?* And here's me nattering on when I've got an early shift tomorrow! Sorry, Alfred and Amy: we *love* your company but not your hours. Lots of things I must do before bedtime, I'm afraid. Why, it's almost… six o'clock…'

※

Multiply satisfactory skirmishes such as that by… however many it took, and Ayling finally got the message. Thereafter, aside from an unfailing 'good morning' on first sighting and bookend 'good night' should our paths cross, he left me alone.

Whereas I wasn't so standoffish and unneighbourly. On sunny days, when windows were open or they were in their garden (and my Wife out), I graciously decided to teach Ayling *'The Armes Prydein'*—or *'Prophecy of Britain'* in usurper-speak. Which is something he and his nation *jolly'* well ought to know. To broaden their outlook.

I usually started off with that bit where the tenth century bard says:

JOHN WHITBOURN

'The warriors will scatter the foreigners as far as Durham,
They will rejoice after the devastation,
And there will be reconciliation between the Welsh and the men of Dublin,
The Irish of Ireland and Anglesey and Scotland,
The men of Cornwall and of Strathclyde will be made welcome among us,
The Britons will rise again...'

Though I say so myself, I have a good declamatory voice, well able to penetrate Castle Ayling even after they'd retreated indoors and raised the drawbridge. *And*, for my favourite bit, about how the Celts reunite and chuck out all bloody foreigners, I found it in myself to step up a decibel or ten.

'There will be widows and riderless horses,
There will be woeful wailing before the rush of warriors,
And many a wounded hand before the scattering of armies.
The messengers of death will gather
When corpses stand one by another.'

as Arthur's people reclaim Britain from *'Manaw Gododdin'* (southern Scotland to you) *'to Brittany, from Dyfed to Thanet.'* Whereafter:

'Let them be as exiles,
For the English there will be no returning.
The Gaels will return to their comrades.
The Welsh will arise in a mighty fellowship—
Armies around the ale, and a throng of warriors—
And chosen Kings who kept their faith.
The English race will be called warriors no more...'

And so on and on, for many more fine lines. More prophecy than poetry, I concede, and not exactly in the Philip Larkin league; but any lack in rhythm and rhyme is more than made up for by its moral.

Wherefore I spoke loud and hearty to do the vision of delayed justice justice.

Although, being a reasonable man, I did occasionally vary the program. Say with a rendition of *'Song of the Western Men'*: Cornwall's unofficial national anthem. Even though it was written by an Englishman—which proves I'm not prejudiced.

> '*A good sword and a trusty hand!*
> *A merry heart and true!*
> *King James's men shall understand*
> *What Cornish lads can do!*
> *And have they fixed the where and when?*
> *And shall Trelawny die?*
> *Here's twenty thousand Cornish men*
> *Will know the reason why!*'

There's myriad verses to it, so no one could complain I was being monotonous. Not to mention a really rousing chorus.

> '*And shall Trelawny live?*
> *And shall Trelawny die?*
> *Here's twenty thousand Cornish men*
> *Will know the reason why!*'

On the umpteenth occasion (after less than half an hour!) Ayling did his 'Chad' act. First residual locks, then creased brow followed by appealing (as in begging) eyes appeared over my fence.

'Um...,' he said, as he always prefaced everything, doubtless many years before even saying '*Um..., will you marry me?*'. 'Um, I wonder if I could ask you to keep your voice down?'

And I replied: 'Well, you could *ask*...'

'And change the tune!' shouted Mrs Ayling, unseen from offstage. Me and she 'no longer spoke' in any other way.

'It's just that our Rose, our youngest granddaughter, is staying,' Ayling went on. 'Revising for her A levels. Next week. Because it's a bit hectic at home, what with all her brothers and sisters. We thought it would help her to have a bit of peace...'

I dare say it would: doubly so in such a good cause. Ayling made a compelling case. My apparent acquiescence—or leastways pause—emboldened him to demand more. Give some people an inch...

'And, whilst I mention it,' he said, 'your flag—it's very nice and all that...'

'It is, isn't it?' I answered, happy to have something we could agree on. 'Cost a bomb too, including the *pukka* flagpole and everything. But worth it. About time St Piran's black and silver was flown this side of the Tamar again! Makes a point, don't you think?'

'And a ruddy racket too!' chipped in invisible Mrs Ayling.

'Um, well, yes, because it's so *big* you see,' said Ayling, pouring dilute balm on his wife's whinge. '*Huge*. Plus right up against our house. Which blocks the light. And smacks the spare bedroom window all the time. Where Rose is. *Flap, slap, flap, slap*... Never stops. Due to the wind off the estuary...'

I smiled reassuringly at him.

'Leave it with me,' I said. 'I'll see what I can do.'

Ayling heaved a sigh of relief. He plainly hated confrontation, let alone 'scenes.'

A conundrum: how did his kind ever carve out an Empire?

'Oh good, *thank* you, thank you,' said Chad-Ayling, and quit the field of battle.

'I'll see,' I continued, to myself and for my benefit only, 'what I can do about turning down the wind...'

Meanwhile:

> *'The warriors will scatter the foreigners as far as Durham,*
> *They will rejoice after the devastation,*
> *And there will be reconciliation between...'*

❀

> *'We have tried our best to be friendly and good neighbours, but you....*
> *... We are very sorry but you leave us with no option but to make formal complaint to the proper authorities...*
> *Yours sincerely and in sorrow—Alfred Ayling.*

❀

ALTERED ENGLANDS

I didn't show the Wife that note, and happily her shift patterns made it easy for me to intercept any 'letter from the council' or whatever feeble English apocalypse Ayling intended. So I felt pretty sanguine about the prospect of race-war. In fact, the outbreak of active hostilities would enliven things here until my nagging bore fruit and the Wife got a new, better, job back over the border. Concerning which, as I've said, speed the day. Especially since my own employment was starting to go septic. Then gangrenous. Then drop off.

I blamed overwork. And over-taxed eyes. Even though *siestas* and stronger specs failed to cure things. Extraneous full stops—always in double-vision pairs and strained-vision angry red—continued to burn up from every page I proofread. The avoidance of which caused my gaze to skip lines and produce... lapses.

At first, minor mistakes went unmentioned: not worth a phone call or amended invoice. But then the slip-ups and solecisms grew so as to be 'brought to my attention'. In e-mails growing ever more peevish. Leading to penal deductions from my bill. And finally the phone call no proofreader wants.

The *Exeter Herald*'s Editor was *incandescent*. He could hardly speak. Up till then I had contracted-out oversight of many of his pages, including the vital-there-be-no-blunders death notices. Now he gave me to understand—in staccato sentences peppered with Anglo-Saxon—that that gig was gone. Plus I was on final notice for the rest.

'*No*,' went his parting worlds to me. '*You* get on the phone and apologise to them. And explain. *If* you can...'

So I did. But I couldn't. It is no easy thing to convey to a grieving family how their tragically-taken-from-them and beloved *son* came to be called:

'*A TRUE SOD*'

in twenty-three-point-title-font in cold print to hundreds of thousands of readers. My 'sorry' and offer of a free second insertion didn't really cut it. So I even proposed coming round to grovel in person. They said they couldn't guarantee my safety...

After which trauma I took extra-special, burning the midnight oil, burning my eyes red-raw, painstaking care. But by then there were reinforcement red dots too; multiple other '*eyes*' than mine. Whose stare up at me I found strangely hard to meet. A series of opticians, costing me a packet I could no longer afford, were unable to either account for or dispel them.

Which must be how, in their expensive, full page, full colour, advert, Exeter's prestigious two Michelin star (till then) Swiss Restaurant came to be dubbed:

'THE SWILL RESTAURANT'

throughout.

The owner told the Editor that howlers like that took decades to be forgotten by long-memoried local wags. And that trade was already down. And that henceforth he'd be taking his business elsewhere. *And* suing. Not that that was any concern of mine, because by then I'd been sacked.

My academic work took longer to die, since publishing schedules are stately and errors only filter through at spaced intervals. Like delayed detonations. Yet I suspected they were there and en route, although powerless to prevent arrival. Like some submariner hunkering down in the deep dark silence, awaiting depth charges, the tenterhooks anticipation was exquisite agony.

Then *BOOM!*

Oh, *how* reviewers leapt like salmon on finding my half-cocked amendments and allowed-past blunders in their 'colleagues'' works! Or better still, someone's life-work *magnum opus* or *festschrift*. The trumpeted and ill-concealed joy they took in university internecine bitchiness should not have surprised me—but still did.

The concluding gaffe that killed my career dodo-dead went national. *'Among the remarkable revelations to be found in distinguished Professor X's 'A New History of England','* said the *Times Literary Supplement*, *'is the bombshell that the Battle of Hastings was won by one 'Norman the Conqueror' (sic). And in 1666—which is somewhat later than hitherto conventionally thought…'*

I'm told that the mortified 'Professor X' actually came to fisticuffs with his publisher about it. Not that that was any concern of mine, because by then…

Within a short space I perforce became a 'kept man'. The Wife was good about it: didn't say anything. She didn't need to. I was still meeting the mail to head off any 'complaint' from Ayling. A by-product of which was that I got first sight of all the bills. The rapidly reddening bills…

And thus coincidentally akin in colour to the *eyes* now ever sparkling before me. For I could no longer pretend they were any mere impairment of mine. Liberated from my proofreading pages, they now flew solo and stared at me from mid-air, from the TV screen: from the very headboard of my bed. Meaning I must assume they even kept watch as I slept.

Once, in the fitful early hours and 'in my cups' (the Devil finding work for idle, workless, hands), I tried to reason with them. I confess to an edge of desperation entering my voice.

'What do you *want* of me?' I asked the *eyes*. 'What do you want me to do?'

And a voice from no mouth *I* could see replied:

'Die!'

※

Anxiety has the motivational *oomph* to make you do things you'd prefer not. Things you'd almost rather *'die'* than do. Like talk to despised neighbours.

From upstairs I saw Ayling pottering round his garden. Out of nowhere, I suddenly knew what was needful, no matter how humiliating. I had to ask if he'd ever heard our house was haunted. Or the abode of unclean spirits. Or perched atop a Hell-mouth. Or some such Dark Age balls. For that's how embarrassing things had got: I'd lost all sense of embarrassment.

As I issued into the garden all composure went too. The neighbourhood dogs started barking: from silence to *Hound of the Baskervilles* choir in seconds, synchronised round my scent. All of them wanting to *meet* me—and not for wags or walkies either.

Then a roof tile saw fit to desert its post and crown me.

Bop!

Bullseye: centre pate. It was *hard*, edge on. Knees buckled and blood was shed. Nevertheless, my main hurt was to dignity. Even though none but accompanying *eyes* saw.

Being robust I recovered and strode on. Likewise, being of blacksmith-build, I didn't have Ayling's Chad-act problem. I showed up over the fence without stretching.

He'd heard my *'Ouch!'* and was heading indoors rather than converse.

'Wait, Alfred! Please!'

Despite all the bad omens, my instinct proved spot on. Straightaway, I could see I'd selected the right man. Ayling's guilty face told all without need for words. He *knew*.

He also somehow knew what I was going to say.

'Sorry,' he said, setting down his secateurs. 'I'm *so* sorry! But there's nothing I can do. I *can't*. I would if I could. Really I would…'

It was easily within my powers to have the fence down and be wringing his neck within seconds. Yet Ayling's confession hinted at some useful influence. Which constrained me—that and a tree branch swooping.

Sock!

Right hook! Full face! Over I go!

The windpower behind it was bespoke: tailor-made. No other foliage stirred. Ditto only an extremity getting involved. Enough to down a man and imprint a temporary twig-and-leaf tattoo, but nowhere near lethal force. Not this time. Just a personalised present from an English oak.

Then the rest of my face coloured up to match that arboreal kiss. Because Ayling's *fizzog* appeared over the fence to see me spread-eagled: adorning my lawn like some daytime drunk.

When I say 'lawn' I actually mean gravel. Given my gainful employment pickle, funds hadn't stretched to the original concreting-over plans. Bear with me—it *is* relevant.

'Are you all right?' Ayling looked genuinely concerned. 'Shall I come round?'

I was only just coming round myself. Was I at all 'right', let alone 'all right'? I couldn't say. Literally. Other matters intruded.

In the ordinary course of things, say after a game of Cornish rugby or Celtic wrestling match, I like a massage. Yet the one I was now 'enjoying' from my gravel failed to please. Mother Earth and her stony shroud were both breathing heavily and mobile beneath my back. Not in any attempt to soothe, but rather to *reject*. As in heaving and retching, pre *'parking the tiger'* and a *'technicolour yawn'*. Or 'vomit' to you non-rugby-playing types.

I was inspired to get upright in a single bound. No mean feat for a desk-bound computer-jockey no longer in his prime. Ayling backed away. Not out of fear but guilt.

'Sorry…,' he repeated. Again, in my estimation, sincerely so. 'I did directly think better of it, honestly. I tried to cancel. *Pleaded*. Too late. I'd made the call, you see: blown the horn. Said the *'Ut! Ut! Ut!…'*

ALTERED ENGLANDS

'Said the *what?*'

'Doesn't matter.' Ayling was discomfited: had disclosed more than he should. 'Just something in the *Old Tongue*. But the point *is* that once... certain matters are set in motion... Well, you know what *families* are like...'

Did I? I didn't have time to think. For just then a gull messed on me. Copiously, *abundantly*. A precision *Stuka*-style dive-bomb and then *splat!* One off-white direct hit to the middle of my mullet. Where it mixed but not matched with the bloodstains already present to make (a mirror later revealed) a sort of *Mardi-Gras* meets raspberry-ripple hair-do

Then another bird emptied its bomb-bay bum on me, then another; then another: a sequence that felt *ad infinitum*. And also *ad nauseam*. With a squadron that size overhead Ayling should have got his proper portion too. But no. This was pinpoint precision bombing solely on and for me.

Needlessly, in words as redundant as I currently was, Ayling pointed out my *guanoed* state. I suppose he was, as ever, in search of something positive to say.

'Um, I think a bird's messed in your hair,' he said. Then: 'Some people say that's good luck...'

☸

'*A DICTIONARY OF ENGLISH SURNAMES.*'
Lady Caroline Callipyge Gale. Pevensey Castle Press. 1897.

'... AYLING: Anglo-Saxon origin. First attested in the *Rotuli Litterarum Clausarum*, (ed. T. D. Hardy, 2 vols. Record Commission, London 1833-44) c. 937 AD. Signifying the '*SUNA*' or sons or otherwise descendent ('*-ing*') of Aelle (*floruit* 477-514? AD), king of the South Saxons and also inaugural 'BRETWALDA' or pre-eminent ruler of the early English Heptarchy.

Initially acquired solely by right of claim in the Darwinian Dark Age struggle for supremacy, the Bretwalda honorific was later adopted by legitimate and recognised monarchs such as Alfred the Great and Aethelstan and their lines. Accordingly, bearers of the Ayling nomenclature were once attributed quasi-royal status and legal privileges...'

JOHN WHITBOURN

✸

So that was that. It came down to who-you-knew and family connections. I might well be *Mebyon Kernow*, but Alfred Ayling was *Suna* Aelle. And *Suna* Aethelstan and *Suna* Alfred *et al* (or *et Aelle*). Which here, on this soil, in this place, was trumps.

'Lady Caroline's dusty labour of love, dredged up from Exeter University Library's reference section, was the first book I'd cracked in weeks. Nevertheless, the *eyes* awaited me within. Their peering out from every page made the exercise a misery, costing me dear. Consulting the 'A' section alone was almost too much to take. Plus the whimpering and wincing noises any attempt at reading wrenched from me nowadays nearly got me chucked out. A librarian loudly accused me of indulging in furtive self-abuse. *'Our books are here for consultation,'* she said. *'Not for unnatural intercourse!'*

As if I didn't have enough on my plate. There simply wasn't room for public humiliation too. Not with my mind being perpetually fugged: incubated to fever pitch by the Old-Folks-Home-style heatwave I carried round with me. Such that milk curdled and food corrupted in my proximity. Leaving me *persona non grata* in every shop that sold perishables. And so starving.

Likewise, people shunned sharing my personal, portable, sauna. Granted, the guaranteed seat to myself on buses and trains was nice, but the Wife said it was like being in bed beside a barbeque. So, no more joint sleeping arrangements…

I'd gone to the University in search of work but my fame or infamy preceded me. I saw a photocopy of my 'Norman the Conqueror' masterpiece pinned to a departmental noticeboard. Proving I was already well known: but not in any work-recommending way. Therefore I didn't even ask. Derisory laughter often offends.

Exiting via the foyer, I stumbled over what felt like an invisible stuck-out foot. Flailing for support to stay upright, I brought down to destruction a displayed Grayson Perry vase—or:

'Objet d'art céramique sadomasochiste'

as per its proud placard.

ALTERED ENGLANDS

Purchased by the University for 'a five-figure sum', I thus acquired its shards for the same amount—or so a swarm of security guards and University bigwigs assured me. Prior to the police arriving to *'take my details'*. The boys in blue said I might get off with a caution. Maybe.

Exeter is a bumpy place and its University sits atop what students call 'Cardiac Hill'. So, my way home, of necessity, involved descent. Which seemed appropriate and in keeping with my career. The alternative was laying down to die. Which had its attractions too, but felt a tad defeatist. Not the sort of thing a stout *Mebyon Kernow* should do.

So off I set, on foot. Even if we hadn't had to sell my car I no longer trusted myself behind the wheel. Several times recently unseen hands had sought to seize control. That, plus the notion of my shot-nerves propelling a ton-plus weight capable of ton-plus speed, ruled motoring RIGHT OUT. Botched books, ruined restaurants, offensive obituaries, even obliterated 'five-figure' *objet d'art*, were bad enough, but bus queue massacres were a quantum leap I wasn't willing to risk. Yet.

Externally, intrinsically, it was a lovely day. Morning dew still laced the grass in places and flights of daddy-longlegs lifted off from the lawns around student accommodation bunkers. The sun shone down impartially on all—or almost all. For it was definitely dimmer wherever I went. In the face of my designer *Jonah-field* the laws of physics faltered, and light meant for me instead slowed and then stalled.

As did I upon beholding red *eyes* at head height blocking my path.

I shifted left. So did they. I moved right and—well, guess what...

This pair were exceptional(!), glittering with fanatic intent. And, I saw, every intention of acting upon it. *Now*.

I'd arrived at the climactic. Appropriately enough, my private micro-climate stepped up a notch in recognition. Sweat—implausibly both hot *and* cold—poured off me. I was, as the somewhat basic English saying says: 'flooding my boots'...

And yet, irate orbs aside, all around still looked so prosaic. Passersby passed by, not noticing. Across the road, the *Red Cow*, famous for its 'Wally's Special' cider (*'No Patron Shall Be Served In Excess Of A Quart'*), was open for business. Awaiting my order for a gallon.

And looming high above all was the Cathedral. Where I (an ardent atheist until a moment ago) wanted to seek sanctuary. However, all that alluring loveliness, including my house, lay *before* me. In-between, angry *eyes* interposed.

Whereas behind lay a clear—and left-clear—escape route to *Kernow*. Where I should be, apparently. Where all present thought I really should be. *Really*.

I'd had my warnings—a plethora of warnings *way* beyond what was reasonable—and chosen to ignore them. So, a senior figure was now here to insist.

Whoever it was shifted position, suggesting the hefting of a unseen sword held in ditto hands.

I proved less fearless than I thought and always said I was. Which, down the line, would provoke major self-image revision and distress. But back then I merely feared a sharp edge I couldn't see. Survival instincts surfaced and demanded—*demanded*—I address one threat-to-life at a time…

'Can't I go home to pack?' I asked. 'And let the Wife know? Please?'

It sounded even more pathetic than it reads.

Perhaps I should have appealed to Aethelstan and co.'s better nature. *'I mean,'* I might have said, had my usual eloquence not failed me, *'when all's said and done, that law of yours is ancient history. And so surely doesn't apply to modern me…'*

I could also have dwelled on how the English were supposedly keen on 'fair play'. Weak, weasel words along those lines...

Too late for words. The *eyes* slitted. A line of lightning from another universe slashed into mine. Slicing off my right ear. Kindly cauterising the wound at the same time.

I suppose I should have been thankful—over and above the agony. I *was* a wilful lawbreaker after all, and my offence a capital crime. Strictly speaking, it should have been my throat that was severed, not merely a single *shell-like*. So, maybe fair play and moderation *had* saved me…

Oddly enough, once again gratitude 'no-showed'.

Instead, *I* departed. As in about-turning and conquering Cardiac Hill in surely Exeter University 'all-time-best' beating style. Directly away from my aural-amender in any old direction, before settling on the shortest route to Cornwall.

All the way there my shoulders were hunched, any second expecting a bisecting blow. Leaving me conveniently autopsy-ready beside the A30. A transitory Police and Press puzzle. Then a 'still open' file. Finally an 'unsolved case'.

The doctor I saw at Launceston General said he'd never in all his career encountered such knotted neck and back muscles. Even months of physiotherapy failed to fully unclench them. So they're still much that way today, giving me a hunched, haunted look. As does the unpaid physio's bailiffs-and-bankruptcy debt-collection *jihad*. Yet another souvenir from my stay in England. Alongside fifty-percent shortfall in the standard ear quotient and consequent keeping-hats-and-sunglasses-on issues.

In sum, hardly the 'See the conquering hero come!' triumphal return to Kernow I'd envisaged...

☸

Still, all that was like a lover's kiss compared to the necessary 'phone call to the Wife'.

She didn't slam the phone down. She listened attentively whilst I was as honest as possible. Yet at confession's end only ominous silence ensued. Concluding in a *click*.

I'd no confidence she'd follow in my footsteps. Wherefore I became single again for a spell; embracing all the associated sad freedoms. Wherein I consoled myself.

Bottles mostly. And other curvaceous items.

Yet eventually she came. Packed up her job, packed up the house and then drove to my—now our—pokey Cornish bedsit.

Fortunately, belief in my tale and her consequent decision had been helped along. Not by my silver-tongued Celtic blarney but by the 'Law' now proceeding against her too. Albeit mildly and mercifully: not enforced with the full rigour I'd felt. Her England-quitting car was reportedly buffeted all the way by a customised evil weather-front just a bumper-span behind. Whose wicked winds cried not *'Mary'* but assurance of awaiting her at storm-strength should she ever darken east-of-the-Tamar doors again.

And guess who got the blame for that? Correct: yours truly! Which was *so* unfair! The eviction and expulsion, her crocked career and missed shopping-and-a-show trips? Apparently all *my* fault!

Some reunion! Believe me, *'Heathcliff! Cathy!'* it wasn't! Not by a long chalk.

For days I barely got a kind word out of the woman as she did the laundry and binned empties.

☸

So, welcome back to right now and us at *Welcombe*. The Wife and I studying the lost prospect.

From our permanent-exile-perspective England looked idyllic. A lost *Lyonesse*. Which was a thought I never thought I'd think.

At the *Olde Smithy Inn* the inept pub-luncher had finally acquired sufficient Cumberland-sausage-control to tuck in. He and his gaggle hadn't even noticed us two nosey-parker passersby not actually passing by but lingering longer and looking more longingly than was polite.

Not so the sentinel *eyes*, red and vigilant. *They* noticed. Unseen save by us, they watched over these oblivious Englishfolk. Whilst watching us. Like hawks. Waiting, wanting, *ravenous*.

One cross-Tamar step was all it would take. Then these post-human, pre-human-rights-era, immigration officers would step in to do their Dark Age stuff. Or, as they doubtless saw it, simply enforce the Law. Aethelstan's never-repealed law.

Nothing personal.

Unlike the Wife's verdict on all this and me.

She turned to (and on) me. To say:

'You *stupid* Celt…'

At least I think that's what she said.

Yet, as *I've* said, she's generally soft-hearted. Many's the time she's said I'd have to leave her before she ever left me.

Which must account for her snapping. And snap decision. And shoving me into England.

☸

ALTERED ENGLANDS

35~

YOU MUST BE COLD

☸

INTRODUCTION

I was an archaeologist once, but have successfully (well, OK: a few lapses maybe; I'm only human…) been going straight for decades now. Other than to confess that, I draw a veil of obscurity over the affair. Everyone deserves a second chance.

Except that I feel a valedictory compulsion to impart and so perpetuate my experience that on the whole, by and large (especially large), and all other things being equal, British lady archaeologists really are quite *lovely*. Up to and including *exquisite* in many cases. Futurity should know this.

And, lest it be necessary to disabuse the more… low-minded reader, I stress that I speak here of persons and connections of *unimpeachable propriety*. *Honi soit qui mal y pense.*

So, to: Amy, Anne, Ann, 'Blond Betty-Boop', Diane, Ellie-the-cook, Garden Hill's raw pastry chef, Hascombe 'T. A. Lady', Jayney, Joy, Linda, Lizzy-B, Lorraine, Lynne, Mary, Melissa, Sally, Sue-of-Hascombe, Thelma… and *et al.* Good on you and *bless* you. Ladies like you make the world a better (or leastways more tolerable) place.

Less happily, I feel I should apologise in advance to a certain someone herein, who, for 'spoiler' reasons, shall presently remain nameless—but let's call them JM. I little doubt I've done JM an undeserved disservice here, even though, at the time, they'd probably have had me shot. So now we're equal—no hard feelings.

If both of us should chance to make it to Heaven, I'll buy JM a double ambrosia.

YOU MUST BE COLD

'*You* must be cold!'

The Director spoke not to me but the brave soul atop Dunadd. There was no chance the distant figure would hear: he was a mini-mountain and good quarter-mile away. Even so, we could plainly see he was in his shirtsleeves, so he got co-opted into my briefing.

'I'm not your mummy,' the Director continued, back to me and only me again, 'but I'd advise you wrap up warmer than that twit when you're atop. It blows a breeze there 24/7. You'll sweat during the heavy work, then chill. That way you get colds. I don't hold with colds or days off sick—save maybe for mortal wounds. *Maybe*. And even then I expect you to wait till lunchtime to get an ambulance.'

I'd heard tell this dig was hard-line, though I think the last bit was an attempt at humour. I reviewed it by failing to smile and keeping strictly to business.

'Where will I be?' I asked.

I saw three separate trenches opened on Dunadd, plus a fair start on sectioning the ramparts. All looked equally promising and my settled stance was not to care. From finds-washing and finicky whisk-work, right through to brute-force-and-ignorance pickaxe stuff: it was all the same to me nowadays: all archaeology—the only thing I had left to love.

'You've been around,' the Director conceded. 'Your references are good. So…, the summit I reckon, plus your fair share of the ramparts, naturally. Every hefty bloke takes their turn there. But up top is where I mostly see you: that's where I've greatest hope.'

JOHN WHITBOURN

I think he wanted me to ask *'of what?'* but I passed on that, boss or no. I knew his reputation as he knew mine. Like he said, I'd been around: a *'nomad'* as we're termed, a pittance-paid professional digger, at home on any site from Palaeolithic to post-Medieval, from Afghanistan to Argyll, as now. My 1990s-spanning *CV* spoke for itself. I'd earn my money, such as it was.

The Director accepted I wasn't another of his archaeology undergraduate conscripts doing their compulsory fieldwork, nor yet some volunteer from the local leisured bourgeoisie. Not only did I have a decade or two on the former, but my skills could command payment, unlike the latter. There were plenty of other places who'd have me and be glad of it. So, he'd have no fun from psychological games with (or from) me—only competent graft. Of course, he wasn't privy to my cheap scotch habit: that was an in-my-tent-only secret. In public I was staunch teetotal.

I don't think he was disappointed as such. Every excavation needs a leaven of *'leave 'em alone and let 'em get on with it'* types. All the enthusiasm and *joie de vivre* can be delegated to the far greater number of youngsters (of all ages).

'OK,' he said, still surveying his site, seeking out imperfections after having failed with me. 'Start this afternoon. Pitch your tent: settle in: help yourself to some lunch. We kick off again at 14:00—sharp. Report to Duncan on the summit. Tell him I said you can jump straight in.'

Viewing where I'd soon be made us both notice the lone figure again. He was still at the very top of Dunadd, indifferent to the elements. I presume the view was distracting him: the dig prospectus said it was spectacular—over to Mull and Jura, even across to Ireland on a clear day (i.e. rarely).

'Twit!' the Director repeated. 'He'll catch his death—though maybe that's what he wants...'

There was a definite hook in his words that he really hoped would be bitten. Gruff might be my chosen default, but rarely rudeness—so I bit.

'What do you mean?'

The Director did his 'sort-of' smile that *hinted* at a human side yet didn't commit him further.

'Well,' he said, still wearing that annoying 'man of the world' smirk. 'Dunadd sometimes gets used for flying lessons, y'ken...'

I could guess, but wanted him to spell it out—just so all the crassness should be on his shoulders alone. It also didn't help that his overdone, *'have I mentioned I'm Scottish?'* accent had started to grate. I'm born and bred myself but never felt the need to provocatively roll my *rrrrs* all over the place like that. The next station along was mangling *'Rabbie'* Burns and wearing a kilt other than under duress at weddings. Include me out.

'What?' I pretended to be slow, even trying to sound English. 'Hang-gliding do you mean?'

A snort of pseudo-amusement. '*Och* no; I mean the free, solo, amateur sort. *Failed* and once-only flying lessons. Fine take-offs but crap landings…'

My, *how* I laughed. *Not.*

That accent didn't only soar, from time to time it also slipped. I suspected this born-again was actually born in Birmingham. Another bandwagon-boarding *'bonnie-prince-shortbread-tin'* Scot slapping down the ethnic trump card.

'Don't worry,' I told him—*told* him, and with his own words too. 'I'm here to *'jump in'*, not jump off. Anyhow, whereabouts in Wales do you come from?'

⚘

'Dunadd,' said the Director, 'as a hilltop stronghold has its origins in the Iron Age, but only really achieves prominence from the seventh century CE—that is to say, *Current Era*—onwards. Its name derives from the Goidelic Gaelic—*not* '*Celtic*', if you please…'

Polite titters met this scornful reference to common if misplaced parlance. He and his informed audience were at self-congratulatory one regarding discredited and racially tinged terminology.

The Director's *Braveheart* meets am-dram *Macbeth* accent had gone down a notch or four for this spiel to distinguished guests. They were, after all, *distinguished*. Who knows, maybe some of them carried keys to *funding* in their pockets or purses (not sporrans). Or even *recommendations*, and thus the Holy Grail of *tenure*. It was important he be inclusive and *sensible*.

'… meaning fort on the River Add: hence *Dún Add*. The site is notable for its—count 'em: one, two, three, four—successive circuits of cyclopean dry-stone ramparts, and for featuring in so-called 'Dark Age' chronicles as the capital, for want of a better word, of the Kingdom of Dál Riata. Popular attention is also caught by the famed 'coronation stone', complete with footprint-shaped indentation, which we shall see on the summit. I shall also point out the highly significant Pictish incised boar symbol and the Ogham inscription.'

Us foot-soldiers knew this stuff from the dig prospectus or else had heard it all before. So we just carried on scraping away on our hands and knees, pretending we weren't being observed like zoo animals and the more shapely raised arses covertly admired.

I was pretty safe in that last respect, but still felt the creepy caress of *'wonder what's he doing?'* looks along the spine. It is the one thing even veteran diggers never get used to: being conscript mime-artists performing for free. It might help if the audience brought bags of buns along to throw. Especially since tea break times were strictly enforced on this excavation, and dinner often seemed stomach-rumblingly distant.

But no buns flew, only guilty glances at bums, so there was nothing for it but to pretend we occupied separate realities. I turned my back on the invaders from planet Academia.

And thus towards my companion in this section of *'Trench Two'*. Flora was a sweet old soul, not, I soon discerned, exactly overtaxed by playing housewife to the retired Mathematics professor who'd heard about Dunadd on the departmental grapevine and suggested she volunteer. I could almost hear the conversation over breakfast that brought her here and into my less-than-convivial company: *'Might get you out of the house, old girl: give you an interest. Leave it to me, my dear; I'll have a word with the Head of Archaeology...'*

So he had and here she was. But no one had told her that buying a *riveted* trowel was no good—they don't last five minutes. And though someone had loaned her a proper one and devoted all of five seconds to demonstrating its use, she was left in the dark about why and what for. Why scrape so slowly down through the mantle of Mother Earth? What might be revealed that a spade couldn't tell you ten times quicker?

I'll admit the milk of human kindness has pretty much curdled in me, but I felt sorry for Flora, who meant well yet hadn't turned out as she'd once upon a time hoped. The ghost of her girlish smile now had a gravitational pull towards '20 past 8'. That much I could readily empathise with.

'Here,' I chose then to say—even though the Director was still in full flow and conversation was *'discouraged'* during working hours, 'try it this way: sweep *towards* you—and with the fingers, not the wrist. That way you get more control in it and don't go home sore. *That's* the ticket: good. See that chocolate colour layer coming up through the lighter stuff? Gently scrape at the edges of it and get some more. Reveal the shape like it's a puzzle. Right? Now, that's *fill* you're revealing: a back-filled pit no one but you has seen since it stopped being useful a millennium ago…'

Us nomad-diggers no longer leap like salmon at the *'Chasms of Time'* aspect of the job, but I could see Flora was—why mince words?—*thrilled*. Over this evening's sherry *aperitifs* she'd have something to tell hubby about what *she'd* done today.

I sensed bad vibes bathing the back of my neck and guessed the Director wasn't digging (if you'll excuse the pun) my little seminar. Not only was I breaching the no chitchat rule and distracting from his spiel, but he hadn't forgiven me for the *Wales* crack last week either.

'As I was *trying* to say, ladies and gentlemen,' he said, voice raised, 'Dunadd has been excavated on a number of occasions: in 1904-5 and 1929 and, most professionally, in 1980 by the then University of *Wales*…'

Was it my neck hairs' imagination, or was someone dancing on my grave, inspired by that last word?

'Accordingly,' he pressed on, 'the primary purpose of our 2001 digging season is to ascertain if there remain any significant areas undisturbed by those previous investigations, and to seek evidence, such as firing or deliberate demolition, of the two attested sieges of the site, in 683 and 736 CE, as per the Annals of Ulster. This will primarily be tested, as you can see, by a thorough sectioning of each of the ramparts…'

And somehow I knew, with all the faith of a saint in Christ, that I would be working on the ramparts that afternoon, even though it wasn't my turn—and doubly sure if it came on to rain as the clouds threatened. Meaning moving monstrous rocks in inadequate wheelbarrows until, by knocking off time, I resembled Argyll's answer to *The Beast from Fifty Fathoms'*.

So be it. I no longer expected any day to be my day. In the immortal words of my hero, Ho Chi Minh, *'So much of misfortunate have I seen that I have set my face like stone'*. No one would ever know what I thought of extra ramparts work—or anything else.

'What should I do about this?' Flora had leant across and whispered in my ear, so keen was she to avoid Directorial reproof. 'There's a stone in my—the—pit…'

And then I saw that today could never have been my day—or anyone else's bar Flora's. There, revealed by her timid scrapes, was a slab of slate: non-native to Dunadd geology but precisely what the Picts favoured for their enigmatic (*le mot juste* coming up) pictograms.

I went over and reverently puffed the remaining crumbs of earth away, never really doubting what I would see. Sure enough, though still begrimed, there were the etched lines, white on grey: swirls of surprising calligraphic skill.

Before the invading Scots (probably) wiped them out, the Picts had sealed Flora's pit with this last token of… something or other. It was one of the extra-enigmatic kind: a *'swimming elephant'* symbol: the headlines-worthy find of a lifetime.

I indicated Flora should look closer. So she did and she saw—but yet didn't.

'Oh, God!' she said, actually *scared*. 'Those marks—have I scratched it?' I'm *so* sorr-…'

'*'Sorry'* is it?' I echoed—but for her ears only. *'Au Cointreau*, hen: in the immortal words of that witch Thatcher: *'Rejoice! Just rejoice!'* Now, prepare to bask in glory…'

I backed off and whistled, high-pitched like a shepherd, suggesting the Director should shut up and come over. It was another total certainty that his frown would be turned upside down (and stay pinned that way for days) the second he got here.

'Look what Flora's found!' I told all promiscuously, from Director to lowest pickaxe-pleb (just so that it couldn't be… *nuanced*—or even *'och-aye-the-noo'-anced*—later). 'And cleaned off perfectly too! She's gonna be *famous!*

Then, without asking for permission, I adjourned for a smoko, knowing there'd be no more work on Trench Two that glorious Flora-made morning.

☸

I suppose I could have stayed to share the joy, and hear the honeyed words poured over a stunned Flora, but bright scenes like that were no longer my scene. I took myself away from humanity and left them to their happiness. At least then I wouldn't spoil things with my brooding presence.

On Dunadd's summit I stood beside (not *on*—I was still an archaeologist) the pseudo foot-imprint stone used in the coronation of Dark Age kings, drawing on a menthol-tipped 50-50 baccy/weed roll-up. The view over the Add and its *'Great Moss'* bog, the little farms and hamlets all the way to Lochgilphead and the Crinan canal, and then the horizon-forming pine-twilight of Kilmichael forest—it was *splendid*. Even the storm clouds did the decent thing and made way for a rare bit of sunshine. Aside from the omnipresent biting midges (probably proof against *ack-ack* guns, never mind mere smoke) things looked and were as good as they were ever going to get.

But not for me. How could I feel joy when Joy had definitively said *'No'*? And how to get into the party spirit when the Party was no more?

High up—washed up—atop Dunadd at the tender age of forty, I realised I was high and dry.

✹

Communists are often at a loose end on Sundays. Especially since their Party dissolved itself (or committed suicide) in 1991. And you'll not be surprised to hear that church-going isn't high on the alternative to-do list—though it *may* amuse to learn that many have taken up bird-watching since. And no—I don't care to analyse that for fear of what it might say about *me*. For the record, I've no intention of emulating them. Where's the pleasure in living under a cloud of suspicion of being a peeping tom?

And, as with my life-long cause, likewise with the love of my life. Joy was (at best I knew since we no longer spoke) hundreds of miles and a routine I knew nothing of away. Our last—still searing—conversation has cauterised any lingering hopes I had on the *'us'* front. That's what happens when you only get to meet a (and also THE ONE!) woman via being already engaged to her sister.

This excavation started late on the Sabbath. Some reactionary diggers went to Mass, others had a lay-in and nursed their hangovers. Me? Oblivion in a bottle being out of the question, my round-and-round-about thoughts drove me out of my sleeping bag bright and early.

The nearest farm to Dunadd had a Sabbatarian *'Wee-Free'* tenant, but a workaholic sheepdog. The latter couldn't abide idleness and so, whilst his master attended chapel, read the Bible or did whatever it is Calvinists do when God calls, he went out *looking* for work. This took the form of shepherding flocks of walkers, whom he'd guide, darting, barking and nipping as he did with four-legged sheep, up to the top of Dunadd, and then back down again. I'd seen him do it from Sunday dawn to dusk, amusing or annoying folk according to type.

That morning all he could find was me, but a flock of one is better than nothing. Being ever fonder of animals the more I learned of humans, I swallowed my pride and allowed myself to be herded aloft. It was where I was going to bide a while in any case. This way at least someone would get a little pleasure out of it.

Then, near the top, workaholic-dog suddenly changed his mind. Instead of urging me on he counselled retreat. In fact, he tried to enforce it, placing jaws round my jeans, trying to draw me back. That was the stick: his carrot was whimpering, tugging at the heartstrings as he did my trousers. *'Humour me, oh two-legs,'* he was saying. *'Don't make a hard-working hound unhappy just because you can…'*

I fully approve of overturning human hierarchies but that's as far as it goes. Giving in to him would be taking animal rights consciousness (a *petit-bourgeois* deviation in any case) a step too far. So I took *contrary* steps and said something not for delicate ears and shook the moody beast off and away. Its advice slighted, it soon showed me a clean set of pads.

Whereupon I reached the top and saw that the 'fresh air freak' was back, still only shirt-sleeved. Yet somehow the man was managing to keep his old-style trilby on without having to clamp it down. The wind blew and buffeted him and me but kindly relented re his headgear. Odd.

Thoughts of how that might be reminded me of the weather. I was in my parka and glad of it too, unfashionable fur trim and all. Whereas my surprise (and unwanted) companion was high-summer clad.

There was no escaping conversation: we'd happened on each other at point-blank range. To say nothing at all would be tantamount to rudery. So:

'You must be cold…'

I didn't mean to take him by surprise. I assumed my arrival, complete with towed cur, had been heard but politely ignored. Yet when he turned the middle-aged man was a picture of horror. He didn't expect to see me. He didn't see *how* he could see me.

And then I couldn't see him because he vanished.

ALTERED ENGLANDS

Back at the tent lines the Director caught me and started to say what I could do today. Still in shock, I told him precisely what *he* could do.

And then I arbitrarily took the day off, heading for habitations and people and noise and anywhere *not*-Dunadd, meanwhile telling myself repeatedly:

'That did *not* happen. That did *not* happen…'

※

But it *did* and nothing I could say, however often, could shake that. So when I got off the bus in Tarbert I headed for the nearest pub.

Soaking in four pints of *'heavy'* made me feel a little better, maybe even made me look better, because the landlord then engaged me in conversation, which I'd seen him decide against before.

'What brings you to Tarbert, pal?' he asked, skipping the pointless *'You're not from round here, are you?'* foreplay. He meant well—but thereagain so did Stalin.

'Archaeology' was just too complicated, and sometimes even controversial ('grave-robbing' and all that), so I said I was a dry-stone waller. I saw him check out my hands but they fitted the bill, meaning the bogus conversation could stumble on a few more clauses. I don't even remember what other lies, if any, I told.

Afterwards I went and explored the town—which occupied all of ten minutes, including a fair while staring entranced into a recordshop window display of antique Andy Stewart and Moira Anderson *'White Heather Club'* LPs. *'Warning!'* said the cheeky placard placed above. *'These records may include phrases such as "Hoots Mon!" and "D'ye no ken?" May also contain traces of tartan-tomfoolery.'*

Then I bought a *bridie* and chips and went and sat by the harbour, watching the fishing boats. Having been bitten before I should have known better. Blame the beer. The mutton (maybe) and greasy pastry *atrocity* was rejected by every taste bud even before I chewed. That first and last mouthful went into a handy bin and the balance got chucked onto the beach. A vigilant seagull swooped, sniffed—and then flew away empty-beaked! Which is something I have never seen before in my entire life, anywhere in the world…

Whereas my new companion sitting beside me: him I'd met before. He wasn't there a moment ago; now he suddenly was, though how I couldn't tell. The half-gallon of *heavy* evaporated instantly.

Shirtsleeves from Dunadd recognised me.

'Oh, you again,' he said. 'How d'you do?'

There was surprise at seeing me—or at me seeing him—but not the previous dismay. He now seemed reconciled to the encounter.

I couldn't say the same. I couldn't say anything at all. Yet hardwired behavioural traits made me match the friendly hand he extended.

Mistake: worse than the *bridie*. His hand was so frigid that when I shook it my skin stuck.

I was able to tear myself away from that grip, but not, alas, from the bench and *off*. That was asking too much of my trembling legs.

He studied the little patches of me I'd left adhering to his palm.

'We seem connected in more ways than one,' he said. 'Sorry about that, my friend.'

Again, ancient engines cut in to say something polite instead of what I felt.

'That's okay...'

'I'm John, by the way. John Maclean. Nice to meet you.'

And in a funny, totally implausible, way, it actually *was*. *Now* I knew why that open, friendly face seemed familiar. He was someone I'd long admired but never thought to meet. What with him dying in, what was it—1923? I'd sort of ruled it out.

The warm flood of data was now the sole thing that kept me there in that frost-generating presence. Otherwise, I'd have been away down Harbour Street wailing like a banshee. As it was, I *had* to know...

'What?' I asked, through chattering teeth. '*The* John Maclean? Hugh MacDiarmid *poem* John Maclean? *'Red Clydeside'* and all that? *'Scotland's Lenin'?*'

He smiled. 'I'd not go that far, though I'm flattered to be compared to the great man. But MacLenin? No: though the Bolsheviks were kind enough to make me their Scottish consul...'

And... and I believed it. Believed *him*. The modesty, the charm, accorded with all I'd read. He fitted every grainy photograph I'd seen. Even the shirtsleeves detail was spot on. I remembered now: he died young, before his time and way before he ought—of pneumonia. It was part of the Maclean legend and typical of the (living) man. Though weakened by prison hunger-strikes and forced feeding, he'd loaned his only overcoat to a Jamaican comrade suffering in a Scottish winter. Whereof he died…

Died. John Maclean was *dead*. Did that mean…?

'No,' he told me, still looking straight ahead at the same scene as me—or so I then thought. 'You're all right, my friend. Or so-so anyway. Although obviously in some sort of trouble if you can see me. Mebbe that's what drew me here. I always had a habit of heading towards trouble….' He suddenly turned to me and, faced with that sincere countenance, I felt ashamed for feeling fear. 'But only ever to help, mind,' he added to reassure me. 'Only ever for the Cause…'

Wasn't that the truth! He was *our* hero; of Highlands stock, in and out of prison till it was a second home; fearless before raw power in the second *'Killing Time'* of WW1. A proletarian internationalist to his fingertips, but a better Scottish patriot than Wallace or Bruce ever were!

So I stayed. My coat was crisped on one side by the chill he radiated, but I stayed because here was a *man*…

Was… Second-thoughts time. I didn't believe in ghosties or *any* mumbo-jumbo. To do so would require a revolution in everything that made up the nation state of *Me*. A dilemma.

John Maclean sensed and solved it.

'Don't fret,' he said. 'Just accept there's a Court of Appeal—justice arriving eventually. I don't even *try* to think it through any more. I'm just grateful…'

It was no longer possible to resist hugging myself. His cold had entered my bones.

'How do y'mean, Mr Maclean? What court-…'

'It's *John*, please,' he cut in. 'And have you no heard a picture's worth a thousand words? Look about. Tell me what you see.'

For a teacher by trade he had brawn in his arms. He waved one to encompass Tarbert.

I looked and duly reported. An alleged town little bigger than a village. Water to two sides. A withered fishing fleet. The chippie where my *bridie* was born, that jokey recordshop…

And yet, truth to tell, all that seemed less… clear than before. Squinted at just right, some other scene slipped in and out of sight behind *my* panorama. Something busier: and better?

Maclean nodded.

'You can almost glimpse it, can't you, son? Which means you're sharing my vision. And shall I tell you what that is? It's *Socialist* Tarbert, in collectivised Argyll, part of the *'Red Highlands'* and SSSR: the good old Scottish Socialist Soviet Republic! Which is in turn not the least part, if I may say so, of the USSE…'

Because he wanted me to I played 'guess the acronym'.

'The USS… Europe…?' I ventured.

Maclean grinned. He had better news than that even.

'*Earth,*' he told me.

I looked again and now saw more. When the vision chose to firm up, I viewed superior, safer, trawlers. Red flags flew from church and kirk spires; and all the workers' towerblocks too. Passersby looked healthier, *happier*; less abraded by Capitalism's relentless war of all versus all.

A part of me is incurably frivolous: it's why I never aspired to Party office when it was still around. At that sublime moment I saw fit to wonder if there were *bridies* in that ideal world. If so, likely they were *delicious* ones…

'Remember?' said my companion—*'friend'* even. 'A Court of Appeal, like I told you.'

And now it was staying with me for whole seconds at a time. I saw the world the great John Maclean had fought and, aye, *died* for. And now had to hand. For those snippets of time I stopped wanting to scream or flee.

Yet, still a residual rationalist, I tried to rationalise things.

'It could be the *'Many Worlds Theorem'*,' I suggested. 'Modern Physics, you know. That every *possible* world actually does exis-…'

Maclean shrugged.

'Och, who knows? Or cares?' he said, impassioned into dialect, 'I dinnae want to analyse it. All I know is this: I may have nae overcoat, but as recompense I've got a whole world instead!'

Heady stuff! Even as all feeling left the side of me nearest to him, I felt the glow of something so unfamiliar this last arid decade I didn't initially recognise it. Without first introducing itself, *hope* just felt… weird. Weird but warming…

Words failed me—but something seemed expected. So:

'So…?'

Maclean again turned to me full-face, focussing the personal force that had made him a giant of his time.

ALTERED ENGLANDS

'Gift horse, son,' he counselled. 'Leave its mouth alone: that's my advice. Here's a world as real as any other, but a bloody site better than most—excuse my language. And everyone gets their own tailor-made world! I can get you into yours…'

Abruptly, Maclean's face fell. If forced to interpret, I'd read it as realising he'd gone too far.

Equally abruptly, he was also gone. I sat alone again in… *okay*, I suppose, but basically business-as-usual Tarbert. Which would no longer *do*.

That morning I'd thought my reality was all there was, and had been sort of resigned to it. Now, around midday the same day, it just left a sour taste in the mouth that was nothing to do with *bridies*.

❈

My performance slipped, the Director turned (still more) sarky. I took to taking long lone walks in Kilmichael Forest.

Which is a dead and commercial place. Just rows of £s & pence pines, ringed with logging roads designed to carry really big rigs. You learned to give a wide berth to those—once going fully laden with slaughtered trees they weren't stopping for anyone.

Yet, for all its faults, it would do for me, for now, for brooding in. It had been real once, you could see that much. There was a proper deserted village from the *'Clearance'* days, and a WWII POW camp where Glaswegian lumberjacks now slept off their work and play. I even found a 'secret' waterfall set in its own little canyon, which I bet no one bar me had stopped to admire since the forest was founded. Like with everything and everywhere else, there were *just* sufficient remnant scraps to keep me going.

Those evening strolls-more-like-marches were meant to steel me. Or heal me: the good old 'walking cure'. As in so many things, the Romans had it sussed: *solvitur ambulando*: *'It is solved by walking.'*

And it *almost* was. That particular slog, striding along in twilight silence with only my own personal midge cloud for company, I nearly sorted things. John Maclean? Deceased 1923? What a load of…. That Tarbert beer must have been stronger than I thought. And, before it, the air atop Dunadd rarefied and head-deluding. Lord alive, *New Labour* was easier to believe in than any of this supernatural stuff.

Then the forest beside me spoke. At that point the logging road narrowed to a darkening tunnel of trees. To either side, the pine shade was profound; I couldn't tell what was happening mere feet from me—but something was. The tree cover at my shoulder groaned and heaved as a more-than-human happening headed my way.

I had a long second to prepare, and in that time all my flimsy barricades fell. I knew it was *him* and that I'd been a bairn to deny my own five (maybe six) senses. Only children and cowards cling to delusion. I accepted and surrendered.

I *had* conversed with Scotland's greatest Communist, even though our lives did not coincide. And I *did* want Joy—joy with Joy. Of course I did. Every molecule of me did. Marriage and babies and all the trimmings. Forever, till I died in her arms. And, yes, I did hunger for Peace and Socialism: worldwide human solidarity and mutual assistance. *'From each according to their abilities, to each according to their needs.'* With a vanguard Party to guarantee it. Those things were my entire world, my real one, and I *did* want a world with them in it Why prolong the deadly drought of the last decade?

So, in that short space I decided. If a dead man offered me miracles I'd not inspect that aforementioned equine oral cavity. I'd damn well take my due—and sod the implications.

Whereupon a red deer: a huge *'Monarch of the Glen'*-style stag, emerged from the forest edge. He was every bit as stunned to see me as I him. It was 'just' him, no one else, minus the harem he probably had somewhere near, but a big enough commotion-causing old boy all the same.

'Struck comical' as I was, His Majesty could had trampled me, maybe even speared me with his probably (I didn't count) sixteen-point tines, for spoiling his evening promenade. In the event, he just graciously progressed by. Crossing the road (without looking), His Highness then barged through the opposite tree cover and out of my life.

But not without leaving his mark. Before the noise of that departure died away, even before I'd metaphorically crammed my heart back down where it belonged, this crossing of paths had settled things. In the Party Congress of my mind my earlier 'decision' was formally proposed, seconded, voted on, and then passed unanimously to tumultuous acclaim.

'Democratic Centralism' now dictated that all comrades should follow the new Party line.

ALTERED ENGLANDS

I hit the hill at first light, knowing—*knowing*—he'd be there. En route I met the Director, an early riser who'd already been out and got his *'Guardian.'*

It was a blustery day and my face must have matched it. Seeing me was shock enough to make him drop the plump *'Public Appointments'* supplement.

'Oh—I mean *och*,' he said. 'What's up? Where are you go-…'

'I quit!' I told him.

'But your contract… notice…'

I didn't even pause on the path up.

'Tough. What you gonna *do* about it, Taffy?'

Nothing was what—you could bet the farm on it.

John Maclean was waiting at the summit. Always Mr Dependable: as in life so in… whatever.

Unfortunately, also present were a primary-coloured gaggle of *cagoul*ed hikers—early birds who saw and heard me—but not him, I think. Which explains their *looks* at me, and then swift leaving when conversation started.

'Why here?' I asked, without preamble. Incredibly, it was the one thing still puzzling me. 'Why survey the scene from Dunadd?'

Maclean smiled at the scenery. Answer came easy.

'Because of you, I presume,' he said. 'We seem to be fated: linked like with handcuffs. But also for the *contrasts*: I sometimes bide here for them.'

I looked but couldn't see anything. The Crinan peninsula was pretty monocultural till you got to Glasgow. Maclean took pity.

'Beginnings and ends,' he explained. '*Alphas* and *Omegas*. There's so much to relish. *Progress*. Think about it, son: from here, home of kings—and barbarian warlord kings at that—to…,' he waved at the—his—*'Red Highlands'*, 'to Human Liberation Day!'

It was a thought. Though I also had another one.

'But don't barbarian kings get their own—horrible—heavens too? What do *those* look like?'

Maclean shrugged his shirt. 'Don't know. No idea. I've never so much as glimpsed one. They probably don't get to go there…'

I could have baulked at that, this blush-birthing brush with theology. I could have brought out my fig leaf *'Many Worlds Theorem'* again, but, characteristically, Maclean wouldn't take the easy way out.

'Aye, I know,' he said, as near to tetchy as I'd heard him, 'it's getting close to *'God'* and all that Kirk cack. Well, I didnae believe in him or them in Life and I'm damned if I will now. So what? Mebbe the Big Man's love is infinite like the pastors said—but so are all his worlds. That'll do for me.'

Why did I maintain my life-membership of the awkward squad, even on the threshold of Paradise? Joy was calling me and yet here I was quibbling. I realised now what a fool I was—and always had been.

'So you can even ignore *Him*,' I said, 'if that's your thing—to keep sort of honest… consistent…'

Maclean gave the curtest of nods. 'He doesnae mind—he's no touchy.'

And then John had had enough of 'that sort of talk'. He turned and put a cold hand on my shoulder.

'So, what *is* your problem, man? Tell me. Cough it up…'

And, amazingly, I did. It all came blurting out. Joy, the Party, the fall of the Wall; ten years of wandering the world wounded. I sobbed the lot up like a great big *Jessie*.

Maclean didn't judge (though I saw him shudder when I said about the USSR). He just rested a fatherly (and anaesthetising) palm on me, and endured the Olympic-gold whine.

Then, when I'd done:

'You too, eh?' he said, kindly avoiding my red eyes, back to looking out over *his* world again. 'D'ye know, the only folks I seem to meet these days are in despair. One foot in the grave…'

That struck a cord—or maybe alarm bell. But I couldn't recall why.

'I won't show you,' he said, 'but I can see it, plain as anything: your future here. It's not much. Two years from now you'll be unemployable: even as a *'nomad digger'*—whatever *that* is. Alcoholism, unreliability, *delirium tremens*. A couple of criminal convictions even: *silly*, boozed-up, crimes. And you'll never have another woman…'

'I don't want one!'

'Aye, I know. You only want *one*. Because you've a good heart. Your sort often suffer the worst. But now there's no need. I can give her to you.'

Wow! The utterly impossible and irrecoverable—all lined up waiting for me!

I was *gagging* for it—but still a well brought-up boy. Highland homes of my vintage had 'manners' on the core curriculum. No *'please'* got ignored; no

ALTERED ENGLANDS

'*thank you*' got whatever you'd been given snatched back. And maybe a clipped ear too. Too late to change now.

'Thank you; Oh Christ, *thank you*, Mr Mac-... John. But how? No, *why?* Why do you do this?'

John Maclean turned his head to smile: a real thirty-two teeth dazzler.

'I just want to do good, lad; to make things better. Like I did in life. Like with that coloured comrade...' He tugged one shirtsleeve to remind me. 'Its just a shame Life makes you use death to do it.'

Screech of brakes. Emergency stop.

'What?'

Mr Maclean held my shoulder all the firmer. A death-grip.

'Well, *obviously*, son,' he said, 'you can't get into your perfect world alive. There's a wee entry fee to be paid.'

'But...'

'Steady on now; you're one of us: a comrade. You know what the great Vladimir Ilyich said: you cannae make an omelette without breaking a few eggs...'

For the first time in my adult life I no longer cared what Lenin said.

'No!'

'S'true. Omelettes and eggs; revolutions and heads...'

I now saw John Maclean's world plain. Saw *exactly* what he did. The landscape I'd known was gone.

'No!'

The collectivised farms were famine factories. It wasn't just sheepdogs who worked seven days a week all their short lives. In the hamlets there were scaffolds: they sagged with *examples* bearing placards strung round stretched necks. From Lochgilphead I heard the crackle of a distant firing squad. Dunadd was now crowned with a statue of Stalin. We two stood in its titanic shadow.

And, *somehow*, I could see Joy. She scowled at me—and everything. Joy was in uniform, a dead-eyed commissar buttoned up to *here*. Completely contemptuous of bourgeois deviations like '*Love.*'

John Maclean saw too. 'It's for their—and your—own good,' he said. '*False consciousness*' must be crushed. Mercy is just milksop sentiment. The proletariat requires firm guidance by a vanguard! A steel vanguard. Hard as steel. Cold as steel. You must be cold! *You must be cold!*'

This last was delivered in a rising scream, touched by what only the kind would call madness. But screamed with a *smile*.

Finally it occurred to me to wonder just who was this *'He'* we'd been talking about. Who precisely was it that had created this world for Mr Maclean?

Or part of him. I now knew what portion of John Maclean had survived to meet me. The majority best bits were long gone elsewhere.

The dead are supernaturally strong. I was picked up like a toy (which to him I suppose I was) and aimed at rocks far below.

I expect the coroner blames a freak wind for hurling me off the hill. Or yet another Dunadd *'failed flying lesson.'*

ALTERED ENGLANDS

JOHN WHITBOURN

THE BINSCOMBE TALES: CODA & COMPLETION

✸

COMPRISING:

'PUBLISH & BE DAMNED!'
'UP FROM THE CELLAR' or 'ENGLAND EXPECTS!'

INTRODUCTION

Herewith two stories which should speak for themselves—and so they jolly well ought, allowing their poor old Dad to have a rest. However, being 'Attitudinally challenged' like so many of my offspring, they won't. Therefore I'll have to rouse myself.

'Publish & Be Damned' is a case of real life intermingling with fiction—or possibly vice versa. Which makes your think… Barbara and Christopher of the *Ash-Tree Press* are best placed to recount the background. Whereafter I 'go off on one' yet again.

'Up from the Cellar' aka *'England Expects!'* forms the very last (canonical number 26!) and semi-explanatory Binscombe Tale. It was published in *'More Binscombe Tales—Sinister Sutangli Stories'* in 1999,[124] but not in any of the subsequent reprints. For no real reason I can recall at this remove. *'Blame it on the boogie.'*

---

[124] The widely feared spectre of *'Yet More Bloody Binscombe Tales!'* (2000) never materialised.

ALTERED ENGLANDS

Aficionados and/or survivors of the *'Binscombe'* sequence who might in the past have yearned to get ahold of Mr Disvan's lapels and drag a straight answer out of him, may—I only say *may*—find some or other closure therein.

Though never underestimate the man (if man he be…)

JOHN WHITBOURN

36~

PUBLISH AND BE DAMNED!
Or
THE SUPPRESSED (& DEPRESSED) EDITION.

✸

INTRODUCTION

What on earth possessed me to say such things? Why should a Dr Frankenstein be surprised to see the monster he'd created get up and dance the *'Monster-mash'* before his very eyes?

In my tirade-cum-introduction to *'More Binscombe Tales—Sinister Sutangli Stories'* (Ash-Tree Press 1999), called *'An Overview and Cheerio, or, 'A Sutangli Speaks!'*) I was ill-advised enough to say:

'The Binscombe Tales series is now at an end. To mark that drawing of the line, I composed an unexpectedly vast 'Stories I'll Never Get Round To' essay concerning all the unused plots and ideas collected with 'Binscombe' in mind. It seemed kindest to allow them at least a little glimpse of the light if they were fated never to be born.'

And:

'As far as I'm concerned though, the Binscombe Tales are no more, because, in life as in art, there are only two occasions for ending a project: too soon and too late. I'm not sure which side of that frontier I finally skidded to a halt. Similarly, I am reminded of the <u>two</u> great iron-rules of writing:

1) Always leave your audience wanting more...'

ALTERED ENGLANDS

As you may see, though the occasion was nominally sad, it did at least supply the chance to give one of my favourite old jokes an outing...

Then, at the end of that same volume were the unwise words:

'So, in a way, the Binscombe Tales are no more—but only 'in a way'. Perhaps, in another time stream thinly divided from our own, a parallel me taps on, churning out all the above tales for better or for worse. Mr Disvan would doubtless know of a communicating doorway between here and there, but it won't be me that troubles him for it. If others should care to do it, let <u>them</u> enquire for the key...'

Such hubris! That parallel time stream didn't mind its own business for long. Never mind politely knocking at the *'communicating doorway'*: it kicked the thing down and invited itself and its yobbo mates in for a party!

As to ensuing events, I can do no better than turn to the *Ash-Tree Press'* own words at the time (2003):

'THE SUPPRESSED ASH-TREE

Even in the most well regulated of circles, things sometimes go wrong. The well-regulated circle of Ash-Tree Press is no exception; and, as we approach the publication of our one hundredth title in December 2003, the time is right to release details of the *'Suppressed Ash-Tree.'*

In mid-January 1998 we were awaiting delivery of *'Binscombe Tales— Sinister Saxon Stories'* by John Whitbourn. The telephone rang. The familiar voice of our printer, a little less cheery than usual, faltered: 'Er, Binscombe Tales. We've just begun casing in. Er, unfortunately, there's been a cock-up with the pagination of the prelims...'

'Cock up? How bad?'

'Oh, not too bad, it's just that page xiii is printed on the back of page vii, and what should be xiii—you know, after xii, and before xiv, is now blank. Will this be a problem?'

'Well, it won't be a problem to us... but it looks like it's going to be a problem for you... Can anything be salvaged?'

'No, the whole thing is sewn and ready for casing. We can't get away with just printing new prelims...'

His voice faded to silence, expectantly awaiting me to accommodate his problem by agreeing to accept the job as it was.

'Looks as if you'll be reprinting the whole book then, doesn't it?'

'Oh... you won't take it as it is, then?'

'No, I won't take it as it is then.'

'Oh... That's going to cost me, then.'

'Looks like it... Oh, and by the way, we still need it by the 31st. OK?'

'Oh.'

'And how many copies have you already cased in?'

'Just ten before they noticed the problem.'

'Ah, well at least you won't have the cost of extra bindings. Perhaps you'd send me those ten copies as a souvenir? And just so that I can ensure they don't get released...?'

Click.

The ten copies duly arrived, and so did the correctly paginated edition of Binscombe Tales, just a few days late, giving many Ash-Tree readers their first taste of life in Binscombe. Subsequently, a second volume, *'More Binscombe Tales—Sinister Sutangli Stories'* was released, thus ending the cycle of Binscombe stories. There would be no more tales of Mr Disvan and Mr Oakley, no more visits to 'The Duke of Argyll.' Well, that was the intention...

For something so major to have happened to an Ash-Tree production, strange forces had to have been at work... somewhere. And where other than in Binscombe itself?

In celebration of Ash-Tree 100, John Whitbourn has resurrected his Binscombe characters, and we are at last able to bring you the full story behind those events of January 1998 in *'Publish & be Damned!* or *'The Suppressed (& Depressed) Edition.'*

For purists, and completist collectors, of the ten copies of the suppressed edition, one is in the hands of a private collector; one forms a part of the Ash-Tree library; and eight remain in their pristine green cloth on a shelf of our stock room. They would, of course, command absolutely outrageous prices were they ever to be offered for sale (we are open to persuasive approaches!)

Ash-Tree Press 2003'

ALTERED ENGLANDS

PUBLISH AND BE DAMNED!

✵

'Oh yes they will!'
'Oh no they won't!'
'Oh yes they will!'
'Oh no they won't!'

I was too young and cool to appear in panto and so desisted. Let Disvan be content with contradiction. *I* had the written evidence. It was waved in his face.

Then temptation overwhelmed me—as it so often did.

'Oh *yes* they will!'

Now I also had the final word. For once he had no reply—save to read out my *coup de grâce*. The *Argyll* clientele listened avidly. If Mr Disvan truly *had* been bested then they wanted to drink it in and acquire the details to tell their grandchildren.

'*'Ash-Tree Press presents'*,' he read from the flyer, *''The Binscombe Tales': Sinister Saxon Stories by... this other Binscombe is a place rich in history, where strangers are welcome-...''*

'I dunno about that,' said the Landlord, who made some outsiders about as welcome as rabies in a guide dogs' home. 'I mean, there's strangers and *strangers*. There was this lawyer once, right? Comes in here, just like a normal human and-...'

Disvan waved him to sullen silence and pressed on.

'*'.. but not always safe. We see Mr Disvan and Binscombe life through the eyes of Mr Oakley, a newcomer whose family has long had roots there...''*

'Don't look at me!' I protested—as everyone did. 'Nothing to do with me!'

Happily, that got Disvan's backing, thus defusing the hostility bomb.

'No,' he told the *Wicker-Man* extras. 'This is nothing to do with Mr Oakley. Apparently, it's quite intelligently written.'

'Oh, *thank* you!'

'Don't mention,' smiled Disvan, and then—sort of—softened the blow by recounting some of the high praise heaped on the book.

'*'Advance reviews of 'The Binscombe Tales': 'Bloody well buy it, you bastards!'* Would the *Times* really say that? Even nowadays? '*As sleek and stylish as a supermodel's bottom*': *The Catholic Herald*. Honestly!'

He'd really got them going now (to cite his favourite band, *The Kinks*) and was barely ahead in the outrage stakes.

'*'To be published on St George's Day'*. Oh *will* it now...'

'Oh yes it will,' I said to annoy him, retrieving the grievously scrumpled brochure and passing it round. This was where we'd come in. 'It says so here and there's nothing you can d-...'

The mid-syllable skid was caused by hearing myself boast I knew what he could and couldn't do. And I knew I didn't. Like Judge Jeffreys when his gall stones played up, Disvan was capable of anything.

Meanwhile, the news was getting ever wider spread, the leaflet snatched from hand to hand.

'They're going to release it in America!' cried one. Eyes widened, *Barbour*ed shoulders clenched.

'There's a map on the front,' lamented another ('*One*'s brother-in-law). 'To here!'

'That'll be the end of us: tourists! PhD students!'

'*Furriners! Londoners* even!'

'It'll all come out—Cromwell's head, the *Concrete Fund*, Reggie Suntan's Doomsday plan: everything!'

Disvan didn't rush to comfort them—which was a very bad sign.

'Kindly say who is this... author?' asked Mr Limbu (former Gurkha *Havildar*), silkily calm—and knowing him that boded ill.

'Yeah, do tell,' echoed Bridget Maccabi—ditto squared.

Mr Disvan said and the lynch mob got out their *me-no-understandee* looks.

'Never-'eard-of-'im,' snapped Mr Patel.

ALTERED ENGLANDS

'*Nevererdovim*'?' queried the Landlord, contentedly puzzled. 'Weren't he a Russian shot-putter? At the last Olympics? But what's that got to do with anyth-...'

'You know what I meant,' said Patel, the irascible Immigration Officer—and then in mind-you-don't-cut-yourself crystal-clear BBC English: 'I have never heard of him.'

'No, nor me,' agreed the Landlord, back up to speed again and as though that settled the matter. Not to be '*heard of*' was to be beyond whatever's beyond the Pale.

'Unless...,' muttered Dr Bani Sadr—and stilled the hubbub. His razor-sharp intellect was highly rated—in marked contrast to his morals.

'Yes...?' A Greek chorus from around the bar.

'Recall that mystery chap? He was *Whiteburgh*, wasn't he? Or *Whatsburn*? Always sat over by the charity pile of pennies. Quiet as a mouse; unstable looking. Kept himself to himself. Drank lager...'

'Oh *yes*,' said the Landlord. His lip curled to quite extraordinary extent, better than the 1950's Cliff Richard. 'I remember *him*.'

'He was always scribbling in a little book,' recalled Ms Maccabi. 'Said he was doing his accounts.'

'A lager drinking accountant,' wondered the Landlord aloud. 'How did *he* get in here?'

'It's worse than accountancy,' said Mr Disvan, in deadly earnest—and *that* raised some eyebrows. 'It's publicity!'

'No publicity is bad publicity!' I quipped—and there's nothing sadder than the humiliation of an entire room passing over your comment in pity.

'*I* know the man,' Disvan pressed on, as though someone hadn't just courted social suicide. 'Should be ashamed of himself. The Whitbourns are old blood: the oldest—and coldest too, as it turns out. Good job he left for that military attaché job at the Cornish Embassy: otherwise... Wait till I see his mum!'

To thine own self be true. I've always had defective brakes—that *is* my trouble. In the City or in bed—or indeed, in *The Duke of Argyll*—the red lights installed by society for our safety seem invisible to me. Likewise, whether raiding vulnerable Third-World currencies or pleasuring the boss's wife at the office Christmas party, I can't help but burst that Biblical '*triple tied cord*' of family, church and country which seems to keep the majority within bounds. So I said some more.

'Does it really matter? I mean, so what? This bloke sits in the corner for years, eavesdropping; taking notes, and now he's turned Judas. Well, big deal! No one will believe him anyway. Let this *Gnash-Tree* bunch-...'

'Ash, Mr Oakley. *Ash.*'

'Whoever. Let them publish. Relax! Stop being so English. Loosen up. Go with the flow!'

I blessed the Landlord for injecting words into the horrible silence that followed—even his kind of words.

'I went out with a girl called Flo once,' he told us—though our indifference knew no bounds. 'And my oath, *she* was a goer...!'

Lottie the landlady, who he'd momentarily forgotten, clipped his ear.

Also and unhappily, the great script writer in the sky chose that moment for someone to audibly flush the pub loo. I was getting all the wrong *'flow'* references.

'That'll serve as better comment than any I could make,' said Disvan, regarding me with genuine compassion. 'Now, whilst Mr Oakley makes amends and gets some drinks in, I'll just sabotage this book...'

❈

I feared and hated Mr Disvan 'quiet smiles of satisfaction' more than I did redundancy notices and letters from clinics. They always attended his modest pleasure at 23-0 victories over my world view.

For the umpteenth time and by popular demand, the Landlord crowed aloud from the *'Ash-Tree Update'* print-out:

"We regret that due to printing problems the projected Binscombe Tales volume has been postponed until further notice..."

I silently deplored the applause and the free drinks which flowed like... well, drinks. They and the news earned only a pout from me. Though I now kept it to myself, I'd been rather looking forward to seeing my adventures in print. I felt confident that my constant moral victories over Binscombe's pre-Enlightenment values would be faithfully depicted, my dogged defence of the modern world vindicated. The author, plainly a sympathetic soul and fellow rebel against Binscombe *mores*, would surely skip over the occasional minor embarrassments...

Also, truth be told, the notion of casually dropping the tome in some desirable lap had more than once entertained my commuting hours. *'Hey, baby,'* I'd say, *'read the advertisement.'* Then: *'Come to Oakley...'*

'I expect you're relieved,' said Disvan, handing me a *Babycham* I hadn't ordered. 'Imagine if it had come out about when you tried it on with Linda Disch!'[125]

'Yeah,' laughed Mr Patel, 'first time I've ever seen a fawn suit go dark with sweat.'

'Or that time you wore make-up and wrote poetry...'

'Bloody grim poetry,' said the Landlord—as if he were any kind of perceptive critic.

'... and hit Mr Bretwalda,' continued Mr Disvan.

'And he didn't notice!'[126] chortled Dr Bani-Sadr.

'Yeah, yeah, yeah; all right, all right.' There *had* been trifling incidents, I freely admitted. I just didn't want them broadcast round the tribal campfire unto the fifth generation—and particularly that last little slip. The Bretwaldas—all built like King Kong and about as forgiving—were in tonight.

I released one of my *to-understand-all-is-to-forgive-all* sighs, a magnanimous concession that usually appeased the barbarians—for a spell. The chanting of some less flattering sections of my *CV* ceased. I took advantage of the conversational lapse.

'So, Mr D, why? No, no, forget that: that one always leads to tears—of frustration, mostly. Try how: *how* did you?'

'Oh, easy,' he replied, amplified by a *it-was-nothing* shrug of the shoulders. 'No subtle or arcane forces, I assure you. Just the good old *'52-card shuffle'* of the proofs on the floor immediately before printing. Then a distracted page checker: that sort of thing. Effective, untraceable, *'accidental'*: just like the best assassinations—or so Reggie Suntan[127] tells me. Anyway, it worked. You can't sell a book with transposed pages, can you? They had to pulp the lot.'

---

[125] For which *dangerous liaison* and seduction scene see *Binscombe Tale* number 18: *'Hello Dolly'*
[126] For all of which see *Binscombe Tale* number 25: *'I could a Tale Unfold...'*
[127] Eponymous subject of *Binscombe Tale* number 11. A... colourful character and Binscombe-expat, generally resident in Spain.

I felt sorry for the poor, put-out, *Asphalt-Tree* people. It was so unfair. I cloaked my outrage in pointless questions—just to inconvenience Disvan and see how he liked it.

'How did you arrange it? Who do you know in Canada? Have they got the Mafia out there?'

Disvan looked offended: which was a small—well, petty, actually—result.

'Certainly not. And if they did I wouldn't... No, we've got good friends out in Free North America. I—I mean we—did favours for them after the war...'

By now I was attuned to such things: in Binscombe that wasn't necessarily a plain statement.

I interrupted. '*Which* war?'

It put him on the spot. Disvan wouldn't downright lie—not to *blood* families anyway.

'Oh... um...,' he huffed, colouring up. He didn't like being caught out in acts of kindness or holding knowledge he'd no business to. 'Well, not the last one. A long while back. The colonists rebelled or something. And Loyalist English moved north.'

'50,000 of 'em,' expanded the Landlord—whose random, unsolicited, historical wisdom often disturbed me. 'The Americans took everything save the clothes on their backs, poor devils. It seemed only brotherly to help.'

'Yes, yes,' Disvan curtailed him: taking his turn to be the urgent abortionist of discourse. 'Anyway: there's still people out there with honour and long memories. I'd refer you to what that Welsh friend of yours wisely said, Mr Oakley.'

'Just before he was sick over my doorstep,' said Lottie.

'And ripped my skirt,' added Ms Maccabi.

'Professor Griffiths?'[128] I hazarded, warily. 'He *was* under a lot of stress at the time...'

'*Under stress*?' queried Bridget, a stickler for accuracy, however untimely. 'More interested in getting me under him, I reckon...'

---

[128] Surely *not* to be identified with the classicist, philosopher and *'Celtic Marxist bon viveur'* (and patron of *The Binscombe Tales*), whose introductory words graced Vol. 1 thereof: *'Sinister Saxon Stories'*, Ash-Tree Press 1998. And also the book you hold.

'He *said*,' Disvan gamely persisted, '*'when debts of honour are forgotten, then we are all diminished and ever after the stars shine less bright'.*'

'Commie windbag,' commented Mr Patel, in bile-rich tones. His lovely daughter, Lucretia, had gone *AWOL* with the visiting professor (*'mushroom picking'*) and returned all shiny-eyed.

'Well, *I* thought it was an admirable sentiment,' answered Disvan—and then spoilt it. 'For a Celt.'

'So then,' exulted the Landlord, throttling the top off another bottle of champagne (Hascombe *'Elderflower champagne'*). Which always cheered him (and his profits) up. 'That's the end of that!'

'Amen,' chorused the Binscomites and raised their glasses high.

I kissed literary immortality goodbye.

'Bastards! Buggers!'

Disvan brow was furrowed—and not just at Patel's profanities. He handed the print-out back to the Reverend Jagger, our appointed *Internet* spy.

'I'd no idea colonials could be so dogged,' he lamented.

I snatched at both paper and joy, to read it again: aloud.

''Ash-Tree proudly present 'The Binscombe Tales'—a first edition that's a second printing! Undeterred and only a little late, we can again offer entry to the world of Binscombe—a place rich in history, where strangers are welcome-...''

'...*'But not always safe'*,' recited Mr Bretwalda, lumpenly. 'Well, they bloody well won't be if they show their faces in here, I tell you!'

He was volcanic at the best of times, but also had a lot to lose. If news got out about *'The Binscombe Scholarship'* and a certain chatty—and deceased—severed head, bang went Vladimir Bretwalda's precious place at Cambridge.[129]

Mr Disvan mused over his untouched Guinness.

'They're persistent: I'll give them that.'

It seemed a tribute but his already sharp profile had hardened. My backbone (which I *do* own, whatever Bretwalda says) chilled. There was more. There always was in Binscombe.

129 For which see the shocking—*shocking!*—revelations of *Binscombe Tale* number 14: *'No Truce With Kings'*.

'And I'll give them something else as well...,' he added, like some hanging judge.

I'd no idea what it might be but could be confident I wouldn't like it. It'd be the sort of thing that involved *Interpol* and not getting into heaven—not that I believed in either you understand, save on the 'just in case' principle...

The field mouse squeaked its protest before the combine harvester.

'But... but... but...,' I said. The best I could muster at short notice.

'But me no buts, Mr Oakley.' Disvan quashed my timid litany. 'This is Guy Fawkes time...'

I puzzled. 'November the fifth? *Bonfire Night*? No it's not—that's miles off.'

Mr Disvan was patient with me—and I was grateful for that. The rest of the faces in the bar had suddenly became... thinner, less familial.

'My reference is to the great English patriot—and should-be saint, by the way. I speak of his famous words to King James I.'

'What?' queried the Landlord, concerned at finding himself adrift, *"I wished to blow you and all you Scottish beggars back to your mountains"?'*

'No, not that one,' answered Disvan, although plainly pleased to hear it spoken. 'I mean what he said when asked about his methods.'

'Oh, *yeah*,' roared the Landlord, glad to be back on track, delving yet again into his incongruous larder of erudition. '*That* one!' He fixed me with a basilisk stare, enjoying every second.

'*'Desperate situations'*,' I was told—and one by one the regulars chimed in, turning it into a tribal hymn—'*"merit desperate remedies"!*'

※

I'd wrestled with my conscience (after locating its hiding place) and was resolved. If they proposed anything in the bomb line then I was reporting them to the authorities. I would actually *grass*—and so cast myself and all my descendants till Doomsday into the outer darkness.

Happily, there was no need. I drew from my repertoire of bird impressions and watched them like a hawk. A missive *was* posted to *Ash-Tree* but a slim one, incapable of holding anything more lethal than a stiff letter.

Imagine my surprise then, when Mr Disvan freely admitted its rigidity only arose from an enclosed cheque. My jaw hit the knot of my silk tie. It was not in their nature to pay *Dane-Geld*[130]—or so Disvan always maintained. The lessons of King Alfred the Great and Rudyard Kipling[131] were supposedly well absorbed over the last millennia. And how dare they just assume the *Slash-Tree* people could be bought off? I had *doubts* and let them out to play.

They ought to have stayed safe at home in my head, thus saving a smirk-in at my expense. It transpired the only thing being *bought* was a copy of the book. That envelope-of-much-concern contained not only payment but an order-form!

It got prompt reply. Next Saturday lunchtime in the *Argyll*, Mr Disvan dragged the bound volume from its *jiffy-bag* and held the thing aloft.

Everyone else in the bar seemed to be treating it with excess caution, so I saw opportunity to salvage some bravado points.

'Let's have a butcher's then...'[132]

For once, Disvan forgot to feign ignorance of *Mockney*. I should have been warned, I *really* ought to have guessed. He let me have it—in more ways than one.

'Ah, nice cover,' I mused. 'And green boards: very ethnic. Looks good.'

I waved it at them. They shied back. I worried.

'I expect you wonder what all the fuss was about now, eh?'

They didn't look terribly reconciled or relaxed. The book and I were the focus of all attention. Sometimes I like that. There were memories of scoring some winning runs at prep school—and also the incident with matron (but that's another story). Right now I was less enamoured.

'Let me have a read over lunch,' I said, hoping that would fend them off. Eating was one of those times when Binscombe lore respected a wish for privacy, and my ordered *Argyll 'Turbo-curry + poppadums'* was on its way. 'Then I'll let you know what I think.'

They seemed agreeable and turned away to their darts and tall-tales and whatever else it was they did when I wasn't watching. Right on time, Lottie the landlady turned up with the piping plateful.

---

[130] Tax levied by some Old-English kings to provide protection money against Viking invaders.
[131] *'We never pay <u>any</u>-one Dane-Geld, / No matter how trifling the cost, / For the end of the game is oppression and shame, / and the nation that plays it is lost!'* 'Dane-Geld', 1911.
[132] *'Butcher's hook'* = look. City financiers employ Cockney and its 'rhyming slang' as their demotic, tribal language. Hence *'Mockney'*.

'Um... what's this?' I said.

Lottie smiled. Part of her life destiny, her *'Wyrd'* as Disvan called it, was the 'feeding-up' of people deemed in need of it. She couldn't abide *'skin and bones'*.

'Venison curry, my love. Fresh in, courtesy of Reverend Jagger's gun. Eat it up: do you good.'

'Um... right. Only, um... I really wanted vegetarian, you see...'

'That's okay, sweetness,' she 'answered'. 'Deer *are* vegetarian.'

I... couldn't answer that. And I was hungry: not just for poor Bambi lately poached off Binscombe Ridge, but also references to myself in the pristine volume. I revel in reading about myself and, as mentioned, hadn't had much chance since my old school's sports reports. The growls of my stomach and vanity combined to drown out ethics. *'Grub first, then morals'* as Bertolt Brecht said (and lived).

Propping the book up before my meal I tucked into both.

'Binscombe Tales—Sinister Saxon stories by... Contents: page xi: 'Introscript...'

For a second I had the overwhelming urge to take a walk or a women—or *anything*. And then I took a little holiday from the world.

※

'Funny how curry burns and stains, isn't it?'

Mr Disvan meant both funny/strange and funny/ha ha. I failed to appreciate either.

'There, that's got most off,' said Lottie, wielding the last of a whole pack of *'moisty lemon wipes—for those sticky moments'* over my face and front and hair. Her voice lacked all conviction. Expert maternal hands fingered my suit lapels. 'It *might* come out—with a few dry-cleans...'

'Your fringe has gone two-tone though,' said the Landlord, observing me like a side-dish he'd didn't recall ordering. 'I don't know whether to suggest dyeing the rest red or that bit natural mousy...'

They'd left me face-first in my curry for far longer than necessary: I was convinced of it. Did they really think I ate like that—however famished? Even starving men don't try to get nourishment by osmosis.

'What...?' I spluttered—and everything tasted of revisited dead deer.

ALTERED ENGLANDS

'We believe in freedom of speech,' said Mr Disvan, answering a question I hadn't posed. 'It's a right and triumph dear—no pun intended, Mr Oakley—bought. People from here gave blood to see it won.'

We'd been through this before: the role of Binscomites in the struggles for Liberty, from Cromwell to the Falklands. I just couldn't see the relevance to my recent guillotine-descending coma. My curried face conveyed that.

'And so,' Disvan continued in his *bear-with-me-I'm-getting-somewhere-with-this* mode, '*Ash-Tree* can print anything they like and good luck to 'em.'

'They'll need it!' rumbled Mr Bretwalda. Even his laughter sounded like death threats.

Disvan evidently agreed but wouldn't phrase it that crudely. He hid his hesitation in a sip of black beer.

'Like I say, Mr Oakley, they can print what they like but they can't make it *read*. *'You can drag a horse to water...'* and all that. Post-composition interference isn't so wicked...'

'How...?'

First *'What'*, now *'How'*; I was progressing up the evolutionary chain of interrogatives.

'Doubtless you know of Leech, Bore & Co.?' Disvan seemed to say the words speedily.

'No. Should I?'

'Perhaps not, on reflection: they're hardly the most flamboyant of locals. An accountancy firm, Mr Oakley, up the road in Goldenford; been there donkey's years.'

'If you say so.' Actually, the name did now—dimly—call to mind a brass plate beside an office block—and grey-suited, slope-shouldered men and women traversing its portals.

'They handle my accounts,' volunteered the Landlord. 'Ever since I arrived. And the man before me and the one 'afore him I expect. Very efficient: shave tax off like mad axemen they do—but dull: very *dull*. *'Do my books,'* I says to 'em, *'but, please, no conversation...'*'

'Me too,' agreed Disvan. 'Collectively, we've put a lot of money their way over the years—and covered up a few dry scandals. They owed us a favour.'

'Really?' The idea was to inch towards that prince of questions: *'Why?'*, meanwhile keeping it staccato to deny Disvan's grappling-hooks-ofprevarication any purchase. Also, every syllable was stale curry tinged. I had powerful incitements to brevity.

'Books need paper, Mr Oakley,' replied Dr Bani-Sadr, stating the obvious—which was suspiciously unlike him. 'Without it they're just electronic dreams in a word processor.'

'And likewise, *accounts* need paper,' added Disvan, 'if they're to spring into life.' He re-considered and repented his words. 'Not that they really can, you understand; they more sort of shuffle at a sensible pace rather than stroll or dance, but you get my drift: you see the connection?'

'Nope!' I was damned if I was going to use my intellect and make things easier for them: not after they'd curried me.

'Paper, Mr Oakley,' said Disvan. '*Paper*. Leach, Bore & Co. carry a heavy stock: *'just to be on the safe side'* as one partner told me. It's there piled up in their basement: great pale mountains of the stuff. And, of course, you know what people are like—even accountants. They take the easy way every time: the top pack from the pile. Some of the stuff at the bottom has been there since the fifties!'

'Picking up the vibes,' grimaced Mr Patel.

'Absorbing decades of their office atmosphere into its pores,' expanded Bridget Maccabi.

'Deadly stuff,' summed Sigismund Maxted, the bookie. 'I went to help fetch it and caught a whiff. Couldn't shake off dreadful lethargy for days—the world went *banal*.'

Disvan transcended the... unfortunate mispronunciation of that word.

'It was easy to place it with *Ash-Tree*'s printers,' he said. 'Their management never knew.'

'Friends...,' I snapped and supposed. 'People in place...'

Disvan couldn't or wouldn't perceive my disenchantment. He was still rapt, describing the glory of it all.

'S'right,' came confirmation. 'We're myriad: *legion* even—like the stars of the sky: a debt of honour here, a descendant there. Wherever England went Binscombe rode tandem. I tell you, Mr Oakley, we're human Plantain herb: *'Waybroad'* or *'English Man's Foot'* as the Red Indians call it. Just like that herb our seed spreads stuck to history's boots!'

I saw it more prosaically.

'What you mean is you've more corrupt contacts than the Masons!'

Courteous as always, he declined to press the point on an unwilling public. There was a verse from his precious *Koran* he generally chucked at me when we reached that stage.[133] For once I was spared it.

'*Anyhow*,' he continued, 'the deed was done and here we have it.'

He handed the book to me but I shrank away.

'No chance!'

Disvan nodded sagely. 'That'll be the usual reaction amongst the more sensitive or once-bitten. The aura will deter them. Stronger souls might penetrate a few pages in but we'll still be safe. I reckon some'll just rave and praise it to the skies rather than read it. Doesn't matter. We can live with good reviews. Either way, readers will be lead-eyed or compelled to do something else long before they've learnt anything of us. It's only the hardcore persistent who'll be stunned to sleep. I just hope they'll be in company—to rouse 'em afterwards. I mean, what if there's a solitary type and he flakes out direct into his soup...? Well, it doesn't bear thinking about. Heaven knows, we don't want fatalities but-....'

"*Desperate situations'*,' I recited, "*merit desperate remedies.*"

Disvan beamed upon me: a slacker who'd learnt to sing the company song.

'*Exactly*, Mr Oakley. We're all of us driven by necessity—and she can be a harsh old boss. I reckon it's enough just to try and not harm *too* many people, don't you?'

I damned well didn't. I also didn't want him to win. I'd really looked forward to reading about my exploits and victories over Binscombe life. Now I'd never know—and nor would anyone else. If I dropped the wretched book in some girl's lap she'd just nod off—which had possibilities of its own, granted—but was way off my hopes and plans. I rebelled. I wouldn't *have* it. Or her.

'There'll be some who'll finish; you see. You rate people too low.'

Again Disvan swerved the feeble thrust. The prospect failed to daunt him.

'Doubtless,' he agreed with me—the swine. 'Though it'll take high intellect and indomitable will. Those who glimpse *'THE END'* will have to be titans of the imagination. How far did you get by the way?'

'The *'Contents'*.'

---

[133] Probably Surah 109, *Al-Kafirun* (The Unbelievers): *'You have your own religion, and I have mine.'*

'There you are then. My point exactly.'

I clenched my curry-coloured teeth.

'Yes, thank you *so* much.'

That supplied the iron-in-the-soul to still try and blow out the candles on his cake before he got to them. A mean-spirited impulse I admit—but I was getting to believe that's the way the world was.

'They'll arrive,' I tried to crow, 'you mark my words. 'Your cover's blown. There'll be those who can read and learn!'

'Good,' he said—and again floored me. The trouble with these bouts was the lack of a referee to stop the unequal punishment; no Marquess of Queensberry to enforce some humane rules.

'Eh?'

'Think about it, Mr Oakley. There's some we don't *mind* knowing...'

I put down my drink. It tasted of you-know-what anyway.

"Don't you?' At long last I got there and posed the ultimate question, even if only in negative form. '*Why* not?'

'I've got just one word for you, Mr Oakley,' said Disvan, and raised his glass to me in mockery or triumph. '*Recruits!*'

ALTERED ENGLANDS

37~

UP FROM THE CELLAR
Or
ENGLAND EXPECTS!

☸

'Bastards!'

Fortunately, my blessing was lost, diluted and drowned—what you will—in the sea of laughter. Enormous patience and—to maintain the watery metaphors—an ocean of words had been devoted to getting me on stage for the *'Duke of Argyll'*s 'Karaoke Night'. Aware of my particular weaknesses, Lucretia Patel and a bevy of the Bretwalda amazons, deployed unfair feminine wiles to charm me into the limelight. Likewise, Bridget Maccabi (home on leave from Israeli Army basic training) tugged puppeteer-style on the strings of lust and terror to propel me forwards.

The inner defence lines were also betrayed. *'Directors* bitter'—freely imbibed, I admit—treacherously drugged my inner voices of caution to a whisper. Judas impulses from mankind's dawn and African savannah days caused my legs to walk. I was mug enough to think the cheers were genuine.

Then, with a grin like an ice-crevice opening beneath my feet, the Landlord selected me *'Good Vibrations'* by The Beach Boys.

Not possessing six or seven falsetto, octave-ranging separate voices, it's fair to say my performance... lacked a certain something. I couldn't quite do the song full justice. It went down well though—alongside the flaming wreckage of my dignity. I may even have hit one or two of the right notes: just: by my vocal fingertips. Of course, at the time I'd have far rather hit the beaming faces of some of my tormentors, but for reasons of courage etc. that wasn't, alas, on.

It isn't that often you see a whole room full of people in tears of laughter. There was nothing the aboriginal Binscomites liked so much a good old-fashioned ambush. As my social suicide drew to an end, I imagined Hogarth at his most jaundiced, depicting them on a day out at a hanging.

After walking the million miles back to my seat, I was joined by Mr Disvan.

'Bastards!' I repeated.

At first he seemed surprised but then looked coolly round.

'A few,' he conceded at last. 'Mr Medici has no idea who his father was. I recall him saying his mother put 'some sailors—but it was dark' on his birth certificate. And, oh yes, the Bretwaldas jumped the gun a bit in having their Vladimir. Still, I wouldn't have put you down as the type to worry about such things...'

'Don't you muck me around. You know *exactly* what I mean.'

He made sure the table top was dry before setting down his *Koran*. Swift and ghost-like, Lottie the Landlady appeared briefly with a jug to top up his glass of beer.

'Obviously not, Mr Oakley,' he finally answered, looking concernedly at me. 'If you've no problem about people's legitimacy then I accept that. We'll let the subject drop. I liked your song by the way. I'm a great fan of Kate Bush: that was one of her best.'

'Oh, very funn*ee!*'

Actually he'd seemed deadly serious—and now rather lost.

'Was it? Well, if you say so, Mr Oakley.'

A fairly frosty silence fell between us and I was half minded to take my sulk home to treasure and polish it. Just then however, the Butt twin-sisters stepped up to render a very... absorbing interpretation of Robert Palmer's *'Addicted to Love'* and, in the grip of powerful emotions, I graciously decided to linger on a while.

'Very nice dresses they're almost wearing,' commented Disvan, innocently. 'A mite cold for outdoors though.'

'They ought to be nice,' I answered, largely on auto. 'Pure silk doesn't come cheap: cost me a bomb!'

'Really?' asked Disvan, sounding unaccountably pleased with me—not that I could spare the time or attention to check. 'Now, that *was* kind of you. I doubt the twins' wages at Sainsbury's stretch to many luxuries but they deserve them all the same. They're much loved figures round here, you know.'

I was in no position to deny that. Besides, when he chose, Disvan's statements could be such minefields of multiple meaning that they were often best skirted round, rather than probed. Right then, for instance, I had the uncomfortable feeling that he was privy to all my secret dealings (an appropriate choice of word vis-à-vis the Butts' dresses), looking remote, amused and tolerant, down on them, like a man observing mayflies.

'You have your hobbies,' I said defensively, 'I have mine...'

'Hmmm...,' replied Disvan—and I couldn't help but tear my eyes from the performance, a memory-rich feast though it was, to query the infinite variety of that simple affirmative. My companion, the closest acquaintance of all my Binscombe years, was studying me. His blue eyes were as cold and implacable as an advancing glacier.

'But then,' he said, softly, though still strangely audible through the music maelstrom, 'pastimes... pass... and pall. There comes a time when men must work.'

'Do you have to?' I protested. 'I'm back there on Monday and don't want reminding.' My job was all very diverting and that, filling in the hours and saving me from thought. It was likewise lavishly rewarding in strict *dosh* terms, paying for all sorts of toys and games. Even so, life in the City fast lane was like time in an iguana-pit. Everyone writhed over everyone, seeking the clear sky at the top, and everyone *bit*. Of late it had got a bit wearing. I wasn't getting any younger and appearing more hard-eyed than the rest had lost its novelty..

'As ever,' Disvan observed placidly, 'you surge forward to seize the wrong end of the stick. What I meant was that I've got to do my turn soon.'

That seemed highly unlikely. Next in succession had been the males of the Bretwalda clan, giving-it-some (and threatening the stage) along to Status Quo's *'Rockin' all over the World'*. Truth to tell, I'd never actually considered what a growth-hormone enhanced, violence prone, Neanderthal version of the 'Quo' would look like—but now I knew all the same. Mr Disvan didn't seem to fit, however far down, on that sort of bill. He anticipated my words of doubt.

'It gets more sedate later on, Mr Oakley.'

And so it did in fact, much to my—if no one else's—surprise. The evening gradually, gracefully ascended (or declined, depending on your point of view) up the evolutionary scale, transforming itself into a different beast entirely. Esther Constantine interpreted the change according to her lights, invoking *'the quantitative becoming qualitative'* or some such Marxist magic, and being somewhat frightened of her 30's vintage, Stalinist zeal, I pretended to agree. However, she seemed alone in her desire to explain (and thus deny) the ineffable. Every other heart appeared ready for the ride.

The Karaoke machine was now neglected in favour of individual inspiration. Mr Jarman got up and sang a sort of Goth-ecised version of *'Jerusalem'*, to the accompaniment of Phil the ambulance man's accordion. Our local/lovely District Nurse, Magali Williams—dying in whose arms was the only way I'd ever agree to go—gave us *'Waterloo Sunset'*, assisted by green-clad 'Mr R. Hood' on bass. Mr Disvan, on record as regarding 'The Kinks' Ray and Dave Davies as *'geniuses both'*, stood to applaud.

Tears adorning her wrinkled face, Esther Constantine sang the *'Internationale'* and even I, a Hayek fan and free-marketeer, forgot my brimming pint, amidst the might-have-beens of history. Tania Knott (who well knew how to speak of it) then softly sang a Wessex story of lost love and separation. The Reverend Jagger slew us with Macaulay's *'Jacobite Epitaph'* and Sigismund Maxted the bookie surprised all assembled by showing he knew—and understood!—Gray's *'Elegy in a Country Churchyard.'*

Sammy Patel got up and said 'Right, this one's a song about the English killing-fields,' and then brought moisture even to my cold eye with Eric Bogle's *'No Man's Land'*. Bob Springer, of bus-stop fame, decorously, delicately, accompanied him on the squeeze-box, a jolly-dog, sea-shanty instrument converted to sing pity.

For a space we were all in Flanders field—and *'Wipers'* and Loos—where my newly-wed great-uncle Jack and other sundry Oakleys died in swathes and have their unknown graves, leaving my aunts to mourn long lifetimes afterwards. They'd been mere yellowing bedside photos to the junior Oakley but now I knew. *'A whole generation that was butchered and damned'*—England dying on the wire.

It was a relief therefore, and opportunity to discreetly swipe our eyes, when the Landlord next took us two steps forward and one step back, first with Kipling's *'Recessional'*, and then Marie Lloyd's *'A Little Of Wot You Fancy Does You Good!'*

Doctor Bani-Sadr (who was living proof of those last sentiments) wowed everyone with a high, brittle-voiced rendition *of 'The Sash My Father Wore'*. Mr Limbu melted the most accountant-ish hearts present with a Gurkha ballad about love and murder mixed. Bridget Maccabi then terrified us with the 137th psalm (arranged: *'Boney-M'*). For a few precious moments we were exiles beside the Rivers of Babylon, subject to the sorrow of attempting the Lord's song *'in a strange land'*.

Somehow, imperceptibly, a gear had switched and what was an evening of fun and frivolity had gone into supercharge, becoming a service of sorts. The entity that was Binscombe was reciting its core beliefs, sharing various views that conjoined to make a creed, and communing with that which is beyond and... better.

I'd not seen the like since the massed chorus that greeted each Rollover Night. Now I knew why this was an all-ticket gig.

Then Mr Disvan got up and the *Argyll* was one collective mind focused.

'Testing-one-two-three,' he said, tapping the microphone, partly spoiling everything. The spell lapsed and people remembered their drinks and smokes.

'It is a terrible thing,' he pronounced eventually, in his distinctive slow, thin voice, 'to die under an axe.' Suddenly he had our attention again. 'Or so I should imagine. That is the prospect the Saxons I shall speak of faced, for all their hopes were gone. Their Lord, Byrhtnoth, had fallen; the Viking invaders had prevailed, but still the survivors did not falter. Save for a few... normal types who had fled, Byrhtnoth's household troops, his oath-sworn huscarls, steeled themselves for the final act. We do not know the poet's name—he cannot have been at Maldon else he would not have lived to write these words...

'I've read somewhere that the true heart, the obsession almost, of early English verse is the stout outfacing of despair, vast odds and certain death. I think that's right and in my humble opinion when men manage that, they overcome the flesh's command, their baser nature, and aspire to the status of angels. Their last thoughts are likewise breathed on by God. And if that's so, let us hope their final words were reported right, for nowhere in literature have I heard more glorious sentiments expressed.'

And so Mr Disvan read us *'The Battle of Maldon'* by the famous and prolific *'Anon'*. Even I, who simultaneously disapproved of, and disbelieved in, death—and especially provocative gestures in its face—was drawn in. The rest of the audience were equally rapt and temporarily somewhere else than a pub in a village in the south-east portion of a plain and simple nation of humans. We were hearing the words of the best of men when at their best, and the boldest of discourses with someone who—I suppose I must admit—we all will meet one day.

> '... Then Byrhtwold spoke, shook ash-spear,
> raised shield-board. In the bravest words
> this hoar companion handed on the charge:
> 'Courage shall grow keener, clearer the will,
> and heart the greater, as our might grows less.
> Here lies our lord levelled in the dust,
> cut down in battle. Ever must he mourn
> who thinks to go home from this battle-play.
> Though I am white with winters I will not go,
> for I think to lodge me alongside my dear one,
> lay me down by my lord's right hand.'

I cannot say we left in silence—but we were hushed.

❦

'It was a good spell whilst it lasted—which thankfully wasn't long. By the middle of next morning I was back to normal.'

'Oh, I'm sorry to hear that,' answered Mr Disvan, affably, rather putting a spike in my guns before they'd all fired. In addition, he'd annoyingly passed my little test. Without prompting he'd known I was referring to last week's Karaoke evening, and I wasn't pleased that he should be so aware of its effect on me.

I hadn't seen him since, the intervening period being one of his unexplained absences which no one else appeared to find curious or question-worthy. In past times, whilst I still bothered, it always seemed like my enquiries were phrased in Cornish or Martian for all the straight answers they got.

Today I was confident he'd be around, for Mr Disvan rarely missed a Binscombe funeral, and then invariably returned to the *Argyll* to formulate a consensus obituary. Esther Constantine, when she at last broke, had gone down fast—which just goes to show even little old ladies can die of a broken heart.

'I think it was Cuba going that finished her,' Disvan had told me, after describing a pretty savagely secular crematorium service. 'That was the remaining domino and final straw. I mean, you can see her point: what's the use of being a *Spetsnaz* if the Red Army's never going to come?'

Apparently, all the surviving factions of the Communist Party of Great Britain, from Stalinist 'tankies' to polytechnic-polysyllabists sent representatives to the obsequies. Hostilities were not suspended for the duration however, and two luxuriantly bearded Marxists, paladins of either the nostalgic or tedious factions, traded ineffectual blows in the car park afterwards.

'You oughtn't to laugh at a funeral,' commented Disvan, decapitating a bottle of Guinness, 'but it was touch and go at that point. Luckily, Father Wiltshire was around, waiting for the next lot in, and he restored order. Wonderful right hook for a priest, that man has.'

'Oh... really?' I didn't like the sound of that. Inspired by ale I'd cracked the old 'Why did God give Negroes natural rhythm when it's the Catholics who need it?' 'joke' to him only a few days back. He's laughed at the time but now I wondered if he bore grudges...

'Anyway, you were saying, Mr Oakley: you feel normal again...'

I put images of the death throws of socialism and priests lurking in dark alleys from my head.

'That's right. I soon got safely back to the real world.'

'Entirely? Unaltered?'

I don't know what made me provoke him; given our track record it can only have been some distant cousin of the death-wish.

'Absolutely. You know, glorious last stands and all that... well, they're... quaint to hear about, but you can't believe in them. Those sort of things belong in Narnia. People delude themselves if they think otherwise.'

Disvan didn't take offence—though he rarely, visibly, did. Thus that was little comfort.

'So you'd have been on the first horse home, would you, Oakley?' laughed the Landlord. I'd thought he was out of our hair, marshalling his bottle parades in the cellar. I could have done without such carpet-bombing style humour as witness to the point I was trying to make.

'Yes: of course—assuming you'd have got me there in the first place,' I replied, cautiously keeping it jocular. 'People should weigh the odds before they venture into things.'

The circle at the bar gave that more consideration than I'd ever intended them to. The quiet dragged on.

'Well, *shouldn't* they?' I prompted.

'Let's have some 'ush,' said the Landlord, adopting an exaggerated 'The Thinker' type pose. 'We're weighing the odds afore answering.'

That gave birth to a minor grin-fest which lightened the atmosphere, though for once Dr Bani-Sadr declined to join in.

'I'm not so sure,' he said, setting down his barley wine. 'We've all got to go sometime. Zeus knows I've seen there's enough undignified ways to go. It's not like Dickens you realise, Mr Oakley: our leaving this world isn't always a pretty sight. Maybe that old Saxon wasn't so daft in copping an axe. At least he went with dignity, looking the Reaper in the eye. You try doing that if you're all drugged up and chained to a life-support, with your relatives looking at their watches. It's not so easy then I can tell you!'

He paused, momentarily abstracted, peering with an inner eye (or so it seemed to me) at some less than pleasant memories. I hardly expected more, for it was already the longest sarcasm-free speech I ever recalled from him—and yet it transpired the Doctor hadn't finished.

'And another thing,' he went on, 'at least we remember old Bert-what's-his-name and think well of him. You can't say that about the old-time Oakleys who scarpered or never even turned up. If all we're doing down here is weaving a story for our descendants to tell, why not make it a rousing yarn, eh?'

That rather shocked me. I'd always deemed Bani-Sadr an arch rationalist and solid chap, entirely dismissive of whimsy. And yet here he was apparently lining up with the 'good old Dark Ages' *Fuzzy-wuzzies*.

'You speak for yourself,' I countered, bolder than strict courtesy dictated. 'My *'story'*'s just for me. I shan't hear it so I don't much care how it's received.'

'Such faith!' marvelled Mr Patel. I'd always suspected him of being closet *Opus Dei*.

By now I was unclear if I was winning this or not, if I was a voice in the wilderness or *vox populi*.

'Oh, come on!' I persevered. 'You must be with me really. You've all been around. You know that if you go about with your head in the clouds it only leads to disappointment. Those sort of people get all bitter and twisted when life doesn't match up to their imaginings. I mean, it's obvious, isn't it? There's the world as it is—and that's *all* there is! And that's more than enough, surely?'

ALTERED ENGLANDS

Mr Disvan sighed. 'And after all you've seen,' he said, frowning slightly. 'Do you still believe *that*?'

'None so blind as *won't* see,' said the Landlord—and wrung his barcloth like it was my neck.

'There's been some odd things,' I agreed: I could hardly say otherwise, much as I'd like to. 'But they're just weeds along the way: freaks and survivals and... you know, last of the line sort of stuff. The *real* world's still there, unaffected. That's the only thing you've really got to take notice of. Whatever weird things may have happened to me I still know the score...'

Disvan grimaced. 'If you do,' he said, as harsh as I'd ever heard him, turning my spine as frigid as a fiancée, 'then it's the score in a fourth division, pub Sunday-side game, a relegation play-off somewhere up north, near... *Staly*bridge, on a cold and drizzly day. The spectators are someone walking their dog and two sad divorced men with nowhere better to be. In short, Mr Oakley, it's not a match I'd travel far for!'

I reeled in this unprecedented frankness, chewed on it but failed to make so much as a toothmark. Some barrages are just best sheltered from, too devastating for a reply.

'Don't hold back any,' I said, abashed. 'Feel free to speak your mind...'

Disvan shook his head sadly. 'I'm sorry, Mr Oakley, but you've only yourself to blame. I shall have to speak plain. Time's getting on and I can't decide whether you're like a sieve or made of *Teflon*. Nothing seems to make a lasting impression on you. Come with me.'

And, most unlike him, peevish and impatient, he tapped me on the forehead.

☸

'Where am I—are we?'

Actually, I thought I did well to say that, instead of the more favoured option of unconditional surrender to howling panic.

'Where I always am,' Disvan replied, matter of factly. 'In my memory.'

'But... how come I'm here too?'

'I've got a very strong memory, Mr Oakley.'

I slowly, reluctantly, looked about but refused to accept delivery of the signals to my optic nerves.

'That doesn't make sense.' I sounded like a little child, trying to find a logical flaw in Dad's plans to visit frightening old Aunt Maud.

'And this does?' countered Disvan—and he had a point. We were high up, overseers of the landscape below, confined to one small corner of the scene, like a sign linguist on some early hours *Open University* broadcast. It shouldn't have been possible—but it was.

'Just enjoy the show, Mr Oakley: I though you enjoyed films.'

Well, so I did: but I never planned on being in one, certainly not one that looked so worringly real. At the very least I'd have wanted my contract to specify a happy ending. Also, now I came to—wildly inopportunely—think about it, an input re casting the female romantic interest would be nice too. However, the prospect before us looked horribly unresolved and open-ended. I didn't care for that sort of improvised, *avant-garde* effort at the best of times—and this was hardly...

'Ah, yes: *time*,' said Disvan, entirely failing to apologise for trespassing in my thoughts. 'I suppose I ought to specify that: seeing how your poor father was robbed over your private education. We're almost a millennia back. This is Senlac Field—the Battle of Hastings to you.'

It did look awfully like it: all madmen in armour, blood and screams and similar. I averted my gaze.

'You can't remember that,' I protested, hoping sweet reason would make it all go away.

'I most certainly *can*,' answered my 'friend', at the most melancholy I'd yet heard him. 'Would it were otherwise.'

I looked down again. A wave of metal-draped men were bullying their sensibly reluctant horses up the steep slope. Long lines of axe waving bearded types were atop the crest just dying to meet them. A hypnotic chant of *'Ut! Ut! Ut!'* rose from the waiting shieldwall. The Normans were too puffed or preoccupied to reply.

"Out, out, out'—or just 'go away',' interpreted Disvan helpfully.

Aside from some all too rare erotic occasions I'd never been so swift to accept an invitation.

'Fair enough. I will. Let's not upset them. Away we go then.'

Mr Disvan smiled distantly. 'You and your jokes, Mr Oakley. Nothing worries you, does it? No, they don't mean us; we can't be seen. It's just the traditional English chant against an invader.'

ALTERED ENGLANDS

I wasn't going to release my grip on any half-promising way out as easily as that.

'Even so, we shouldn't be here. I'm too polite to nose in on people's private moments. Let's be off. This isn't any of our business.'

'Now that,' said Disvan, turning to face me in our little commentary box in the sky, 'is where you're wrong. I'll show you...'

And then the swine, the evil, tormenting, heartless, ice-veined, *ratbag* pushed me out. His old man's arm proved to be like an oncoming scrum. I was expelled like Adam from what was, I now realised, the delectable safety, the veritable Eden, of the corner seat.

'Aaaaaarrrggghh!' I said, as befitted a falling man—and then found that was not the case. My feet were on solid ground, though not solid in the lovely concrete paving sense of modern Binscombe. To find myself intact, on my own two feet, was, I admit, preferable to the squelchy hard landing I'd expected. However, I was still a league short of happiness. This springy turf was a mite extra springy today as it shuddered under the impact of oncoming horsemen.

'*Aaarrgh*?' queried my neighbour in the shieldwall. 'What sort of a strife-greeting is that?'

It wasn't—modern—English he was speaking but, dammit, I comprehended him. Disvan's voice was also still with me even if he was not.

'There you are, Mr Oakley,' came his calm, friendly tones inside my head, 'I told you there was some connection. Your ancestor was at Hastings—and now so are you. You'll be able to see and experience what he did: no, don't thank me, just enjoy yourself. Rest assured, Great-great-great etc. Grandfather Oakley can't perceive you're riding alongside him.'

'*Inside* him! *Inside*, you ******!' I screeched, thinking the correction rather important. 'You've gone too far this time. It's not safe!'

'Are you well?' queried my neighbour again, diverting part of his attention from the imminent nightmare of horseflesh and lance-points to eye me suspiciously.

Terrified and enraged, I gestured wildly up at where Disvan was still visible in his little corner of the heavens.

'Look, a spy!' I told the soldiers all around me. 'Shoot him!'

Contemporary English thoughts came out as spoken Saxon. My unsolicited comrades understood my words but not my purpose. Some looked but saw nothing.

'Sort yourself out!' said one. 'Or else I'll-...'

He didn't confide the rest of his plans to me because he was dead. A great big arrow came down from the sky and spitted the face which I'd caused to be upturned.

'I shouldn't do that,' came Disvan's voice again. 'Like I said, they can't see me.'

'I don't *like* you,' I answered, but then had to forget that as I found I liked the Norman knight before me even less. Unaware I was an out-of-place 'Equities and Currencies trader', with no interest in disputing his territorial claims, he tried to ride his steed up the slope and right over me.

Even I realised the time for rational discussion and compromise was past. Great-great etc. Granddad's axe was handy and so I used it to save myself. Back (or forward) in my prep school Officer Training Corps 'manoeuvres', and at cub-scout 'camps', I'd had occasion to chop a log or two, to feed the fire. The technique, once learned never forgotten, proved to work just as well on Norman skulls.

'*Eeerrr!*' I protested at the ensuing sights, wrinkling my nose. That reaction put me in a minority of one, as my surrounding companions gave rave reviews.

'*Yowsa!*' they cried—or the Anglo-Saxon equivalent. Then they frowned as, somewhat ladylike I suppose to their eyes, I tried to clean the yuck off the axe-blade on a tussock.

The loss of their leader put the following horsemen in two minds (rather like said leader in fact: ho ho) about pressing their attack. They threw some lances and the English responded in kind. The assault sort of blanded away.

'Good man!' boomed a familiar voice, whilst simultaneously a mighty paw clapped my back. I looked round—and up—and up—and found myself greeting none other than Mr Bretwalda. Only it wasn't him. This King was the right monster size and appearance and everything, but he wasn't the demolition-contracting, *'Directors'*-swilling, proud father of Hengist, Horsa, Vladimir, Kylie *et al* and *Argyll* regular that I knew and... was rather nervous of. Somehow I guessed who this titan really was in this slice of history and managed to look suitably dutiful.

'Oak of Budenescumbe,' King Harold addressed me, 'you are well named: my sturdiest huscarl!'

'This oak sets itself by you, Lord,' I heard myself saying, my cursed ancestor hijacking my/his tongue. 'It shall not be uprooted.'

Harold/Bretwalda looked down on 'me', and for the merest second his face of fury eased. Here at the end of things it heartened him to find that not everything came down at last to treachery and shabbiness.

All about, the surviving huscarls raised their blades and cheered, and Harold strode off towards the thorn tree that was the centre of his line, to where his 'Fighting Man' standard and the golden Wyvern of Wessex were planted. At the same time I seized back the wheel re my powers of speech.

'Hang on!' I blurted out—presumably to my forefather's surprise. I was anxious to insert a more modern, appraising viewpoint into all this. Standing under a growing arrow storm, awaiting death or, at the very least, anaesthetic-free medical treatment seemed... old-fashioned and inadvisable to someone with unresolved career aims.

And then suddenly it didn't any more. The King turned back to me—and I couldn't disappoint him.

'Yes?' he asked. 'Speak and you shall receive.'

'Nothing... majesty.'

He looked puzzled but I got away with it and part of me, presumably the ancestral Oakley, was glad.

'Damn, damn, damn!' I lamented to myself.

'Mr Oakley!' came Disvan's voice, as ambivalently received as a broken birthday present. 'I'm surprised at you!'

'Don't crow: just *don't* crow!'

'I wasn't going to,' he countered unconvincingly from up in the remote, safe, sky.

'Okay, all right. So now get me out of here.'

'I should stay for the end, Mr Oakley.' It was an order wrapped in a suggestion's clothing. 'There's not long to go and you can't come to any harm.'

What proved to be the penultimate attack arrived just then, to give his words the lie. A lancehead tracked a red motorway map on the flesh of my arm, chainmail protection notwithstanding. It felt like a new sun was flaring into life in my left bicep.

Thus inspired, it was no chore to whack the bloke-wot-dun-it. Then, when his severed head was still wondering which way to fall, I bashed his horse for good measure. It said its final French *neigh* and died, breathing its last right in my face.

'Crowbait!' I howled. 'I hope you—both—burn all the way down!'

The dead man's close companions were plainly making similar harsh judgements about me—but they steered well clear. I rather liked that. Whereas ordinarily I'd now be thinking in terms of fainting and hospitals, not to mention soft-palmed and full-bottomed nurses, the sight of the enemy wheeling away inspired me to fresh madness.

I leapt forward and *bopped* one of the nearest knights. Let's see how he liked having an arm on fire!

He didn't. He said *'Merde!'* and rode off *tout de suite*. Someone else prodded a lance at me but I made short work of both it and then him. After that I was fairly safe, being shielded by potential horsesteaks and portioned Normans.

'I *like* this! I exulted to no one in particular—and then gasped to hear myself say such a thing. I honestly couldn't be sure if had been Great (etc.) Granddad or me.

'Well, *you're* a dark horse,' commented Mr Disvan from his god-like distant perspective. 'And to think Bridget Maccabi called you a *Guardian* reader! Do you still want to leave?'

I didn't get the chance to answer: well, not really, because it was then—or quite soon after—that the last attack went in. The Normans committed everything they had, foot as well as horse, and preceded all with a barrage of high arrows.

I saw Harold take one in the eye and I forgot my own pain, as my heart shook. The stricken King grasped the Wyvern standard and just, at unimaginable cost, managed to stand.

'England!' he cried, in a voice shot through with the lightning of agony. 'For England!'

Then he was lost to my sight as Norman knights at last broke through our line.

And I thought... *'Stuff* being a commuting, calculating, *Independent*-perusing accountant of a human! To hell with being ever-reasonable and moderate and self-limiting and every other sort of *'oo: are you sure?* sort of tendency!

ALTERED ENGLANDS

Adrenaline drowned out the messages from my torn limb. Brother body was receiving unfamiliar transmissions from parts the sensible, secular 20th century never normally reached—and it rather liked them.

'To me!' I hear myself saying. 'Binscombe! Binscombe!'

It was a feeling from out of mundane time that both was, and wasn't, me, that came from the same place as I did.

I headed for where the action was and for the first time in my existence people were inspired to follow me. I recognised some faces from the *Argyll*.

It all goes a bit fuzzy after that; memory being shrouded in a reddish mist. I do recall seeing my King hacked to bits, I mind clearly taking a horse's head off in one—a neat trick if you can do it: or so at least his rider seemed to think in the fleeting seconds left to him

For a while I even held the Wyvern standard aloft, before surrendering it into the custody of a less injured man. I rallied the loose fringes of the huscarl stand. The diminished shieldwall shrank ever inwards—but it stood. No one chose to run off to a longer-but-lesser life beyond this closing day. I saw the end to which we were surely proceeding but it made no difference. I also suddenly realised, with a shock, I was actually, properly... *happy* for the first time in my life.

'Time to go,' said Disvan via his private waveband within my skull.

'*Ut!*' I answered. 'I stay!'

He paused for a second before, without reproach, formalising my inmost thoughts.

'"*Courage shall grow keener, clearer the will*" he recited, "*and heart the greater, as our might grows less... I will not go, for I think to... lay me down by my lord's right hand.*"

'Below the belt, Disvan. It's not that. It's... I've just no wish to live on in an England gone under...'

Mr Disvan was suddenly all comfort and reassurance.

'It never did, Mr Oakley. The object of your concern faltered—but revived—and prevailed: too strong a story to be extinguished. We should move on to see how that was...'

I was consoled, but also stayed and in due course died. I was there at the last, down on the ground but not out, and saw the Wyvern fall—as I bit a Norman ankle. Dark and merciful clouds then came to hide the view.

To my surprise I woke again, still flinching from the final lance. Disvan and I were reunited up in his little 'window upon history', observing another, altogether different, scene.

'You even look altered,' was his only comment. I didn't reply.

And then I had an educational day, although we did not greatly linger in any one place or time. Hastings had been my introductory lecture and subsequent lessons could be more speedily absorbed.

It transpired, for instance, that I—or my kin—served with Hereward the Wake and saw the circumstances of his passing into legend. I was privy to the amazing truth about 'Robin Hood' and watched the sky turn black with arrows at Agincourt. Disvan pitched me into the tumultuous cauldron at Flodden, when an invading Scottish King's head was made into a football. I saw the triumph of capitalism and... nastiness when the monasteries tumbled and a civilisation died. A tear(!) adorned my eye to see the devil enthroned at Walsingham.

I was prey to mixed feelings at seeing the Armada repulsed and was betrayed along with Guy Fawkes. There proved to be a Mr Oakley in Sykes Close at Marston Moor, where the Earl of Newcastle's *Whitecoats* died to the last man for—who knows or cares?—some or other cause. Riding with the opposing side in a variant family incarnation, I had the honour to charge as an *'Ironside'* alongside Cromwell; and be beside him when he cleared Parliament, telling them to *'make way for better men'*—who never came.

I stood by what I now know to be the last legitimate King of this land, when James II took ship, broken-hearted, for France. I lost everything in attempting to restore him: as did my sons and grandsons for his son and grandson. Someone looking like me tried to urge Charles Stuart, Charles III by right, to press on from Derby and find either death or glory.

I chanced to be in court that day in 1712 when a terrifying judge ruled that no man could be a slave upon the soil of England—and freed the escaped Negro who had hardly expected justice.

As I've said, a lot of Oakleys died on the wire in France, at places they could barely pronounce, and those that lived, whole or maimed, saw in that shaking of the foundations the start of another long slide into the dark. To my amazement, I served the wrong masters in the right cause in the 'International Brigade.'

ALTERED ENGLANDS

Light flared briefly again and my line saw Britain stand wondrous and alone against... pure evil, whilst I wheeled across southern skies, as free and deadly as a hawk, in the summer of 1940.

An Oakley held command amongst the partisans in another, later, summer, amidst the inferno of Downing Street, when the European Union quisling troops tried—and mostly failed—to 'reincorporate' us. I helped raised the giant cross of St. George on Dover cliffs, and travelled to ruined Brussels to negotiate a better understanding.

I was in Wessex when the crop circles finally bore fruit and were interpreted, and it became clear we really were not... alone. I even had the briefest glimpse of Pluto from the bridge of the *'Eng. S.S. Glastonbury'* before spoilsport Disvan called me back.

Left to myself I would have travelled on, to the heat death of the Universe, or Judgement Day or the ending of my nation, had not Mr Disvan reined me in. I had lost all awareness that he was conducting my grand tour, even though I glimpsed him on the sidelines from time (sic) to time. Whether those sightings were actually him or not I couldn't say; being too preoccupied to check. Mostly however, he remained in spectator mode, an overlooker who was easily overlooked. I do recall mentioning Disvan to Thomas More who, unable to actually see what I could up in the sky, interpreted him as an analogy to the eternal eye of Almighty God. Even the greatest and most saintly minds can still misunderstand...

The final jaunt was into a dark and gloomy place which I took to be the end of the world.

'Not exactly,' Disvan told me. 'Though it's the be-all-and-end-all of the world for some. Don't you recognise the Duke of Argyll's cellar, Mr Oakley?'

'Oh yeah! But *when* are we?' I was fully expectant of being pitched into another nexus.

'About a hour after we—or you—left.'

'Oh... right. So what now?'

'I shall be seeing you,' he replied, not too helpfully, and vanished from my mind's eye, leaving me to the dank and dark.

It was only then that I discovered I couldn't move my arms, finding them to be securely wrapped round my chest. Some close confining coat had rendered me effectively armless.

Accept my word that it's no laughing matter to try and negotiate a treacherous set of steps in inky blackness: especially so when your head is fizzing with infinite new notions and an even greater number of questions. However, that taskette proved to be nothing compared to unlatching an eccentric, rusty cellar door catch with your nose. I was privileged to explore in depth a whole fresh cosmos of frustration.

At last though I emerged, like a babe from the womb or a born-again from the Jordan, blinking into the *Argyll*'s light of day. I'd rather expected some kind of acclamation but instead had to settle for gales of laughter. Perhaps it was the (shocking) pinkness of the straitjacket that did it.

'Bastards!' I said to the assembled regulars (this was becoming a habit). 'You've no idea what I've been through!'

Mr Disvan, who gave every impression of having never shifted from his seat, saluted me with his glass.

'On the contrary, Mr Oakley,' he stated, cheerfully. 'Everyone who should be is only all too aware!'

And as I checked each pair of eyes I saw that he spoke the truth.

'Be gentle with him,' Disvan instructed them. 'Re-indoctrination can be a touch traumatic. He's left his brainwashing behind him and it'll feel comical for a while.'

'I thought Monday was wash-day,' joked Mr Patel. For some reason I didn't chuckle.

'You were writhing about like you were in battle,' Doctor Bani-Sadr 'explained' in his best bedside manner, indicating my new stylish jacket. 'I trussed you up and put you down there for your own safety.

'I said not to!' chipped in the Landlord. 'Best mime act I've ever seen: laughing fit to sick ourselves we were!'

My response to that must have been clear on my purpling face—for I didn't trust myself to speak. The Doctor strolled leisurely over to release me.

'Sorry it was the ladies' model,' he said, not sounding repentant at all. 'That was the only one I had by me...'

'Now, now,' counselled Disvan, defusing by tone alone the nuke of temper that would have surely followed. 'You're still their Mr Oakley for a little longer. You must expect them to make the most of last opportunities...'

'I'm being treated different. There's less and less abuse and mickey-taking.'

'Get used to it, Mr Oakley. They're adapting to you gradually.'

I shook my head as if in pain, looking vainly amidst the nearby trees as though they could supply enlightenment.

'I don't *understand*,' I protested, almost pleading with him.

'Not at present, no,' replied Disvan. 'But you will, never fear—and very soon. How do you feel?'

I shrugged my shoulders. Actually, I'd never felt better, both within and without, but I was damned if I was going to admit that to the mazemaster.

'You mean generally?'

'Of course.'

I leant back against the stile, looking over the 'Rollover Night' field sloping away before us. My head rested against the cool and much scratched standing stone which recorded each of those unnerving evenings. It seemed a bit pointless not to confess *anything*.

'I'm still the same me,' I said, 'but more... centred. Something or other's changed: I used to believe that today is all there is.'

'And now?'

'I don't.'

Disvan nodded, evidently well satisfied.

'I should think not, Mr Oakley. How can people look at a beautiful tapestry and only see thread? Even so-called 'primitives' don't make such mistakes.'

It went against the grain to just agree with him but I saw no other honest course.

'I'm a child of my age—or was.' I suppose I was speaking in my defence, but Disvan judged it a pretty poor excuse.

"First Corinthians, 13, 11" he told me. "*When I was a child... I thought as a child: but when I became a man, I put away childish things*.' What verdict can you pass on an age that teaches its people to prefer toys and blindness?'

Inexplicably, I just seemed to know the continuance of Disvan's text and could fire further lines back at him.

'First Corinthians, 13:12*: 'For now we see thorough a glass, darkly: but then face to face: now I know in part: but then shall I know even as also I am known*'.'

Speaking of 'knowing', I don't know who should have been more shocked to hear my spouting of holy writ: him or me, but, strangely, neither of us were. Public School Anglicanism and adult agnosticism were hardly calculated to have stocked my mind with scripture. Something was going on here, but somehow it seemed easiest—and right—to just go with it.

Likewise, once upon a time I might have contended with him about his pronouncements, or (vainly) asked for elaboration. Now there was no need. In the months succeeding my historical holiday with him, I found that Disvan's every word stayed with me, crystal clear for all time, surrendering their layers of meaning in the watches of the night.

'You were about to ask 'why here'?' he said. It was true: I was, though I'd given no sign of it.

Mr Disvan looked at the valley before us, the red-roofed village and estate within its fold, and out into the green distance towards the 'Hogs Back' ridge; the edge of his closely delineated world. I was also confident that, if only with an inner eye, he simultaneously viewed the barrow-dotted wooded hill behind him.

'It's as good as place as any,' he said, answering his own, borrowed, question. His tone belied the casual reply, for he was speaking as of a beloved. 'It also so happens that I first saw this place from here. The valley floor was cleared by a fire: or was it a flood? Do you know, I can't quite recall: it was a fair while ago.'

I was stunned. For Disvan to mention his—as opposed to *the*—past was the deepest blue of blue moons. I proceeded cautiously, like I was stalking a shy prey.

'And... when was that?'

He just... replied straightaway, without the usual defence in depth, trip-wires, fallbacks and false trails.

'Well, there was no record of years then, Mr Oakley: not as you'd understand it. I suppose we're talking about the late Mesolithic—nudging on the Neolithic.'

There was the option of donning lead diver's boots and saying something like 'but you can't be-...' or 'how could that be poss-...', but all that bank-clerkish stuff had been rinsed out of me by events. Instead, being on a roll, I decided to home in for the kill.

'Then *what* are you?'

Once again he smiled upon the panorama that was his everything.

'I was... a man like you, Mr Oakley. And then I got another job. It seemed like an excellent offer at the time: not that there was all that much choice about it; as little as you're being given. Just lately though, over the last few centuries, I've begun to have doubts—or maybe just tire: like my predecessor did. Even the sweetest tune palls after thousands of hearings. Presumably you'll be the same...'

'I'll *what?*'

Disvan leapt into and onto and all over my exclamation.

'A *'Genius Loci'*, Mr Oakley. Look it up in your old school Latin dictionary. *'The Spirit of the Place'*. That's the short answer to your question. Each place and—most—nations have them. The Romans erected altars to us: though that's overformal if you ask me—being who and what I am and represent. I'll give you an instance: Croydon's spirit is a grey and poisoned predatory beast; Belgium's genius died a few years back and left no replacement. Do you get the picture? We come and we go. That being so, these are for you...'

He drew out two thickish books from the depths of his jacket. One I directly recognised as his *Koran*.

'Yes, you'll be needing that,' he confirmed. 'But the other's more immediately important.'

I just... took both, rushing in for reasons not readily fathomed, where the most martial angels would have reconnoitred first. The second tome, though professionally bound, contained reams of close-set script.

'The 'Collected Wisdom', that's all,' he said. 'Mine and my predecessor's—though his grunts took some deciphering. You'll refer to it less and less as time goes on and you get the hang of things. And take heart, once you understand all, you find the strength to forgive all...'

Sensing that King Time was no longer quite the tyrant he once was, I dipped within:

'... residual energies, stone and soil memories of the lives lived there, are subject to their own laws and acquire resonance in tune to the mundane time-stream and once again step forth.'

...

'... these echoes (being conjoined with the perceptions of those who follow after) transpose the past to the present—or the present to the past—creating, however briefly, a new and mutually-influential stream.'

...

'There are, however, dark streams...'

...

'Dogs and children and horses see them first and best...'

...

'The past lives, sometimes invisibly, alongside and therefore does not fail...'

...

'Paths and roads traverse more than distance... they can also connect times, tides and lives... Most are dual purpose (though unintendedly so), leading to both a 'real' place and through variant dimensions.'

...

'Beware of what are known as 'Heavy' objects, inconsequential in this world, but perilous to move or dispose of, for their tumultuous significance in others. I recall Mrs Eyeions dressing gown, which caused war and natural disaster throughout the higher planes. It must stay on her second from left clothes-hook.'

...

'Just as hardy plants appear in most unlikely places, flowers blooming from pockets of soil accumulated in nooks and crannies, just as grass can sunder suffocating tarmac, so do the ebbs and tides of universal energy leave rock pools behind... Ruined walls are particularly prone...'

...

ALTERED ENGLANDS

'As even reductionists admit, energy is indestructible... the vibrations of lives lived gain independence when the body is sloughed off... ...their own rules but best prefer the very threshold of normal perception. One need hardly add that thresholds are for crossing, either invited in or as a trespasser...'

...

'As the right note shatters a wineglass so a certain resonance releases hidden energies into our world. It is often preceded by sunshine and you will come to detect its silent approach...'

...

'The membranes between the worlds are semi-permeable...'

...

'... specifically there are the elves of the hills, Dun-elfen; of pools and rivers, the Water-elfen; amidst the trees, Wudu-elfen; from the sea, Soe-elfen, and, of course, out on the moors, Wylde-elfen. ... they may sometimes assist but beware them, for they are cool-hearted and have a different patron from our own...'

...

'Some things cannot die... Acts and facts may be forgotten but they do not cease.'

...

'A dark, unseen tide flows from points of remembrance out into the fields and days beyond. There is surprisingly little dividing then from now...'

...

'The meaning of existence is...'

'It's just a mishmash of advice and observation,' advised Disvan, reminding me of his presence. 'But I suggest you start with chapter twenty-three. That's the one about God. Yes, certainly read that one first...'

'I'm...'

'True, Mr Oakley. That's right. You *are* now—or very nearly. You were the natural choice. Your line tracks back to the beginning of Binscombe, though latterly they strayed. Now you're back for good—in every sense of the word. If you'd just kindly permit me a moment more... Then you can have the rest—and *I* can rest.'

I'd have gladly permitted him an eternity but that was precisely what he no longer required

'They're good people,' he told me, gesturing to the village—or perhaps much wider afield, 'more or less. By and large they don't murder and hate; kindness is still generally admired. There's no shortage of times and places you couldn't say that of, you know.'

I found that I did know it.

'And they're gentle through hard-won wisdom, not softness,' he went on. 'Never forget that. There's cold iron under the surface that can cut and bruise. See if you can keep it mostly covered. Likewise those who'll follow them. There'll be bad years now and then, but I think you'll enjoy your time here: I certainly did. Though of course, in one sense, I'll still be with-...'

And with a smile he just... merged into the landscape, gilding it as he went. For a final second, before he and it were too diluted, both were noticeably enriched.

I had other things to think about right then, but instead suddenly recalled Belloc's *'Duncton Hill'*, as drummed into me for 'O' level. Feeling as he did, perhaps the poet would forgive me my tiny, concluding, amendment:

> *'He does not die that can bequeath*
> *Some influence to the land he knows,*
> *Or dares, persistent, interwreath*
> *Love permanent with the wild hedgerows;*
> *He does not die, but still remains*
> *Substantiate with his darling plains.*
>
> *The spring's superb adventure calls*
> *His dust athwart the woods to flame;*

ALTERED ENGLANDS

His boundary river's secret falls
perpetuate and repeat his name.
He rides his loud October sky:
He does not die. He does not die.

The beeches know the accustomed head
Which loved them, and a peopled air
Beneath their benediction spread
Comforts the silence everywhere;
For native ghosts return and these
Perfect the mystery in the trees.

So there, though myself be crosst
The shuddering of that dreadful day
When friend and fire and home are lost
And even children drawn away—
The passerby shall hear me still,
A boy that sings on Binscombe Hill.'

By then he was gone, leaving only his hat and his smile—and his task—with me.

Also by that time, I was no longer entirely plain and simple Mr Oakley, a 'child of his time' and cheerful conscript of the money machine; no longer exactly... human.

And from then on it was my turn to look upon—and after—Binscombe valley and its enfolding hills. I... consumed and absorbed the view, and thus came to understand everything—within limits.

THE END

✦

JOHN WHITBOURN

38~

AFTERWORD & FAREWELL

Or

'SUMMA WHITBOURNIA'

✡

I've always thought it a sad anticlimax, not to mention ungenerous,[134] to end an anthology with merely the last line of the last happenstance story. Which, let's face it, could be just any old nonsense.

So, instead, to end with a bang not a whimper,[135] herewith an idiotsyncratic[136] bittersweet farewell. Or what you might call the *'Summa Whitbournia'*...

Pretentious? *Moi?*

Thank you for your company.

Fare well.

✡

---

[134] I said *not* to mention ungenerous! *Why-you-no-listen?* (Hat tip: Benny Hill's *'Chow Mein'*).

[135] Sound advice to any person of spirit.

[136] A wilful typo, inserted as a *'Persian Flaw'*. Perfection belongs to G-d alone. Although doubtless there's others. Which only reinforces the point.

'I <u>believed</u> life was a vale of tears and hard on failure... I <u>hoped</u> that what the Church taught was true, but I <u>feared</u> that nothing was true and everything was permissible.'
Admiral Slovo, *floruit* 1460?-1525? Quoted in *'Popes & Phantoms.'* Gollancz. 1993. p278.

...

'Do not fret at anything... I wish I never had.'
Horatio Nelson. (1758-1805).

...

'All that is on earth will perish:
But will abide (for ever) the Face of thy Lord.'
The Qur'an. *Ar-Rahman* (The Merciful) 55:26-7.

...

'Be ye therefore wise as serpents, and harmless as doves.'
Matthew 10:16.

...

'I suppose we just have to do the best we can...'
Mrs Elsie King of Binscombe (1915-2004).
Said shortly before her death.

THE END

Printed in Great Britain
by Amazon